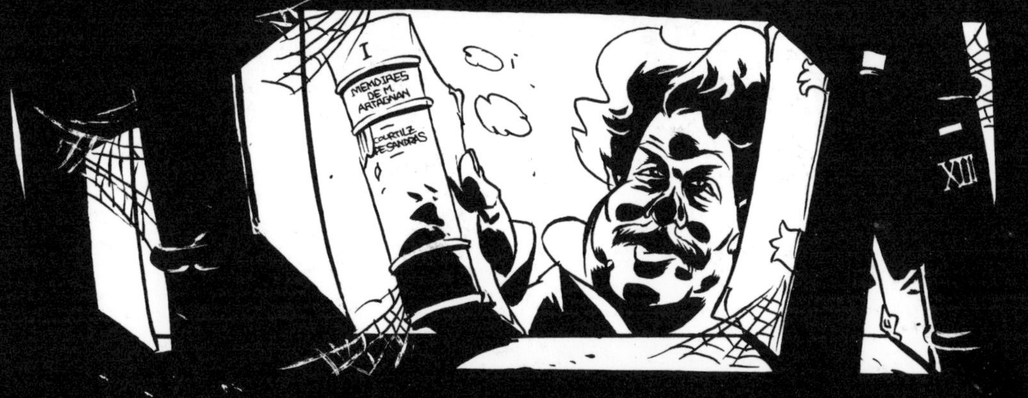
I
MEMOIRES DE M. ARTAGNAN
COURTILZ DE SANDRAS
XIII

We confess, these three strange names struck our imagination, and it immediately leapt to mind that they were but pseudonyms by which d'Artagnan had masked what may have been illustrious names, if indeed, the bearers of those borrowed names hadn't themselves chosen them on that day when, through caprice, by some discontent, or for want of better luck, they'd donned a musketeer's simple cloak.

Afterwards, we couldn't rest until we found, in contemporary works, any trace at all of those extraordinary names that had so stoked our curiosity.

A simple list of the books we read to achieve this goal would fill an entire chapter, which might prove instructive, but hardly amusing for our readers. We'll content ourselves therefore with telling them that, at the very moment when, discouraged by so much fruitless investigation, we were going to abandon our research, we finally found, guided by the advice of our illustrious and learned friend Paulin Paris, an in-folio manuscript, marked number 4772 or 4773— we no longer remember exactly —having as a title: "Memoirs of M. le Comte de La Fère, concerning some of the events that occurred in France near the end of King Louis XIII's reign and the beginning of King Louis XIV's reign."

One can imagine how great was our joy when, while leafing through that manuscript, our last hope, we found on the twentieth page the name of Athos, on the twenty-seventh the name of Porthos, and on the thirty-first the name of Aramis.

The discovery of a heretofore unknown manuscript, in an era when historical research has reached such a high degree, seemed almost miraculous to us. Thus we hurriedly sought permission to have it printed, with the goal of one day presenting ourselves with the literary baggage of others at the Académie des inscriptions et belles-lettres, if we didn't succeed, as seemed very likely, in entering the Académie Française on the strength of our own. This permission, we should note, was graciously granted to us, which we note here to make a public refutation to those malevolent souls who claim we're living under a régime poorly disposed towards men of letters.

In the meantime, as a godfather is a second parent, we invite the reader to blame us, and not the Comte de La Fère, for his pleasure or his boredom. That being said, let's get on with our story.

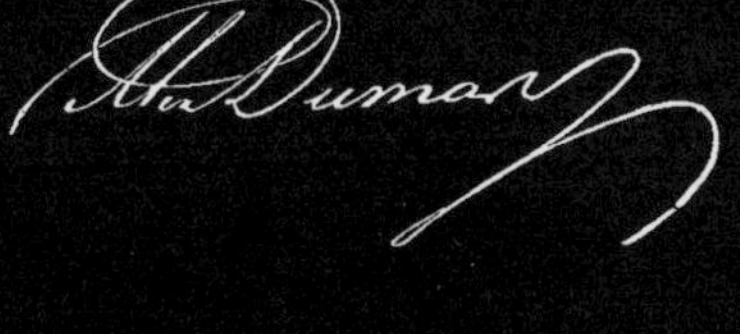

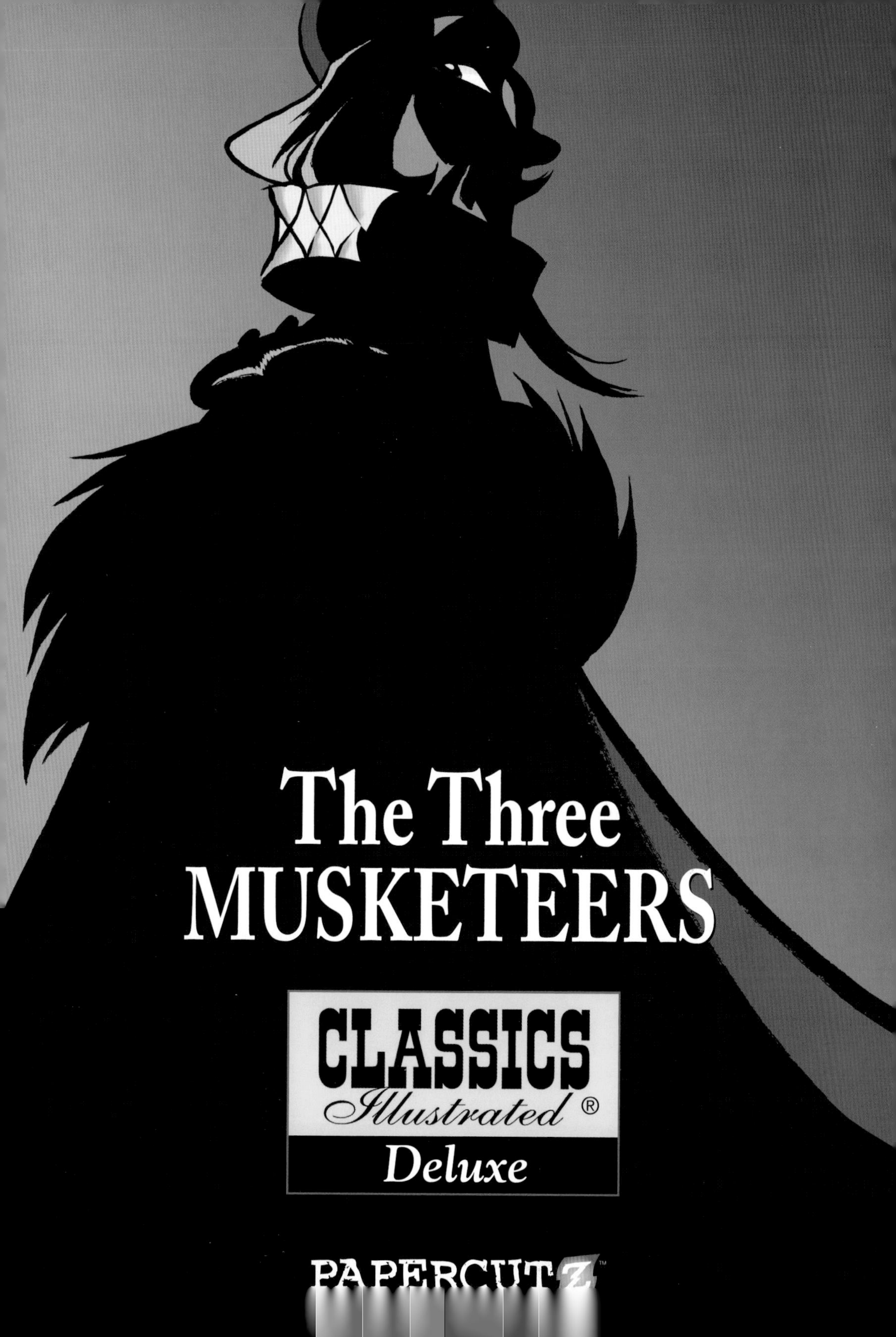

The Three MUSKETEERS

Classics Illustrated® Deluxe

PAPERCUTZ

CLASSICS ILLUSTRATED DELUXE

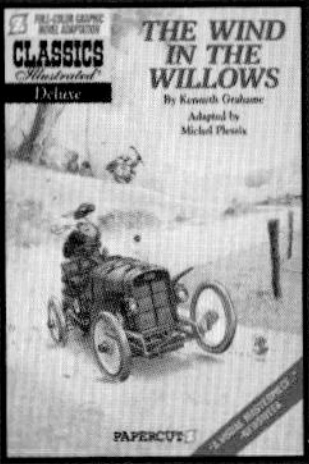
CLASSICS
Deluxe
THE WIND IN THE WILLOWS
PAPERCUTZ

#1 "THE WIND IN THE WILLOWS"

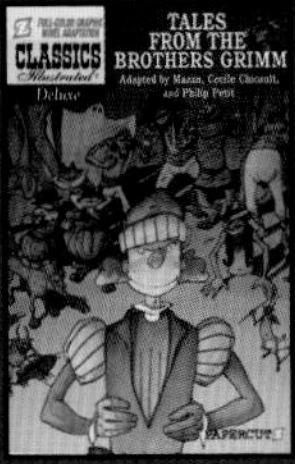
CLASSICS
TALES FROM THE BROTHERS GRIMM
PAPERCUTZ

#2 "TALES FROM THE BROTHERS GRIMM"

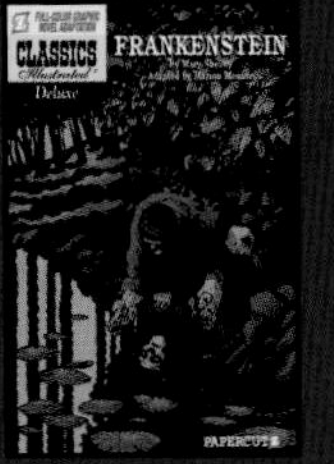
CLASSICS
FRANKENSTEIN
PAPERCUTZ

#3 "FRANKENSTEIN"

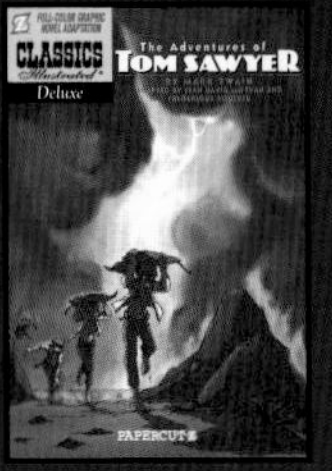
CLASSICS
The Adventures of
TOM SAWYER
PAPERCUTZ

#4 "THE ADVENTURES OF TOM SAWYER"

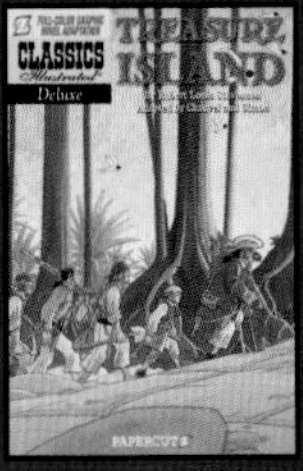
CLASSICS
TREASURE ISLAND
PAPERCUTZ

#5 "TREASURE ISLAND"

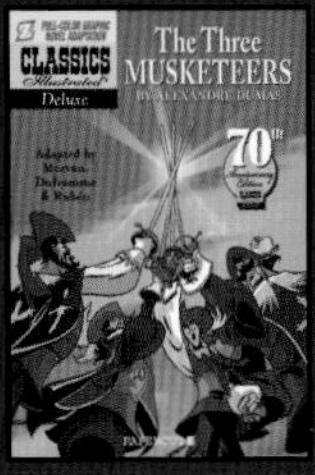
CLASSICS
The Three MUSKETEERS
BY ALEXANDRE DUMAS
70th

#6 "THE THREE MUSKETEERS"

CLASSICS ILLUSTRATED

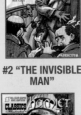

CLASSICS ILLUSTRATED GRAPHIC NOVELS AVAILABLE FROM PAPERCUTZ

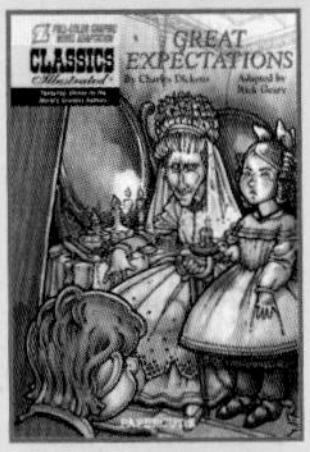
CLASSICS
GREAT EXPECTATIONS
PAPERCUTZ

#1 "GREAT EXPECTATIONS"

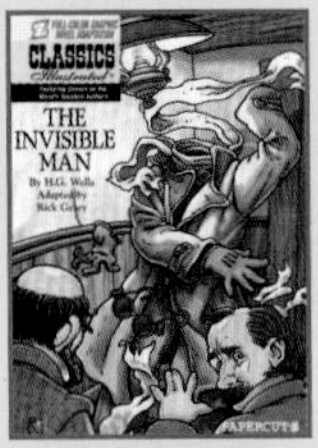
CLASSICS
THE INVISIBLE MAN
By H.G. Wells
PAPERCUTZ

#2 "THE INVISIBLE MAN"

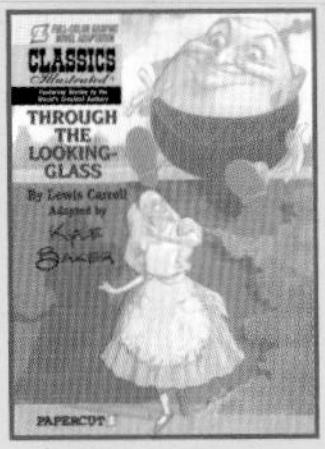
CLASSICS
THROUGH THE LOOKING-GLASS
By Lewis Carroll
PAPERCUTZ

#3 "THROUGH THE LOOKING-GLASS"

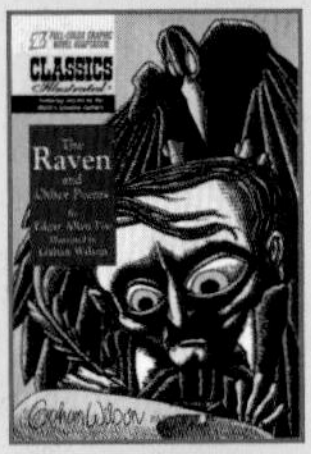
CLASSICS
The Raven and Other Poems

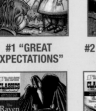

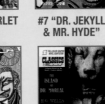

#4 "THE RAVEN AND OTHER POEMS"

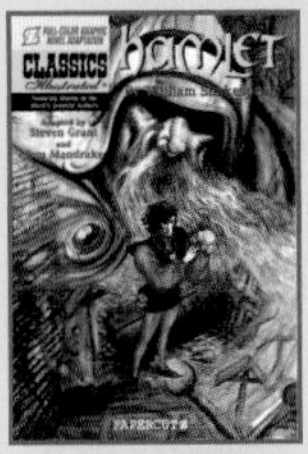
CLASSICS
Hamlet
PAPERCUTZ

#5 "HAMLET"

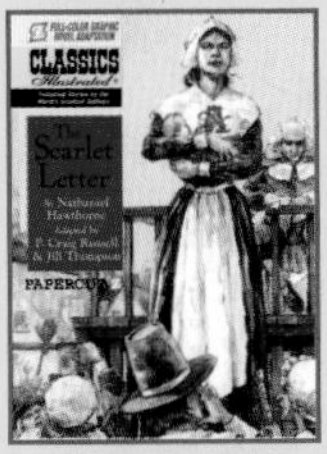
CLASSICS
The Scarlet Letter
PAPERCUTZ

#6 "THE SCARLET LETTER"

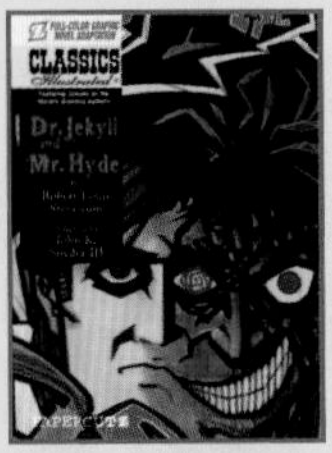
CLASSICS
Dr. Jekyll and Mr. Hyde
PAPERCUTZ

#7 "DR. JEKYLL & MR. HYDE"

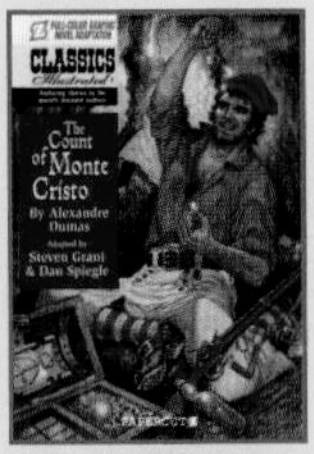
CLASSICS
The Count of Monte Cristo
By Alexandre Dumas
PAPERCUTZ

#8 "THE COUNT OF MONTE CRISTO"

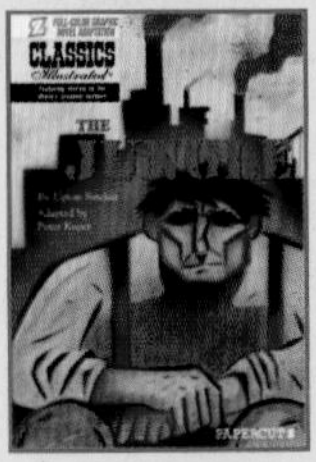
CLASSICS
PAPERCUTZ

#9 "THE JUNGLE"

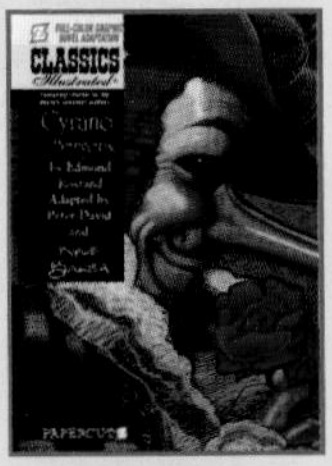
CLASSICS
PAPERCUTZ

#10 "CYRANO DE BERGERAC"

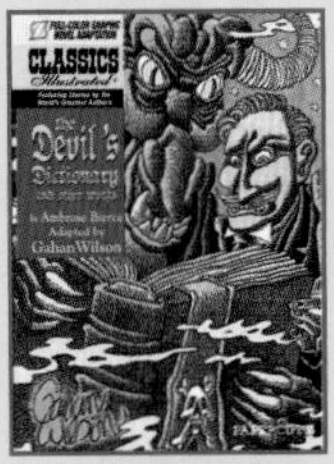
CLASSICS
The Devil's Dictionary
PAPERCUTZ

#11 "THE DEVIL'S DICTIONARY AND OTHER WORKS"

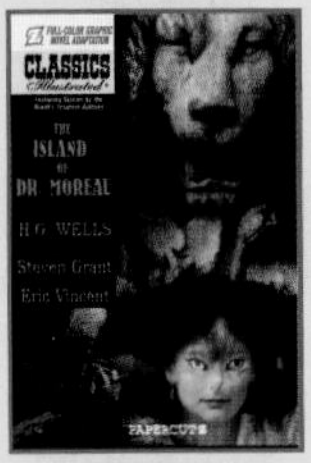
CLASSICS
THE ISLAND OF DR MOREAU
H.G. WELLS
PAPERCUTZ

#12 "THE ISLAND OF DOCTOR MOREAU"

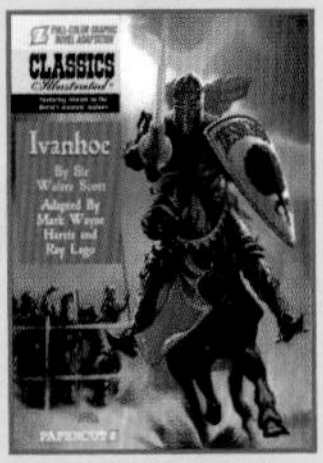
CLASSICS
Ivanhoe
By Sir Walter Scott
PAPERCUTZ

#13 "IVANHOE"

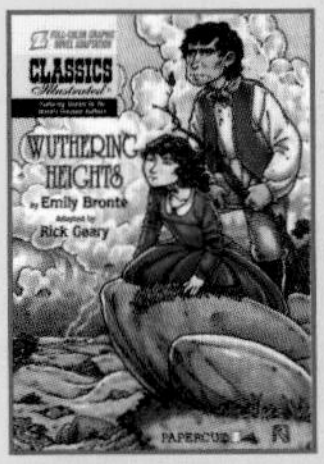
CLASSICS
WUTHERING HEIGHTS
by Emily Bronte
Adapted by Rick Geary
PAPERCUTZ

COMING AUG. '11 #14 "WUTHERING HEIGHTS"

CLASSICS ILLUSTRATED DELUXE graphic novels are available for $13.95 each in paperback and $17.95 in hardcover, except #6 which is $16.99 pb, and $21.99 hc.
CLASSICS ILLUSTRATED graphic novels are available only in hardcover for $9.95 each, except #8-14, $9.99 each. Available from booksellers everywhere.

Or order from us. Please add $4.00 for postage and handling for the first book, add $1.00 for each additional book.
MC, Visa, Amex accepted or make check payable to NBM Publishing.
Send to: Papercutz, 1200 Rte. 523, Flemington, NJ, 08822 • 1-800-886-1223

www.papercutz.com

CLASSICS
Illustrated ®
Deluxe

#6

The Three
MUSKETEERS

By Alexandre Dumas
Adapted by Jean David Morvan, Michel
Dufranne, Rubén, and Marie Galopin

PAPERCUTZ™
New York

For Marino Del Rincón, captain of the King's Musketeers, and thanks to my dear Sara, for having put me in contact with Alexandre Dumas, bowing before his studio at the Château d'If.
Rubén.

To Gisèle, Nicole, and Maria... the three women in my life.
Thanks to Monsieur de Morvan for the battle plan and to his
Lordship Rubén for putting it to work.
Thanks to Lady Marie for her colorful intrigues.
Thanks to all the musketeers met during the adventure:
Patrick "Lucha" Lehance, Caroline "Dico" Moreau, Benoît
"Édito" Cousin, Franck "Typo" Debernardi, Guillaume
"Montage" Lavergne... and all those who worked in the shadows
in the King's service.
M.D.

When he was a kid, Rubén loved two things: drawing and fighting with wooden sticks. Luckily for him, he chose to blacken the page rather than continuing to disguise himself as D'Artagnan. He took his first drawing classes at the age of four in the little village where he lived with his parents, before joining, some years later, the JOSO of Barcelona, Spain's most reputable comics school. It was during this time that he produced several short stories for sundry Hispanic magazines, one of which caught Jean David Morvan's attention. He contacted Rubén, and from that meeting would be born the series Jolin la teigne, the majority of the stories in the third volume of Sir Pyle, and this adaptation of "The Three Musketeers," which thus allows the two passions of his youth to finally be brought together!

"I was three years old when I fell in love with an animated TV series. It was about The Three Musketeers, but in a version where the characters were dogs!! Even now, for me, the main character, 'D'Artacan,' (in Spanish) seems more familiar to me than the real D'Artagnan. But the essence of what made this series a myth in Spain (History, adventure, feelings, etc.) also inspired me to read Dumas's original text... which moved me, which I admired, and whose sequels I discovered, including the characters' deaths.

"One day, after the umpteenth rereading of 'The Three Musketeers,' I got the idea for a story in the Sir Pyle series of working in Milady. Jean David, the script writer, liked the idea, so I drew the story. After seeing the pages, Jean David then told me, in his usual easy-going way, 'Hey, that's cool. Why not do the adaptation of 'The Three Musketeers' in comics?' So, I answered him: 'That's crazy, there must already be a thousand adaptations in France!' When he responded: 'No, there aren't any,' I was speechless. It's still a huge mystery to me...There aren't any adaptations?!

"Now, I have the gratification of being able to return the enormous gift given to me by the television series and the great Dumas."
Rubén

"The Three Musketeers"
By Alexandre Dumas
Adapted by...
Jean David Morvan & Michel Dufranne – Writers
Rubén – Artist
Marie Galopin – Colorist
Joe Johnson – Translation
Bryan Senka & Ortho – Lettering
Ortho – Production
John Haufe and William B. Jones Jr. – Classics Illustrated Historians
Michael Petranek – Associate Editor
Jim Salicrup
Editor-in-Chief

ISBN: 978-1-59707-252-6 paperback edition
ISBN: 978-1-59707-253-3 hardcover edition

Printed in China
March 2011 by New Era Printing LTD
Trend Centre, 29-31 Cheung Lee St.
Rm.1101-1103, 11/F, Chaiwan

Distributed by Macmillan.

First Papercutz Printing

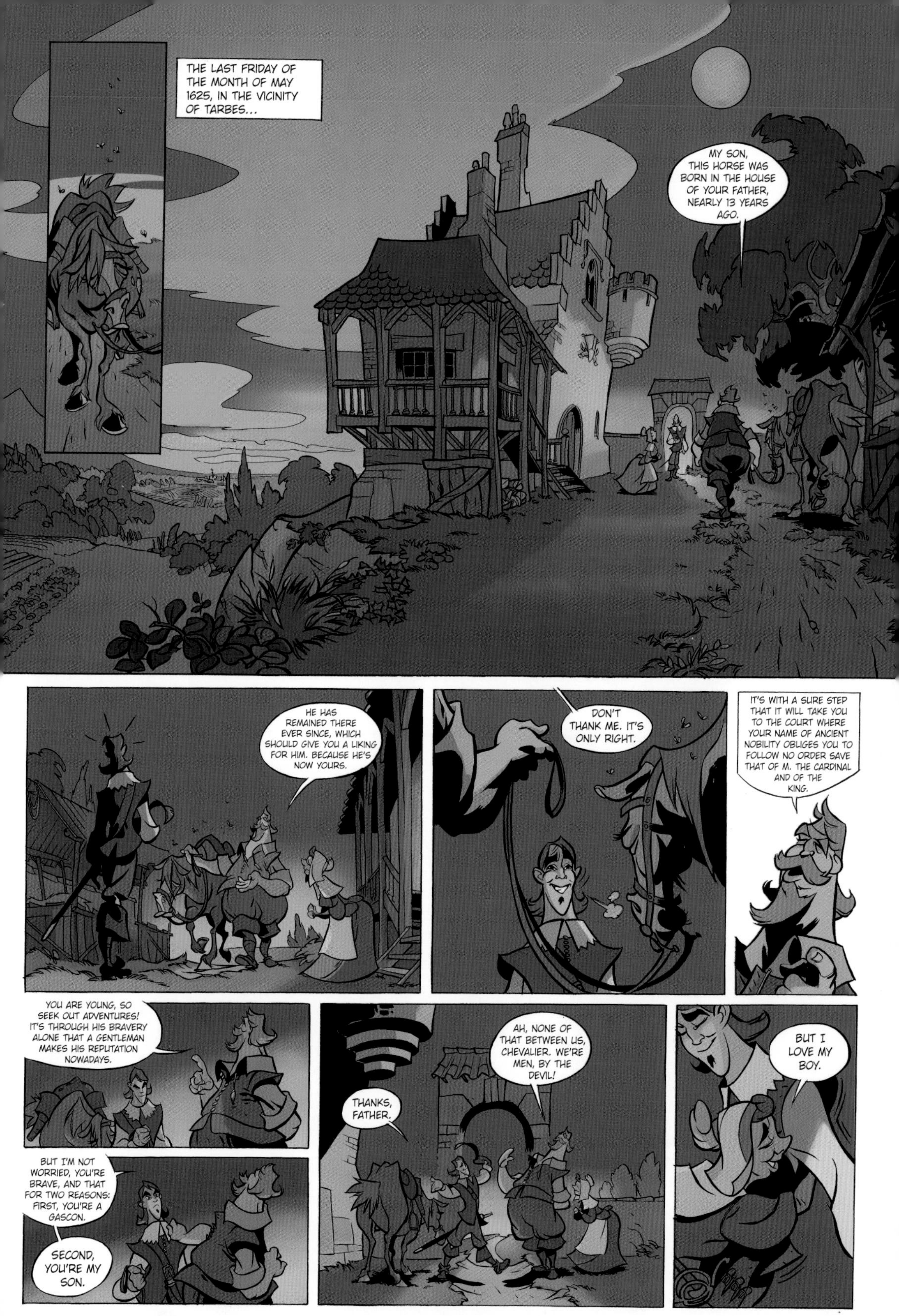
THE LAST FRIDAY OF THE MONTH OF MAY 1625, IN THE VICINITY OF TARBES...
MY SON, THIS HORSE WAS BORN IN THE HOUSE OF YOUR FATHER, NEARLY 13 YEARS AGO.
HE HAS REMAINED THERE EVER SINCE, WHICH SHOULD GIVE YOU A LIKING FOR HIM. BECAUSE HE'S NOW YOURS.
DON'T THANK ME. IT'S ONLY RIGHT.
IT'S WITH A SURE STEP THAT IT WILL TAKE YOU TO THE COURT WHERE YOUR NAME OF ANCIENT NOBILITY OBLIGES YOU TO FOLLOW NO ORDER SAVE THAT OF M. THE CARDINAL AND OF THE KING.
YOU ARE YOUNG, SO SEEK OUT ADVENTURES! IT'S THROUGH HIS BRAVERY ALONE THAT A GENTLEMAN MAKES HIS REPUTATION NOWADAYS.
BUT I'M NOT WORRIED, YOU'RE BRAVE, AND THAT FOR TWO REASONS: FIRST, YOU'RE A GASCON.
SECOND, YOU'RE MY SON.
THANKS, FATHER.
AH, NONE OF THAT BETWEEN US, CHEVALIER. WE'RE MEN, BY THE DEVIL!
BUT I LOVE MY BOY.

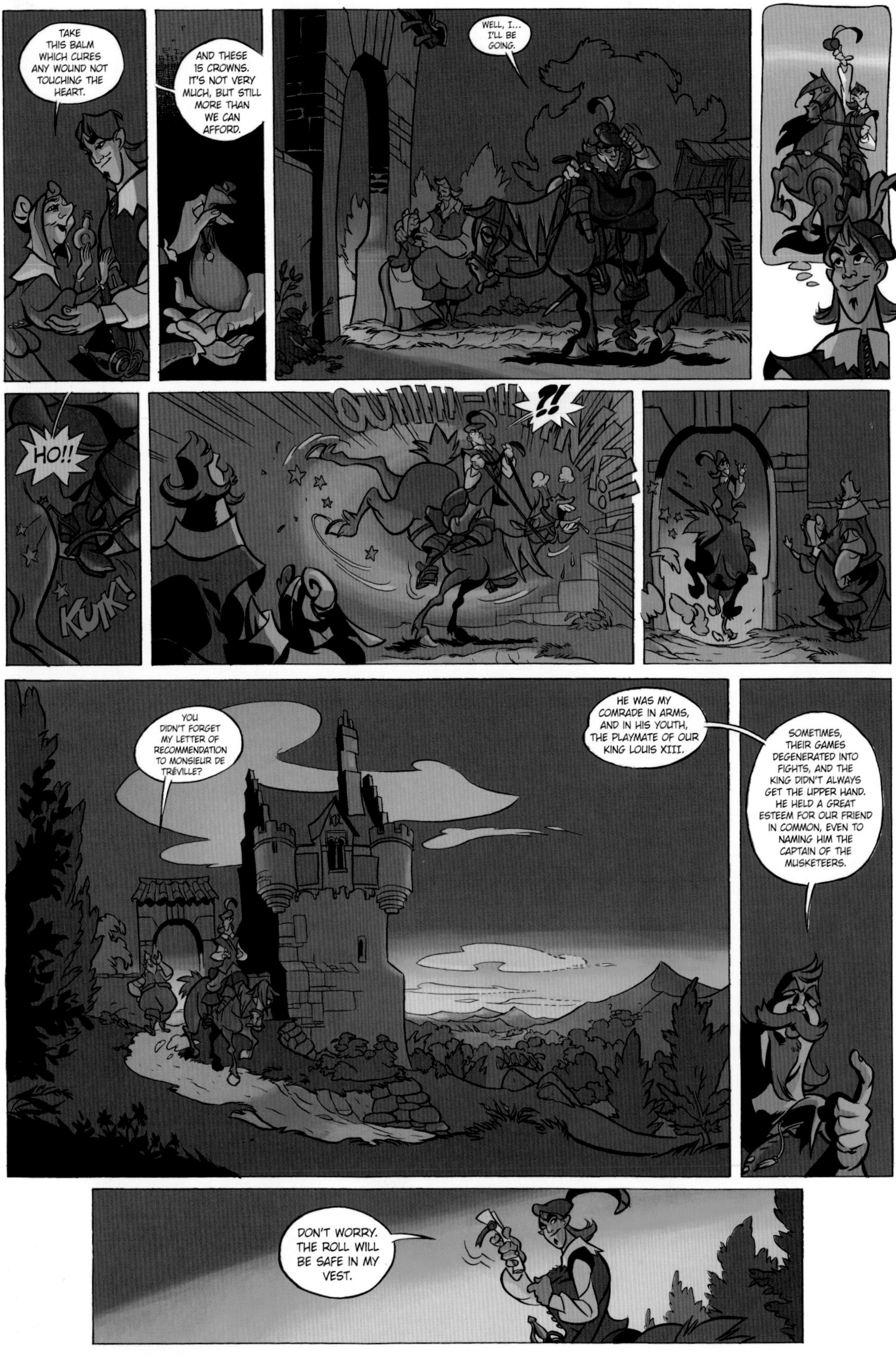
TAKE THIS BALM WHICH CURES ANY WOUND NOT TOUCHING THE HEART.
AND THESE IS CROWNS. IT'S NOT VERY MUCH, BUT STILL MORE THAN WE CAN AFFORD.
WELL, I... I'LL BE GOING.
HO!!
KUIK!
?!
YOU DIDN'T FORGET MY LETTER OF RECOMMENDATION TO MONSIEUR DE TRÉVILLE?
HE WAS MY COMRADE IN ARMS, AND IN HIS YOUTH, THE PLAYMATE OF OUR KING LOUIS XIII.
SOMETIMES, THEIR GAMES DEGENERATED INTO FIGHTS, AND THE KING DIDN'T ALWAYS GET THE UPPER HAND. HE HELD A GREAT ESTEEM FOR OUR FRIEND IN COMMON, EVEN TO NAMING HIM THE CAPTAIN OF THE MUSKETEERS.
DON'T WORRY. THE ROLL WILL BE SAFE IN MY VEST.

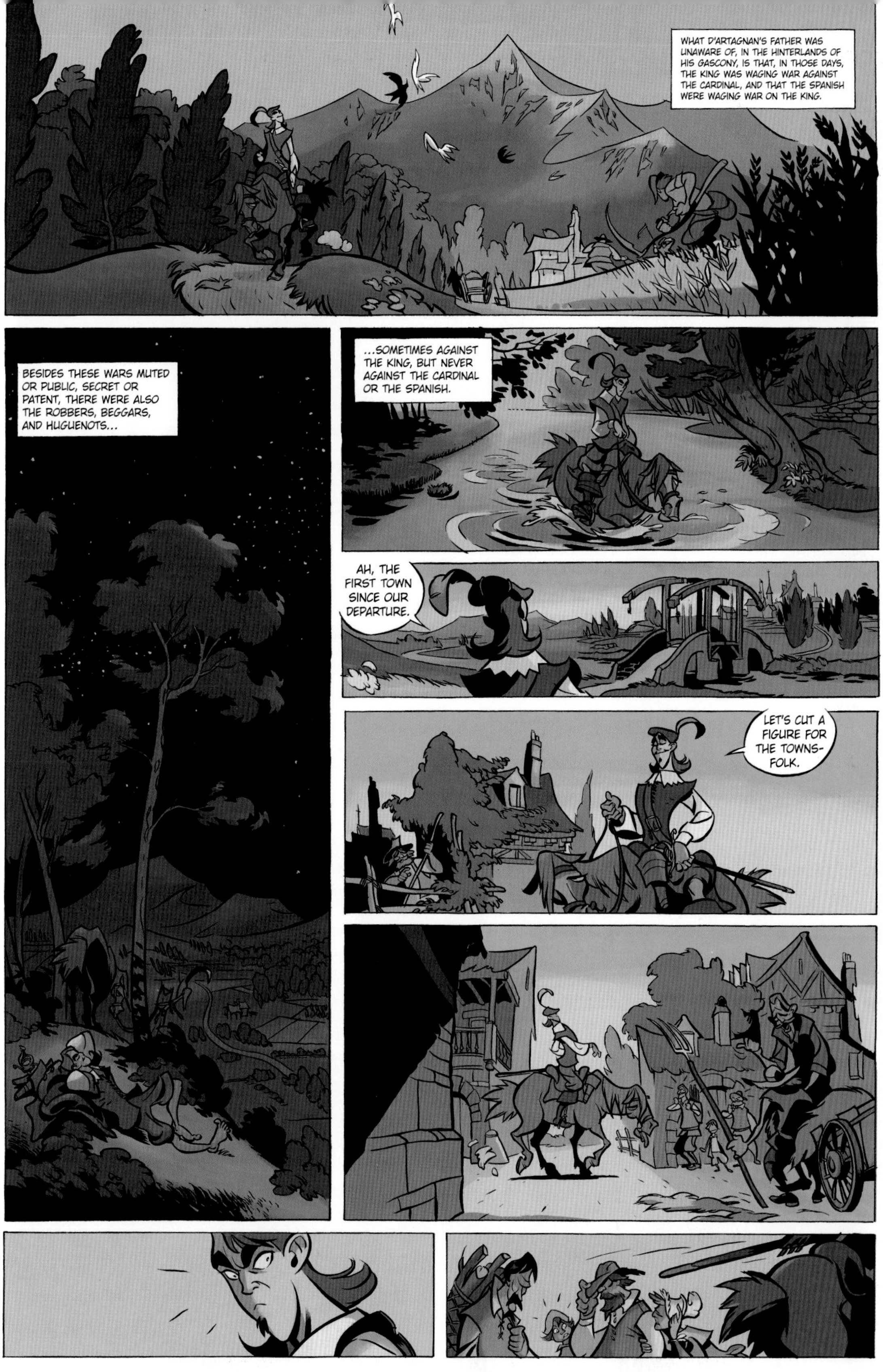
WHAT D'ARTAGNAN'S FATHER WAS UNAWARE OF, IN THE HINTERLANDS OF HIS GASCONY, IS THAT, IN THOSE DAYS, THE KING WAS WAGING WAR AGAINST THE CARDINAL, AND THAT THE SPANISH WERE WAGING WAR ON THE KING.
BESIDES THESE WARS MUTED OR PUBLIC, SECRET OR PATENT, THERE WERE ALSO THE ROBBERS, BEGGARS, AND HUGUENOTS...
...SOMETIMES AGAINST THE KING, BUT NEVER AGAINST THE CARDINAL OR THE SPANISH.
AH, THE FIRST TOWN SINCE OUR DEPARTURE.
LET'S CUT A FIGURE FOR THE TOWNS-FOLK.

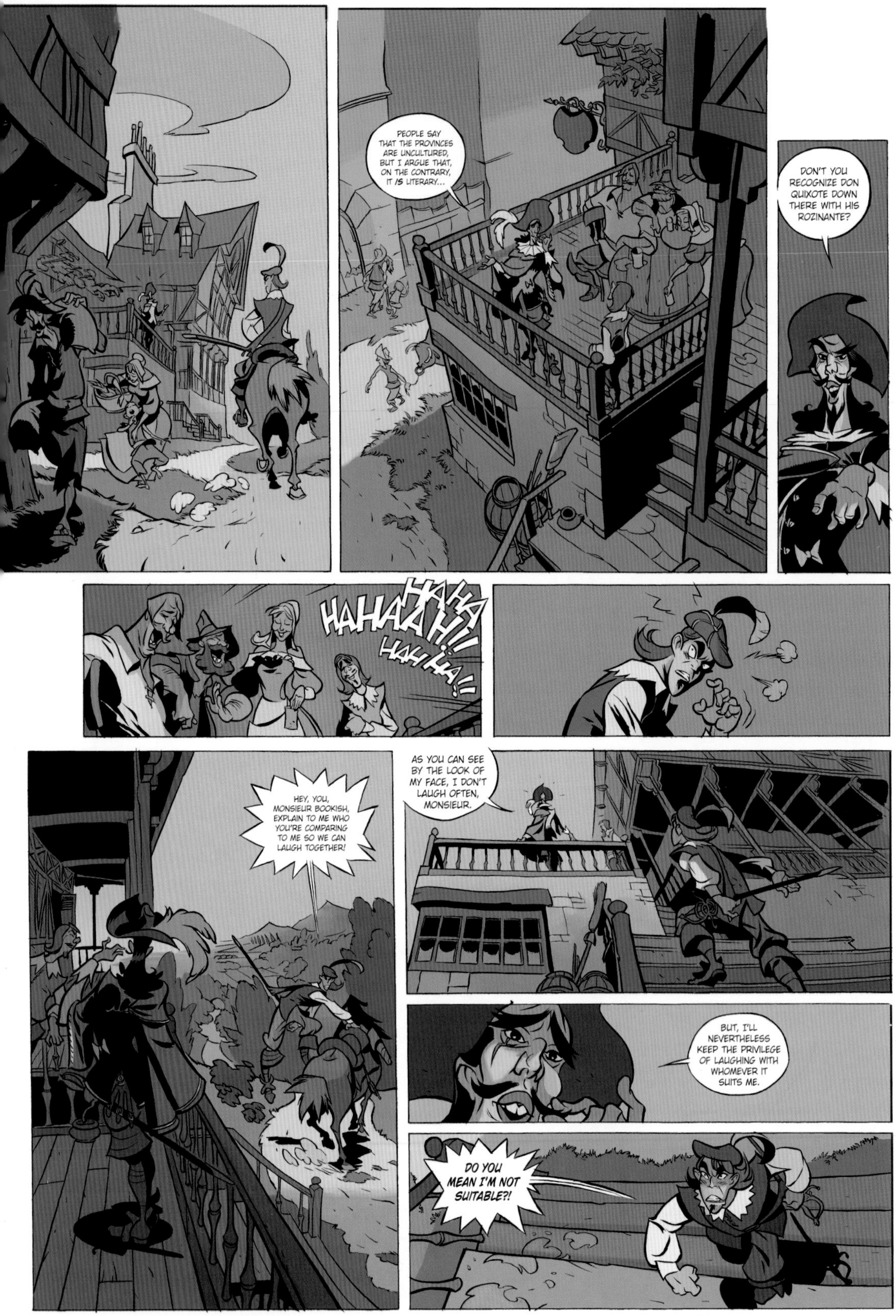
PEOPLE SAY THAT THE PROVINCES ARE UNCULTURED, BUT I ARGUE THAT, ON THE CONTRARY, IT *IS* LITERARY...
DON'T YOU RECOGNIZE DON QUIXOTE DOWN THERE WITH HIS ROZINANTE?
HAHA HAHAAH!! HAHAHA!!
HEY, YOU, MONSIEUR BOOKISH, EXPLAIN TO ME WHO YOU'RE COMPARING TO ME SO WE CAN LAUGH TOGETHER!
AS YOU CAN SEE BY THE LOOK OF MY FACE, I DON'T LAUGH OFTEN, MONSIEUR.
BUT, I'LL NEVERTHELESS KEEP THE PRIVILEGE OF LAUGHING WITH WHOMEVER IT SUITS ME.
DO YOU MEAN I'M NOT SUITABLE?!

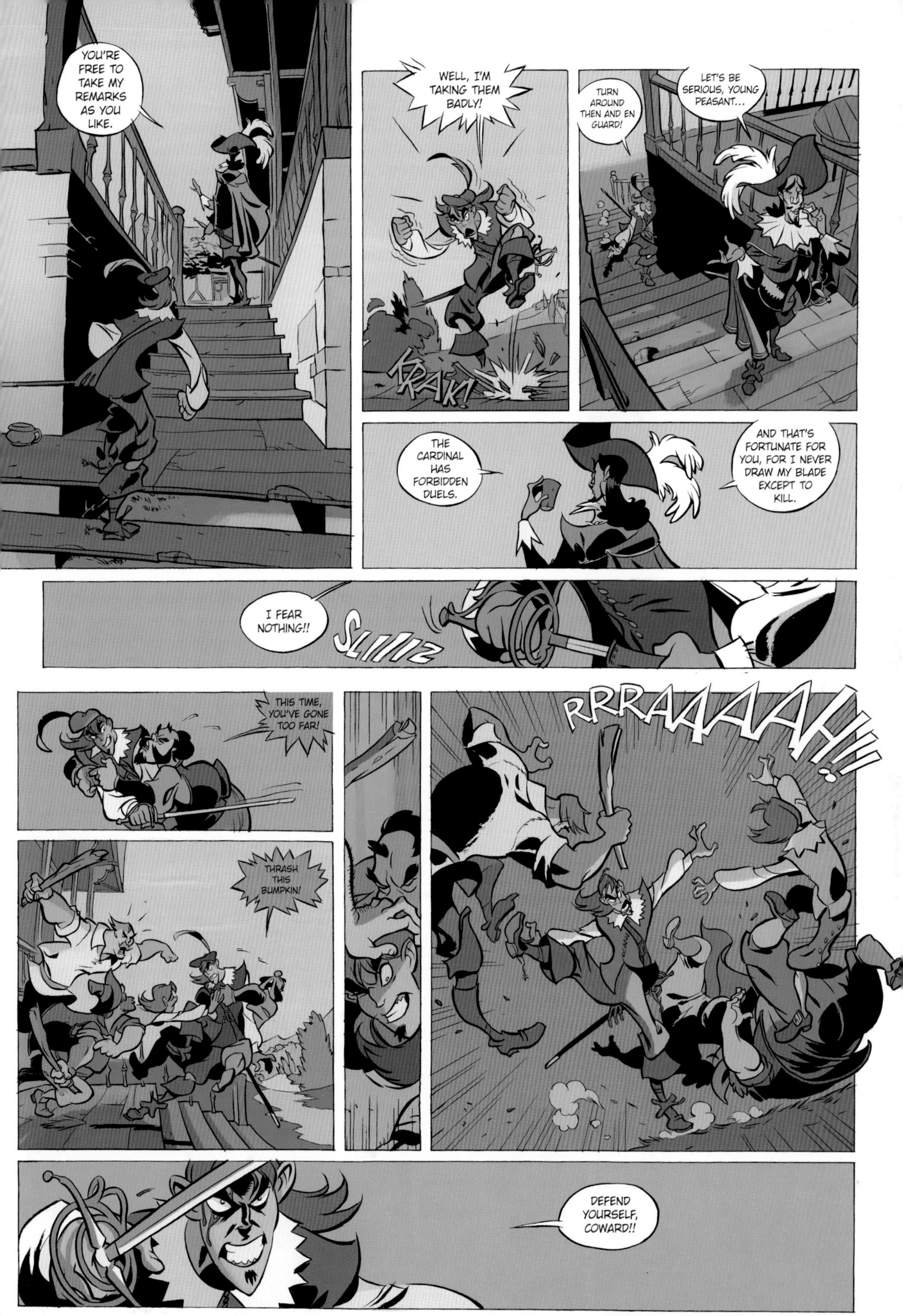
YOU'RE FREE TO TAKE MY REMARKS AS YOU LIKE.
WELL, I'M TAKING THEM BADLY!
KRAK!
TURN AROUND THEN AND EN GUARD!
LET'S BE SERIOUS, YOUNG PEASANT…
THE CARDINAL HAS FORBIDDEN DUELS.
AND THAT'S FORTUNATE FOR YOU, FOR I NEVER DRAW MY BLADE EXCEPT TO KILL.
I FEAR NOTHING!!
SLIIIZ
THIS TIME, YOU'VE GONE TOO FAR!
THRASH THIS BUMPKIN!
RRRAAAAAH!!!
DEFEND YOURSELF, COWARD!!

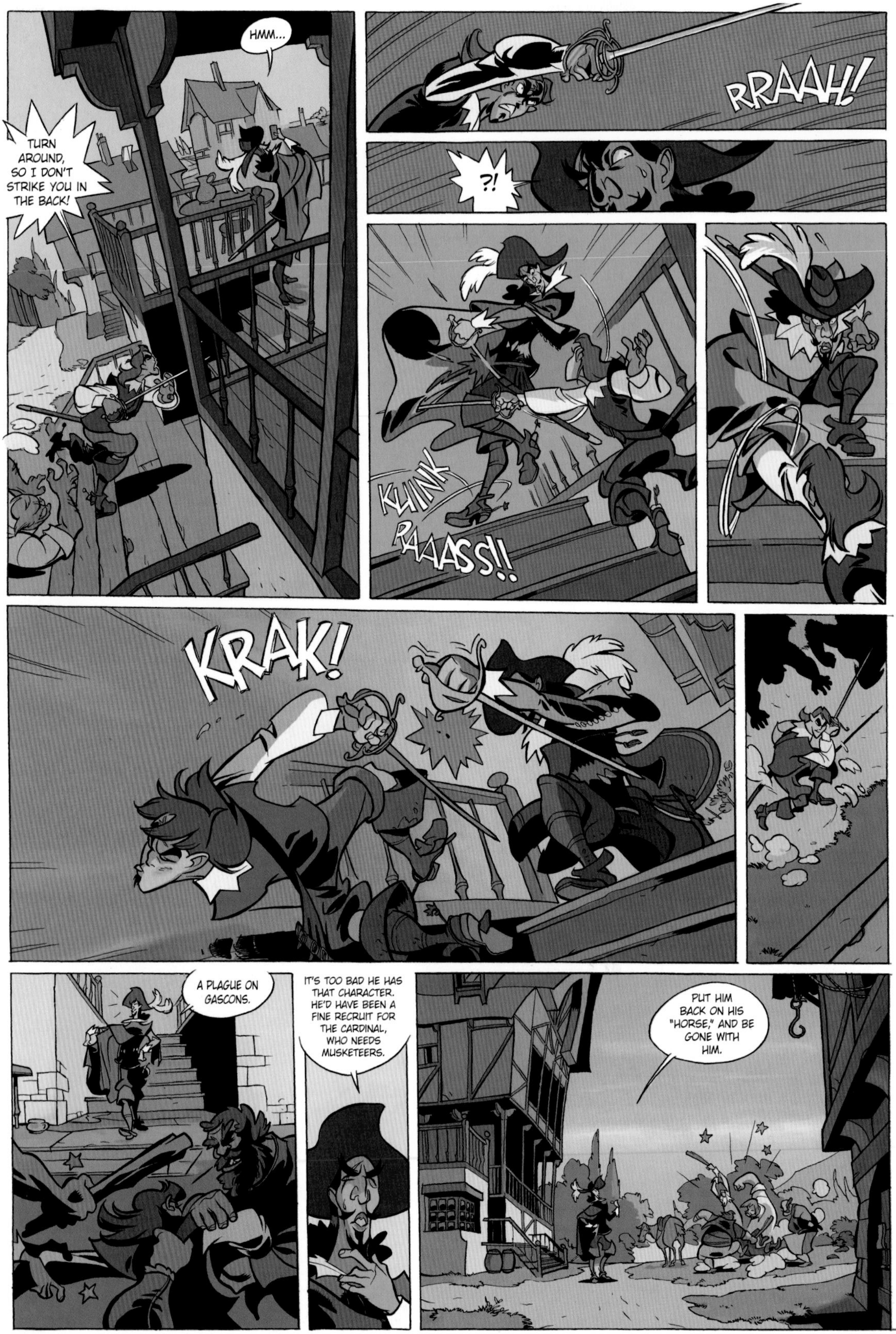
HMM...
TURN AROUND, SO I DON'T STRIKE YOU IN THE BACK!
RRAAH!
?!
KLINK
RAAASS!!
KRAK!
A PLAGUE ON GASCONS.
IT'S TOO BAD HE HAS THAT CHARACTER. HE'D HAVE BEEN A FINE RECRUIT FOR THE CARDINAL, WHO NEEDS MUSKETEERS.
PUT HIM BACK ON HIS "HORSE," AND BE GONE WITH HIM.

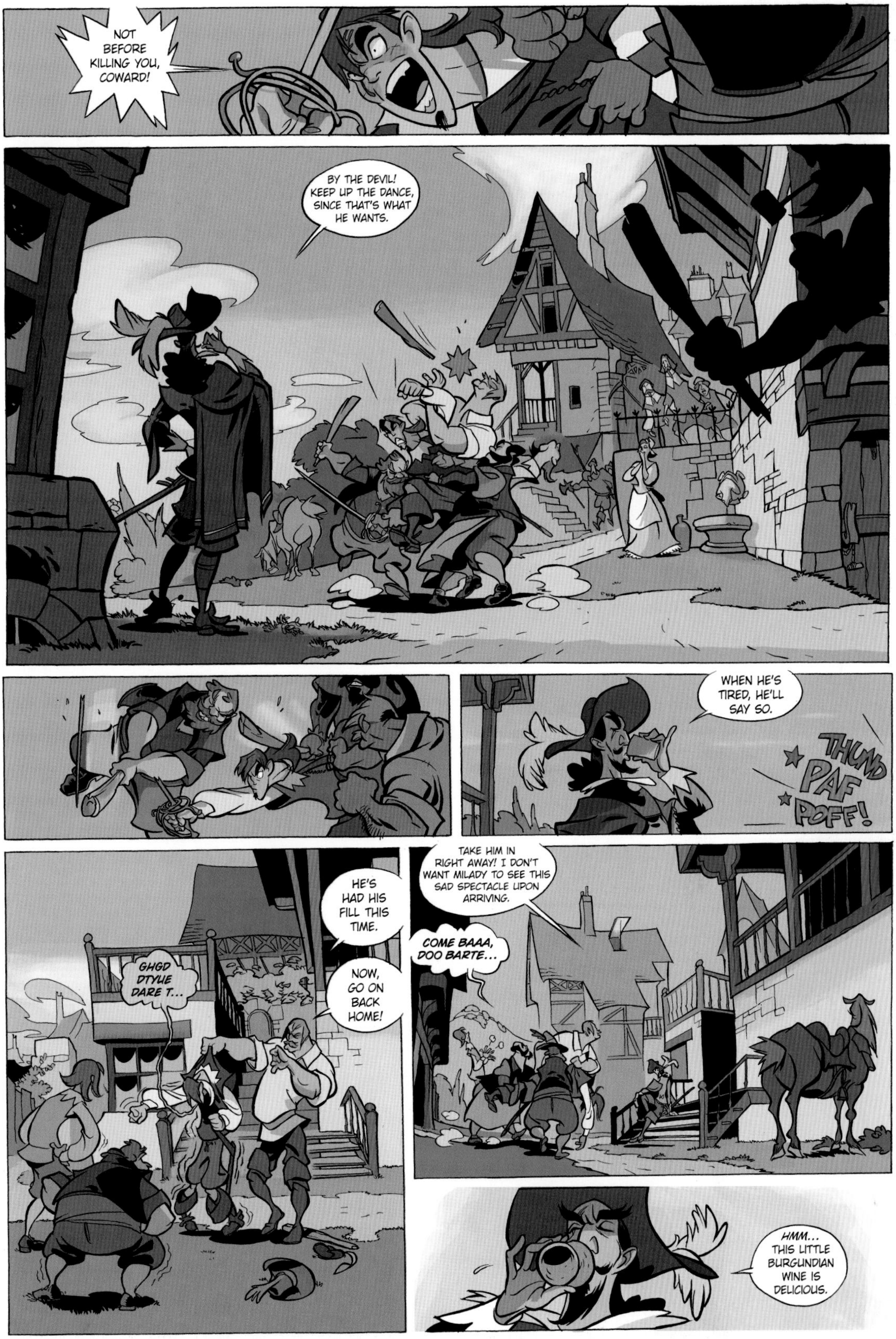
NOT BEFORE KILLING YOU, COWARD!
BY THE DEVIL! KEEP UP THE DANCE, SINCE THAT'S WHAT HE WANTS.
WHEN HE'S TIRED, HE'LL SAY SO.
THUND
PAF
POFF!
HE'S HAD HIS FILL THIS TIME.
NOW, GO ON BACK HOME!
GHGD DTYUE DARE T...
TAKE HIM IN RIGHT AWAY! I DON'T WANT MILADY TO SEE THIS SAD SPECTACLE UPON ARRIVING.
COME BAAA, DOO BARTE...
HMM... THIS LITTLE BURGUNDIAN WINE IS DELICIOUS.

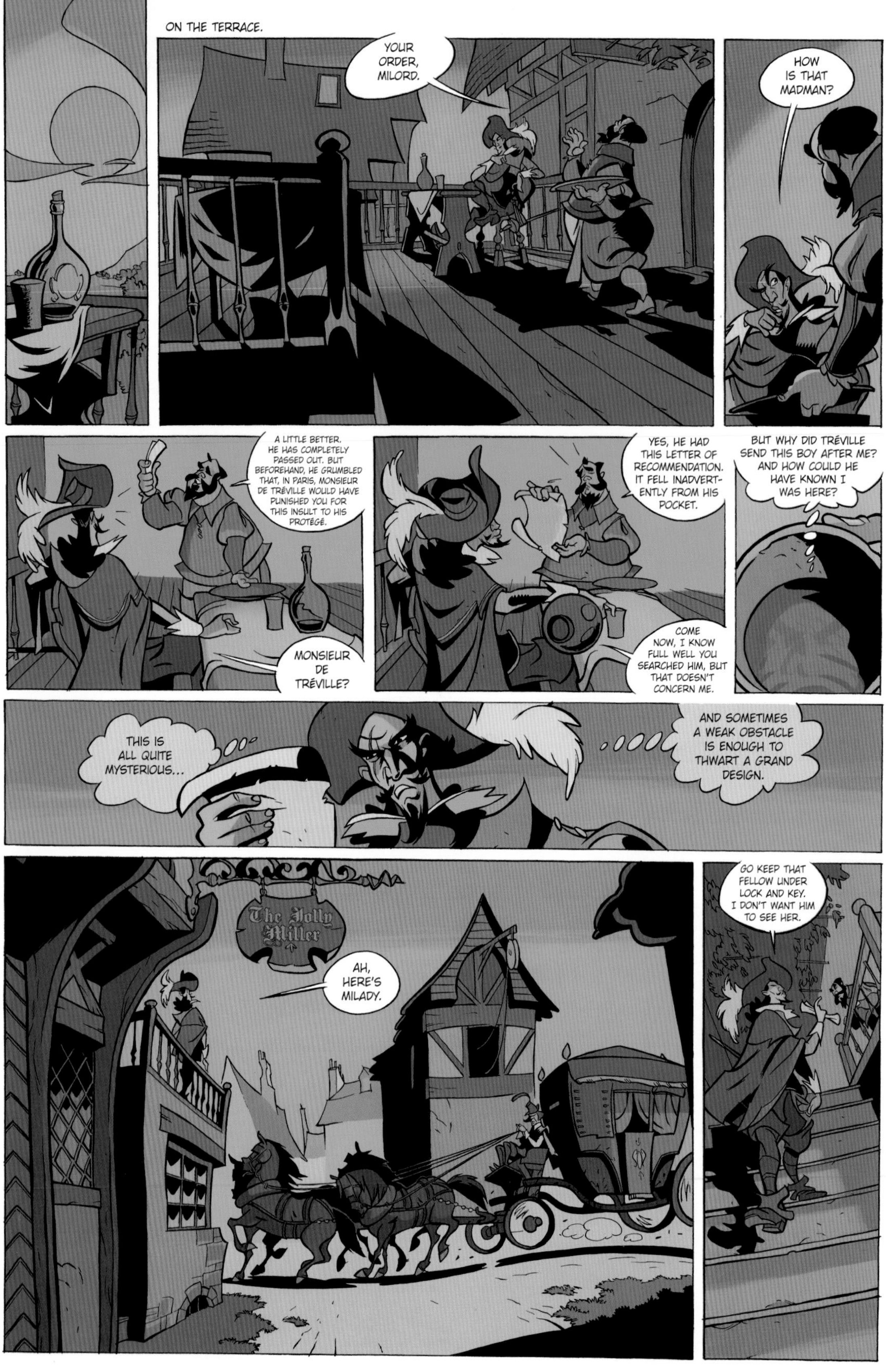
ON THE TERRACE.
YOUR ORDER, MILORD.
HOW IS THAT MADMAN?
A LITTLE BETTER. HE HAS COMPLETELY PASSED OUT. BUT BEFOREHAND, HE GRUMBLED THAT, IN PARIS, MONSIEUR DE TRÉVILLE WOULD HAVE PUNISHED YOU FOR THIS INSULT TO HIS PROTÉGÉ.
MONSIEUR DE TRÉVILLE?
YES, HE HAD THIS LETTER OF RECOMMENDATION. IT FELL INADVERTENTLY FROM HIS POCKET.
COME NOW, I KNOW FULL WELL YOU SEARCHED HIM, BUT THAT DOESN'T CONCERN ME.
BUT WHY DID TRÉVILLE SEND THIS BOY AFTER ME? AND HOW COULD HE HAVE KNOWN I WAS HERE?
THIS IS ALL QUITE MYSTERIOUS...
AND SOMETIMES A WEAK OBSTACLE IS ENOUGH TO THWART A GRAND DESIGN.
The Jolly Miller
AH, HERE'S MILADY.
GO KEEP THAT FELLOW UNDER LOCK AND KEY. I DON'T WANT HIM TO SEE HER.

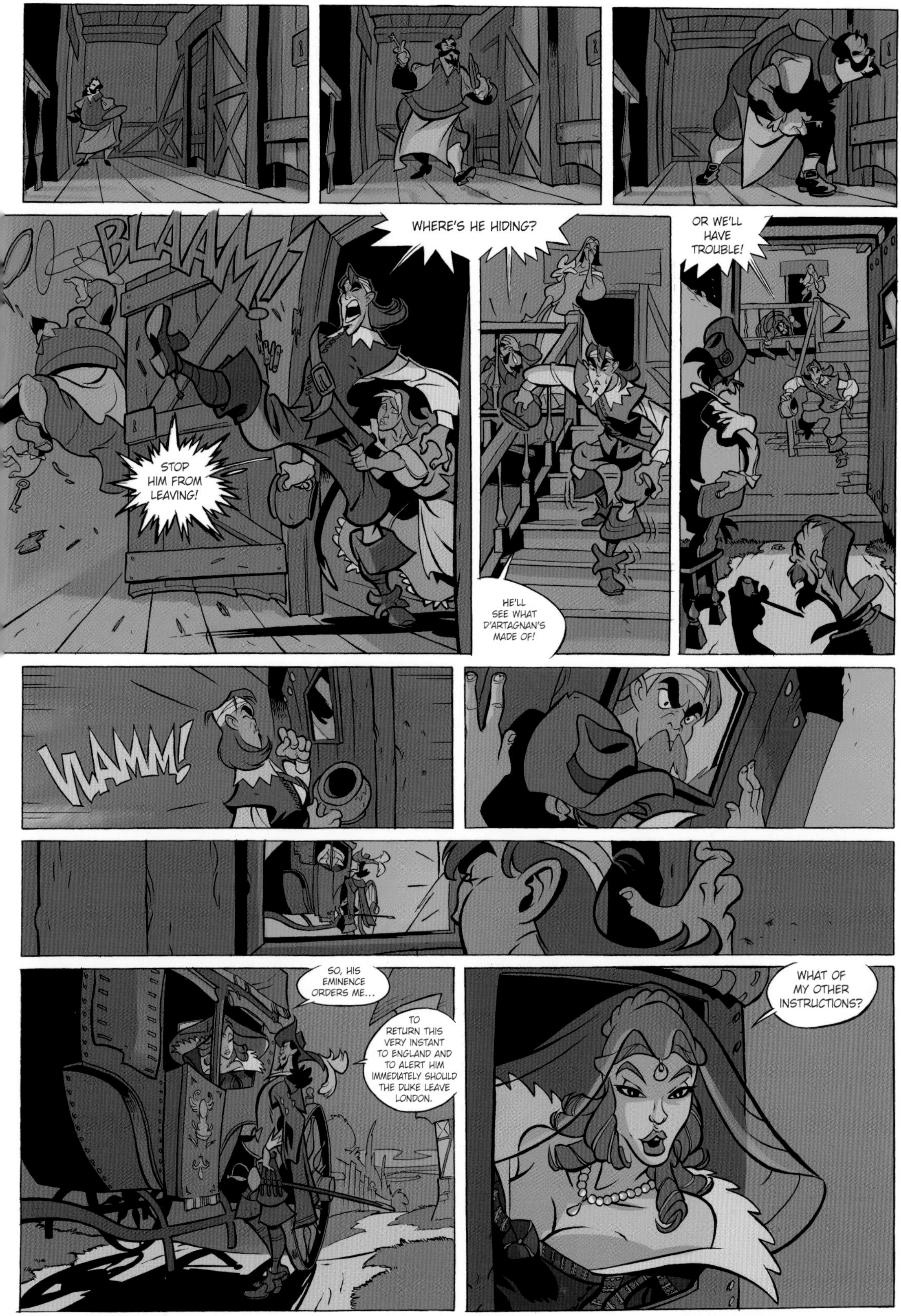
BLAAM!!
WHERE'S HE HIDING?
STOP HIM FROM LEAVING!
HE'LL SEE WHAT D'ARTAGNAN'S MADE OF!
OR WE'LL HAVE TROUBLE!
VLAMM!
SO, HIS EMINENCE ORDERS ME...
TO RETURN THIS VERY INSTANT TO ENGLAND AND TO ALERT HIM IMMEDIATELY SHOULD THE DUKE LEAVE LONDON.
WHAT OF MY OTHER INSTRUCTIONS?

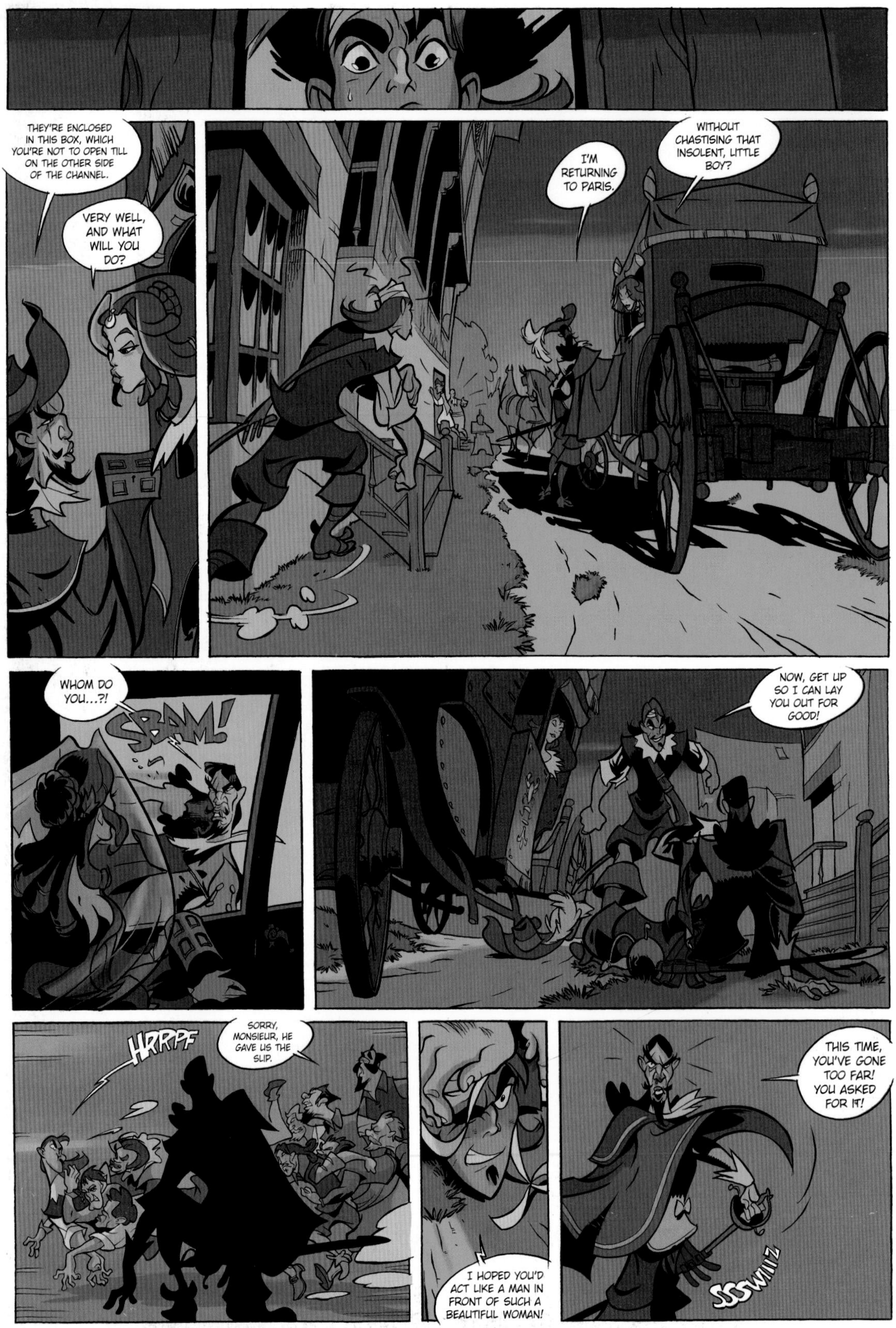
THEY'RE ENCLOSED IN THIS BOX, WHICH YOU'RE NOT TO OPEN TILL ON THE OTHER SIDE OF THE CHANNEL.
VERY WELL, AND WHAT WILL YOU DO?
I'M RETURNING TO PARIS.
WITHOUT CHASTISING THAT INSOLENT, LITTLE BOY?
WHOM DO YOU...?!
SBAM!
NOW, GET UP SO I CAN LAY YOU OUT FOR GOOD!
HRRPF
SORRY, MONSIEUR, HE GAVE US THE SLIP.
I HOPED YOU'D ACT LIKE A MAN IN FRONT OF SUCH A BEAUTIFUL WOMAN!
THIS TIME, YOU'VE GONE TOO FAR! YOU ASKED FOR IT!
SSSWIIIZ

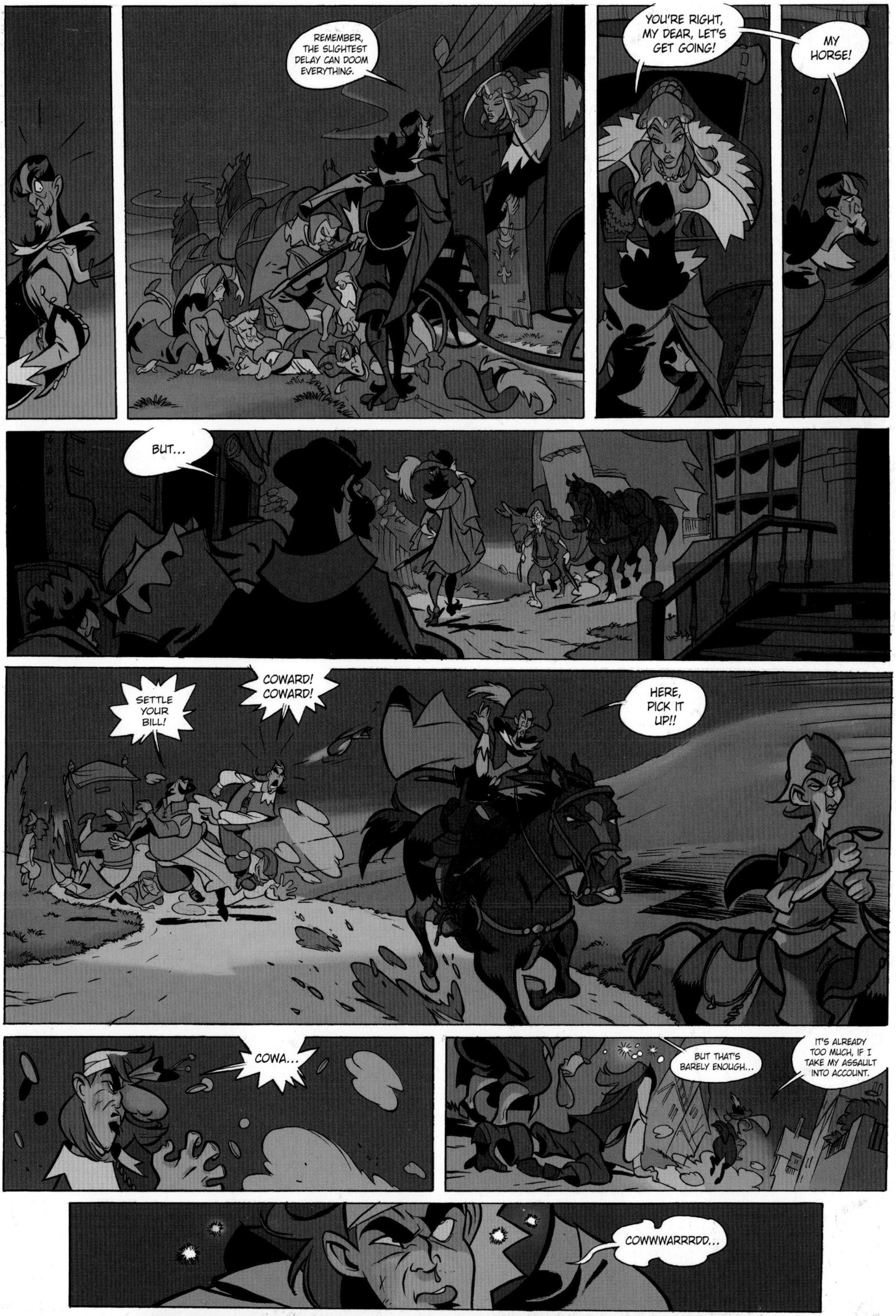
REMEMBER, THE SLIGHTEST DELAY CAN DOOM EVERYTHING.
YOU'RE RIGHT, MY DEAR, LET'S GET GOING!
MY HORSE!
BUT...
SETTLE YOUR BILL!
COWARD! COWARD!
HERE, PICK IT UP!!
COWA...
BUT THAT'S BARELY ENOUGH...
IT'S ALREADY TOO MUCH, IF I TAKE MY ASSAULT INTO ACCOUNT.
COWWWARRRDD...

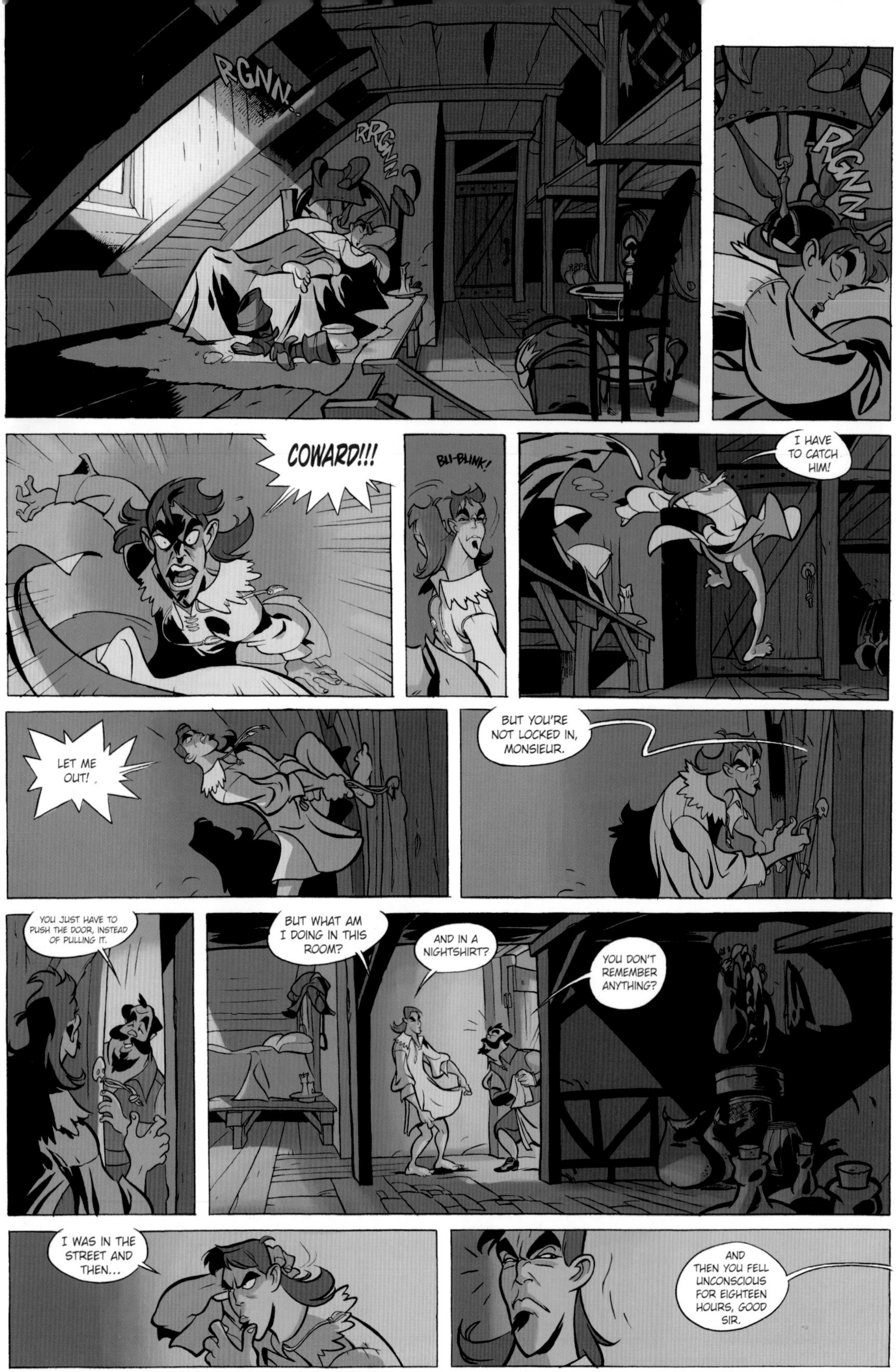
RGNN.
RRGNN
RGNN
COWARD!!!
BLI-BLINK!
I HAVE TO CATCH HIM!
LET ME OUT!
BUT YOU'RE NOT LOCKED IN, MONSIEUR.
YOU JUST HAVE TO PUSH THE DOOR, INSTEAD OF PULLING IT.
BUT WHAT AM I DOING IN THIS ROOM?
AND IN A NIGHTSHIRT?
YOU DON'T REMEMBER ANYTHING?
I WAS IN THE STREET AND THEN...
AND THEN YOU FELL UNCONSCIOUS FOR EIGHTEEN HOURS, GOOD SIR.

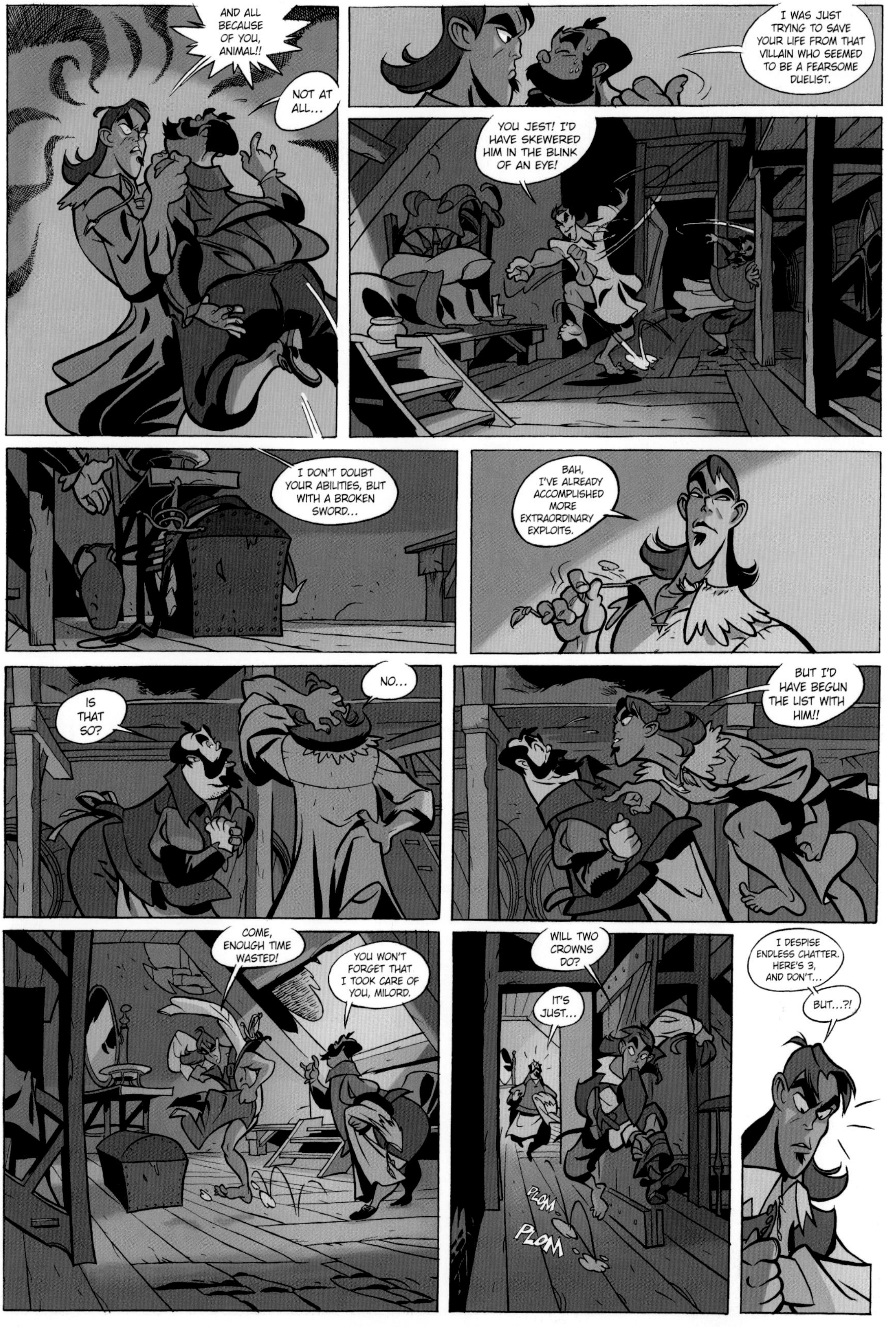
AND ALL BECAUSE OF YOU, ANIMAL!!
NOT AT ALL...
I WAS JUST TRYING TO SAVE YOUR LIFE FROM THAT VILLAIN WHO SEEMED TO BE A FEARSOME DUELIST.
YOU JEST! I'D HAVE SKEWERED HIM IN THE BLINK OF AN EYE!
I DON'T DOUBT YOUR ABILITIES, BUT WITH A BROKEN SWORD...
BAH, I'VE ALREADY ACCOMPLISHED MORE EXTRAORDINARY EXPLOITS.
IS THAT SO?
NO...
BUT I'D HAVE BEGUN THE LIST WITH HIM!!
COME, ENOUGH TIME WASTED!
YOU WON'T FORGET THAT I TOOK CARE OF YOU, MILORD.
WILL TWO CROWNS DO?
IT'S JUST...
PLOM
PLOM
I DESPISE ENDLESS CHATTER. HERE'S 3, AND DON'T...
BUT...?!

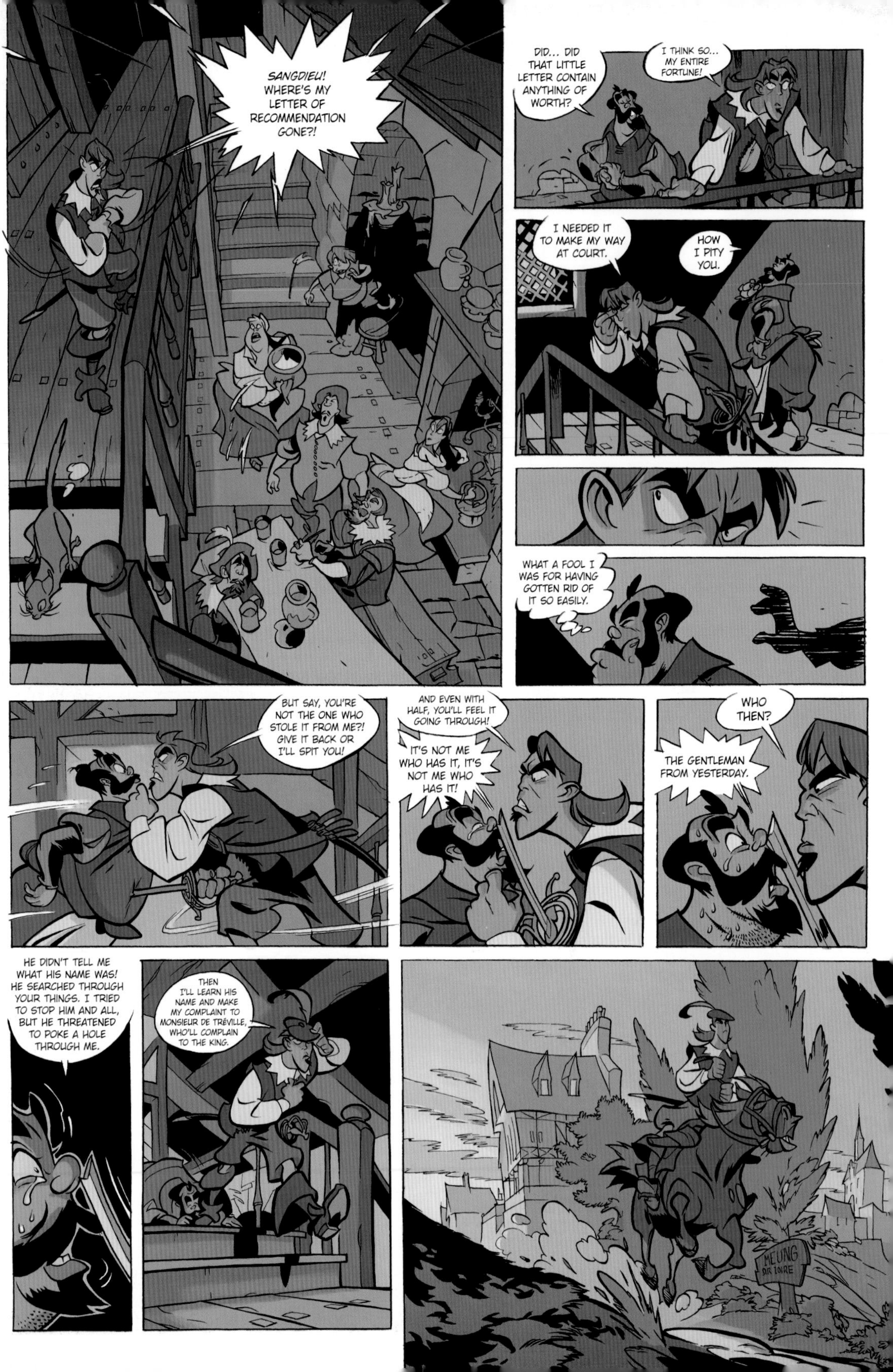
SANGDIEU! WHERE'S MY LETTER OF RECOMMENDATION GONE?!
DID... DID THAT LITTLE LETTER CONTAIN ANYTHING OF WORTH?
I THINK SO... MY ENTIRE FORTUNE!
I NEEDED IT TO MAKE MY WAY AT COURT.
HOW I PITY YOU.
WHAT A FOOL I WAS FOR HAVING GOTTEN RID OF IT SO EASILY.
BUT SAY, YOU'RE NOT THE ONE WHO STOLE IT FROM ME?! GIVE IT BACK OR I'LL SPIT YOU!
AND EVEN WITH HALF, YOU'LL FEEL IT GOING THROUGH!
IT'S NOT ME WHO HAS IT, IT'S NOT ME WHO HAS IT!
WHO THEN?
THE GENTLEMAN FROM YESTERDAY.
HE DIDN'T TELL ME WHAT HIS NAME WAS! HE SEARCHED THROUGH YOUR THINGS. I TRIED TO STOP HIM AND ALL, BUT HE THREATENED TO POKE A HOLE THROUGH ME.
THEN I'LL LEARN HIS NAME AND MAKE MY COMPLAINT TO MONSIEUR DE TRÉVILLE, WHO'LL COMPLAIN TO THE KING.
MEUNG SUR LOIRE

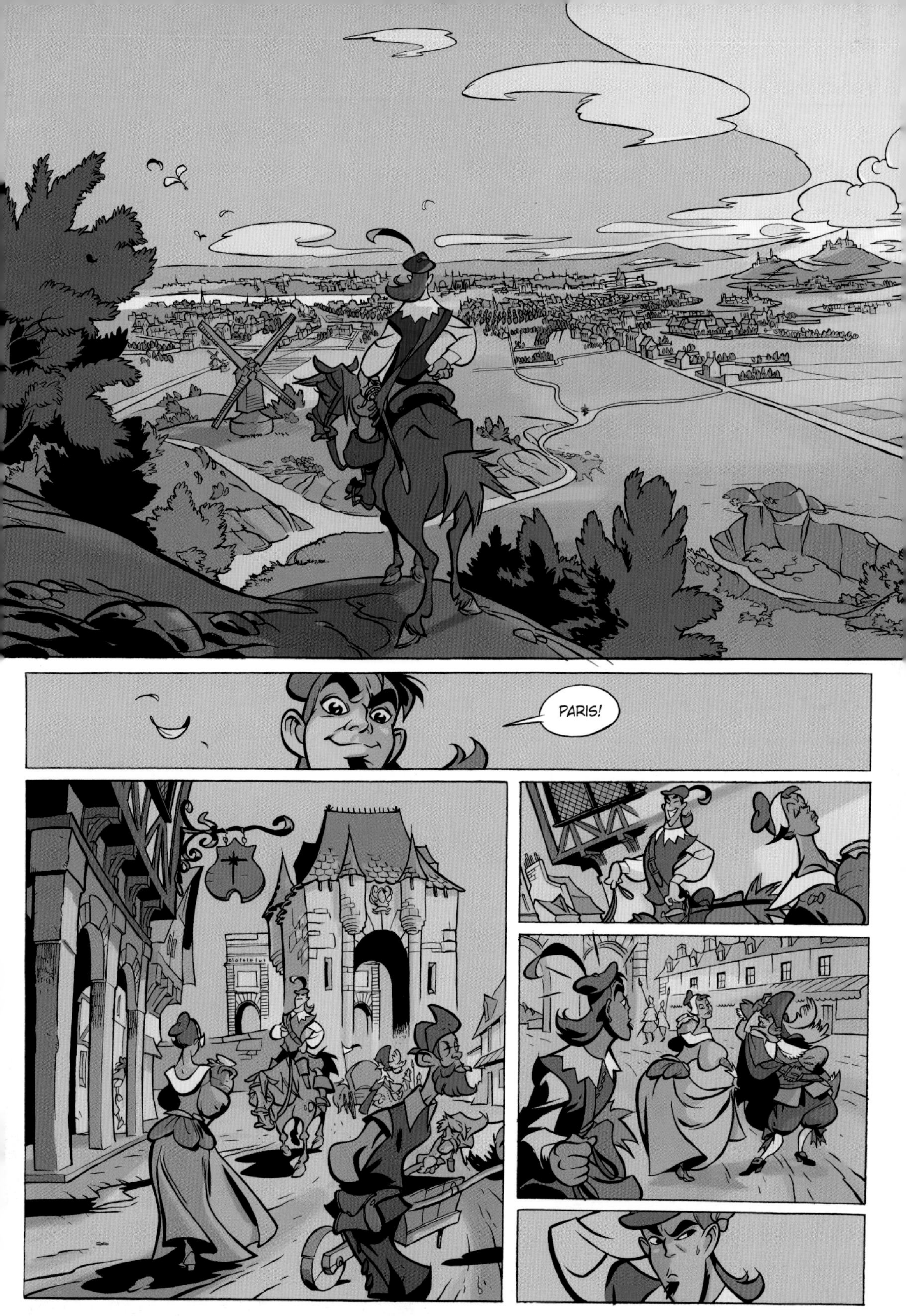
PARIS!

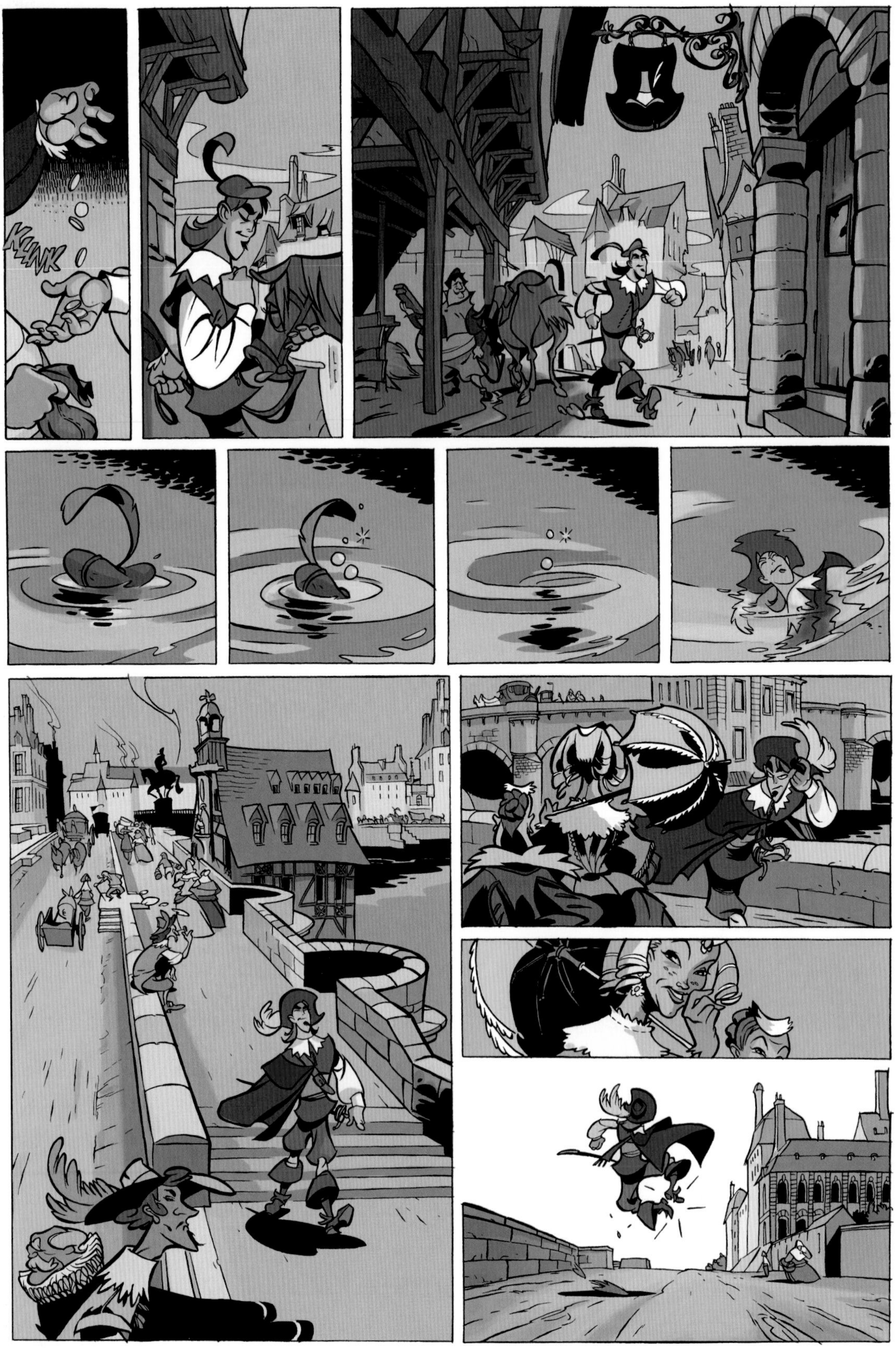
KLINK

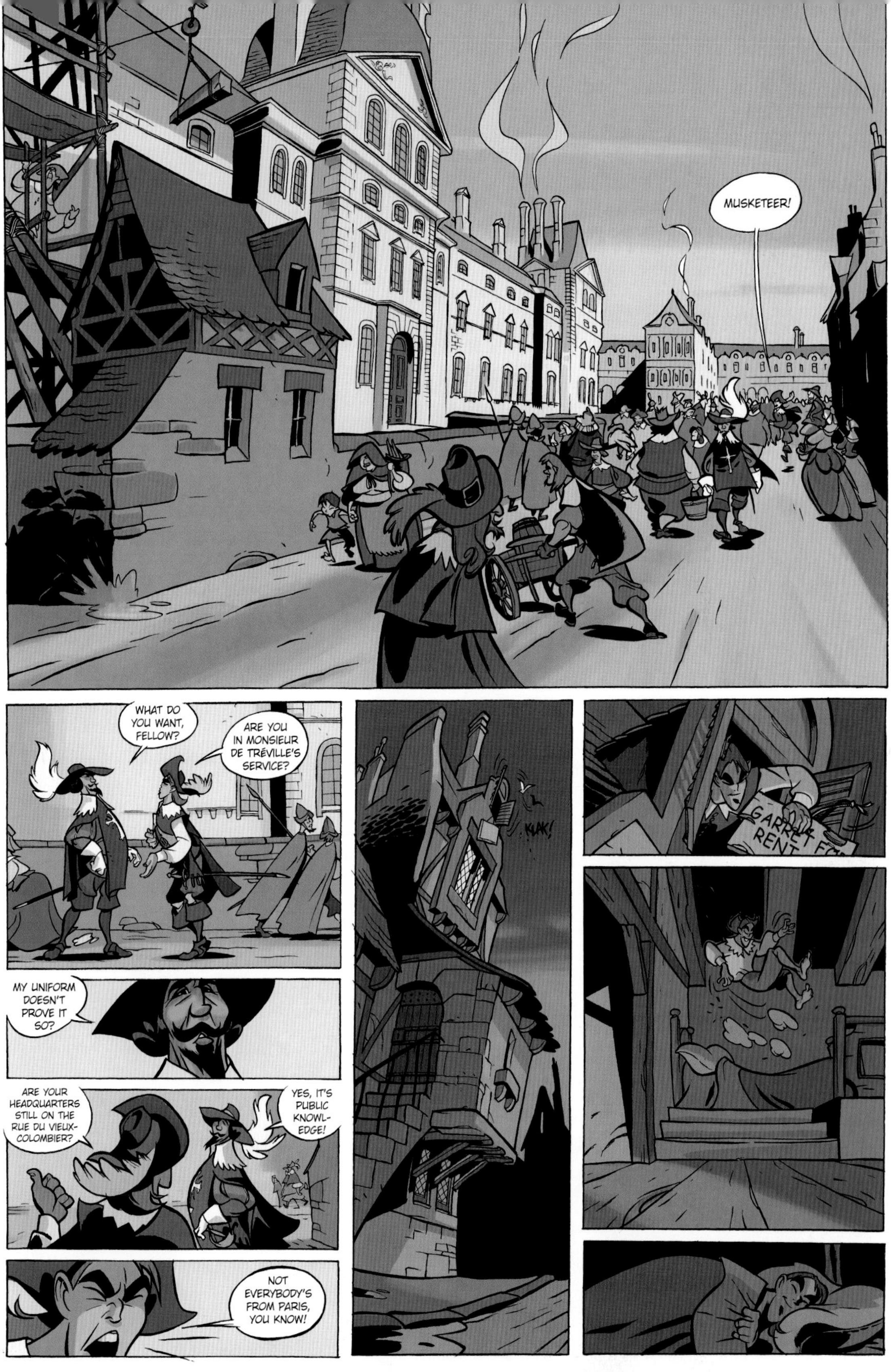
MUSKETEER!
WHAT DO YOU WANT, FELLOW?
ARE YOU IN MONSIEUR DE TRÉVILLE'S SERVICE?
MY UNIFORM DOESN'T PROVE IT SO?
ARE YOUR HEADQUARTERS STILL ON THE RUE DU VIEUX-COLOMBIER?
YES, IT'S PUBLIC KNOWL-EDGE!
NOT EVERYBODY'S FROM PARIS, YOU KNOW!
KLAK!
GARRET FO RENT

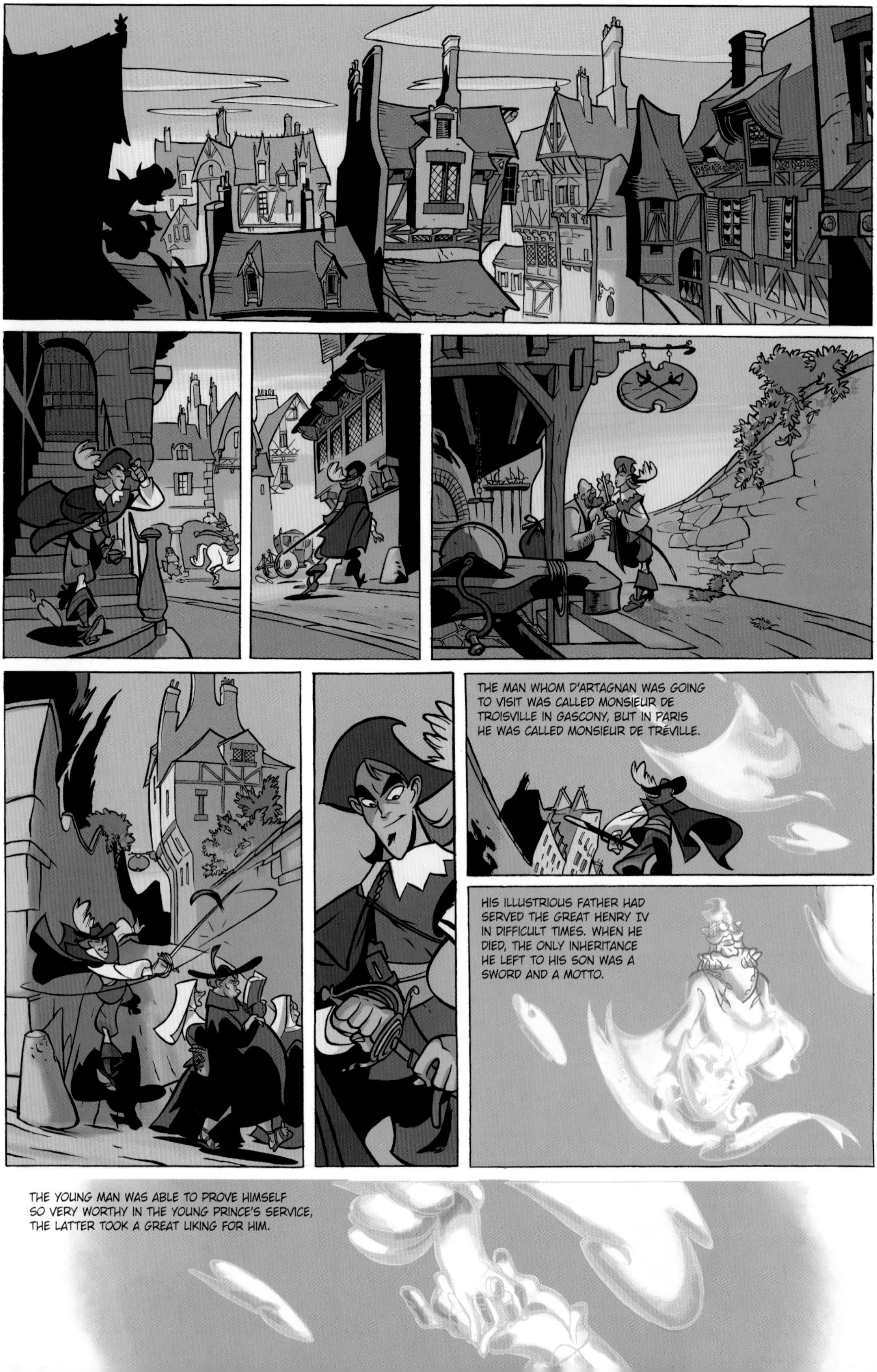

THE MAN WHOM D'ARTAGNAN WAS GOING TO VISIT WAS CALLED MONSIEUR DE TROISVILLE IN GASCONY, BUT IN PARIS HE WAS CALLED MONSIEUR DE TRÉVILLE.
HIS ILLUSTRIOUS FATHER HAD SERVED THE GREAT HENRY IV IN DIFFICULT TIMES. WHEN HE DIED, THE ONLY INHERITANCE HE LEFT TO HIS SON WAS A SWORD AND A MOTTO.
THE YOUNG MAN WAS ABLE TO PROVE HIMSELF SO VERY WORTHY IN THE YOUNG PRINCE'S SERVICE, THE LATTER TOOK A GREAT LIKING FOR HIM.

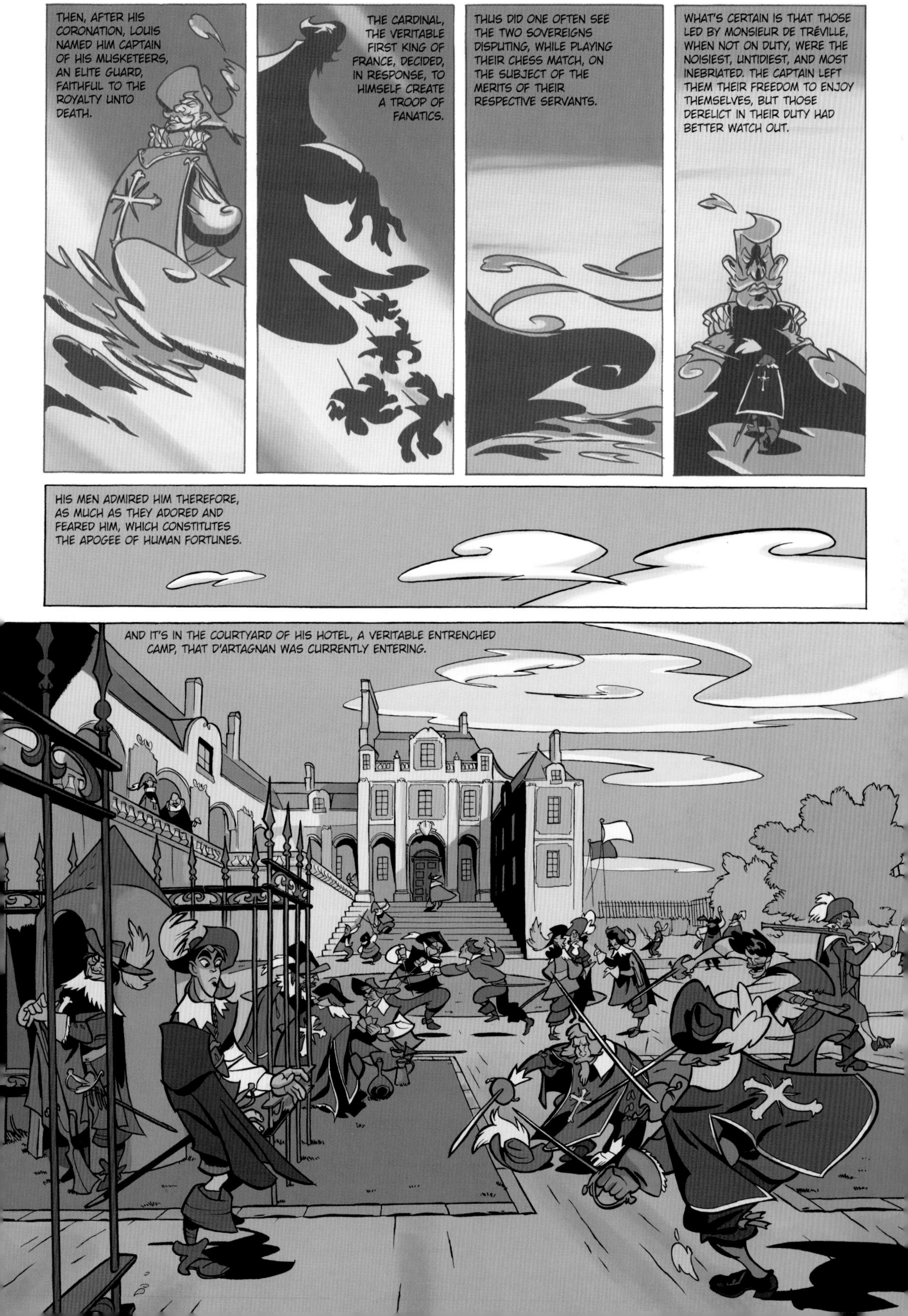
THEN, AFTER HIS CORONATION, LOUIS NAMED HIM CAPTAIN OF HIS MUSKETEERS, AN ELITE GUARD, FAITHFUL TO THE ROYALTY UNTO DEATH.
THE CARDINAL, THE VERITABLE FIRST KING OF FRANCE, DECIDED, IN RESPONSE, TO HIMSELF CREATE A TROOP OF FANATICS.
THUS DID ONE OFTEN SEE THE TWO SOVEREIGNS DISPUTING, WHILE PLAYING THEIR CHESS MATCH, ON THE SUBJECT OF THE MERITS OF THEIR RESPECTIVE SERVANTS.
WHAT'S CERTAIN IS THAT THOSE LED BY MONSIEUR DE TRÉVILLE, WHEN NOT ON DUTY, WERE THE NOISIEST, UNTIDIEST, AND MOST INEBRIATED. THE CAPTAIN LEFT THEM THEIR FREEDOM TO ENJOY THEMSELVES, BUT THOSE DERELICT IN THEIR DUTY HAD BETTER WATCH OUT.
HIS MEN ADMIRED HIM THEREFORE, AS MUCH AS THEY ADORED AND FEARED HIM, WHICH CONSTITUTES THE APOGEE OF HUMAN FORTUNES.
AND IT'S IN THE COURTYARD OF HIS HOTEL, A VERITABLE ENTRENCHED CAMP, THAT D'ARTAGNAN WAS CURRENTLY ENTERING.

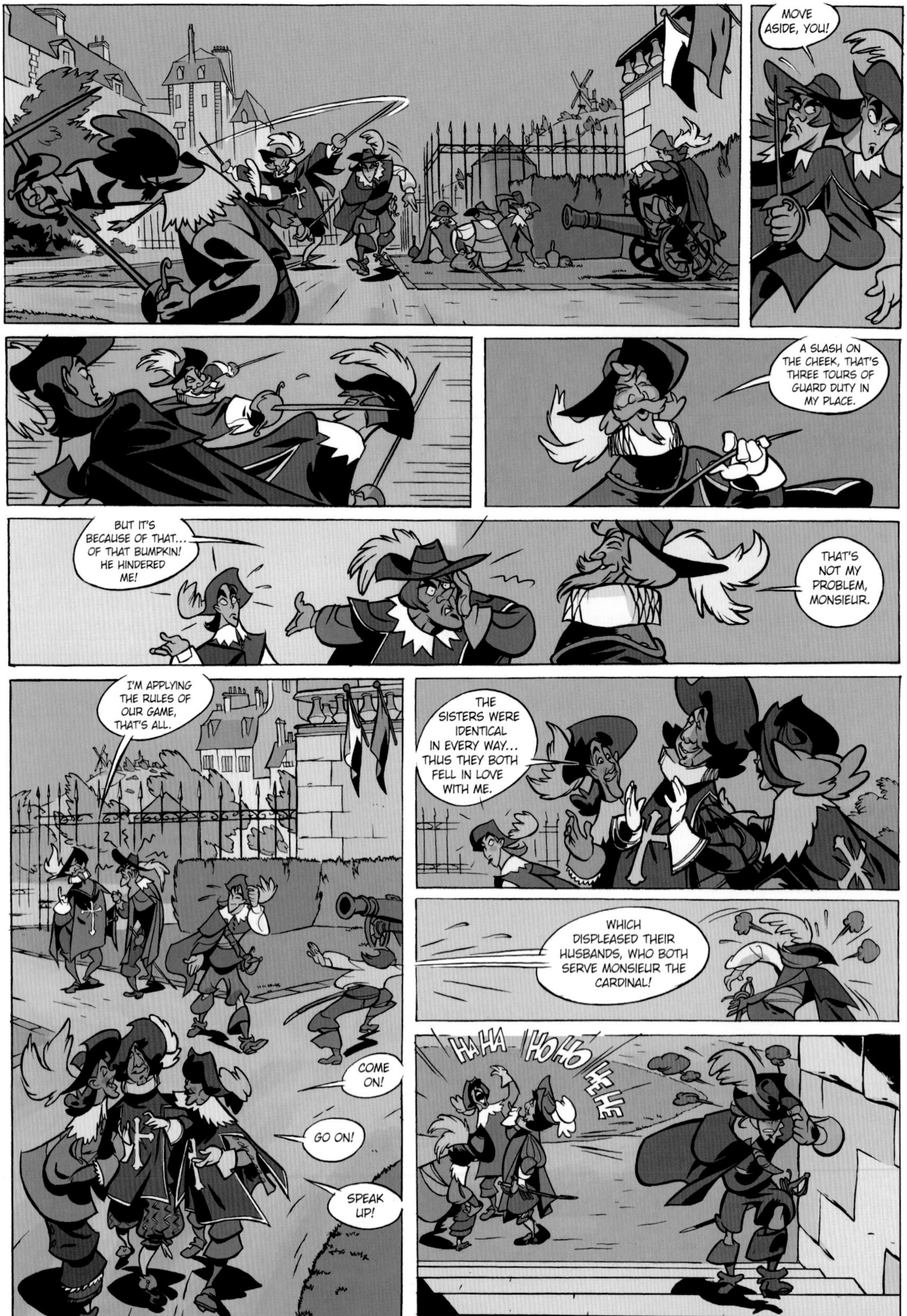
MOVE ASIDE, YOU!
A SLASH ON THE CHEEK, THAT'S THREE TOURS OF GUARD DUTY IN MY PLACE.
BUT IT'S BECAUSE OF THAT... OF THAT BUMPKIN! HE HINDERED ME!
THAT'S NOT MY PROBLEM, MONSIEUR.
I'M APPLYING THE RULES OF OUR GAME, THAT'S ALL.
COME ON!
GO ON!
SPEAK UP!
THE SISTERS WERE IDENTICAL IN EVERY WAY... THUS THEY BOTH FELL IN LOVE WITH ME.
WHICH DISPLEASED THEIR HUSBANDS, WHO BOTH SERVE MONSIEUR THE CARDINAL!
HA HA
HO HO
HE HE

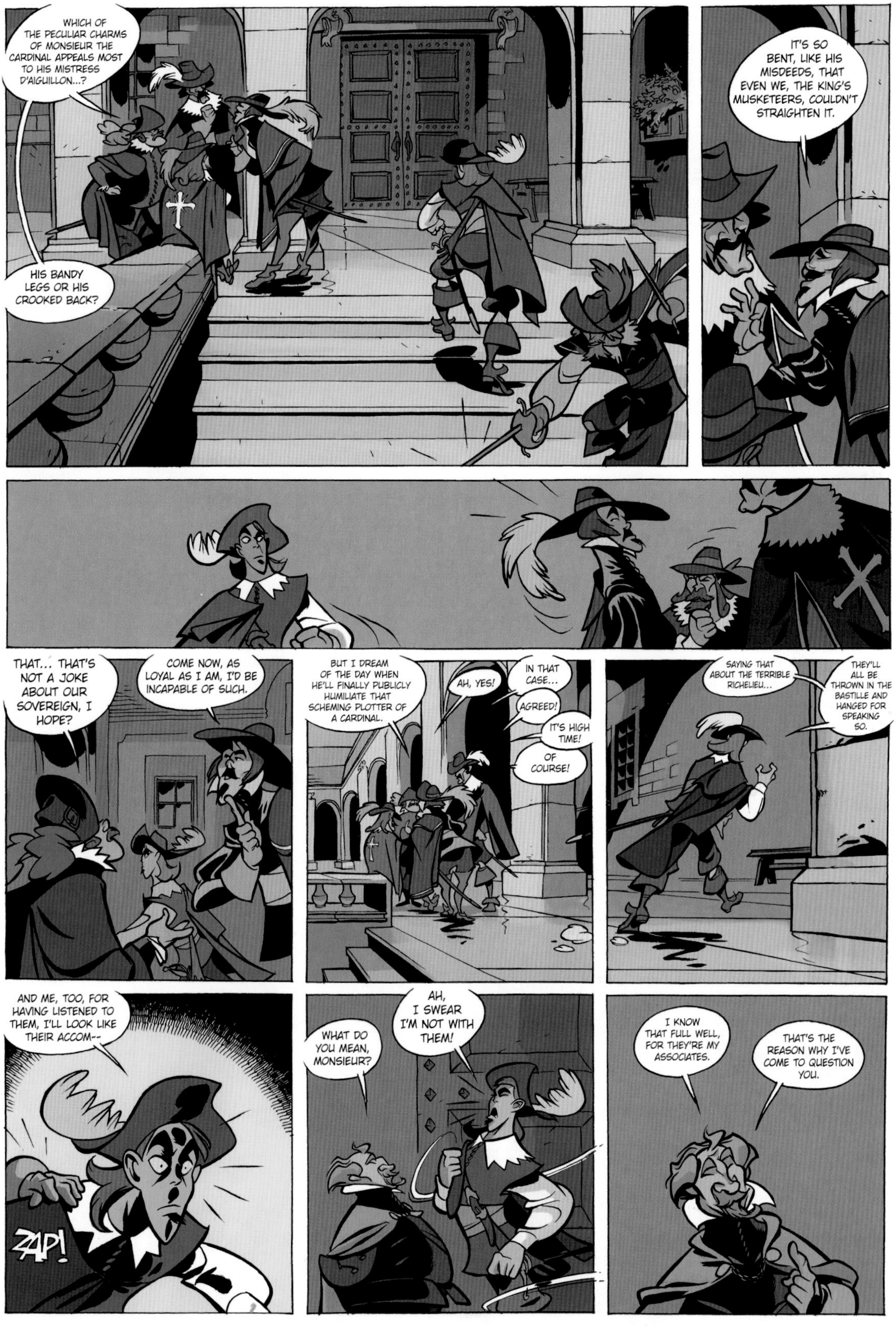
WHICH OF THE PECULIAR CHARMS OF MONSIEUR THE CARDINAL APPEALS MOST TO HIS MISTRESS D'AIGUILLON...?
HIS BANDY LEGS OR HIS CROOKED BACK?
IT'S SO BENT, LIKE HIS MISDEEDS, THAT EVEN WE, THE KING'S MUSKETEERS, COULDN'T STRAIGHTEN IT.
THAT... THAT'S NOT A JOKE ABOUT OUR SOVEREIGN, I HOPE?
COME NOW, AS LOYAL AS I AM, I'D BE INCAPABLE OF SUCH.
BUT I DREAM OF THE DAY WHEN HE'LL FINALLY PUBLICLY HUMILIATE THAT SCHEMING PLOTTER OF A CARDINAL.
AH, YES!
IN THAT CASE...
AGREED!
IT'S HIGH TIME!
OF COURSE!
SAYING THAT ABOUT THE TERRIBLE RICHELIEU...
THEY'LL ALL BE THROWN IN THE BASTILLE AND HANGED FOR SPEAKING SO.
AND ME, TOO, FOR HAVING LISTENED TO THEM, I'LL LOOK LIKE THEIR ACCOM--
ZAP!
WHAT DO YOU MEAN, MONSIEUR?
AH, I SWEAR I'M NOT WITH THEM!
I KNOW THAT FULL WELL, FOR THEY'RE MY ASSOCIATES.
THAT'S THE REASON WHY I'VE COME TO QUESTION YOU.

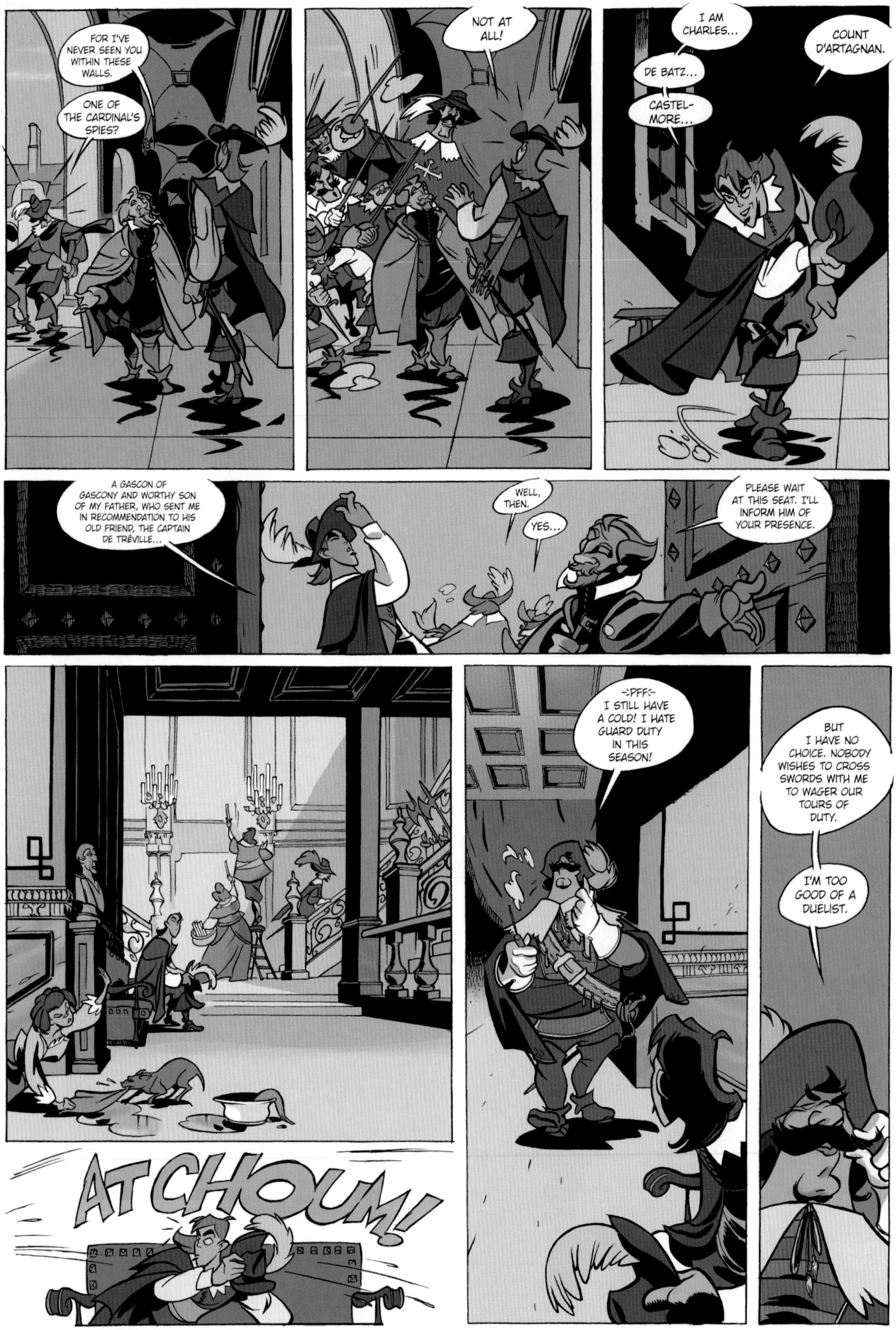
FOR I'VE NEVER SEEN YOU WITHIN THESE WALLS.
ONE OF THE CARDINAL'S SPIES?
NOT AT ALL!
I AM CHARLES...
DE BATZ...
CASTEL-MORE...
COUNT D'ARTAGNAN.
A GASCON OF GASCONY AND WORTHY SON OF MY FATHER, WHO SENT ME IN RECOMMENDATION TO HIS OLD FRIEND, THE CAPTAIN DE TRÉVILLE...
WELL, THEN.
YES...
PLEASE WAIT AT THIS SEAT. I'LL INFORM HIM OF YOUR PRESENCE.
ATCHOUM!
-PFF-
I STILL HAVE A COLD! I HATE GUARD DUTY IN THIS SEASON!
BUT I HAVE NO CHOICE. NOBODY WISHES TO CROSS SWORDS WITH ME TO WAGER OUR TOURS OF DUTY.
I'M TOO GOOD OF A DUELIST.

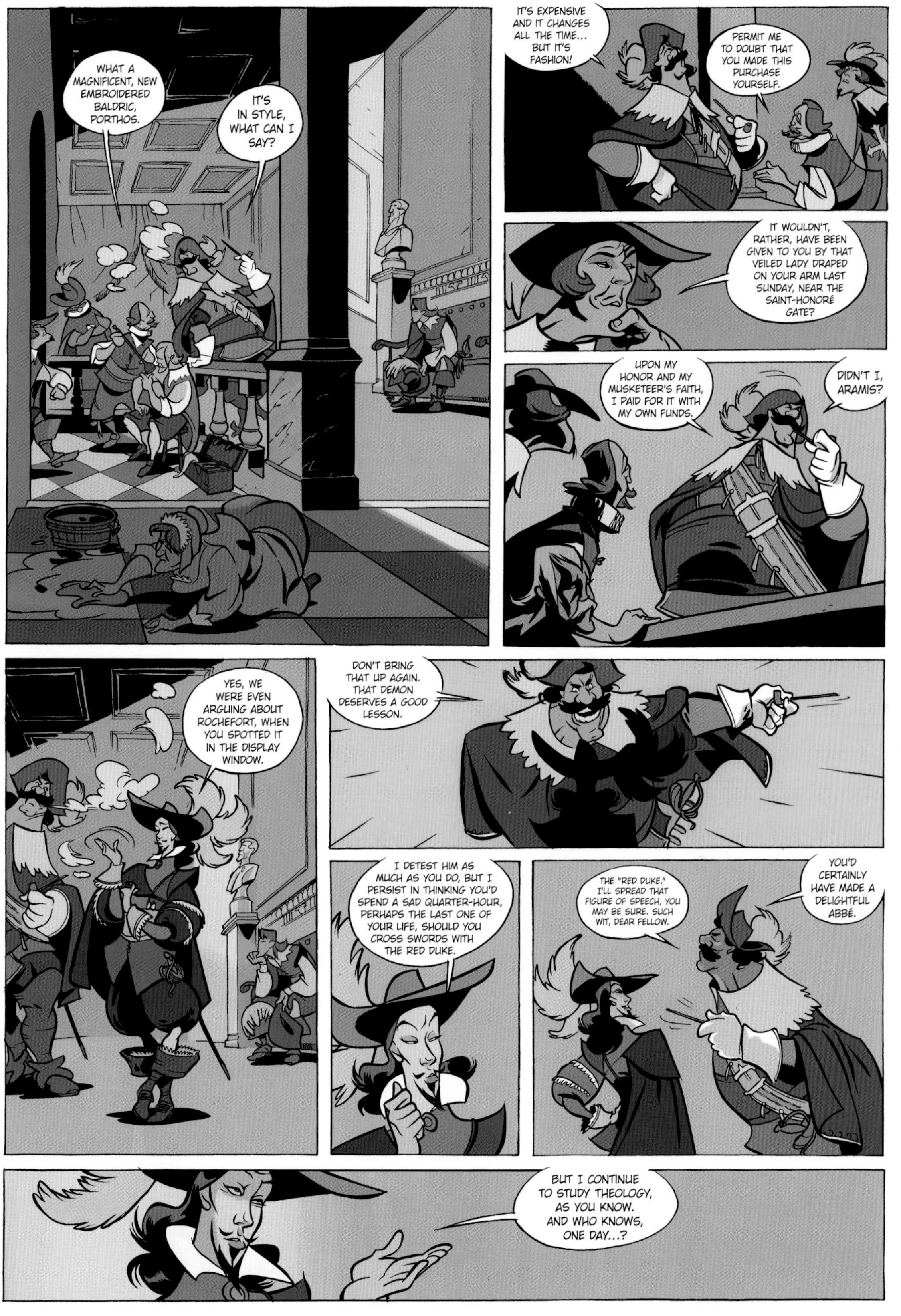
WHAT A MAGNIFICENT, NEW EMBROIDERED BALDRIC, PORTHOS.
IT'S IN STYLE, WHAT CAN I SAY?
IT'S EXPENSIVE AND IT CHANGES ALL THE TIME... BUT IT'S FASHION!
PERMIT ME TO DOUBT THAT YOU MADE THIS PURCHASE YOURSELF.
IT WOULDN'T, RATHER, HAVE BEEN GIVEN TO YOU BY THAT VEILED LADY DRAPED ON YOUR ARM LAST SUNDAY, NEAR THE SAINT-HONORÉ GATE?
UPON MY HONOR AND MY MUSKETEER'S FAITH, I PAID FOR IT WITH MY OWN FUNDS.
DIDN'T I, ARAMIS?
YES, WE WERE EVEN ARGUING ABOUT ROCHEFORT, WHEN YOU SPOTTED IT IN THE DISPLAY WINDOW.
DON'T BRING THAT UP AGAIN. THAT DEMON DESERVES A GOOD LESSON.
I DETEST HIM AS MUCH AS YOU DO, BUT I PERSIST IN THINKING YOU'D SPEND A SAD QUARTER-HOUR, PERHAPS THE LAST ONE OF YOUR LIFE, SHOULD YOU CROSS SWORDS WITH THE RED DUKE.
THE "RED DUKE." I'LL SPREAD THAT FIGURE OF SPEECH, YOU MAY BE SURE. SUCH WIT, DEAR FELLOW.
YOU'D CERTAINLY HAVE MADE A DELIGHTFUL ABBÉ.
BUT I CONTINUE TO STUDY THEOLOGY, AS YOU KNOW. AND WHO KNOWS, ONE DAY...?

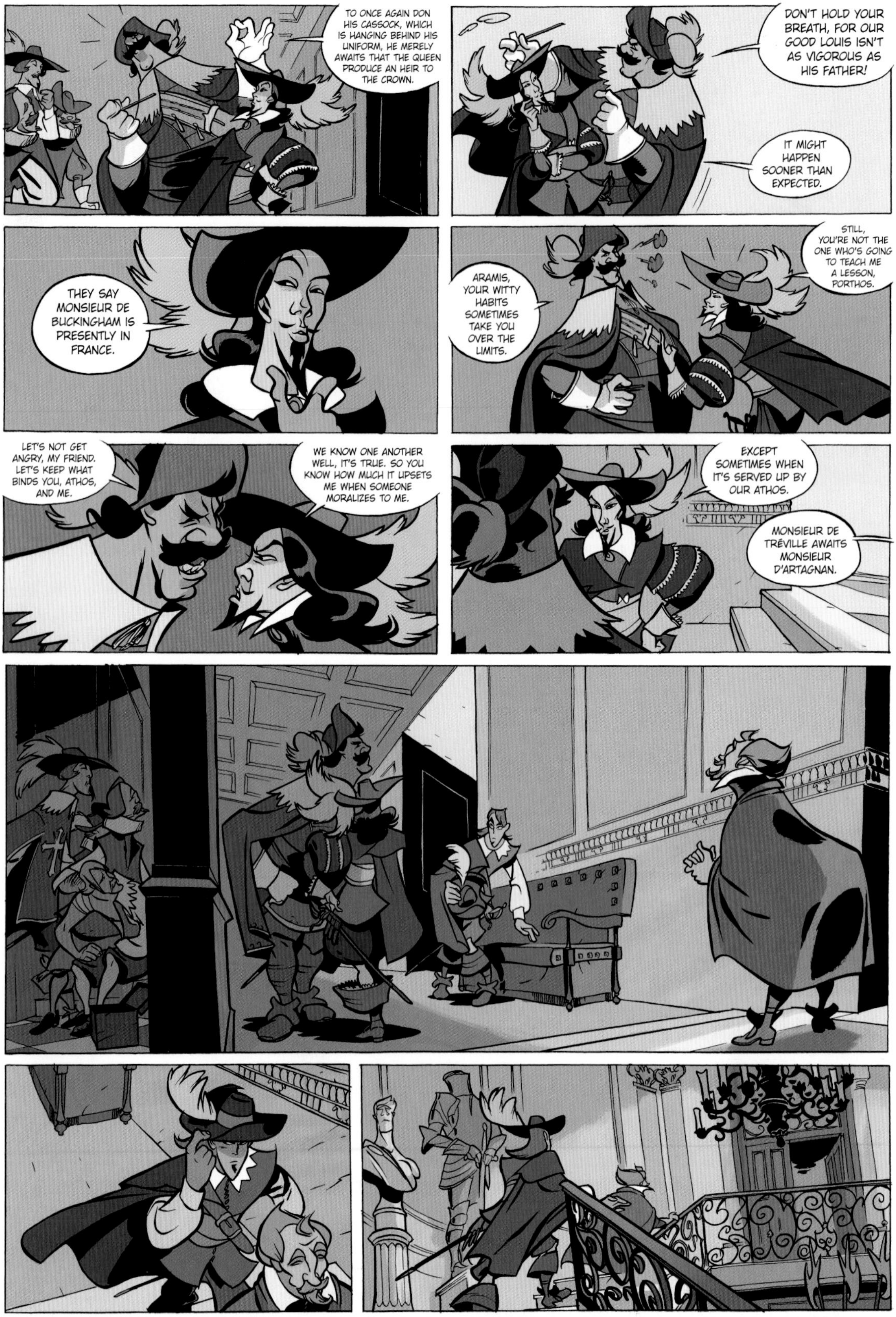

TO ONCE AGAIN DON HIS CASSOCK, WHICH IS HANGING BEHIND HIS UNIFORM, HE MERELY AWAITS THAT THE QUEEN PRODUCE AN HEIR TO THE CROWN.
DON'T HOLD YOUR BREATH, FOR OUR GOOD LOUIS ISN'T AS VIGOROUS AS HIS FATHER!
IT MIGHT HAPPEN SOONER THAN EXPECTED.
THEY SAY MONSIEUR DE BUCKINGHAM IS PRESENTLY IN FRANCE.
ARAMIS, YOUR WITTY HABITS SOMETIMES TAKE YOU OVER THE LIMITS.
STILL, YOU'RE NOT THE ONE WHO'S GOING TO TEACH ME A LESSON, PORTHOS.
LET'S NOT GET ANGRY, MY FRIEND. LET'S KEEP WHAT BINDS YOU, ATHOS, AND ME.
WE KNOW ONE ANOTHER WELL, IT'S TRUE. SO YOU KNOW HOW MUCH IT UPSETS ME WHEN SOMEONE MORALIZES TO ME.
EXCEPT SOMETIMES WHEN IT'S SERVED UP BY OUR ATHOS.
MONSIEUR DE TRÉVILLE AWAITS MONSIEUR D'ARTAGNAN.

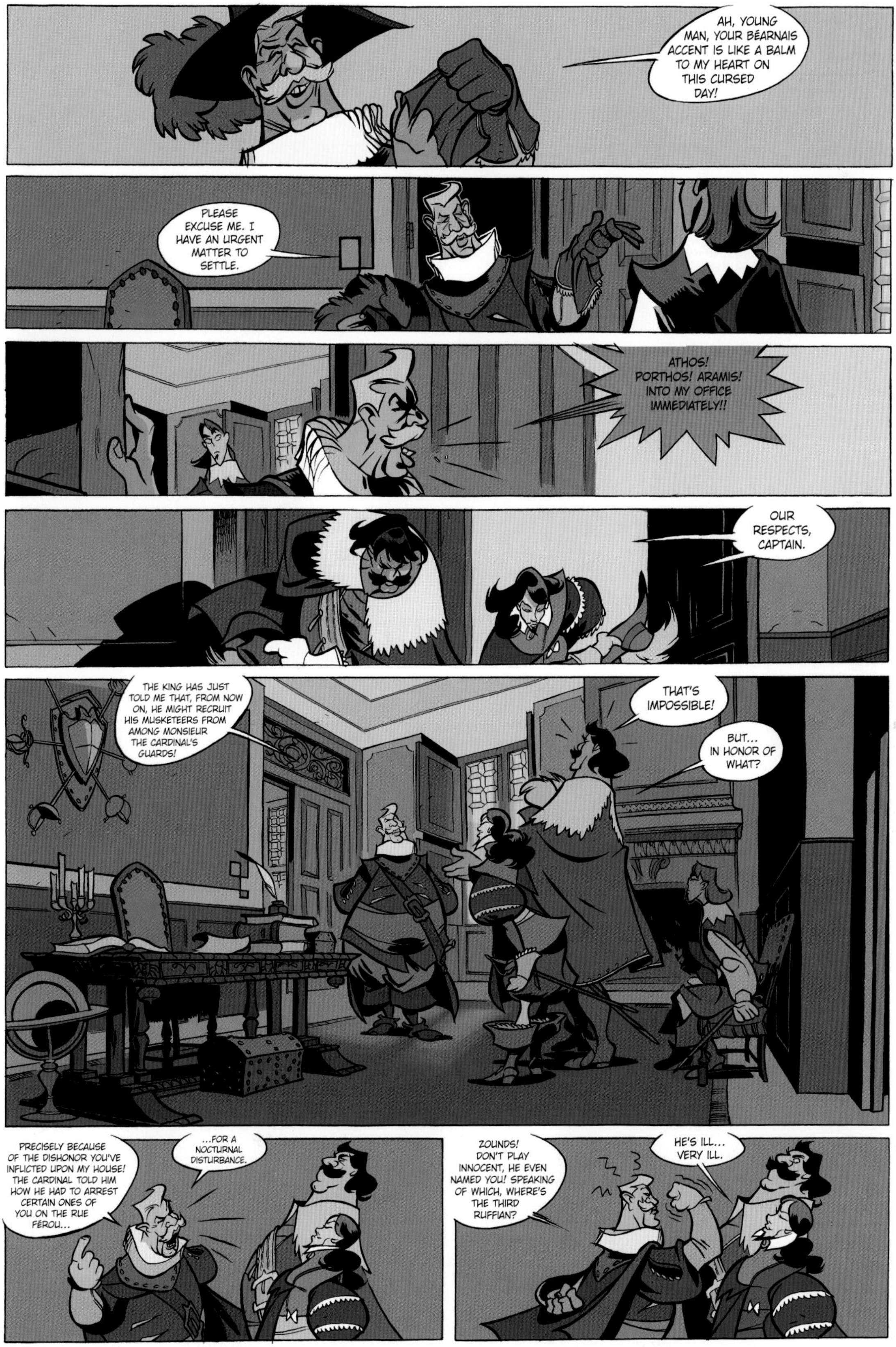
AH, YOUNG MAN, YOUR BÉARNAIS ACCENT IS LIKE A BALM TO MY HEART ON THIS CURSED DAY!
PLEASE EXCUSE ME. I HAVE AN URGENT MATTER TO SETTLE.
ATHOS! PORTHOS! ARAMIS! INTO MY OFFICE IMMEDIATELY!!
OUR RESPECTS, CAPTAIN.
THE KING HAS JUST TOLD ME THAT, FROM NOW ON, HE MIGHT RECRUIT HIS MUSKETEERS FROM AMONG MONSIEUR THE CARDINAL'S GUARDS!
THAT'S IMPOSSIBLE!
BUT... IN HONOR OF WHAT?
PRECISELY BECAUSE OF THE DISHONOR YOU'VE INFLICTED UPON MY HOUSE! THE CARDINAL TOLD HIM HOW HE HAD TO ARREST CERTAIN ONES OF YOU ON THE RUE FÉROU...
...FOR A NOCTURNAL DISTURBANCE.
ZOUNDS! DON'T PLAY INNOCENT, HE EVEN NAMED YOU! SPEAKING OF WHICH, WHERE'S THE THIRD RUFFIAN?
HE'S ILL... VERY ILL.

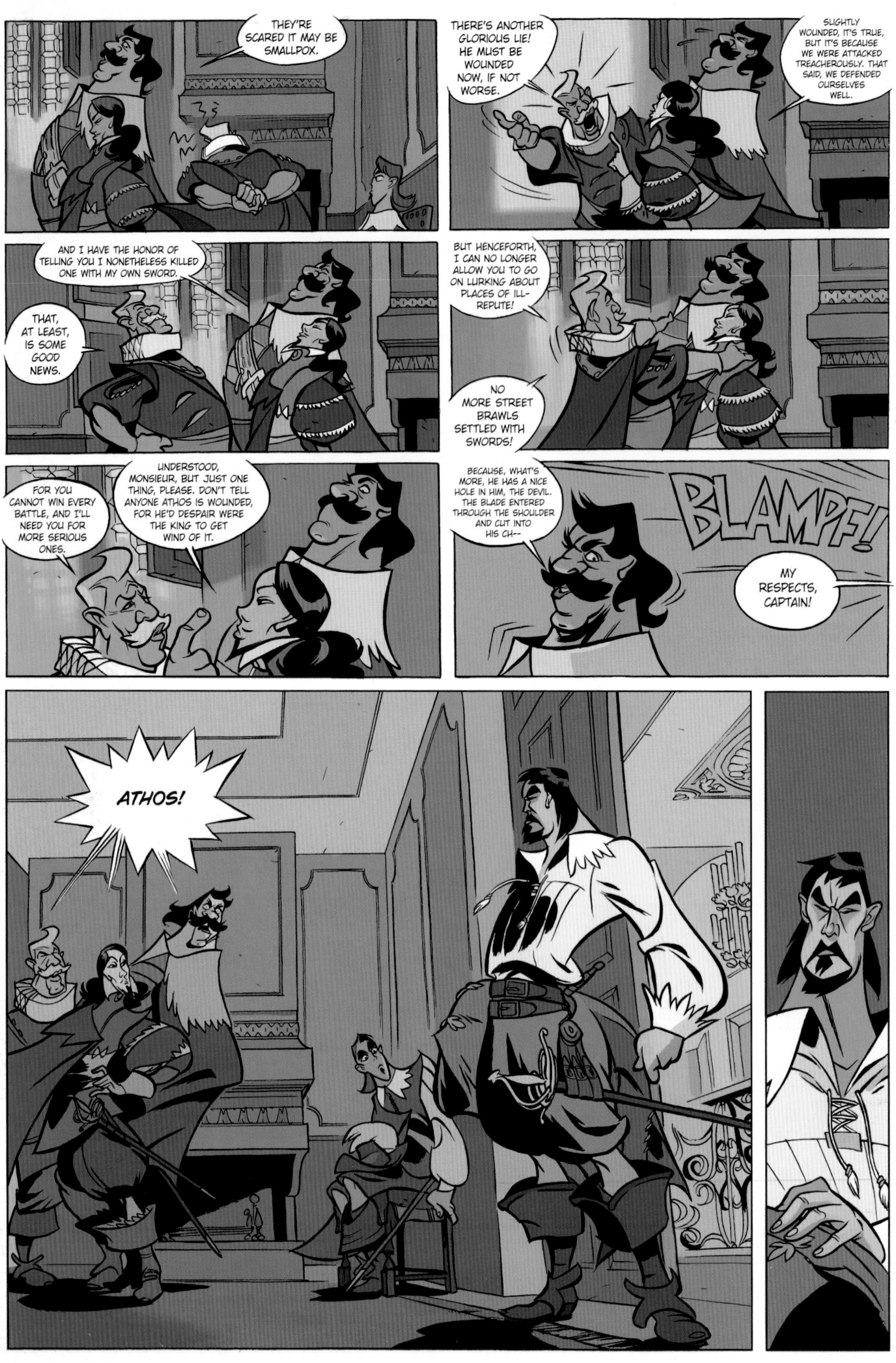
THEY'RE SCARED IT MAY BE SMALLPOX.
THERE'S ANOTHER GLORIOUS LIE! HE MUST BE WOUNDED NOW, IF NOT WORSE.
SLIGHTLY WOUNDED, IT'S TRUE, BUT IT'S BECAUSE WE WERE ATTACKED TREACHEROUSLY. THAT SAID, WE DEFENDED OURSELVES WELL.
AND I HAVE THE HONOR OF TELLING YOU I NONETHELESS KILLED ONE WITH MY OWN SWORD.
THAT, AT LEAST, IS SOME GOOD NEWS.
BUT HENCEFORTH, I CAN NO LONGER ALLOW YOU TO GO ON LURKING ABOUT PLACES OF ILL-REPUTE!
NO MORE STREET BRAWLS SETTLED WITH SWORDS!
FOR YOU CANNOT WIN EVERY BATTLE, AND I'LL NEED YOU FOR MORE SERIOUS ONES.
UNDERSTOOD, MONSIEUR, BUT JUST ONE THING, PLEASE. DON'T TELL ANYONE ATHOS IS WOUNDED, FOR HE'D DESPAIR WERE THE KING TO GET WIND OF IT.
BECAUSE, WHAT'S MORE, HE HAS A NICE HOLE IN HIM, THE DEVIL. THE BLADE ENTERED THROUGH THE SHOULDER AND CUT INTO HIS CH--
BLAMPF!
MY RESPECTS, CAPTAIN!
ATHOS!

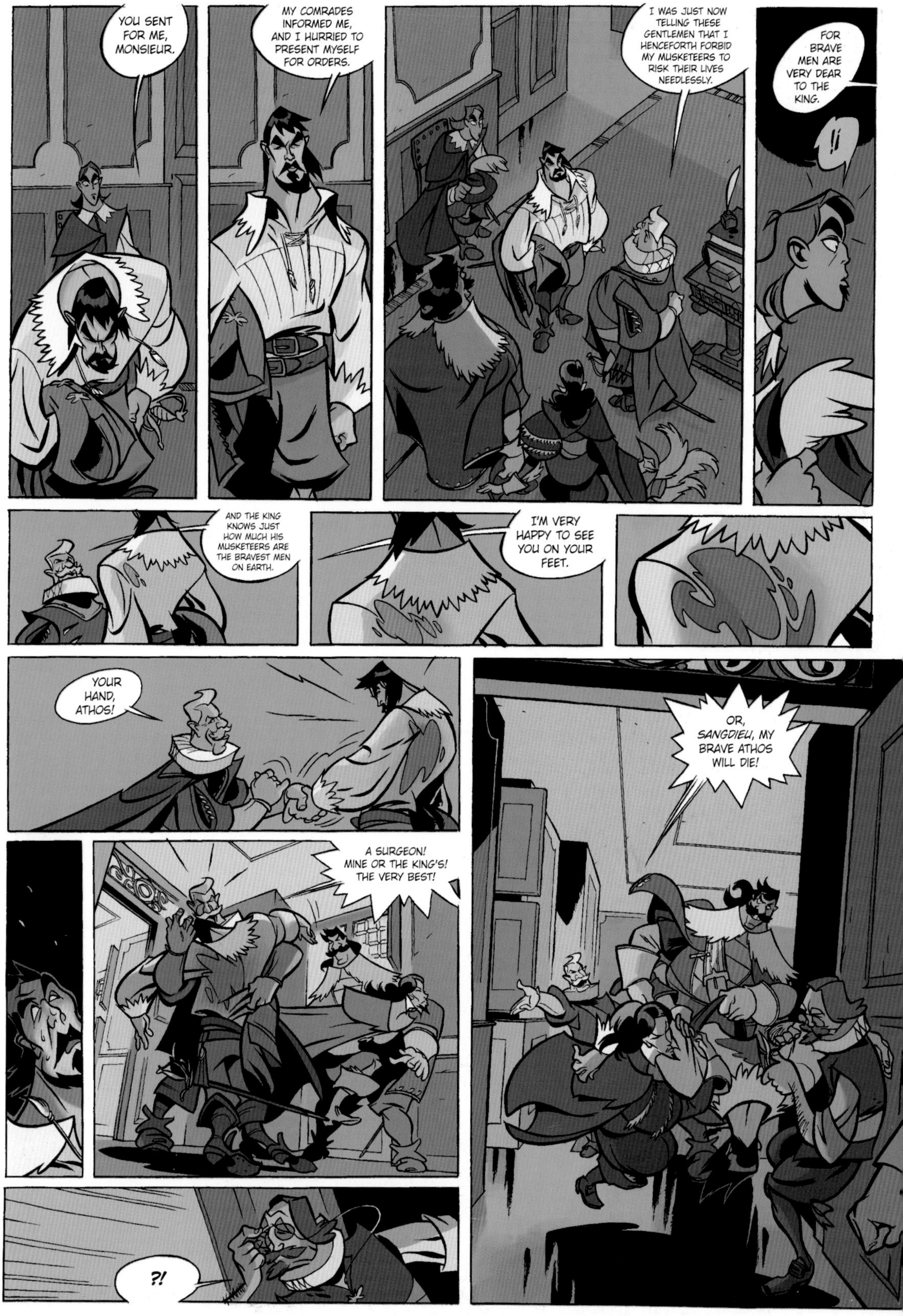
YOU SENT FOR ME, MONSIEUR.
MY COMRADES INFORMED ME, AND I HURRIED TO PRESENT MYSELF FOR ORDERS.
I WAS JUST NOW TELLING THESE GENTLEMEN THAT I HENCEFORTH FORBID MY MUSKETEERS TO RISK THEIR LIVES NEEDLESSLY.
FOR BRAVE MEN ARE VERY DEAR TO THE KING.
!!
AND THE KING KNOWS JUST HOW MUCH HIS MUSKETEERS ARE THE BRAVEST MEN ON EARTH.
I'M VERY HAPPY TO SEE YOU ON YOUR FEET.
YOUR HAND, ATHOS!
OR, SANGDIEU, MY BRAVE ATHOS WILL DIE!
A SURGEON! MINE OR THE KING'S! THE VERY BEST!
?!

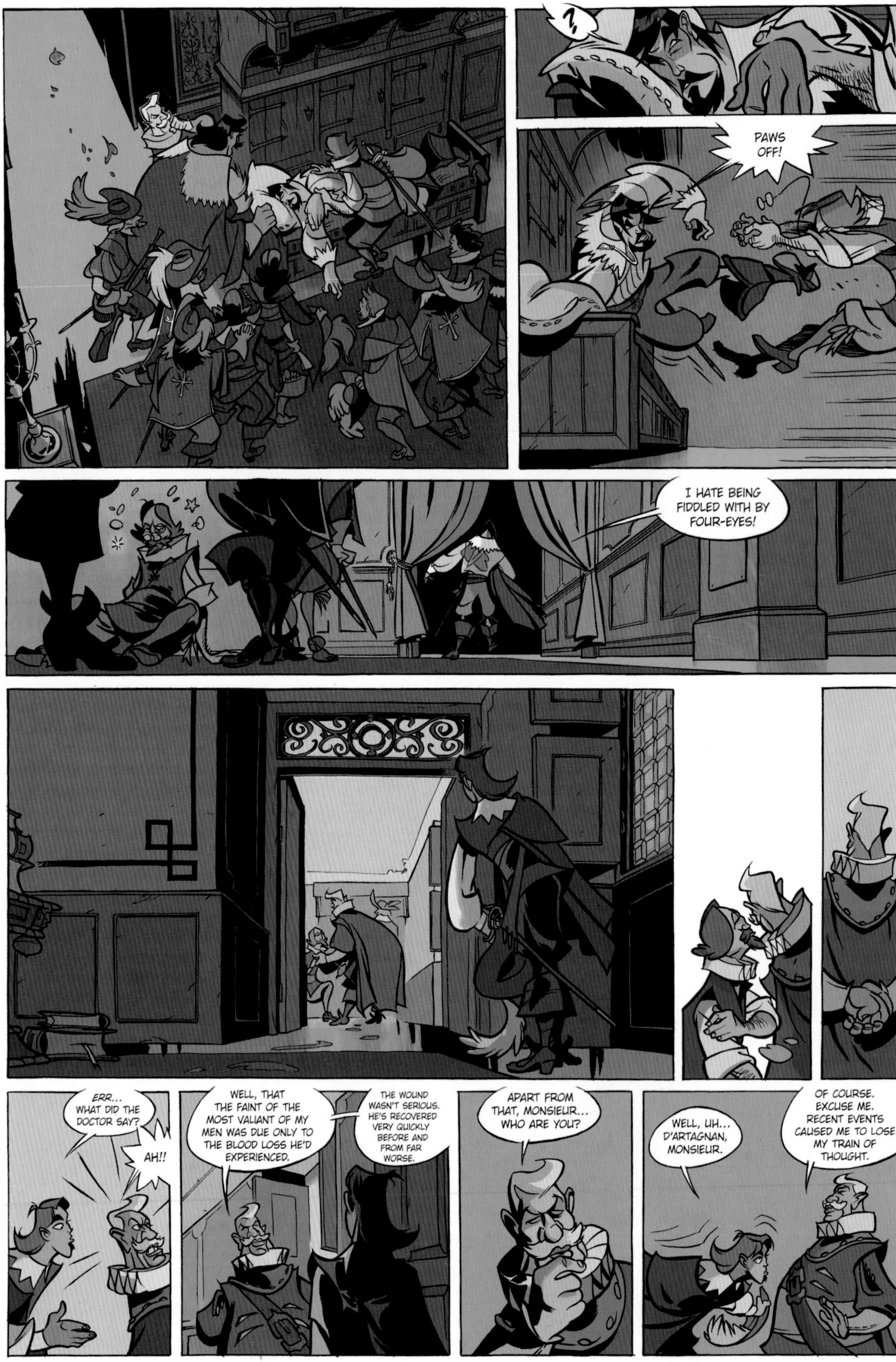
?
PAWS OFF!
I HATE BEING FIDDLED WITH BY FOUR-EYES!
ERR... WHAT DID THE DOCTOR SAY?
AH!!
WELL, THAT THE FAINT OF THE MOST VALIANT OF MY MEN WAS DUE ONLY TO THE BLOOD LOSS HE'D EXPERIENCED.
THE WOUND WASN'T SERIOUS. HE'S RECOVERED VERY QUICKLY BEFORE AND FROM FAR WORSE.
APART FROM THAT, MONSIEUR... WHO ARE YOU?
WELL, UH... D'ARTAGNAN, MONSIEUR.
OF COURSE. EXCUSE ME. RECENT EVENTS CAUSED ME TO LOSE MY TRAIN OF THOUGHT.

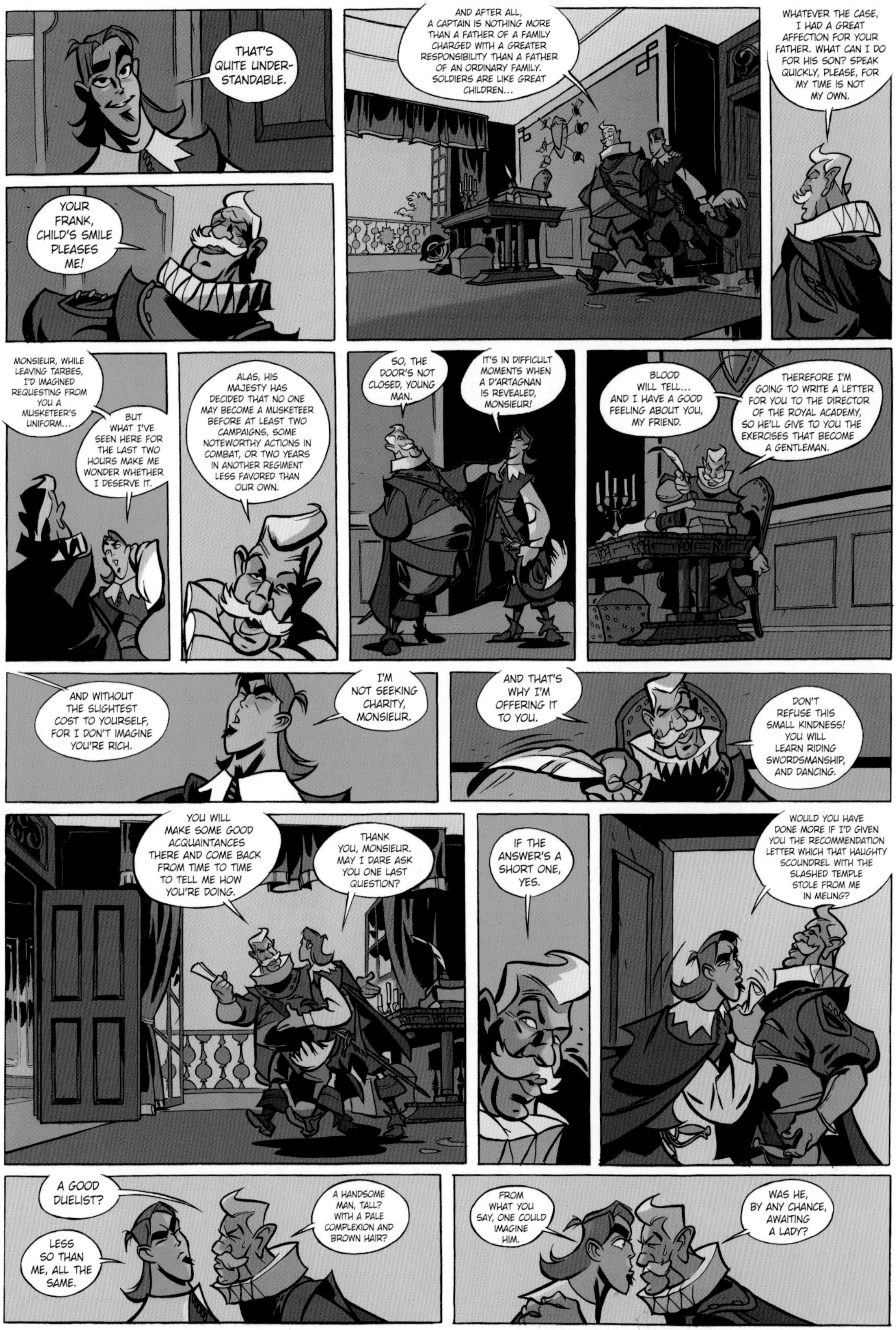

THAT'S QUITE UNDER-STANDABLE.
YOUR FRANK, CHILD'S SMILE PLEASES ME!
AND AFTER ALL, A CAPTAIN IS NOTHING MORE THAN A FATHER OF A FAMILY CHARGED WITH A GREATER RESPONSIBILITY THAN A FATHER OF AN ORDINARY FAMILY. SOLDIERS ARE LIKE GREAT CHILDREN...
WHATEVER THE CASE, I HAD A GREAT AFFECTION FOR YOUR FATHER. WHAT CAN I DO FOR HIS SON? SPEAK QUICKLY, PLEASE, FOR MY TIME IS NOT MY OWN.
MONSIEUR, WHILE LEAVING TARBES, I'D IMAGINED REQUESTING FROM YOU A MUSKETEER'S UNIFORM...
BUT WHAT I'VE SEEN HERE FOR THE LAST TWO HOURS MAKE ME WONDER WHETHER I DESERVE IT.
ALAS, HIS MAJESTY HAS DECIDED THAT NO ONE MAY BECOME A MUSKETEER BEFORE AT LEAST TWO CAMPAIGNS, SOME NOTEWORTHY ACTIONS IN COMBAT, OR TWO YEARS IN ANOTHER REGIMENT LESS FAVORED THAN OUR OWN.
SO, THE DOOR'S NOT CLOSED, YOUNG MAN.
IT'S IN DIFFICULT MOMENTS WHEN A D'ARTAGNAN IS REVEALED, MONSIEUR!
BLOOD WILL TELL... AND I HAVE A GOOD FEELING ABOUT YOU, MY FRIEND.
THEREFORE I'M GOING TO WRITE A LETTER FOR YOU TO THE DIRECTOR OF THE ROYAL ACADEMY, SO HE'LL GIVE TO YOU THE EXERCISES THAT BECOME A GENTLEMAN.
AND WITHOUT THE SLIGHTEST COST TO YOURSELF, FOR I DON'T IMAGINE YOU'RE RICH.
I'M NOT SEEKING CHARITY, MONSIEUR.
AND THAT'S WHY I'M OFFERING IT TO YOU.
DON'T REFUSE THIS SMALL KINDNESS! YOU WILL LEARN RIDING SWORDSMANSHIP, AND DANCING.
YOU WILL MAKE SOME GOOD ACQUAINTANCES THERE AND COME BACK FROM TIME TO TIME TO TELL ME HOW YOU'RE DOING.
THANK YOU, MONSIEUR. MAY I DARE ASK YOU ONE LAST QUESTION?
IF THE ANSWER'S A SHORT ONE, YES.
WOULD YOU HAVE DONE MORE IF I'D GIVEN YOU THE RECOMMENDATION LETTER WHICH THAT HAUGHTY SCOUNDREL WITH THE SLASHED TEMPLE STOLE FROM ME IN MEUNG?
A GOOD DUELIST?
LESS SO THAN ME, ALL THE SAME.
A HANDSOME MAN, TALL? WITH A PALE COMPLEXION AND BROWN HAIR?
FROM WHAT YOU SAY, ONE COULD IMAGINE HIM.
WAS HE, BY ANY CHANCE, AWAITING A LADY?

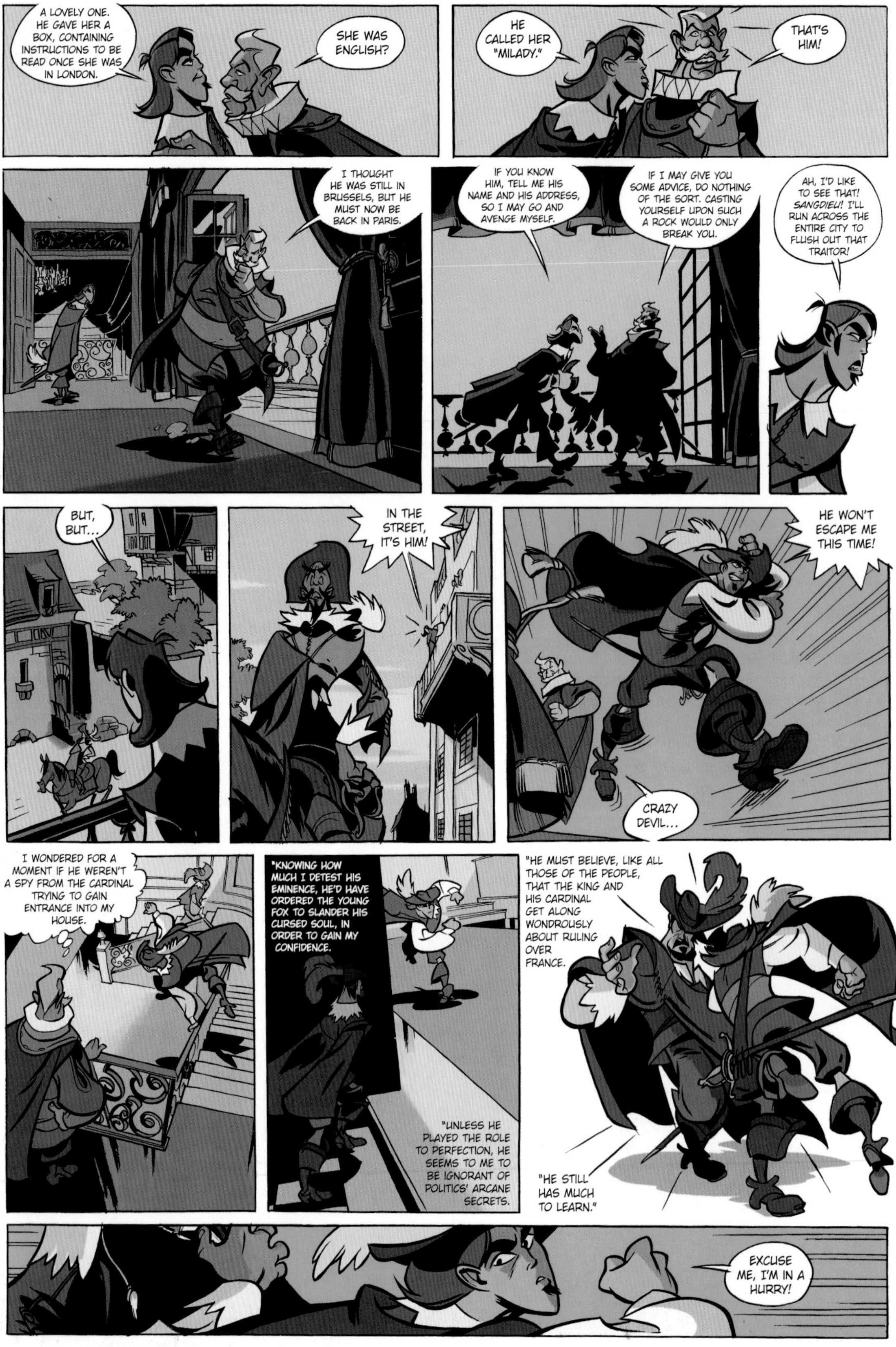
A LOVELY ONE. HE GAVE HER A BOX, CONTAINING INSTRUCTIONS TO BE READ ONCE SHE WAS IN LONDON.
SHE WAS ENGLISH?
HE CALLED HER "MILADY."
THAT'S HIM!
I THOUGHT HE WAS STILL IN BRUSSELS, BUT HE MUST NOW BE BACK IN PARIS.
IF YOU KNOW HIM, TELL ME HIS NAME AND HIS ADDRESS, SO I MAY GO AND AVENGE MYSELF.
IF I MAY GIVE YOU SOME ADVICE, DO NOTHING OF THE SORT. CASTING YOURSELF UPON SUCH A ROCK WOULD ONLY BREAK YOU.
AH, I'D LIKE TO SEE THAT! *SANGDIEU*! I'LL RUN ACROSS THE ENTIRE CITY TO FLUSH OUT THAT TRAITOR!
BUT, BUT...
IN THE STREET, IT'S HIM!
HE WON'T ESCAPE ME THIS TIME!
CRAZY DEVIL...
I WONDERED FOR A MOMENT IF HE WEREN'T A SPY FROM THE CARDINAL TRYING TO GAIN ENTRANCE INTO MY HOUSE.
"KNOWING HOW MUCH I DETEST HIS EMINENCE, HE'D HAVE ORDERED THE YOUNG FOX TO SLANDER HIS CURSED SOUL, IN ORDER TO GAIN MY CONFIDENCE.
"UNLESS HE PLAYED THE ROLE TO PERFECTION, HE SEEMS TO ME TO BE IGNORANT OF POLITICS' ARCANE SECRETS.
"HE MUST BELIEVE, LIKE ALL THOSE OF THE PEOPLE, THAT THE KING AND HIS CARDINAL GET ALONG WONDROUSLY ABOUT RULING OVER FRANCE.
"HE STILL HAS MUCH TO LEARN."
EXCUSE ME, I'M IN A HURRY!

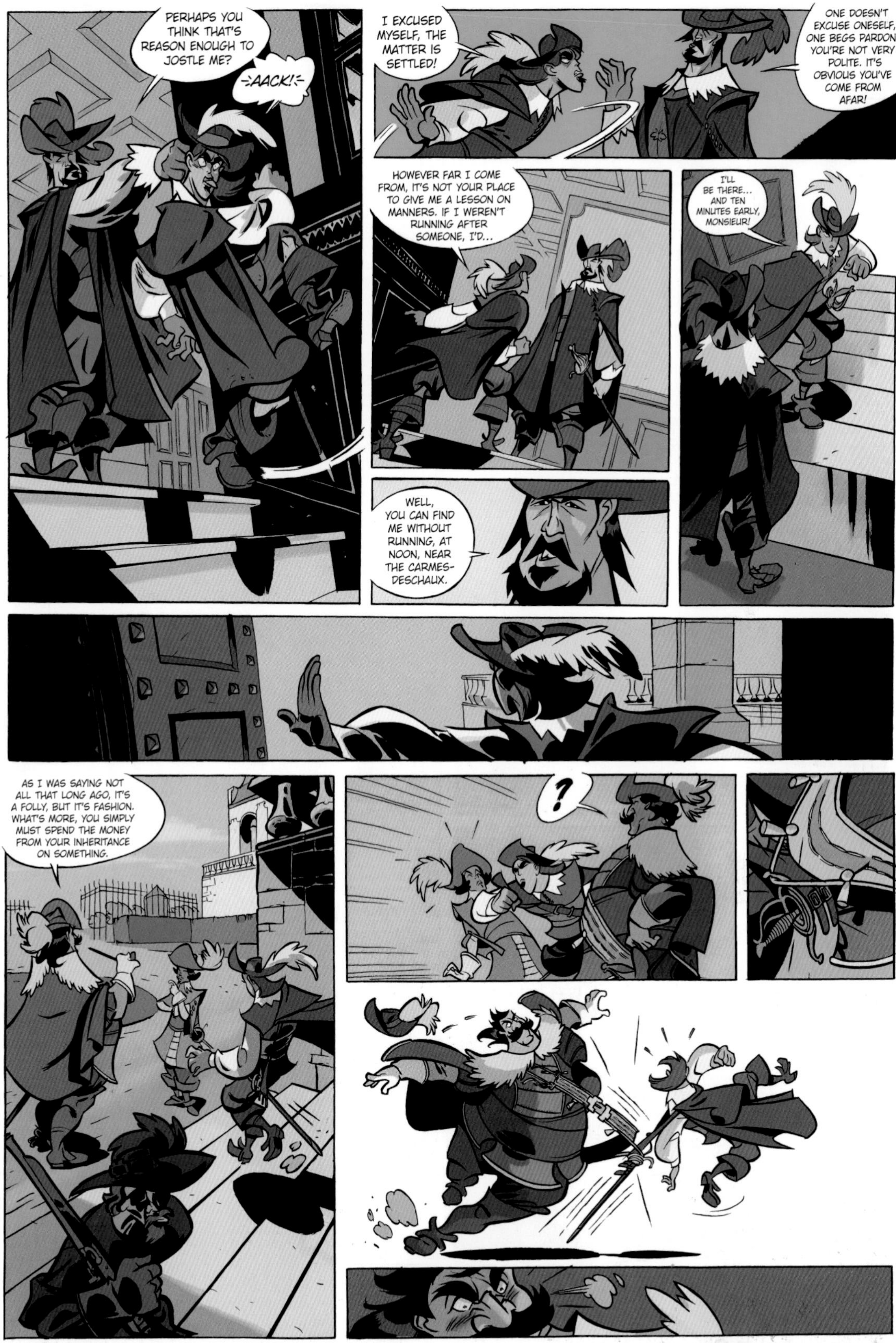
PERHAPS YOU THINK THAT'S REASON ENOUGH TO JOSTLE ME?
-AACK!-
I EXCUSED MYSELF, THE MATTER IS SETTLED!
ONE DOESN'T EXCUSE ONESELF, ONE BEGS PARDON. YOU'RE NOT VERY POLITE. IT'S OBVIOUS YOU'VE COME FROM AFAR!
HOWEVER FAR I COME FROM, IT'S NOT YOUR PLACE TO GIVE ME A LESSON ON MANNERS. IF I WEREN'T RUNNING AFTER SOMEONE, I'D...
WELL, YOU CAN FIND ME WITHOUT RUNNING, AT NOON, NEAR THE CARMES-DESCHAUX.
I'LL BE THERE... AND TEN MINUTES EARLY, MONSIEUR!
AS I WAS SAYING NOT ALL THAT LONG AGO, IT'S A FOLLY, BUT IT'S FASHION. WHAT'S MORE, YOU SIMPLY MUST SPEND THE MONEY FROM YOUR INHERITANCE ON SOMETHING.
?

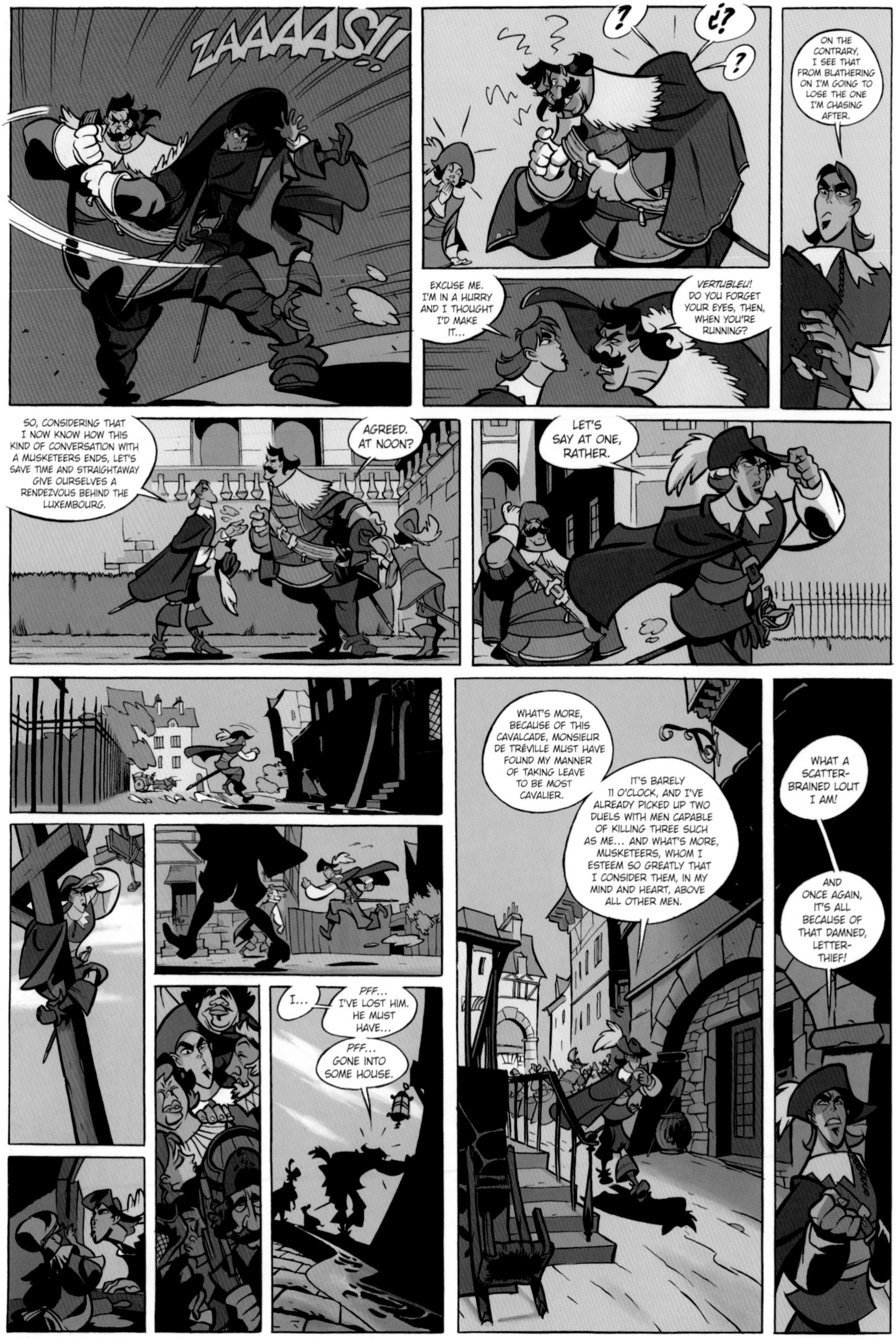

ZAAAAS!!
?
¿?
?
EXCUSE ME. I'M IN A HURRY AND I THOUGHT I'D MAKE IT...
VERTUBLEU! DO YOU FORGET YOUR EYES, THEN, WHEN YOU'RE RUNNING?
ON THE CONTRARY, I SEE THAT FROM BLATHERING ON I'M GOING TO LOSE THE ONE I'M CHASING AFTER.
SO, CONSIDERING THAT I NOW KNOW HOW THIS KIND OF CONVERSATION WITH A MUSKETEERS ENDS, LET'S SAVE TIME AND STRAIGHTAWAY GIVE OURSELVES A RENDEZVOUS BEHIND THE LUXEMBOURG.
AGREED. AT NOON?
LET'S SAY AT ONE, RATHER.
I...
PFF... I'VE LOST HIM. HE MUST HAVE...
PFF... GONE INTO SOME HOUSE.
WHAT'S MORE, BECAUSE OF THIS CAVALCADE, MONSIEUR DE TRÉVILLE MUST HAVE FOUND MY MANNER OF TAKING LEAVE TO BE MOST CAVALIER.
IT'S BARELY 11 O'CLOCK, AND I'VE ALREADY PICKED UP TWO DUELS WITH MEN CAPABLE OF KILLING THREE SUCH AS ME... AND WHAT'S MORE, MUSKETEERS, WHOM I ESTEEM SO GREATLY THAT I CONSIDER THEM, IN MY MIND AND HEART, ABOVE ALL OTHER MEN.
WHAT A SCATTER-BRAINED LOUT I AM!
AND ONCE AGAIN, IT'S ALL BECAUSE OF THAT DAMNED, LETTER-THIEF!

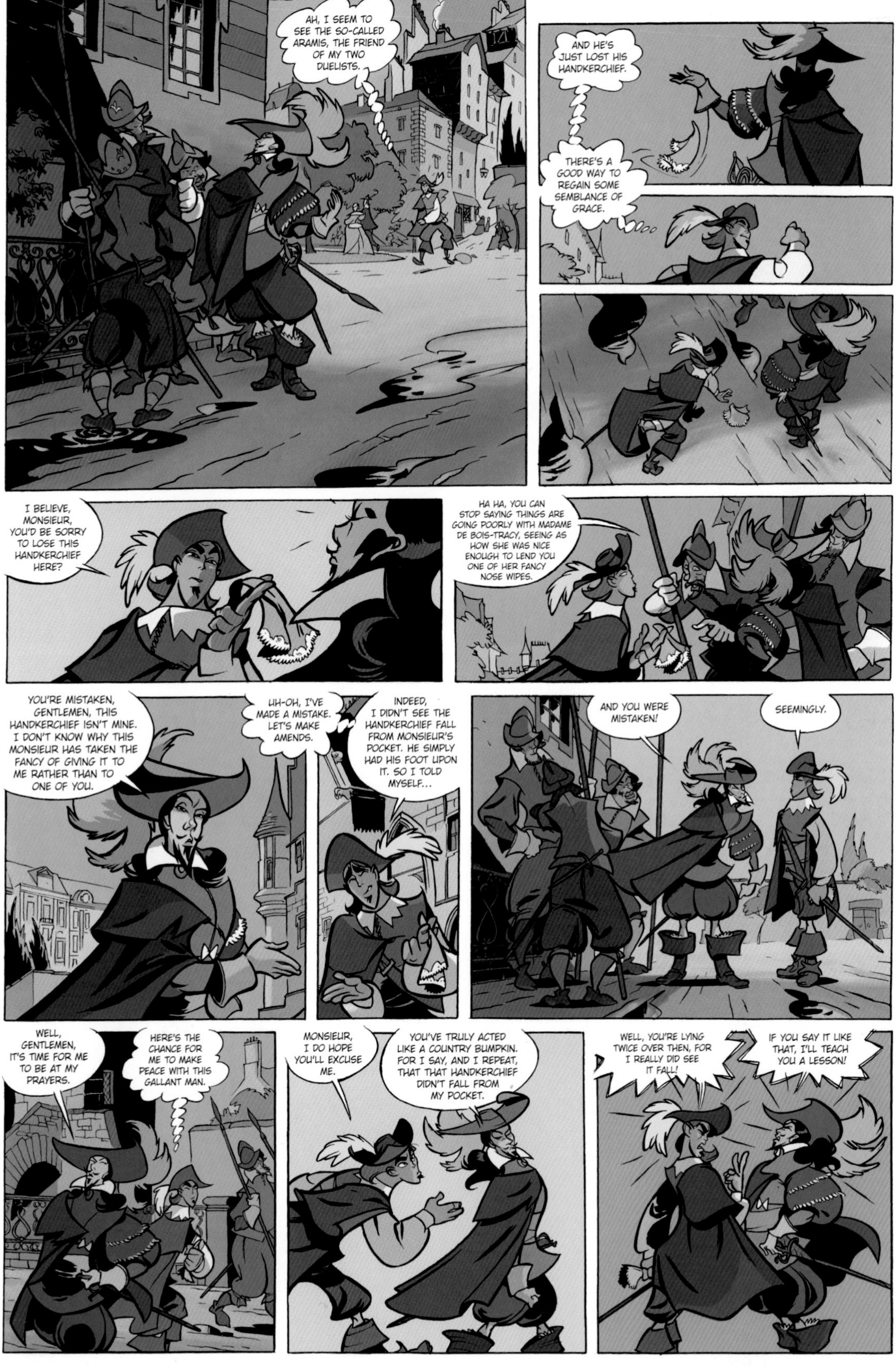

AH, I SEEM TO SEE THE SO-CALLED ARAMIS, THE FRIEND OF MY TWO DUELISTS.
AND HE'S JUST LOST HIS HANDKERCHIEF.
THERE'S A GOOD WAY TO REGAIN SOME SEMBLANCE OF GRACE.
I BELIEVE, MONSIEUR, YOU'D BE SORRY TO LOSE THIS HANDKERCHIEF HERE?
HA HA, YOU CAN STOP SAYING THINGS ARE GOING POORLY WITH MADAME DE BOIS-TRACY, SEEING AS HOW SHE WAS NICE ENOUGH TO LEND YOU ONE OF HER FANCY NOSE WIPES.
YOU'RE MISTAKEN, GENTLEMEN, THIS HANDKERCHIEF ISN'T MINE. I DON'T KNOW WHY THIS MONSIEUR HAS TAKEN THE FANCY OF GIVING IT TO ME RATHER THAN TO ONE OF YOU.
UH-OH, I'VE MADE A MISTAKE. LET'S MAKE AMENDS.
INDEED, I DIDN'T SEE THE HANDKERCHIEF FALL FROM MONSIEUR'S POCKET. HE SIMPLY HAD HIS FOOT UPON IT. SO I TOLD MYSELF...
AND YOU WERE MISTAKEN!
SEEMINGLY.
WELL, GENTLEMEN, IT'S TIME FOR ME TO BE AT MY PRAYERS.
HERE'S THE CHANCE FOR ME TO MAKE PEACE WITH THIS GALLANT MAN.
MONSIEUR, I DO HOPE YOU'LL EXCUSE ME.
YOU'VE TRULY ACTED LIKE A COUNTRY BUMPKIN. FOR I SAY, AND I REPEAT, THAT THAT HANDKERCHIEF DIDN'T FALL FROM MY POCKET.
WELL, YOU'RE LYING TWICE OVER THEN, FOR I REALLY DID SEE IT FALL!
IF YOU SAY IT LIKE THAT, I'LL TEACH YOU A LESSON!

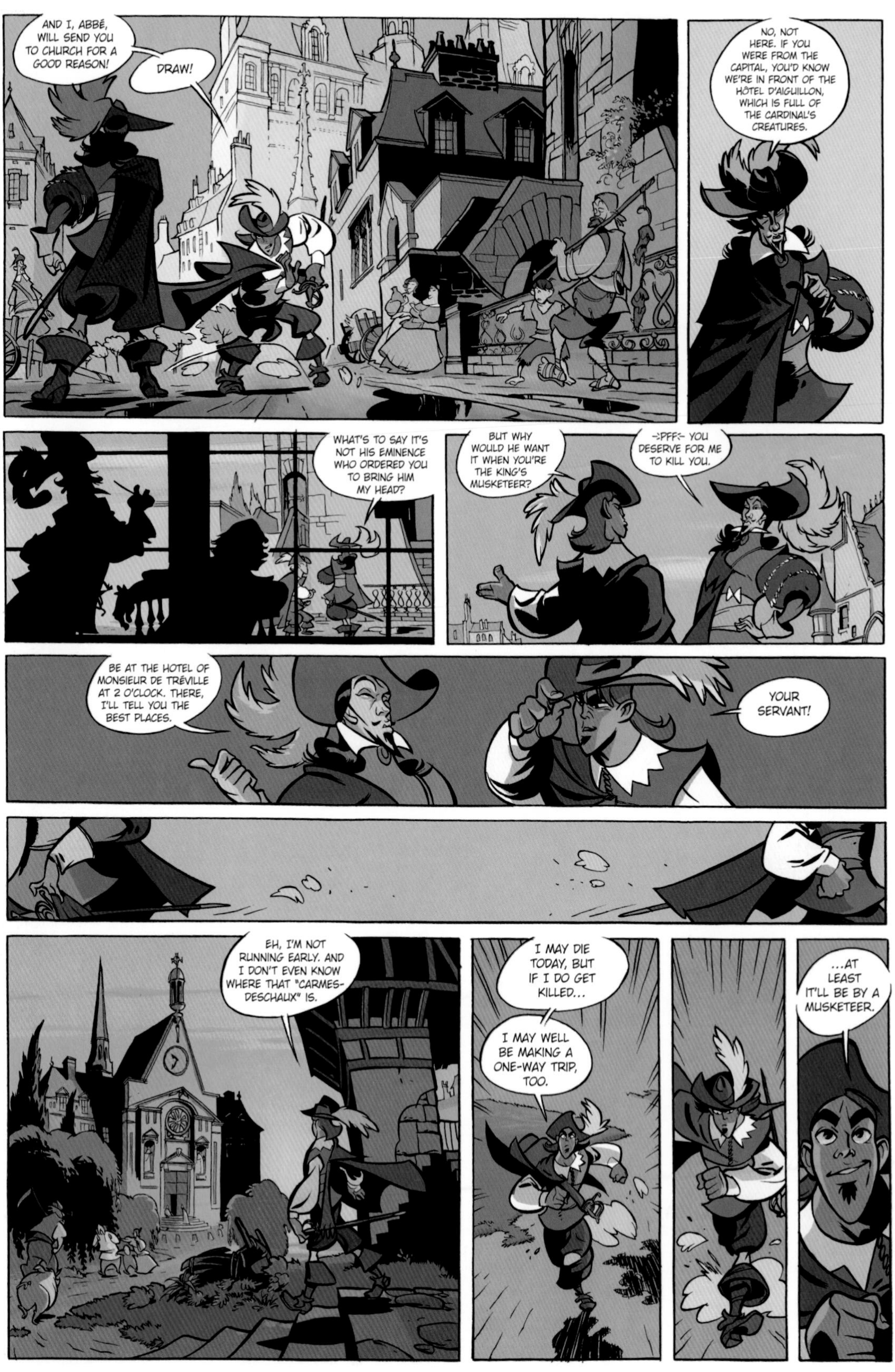
AND I, ABBÉ, WILL SEND YOU TO CHURCH FOR A GOOD REASON!
DRAW!
NO, NOT HERE. IF YOU WERE FROM THE CAPITAL, YOU'D KNOW WE'RE IN FRONT OF THE HÔTEL D'AIGUILLON, WHICH IS FULL OF THE CARDINAL'S CREATURES.
WHAT'S TO SAY IT'S NOT HIS EMINENCE WHO ORDERED YOU TO BRING HIM MY HEAD?
BUT WHY WOULD HE WANT IT WHEN YOU'RE THE KING'S MUSKETEER?
-PFF- YOU DESERVE FOR ME TO KILL YOU.
BE AT THE HOTEL OF MONSIEUR DE TRÉVILLE AT 2 O'CLOCK. THERE, I'LL TELL YOU THE BEST PLACES.
YOUR SERVANT!
EH, I'M NOT RUNNING EARLY. AND I DON'T EVEN KNOW WHERE THAT "CARMES-DESCHAUX" IS.
I MAY DIE TODAY, BUT IF I DO GET KILLED...
I MAY WELL BE MAKING A ONE-WAY TRIP, TOO.
...AT LEAST IT'LL BE BY A MUSKETEER.

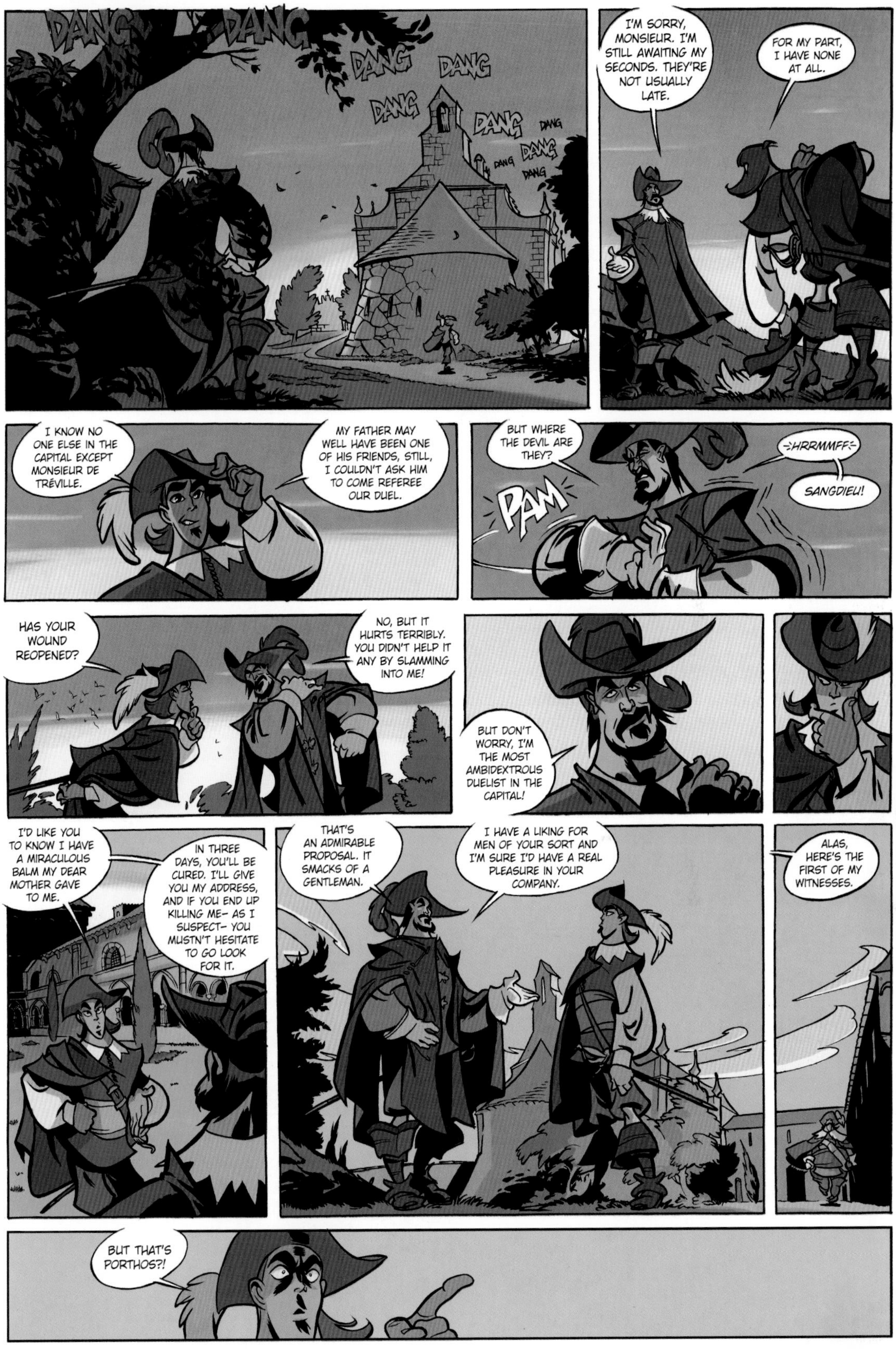
DANG DANG DANG DANG DANG DANG DANG DANG DANG DANG
I'M SORRY, MONSIEUR. I'M STILL AWAITING MY SECONDS. THEY'RE NOT USUALLY LATE.
FOR MY PART, I HAVE NONE AT ALL.
I KNOW NO ONE ELSE IN THE CAPITAL EXCEPT MONSIEUR DE TRÉVILLE.
MY FATHER MAY WELL HAVE BEEN ONE OF HIS FRIENDS, STILL, I COULDN'T ASK HIM TO COME REFEREE OUR DUEL.
BUT WHERE THE DEVIL ARE THEY?
PAM
HRRMMFF
SANGDIEU!
HAS YOUR WOUND REOPENED?
NO, BUT IT HURTS TERRIBLY. YOU DIDN'T HELP IT ANY BY SLAMMING INTO ME!
BUT DON'T WORRY, I'M THE MOST AMBIDEXTROUS DUELIST IN THE CAPITAL!
I'D LIKE YOU TO KNOW I HAVE A MIRACULOUS BALM MY DEAR MOTHER GAVE TO ME.
IN THREE DAYS, YOU'LL BE CURED. I'LL GIVE YOU MY ADDRESS, AND IF YOU END UP KILLING ME- AS I SUSPECT- YOU MUSTN'T HESITATE TO GO LOOK FOR IT.
THAT'S AN ADMIRABLE PROPOSAL. IT SMACKS OF A GENTLEMAN.
I HAVE A LIKING FOR MEN OF YOUR SORT AND I'M SURE I'D HAVE A REAL PLEASURE IN YOUR COMPANY.
ALAS, HERE'S THE FIRST OF MY WITNESSES.
BUT THAT'S PORTHOS?!

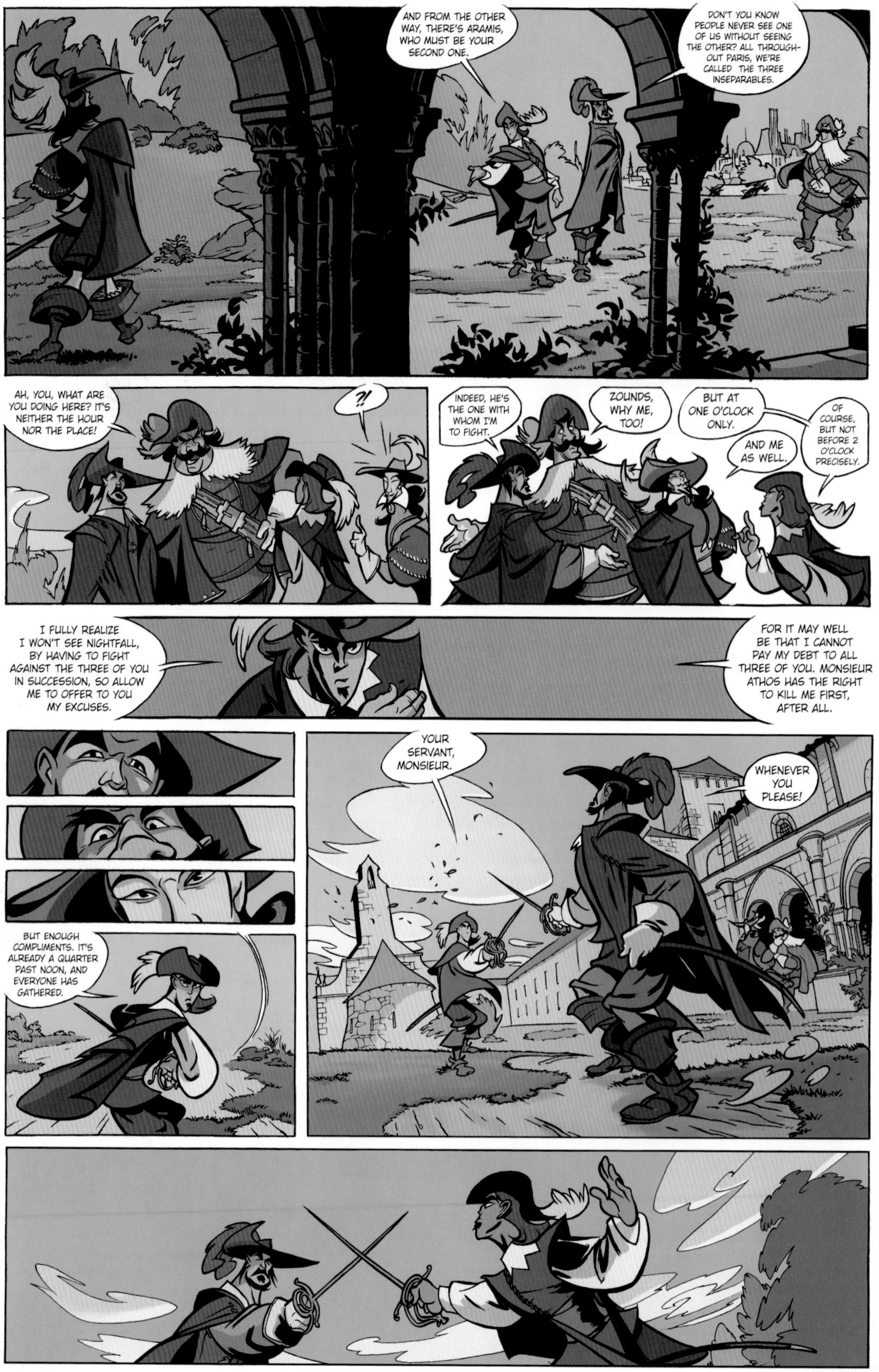
AND FROM THE OTHER WAY, THERE'S ARAMIS, WHO MUST BE YOUR SECOND ONE.
DON'T YOU KNOW PEOPLE NEVER SEE ONE OF US WITHOUT SEEING THE OTHER? ALL THROUGH-OUT PARIS, WE'RE CALLED THE THREE INSEPARABLES.
AH, YOU, WHAT ARE YOU DOING HERE? IT'S NEITHER THE HOUR NOR THE PLACE!
?!
INDEED, HE'S THE ONE WITH WHOM I'M TO FIGHT.
ZOUNDS, WHY ME, TOO!
BUT AT ONE O'CLOCK ONLY.
AND ME AS WELL.
OF COURSE, BUT NOT BEFORE 2 O'CLOCK PRECISELY.
I FULLY REALIZE I WON'T SEE NIGHTFALL, BY HAVING TO FIGHT AGAINST THE THREE OF YOU IN SUCCESSION, SO ALLOW ME TO OFFER TO YOU MY EXCUSES.
FOR IT MAY WELL BE THAT I CANNOT PAY MY DEBT TO ALL THREE OF YOU. MONSIEUR ATHOS HAS THE RIGHT TO KILL ME FIRST, AFTER ALL.
BUT ENOUGH COMPLIMENTS. IT'S ALREADY A QUARTER PAST NOON, AND EVERYONE HAS GATHERED.
YOUR SERVANT, MONSIEUR.
WHENEVER YOU PLEASE!

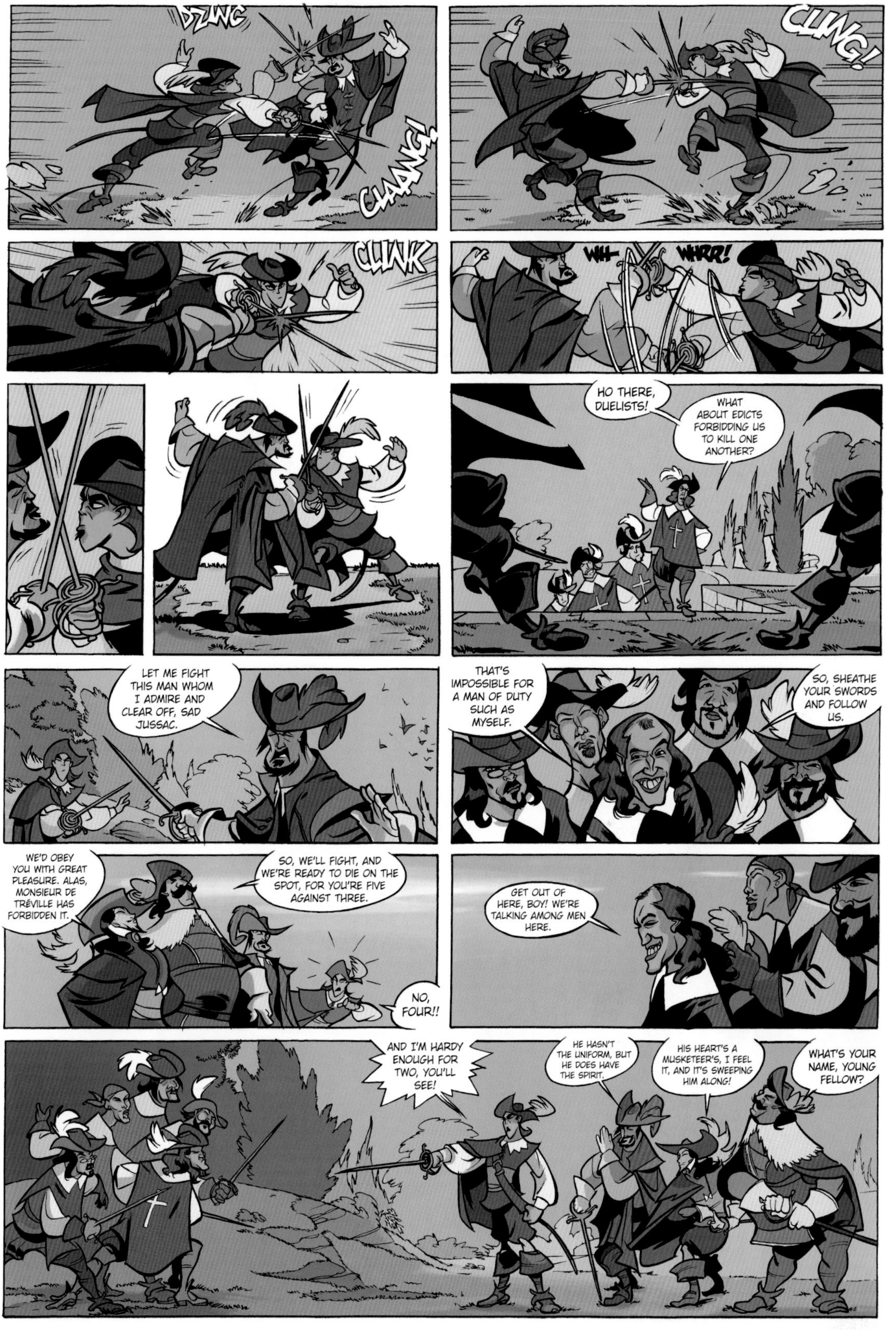
BZING
CLAANG!
CLING!
CLINK
WH
WHRR!
HO THERE, DUELISTS!
WHAT ABOUT EDICTS FORBIDDING US TO KILL ONE ANOTHER?
LET ME FIGHT THIS MAN WHOM I ADMIRE AND CLEAR OFF, SAD JUSSAC.
THAT'S IMPOSSIBLE FOR A MAN OF DUTY SUCH AS MYSELF.
SO, SHEATHE YOUR SWORDS AND FOLLOW US.
WE'D OBEY YOU WITH GREAT PLEASURE. ALAS, MONSIEUR DE TRÉVILLE HAS FORBIDDEN IT.
SO, WE'LL FIGHT, AND WE'RE READY TO DIE ON THE SPOT, FOR YOU'RE FIVE AGAINST THREE.
NO, FOUR!!
GET OUT OF HERE, BOY! WE'RE TALKING AMONG MEN HERE.
AND I'M HARDY ENOUGH FOR TWO, YOU'LL SEE!
HE HASN'T THE UNIFORM, BUT HE DOES HAVE THE SPIRIT.
HIS HEART'S A MUSKETEER'S, I FEEL IT, AND IT'S SWEEPING HIM ALONG!
WHAT'S YOUR NAME, YOUNG FELLOW?

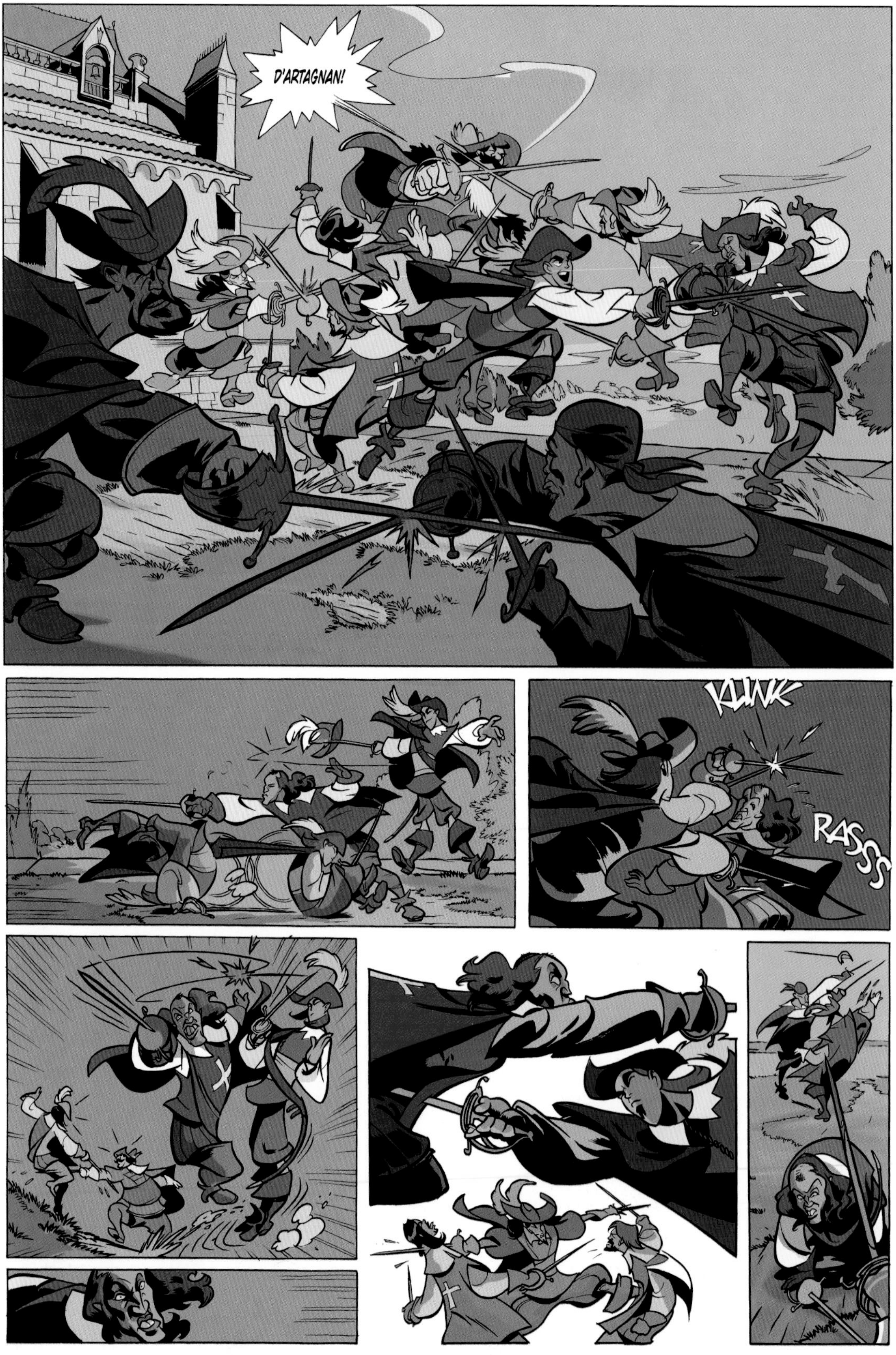

D'ARTAGNAN!
KLINK
RASSS

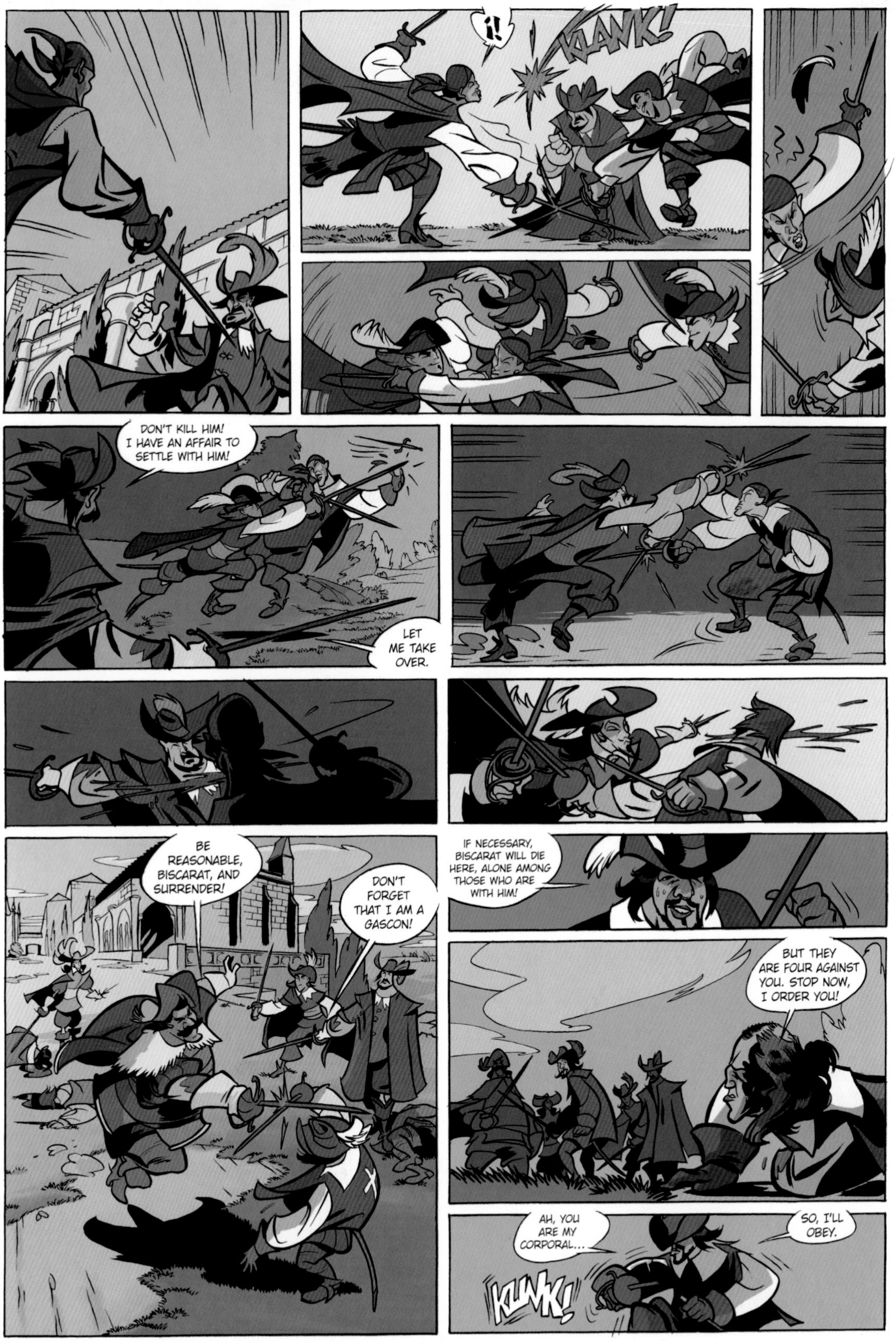
¡!
KLANK!
DON'T KILL HIM! I HAVE AN AFFAIR TO SETTLE WITH HIM!
LET ME TAKE OVER.
BE REASONABLE, BISCARAT, AND SURRENDER!
DON'T FORGET THAT I AM A GASCON!
IF NECESSARY, BISCARAT WILL DIE HERE, ALONE AMONG THOSE WHO ARE WITH HIM!
BUT THEY ARE FOUR AGAINST YOU. STOP NOW, I ORDER YOU!
AH, YOU ARE MY CORPORAL...
SO, I'LL OBEY.
KLINK!

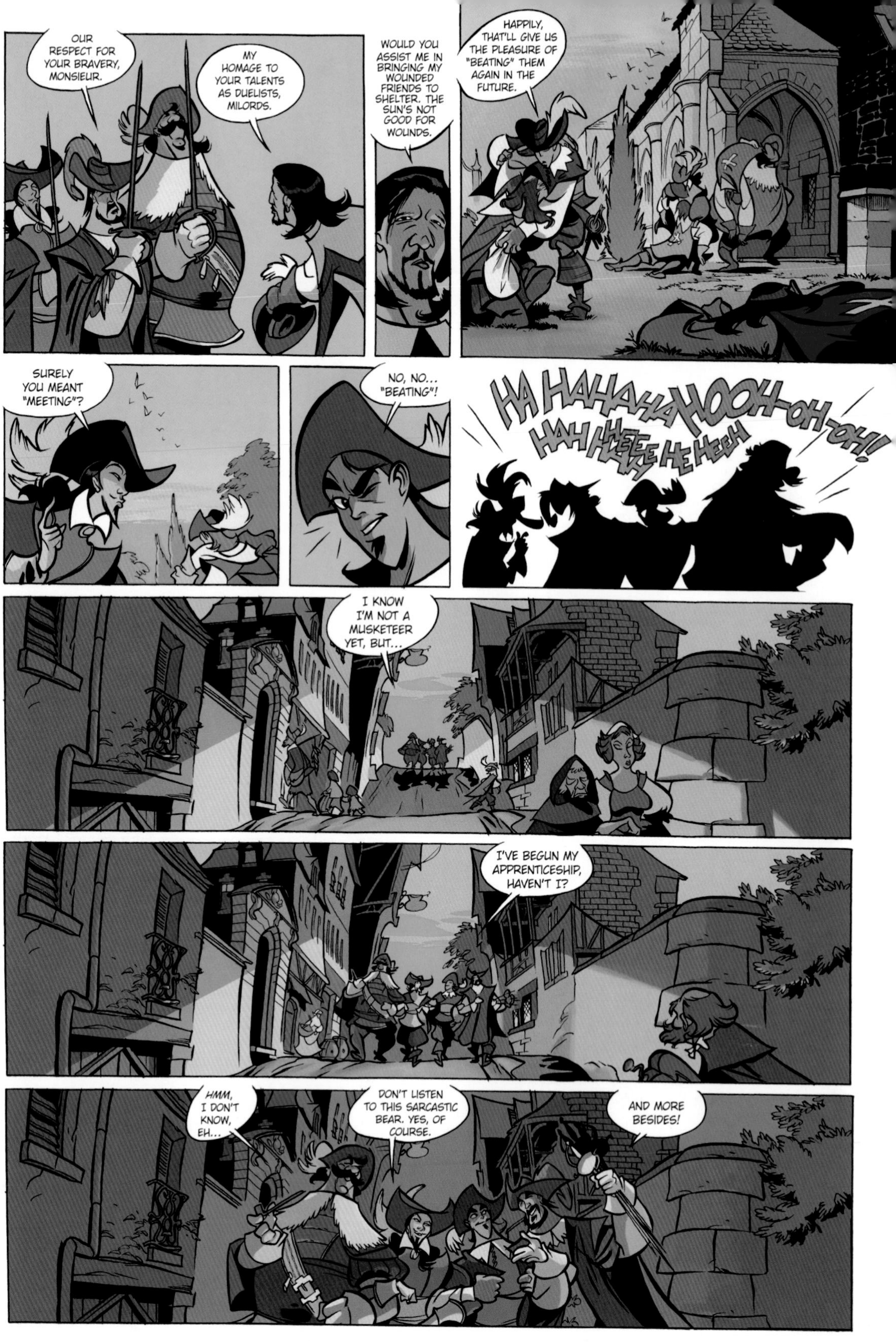
OUR RESPECT FOR YOUR BRAVERY, MONSIEUR.
MY HOMAGE TO YOUR TALENTS AS DUELISTS, MILORDS.
WOULD YOU ASSIST ME IN BRINGING MY WOUNDED FRIENDS TO SHELTER. THE SUN'S NOT GOOD FOR WOUNDS.
HAPPILY, THAT'LL GIVE US THE PLEASURE OF "BEATING" THEM AGAIN IN THE FUTURE.
SURELY YOU MEANT "MEETING"?
NO, NO... "BEATING"!
HA HAHAHAHA HOOH-OH-OH!
HAH HEEEE HE HEEH
I KNOW I'M NOT A MUSKETEER YET, BUT...
I'VE BEGUN MY APPRENTICESHIP, HAVEN'T I?
HMM, I DON'T KNOW, EH...
DON'T LISTEN TO THIS SARCASTIC BEAR. YES, OF COURSE.
AND MORE BESIDES!

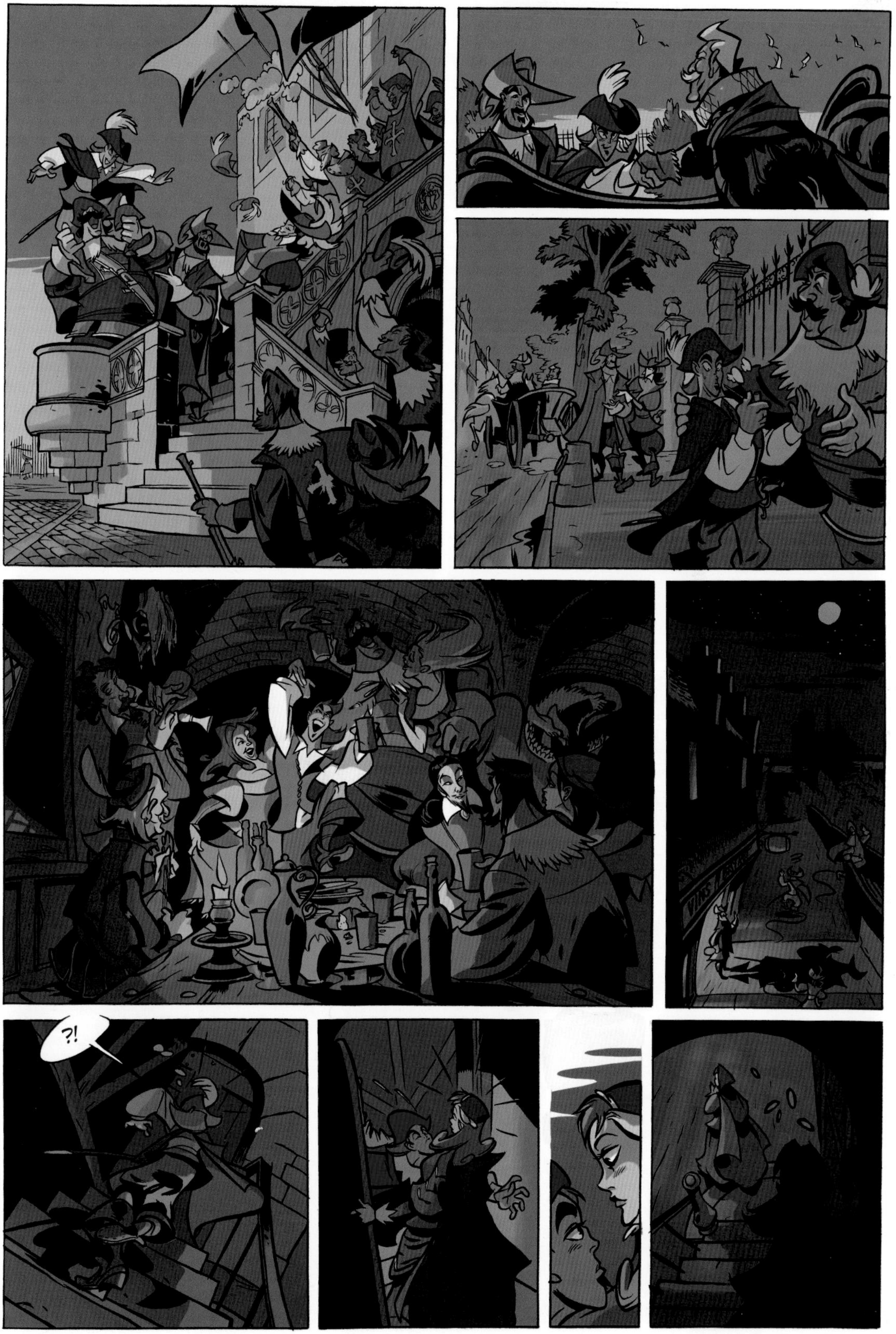
?!

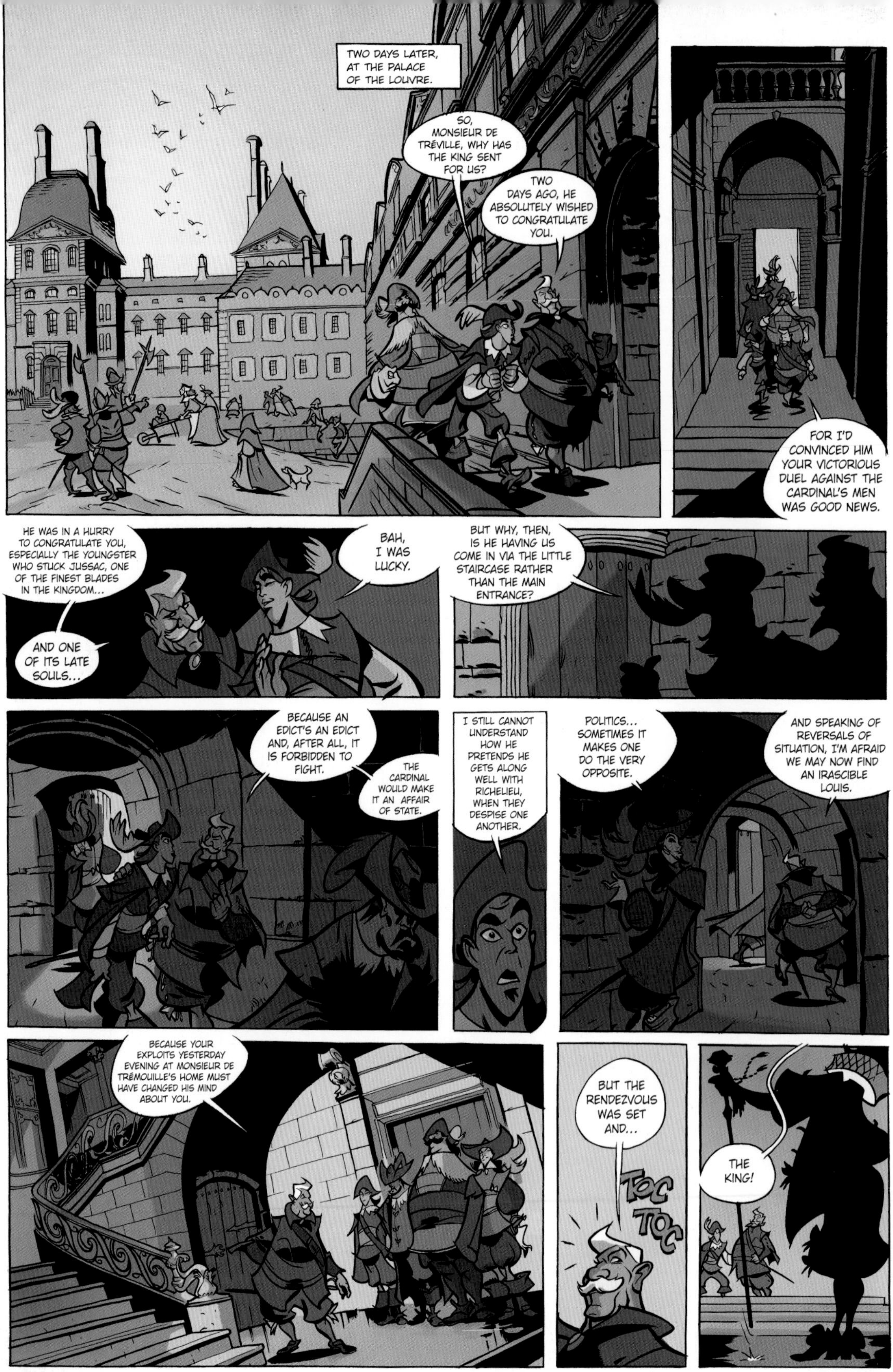
TWO DAYS LATER, AT THE PALACE OF THE LOUVRE.
SO, MONSIEUR DE TRÉVILLE, WHY HAS THE KING SENT FOR US?
TWO DAYS AGO, HE ABSOLUTELY WISHED TO CONGRATULATE YOU.
FOR I'D CONVINCED HIM YOUR VICTORIOUS DUEL AGAINST THE CARDINAL'S MEN WAS GOOD NEWS.
HE WAS IN A HURRY TO CONGRATULATE YOU, ESPECIALLY THE YOUNGSTER WHO STUCK JUSSAC, ONE OF THE FINEST BLADES IN THE KINGDOM...
AND ONE OF ITS LATE SOULS...
BAH, I WAS LUCKY.
BUT WHY, THEN, IS HE HAVING US COME IN VIA THE LITTLE STAIRCASE RATHER THAN THE MAIN ENTRANCE?
BECAUSE AN EDICT'S AN EDICT AND, AFTER ALL, IT IS FORBIDDEN TO FIGHT.
THE CARDINAL WOULD MAKE IT AN AFFAIR OF STATE.
I STILL CANNOT UNDERSTAND HOW HE PRETENDS HE GETS ALONG WELL WITH RICHELIEU, WHEN THEY DESPISE ONE ANOTHER.
POLITICS... SOMETIMES IT MAKES ONE DO THE VERY OPPOSITE.
AND SPEAKING OF REVERSALS OF SITUATION, I'M AFRAID WE MAY NOW FIND AN IRASCIBLE LOUIS.
BECAUSE YOUR EXPLOITS YESTERDAY EVENING AT MONSIEUR DE TRÉMOUILLE'S HOME MUST HAVE CHANGED HIS MIND ABOUT YOU.
BUT THE RENDEZVOUS WAS SET AND...
TOC TOC
THE KING!

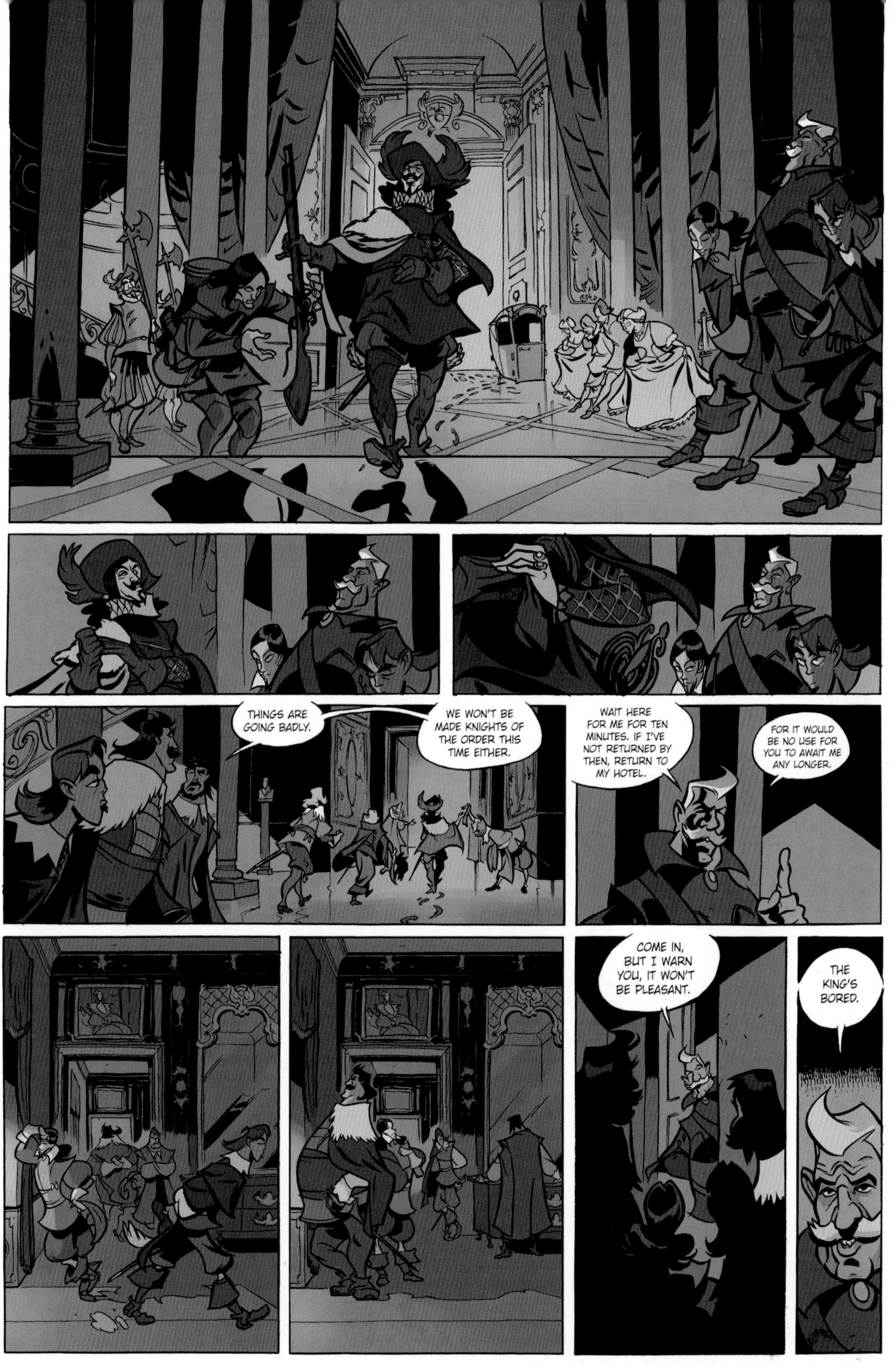
THINGS ARE GOING BADLY.
WE WON'T BE MADE KNIGHTS OF THE ORDER THIS TIME EITHER.
WAIT HERE FOR ME FOR TEN MINUTES. IF I'VE NOT RETURNED BY THEN, RETURN TO MY HOTEL.
FOR IT WOULD BE NO USE FOR YOU TO AWAIT ME ANY LONGER.
COME IN, BUT I WARN YOU, IT WON'T BE PLEASANT.
THE KING'S BORED.

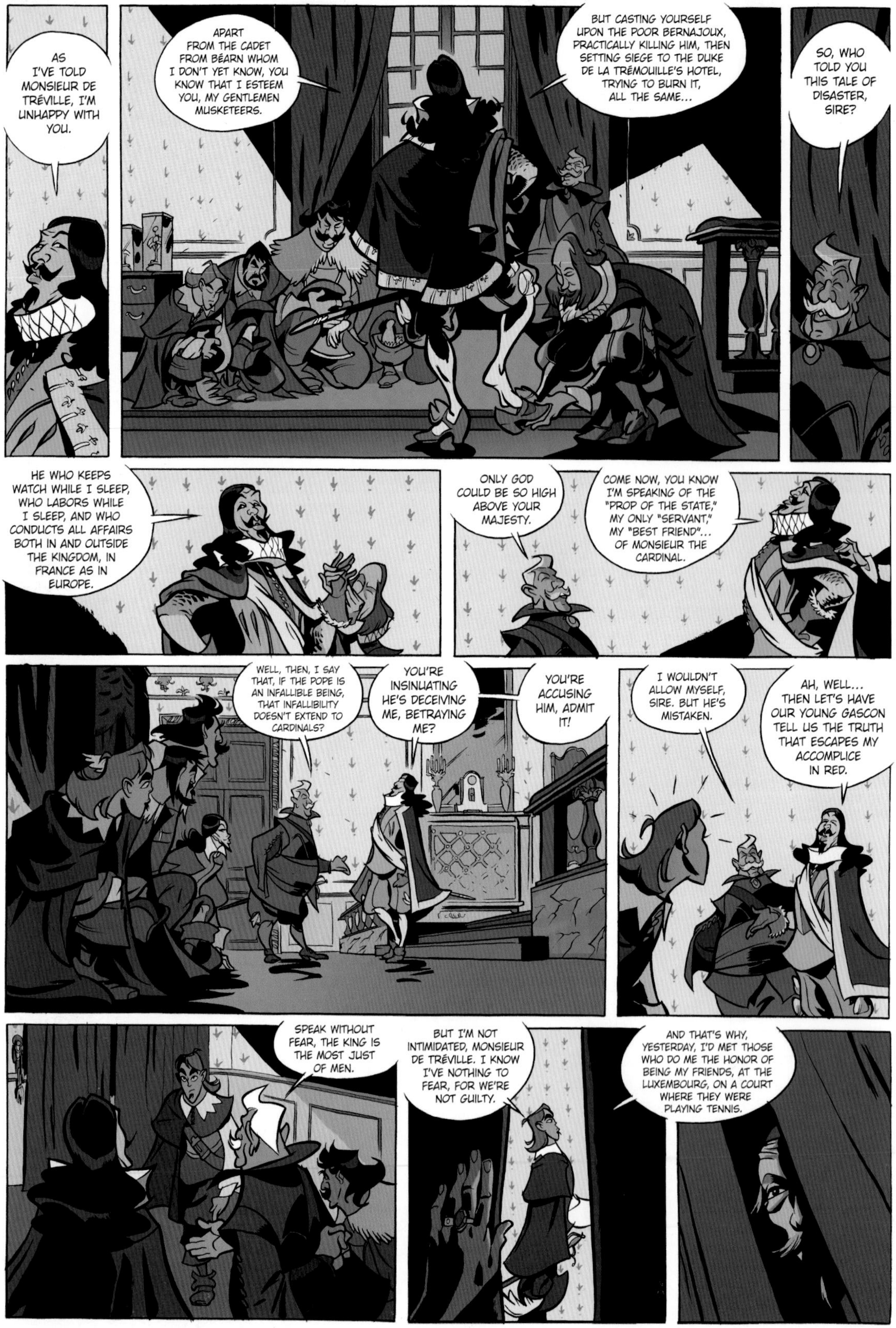
AS I'VE TOLD MONSIEUR DE TRÉVILLE, I'M UNHAPPY WITH YOU.
APART FROM THE CADET FROM BÉARN WHOM I DON'T YET KNOW, YOU KNOW THAT I ESTEEM YOU, MY GENTLEMEN MUSKETEERS.
BUT CASTING YOURSELF UPON THE POOR BERNAJOUX, PRACTICALLY KILLING HIM, THEN SETTING SIEGE TO THE DUKE DE LA TRÉMOUILLE'S HOTEL, TRYING TO BURN IT, ALL THE SAME...
SO, WHO TOLD YOU THIS TALE OF DISASTER, SIRE?
HE WHO KEEPS WATCH WHILE I SLEEP, WHO LABORS WHILE I SLEEP, AND WHO CONDUCTS ALL AFFAIRS BOTH IN AND OUTSIDE THE KINGDOM, IN FRANCE AS IN EUROPE.
ONLY GOD COULD BE SO HIGH ABOVE YOUR MAJESTY.
COME NOW, YOU KNOW I'M SPEAKING OF THE "PROP OF THE STATE," MY ONLY "SERVANT," MY "BEST FRIEND"... OF MONSIEUR THE CARDINAL.
WELL, THEN, I SAY THAT, IF THE POPE IS AN INFALLIBLE BEING, THAT INFALLIBILITY DOESN'T EXTEND TO CARDINALS?
YOU'RE INSINUATING HE'S DECEIVING ME, BETRAYING ME?
YOU'RE ACCUSING HIM, ADMIT IT!
I WOULDN'T ALLOW MYSELF, SIRE. BUT HE'S MISTAKEN.
AH, WELL... THEN LET'S HAVE OUR YOUNG GASCON TELL US THE TRUTH THAT ESCAPES MY ACCOMPLICE IN RED.
SPEAK WITHOUT FEAR, THE KING IS THE MOST JUST OF MEN.
BUT I'M NOT INTIMIDATED, MONSIEUR DE TRÉVILLE. I KNOW I'VE NOTHING TO FEAR, FOR WE'RE NOT GUILTY.
AND THAT'S WHY, YESTERDAY, I'D MET THOSE WHO DO ME THE HONOR OF BEING MY FRIENDS, AT THE LUXEMBOURG, ON A COURT WHERE THEY WERE PLAYING TENNIS.

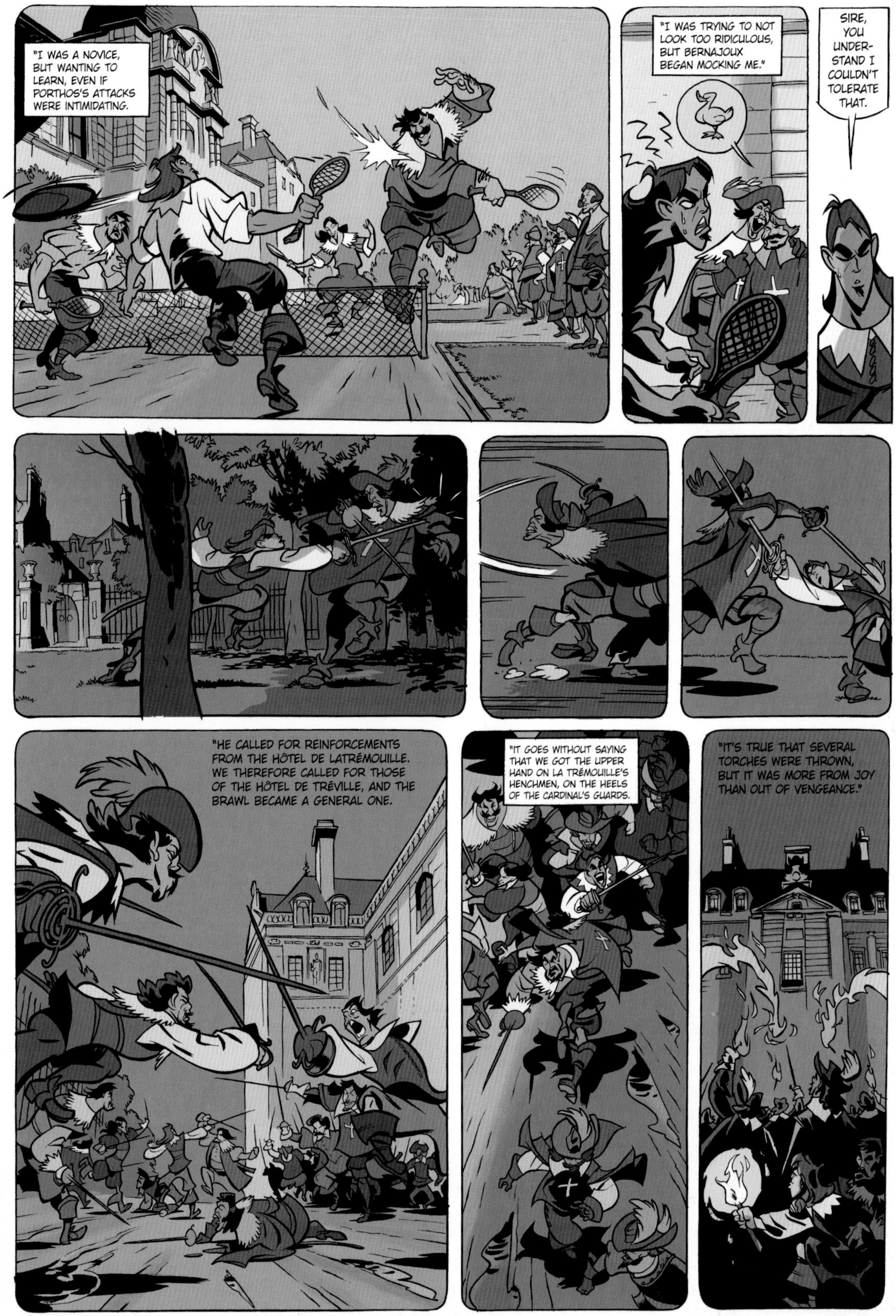
"I WAS A NOVICE, BUT WANTING TO LEARN, EVEN IF PORTHOS'S ATTACKS WERE INTIMIDATING.
"I WAS TRYING TO NOT LOOK TOO RIDICULOUS, BUT BERNAJOUX BEGAN MOCKING ME."
SIRE, YOU UNDER-STAND I COULDN'T TOLERATE THAT.
"HE CALLED FOR REINFORCEMENTS FROM THE HÔTEL DE LATRÉMOUILLE. WE THEREFORE CALLED FOR THOSE OF THE HÔTEL DE TRÉVILLE, AND THE BRAWL BECAME A GENERAL ONE.
"IT GOES WITHOUT SAYING THAT WE GOT THE UPPER HAND ON LA TRÉMOUILLE'S HENCHMEN, ON THE HEELS OF THE CARDINAL'S GUARDS.
"IT'S TRUE THAT SEVERAL TORCHES WERE THROWN, BUT IT WAS MORE FROM JOY THAN OUT OF VENGEANCE."

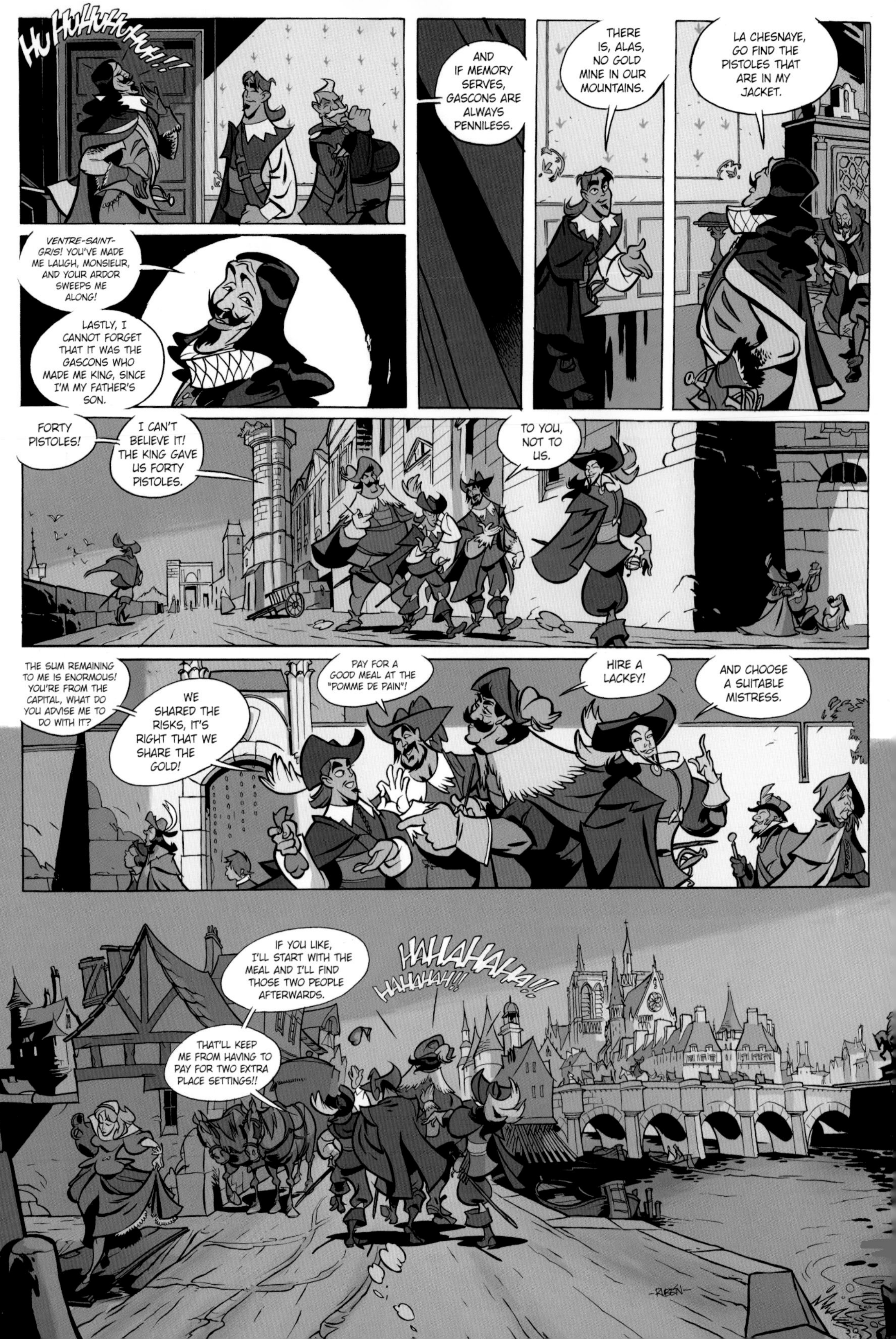
HUHUHUHUHUHUH!!!
AND IF MEMORY SERVES, GASCONS ARE ALWAYS PENNILESS.
VENTRE-SAINT-GRIS! YOU'VE MADE ME LAUGH, MONSIEUR, AND YOUR ARDOR SWEEPS ME ALONG!
LASTLY, I CANNOT FORGET THAT IT WAS THE GASCONS WHO MADE ME KING, SINCE I'M MY FATHER'S SON.
THERE IS, ALAS, NO GOLD MINE IN OUR MOUNTAINS.
LA CHESNAYE, GO FIND THE PISTOLES THAT ARE IN MY JACKET.
FORTY PISTOLES!
I CAN'T BELIEVE IT! THE KING GAVE US FORTY PISTOLES.
TO YOU, NOT TO US.
THE SUM REMAINING TO ME IS ENORMOUS! YOU'RE FROM THE CAPITAL, WHAT DO YOU ADVISE ME TO DO WITH IT?
WE SHARED THE RISKS, IT'S RIGHT THAT WE SHARE THE GOLD!
PAY FOR A GOOD MEAL AT THE "POMME DE PAIN"!
HIRE A LACKEY!
AND CHOOSE A SUITABLE MISTRESS.
IF YOU LIKE, I'LL START WITH THE MEAL AND I'LL FIND THOSE TWO PEOPLE AFTERWARDS.
THAT'LL KEEP ME FROM HAVING TO PAY FOR TWO EXTRA PLACE SETTINGS!!
HAHAHAHAHA!!
HAHAHAH!!
-RUBEN-

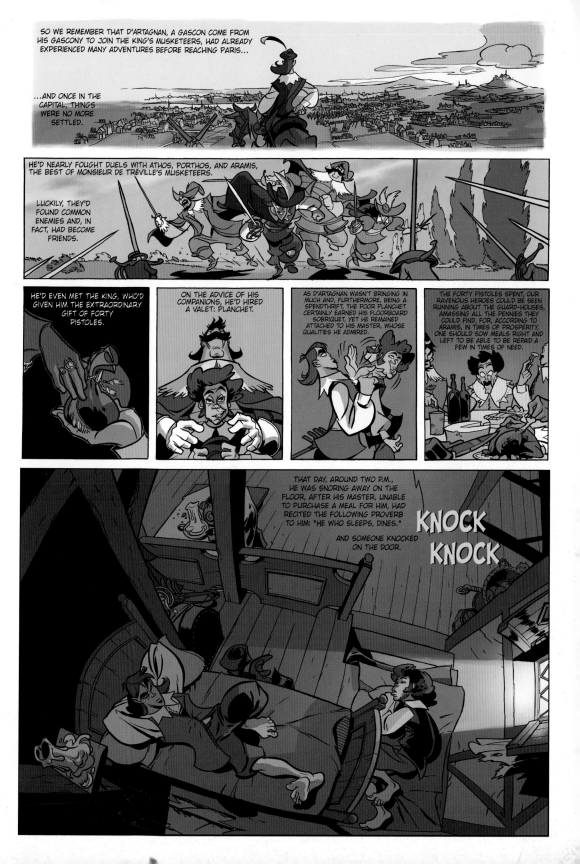

SO WE REMEMBER THAT D'ARTAGNAN, A GASCON COME FROM HIS GASCONY TO JOIN THE KING'S MUSKETEERS, HAD ALREADY EXPERIENCED MANY ADVENTURES BEFORE REACHING PARIS...

...AND ONCE IN THE CAPITAL, THINGS WERE NO MORE SETTLED.

HE'D NEARLY FOUGHT DUELS WITH ATHOS, PORTHOS, AND ARAMIS, THE BEST OF MONSIEUR DE TRÉVILLE'S MUSKETEERS.

LUCKILY, THEY'D FOUND COMMON ENEMIES AND, IN FACT, HAD BECOME FRIENDS.

HE'D EVEN MET THE KING, WHO'D GIVEN HIM THE EXTRAORDINARY GIFT OF FORTY PISTOLES.

ON THE ADVICE OF HIS COMPANIONS, HE'D HIRED A VALET: PLANCHET.

AS D'ARTAGNAN WASN'T BRINGING IN MUCH AND, FURTHERMORE, BEING A SPENDTHRIFT, THE POOR PLANCHET CERTAINLY EARNED HIS FLOORBOARD SOBRIQUET, YET HE REMAINED ATTACHED TO HIS MASTER, WHOSE QUALITIES HE ADMIRED.

THE FORTY PISTOLES SPENT, OUR RAVENOUS HEROES COULD BE SEEN RUNNING ABOUT THE GUARD-HOUSES, AMASSING ALL THE PENNIES THEY COULD FIND, FOR, ACCORDING TO ARAMIS, IN TIMES OF PROSPERITY, ONE SHOULD SOW MEALS RIGHT AND LEFT TO BE ABLE TO BE REPAID A FEW IN TIMES OF NEED.

THAT DAY, AROUND TWO P.M., HE WAS SNORING AWAY ON THE FLOOR, AFTER HIS MASTER, UNABLE TO PURCHASE A MEAL FOR HIM, HAD RECITED THE FOLLOWING PROVERB TO HIM: "HE WHO SLEEPS, DINES."

AND SOMEONE KNOCKED ON THE DOOR.

KNOCK KNOCK

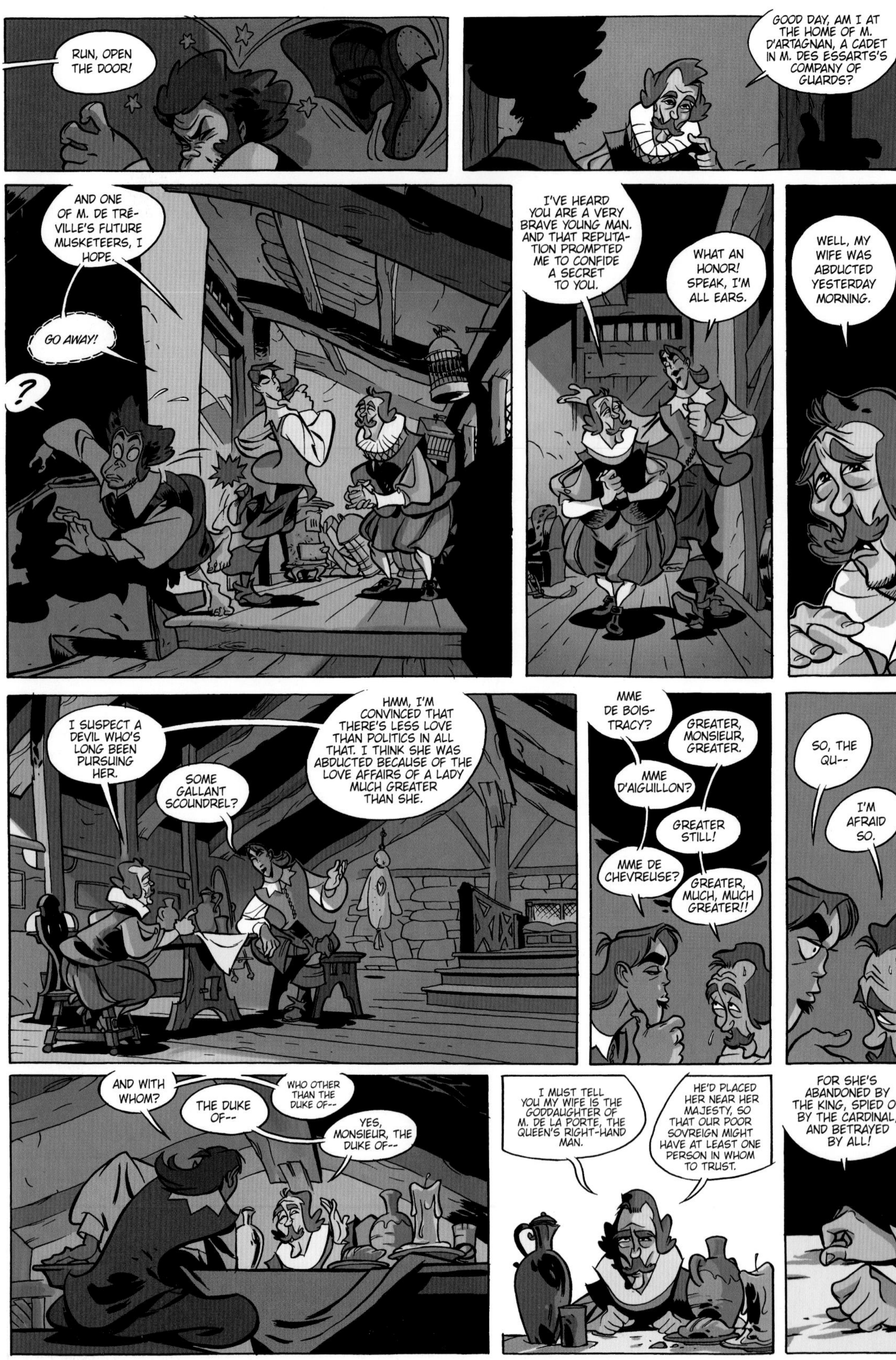
RUN, OPEN THE DOOR!
GOOD DAY, AM I AT THE HOME OF M. D'ARTAGNAN, A CADET IN M. DES ESSARTS'S COMPANY OF GUARDS?
AND ONE OF M. DE TRÉVILLE'S FUTURE MUSKETEERS, I HOPE.
GO AWAY!
?
I'VE HEARD YOU ARE A VERY BRAVE YOUNG MAN. AND THAT REPUTATION PROMPTED ME TO CONFIDE A SECRET TO YOU.
WHAT AN HONOR! SPEAK, I'M ALL EARS.
WELL, MY WIFE WAS ABDUCTED YESTERDAY MORNING.
I SUSPECT A DEVIL WHO'S LONG BEEN PURSUING HER.
SOME GALLANT SCOUNDREL?
HMM, I'M CONVINCED THAT THERE'S LESS LOVE THAN POLITICS IN ALL THAT. I THINK SHE WAS ABDUCTED BECAUSE OF THE LOVE AFFAIRS OF A LADY MUCH GREATER THAN SHE.
MME DE BOIS-TRACY?
GREATER, MONSIEUR, GREATER.
MME D'AIGUILLON?
GREATER STILL!
MME DE CHEVREUSE?
GREATER, MUCH, MUCH GREATER!!
SO, THE QU--
I'M AFRAID SO.
AND WITH WHOM?
WHO OTHER THAN THE DUKE OF--
THE DUKE OF--
YES, MONSIEUR, THE DUKE OF--
I MUST TELL YOU MY WIFE IS THE GODDAUGHTER OF M. DE LA PORTE, THE QUEEN'S RIGHT-HAND MAN.
HE'D PLACED HER NEAR HER MAJESTY, SO THAT OUR POOR SOVEREIGN MIGHT HAVE AT LEAST ONE PERSON IN WHOM TO TRUST.
FOR SHE'S ABANDONED BY THE KING, SPIED ON BY THE CARDINAL, AND BETRAYED BY ALL!

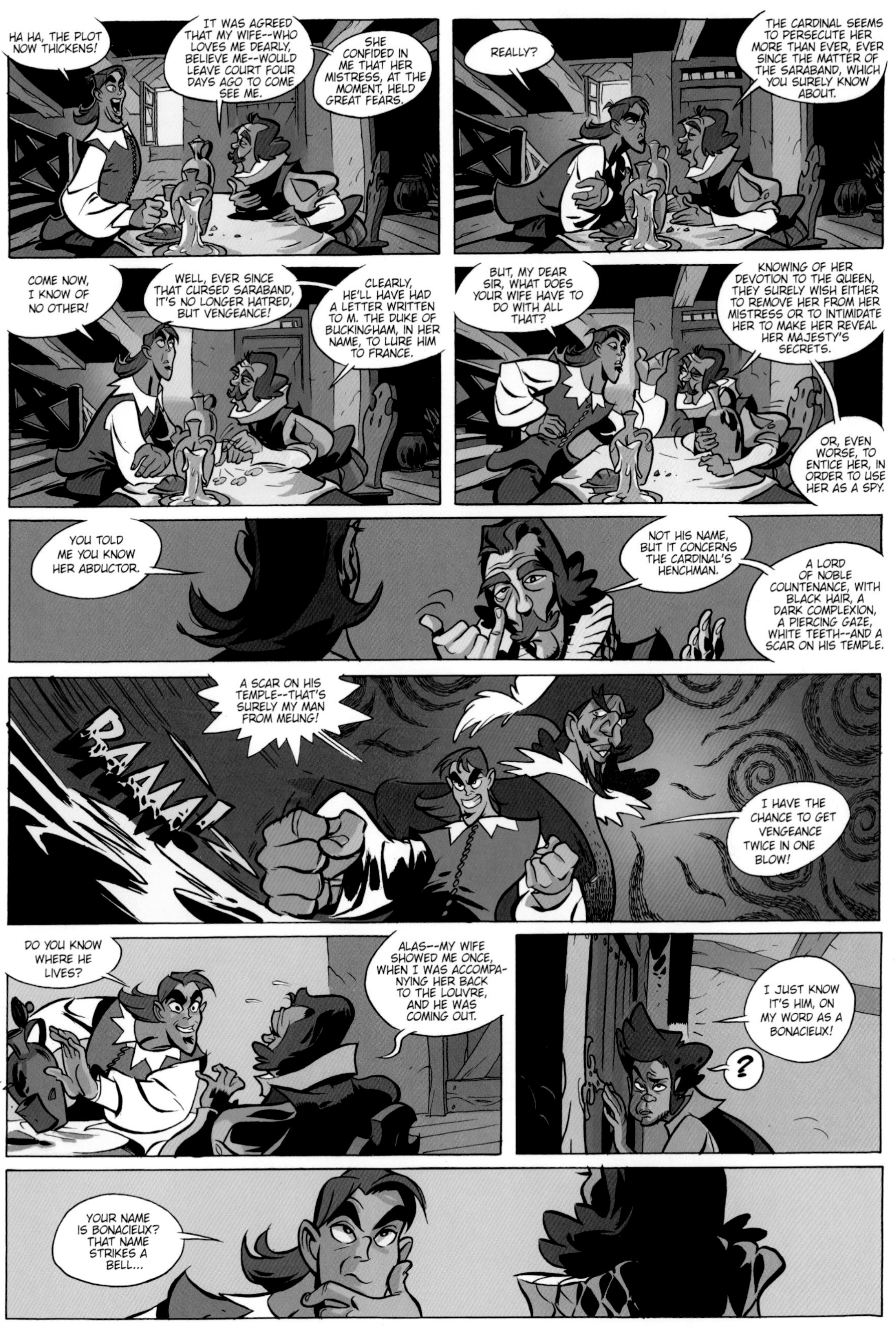
HA HA, THE PLOT NOW THICKENS!
IT WAS AGREED THAT MY WIFE--WHO LOVES ME DEARLY, BELIEVE ME--WOULD LEAVE COURT FOUR DAYS AGO TO COME SEE ME.
SHE CONFIDED IN ME THAT HER MISTRESS, AT THE MOMENT, HELD GREAT FEARS.
REALLY?
THE CARDINAL SEEMS TO PERSECUTE HER MORE THAN EVER, EVER SINCE THE MATTER OF THE SARABAND, WHICH YOU SURELY KNOW ABOUT.
COME NOW, I KNOW OF NO OTHER!
WELL, EVER SINCE THAT CURSED SARABAND, IT'S NO LONGER HATRED, BUT VENGEANCE!
CLEARLY, HE'LL HAVE HAD A LETTER WRITTEN TO M. THE DUKE OF BUCKINGHAM, IN HER NAME, TO LURE HIM TO FRANCE.
BUT, MY DEAR SIR, WHAT DOES YOUR WIFE HAVE TO DO WITH ALL THAT?
KNOWING OF HER DEVOTION TO THE QUEEN, THEY SURELY WISH EITHER TO REMOVE HER FROM HER MISTRESS OR TO INTIMIDATE HER TO MAKE HER REVEAL HER MAJESTY'S SECRETS.
OR, EVEN WORSE, TO ENTICE HER, IN ORDER TO USE HER AS A SPY.
YOU TOLD ME YOU KNOW HER ABDUCTOR.
NOT HIS NAME, BUT IT CONCERNS THE CARDINAL'S HENCHMAN.
A LORD OF NOBLE COUNTENANCE, WITH BLACK HAIR, A DARK COMPLEXION, A PIERCING GAZE, WHITE TEETH--AND A SCAR ON HIS TEMPLE.
A SCAR ON HIS TEMPLE--THAT'S SURELY MY MAN FROM MEUNG!
BAAAM!
I HAVE THE CHANCE TO GET VENGEANCE TWICE IN ONE BLOW!
DO YOU KNOW WHERE HE LIVES?
ALAS--MY WIFE SHOWED ME ONCE, WHEN I WAS ACCOMPANYING HER BACK TO THE LOUVRE, AND HE WAS COMING OUT.
I JUST KNOW IT'S HIM, ON MY WORD AS A BONACIEUX!
?
YOUR NAME IS BONACIEUX? THAT NAME STRIKES A BELL...

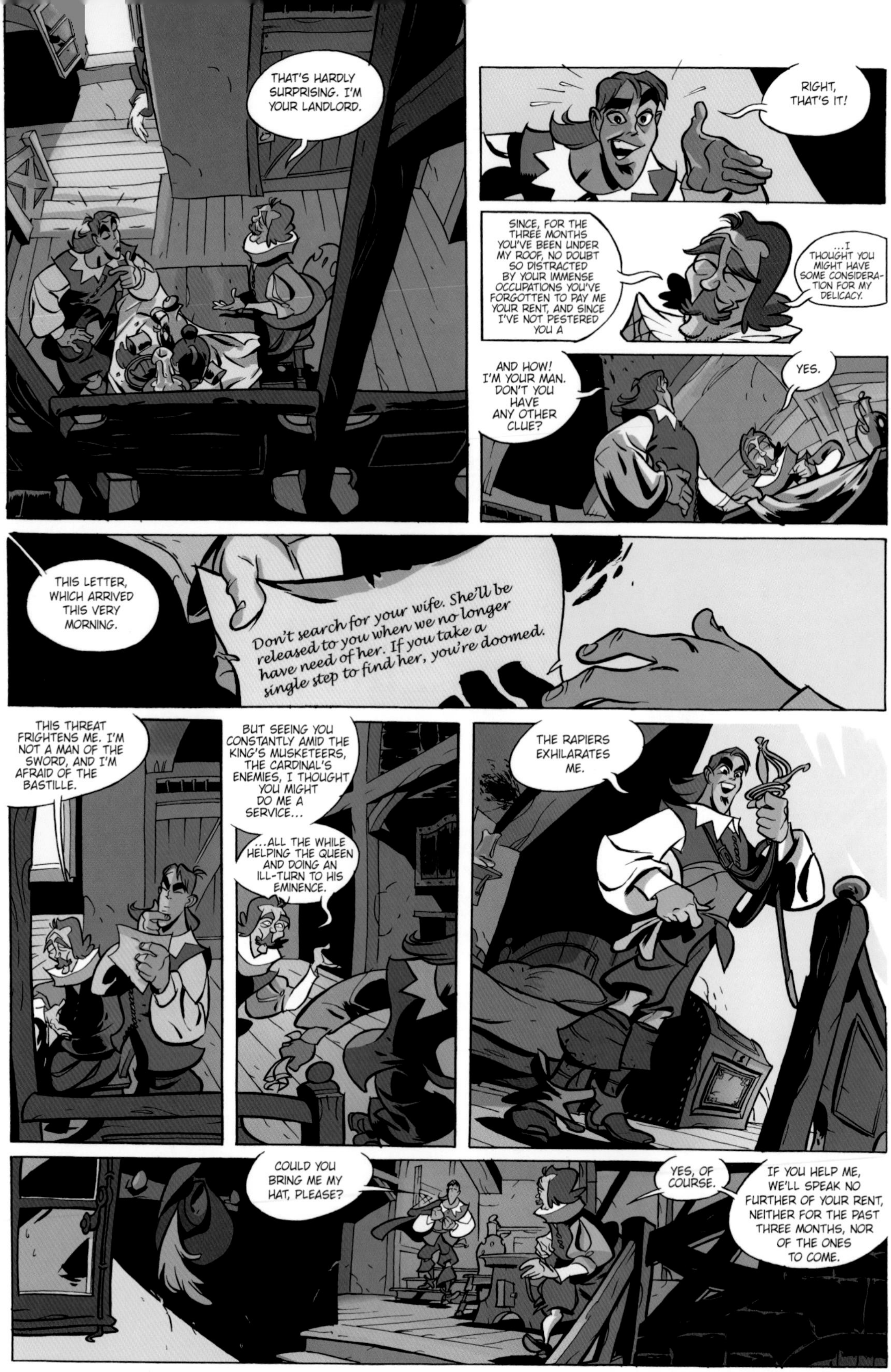

THAT'S HARDLY SURPRISING. I'M YOUR LANDLORD.
RIGHT, THAT'S IT!
SINCE, FOR THE THREE MONTHS YOU'VE BEEN UNDER MY ROOF, NO DOUBT SO DISTRACTED BY YOUR IMMENSE OCCUPATIONS YOU'VE FORGOTTEN TO PAY ME YOUR RENT, AND SINCE I'VE NOT PESTERED YOU A
...I THOUGHT YOU MIGHT HAVE SOME CONSIDERATION FOR MY DELICACY.
AND HOW! I'M YOUR MAN. DON'T YOU HAVE ANY OTHER CLUE?
YES.
THIS LETTER, WHICH ARRIVED THIS VERY MORNING.
Don't search for your wife. She'll be released to you when we no longer have need of her. If you take a single step to find her, you're doomed.
THIS THREAT FRIGHTENS ME. I'M NOT A MAN OF THE SWORD, AND I'M AFRAID OF THE BASTILLE.
BUT SEEING YOU CONSTANTLY AMID THE KING'S MUSKETEERS, THE CARDINAL'S ENEMIES, I THOUGHT YOU MIGHT DO ME A SERVICE...
...ALL THE WHILE HELPING THE QUEEN AND DOING AN ILL-TURN TO HIS EMINENCE.
THE RAPIERS EXHILARATES ME.
COULD YOU BRING ME MY HAT, PLEASE?
YES, OF COURSE.
IF YOU HELP ME, WE'LL SPEAK NO FURTHER OF YOUR RENT, NEITHER FOR THE PAST THREE MONTHS, NOR OF THE ONES TO COME.

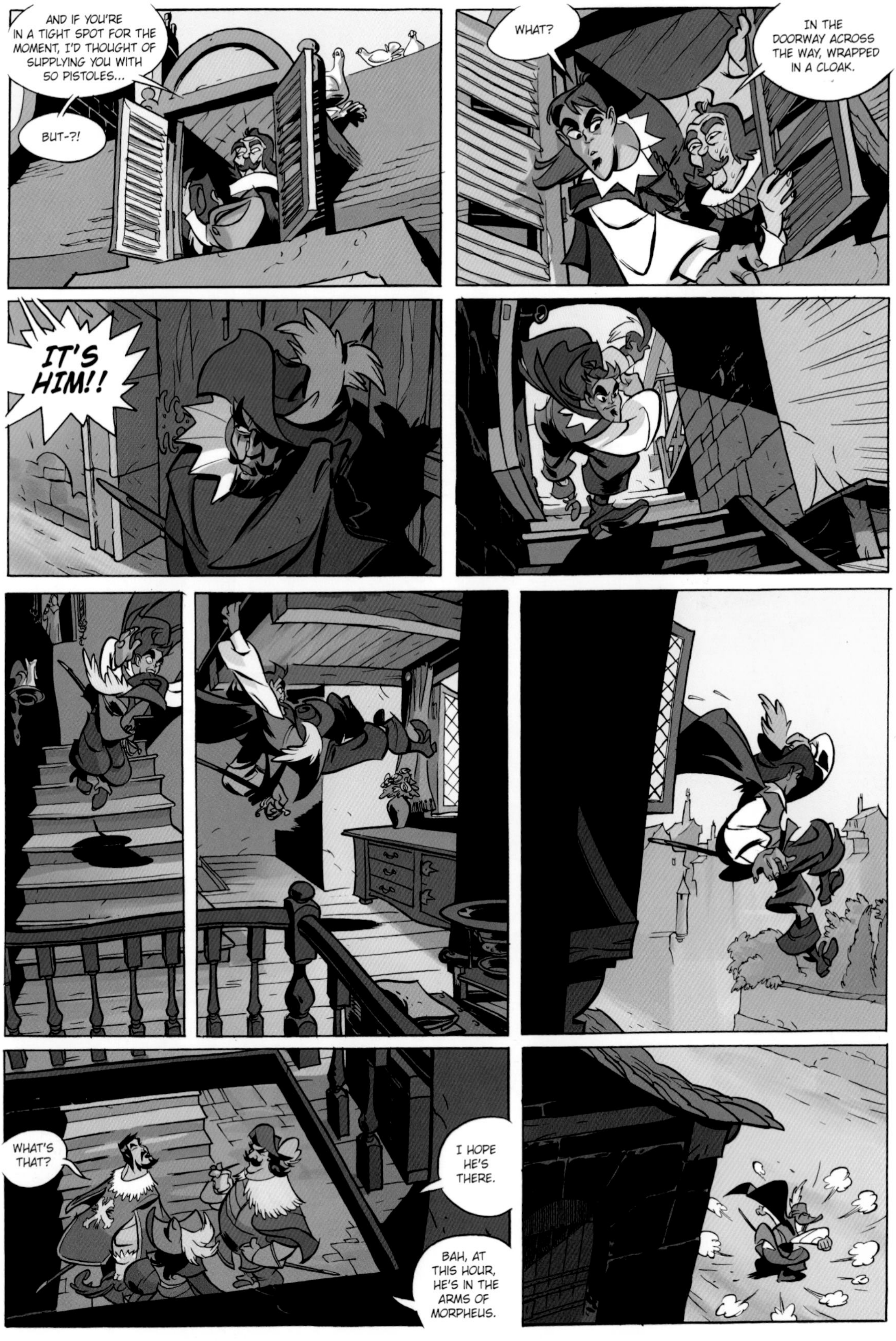
AND IF YOU'RE IN A TIGHT SPOT FOR THE MOMENT, I'D THOUGHT OF SUPPLYING YOU WITH 50 PISTOLES...
BUT-?!
WHAT?
IN THE DOORWAY ACROSS THE WAY, WRAPPED IN A CLOAK.
IT'S HIM!!
WHAT'S THAT?
I HOPE HE'S THERE.
BAH, AT THIS HOUR, HE'S IN THE ARMS OF MORPHEUS.

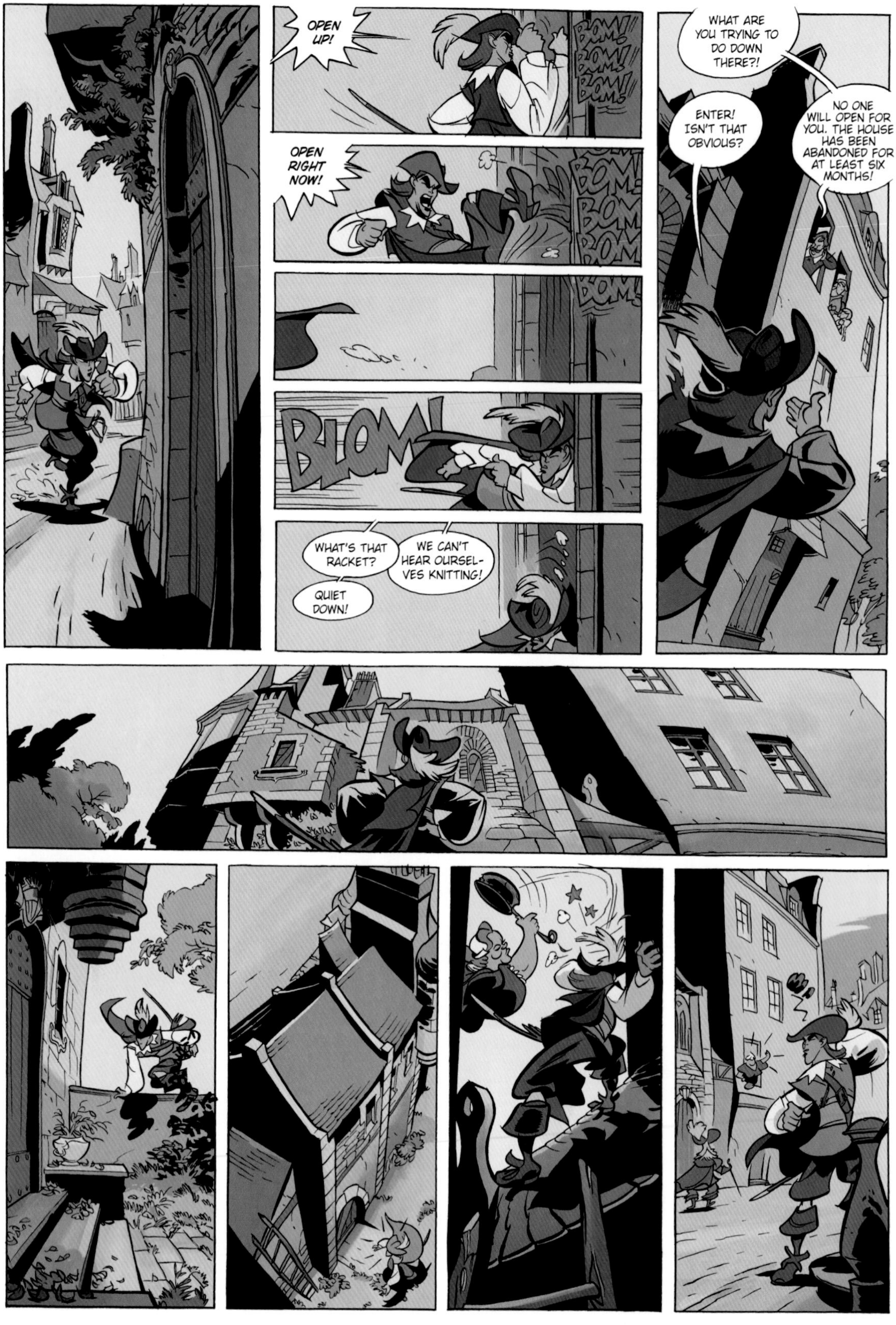
OPEN UP!
BOM! BOM! BOM! BOM!
OPEN RIGHT NOW!
BOM! BOM! BOM! BOM! BOM!
BOM!
BLOM!
WHAT'S THAT RACKET?
WE CAN'T HEAR OURSEL-VES KNITTING!
QUIET DOWN!
WHAT ARE YOU TRYING TO DO DOWN THERE?!
ENTER! ISN'T THAT OBVIOUS?
NO ONE WILL OPEN FOR YOU. THE HOUSE HAS BEEN ABANDONED FOR AT LEAST SIX MONTHS!

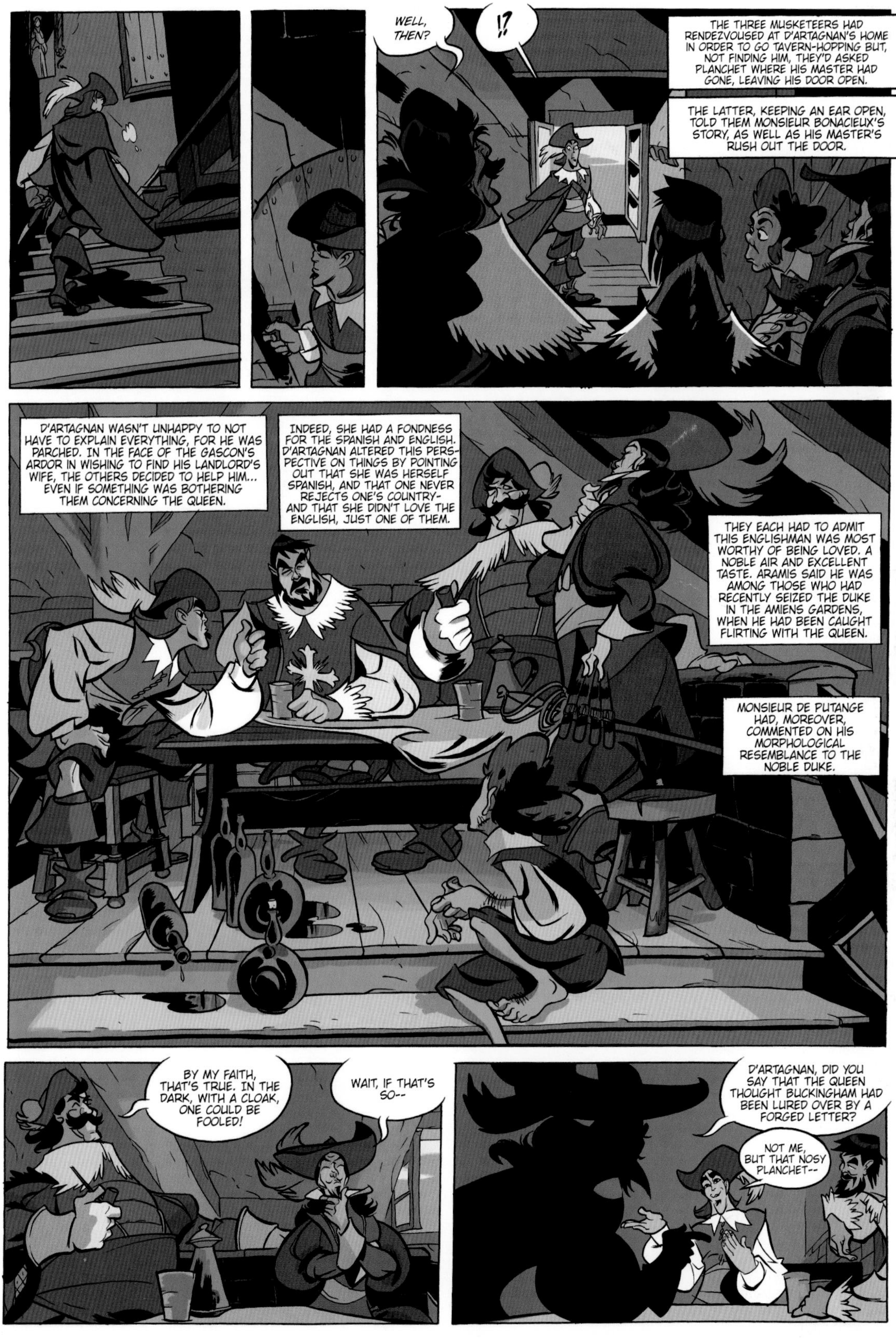
WELL, THEN?
!?
THE THREE MUSKETEERS HAD RENDEZVOUSED AT D'ARTAGNAN'S HOME IN ORDER TO GO TAVERN-HOPPING BUT, NOT FINDING HIM, THEY'D ASKED PLANCHET WHERE HIS MASTER HAD GONE, LEAVING HIS DOOR OPEN.
THE LATTER, KEEPING AN EAR OPEN, TOLD THEM MONSIEUR BONACIEUX'S STORY, AS WELL AS HIS MASTER'S RUSH OUT THE DOOR.
D'ARTAGNAN WASN'T UNHAPPY TO NOT HAVE TO EXPLAIN EVERYTHING, FOR HE WAS PARCHED. IN THE FACE OF THE GASCON'S ARDOR IN WISHING TO FIND HIS LANDLORD'S WIFE, THE OTHERS DECIDED TO HELP HIM... EVEN IF SOMETHING WAS BOTHERING THEM CONCERNING THE QUEEN.
INDEED, SHE HAD A FONDNESS FOR THE SPANISH AND ENGLISH. D'ARTAGNAN ALTERED THIS PERSPECTIVE ON THINGS BY POINTING OUT THAT SHE WAS HERSELF SPANISH, AND THAT ONE NEVER REJECTS ONE'S COUNTRY- AND THAT SHE DIDN'T LOVE THE ENGLISH, JUST ONE OF THEM.
THEY EACH HAD TO ADMIT THIS ENGLISHMAN WAS MOST WORTHY OF BEING LOVED. A NOBLE AIR AND EXCELLENT TASTE. ARAMIS SAID HE WAS AMONG THOSE WHO HAD RECENTLY SEIZED THE DUKE IN THE AMIENS GARDENS, WHEN HE HAD BEEN CAUGHT FLIRTING WITH THE QUEEN.
MONSIEUR DE PUTANGE HAD, MOREOVER, COMMENTED ON HIS MORPHOLOGICAL RESEMBLANCE TO THE NOBLE DUKE.
BY MY FAITH, THAT'S TRUE. IN THE DARK, WITH A CLOAK, ONE COULD BE FOOLED!
WAIT, IF THAT'S SO--
D'ARTAGNAN, DID YOU SAY THAT THE QUEEN THOUGHT BUCKINGHAM HAD BEEN LURED OVER BY A FORGED LETTER?
NOT ME, BUT THAT NOSY PLANCHET--

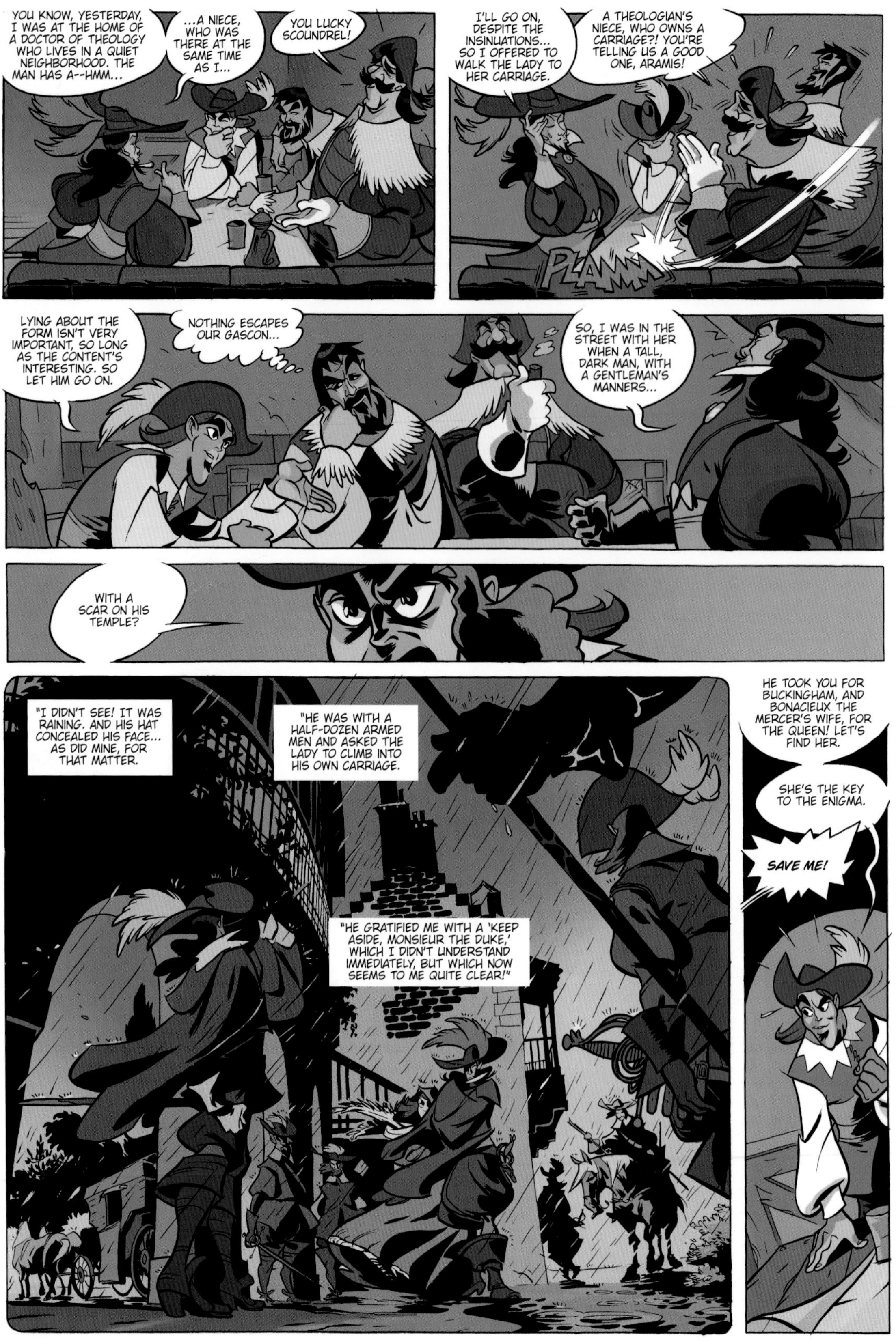
YOU KNOW, YESTERDAY, I WAS AT THE HOME OF A DOCTOR OF THEOLOGY WHO LIVES IN A QUIET NEIGHBORHOOD. THE MAN HAS A--HMM...
...A NIECE, WHO WAS THERE AT THE SAME TIME AS I...
YOU LUCKY SCOUNDREL!
I'LL GO ON, DESPITE THE INSINUATIONS... SO I OFFERED TO WALK THE LADY TO HER CARRIAGE.
A THEOLOGIAN'S NIECE, WHO OWNS A CARRIAGE?! YOU'RE TELLING US A GOOD ONE, ARAMIS!
PLAM
LYING ABOUT THE FORM ISN'T VERY IMPORTANT, SO LONG AS THE CONTENT'S INTERESTING. SO LET HIM GO ON.
NOTHING ESCAPES OUR GASCON...
SO, I WAS IN THE STREET WITH HER WHEN A TALL, DARK MAN, WITH A GENTLEMAN'S MANNERS...
WITH A SCAR ON HIS TEMPLE?
"I DIDN'T SEE! IT WAS RAINING. AND HIS HAT CONCEALED HIS FACE... AS DID MINE, FOR THAT MATTER.
"HE WAS WITH A HALF-DOZEN ARMED MEN AND ASKED THE LADY TO CLIMB INTO HIS OWN CARRIAGE.
"HE GRATIFIED ME WITH A 'KEEP ASIDE, MONSIEUR THE DUKE,' WHICH I DIDN'T UNDERSTAND IMMEDIATELY, BUT WHICH NOW SEEMS TO ME QUITE CLEAR!"
HE TOOK YOU FOR BUCKINGHAM, AND BONACIEUX THE MERCER'S WIFE, FOR THE QUEEN! LET'S FIND HER.
SHE'S THE KEY TO THE ENIGMA.
SAVE ME!

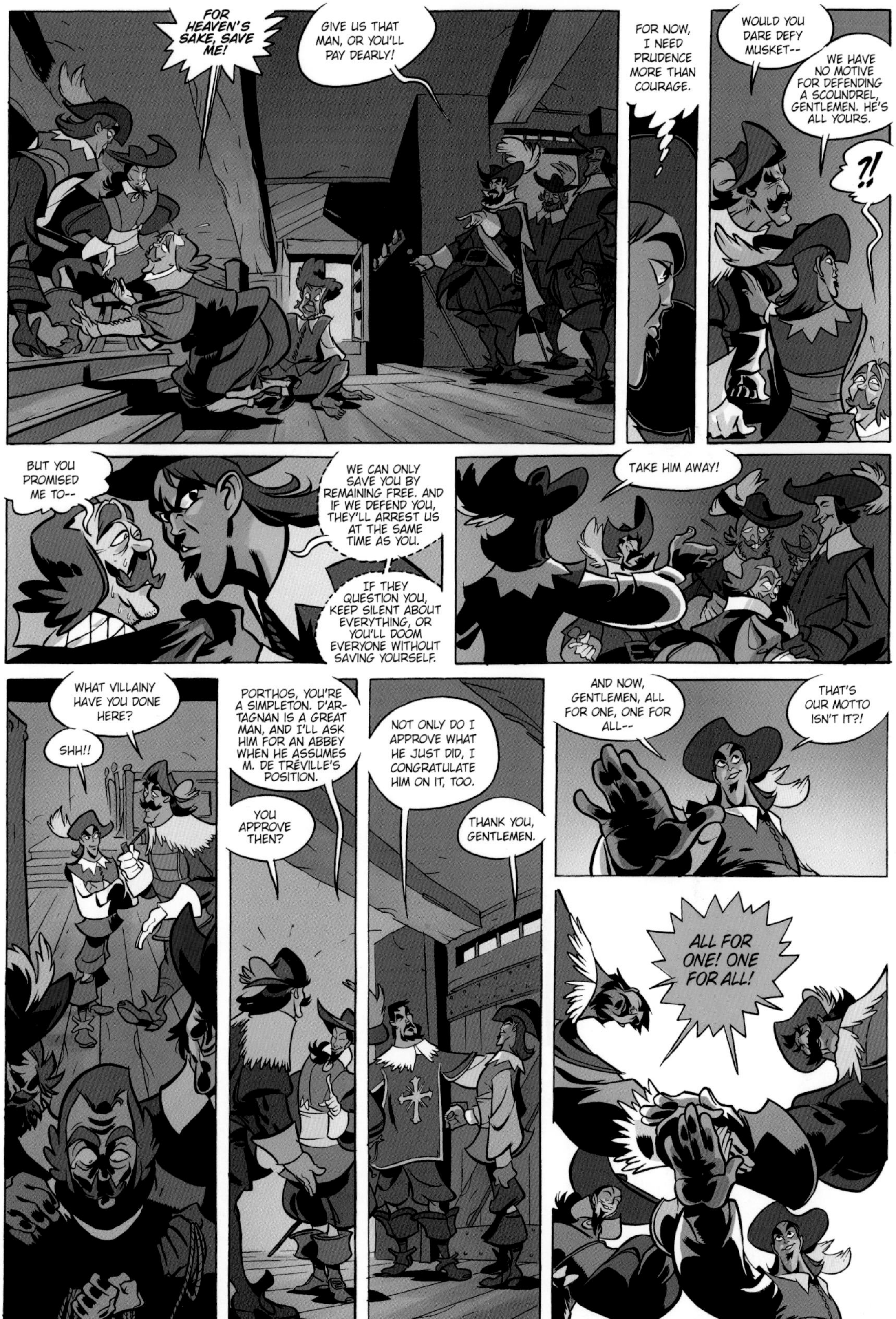
FOR HEAVEN'S SAKE, SAVE ME!
GIVE US THAT MAN, OR YOU'LL PAY DEARLY!
FOR NOW, I NEED PRUDENCE MORE THAN COURAGE.
WOULD YOU DARE DEFY MUSKET--
WE HAVE NO MOTIVE FOR DEFENDING A SCOUNDREL, GENTLEMEN. HE'S ALL YOURS.
?!
BUT YOU PROMISED ME TO--
WE CAN ONLY SAVE YOU BY REMAINING FREE. AND IF WE DEFEND YOU, THEY'LL ARREST US AT THE SAME TIME AS YOU.
IF THEY QUESTION YOU, KEEP SILENT ABOUT EVERYTHING, OR YOU'LL DOOM EVERYONE WITHOUT SAVING YOURSELF.
TAKE HIM AWAY!
WHAT VILLAINY HAVE YOU DONE HERE?
SHH!!
PORTHOS, YOU'RE A SIMPLETON. D'ARTAGNAN IS A GREAT MAN, AND I'LL ASK HIM FOR AN ABBEY WHEN HE ASSUMES M. DE TRÉVILLE'S POSITION.
YOU APPROVE THEN?
NOT ONLY DO I APPROVE WHAT HE JUST DID, I CONGRATULATE HIM ON IT, TOO.
THANK YOU, GENTLEMEN.
AND NOW, GENTLEMEN, ALL FOR ONE, ONE FOR ALL--
THAT'S OUR MOTTO ISN'T IT?!
ALL FOR ONE! ONE FOR ALL!

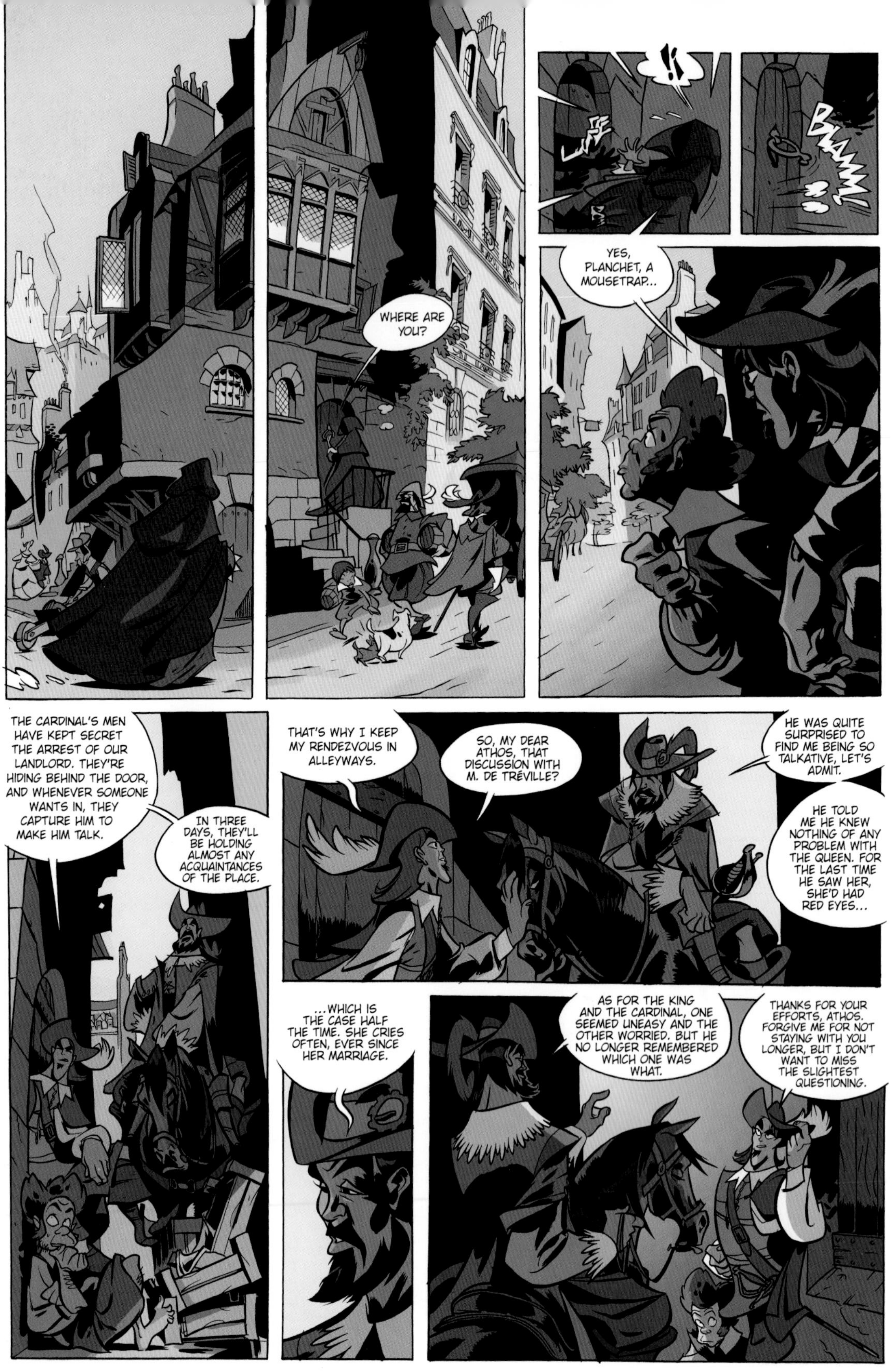
WHERE ARE YOU?
!¡
BLAAMM!
YES, PLANCHET, A MOUSETRAP...
THE CARDINAL'S MEN HAVE KEPT SECRET THE ARREST OF OUR LANDLORD. THEY'RE HIDING BEHIND THE DOOR, AND WHENEVER SOMEONE WANTS IN, THEY CAPTURE HIM TO MAKE HIM TALK.
IN THREE DAYS, THEY'LL BE HOLDING ALMOST ANY ACQUAINTANCES OF THE PLACE.
THAT'S WHY I KEEP MY RENDEZVOUS IN ALLEYWAYS.
SO, MY DEAR ATHOS, THAT DISCUSSION WITH M. DE TRÉVILLE?
HE WAS QUITE SURPRISED TO FIND ME BEING SO TALKATIVE, LET'S ADMIT.
HE TOLD ME HE KNEW NOTHING OF ANY PROBLEM WITH THE QUEEN. FOR THE LAST TIME HE SAW HER, SHE'D HAD RED EYES...
...WHICH IS THE CASE HALF THE TIME. SHE CRIES OFTEN, EVER SINCE HER MARRIAGE.
AS FOR THE KING AND THE CARDINAL, ONE SEEMED UNEASY AND THE OTHER WORRIED. BUT HE NO LONGER REMEMBERED WHICH ONE WAS WHAT.
THANKS FOR YOUR EFFORTS, ATHOS. FORGIVE ME FOR NOT STAYING WITH YOU LONGER, BUT I DON'T WANT TO MISS THE SLIGHTEST QUESTIONING.

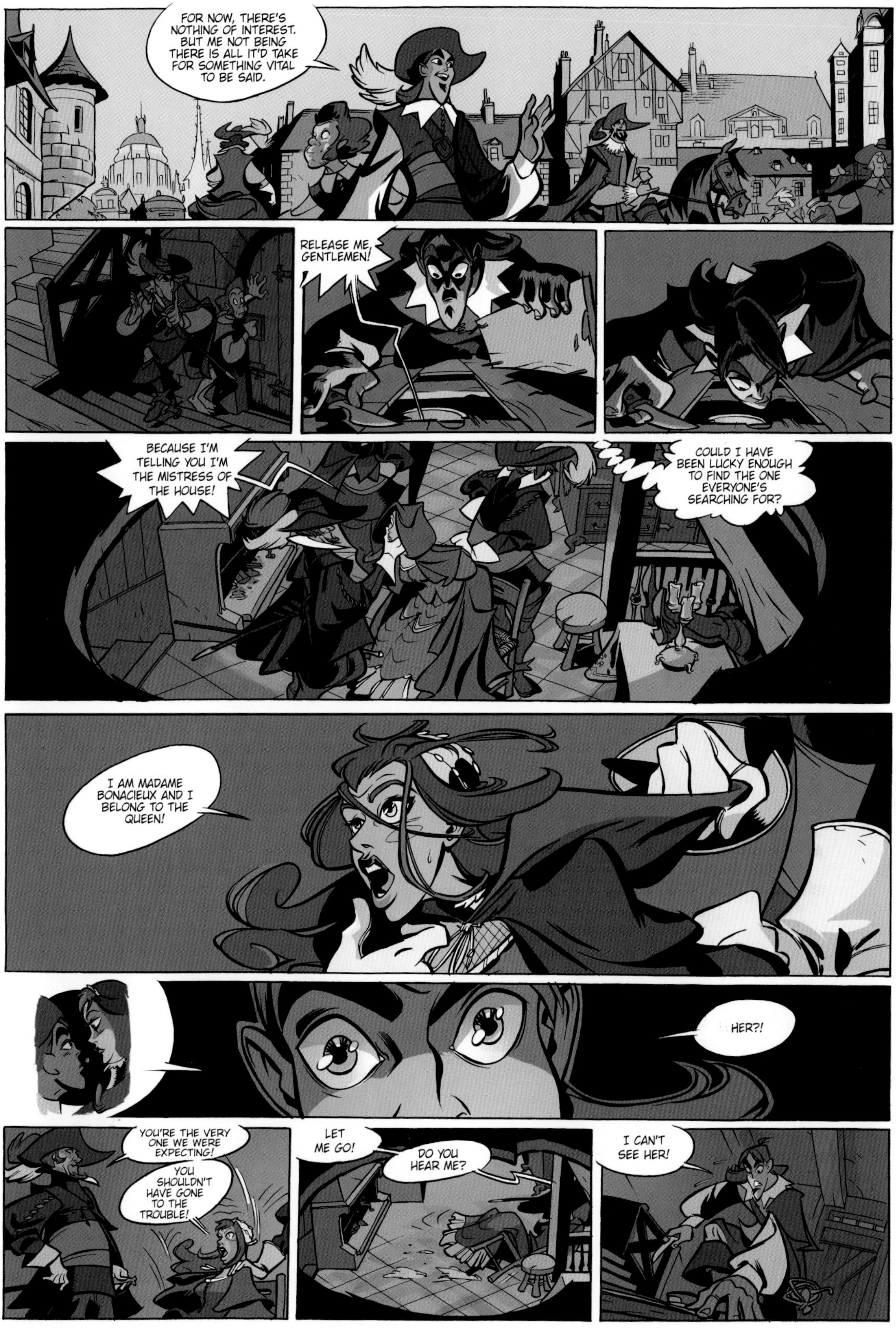
FOR NOW, THERE'S NOTHING OF INTEREST. BUT ME NOT BEING THERE IS ALL IT'D TAKE FOR SOMETHING VITAL TO BE SAID.
RELEASE ME, GENTLEMEN!
BECAUSE I'M TELLING YOU I'M THE MISTRESS OF THE HOUSE!
COULD I HAVE BEEN LUCKY ENOUGH TO FIND THE ONE EVERYONE'S SEARCHING FOR?
I AM MADAME BONACIEUX AND I BELONG TO THE QUEEN!
HER?!
YOU'RE THE VERY ONE WE WERE EXPECTING!
YOU SHOULDN'T HAVE GONE TO THE TROUBLE!
LET ME GO!
DO YOU HEAR ME?
I CAN'T SEE HER!

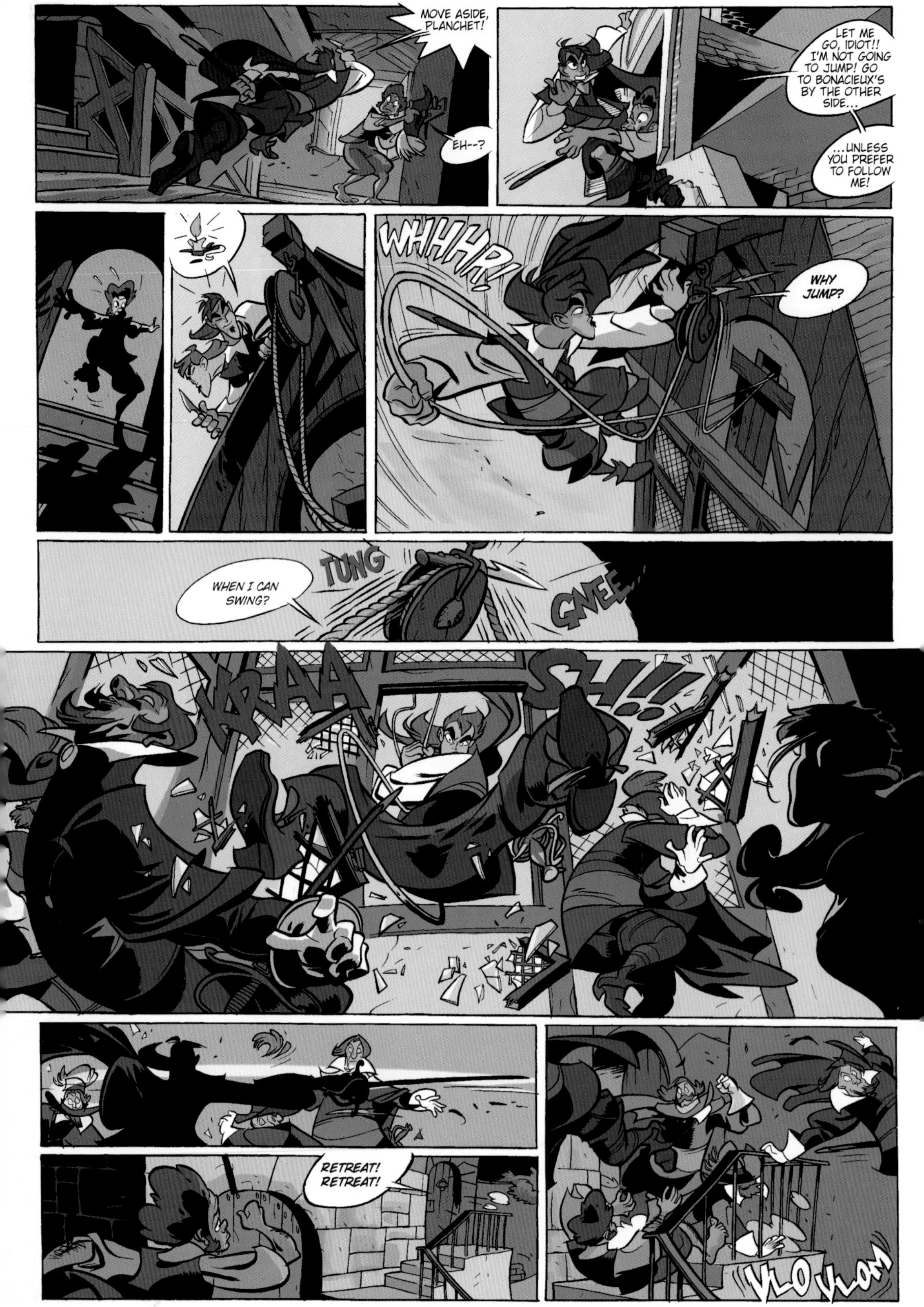
MOVE ASIDE, PLANCHET!
EH--?
LET ME GO, IDIOT!! I'M NOT GOING TO JUMP! GO TO BONACIEUX'S BY THE OTHER SIDE...
...UNLESS YOU PREFER TO FOLLOW ME!
WHHHR!
WHY JUMP?
WHEN I CAN SWING?
TUNG
GNEE
KRAA
SH!!!
RETREAT! RETREAT!
VLO VLOM

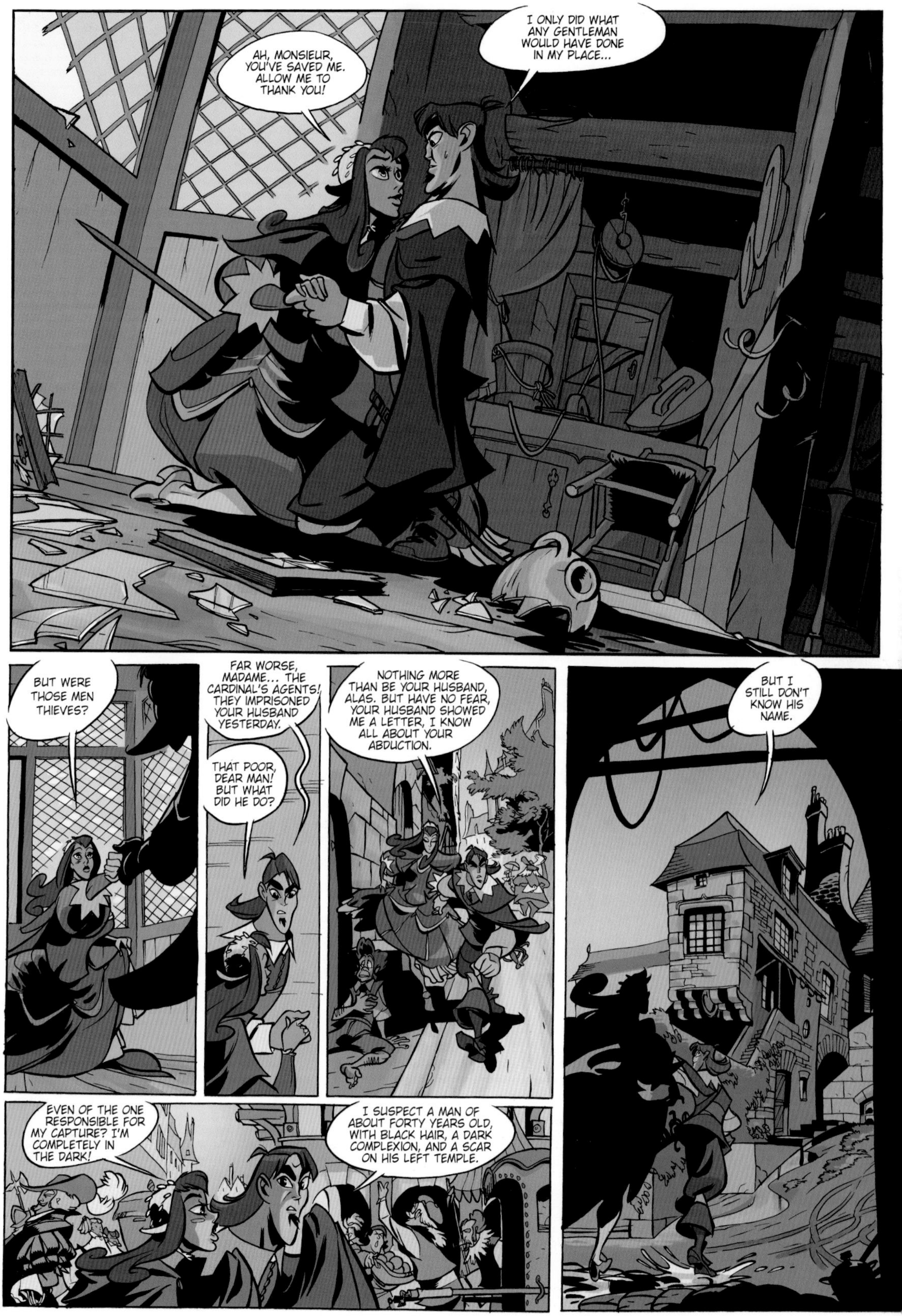

AH, MONSIEUR, YOU'VE SAVED ME. ALLOW ME TO THANK YOU!
I ONLY DID WHAT ANY GENTLEMAN WOULD HAVE DONE IN MY PLACE...
BUT WERE THOSE MEN THIEVES?
FAR WORSE, MADAME... THE CARDINAL'S AGENTS! THEY IMPRISONED YOUR HUSBAND YESTERDAY.
THAT POOR, DEAR MAN! BUT WHAT DID HE DO?
NOTHING MORE THAN BE YOUR HUSBAND, ALAS. BUT HAVE NO FEAR, YOUR HUSBAND SHOWED ME A LETTER, I KNOW ALL ABOUT YOUR ABDUCTION.
BUT I STILL DON'T KNOW HIS NAME.
EVEN OF THE ONE RESPONSIBLE FOR MY CAPTURE? I'M COMPLETELY IN THE DARK!
I SUSPECT A MAN OF ABOUT FORTY YEARS OLD, WITH BLACK HAIR, A DARK COMPLEXION, AND A SCAR ON HIS LEFT TEMPLE.

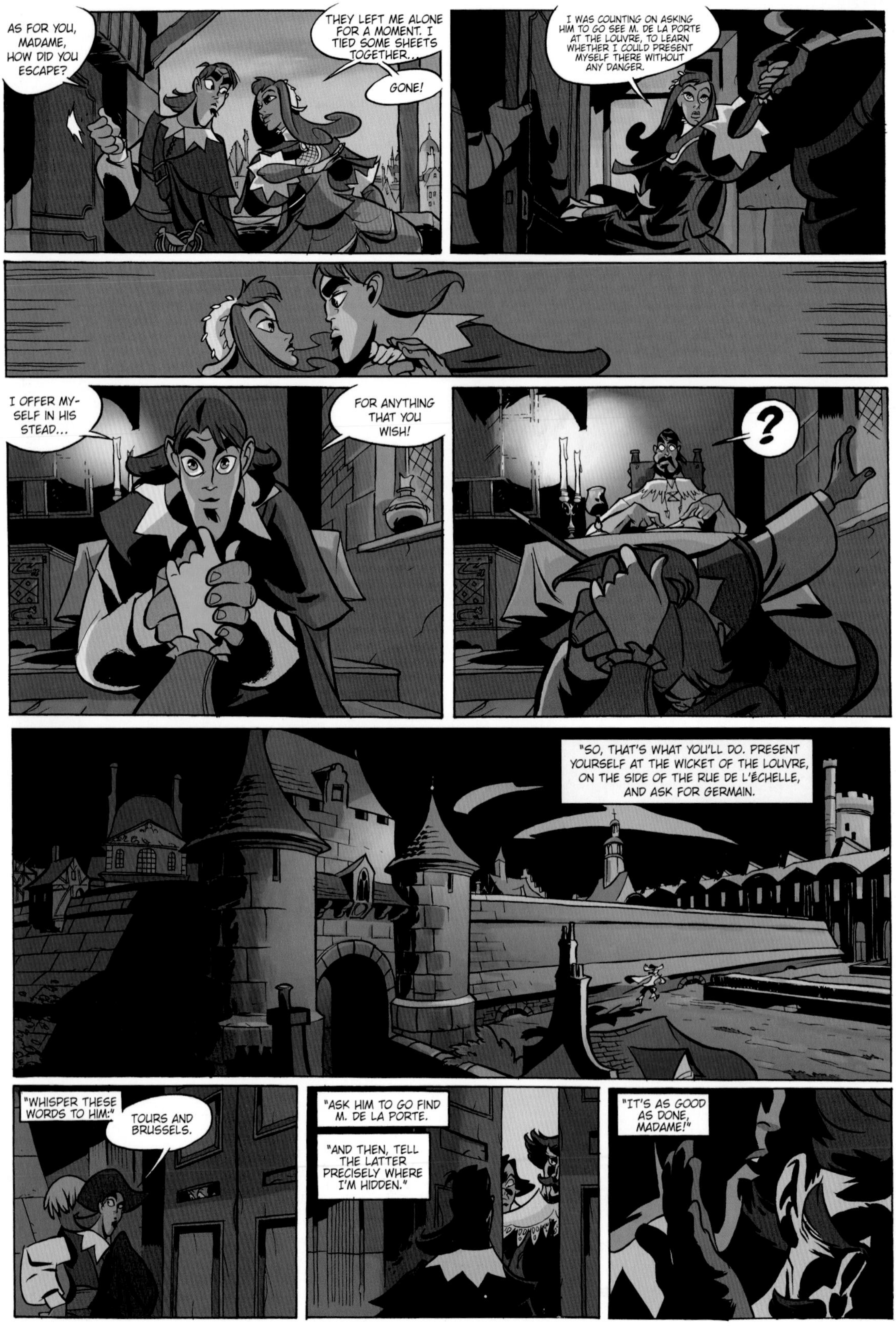
AS FOR YOU, MADAME, HOW DID YOU ESCAPE?
THEY LEFT ME ALONE FOR A MOMENT. I TIED SOME SHEETS TOGETHER...
GONE!
I WAS COUNTING ON ASKING HIM TO GO SEE M. DE LA PORTE AT THE LOUVRE, TO LEARN WHETHER I COULD PRESENT MYSELF THERE WITHOUT ANY DANGER.
I OFFER MYSELF IN HIS STEAD...
FOR ANYTHING THAT YOU WISH!
?
"SO, THAT'S WHAT YOU'LL DO. PRESENT YOURSELF AT THE WICKET OF THE LOUVRE, ON THE SIDE OF THE RUE DE L'ÉCHELLE, AND ASK FOR GERMAIN.
"WHISPER THESE WORDS TO HIM:"
TOURS AND BRUSSELS.
"ASK HIM TO GO FIND M. DE LA PORTE.
"AND THEN, TELL THE LATTER PRECISELY WHERE I'M HIDDEN."
"IT'S AS GOOD AS DONE, MADAME!"

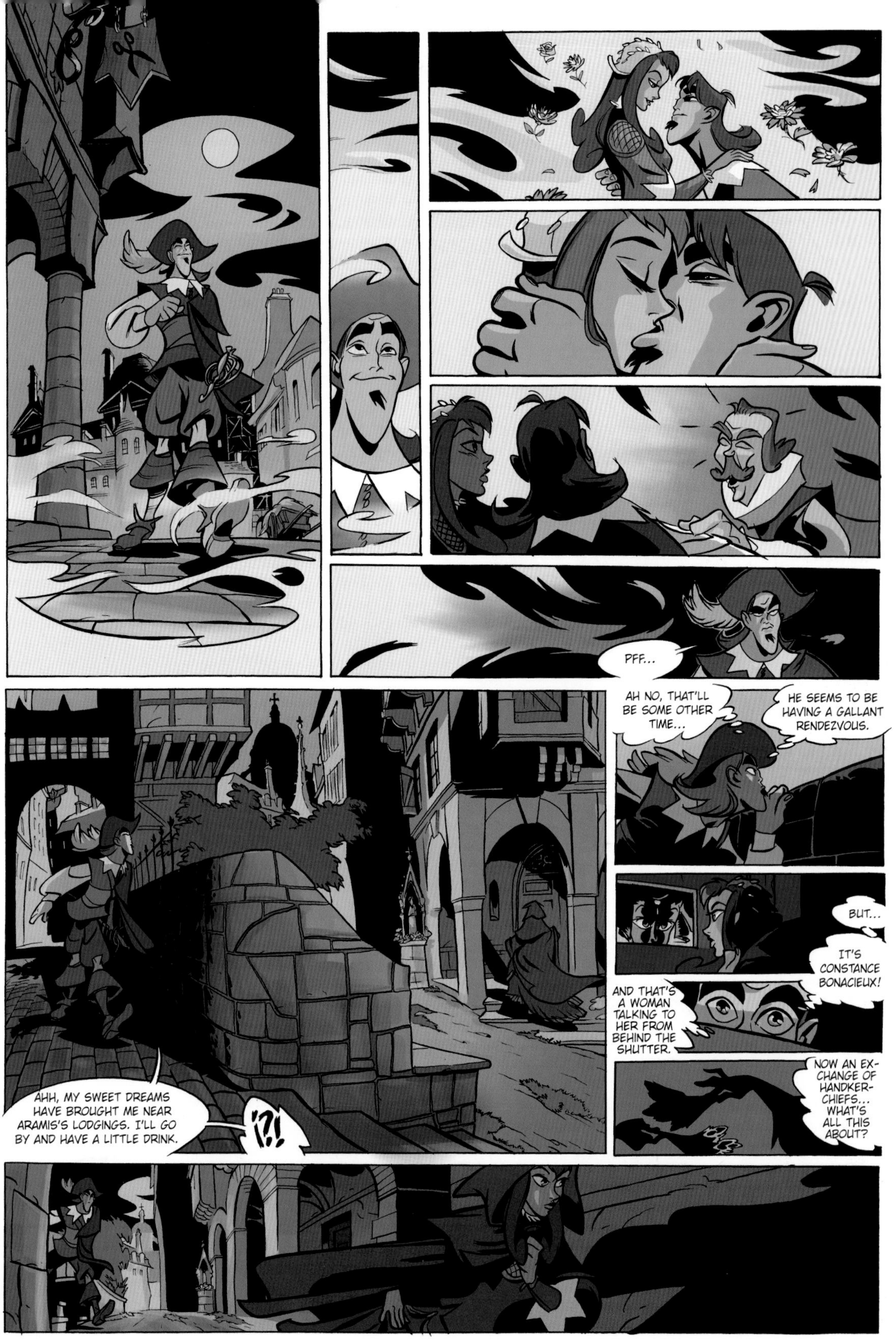
PFF...
AH NO, THAT'LL BE SOME OTHER TIME...
HE SEEMS TO BE HAVING A GALLANT RENDEZVOUS.
BUT...
IT'S CONSTANCE BONACIEUX!
AND THAT'S A WOMAN TALKING TO HER FROM BEHIND THE SHUTTER.
NOW AN EXCHANGE OF HANDKERCHIEFS... WHAT'S ALL THIS ABOUT?
AHH, MY SWEET DREAMS HAVE BROUGHT ME NEAR ARAMIS'S LODGINGS. I'LL GO BY AND HAVE A LITTLE DRINK.
¡?!

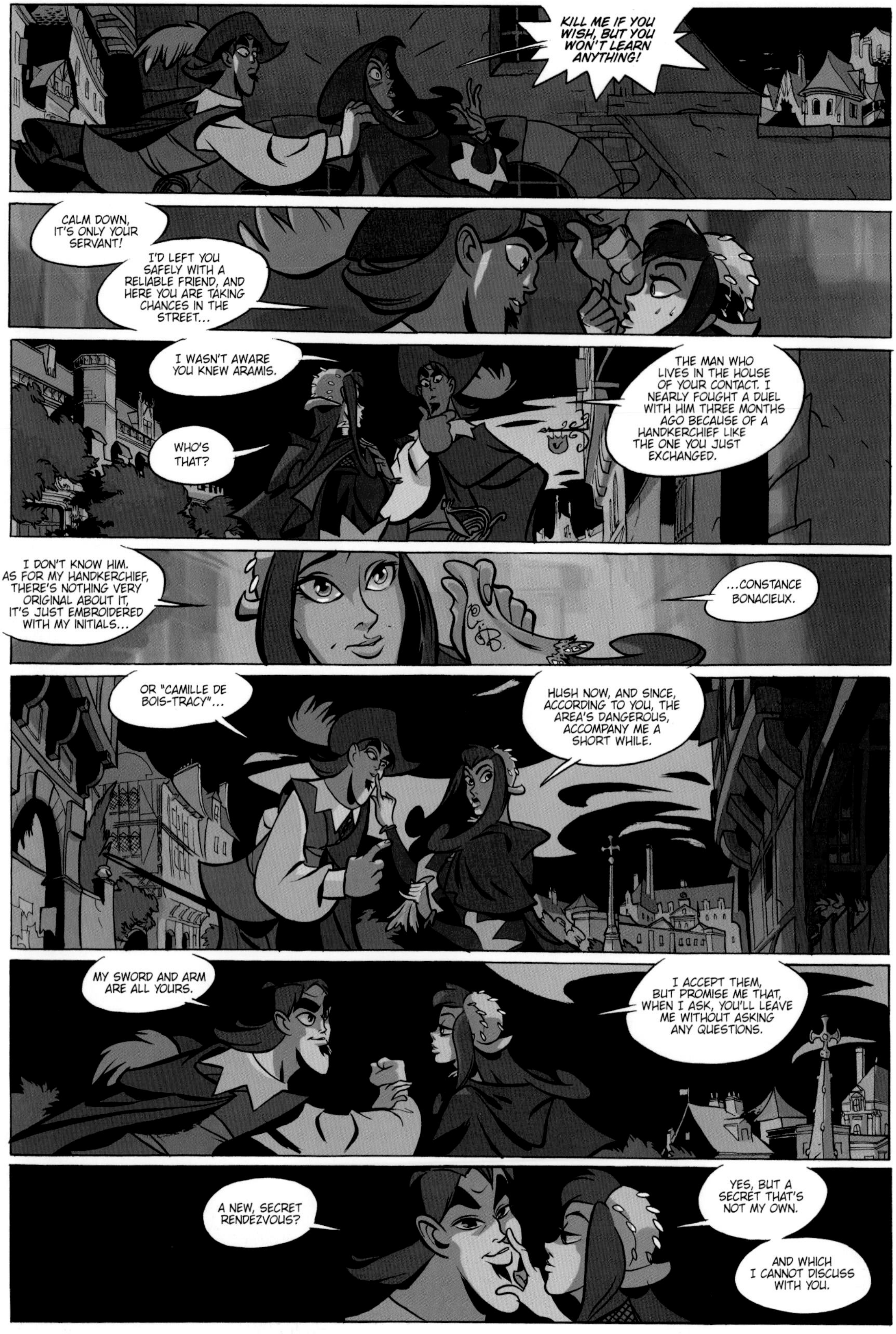
KILL ME IF YOU WISH, BUT YOU WON'T LEARN ANYTHING!
CALM DOWN, IT'S ONLY YOUR SERVANT!
I'D LEFT YOU SAFELY WITH A RELIABLE FRIEND, AND HERE YOU ARE TAKING CHANCES IN THE STREET...
I WASN'T AWARE YOU KNEW ARAMIS.
WHO'S THAT?
THE MAN WHO LIVES IN THE HOUSE OF YOUR CONTACT. I NEARLY FOUGHT A DUEL WITH HIM THREE MONTHS AGO BECAUSE OF A HANDKERCHIEF LIKE THE ONE YOU JUST EXCHANGED.
I DON'T KNOW HIM. AS FOR MY HANDKERCHIEF, THERE'S NOTHING VERY ORIGINAL ABOUT IT, IT'S JUST EMBROIDERED WITH MY INITIALS...
...CONSTANCE BONACIEUX.
OR "CAMILLE DE BOIS-TRACY"...
HUSH NOW, AND SINCE, ACCORDING TO YOU, THE AREA'S DANGEROUS, ACCOMPANY ME A SHORT WHILE.
MY SWORD AND ARM ARE ALL YOURS.
I ACCEPT THEM, BUT PROMISE ME THAT, WHEN I ASK, YOU'LL LEAVE ME WITHOUT ASKING ANY QUESTIONS.
A NEW, SECRET RENDEZVOUS?
YES, BUT A SECRET THAT'S NOT MY OWN.
AND WHICH I CANNOT DISCUSS WITH YOU.

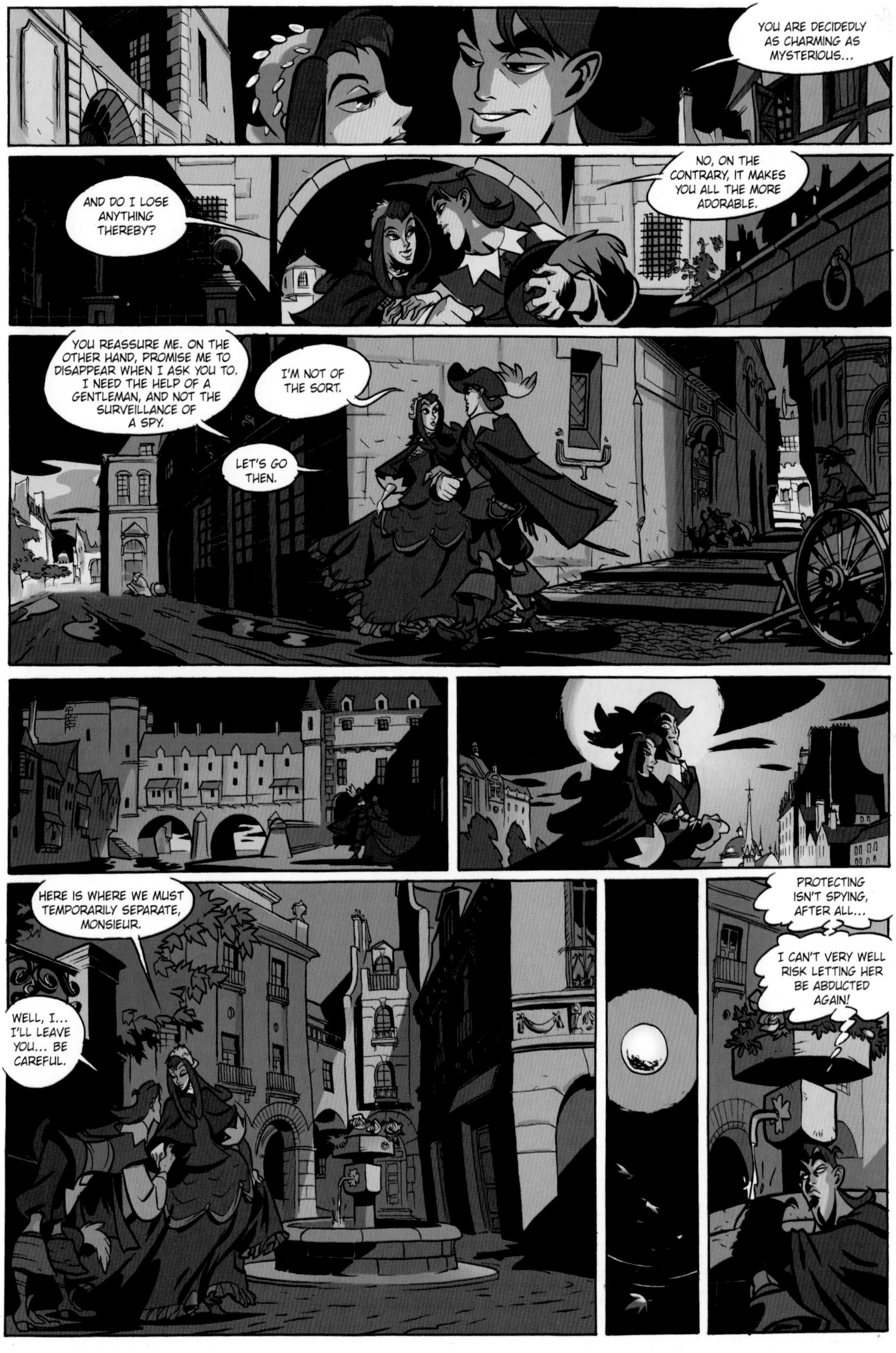
YOU ARE DECIDEDLY AS CHARMING AS MYSTERIOUS...
AND DO I LOSE ANYTHING THEREBY?
NO, ON THE CONTRARY, IT MAKES YOU ALL THE MORE ADORABLE.
YOU REASSURE ME. ON THE OTHER HAND, PROMISE ME TO DISAPPEAR WHEN I ASK YOU TO. I NEED THE HELP OF A GENTLEMAN, AND NOT THE SURVEILLANCE OF A SPY.
I'M NOT OF THE SORT.
LET'S GO THEN.
HERE IS WHERE WE MUST TEMPORARILY SEPARATE, MONSIEUR.
WELL, I... I'LL LEAVE YOU... BE CAREFUL.
PROTECTING ISN'T SPYING, AFTER ALL...
I CAN'T VERY WELL RISK LETTING HER BE ABDUCTED AGAIN!

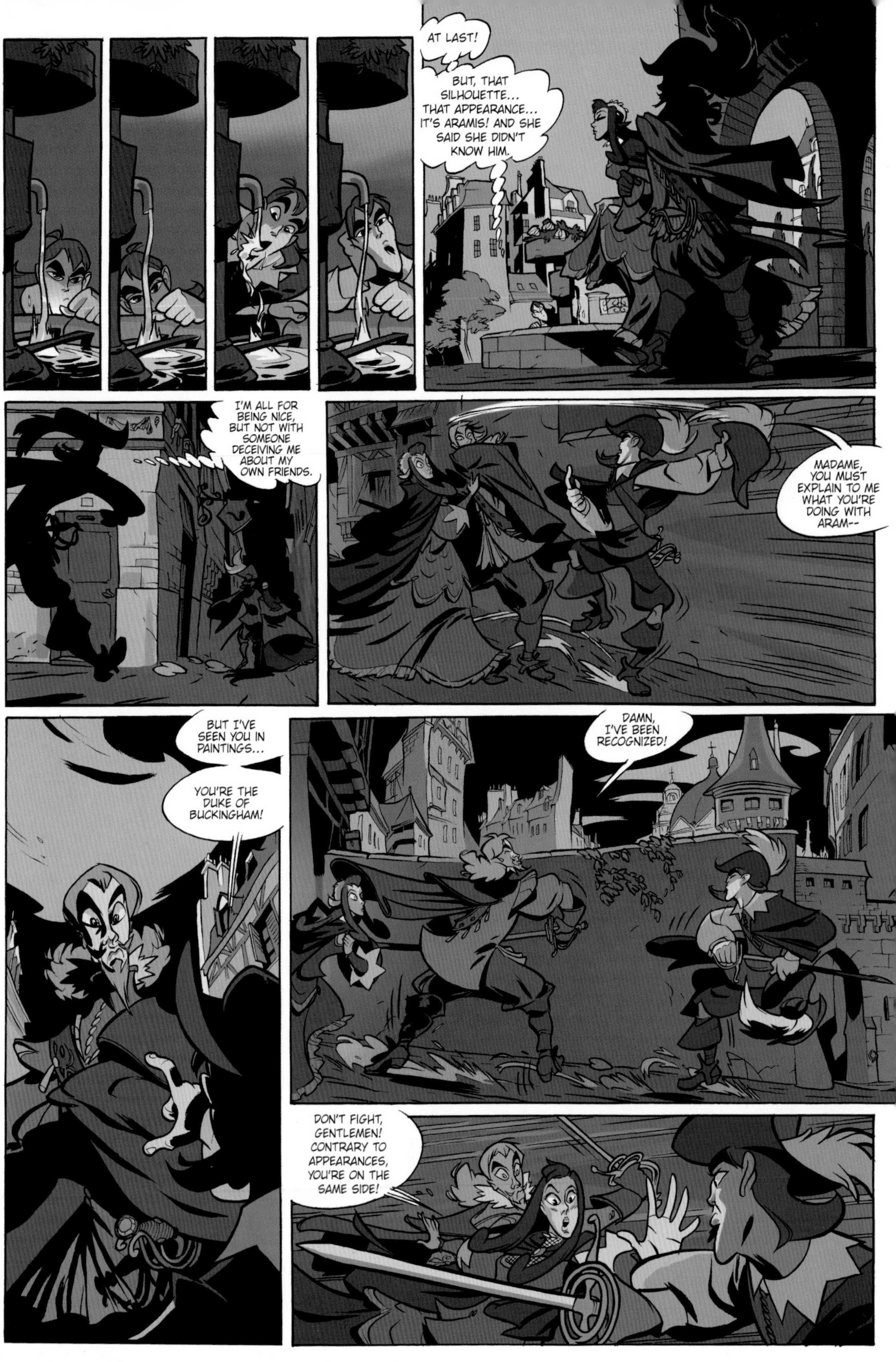
AT LAST!
BUT, THAT SILHOUETTE... THAT APPEARANCE... IT'S ARAMIS! AND SHE SAID SHE DIDN'T KNOW HIM.
I'M ALL FOR BEING NICE, BUT NOT WITH SOMEONE DECEIVING ME ABOUT MY OWN FRIENDS.
MADAME, YOU MUST EXPLAIN TO ME WHAT YOU'RE DOING WITH ARAM--
BUT I'VE SEEN YOU IN PAINTINGS...
YOU'RE THE DUKE OF BUCKINGHAM!
DAMN, I'VE BEEN RECOGNIZED!
DON'T FIGHT, GENTLEMEN! CONTRARY TO APPEARANCES, YOU'RE ON THE SAME SIDE!

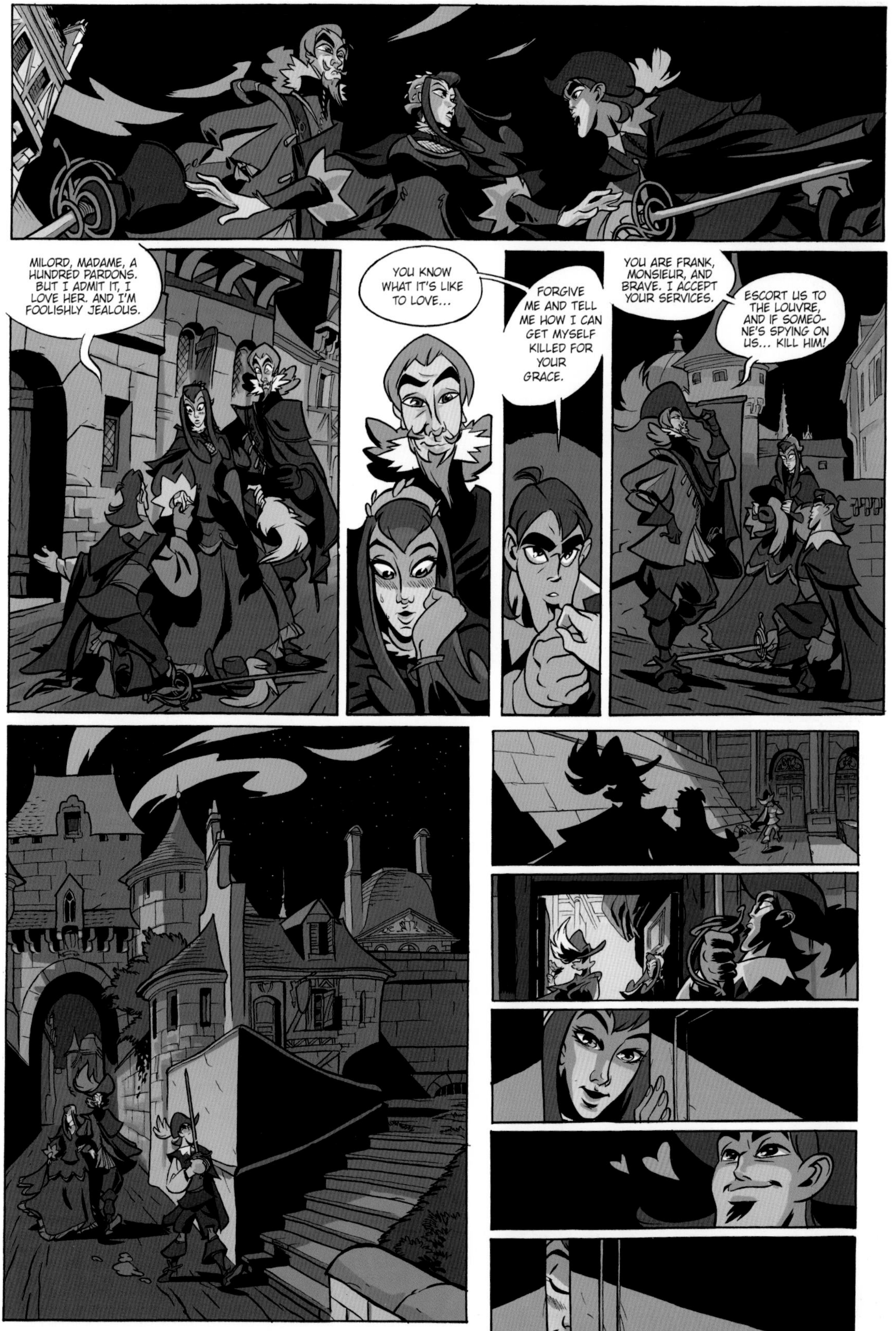
MILORD, MADAME, A HUNDRED PARDONS. BUT I ADMIT IT, I LOVE HER. AND I'M FOOLISHLY JEALOUS.
YOU KNOW WHAT IT'S LIKE TO LOVE...
FORGIVE ME AND TELL ME HOW I CAN GET MYSELF KILLED FOR YOUR GRACE.
YOU ARE FRANK, MONSIEUR, AND BRAVE. I ACCEPT YOUR SERVICES.
ESCORT US TO THE LOUVRE, AND IF SOMEONE'S SPYING ON US... KILL HIM!

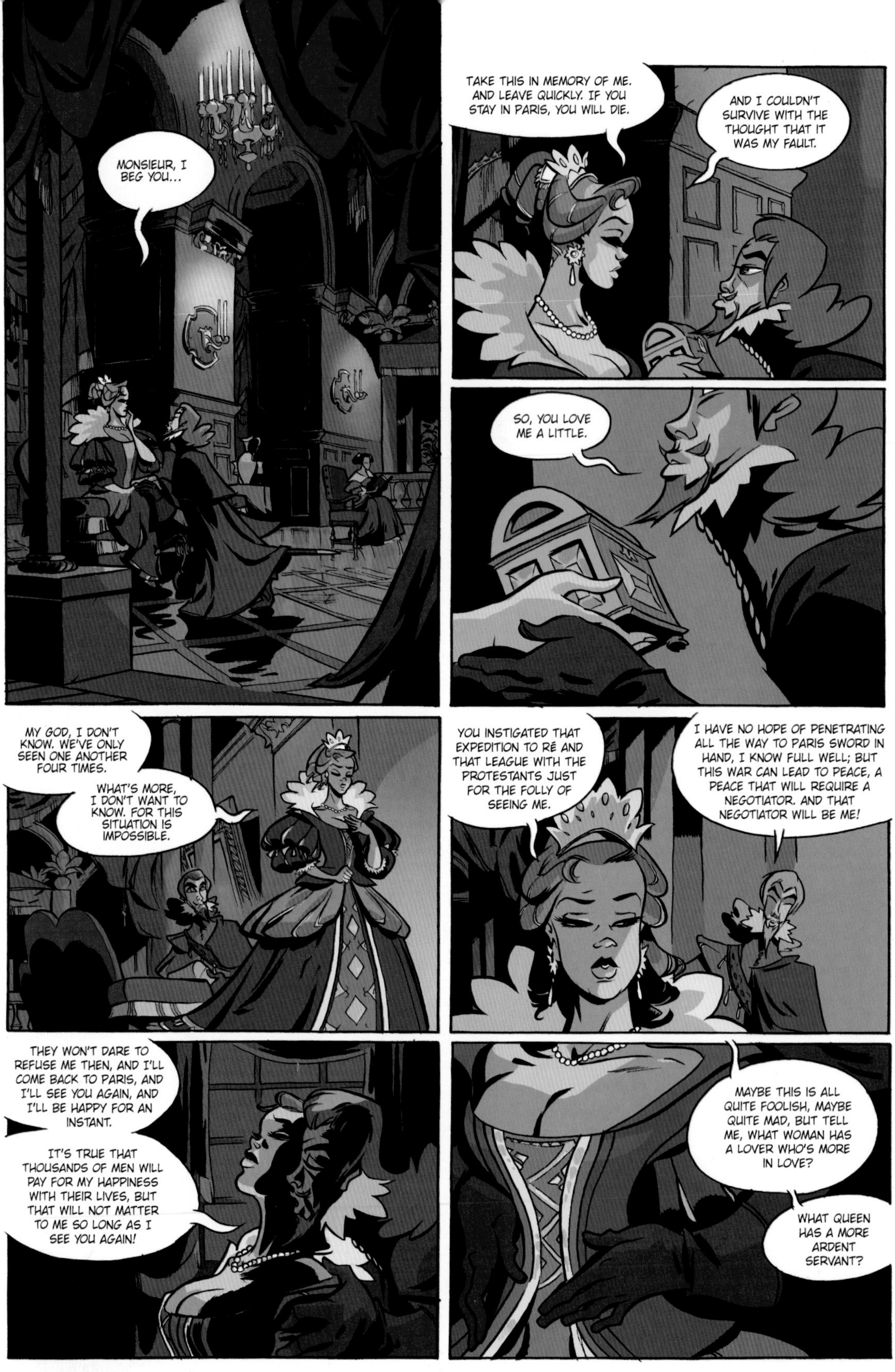
MONSIEUR, I BEG YOU...
TAKE THIS IN MEMORY OF ME. AND LEAVE QUICKLY. IF YOU STAY IN PARIS, YOU WILL DIE.
AND I COULDN'T SURVIVE WITH THE THOUGHT THAT IT WAS MY FAULT.
SO, YOU LOVE ME A LITTLE.
MY GOD, I DON'T KNOW. WE'VE ONLY SEEN ONE ANOTHER FOUR TIMES.
WHAT'S MORE, I DON'T WANT TO KNOW. FOR THIS SITUATION IS IMPOSSIBLE.
YOU INSTIGATED THAT EXPEDITION TO RÉ AND THAT LEAGUE WITH THE PROTESTANTS JUST FOR THE FOLLY OF SEEING ME.
I HAVE NO HOPE OF PENETRATING ALL THE WAY TO PARIS SWORD IN HAND, I KNOW FULL WELL; BUT THIS WAR CAN LEAD TO PEACE, A PEACE THAT WILL REQUIRE A NEGOTIATOR. AND THAT NEGOTIATOR WILL BE ME!
THEY WON'T DARE TO REFUSE ME THEN, AND I'LL COME BACK TO PARIS, AND I'LL SEE YOU AGAIN, AND I'LL BE HAPPY FOR AN INSTANT.
IT'S TRUE THAT THOUSANDS OF MEN WILL PAY FOR MY HAPPINESS WITH THEIR LIVES, BUT THAT WILL NOT MATTER TO ME SO LONG AS I SEE YOU AGAIN!
MAYBE THIS IS ALL QUITE FOOLISH, MAYBE QUITE MAD, BUT TELL ME, WHAT WOMAN HAS A LOVER WHO'S MORE IN LOVE?
WHAT QUEEN HAS A MORE ARDENT SERVANT?

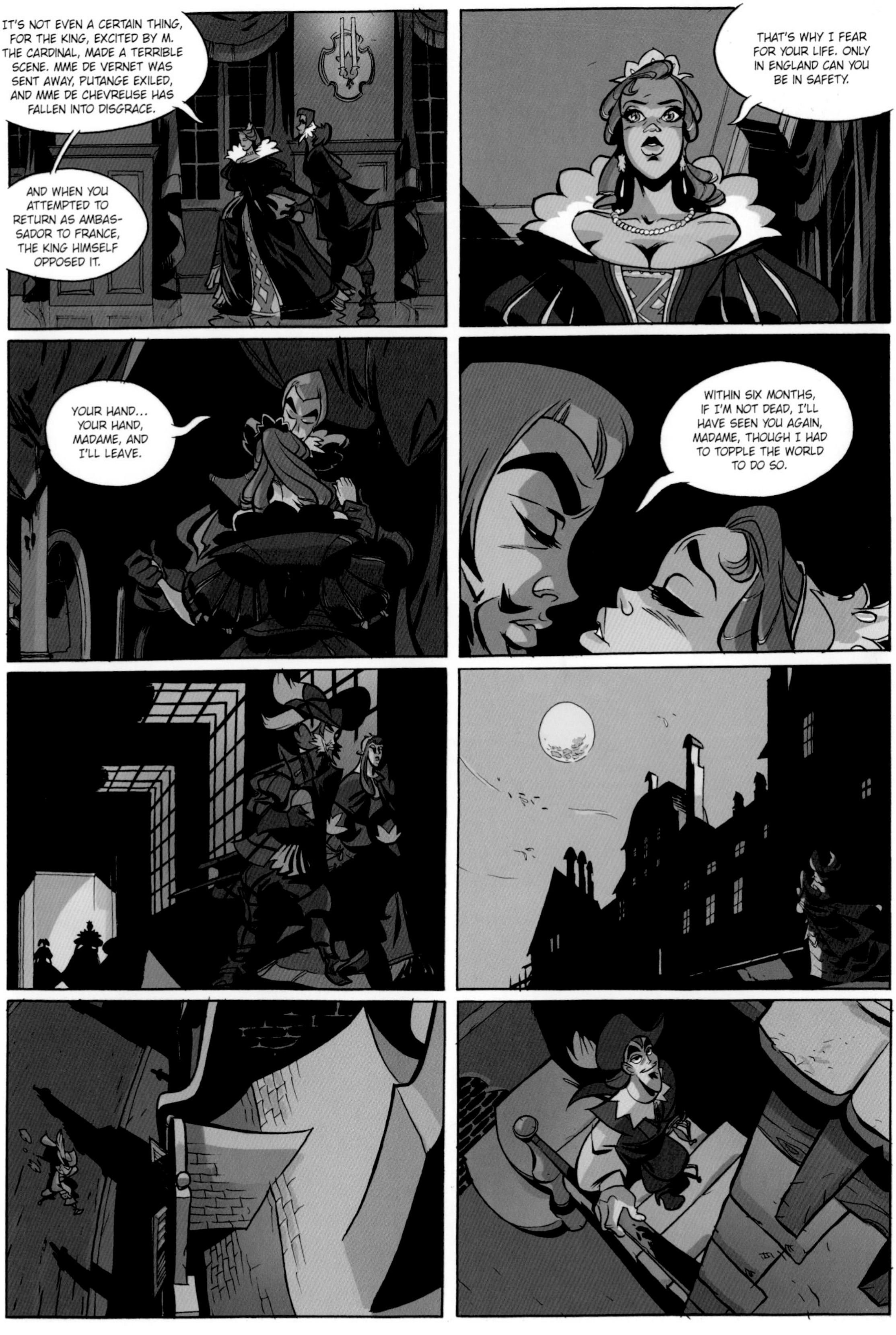
IT'S NOT EVEN A CERTAIN THING, FOR THE KING, EXCITED BY M. THE CARDINAL, MADE A TERRIBLE SCENE. MME DE VERNET WAS SENT AWAY, PUTANGE EXILED, AND MME DE CHEVREUSE HAS FALLEN INTO DISGRACE.
AND WHEN YOU ATTEMPTED TO RETURN AS AMBAS-SADOR TO FRANCE, THE KING HIMSELF OPPOSED IT.
THAT'S WHY I FEAR FOR YOUR LIFE. ONLY IN ENGLAND CAN YOU BE IN SAFETY.
YOUR HAND... YOUR HAND, MADAME, AND I'LL LEAVE.
WITHIN SIX MONTHS, IF I'M NOT DEAD, I'LL HAVE SEEN YOU AGAIN, MADAME, THOUGH I HAD TO TOPPLE THE WORLD TO DO SO.

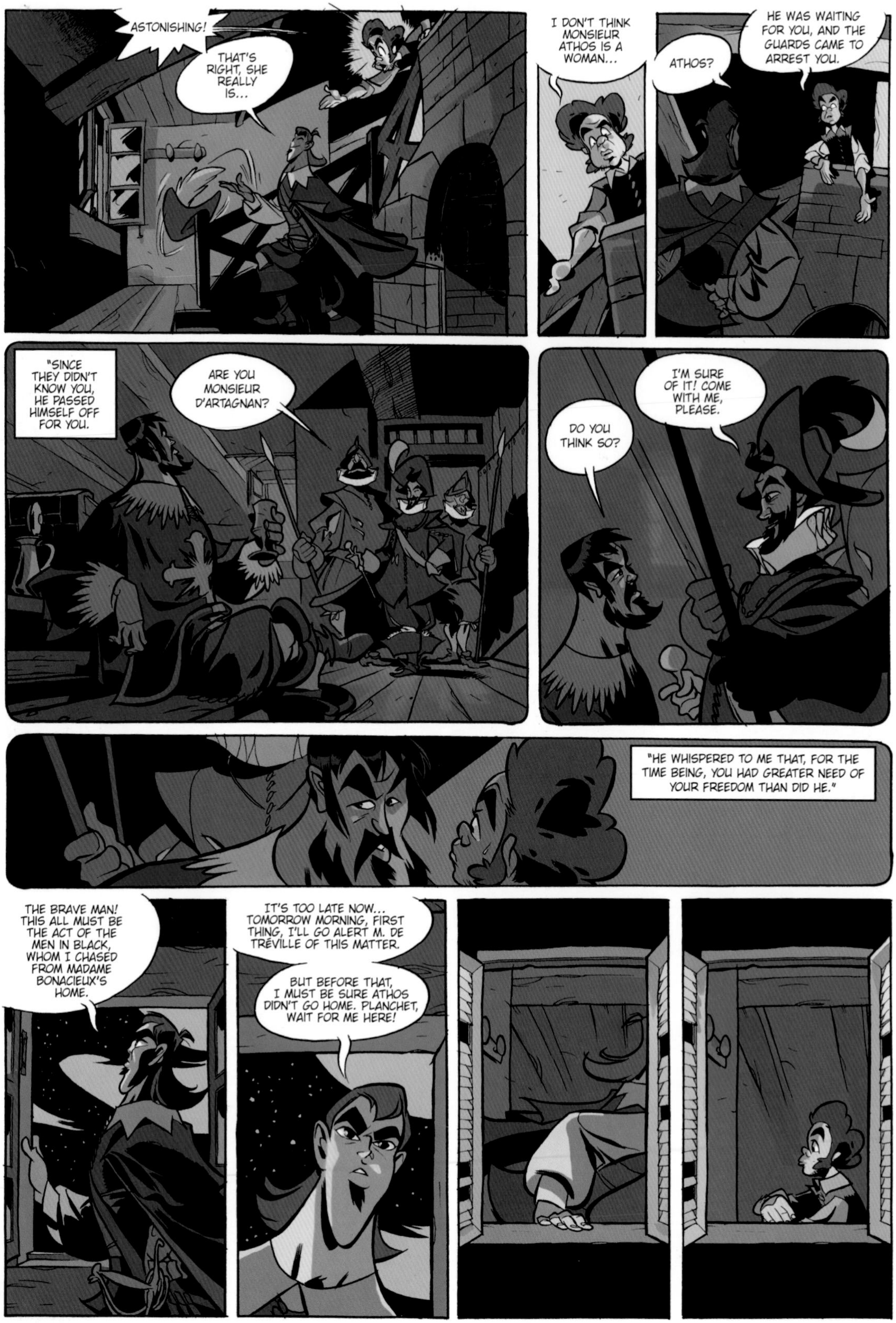
ASTONISHING!
THAT'S RIGHT, SHE REALLY IS...
I DON'T THINK MONSIEUR ATHOS IS A WOMAN...
ATHOS?
HE WAS WAITING FOR YOU, AND THE GUARDS CAME TO ARREST YOU.
"SINCE THEY DIDN'T KNOW YOU, HE PASSED HIMSELF OFF FOR YOU.
ARE YOU MONSIEUR D'ARTAGNAN?
DO YOU THINK SO?
I'M SURE OF IT! COME WITH ME, PLEASE.
"HE WHISPERED TO ME THAT, FOR THE TIME BEING, YOU HAD GREATER NEED OF YOUR FREEDOM THAN DID HE."
THE BRAVE MAN! THIS ALL MUST BE THE ACT OF THE MEN IN BLACK, WHOM I CHASED FROM MADAME BONACIEUX'S HOME.
IT'S TOO LATE NOW... TOMORROW MORNING, FIRST THING, I'LL GO ALERT M. DE TRÉVILLE OF THIS MATTER.
BUT BEFORE THAT, I MUST BE SURE ATHOS DIDN'T GO HOME. PLANCHET, WAIT FOR ME HERE!

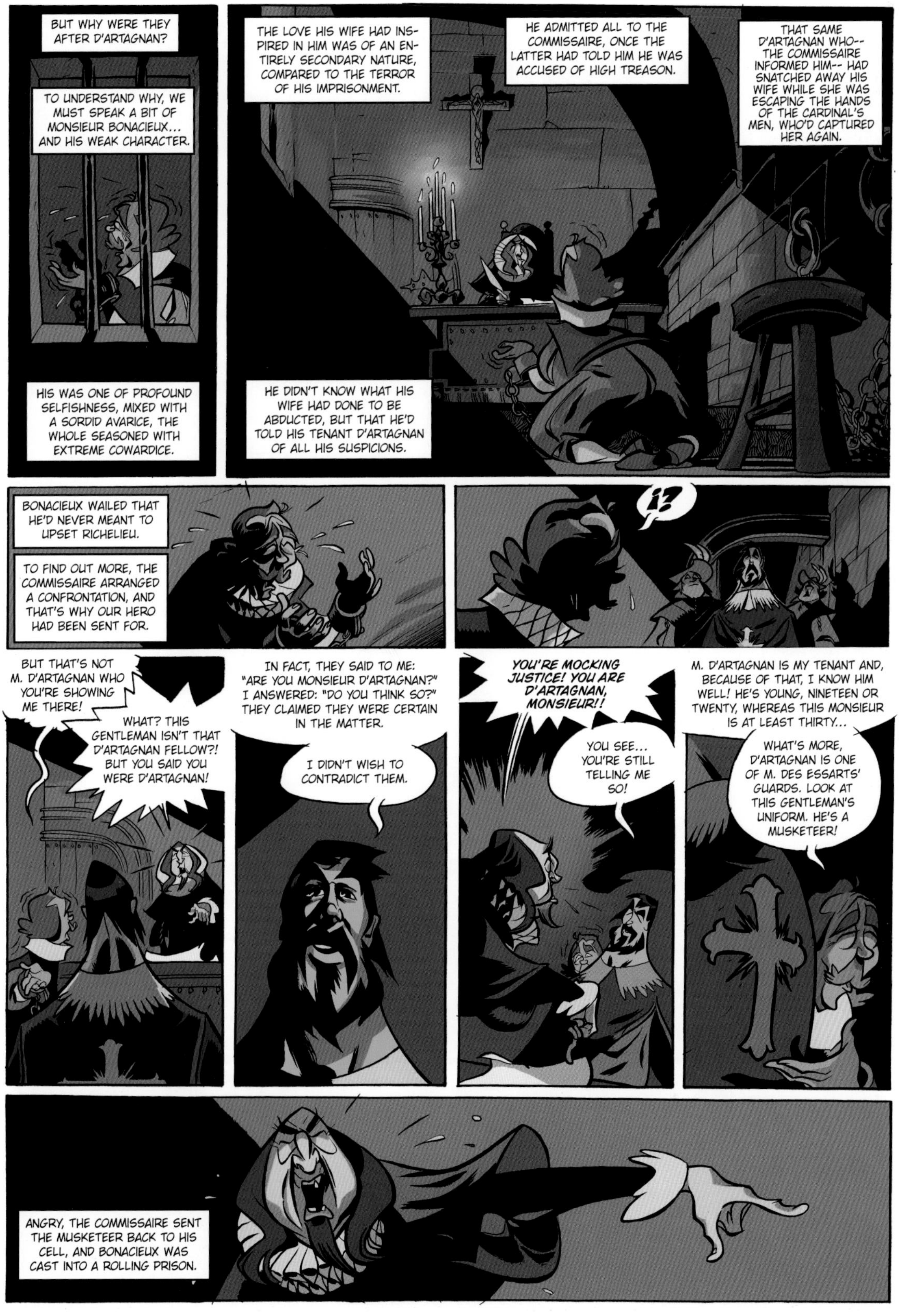
BUT WHY WERE THEY AFTER D'ARTAGNAN?
TO UNDERSTAND WHY, WE MUST SPEAK A BIT OF MONSIEUR BONACIEUX... AND HIS WEAK CHARACTER.
HIS WAS ONE OF PROFOUND SELFISHNESS, MIXED WITH A SORDID AVARICE, THE WHOLE SEASONED WITH EXTREME COWARDICE.
THE LOVE HIS WIFE HAD INSPIRED IN HIM WAS OF AN ENTIRELY SECONDARY NATURE, COMPARED TO THE TERROR OF HIS IMPRISONMENT.
HE ADMITTED ALL TO THE COMMISSAIRE, ONCE THE LATTER HAD TOLD HIM HE WAS ACCUSED OF HIGH TREASON.
THAT SAME D'ARTAGNAN WHO-- THE COMMISSAIRE INFORMED HIM-- HAD SNATCHED AWAY HIS WIFE WHILE SHE WAS ESCAPING THE HANDS OF THE CARDINAL'S MEN, WHO'D CAPTURED HER AGAIN.
HE DIDN'T KNOW WHAT HIS WIFE HAD DONE TO BE ABDUCTED, BUT THAT HE'D TOLD HIS TENANT D'ARTAGNAN OF ALL HIS SUSPICIONS.
BONACIEUX WAILED THAT HE'D NEVER MEANT TO UPSET RICHELIEU.
TO FIND OUT MORE, THE COMMISSAIRE ARRANGED A CONFRONTATION, AND THAT'S WHY OUR HERO HAD BEEN SENT FOR.
¡?
BUT THAT'S NOT M. D'ARTAGNAN WHO YOU'RE SHOWING ME THERE!
WHAT? THIS GENTLEMAN ISN'T THAT D'ARTAGNAN FELLOW?! BUT YOU SAID YOU WERE D'ARTAGNAN!
IN FACT, THEY SAID TO ME: "ARE YOU MONSIEUR D'ARTAGNAN?" I ANSWERED: "DO YOU THINK SO?" THEY CLAIMED THEY WERE CERTAIN IN THE MATTER.
I DIDN'T WISH TO CONTRADICT THEM.
YOU'RE MOCKING JUSTICE! YOU ARE D'ARTAGNAN, MONSIEUR!!
YOU SEE... YOU'RE STILL TELLING ME SO!
M. D'ARTAGNAN IS MY TENANT AND, BECAUSE OF THAT, I KNOW HIM WELL! HE'S YOUNG, NINETEEN OR TWENTY, WHEREAS THIS MONSIEUR IS AT LEAST THIRTY...
WHAT'S MORE, D'ARTAGNAN IS ONE OF M. DES ESSARTS' GUARDS. LOOK AT THIS GENTLEMAN'S UNIFORM. HE'S A MUSKETEER!
ANGRY, THE COMMISSAIRE SENT THE MUSKETEER BACK TO HIS CELL, AND BONACIEUX WAS CAST INTO A ROLLING PRISON.

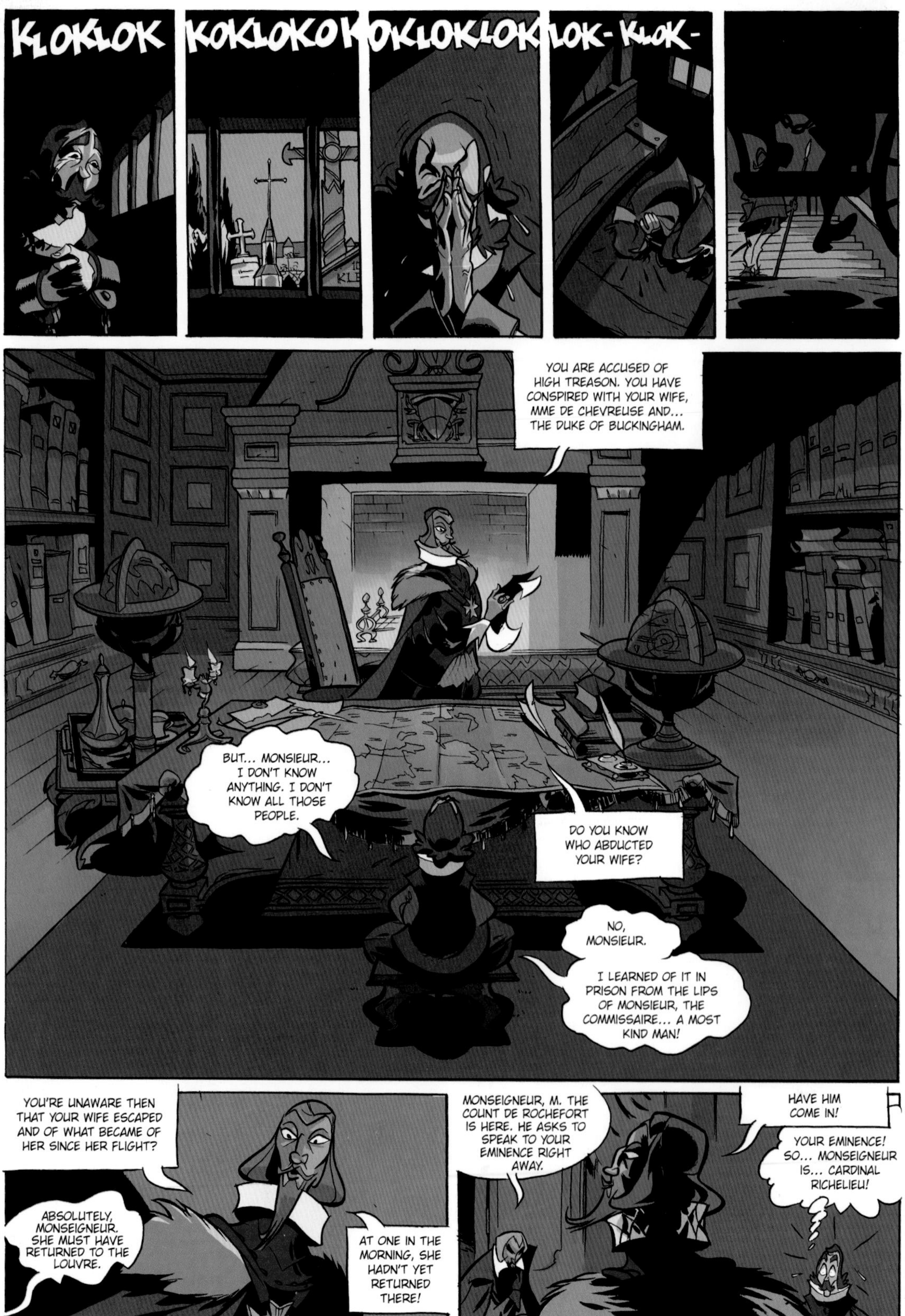

KLOKLOK
KOKLOKO
KOKLOKLOK
LOK- KLOK-
YOU ARE ACCUSED OF HIGH TREASON. YOU HAVE CONSPIRED WITH YOUR WIFE, MME DE CHEVREUSE AND... THE DUKE OF BUCKINGHAM.
BUT... MONSIEUR... I DON'T KNOW ANYTHING. I DON'T KNOW ALL THOSE PEOPLE.
DO YOU KNOW WHO ABDUCTED YOUR WIFE?
NO, MONSIEUR.
I LEARNED OF IT IN PRISON FROM THE LIPS OF MONSIEUR, THE COMMISSAIRE... A MOST KIND MAN!
YOU'RE UNAWARE THEN THAT YOUR WIFE ESCAPED AND OF WHAT BECAME OF HER SINCE HER FLIGHT?
ABSOLUTELY, MONSEIGNEUR. SHE MUST HAVE RETURNED TO THE LOUVRE.
AT ONE IN THE MORNING, SHE HADN'T YET RETURNED THERE!
MONSEIGNEUR, M. THE COUNT DE ROCHEFORT IS HERE. HE ASKS TO SPEAK TO YOUR EMINENCE RIGHT AWAY.
HAVE HIM COME IN!
YOUR EMINENCE! SO... MONSEIGNEUR IS... CARDINAL RICHELIEU!

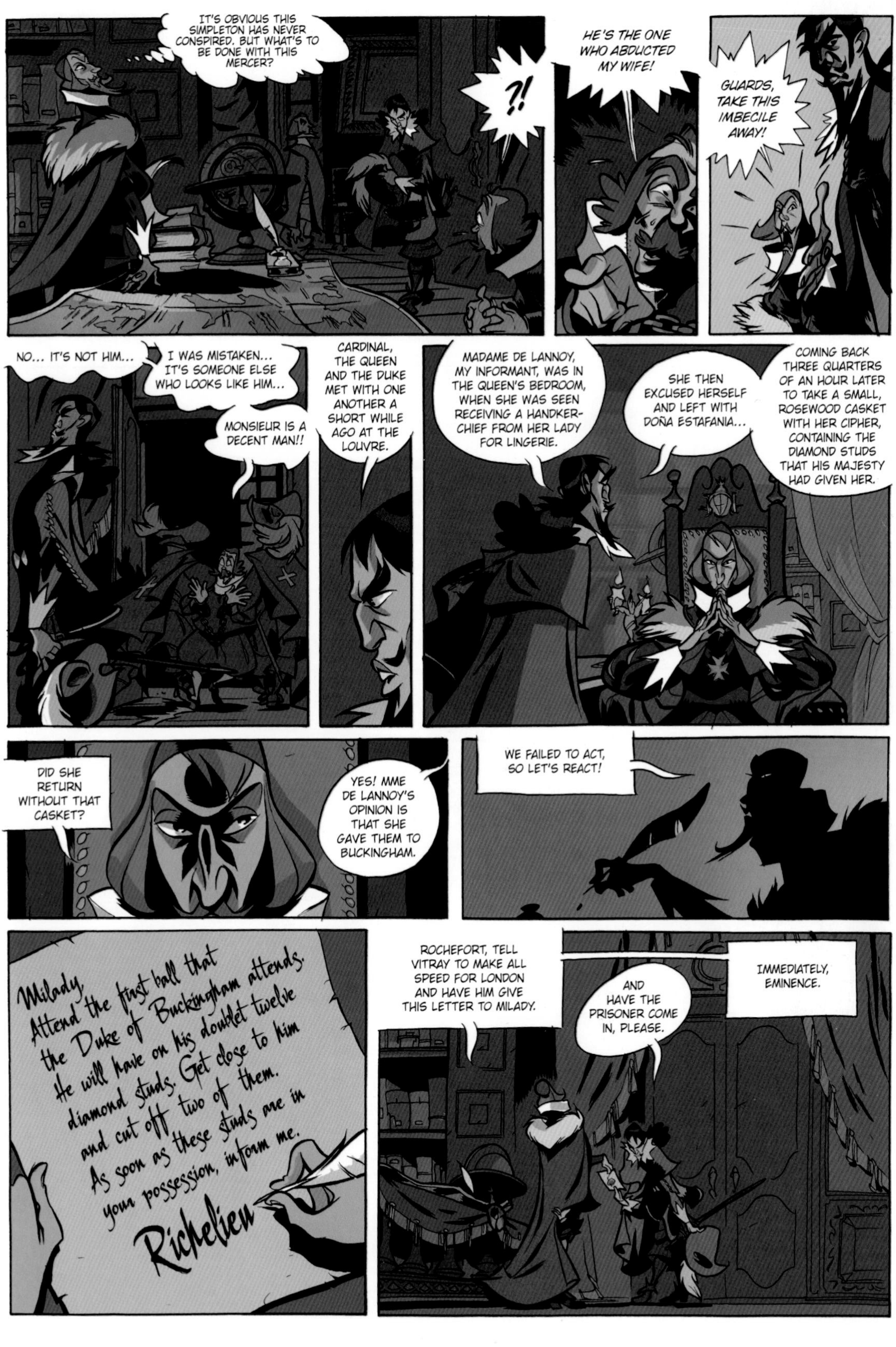

IT'S OBVIOUS THIS SIMPLETON HAS NEVER CONSPIRED. BUT WHAT'S TO BE DONE WITH THIS MERCER?
?!
HE'S THE ONE WHO ABDUCTED MY WIFE!
GUARDS, TAKE THIS IMBECILE AWAY!
NO... IT'S NOT HIM...
I WAS MISTAKEN... IT'S SOMEONE ELSE WHO LOOKS LIKE HIM...
MONSIEUR IS A DECENT MAN!!
CARDINAL, THE QUEEN AND THE DUKE MET WITH ONE ANOTHER A SHORT WHILE AGO AT THE LOUVRE.
MADAME DE LANNOY, MY INFORMANT, WAS IN THE QUEEN'S BEDROOM, WHEN SHE WAS SEEN RECEIVING A HANDKERCHIEF FROM HER LADY FOR LINGERIE.
SHE THEN EXCUSED HERSELF AND LEFT WITH DOÑA ESTAFANIA...
COMING BACK THREE QUARTERS OF AN HOUR LATER TO TAKE A SMALL, ROSEWOOD CASKET WITH HER CIPHER, CONTAINING THE DIAMOND STUDS THAT HIS MAJESTY HAD GIVEN HER.
DID SHE RETURN WITHOUT THAT CASKET?
YES! MME DE LANNOY'S OPINION IS THAT SHE GAVE THEM TO BUCKINGHAM.
WE FAILED TO ACT, SO LET'S REACT!
Milady, Attend the first ball that the Duke of Buckingham attends. He will have on his doublet twelve diamond studs. Get close to him and cut off two of them. As soon as these studs are in your possession, inform me.
Richelieu
ROCHEFORT, TELL VITRAY TO MAKE ALL SPEED FOR LONDON AND HAVE HIM GIVE THIS LETTER TO MILADY.
AND HAVE THE PRISONER COME IN, PLEASE.
IMMEDIATELY, EMINENCE.

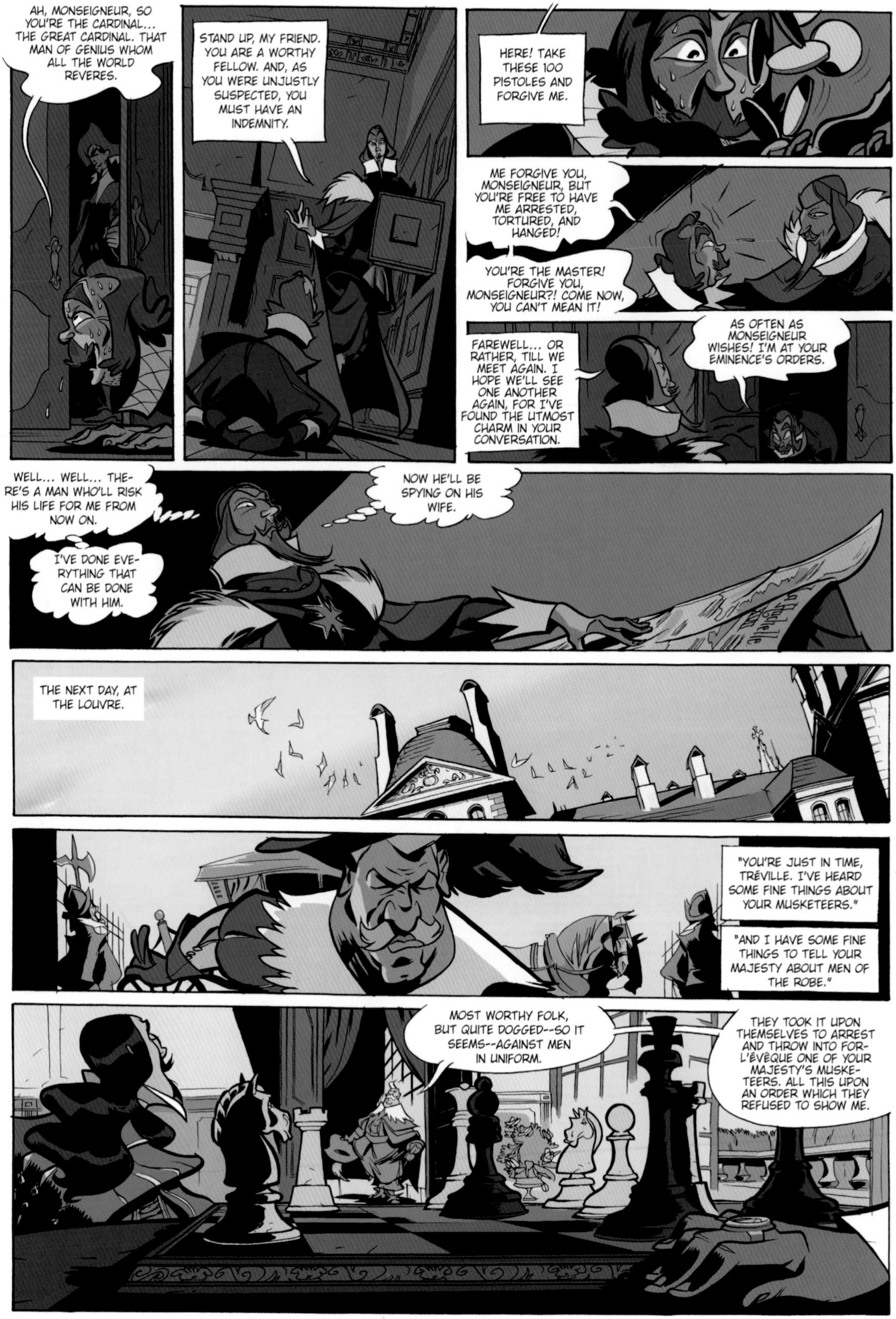
AH, MONSEIGNEUR, SO YOU'RE THE CARDINAL... THE GREAT CARDINAL. THAT MAN OF GENIUS WHOM ALL THE WORLD REVERES.
STAND UP, MY FRIEND. YOU ARE A WORTHY FELLOW. AND, AS YOU WERE UNJUSTLY SUSPECTED, YOU MUST HAVE AN INDEMNITY.
HERE! TAKE THESE 100 PISTOLES AND FORGIVE ME.
ME FORGIVE YOU, MONSEIGNEUR, BUT YOU'RE FREE TO HAVE ME ARRESTED, TORTURED, AND HANGED!
YOU'RE THE MASTER! FORGIVE YOU, MONSEIGNEUR?! COME NOW, YOU CAN'T MEAN IT!
FAREWELL... OR RATHER, TILL WE MEET AGAIN. I HOPE WE'LL SEE ONE ANOTHER AGAIN, FOR I'VE FOUND THE UTMOST CHARM IN YOUR CONVERSATION.
AS OFTEN AS MONSEIGNEUR WISHES! I'M AT YOUR EMINENCE'S ORDERS.
WELL... WELL... THERE'S A MAN WHO'LL RISK HIS LIFE FOR ME FROM NOW ON.
I'VE DONE EVERYTHING THAT CAN BE DONE WITH HIM.
NOW HE'LL BE SPYING ON HIS WIFE.
THE NEXT DAY, AT THE LOUVRE.
"YOU'RE JUST IN TIME, TRÉVILLE. I'VE HEARD SOME FINE THINGS ABOUT YOUR MUSKETEERS."
"AND I HAVE SOME FINE THINGS TO TELL YOUR MAJESTY ABOUT MEN OF THE ROBE."
MOST WORTHY FOLK, BUT QUITE DOGGED--SO IT SEEMS--AGAINST MEN IN UNIFORM.
THEY TOOK IT UPON THEMSELVES TO ARREST AND THROW INTO FOR-L'ÉVÊQUE ONE OF YOUR MAJESTY'S MUSKETEERS. ALL THIS UPON AN ORDER WHICH THEY REFUSED TO SHOW ME.

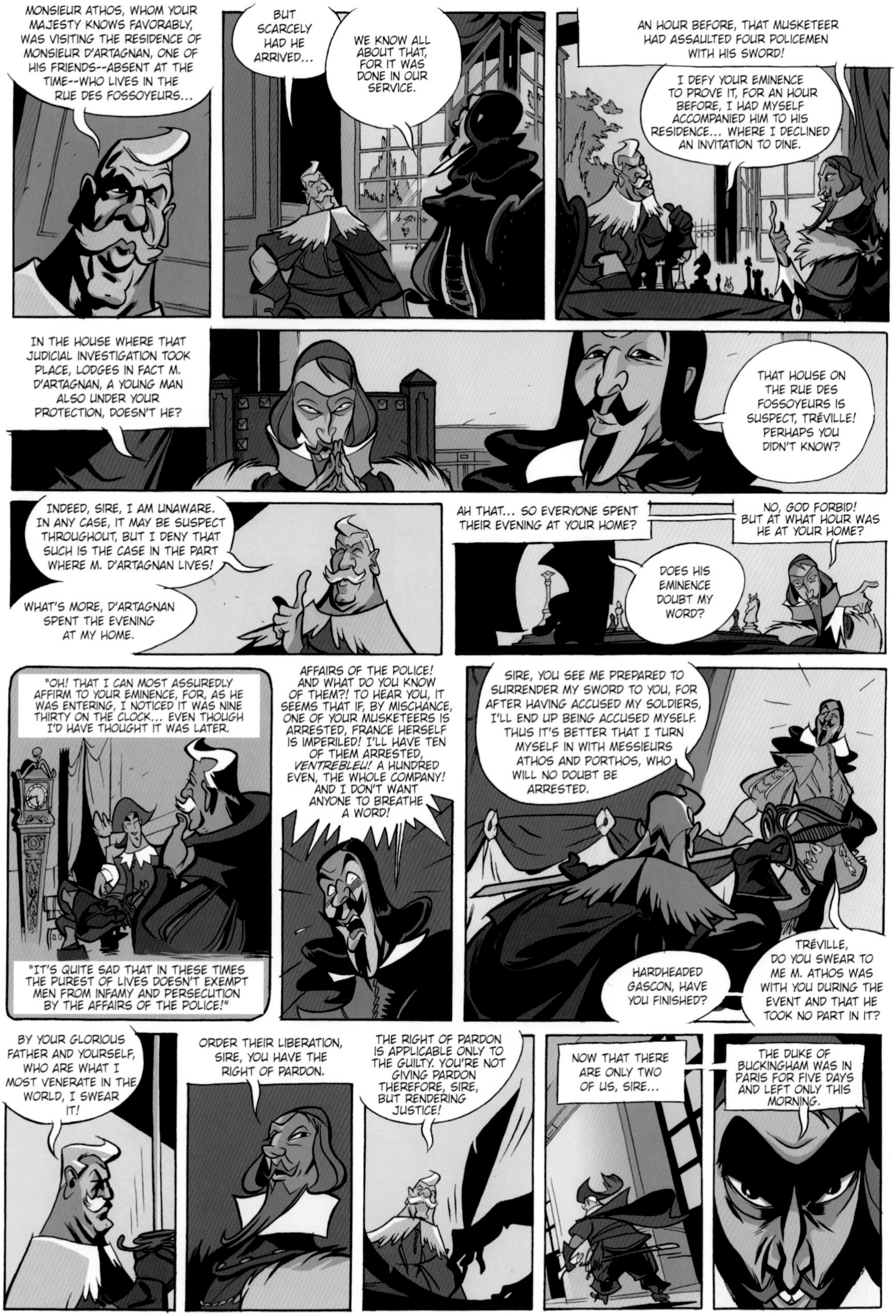
MONSIEUR ATHOS, WHOM YOUR MAJESTY KNOWS FAVORABLY, WAS VISITING THE RESIDENCE OF MONSIEUR D'ARTAGNAN, ONE OF HIS FRIENDS--ABSENT AT THE TIME--WHO LIVES IN THE RUE DES FOSSOYEURS...
BUT SCARCELY HAD HE ARRIVED...
WE KNOW ALL ABOUT THAT, FOR IT WAS DONE IN OUR SERVICE.
AN HOUR BEFORE, THAT MUSKETEER HAD ASSAULTED FOUR POLICEMEN WITH HIS SWORD!
I DEFY YOUR EMINENCE TO PROVE IT, FOR AN HOUR BEFORE, I HAD MYSELF ACCOMPANIED HIM TO HIS RESIDENCE... WHERE I DECLINED AN INVITATION TO DINE.
IN THE HOUSE WHERE THAT JUDICIAL INVESTIGATION TOOK PLACE, LODGES IN FACT M. D'ARTAGNAN, A YOUNG MAN ALSO UNDER YOUR PROTECTION, DOESN'T HE?
THAT HOUSE ON THE RUE DES FOSSOYEURS IS SUSPECT, TRÉVILLE! PERHAPS YOU DIDN'T KNOW?
INDEED, SIRE, I AM UNAWARE. IN ANY CASE, IT MAY BE SUSPECT THROUGHOUT, BUT I DENY THAT SUCH IS THE CASE IN THE PART WHERE M. D'ARTAGNAN LIVES!
WHAT'S MORE, D'ARTAGNAN SPENT THE EVENING AT MY HOME.
AH THAT... SO EVERYONE SPENT THEIR EVENING AT YOUR HOME?
NO, GOD FORBID! BUT AT WHAT HOUR WAS HE AT YOUR HOME?
DOES HIS EMINENCE DOUBT MY WORD?
"OH! THAT I CAN MOST ASSUREDLY AFFIRM TO YOUR EMINENCE, FOR, AS HE WAS ENTERING, I NOTICED IT WAS NINE THIRTY ON THE CLOCK... EVEN THOUGH I'D HAVE THOUGHT IT WAS LATER.
"IT'S QUITE SAD THAT IN THESE TIMES THE PUREST OF LIVES DOESN'T EXEMPT MEN FROM INFAMY AND PERSECUTION BY THE AFFAIRS OF THE POLICE!"
AFFAIRS OF THE POLICE! AND WHAT DO YOU KNOW OF THEM?! TO HEAR YOU, IT SEEMS THAT IF, BY MISCHANCE, ONE OF YOUR MUSKETEERS IS ARRESTED, FRANCE HERSELF IS IMPERILED! I'LL HAVE TEN OF THEM ARRESTED, *VENTREBLEU!* A HUNDRED EVEN, THE WHOLE COMPANY! AND I DON'T WANT ANYONE TO BREATHE A WORD!
SIRE, YOU SEE ME PREPARED TO SURRENDER MY SWORD TO YOU, FOR AFTER HAVING ACCUSED MY SOLDIERS, I'LL END UP BEING ACCUSED MYSELF. THUS IT'S BETTER THAT I TURN MYSELF IN WITH MESSIEURS ATHOS AND PORTHOS, WHO WILL NO DOUBT BE ARRESTED.
HARDHEADED GASCON, HAVE YOU FINISHED?
TRÉVILLE, DO YOU SWEAR TO ME M. ATHOS WAS WITH YOU DURING THE EVENT AND THAT HE TOOK NO PART IN IT?
BY YOUR GLORIOUS FATHER AND YOURSELF, WHO ARE WHAT I MOST VENERATE IN THE WORLD, I SWEAR IT!
ORDER THEIR LIBERATION, SIRE, YOU HAVE THE RIGHT OF PARDON.
THE RIGHT OF PARDON IS APPLICABLE ONLY TO THE GUILTY. YOU'RE NOT GIVING PARDON THEREFORE, SIRE, BUT RENDERING JUSTICE!
NOW THAT THERE ARE ONLY TWO OF US, SIRE...
THE DUKE OF BUCKINGHAM WAS IN PARIS FOR FIVE DAYS AND LEFT ONLY THIS MORNING.

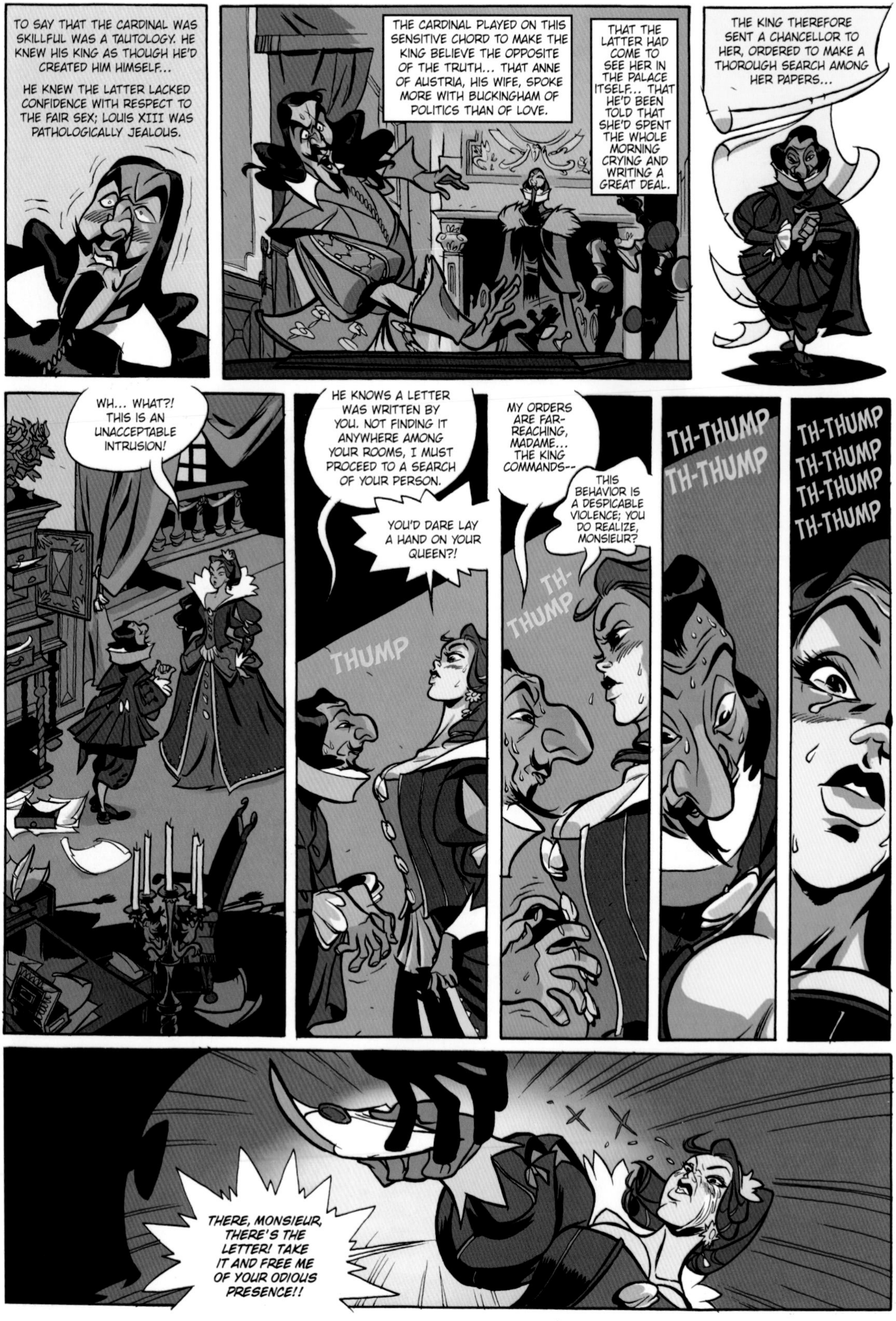
TO SAY THAT THE CARDINAL WAS SKILLFUL WAS A TAUTOLOGY. HE KNEW HIS KING AS THOUGH HE'D CREATED HIM HIMSELF...
HE KNEW THE LATTER LACKED CONFIDENCE WITH RESPECT TO THE FAIR SEX; LOUIS XIII WAS PATHOLOGICALLY JEALOUS.
THE CARDINAL PLAYED ON THIS SENSITIVE CHORD TO MAKE THE KING BELIEVE THE OPPOSITE OF THE TRUTH... THAT ANNE OF AUSTRIA, HIS WIFE, SPOKE MORE WITH BUCKINGHAM OF POLITICS THAN OF LOVE.
THAT THE LATTER HAD COME TO SEE HER IN THE PALACE ITSELF... THAT HE'D BEEN TOLD THAT SHE'D SPENT THE WHOLE MORNING CRYING AND WRITING A GREAT DEAL.
THE KING THEREFORE SENT A CHANCELLOR TO HER, ORDERED TO MAKE A THOROUGH SEARCH AMONG HER PAPERS...
WH... WHAT?! THIS IS AN UNACCEPTABLE INTRUSION!
HE KNOWS A LETTER WAS WRITTEN BY YOU. NOT FINDING IT ANYWHERE AMONG YOUR ROOMS, I MUST PROCEED TO A SEARCH OF YOUR PERSON.
YOU'D DARE LAY A HAND ON YOUR QUEEN?!
THUMP
MY ORDERS ARE FAR-REACHING, MADAME... THE KING COMMANDS--
THIS BEHAVIOR IS A DESPICABLE VIOLENCE; YOU DO REALIZE, MONSIEUR?
TH-THUMP
TH-THUMP TH-THUMP
TH-THUMP TH-THUMP TH-THUMP TH-THUMP
THERE, MONSIEUR, THERE'S THE LETTER! TAKE IT AND FREE ME OF YOUR ODIOUS PRESENCE!!

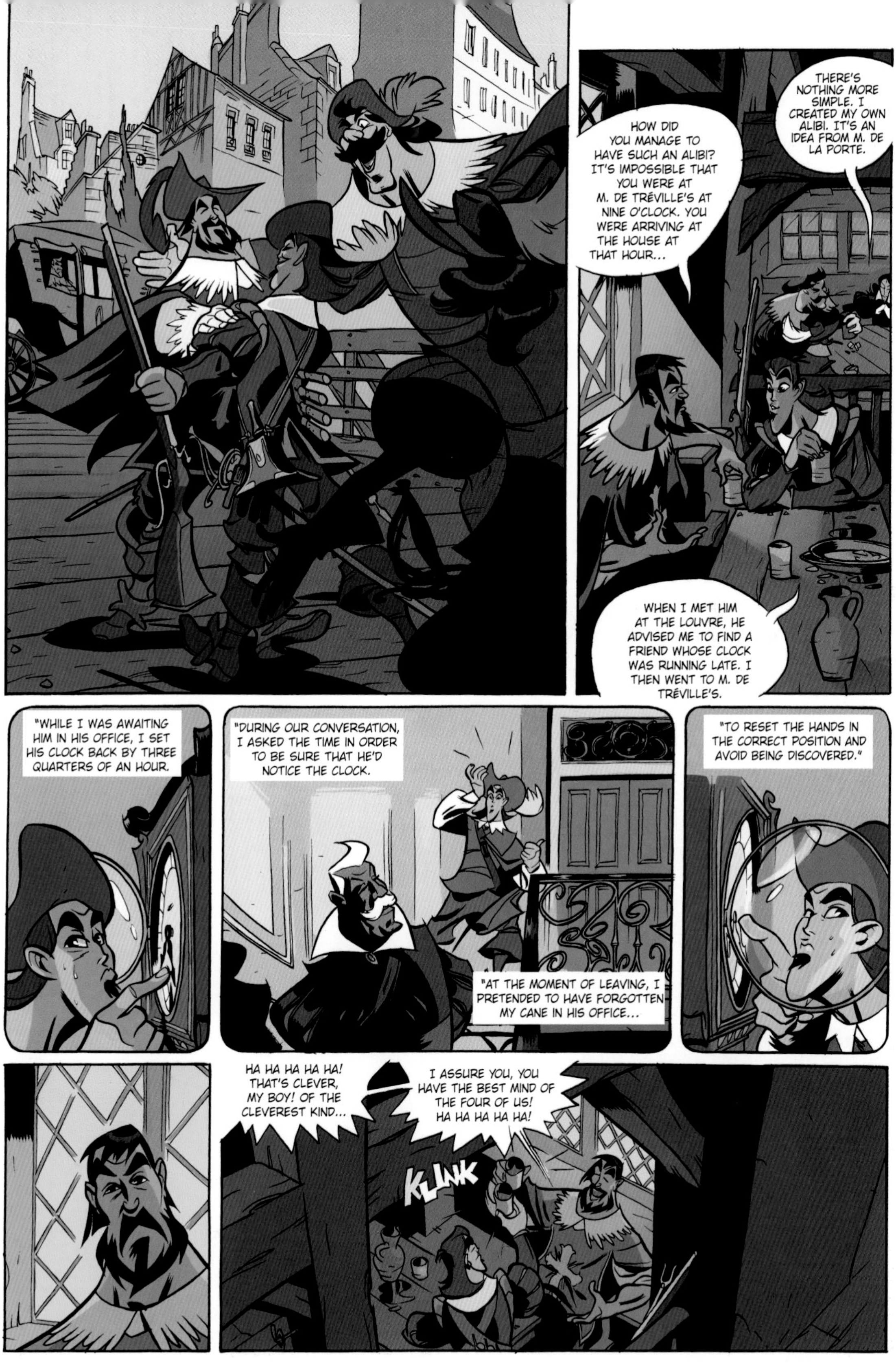
HOW DID YOU MANAGE TO HAVE SUCH AN ALIBI? IT'S IMPOSSIBLE THAT YOU WERE AT M. DE TRÉVILLE'S AT NINE O'CLOCK. YOU WERE ARRIVING AT THE HOUSE AT THAT HOUR...
THERE'S NOTHING MORE SIMPLE. I CREATED MY OWN ALIBI. IT'S AN IDEA FROM M. DE LA PORTE.
WHEN I MET HIM AT THE LOUVRE, HE ADVISED ME TO FIND A FRIEND WHOSE CLOCK WAS RUNNING LATE. I THEN WENT TO M. DE TRÉVILLE'S.
"WHILE I WAS AWAITING HIM IN HIS OFFICE, I SET HIS CLOCK BACK BY THREE QUARTERS OF AN HOUR.
"DURING OUR CONVERSATION, I ASKED THE TIME IN ORDER TO BE SURE THAT HE'D NOTICE THE CLOCK.
"AT THE MOMENT OF LEAVING, I PRETENDED TO HAVE FORGOTTEN MY CANE IN HIS OFFICE...
"TO RESET THE HANDS IN THE CORRECT POSITION AND AVOID BEING DISCOVERED."
HA HA HA HA HA! THAT'S CLEVER, MY BOY! OF THE CLEVEREST KIND...
I ASSURE YOU, YOU HAVE THE BEST MIND OF THE FOUR OF US! HA HA HA HA HA!
KLINK

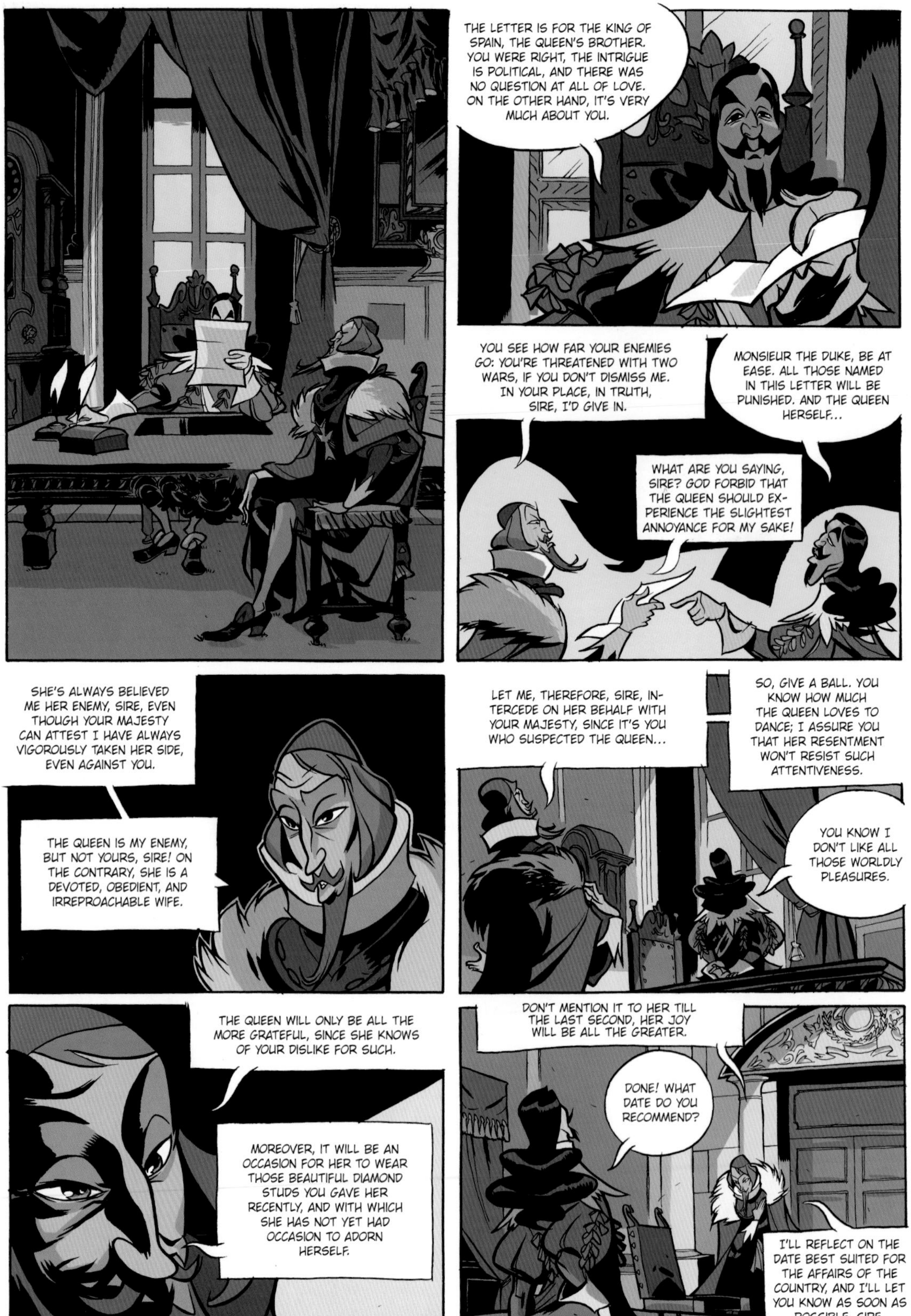
THE LETTER IS FOR THE KING OF SPAIN, THE QUEEN'S BROTHER. YOU WERE RIGHT, THE INTRIGUE IS POLITICAL, AND THERE WAS NO QUESTION AT ALL OF LOVE. ON THE OTHER HAND, IT'S VERY MUCH ABOUT YOU.
YOU SEE HOW FAR YOUR ENEMIES GO: YOU'RE THREATENED WITH TWO WARS, IF YOU DON'T DISMISS ME. IN YOUR PLACE, IN TRUTH, SIRE, I'D GIVE IN.
MONSIEUR THE DUKE, BE AT EASE. ALL THOSE NAMED IN THIS LETTER WILL BE PUNISHED. AND THE QUEEN HERSELF...
WHAT ARE YOU SAYING, SIRE? GOD FORBID THAT THE QUEEN SHOULD EXPERIENCE THE SLIGHTEST ANNOYANCE FOR MY SAKE!
SHE'S ALWAYS BELIEVED ME HER ENEMY, SIRE, EVEN THOUGH YOUR MAJESTY CAN ATTEST I HAVE ALWAYS VIGOROUSLY TAKEN HER SIDE, EVEN AGAINST YOU.
THE QUEEN IS MY ENEMY, BUT NOT YOURS, SIRE! ON THE CONTRARY, SHE IS A DEVOTED, OBEDIENT, AND IRREPROACHABLE WIFE.
LET ME, THEREFORE, SIRE, INTERCEDE ON HER BEHALF WITH YOUR MAJESTY, SINCE IT'S YOU WHO SUSPECTED THE QUEEN...
SO, GIVE A BALL. YOU KNOW HOW MUCH THE QUEEN LOVES TO DANCE; I ASSURE YOU THAT HER RESENTMENT WON'T RESIST SUCH ATTENTIVENESS.
YOU KNOW I DON'T LIKE ALL THOSE WORLDLY PLEASURES.
THE QUEEN WILL ONLY BE ALL THE MORE GRATEFUL, SINCE SHE KNOWS OF YOUR DISLIKE FOR SUCH.
MOREOVER, IT WILL BE AN OCCASION FOR HER TO WEAR THOSE BEAUTIFUL DIAMOND STUDS YOU GAVE HER RECENTLY, AND WITH WHICH SHE HAS NOT YET HAD OCCASION TO ADORN HERSELF.
DON'T MENTION IT TO HER TILL THE LAST SECOND, HER JOY WILL BE ALL THE GREATER.
DONE! WHAT DATE DO YOU RECOMMEND?
I'LL REFLECT ON THE DATE BEST SUITED FOR THE AFFAIRS OF THE COUNTRY, AND I'LL LET YOU KNOW AS SOON AS POSSIBLE, SIRE.

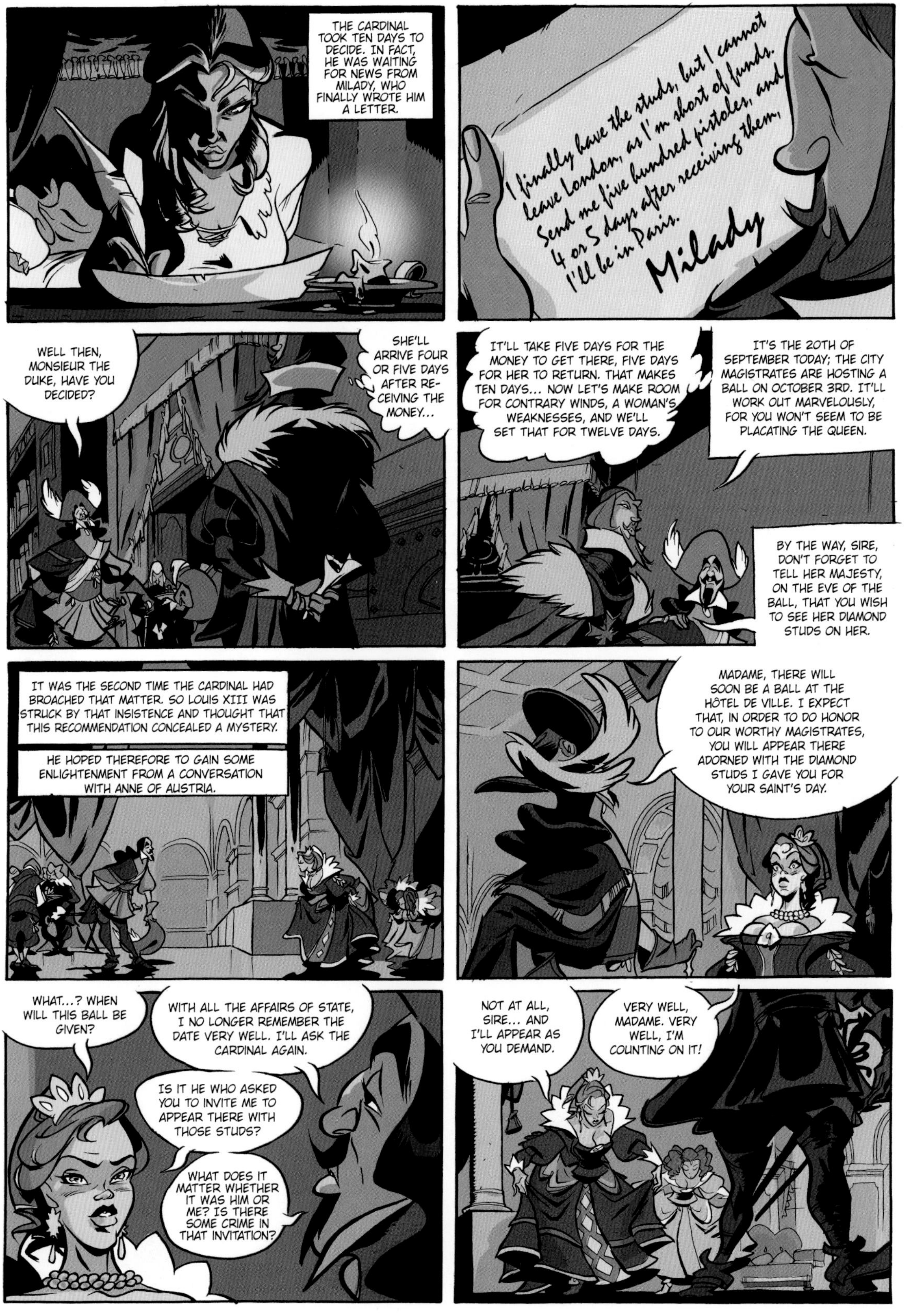
THE CARDINAL TOOK TEN DAYS TO DECIDE. IN FACT, HE WAS WAITING FOR NEWS FROM MILADY, WHO FINALLY WROTE HIM A LETTER.
I finally have the studs, but I cannot leave London, as I'm short of funds. Send me five hundred pistoles, and 4 or 5 days after receiving them, I'll be in Paris.
Milady
WELL THEN, MONSIEUR THE DUKE, HAVE YOU DECIDED?
SHE'LL ARRIVE FOUR OR FIVE DAYS AFTER RE-CEIVING THE MONEY...
IT'LL TAKE FIVE DAYS FOR THE MONEY TO GET THERE, FIVE DAYS FOR HER TO RETURN. THAT MAKES TEN DAYS... NOW LET'S MAKE ROOM FOR CONTRARY WINDS, A WOMAN'S WEAKNESSES, AND WE'LL SET THAT FOR TWELVE DAYS.
IT'S THE 20TH OF SEPTEMBER TODAY; THE CITY MAGISTRATES ARE HOSTING A BALL ON OCTOBER 3RD. IT'LL WORK OUT MARVELOUSLY, FOR YOU WON'T SEEM TO BE PLACATING THE QUEEN.
BY THE WAY, SIRE, DON'T FORGET TO TELL HER MAJESTY, ON THE EVE OF THE BALL, THAT YOU WISH TO SEE HER DIAMOND STUDS ON HER.
IT WAS THE SECOND TIME THE CARDINAL HAD BROACHED THAT MATTER. SO LOUIS XIII WAS STRUCK BY THAT INSISTENCE AND THOUGHT THAT THIS RECOMMENDATION CONCEALED A MYSTERY.
HE HOPED THEREFORE TO GAIN SOME ENLIGHTENMENT FROM A CONVERSATION WITH ANNE OF AUSTRIA.
MADAME, THERE WILL SOON BE A BALL AT THE HÔTEL DE VILLE. I EXPECT THAT, IN ORDER TO DO HONOR TO OUR WORTHY MAGISTRATES, YOU WILL APPEAR THERE ADORNED WITH THE DIAMOND STUDS I GAVE YOU FOR YOUR SAINT'S DAY.
WHAT...? WHEN WILL THIS BALL BE GIVEN?
WITH ALL THE AFFAIRS OF STATE, I NO LONGER REMEMBER THE DATE VERY WELL. I'LL ASK THE CARDINAL AGAIN.
IS IT HE WHO ASKED YOU TO INVITE ME TO APPEAR THERE WITH THOSE STUDS?
WHAT DOES IT MATTER WHETHER IT WAS HIM OR ME? IS THERE SOME CRIME IN THAT INVITATION?
NOT AT ALL, SIRE... AND I'LL APPEAR AS YOU DEMAND.
VERY WELL, MADAME. VERY WELL, I'M COUNTING ON IT!

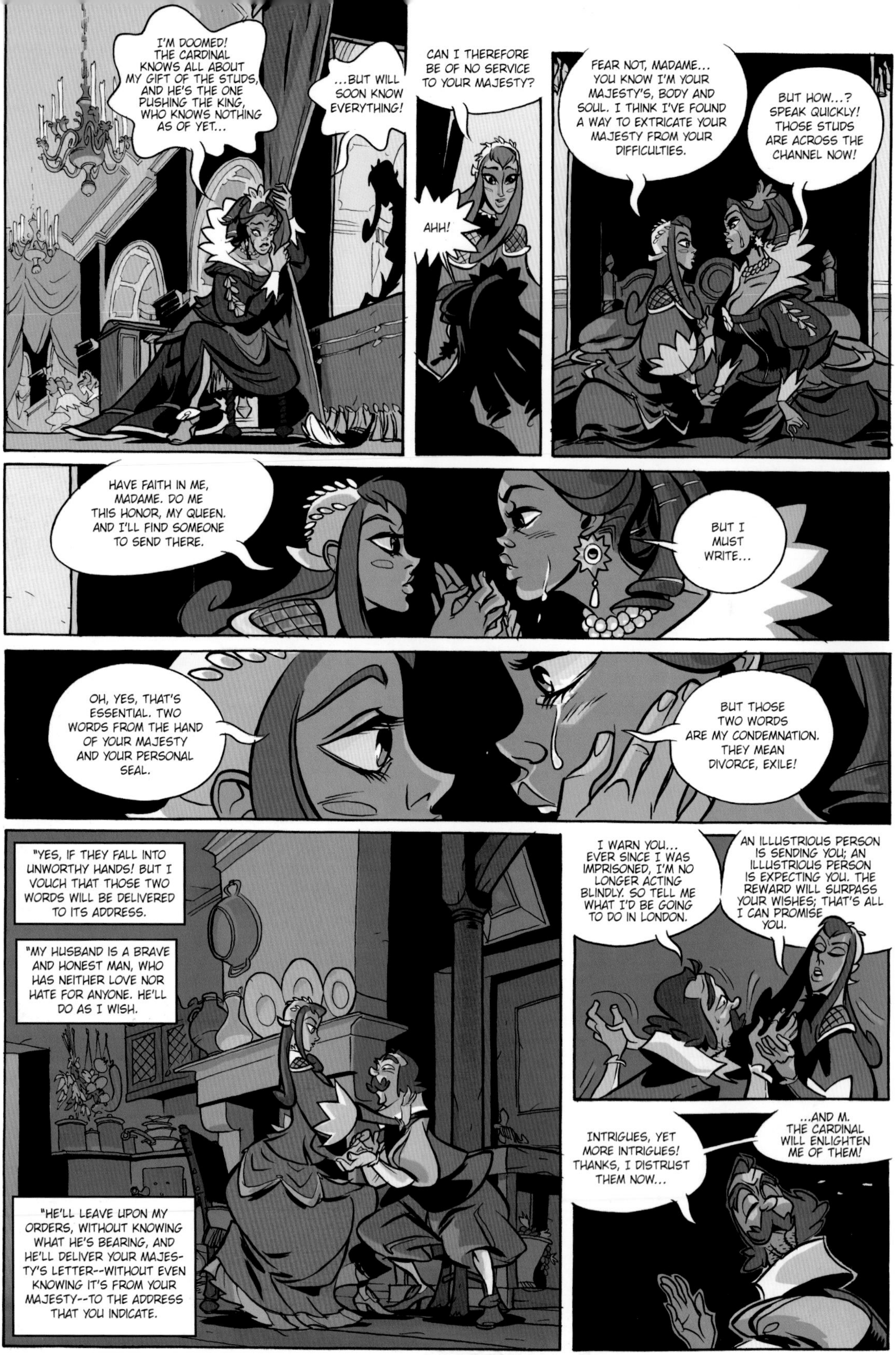
I'M DOOMED! THE CARDINAL KNOWS ALL ABOUT MY GIFT OF THE STUDS, AND HE'S THE ONE PUSHING THE KING, WHO KNOWS NOTHING AS OF YET...
...BUT WILL SOON KNOW EVERYTHING!
CAN I THEREFORE BE OF NO SERVICE TO YOUR MAJESTY?
AHH!
FEAR NOT, MADAME... YOU KNOW I'M YOUR MAJESTY'S, BODY AND SOUL. I THINK I'VE FOUND A WAY TO EXTRICATE YOUR MAJESTY FROM YOUR DIFFICULTIES.
BUT HOW...? SPEAK QUICKLY! THOSE STUDS ARE ACROSS THE CHANNEL NOW!
HAVE FAITH IN ME, MADAME. DO ME THIS HONOR, MY QUEEN. AND I'LL FIND SOMEONE TO SEND THERE.
BUT I MUST WRITE...
OH, YES, THAT'S ESSENTIAL. TWO WORDS FROM THE HAND OF YOUR MAJESTY AND YOUR PERSONAL SEAL.
BUT THOSE TWO WORDS ARE MY CONDEMNATION. THEY MEAN DIVORCE, EXILE!
"YES, IF THEY FALL INTO UNWORTHY HANDS! BUT I VOUCH THAT THOSE TWO WORDS WILL BE DELIVERED TO ITS ADDRESS.
"MY HUSBAND IS A BRAVE AND HONEST MAN, WHO HAS NEITHER LOVE NOR HATE FOR ANYONE. HE'LL DO AS I WISH.
"HE'LL LEAVE UPON MY ORDERS, WITHOUT KNOWING WHAT HE'S BEARING, AND HE'LL DELIVER YOUR MAJESTY'S LETTER--WITHOUT EVEN KNOWING IT'S FROM YOUR MAJESTY--TO THE ADDRESS THAT YOU INDICATE.
I WARN YOU... EVER SINCE I WAS IMPRISONED, I'M NO LONGER ACTING BLINDLY. SO TELL ME WHAT I'D BE GOING TO DO IN LONDON.
AN ILLUSTRIOUS PERSON IS SENDING YOU; AN ILLUSTRIOUS PERSON IS EXPECTING YOU. THE REWARD WILL SURPASS YOUR WISHES; THAT'S ALL I CAN PROMISE YOU.
INTRIGUES, YET MORE INTRIGUES! THANKS, I DISTRUST THEM NOW...
...AND M. THE CARDINAL WILL ENLIGHTEN ME OF THEM!

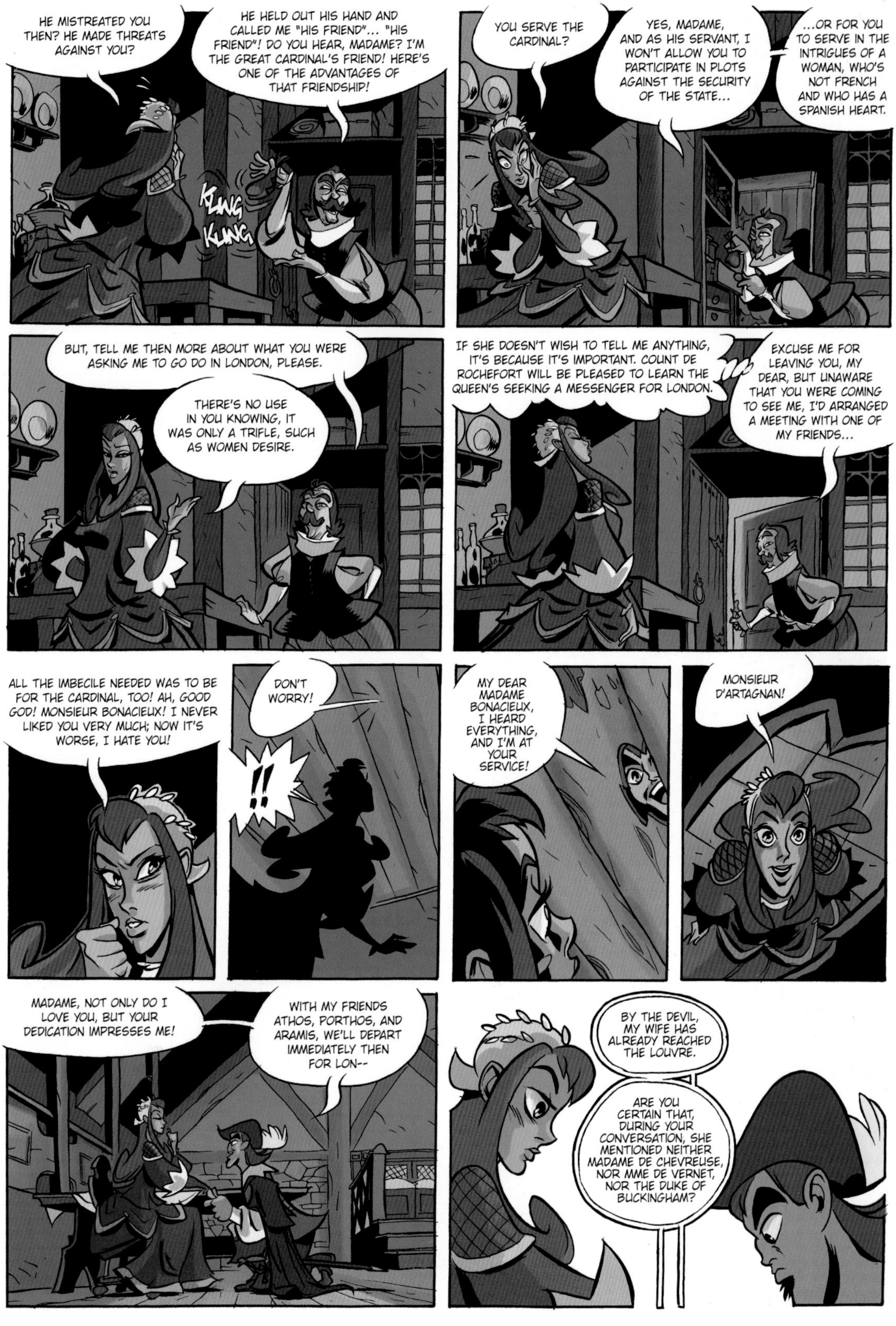
HE MISTREATED YOU THEN? HE MADE THREATS AGAINST YOU?
HE HELD OUT HIS HAND AND CALLED ME "HIS FRIEND"... "HIS FRIEND"! DO YOU HEAR, MADAME? I'M THE GREAT CARDINAL'S FRIEND! HERE'S ONE OF THE ADVANTAGES OF THAT FRIENDSHIP!
KLING
KLING
YOU SERVE THE CARDINAL?
YES, MADAME, AND AS HIS SERVANT, I WON'T ALLOW YOU TO PARTICIPATE IN PLOTS AGAINST THE SECURITY OF THE STATE...
...OR FOR YOU TO SERVE IN THE INTRIGUES OF A WOMAN, WHO'S NOT FRENCH AND WHO HAS A SPANISH HEART.
BUT, TELL ME THEN MORE ABOUT WHAT YOU WERE ASKING ME TO GO DO IN LONDON, PLEASE.
THERE'S NO USE IN YOU KNOWING, IT WAS ONLY A TRIFLE, SUCH AS WOMEN DESIRE.
IF SHE DOESN'T WISH TO TELL ME ANYTHING, IT'S BECAUSE IT'S IMPORTANT. COUNT DE ROCHEFORT WILL BE PLEASED TO LEARN THE QUEEN'S SEEKING A MESSENGER FOR LONDON.
EXCUSE ME FOR LEAVING YOU, MY DEAR, BUT UNAWARE THAT YOU WERE COMING TO SEE ME, I'D ARRANGED A MEETING WITH ONE OF MY FRIENDS...
ALL THE IMBECILE NEEDED WAS TO BE FOR THE CARDINAL, TOO! AH, GOOD GOD! MONSIEUR BONACIEUX! I NEVER LIKED YOU VERY MUCH; NOW IT'S WORSE, I HATE YOU!
DON'T WORRY!
!!
MY DEAR MADAME BONACIEUX, I HEARD EVERYTHING, AND I'M AT YOUR SERVICE!
MONSIEUR D'ARTAGNAN!
MADAME, NOT ONLY DO I LOVE YOU, BUT YOUR DEDICATION IMPRESSES ME!
WITH MY FRIENDS ATHOS, PORTHOS, AND ARAMIS, WE'LL DEPART IMMEDIATELY THEN FOR LON--
BY THE DEVIL, MY WIFE HAS ALREADY REACHED THE LOUVRE.
ARE YOU CERTAIN THAT, DURING YOUR CONVERSATION, SHE MENTIONED NEITHER MADAME DE CHEVREUSE, NOR MME DE VERNET, NOR THE DUKE OF BUCKINGHAM?

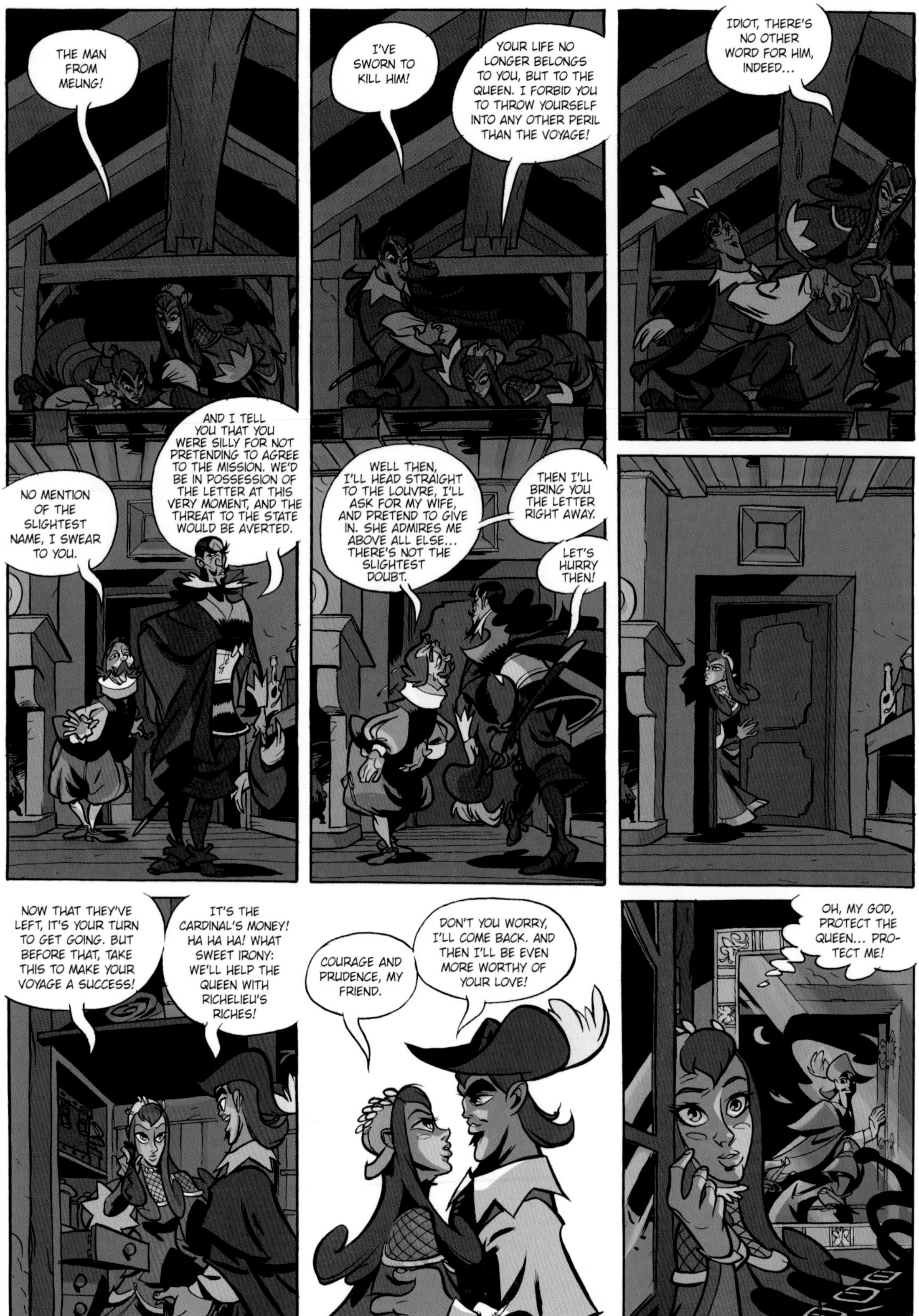

THE MAN FROM MEUNG!
I'VE SWORN TO KILL HIM!
YOUR LIFE NO LONGER BELONGS TO YOU, BUT TO THE QUEEN. I FORBID YOU TO THROW YOURSELF INTO ANY OTHER PERIL THAN THE VOYAGE!
IDIOT, THERE'S NO OTHER WORD FOR HIM, INDEED...
NO MENTION OF THE SLIGHTEST NAME, I SWEAR TO YOU.
AND I TELL YOU THAT YOU WERE SILLY FOR NOT PRETENDING TO AGREE TO THE MISSION. WE'D BE IN POSSESSION OF THE LETTER AT THIS VERY MOMENT, AND THE THREAT TO THE STATE WOULD BE AVERTED.
WELL THEN, I'LL HEAD STRAIGHT TO THE LOUVRE, I'LL ASK FOR MY WIFE, AND PRETEND TO GIVE IN. SHE ADMIRES ME ABOVE ALL ELSE... THERE'S NOT THE SLIGHTEST DOUBT.
THEN I'LL BRING YOU THE LETTER RIGHT AWAY.
LET'S HURRY THEN!
NOW THAT THEY'VE LEFT, IT'S YOUR TURN TO GET GOING. BUT BEFORE THAT, TAKE THIS TO MAKE YOUR VOYAGE A SUCCESS!
IT'S THE CARDINAL'S MONEY! HA HA HA! WHAT SWEET IRONY: WE'LL HELP THE QUEEN WITH RICHELIEU'S RICHES!
COURAGE AND PRUDENCE, MY FRIEND.
DON'T YOU WORRY, I'LL COME BACK. AND THEN I'LL BE EVEN MORE WORTHY OF YOUR LOVE!
OH, MY GOD, PROTECT THE QUEEN... PROTECT ME!

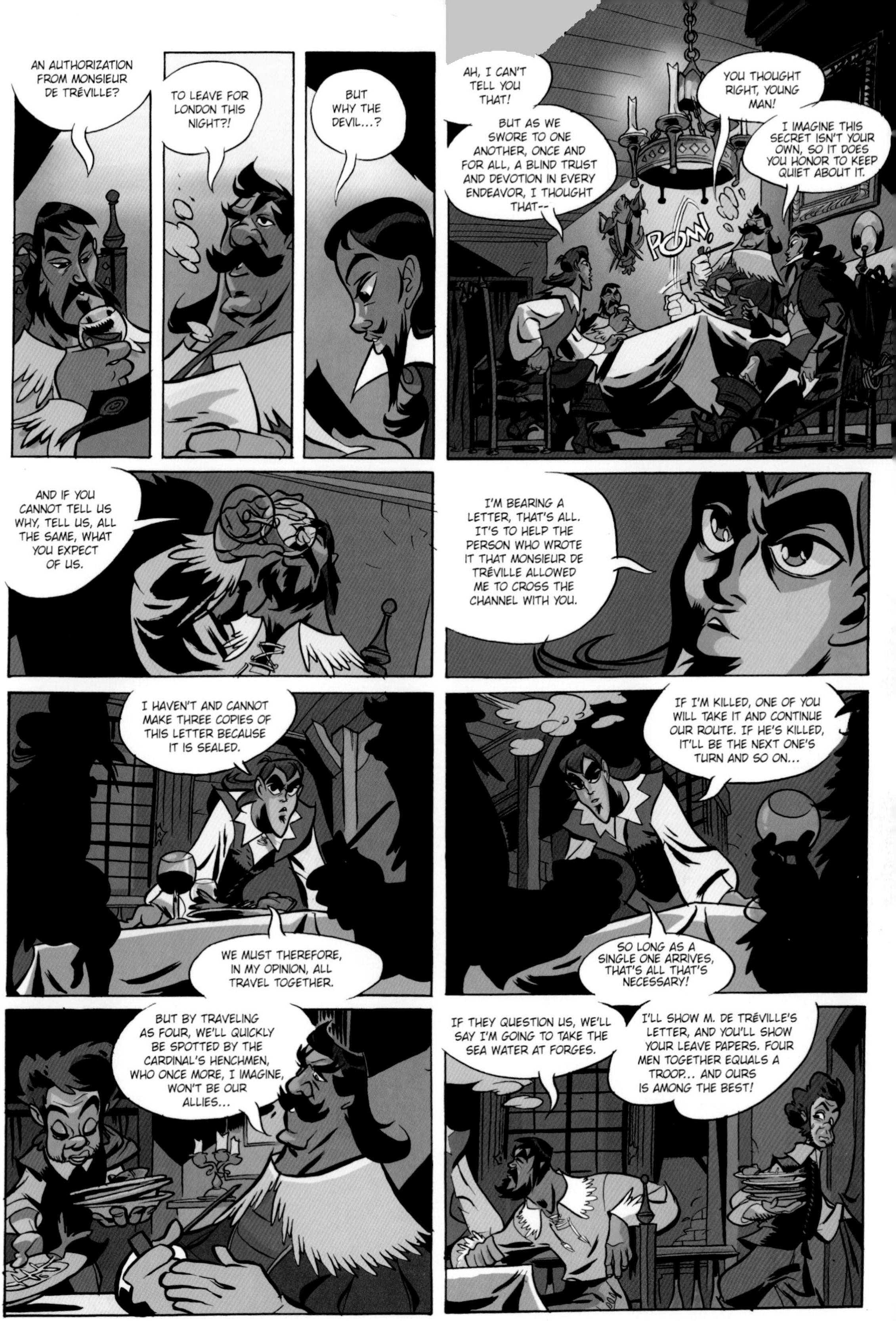
AN AUTHORIZATION FROM MONSIEUR DE TRÉVILLE?
TO LEAVE FOR LONDON THIS NIGHT?!
BUT WHY THE DEVIL...?
AH, I CAN'T TELL YOU THAT!
BUT AS WE SWORE TO ONE ANOTHER, ONCE AND FOR ALL, A BLIND TRUST AND DEVOTION IN EVERY ENDEAVOR, I THOUGHT THAT--
POM!
YOU THOUGHT RIGHT, YOUNG MAN!
I IMAGINE THIS SECRET ISN'T YOUR OWN, SO IT DOES YOU HONOR TO KEEP QUIET ABOUT IT.
AND IF YOU CANNOT TELL US WHY, TELL US, ALL THE SAME, WHAT YOU EXPECT OF US.
I'M BEARING A LETTER, THAT'S ALL. IT'S TO HELP THE PERSON WHO WROTE IT THAT MONSIEUR DE TRÉVILLE ALLOWED ME TO CROSS THE CHANNEL WITH YOU.
I HAVEN'T AND CANNOT MAKE THREE COPIES OF THIS LETTER BECAUSE IT IS SEALED.
WE MUST THEREFORE, IN MY OPINION, ALL TRAVEL TOGETHER.
IF I'M KILLED, ONE OF YOU WILL TAKE IT AND CONTINUE OUR ROUTE. IF HE'S KILLED, IT'LL BE THE NEXT ONE'S TURN AND SO ON...
SO LONG AS A SINGLE ONE ARRIVES, THAT'S ALL THAT'S NECESSARY!
BUT BY TRAVELING AS FOUR, WE'LL QUICKLY BE SPOTTED BY THE CARDINAL'S HENCHMEN, WHO ONCE MORE, I IMAGINE, WON'T BE OUR ALLIES...
IF THEY QUESTION US, WE'LL SAY I'M GOING TO TAKE THE SEA WATER AT FORGES.
I'LL SHOW M. DE TRÉVILLE'S LETTER, AND YOU'LL SHOW YOUR LEAVE PAPERS. FOUR MEN TOGETHER EQUALS A TROOP... AND OURS IS AMONG THE BEST!

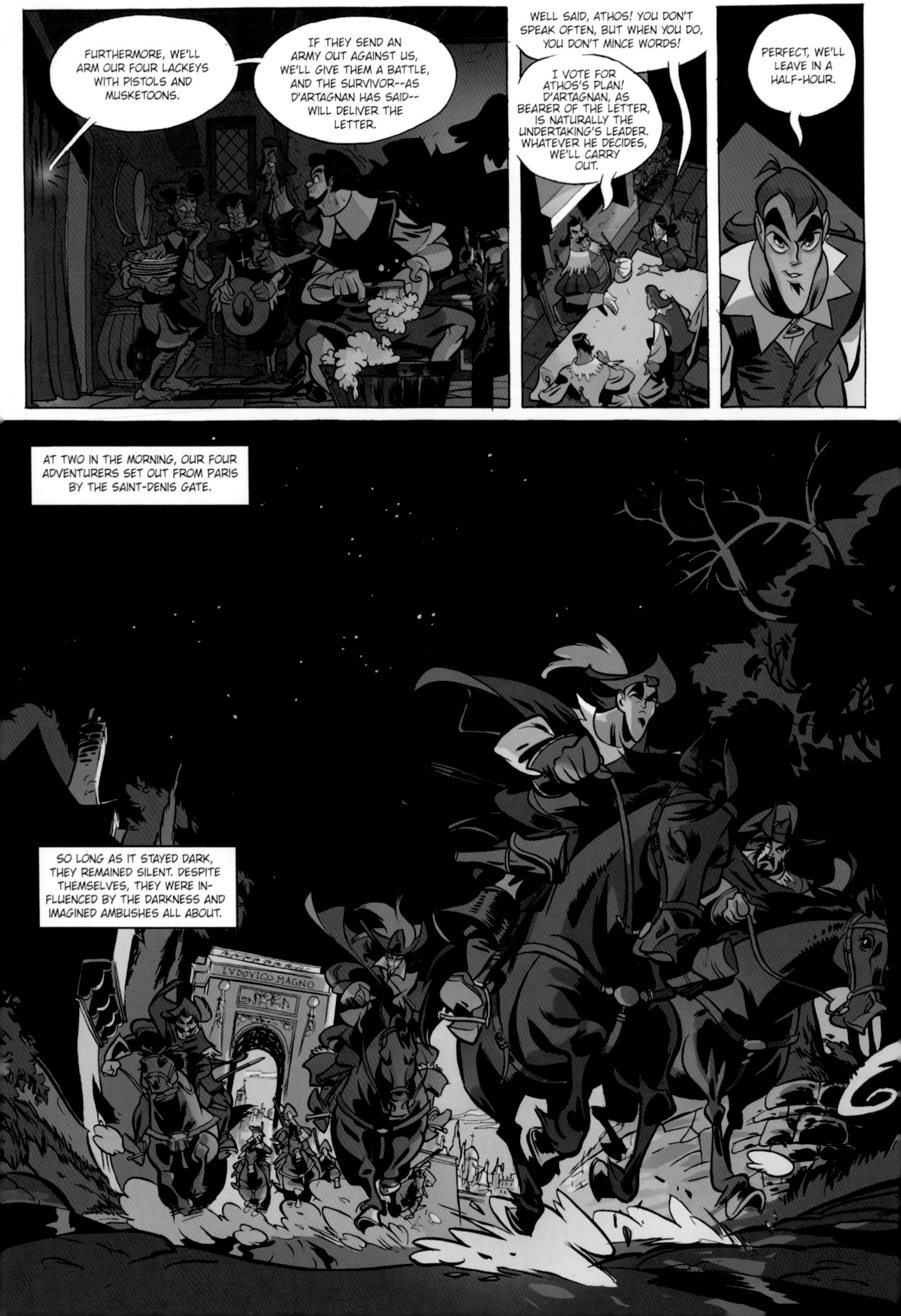
FURTHERMORE, WE'LL ARM OUR FOUR LACKEYS WITH PISTOLS AND MUSKETOONS.
IF THEY SEND AN ARMY OUT AGAINST US, WE'LL GIVE THEM A BATTLE, AND THE SURVIVOR--AS D'ARTAGNAN HAS SAID--WILL DELIVER THE LETTER.
WELL SAID, ATHOS! YOU DON'T SPEAK OFTEN, BUT WHEN YOU DO, YOU DON'T MINCE WORDS!
I VOTE FOR ATHOS'S PLAN! D'ARTAGNAN, AS BEARER OF THE LETTER, IS NATURALLY THE UNDERTAKING'S LEADER. WHATEVER HE DECIDES, WE'LL CARRY OUT.
PERFECT, WE'LL LEAVE IN A HALF-HOUR.
AT TWO IN THE MORNING, OUR FOUR ADVENTURERS SET OUT FROM PARIS BY THE SAINT-DENIS GATE.
SO LONG AS IT STAYED DARK, THEY REMAINED SILENT. DESPITE THEMSELVES, THEY WERE INFLUENCED BY THE DARKNESS AND IMAGINED AMBUSHES ALL ABOUT.
LVDOVICO MAGNO

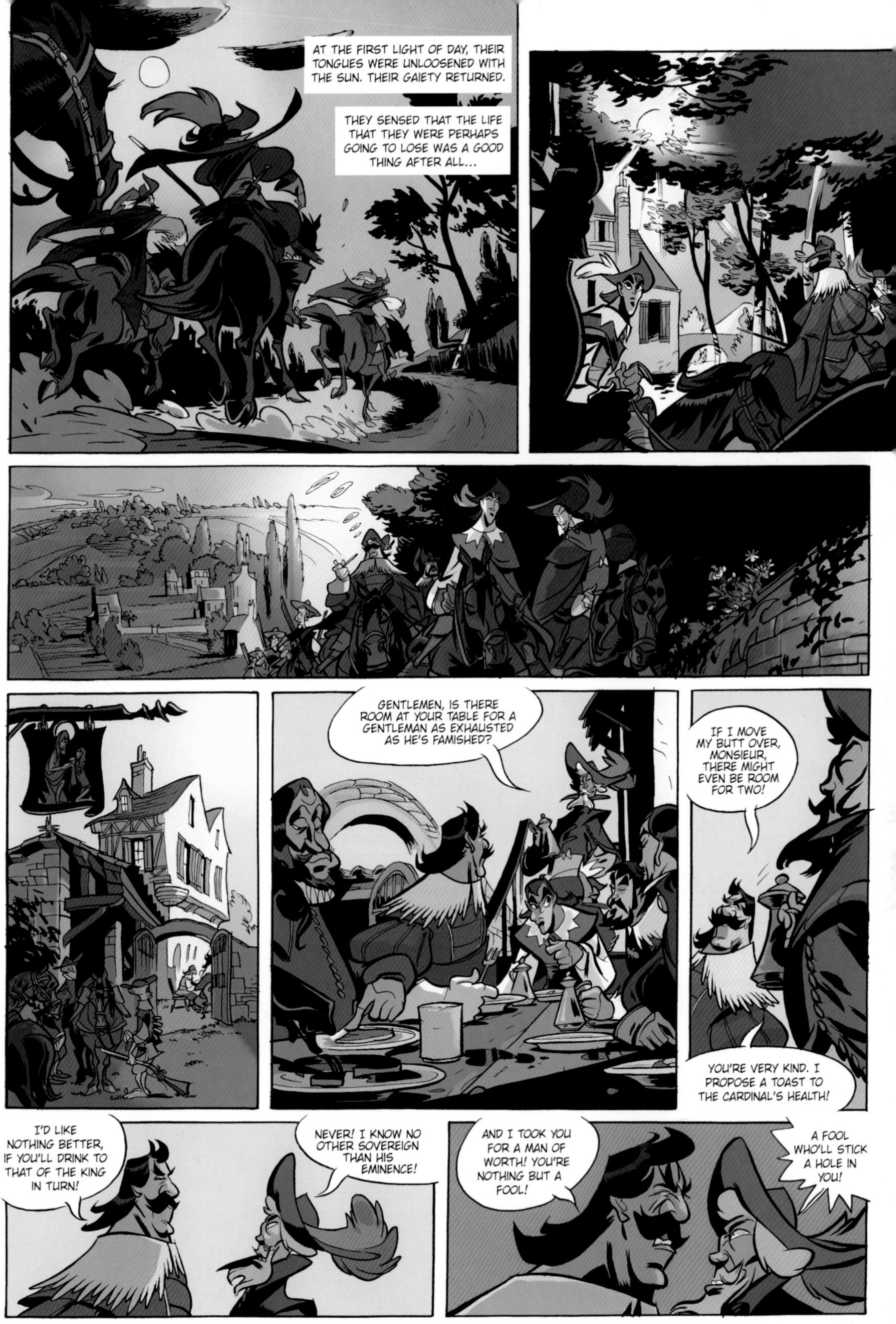
AT THE FIRST LIGHT OF DAY, THEIR TONGUES WERE UNLOOSENED WITH THE SUN. THEIR GAIETY RETURNED.
THEY SENSED THAT THE LIFE THAT THEY WERE PERHAPS GOING TO LOSE WAS A GOOD THING AFTER ALL...
GENTLEMEN, IS THERE ROOM AT YOUR TABLE FOR A GENTLEMAN AS EXHAUSTED AS HE'S FAMISHED?
IF I MOVE MY BUTT OVER, MONSIEUR, THERE MIGHT EVEN BE ROOM FOR TWO!
YOU'RE VERY KIND. I PROPOSE A TOAST TO THE CARDINAL'S HEALTH!
I'D LIKE NOTHING BETTER, IF YOU'LL DRINK TO THAT OF THE KING IN TURN!
NEVER! I KNOW NO OTHER SOVEREIGN THAN HIS EMINENCE!
AND I TOOK YOU FOR A MAN OF WORTH! YOU'RE NOTHING BUT A FOOL!
A FOOL WHO'LL STICK A HOLE IN YOU!

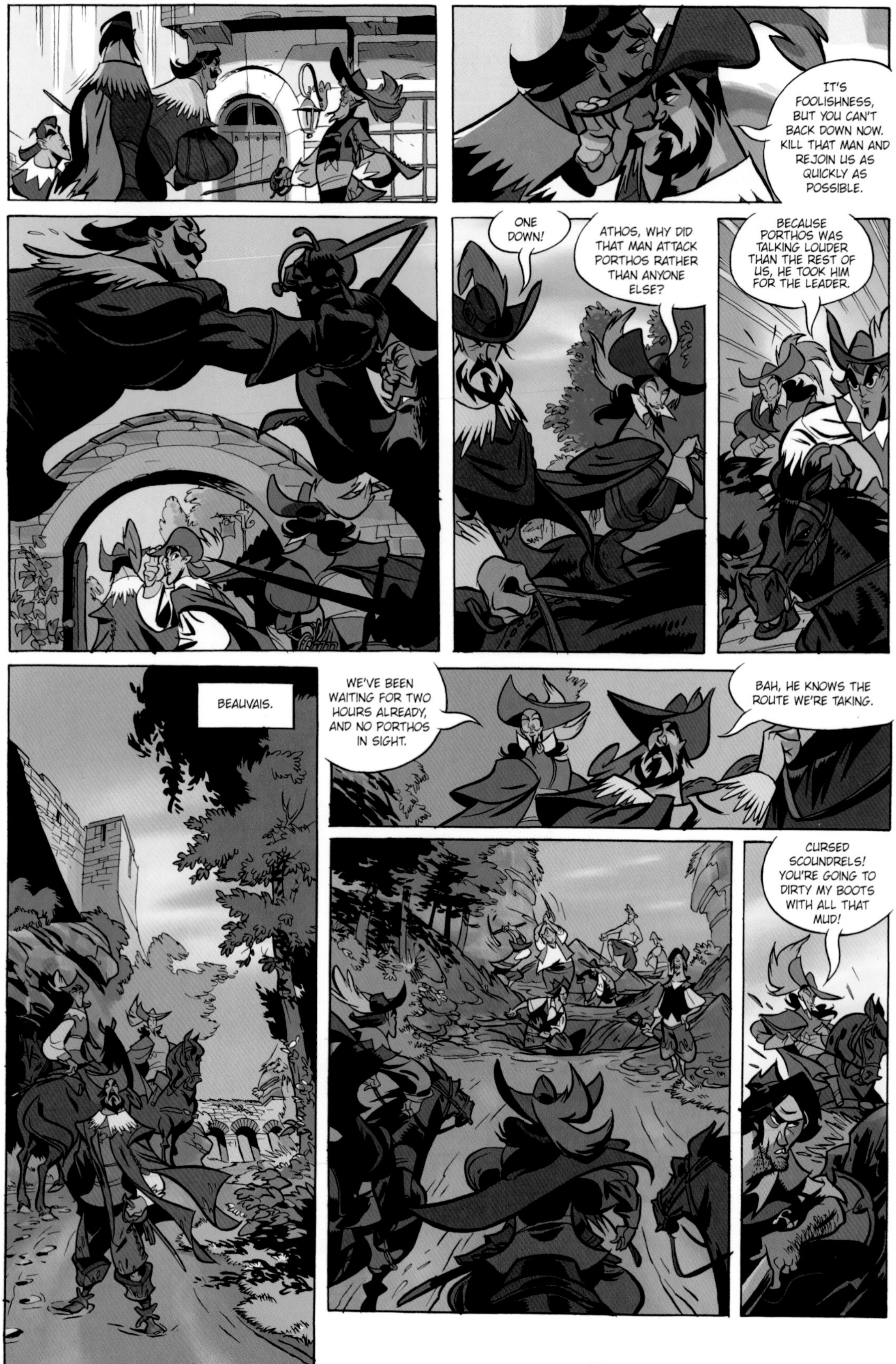
IT'S FOOLISHNESS, BUT YOU CAN'T BACK DOWN NOW. KILL THAT MAN AND REJOIN US AS QUICKLY AS POSSIBLE.
ONE DOWN!
ATHOS, WHY DID THAT MAN ATTACK PORTHOS RATHER THAN ANYONE ELSE?
BECAUSE PORTHOS WAS TALKING LOUDER THAN THE REST OF US, HE TOOK HIM FOR THE LEADER.
BEAUVAIS.
WE'VE BEEN WAITING FOR TWO HOURS ALREADY, AND NO PORTHOS IN SIGHT.
BAH, HE KNOWS THE ROUTE WE'RE TAKING.
CURSED SCOUNDRELS! YOU'RE GOING TO DIRTY MY BOOTS WITH ALL THAT MUD!

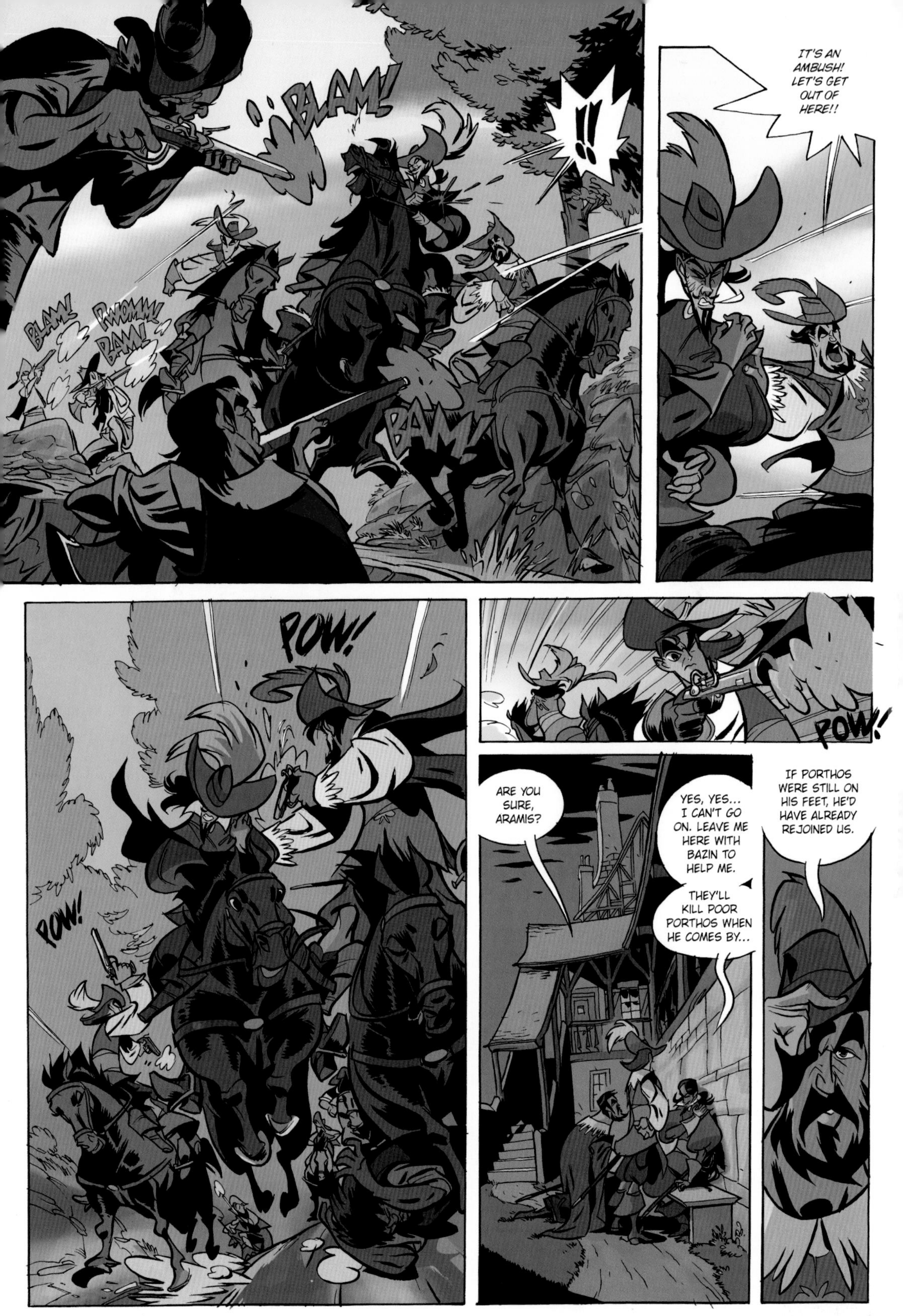
BLAM!
!!
IT'S AN AMBUSH! LET'S GET OUT OF HERE!!
BLAM!
PWOMM!
BAM!
BAM!
POW!
POW!
POW!
ARE YOU SURE, ARAMIS?
YES, YES... I CAN'T GO ON. LEAVE ME HERE WITH BAZIN TO HELP ME.
THEY'LL KILL POOR PORTHOS WHEN HE COMES BY...
IF PORTHOS WERE STILL ON HIS FEET, HE'D HAVE ALREADY REJOINED US.

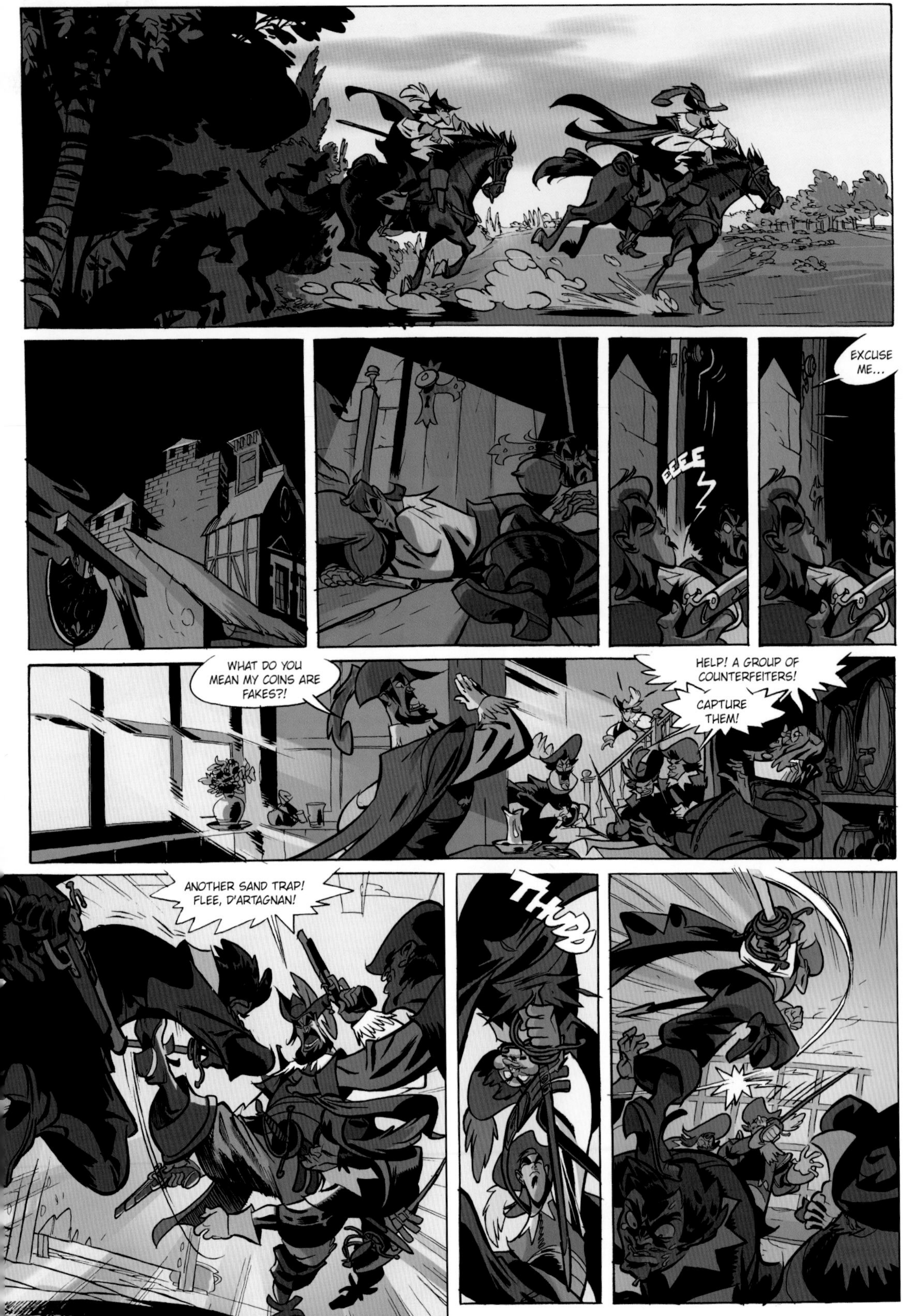
EXCUSE ME...
EEEE
WHAT DO YOU MEAN MY COINS ARE FAKES?!
HELP! A GROUP OF COUNTERFEITERS!
CAPTURE THEM!
ANOTHER SAND TRAP! FLEE, D'ARTAGNAN!
THUD

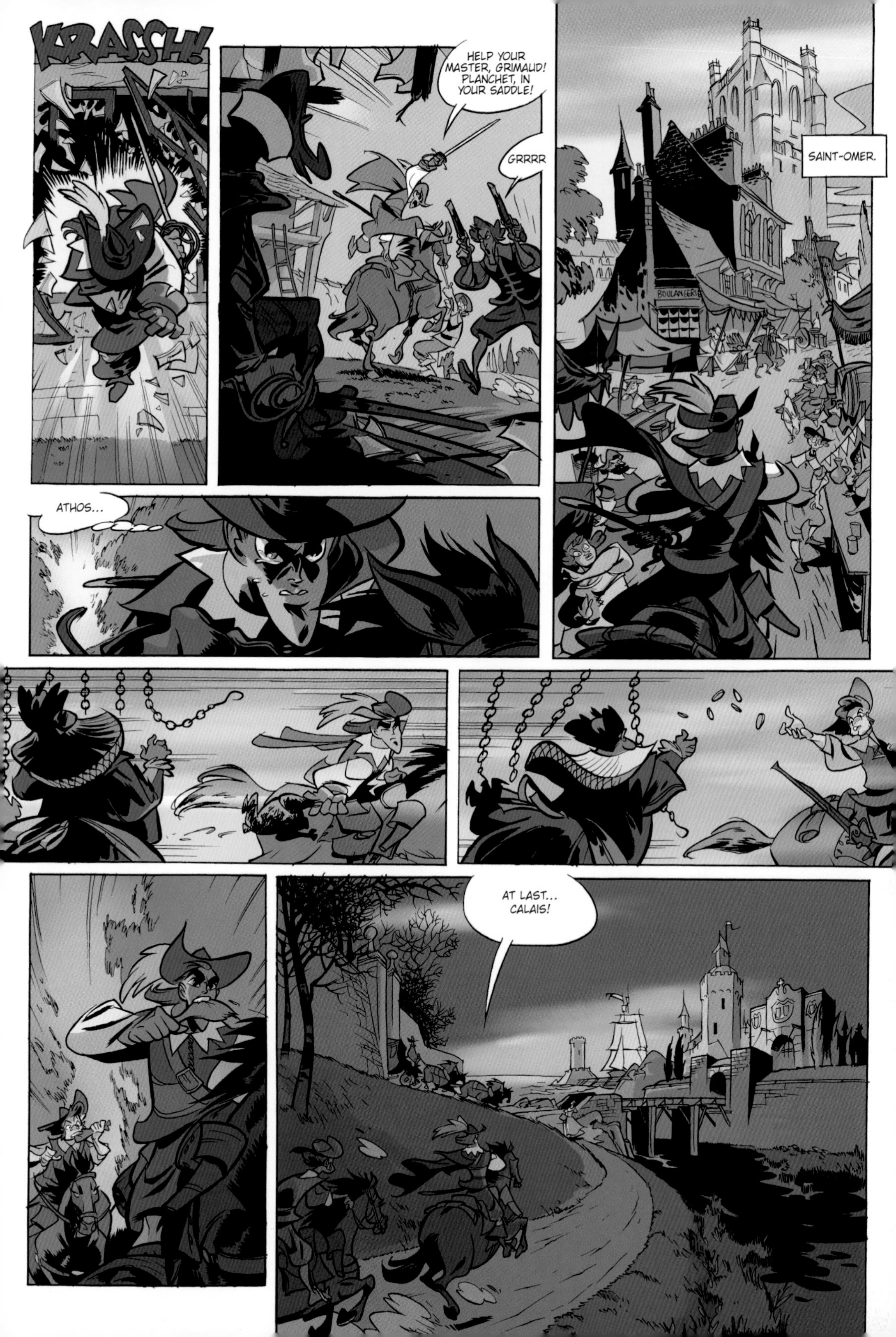
KRASSH!
HELP YOUR MASTER, GRIMAUD! PLANCHET, IN YOUR SADDLE!
GRRRR
SAINT-OMER.
BOULANGERIE
ATHOS...
AT LAST... CALAIS!

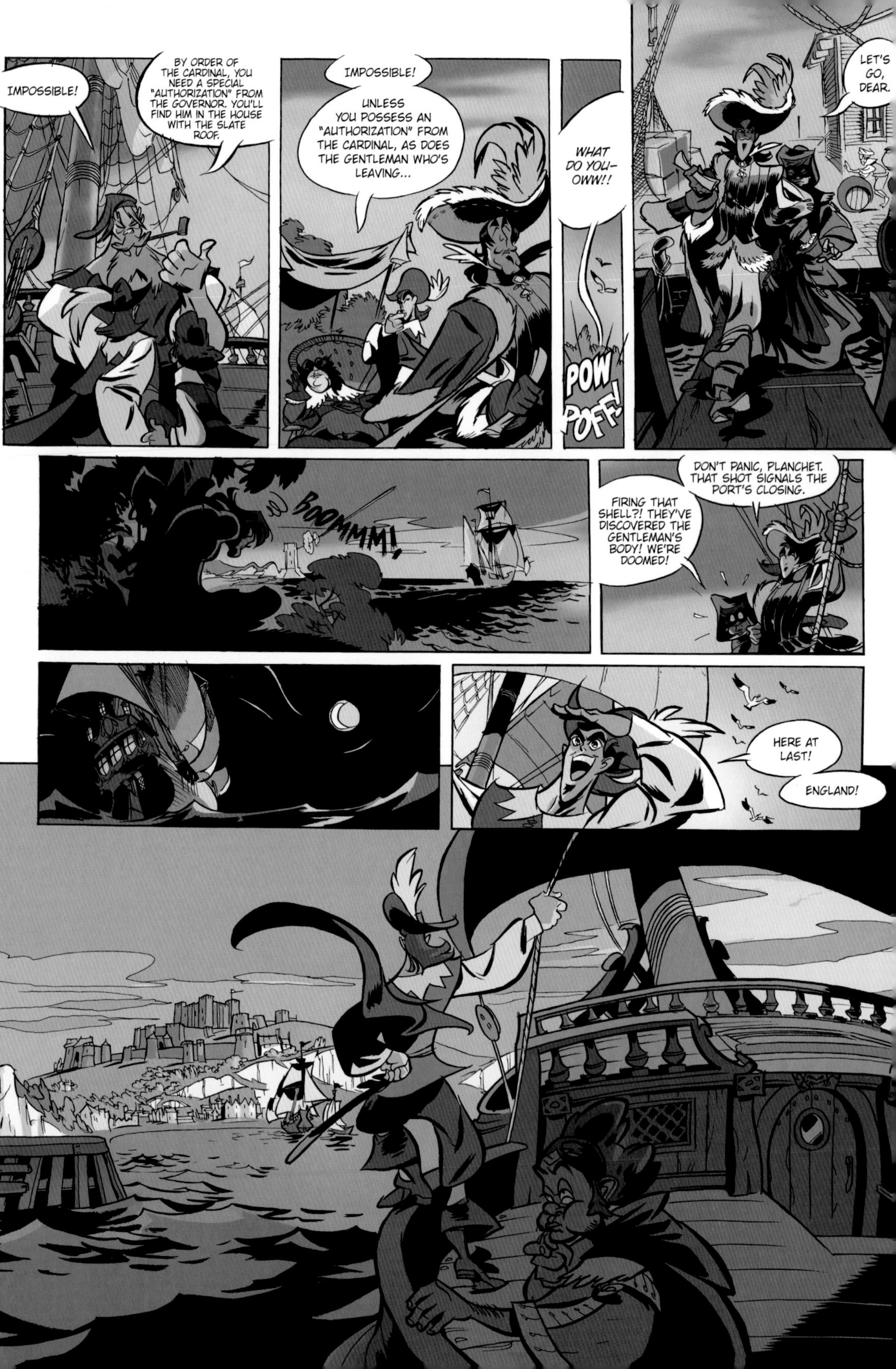
IMPOSSIBLE!
BY ORDER OF THE CARDINAL, YOU NEED A SPECIAL "AUTHORIZATION" FROM THE GOVERNOR. YOU'LL FIND HIM IN THE HOUSE WITH THE SLATE ROOF.
IMPOSSIBLE!
UNLESS YOU POSSESS AN "AUTHORIZATION" FROM THE CARDINAL, AS DOES THE GENTLEMAN WHO'S LEAVING...
WHAT DO YOU– OWW!!
POW
POFF!
LET'S GO, DEAR.
BOOOMMM!
DON'T PANIC, PLANCHET. THAT SHOT SIGNALS THE PORT'S CLOSING.
FIRING THAT SHELL?! THEY'VE DISCOVERED THE GENTLEMAN'S BODY! WE'RE DOOMED!
HERE AT LAST!
ENGLAND!

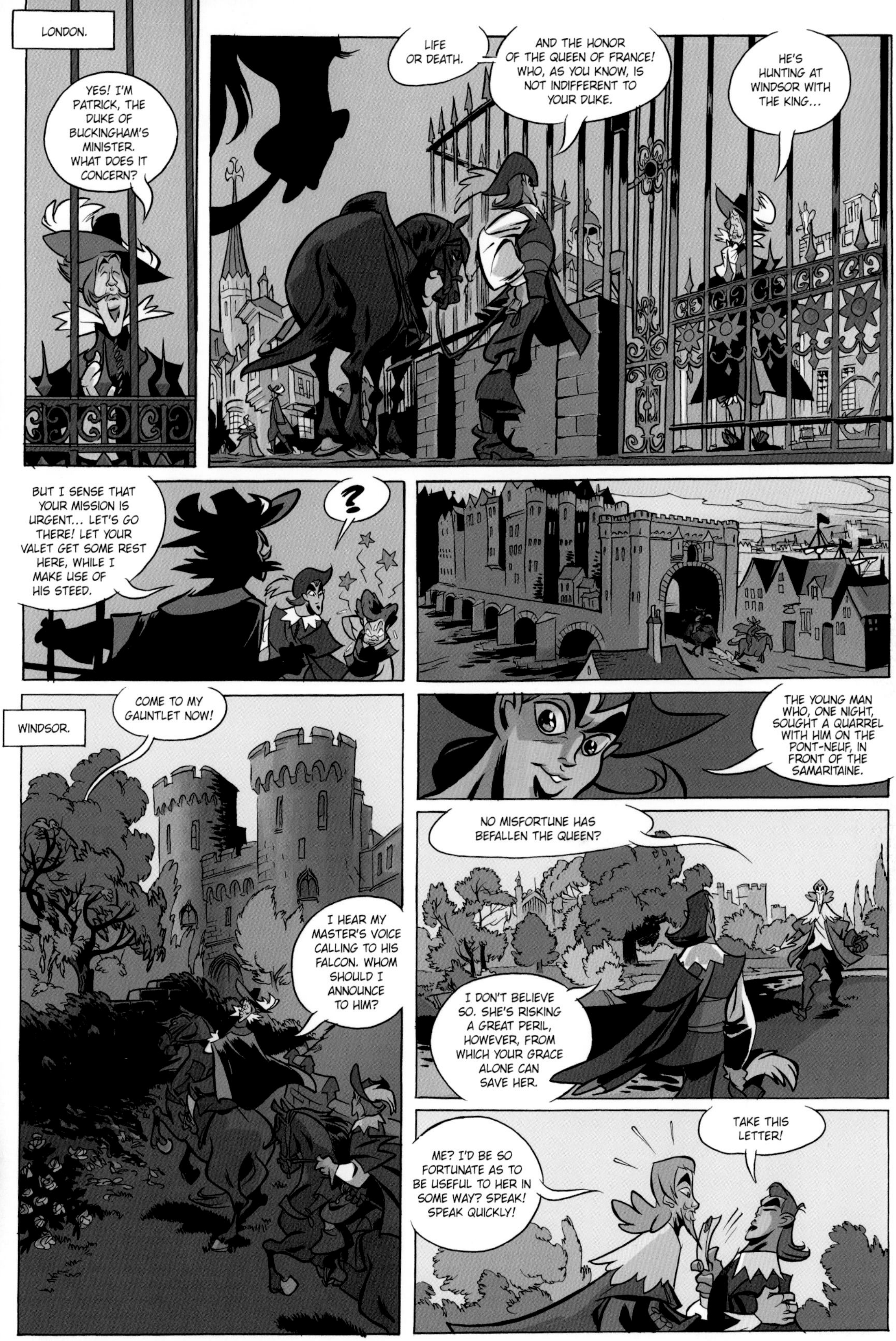
LONDON.
YES! I'M PATRICK, THE DUKE OF BUCKINGHAM'S MINISTER. WHAT DOES IT CONCERN?
LIFE OR DEATH.
AND THE HONOR OF THE QUEEN OF FRANCE! WHO, AS YOU KNOW, IS NOT INDIFFERENT TO YOUR DUKE.
HE'S HUNTING AT WINDSOR WITH THE KING...
BUT I SENSE THAT YOUR MISSION IS URGENT... LET'S GO THERE! LET YOUR VALET GET SOME REST HERE, WHILE I MAKE USE OF HIS STEED.
?
WINDSOR.
COME TO MY GAUNTLET NOW!
I HEAR MY MASTER'S VOICE CALLING TO HIS FALCON. WHOM SHOULD I ANNOUNCE TO HIM?
THE YOUNG MAN WHO, ONE NIGHT, SOUGHT A QUARREL WITH HIM ON THE PONT-NEUF, IN FRONT OF THE SAMARITAINE.
NO MISFORTUNE HAS BEFALLEN THE QUEEN?
I DON'T BELIEVE SO. SHE'S RISKING A GREAT PERIL, HOWEVER, FROM WHICH YOUR GRACE ALONE CAN SAVE HER.
ME? I'D BE SO FORTUNATE AS TO BE USEFUL TO HER IN SOME WAY? SPEAK! SPEAK QUICKLY!
TAKE THIS LETTER!

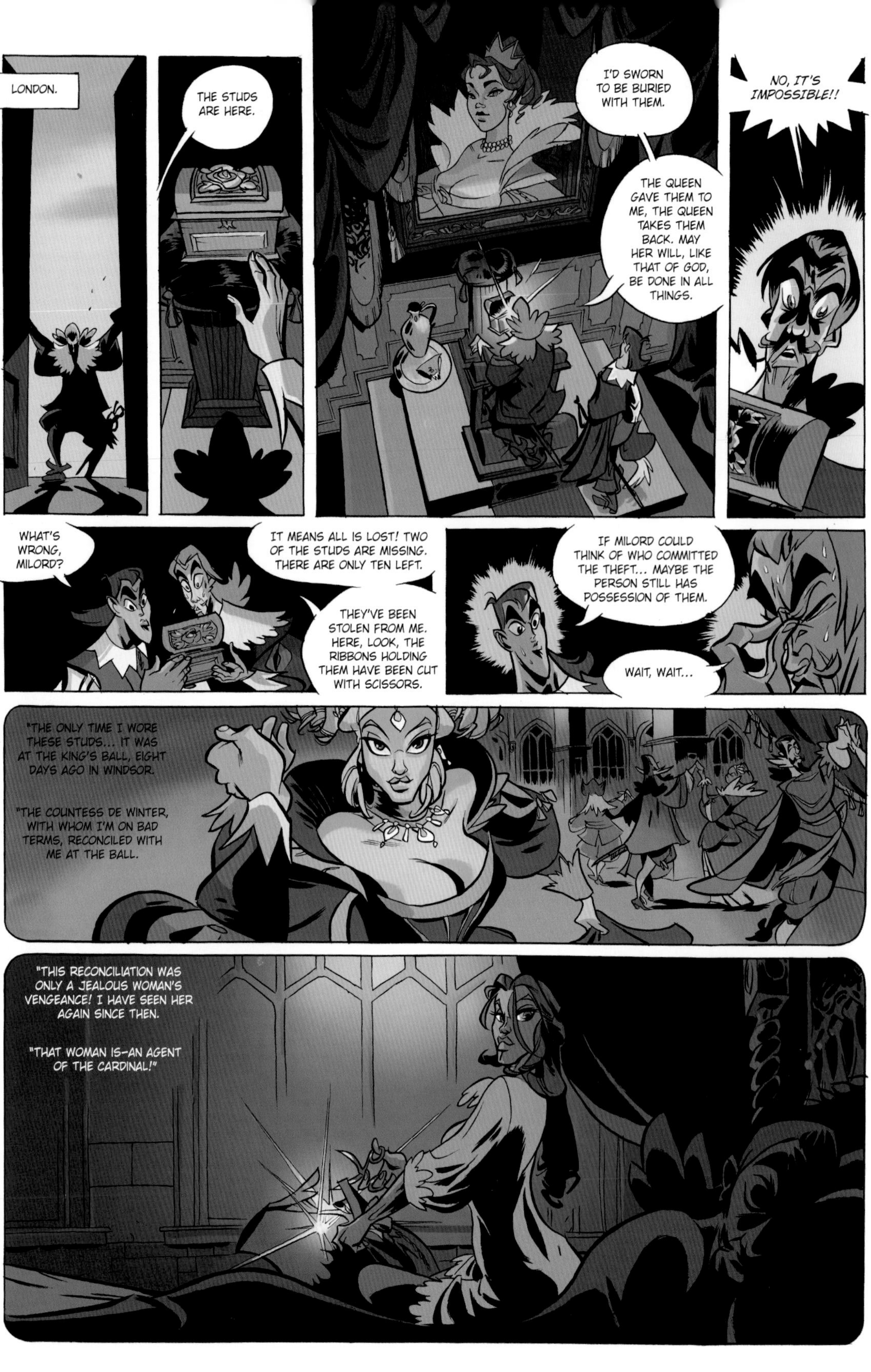
LONDON.
THE STUDS ARE HERE.
I'D SWORN TO BE BURIED WITH THEM.
THE QUEEN GAVE THEM TO ME, THE QUEEN TAKES THEM BACK. MAY HER WILL, LIKE THAT OF GOD, BE DONE IN ALL THINGS.
NO, IT'S IMPOSSIBLE!!
WHAT'S WRONG, MILORD?
IT MEANS ALL IS LOST! TWO OF THE STUDS ARE MISSING. THERE ARE ONLY TEN LEFT.
THEY'VE BEEN STOLEN FROM ME. HERE, LOOK, THE RIBBONS HOLDING THEM HAVE BEEN CUT WITH SCISSORS.
IF MILORD COULD THINK OF WHO COMMITTED THE THEFT... MAYBE THE PERSON STILL HAS POSSESSION OF THEM.
WAIT, WAIT...
"THE ONLY TIME I WORE THESE STUDS... IT WAS AT THE KING'S BALL, EIGHT DAYS AGO IN WINDSOR.
"THE COUNTESS DE WINTER, WITH WHOM I'M ON BAD TERMS, RECONCILED WITH ME AT THE BALL.
"THIS RECONCILIATION WAS ONLY A JEALOUS WOMAN'S VENGEANCE! I HAVE SEEN HER AGAIN SINCE THEN.
"THAT WOMAN IS–AN AGENT OF THE CARDINAL!"

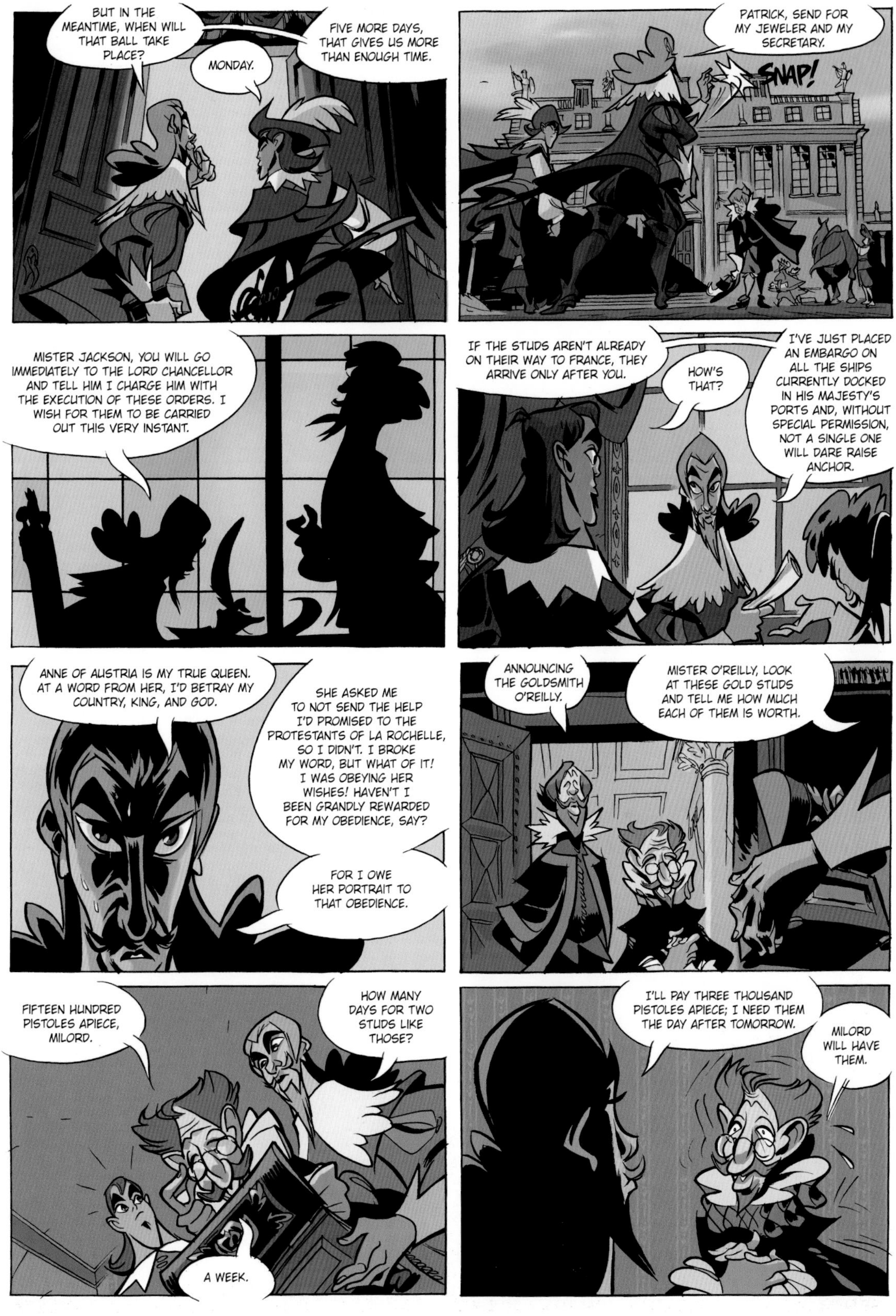
BUT IN THE MEANTIME, WHEN WILL THAT BALL TAKE PLACE?
MONDAY.
FIVE MORE DAYS, THAT GIVES US MORE THAN ENOUGH TIME.
PATRICK, SEND FOR MY JEWELER AND MY SECRETARY.
SNAP!
MISTER JACKSON, YOU WILL GO IMMEDIATELY TO THE LORD CHANCELLOR AND TELL HIM I CHARGE HIM WITH THE EXECUTION OF THESE ORDERS. I WISH FOR THEM TO BE CARRIED OUT THIS VERY INSTANT.
IF THE STUDS AREN'T ALREADY ON THEIR WAY TO FRANCE, THEY ARRIVE ONLY AFTER YOU.
HOW'S THAT?
I'VE JUST PLACED AN EMBARGO ON ALL THE SHIPS CURRENTLY DOCKED IN HIS MAJESTY'S PORTS AND, WITHOUT SPECIAL PERMISSION, NOT A SINGLE ONE WILL DARE RAISE ANCHOR.
ANNE OF AUSTRIA IS MY TRUE QUEEN. AT A WORD FROM HER, I'D BETRAY MY COUNTRY, KING, AND GOD.
SHE ASKED ME TO NOT SEND THE HELP I'D PROMISED TO THE PROTESTANTS OF LA ROCHELLE, SO I DIDN'T. I BROKE MY WORD, BUT WHAT OF IT! I WAS OBEYING HER WISHES! HAVEN'T I BEEN GRANDLY REWARDED FOR MY OBEDIENCE, SAY?
FOR I OWE HER PORTRAIT TO THAT OBEDIENCE.
ANNOUNCING THE GOLDSMITH O'REILLY.
MISTER O'REILLY, LOOK AT THESE GOLD STUDS AND TELL ME HOW MUCH EACH OF THEM IS WORTH.
FIFTEEN HUNDRED PISTOLES APIECE, MILORD.
HOW MANY DAYS FOR TWO STUDS LIKE THOSE?
A WEEK.
I'LL PAY THREE THOUSAND PISTOLES APIECE; I NEED THEM THE DAY AFTER TOMORROW.
MILORD WILL HAVE THEM.

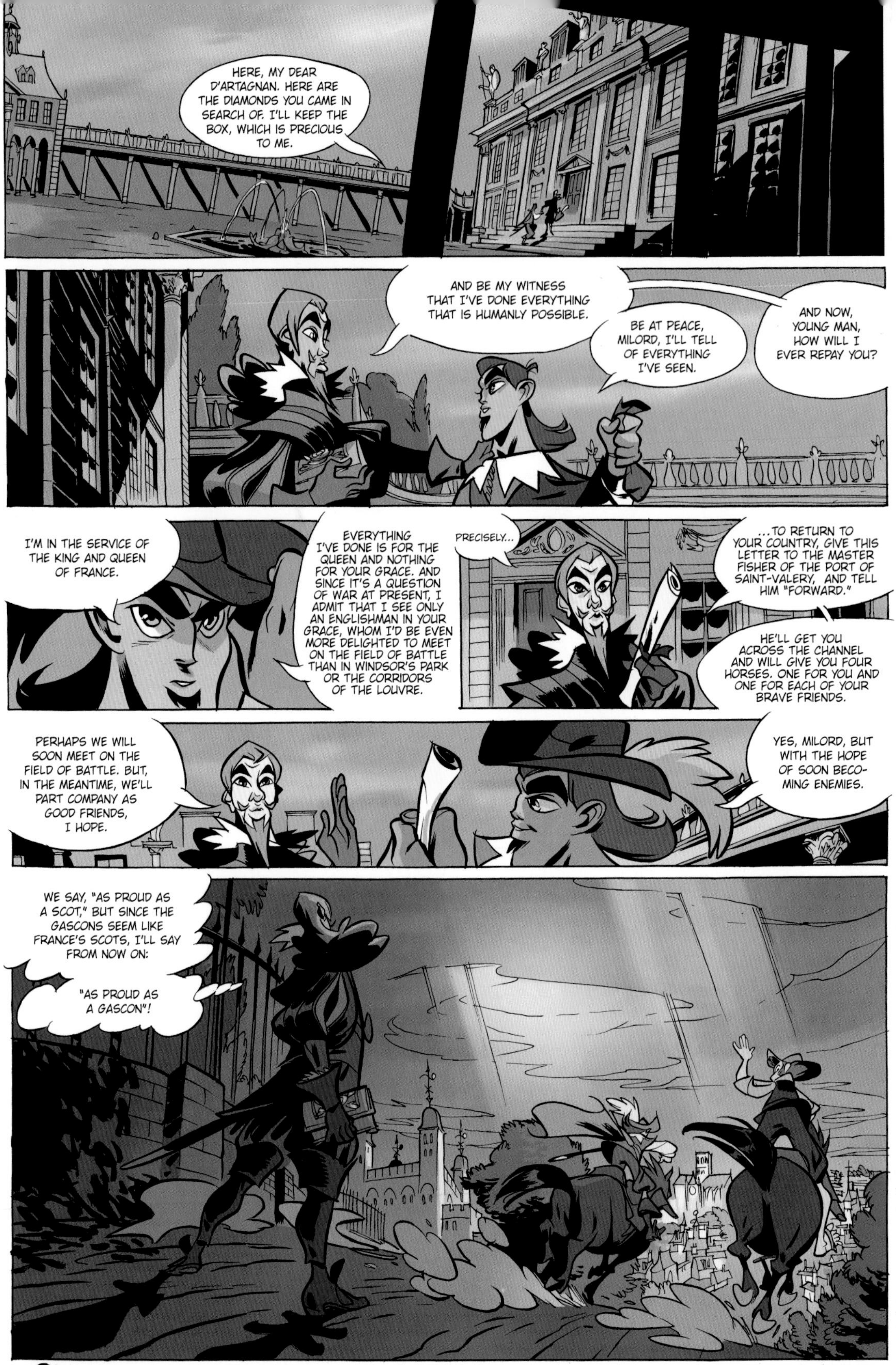
HERE, MY DEAR D'ARTAGNAN. HERE ARE THE DIAMONDS YOU CAME IN SEARCH OF. I'LL KEEP THE BOX, WHICH IS PRECIOUS TO ME.
AND BE MY WITNESS THAT I'VE DONE EVERYTHING THAT IS HUMANLY POSSIBLE.
BE AT PEACE, MILORD, I'LL TELL OF EVERYTHING I'VE SEEN.
AND NOW, YOUNG MAN, HOW WILL I EVER REPAY YOU?
I'M IN THE SERVICE OF THE KING AND QUEEN OF FRANCE.
EVERYTHING I'VE DONE IS FOR THE QUEEN AND NOTHING FOR YOUR GRACE. AND SINCE IT'S A QUESTION OF WAR AT PRESENT, I ADMIT THAT I SEE ONLY AN ENGLISHMAN IN YOUR GRACE, WHOM I'D BE EVEN MORE DELIGHTED TO MEET ON THE FIELD OF BATTLE THAN IN WINDSOR'S PARK OR THE CORRIDORS OF THE LOUVRE.
PRECISELY...
...TO RETURN TO YOUR COUNTRY, GIVE THIS LETTER TO THE MASTER FISHER OF THE PORT OF SAINT-VALERY, AND TELL HIM "FORWARD."
HE'LL GET YOU ACROSS THE CHANNEL AND WILL GIVE YOU FOUR HORSES. ONE FOR YOU AND ONE FOR EACH OF YOUR BRAVE FRIENDS.
PERHAPS WE WILL SOON MEET ON THE FIELD OF BATTLE. BUT, IN THE MEANTIME, WE'LL PART COMPANY AS GOOD FRIENDS, I HOPE.
YES, MILORD, BUT WITH THE HOPE OF SOON BECOMING ENEMIES.
WE SAY, "AS PROUD AS A SCOT," BUT SINCE THE GASCONS SEEM LIKE FRANCE'S SCOTS, I'LL SAY FROM NOW ON:
"AS PROUD AS A GASCON"!

Septembre 2007

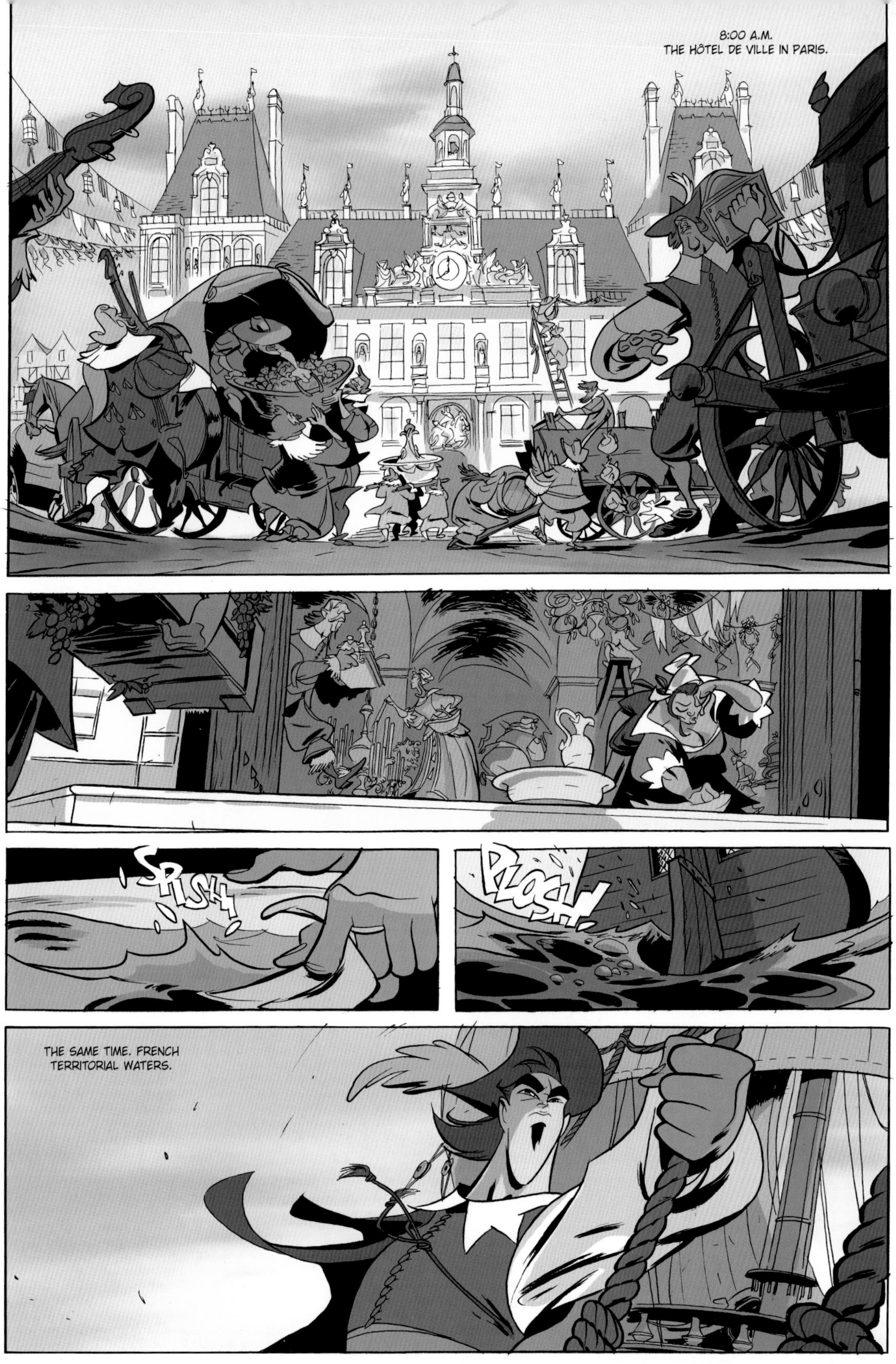
8:00 A.M.
THE HÔTEL DE VILLE IN PARIS.
SPLISH!
PLOSH!
THE SAME TIME. FRENCH
TERRITORIAL WATERS.

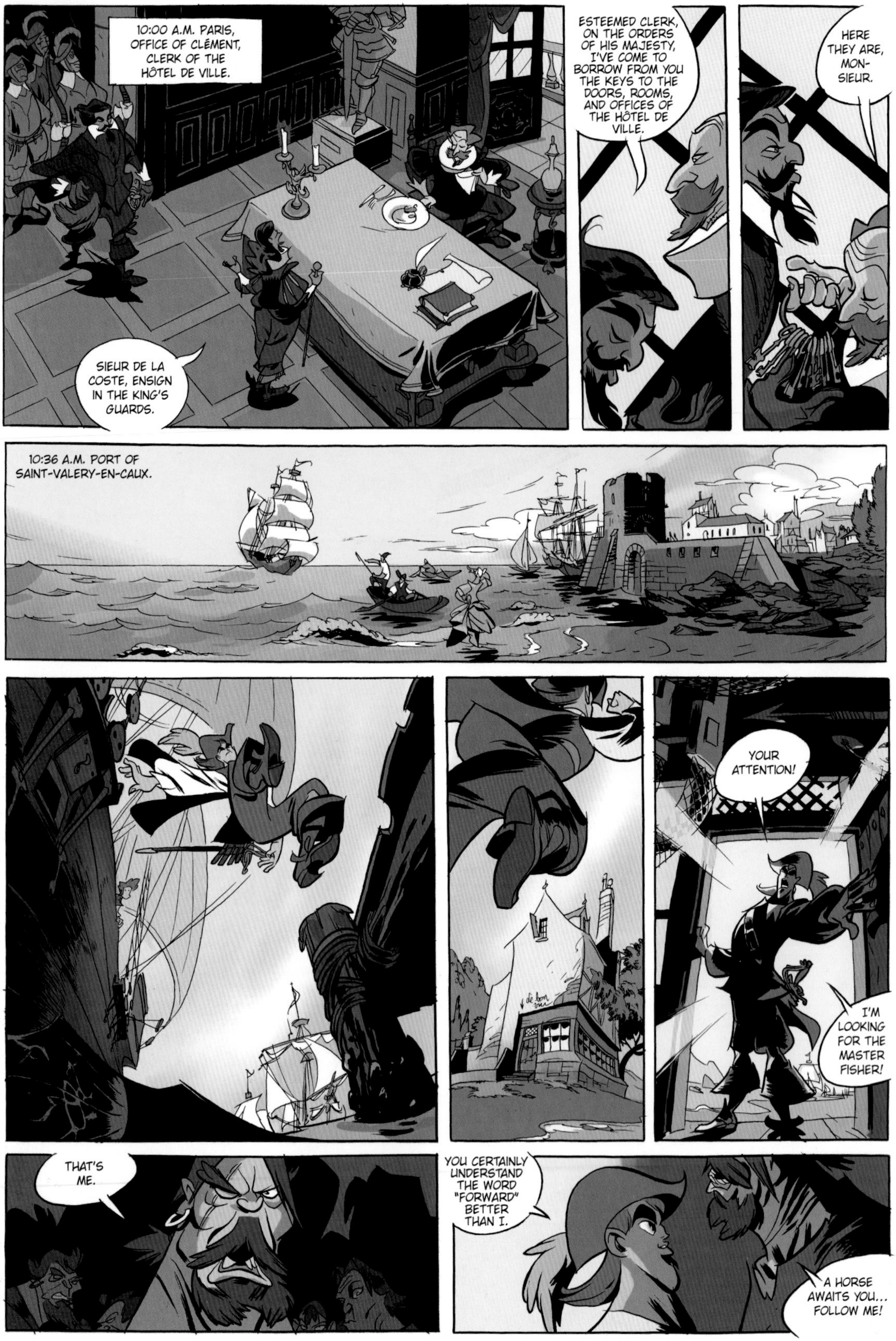
10:00 A.M. PARIS, OFFICE OF CLÉMENT, CLERK OF THE HÔTEL DE VILLE.
SIEUR DE LA COSTE, ENSIGN IN THE KING'S GUARDS.
ESTEEMED CLERK, ON THE ORDERS OF HIS MAJESTY, I'VE COME TO BORROW FROM YOU THE KEYS TO THE DOORS, ROOMS, AND OFFICES OF THE HÔTEL DE VILLE.
HERE THEY ARE, MON-SIEUR.
10:36 A.M. PORT OF SAINT-VALERY-EN-CAUX.
YOUR ATTENTION!
I'M LOOKING FOR THE MASTER FISHER!
THAT'S ME.
YOU CERTAINLY UNDERSTAND THE WORD "FORWARD" BETTER THAN I.
A HORSE AWAITS YOU... FOLLOW ME!

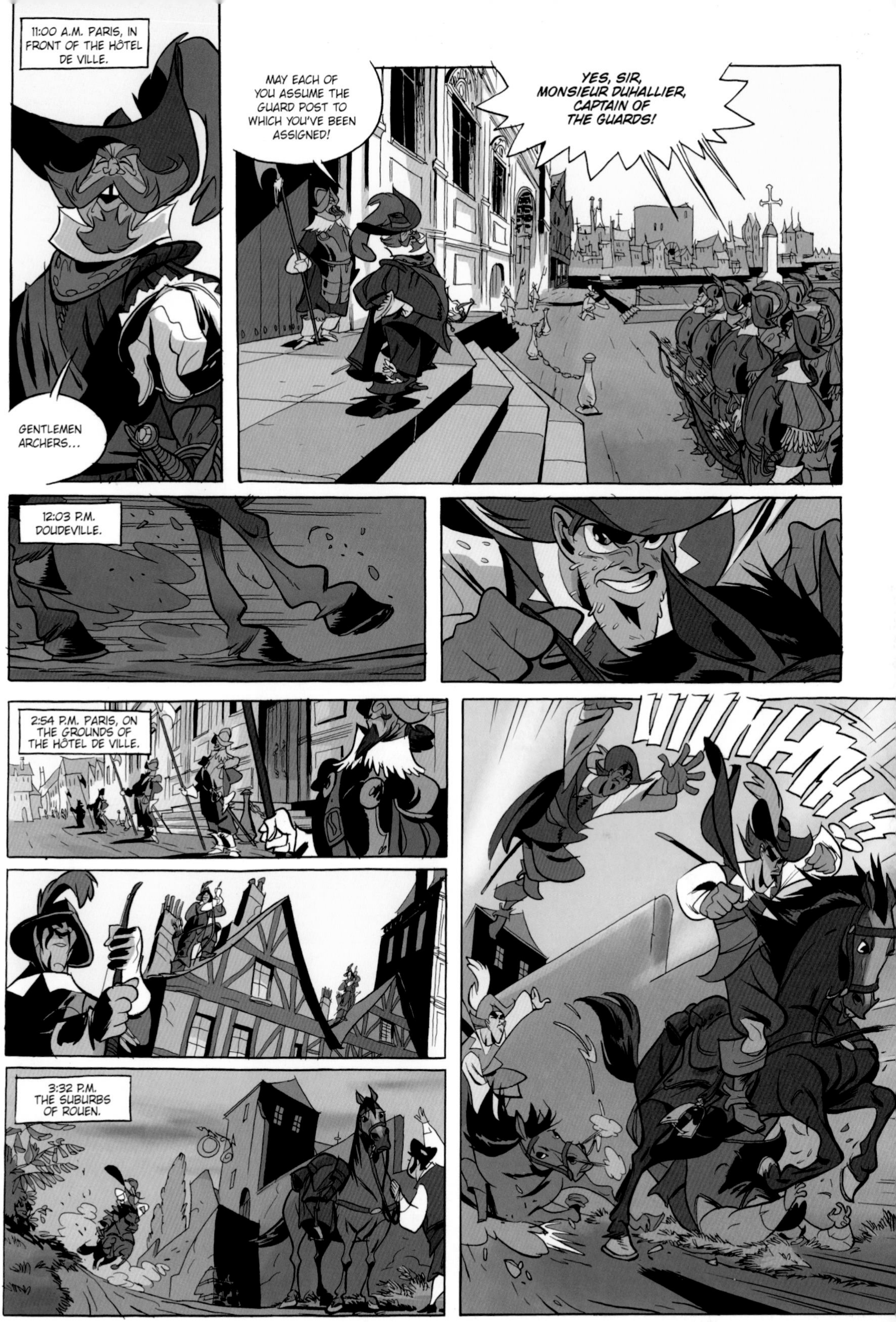

11:00 A.M. PARIS, IN FRONT OF THE HÔTEL DE VILLE.
GENTLEMEN ARCHERS...
MAY EACH OF YOU ASSUME THE GUARD POST TO WHICH YOU'VE BEEN ASSIGNED!
YES, SIR, MONSIEUR DUHALLIER, CAPTAIN OF THE GUARDS!
12:03 P.M. DOUDEVILLE.
2:54 P.M. PARIS, ON THE GROUNDS OF THE HÔTEL DE VILLE.
3:32 P.M. THE SUBURBS OF ROUEN.

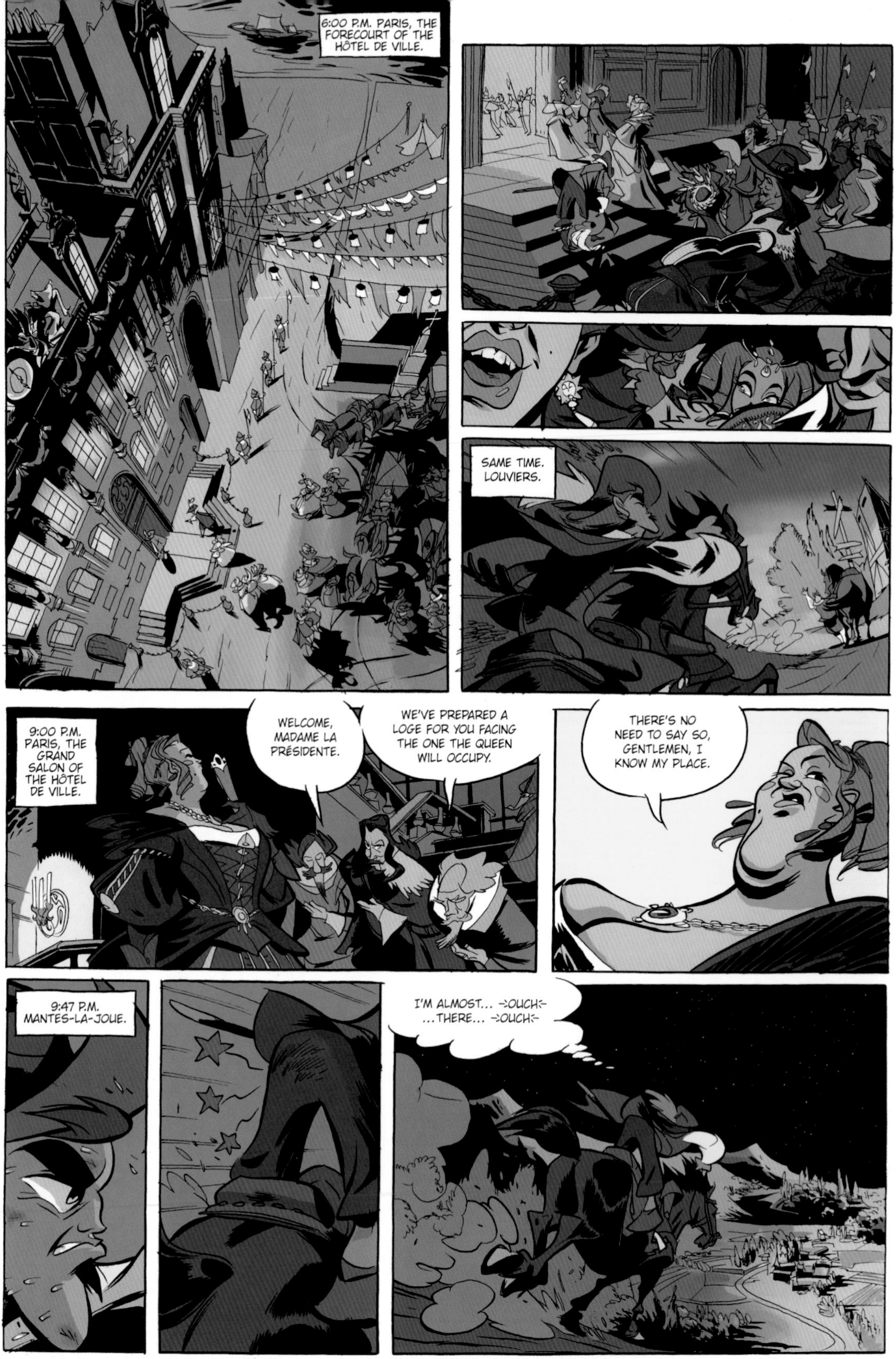
6:00 P.M. PARIS, THE FORECOURT OF THE HÔTEL DE VILLE.
SAME TIME. LOUVIERS.
9:00 P.M. PARIS, THE GRAND SALON OF THE HÔTEL DE VILLE.
WELCOME, MADAME LA PRÉSIDENTE.
WE'VE PREPARED A LOGE FOR YOU FACING THE ONE THE QUEEN WILL OCCUPY.
THERE'S NO NEED TO SAY SO, GENTLEMEN, I KNOW MY PLACE.
9:47 P.M. MANTES-LA-JOUE.
I'M ALMOST... -OUCH- ...THERE... -OUCH-

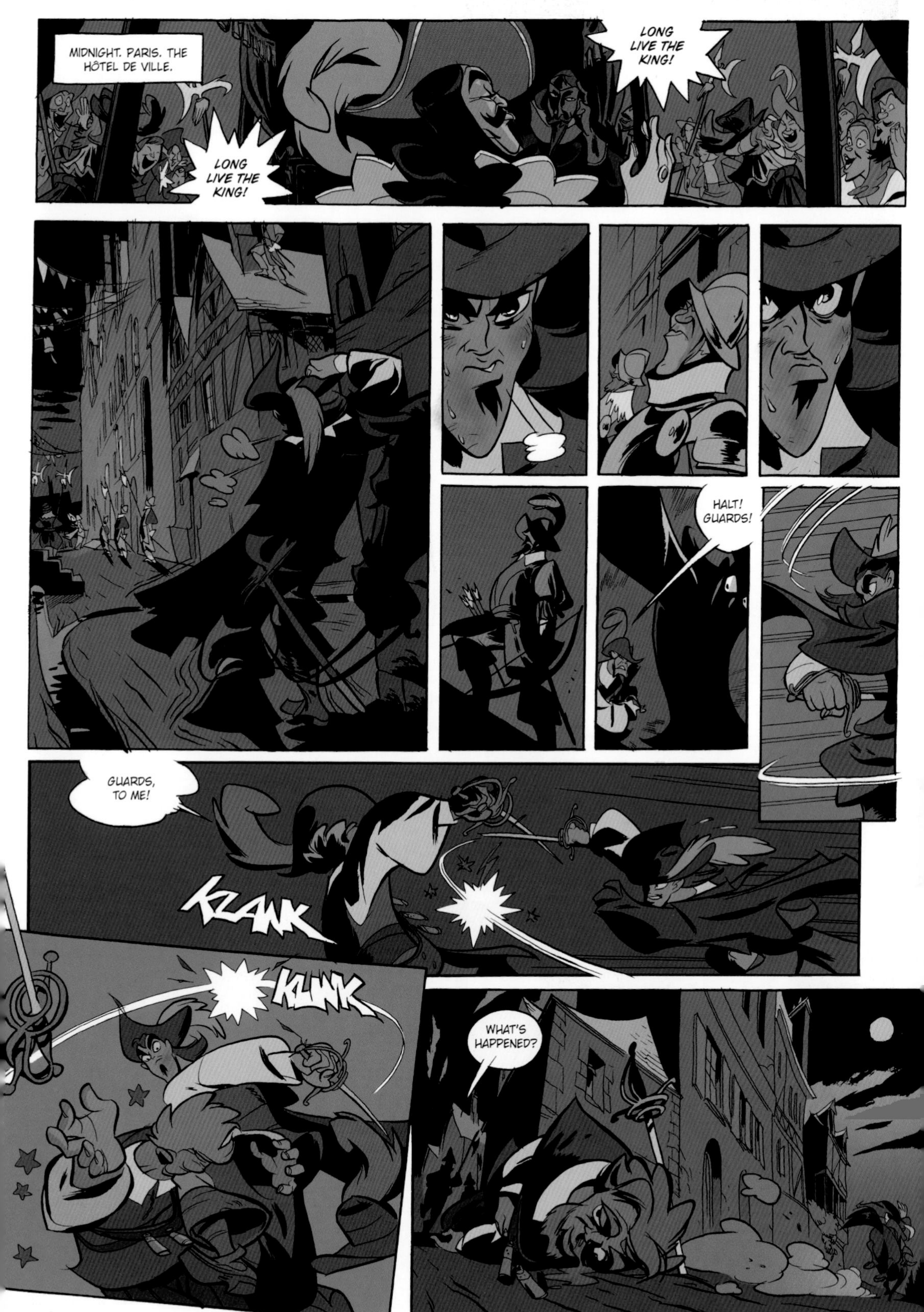
MIDNIGHT. PARIS. THE HÔTEL DE VILLE.
LONG LIVE THE KING!
LONG LIVE THE KING!
HALT! GUARDS!
GUARDS, TO ME!
KLANK
KLUNK
WHAT'S HAPPENED?

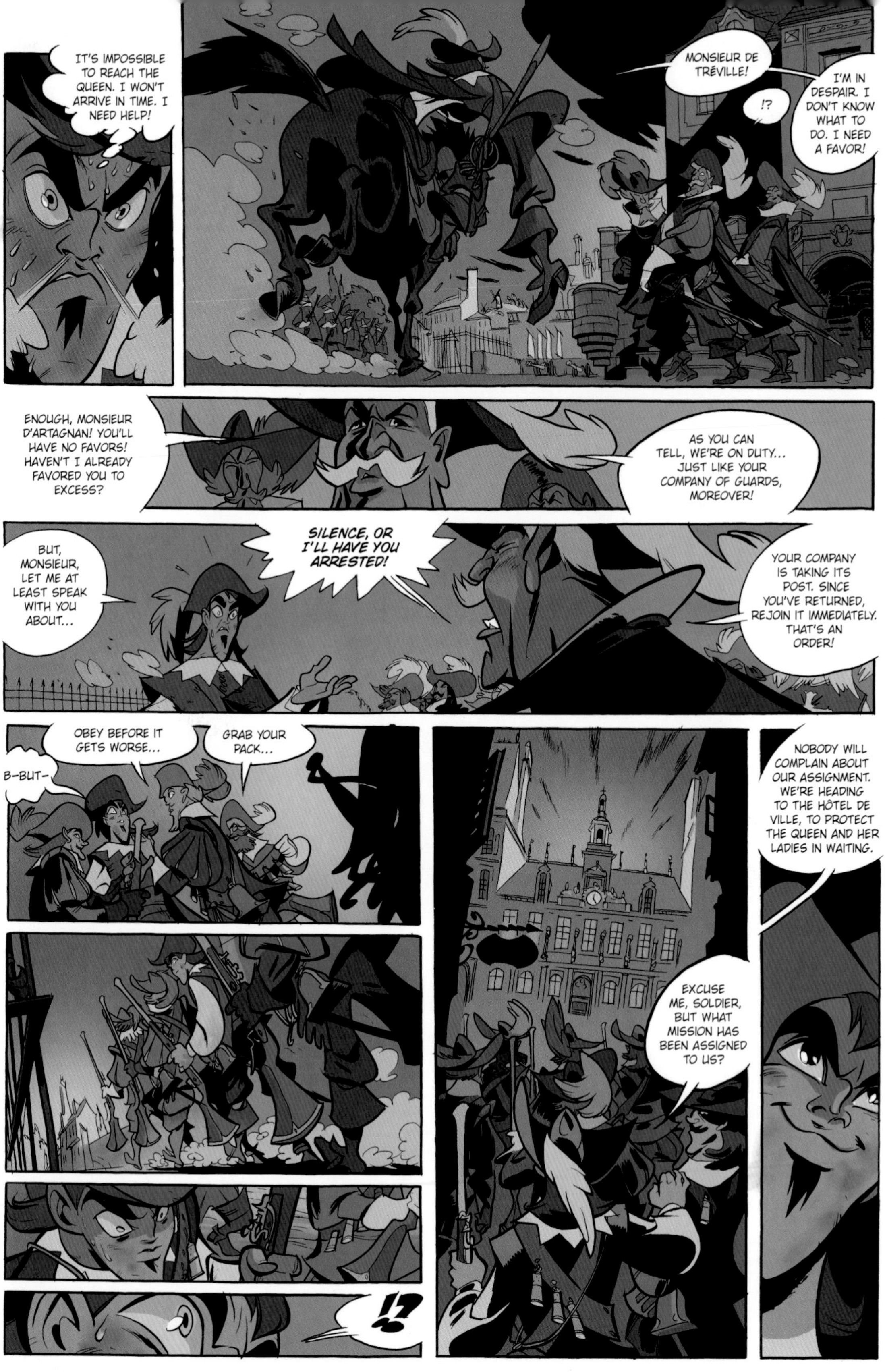

IT'S IMPOSSIBLE TO REACH THE QUEEN. I WON'T ARRIVE IN TIME. I NEED HELP!
MONSIEUR DE TRÉVILLE!
!?
I'M IN DESPAIR. I DON'T KNOW WHAT TO DO. I NEED A FAVOR!
ENOUGH, MONSIEUR D'ARTAGNAN! YOU'LL HAVE NO FAVORS! HAVEN'T I ALREADY FAVORED YOU TO EXCESS?
AS YOU CAN TELL, WE'RE ON DUTY... JUST LIKE YOUR COMPANY OF GUARDS, MOREOVER!
BUT, MONSIEUR, LET ME AT LEAST SPEAK WITH YOU ABOUT...
SILENCE, OR I'LL HAVE YOU ARRESTED!
YOUR COMPANY IS TAKING ITS POST. SINCE YOU'VE RETURNED, REJOIN IT IMMEDIATELY. THAT'S AN ORDER!
B-BUT-
OBEY BEFORE IT GETS WORSE...
GRAB YOUR PACK...
!?
EXCUSE ME, SOLDIER, BUT WHAT MISSION HAS BEEN ASSIGNED TO US?
NOBODY WILL COMPLAIN ABOUT OUR ASSIGNMENT. WE'RE HEADING TO THE HÔTEL DE VILLE, TO PROTECT THE QUEEN AND HER LADIES IN WAITING.

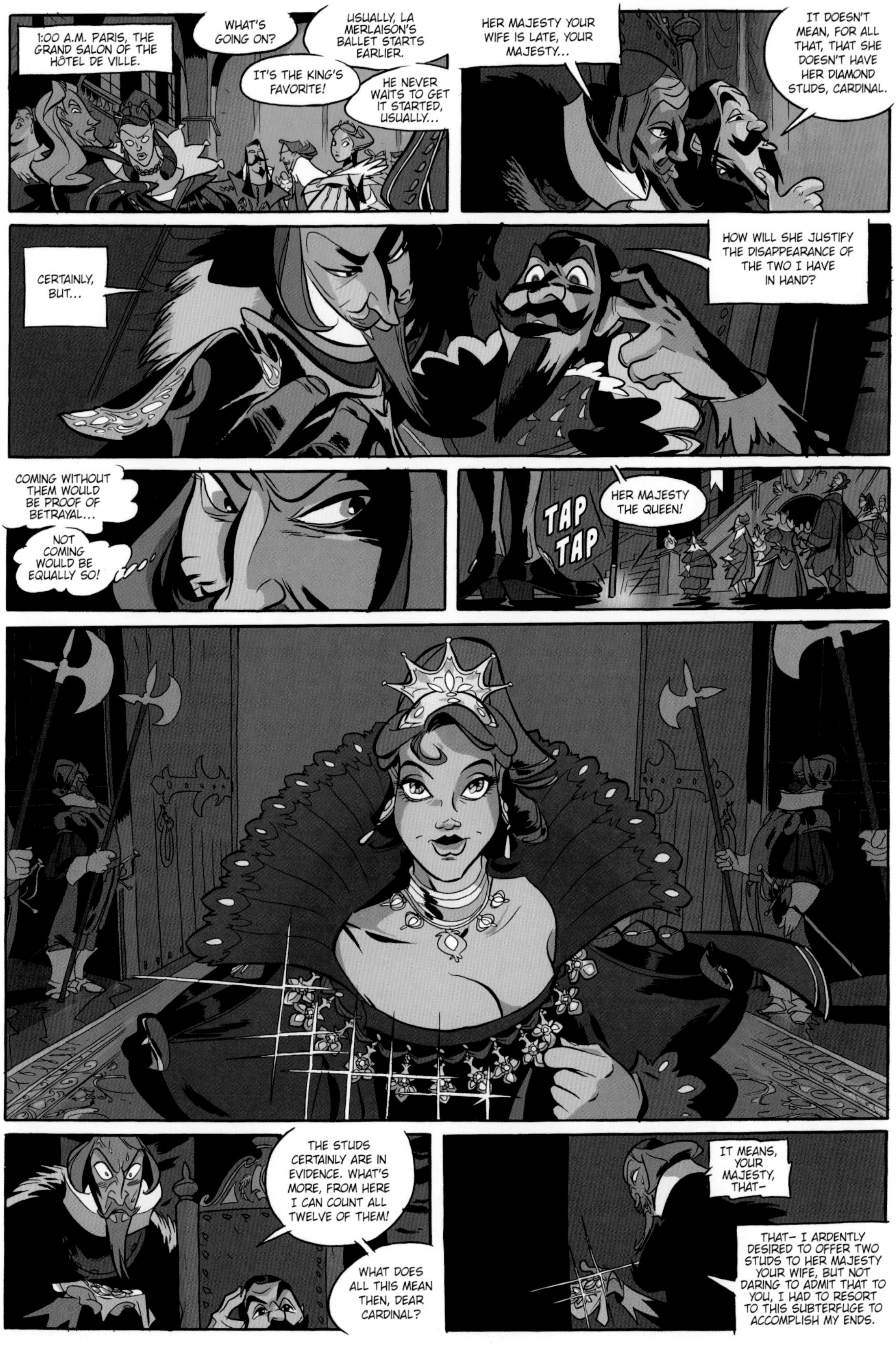
1:00 A.M. PARIS, THE GRAND SALON OF THE HÔTEL DE VILLE.
WHAT'S GOING ON?
USUALLY, LA MERLAISON'S BALLET STARTS EARLIER.
IT'S THE KING'S FAVORITE!
HE NEVER WAITS TO GET IT STARTED, USUALLY...
HER MAJESTY YOUR WIFE IS LATE, YOUR MAJESTY...
IT DOESN'T MEAN, FOR ALL THAT, THAT SHE DOESN'T HAVE HER DIAMOND STUDS, CARDINAL.
CERTAINLY, BUT...
HOW WILL SHE JUSTIFY THE DISAPPEARANCE OF THE TWO I HAVE IN HAND?
COMING WITHOUT THEM WOULD BE PROOF OF BETRAYAL...
NOT COMING WOULD BE EQUALLY SO!
TAP TAP
HER MAJESTY THE QUEEN!
THE STUDS CERTAINLY ARE IN EVIDENCE. WHAT'S MORE, FROM HERE I CAN COUNT ALL TWELVE OF THEM!
WHAT DOES ALL THIS MEAN THEN, DEAR CARDINAL?
IT MEANS, YOUR MAJESTY, THAT–
THAT– I ARDENTLY DESIRED TO OFFER TWO STUDS TO HER MAJESTY YOUR WIFE, BUT NOT DARING TO ADMIT THAT TO YOU, I HAD TO RESORT TO THIS SUBTERFUGE TO ACCOMPLISH MY ENDS.

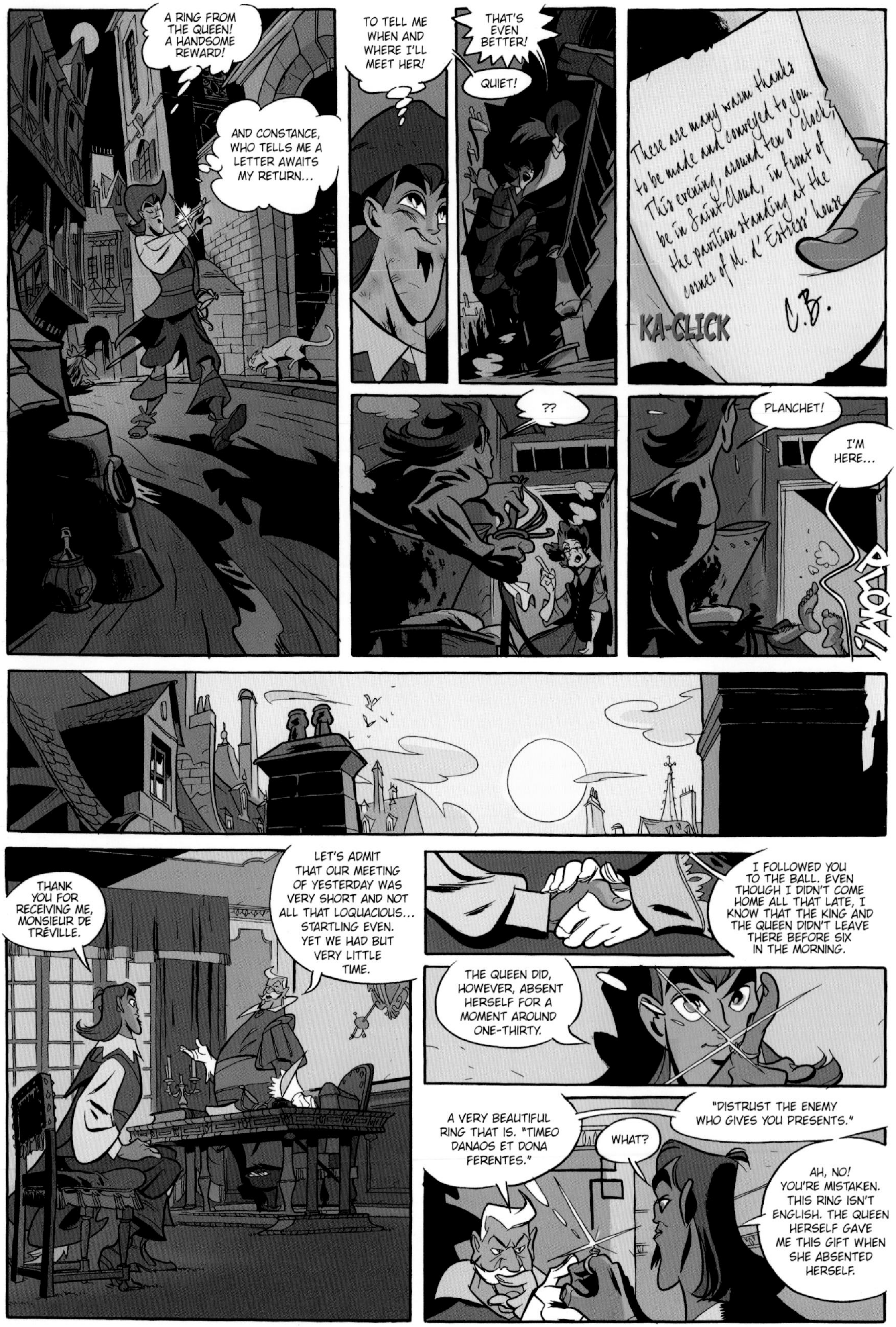
A RING FROM THE QUEEN! A HANDSOME REWARD!
AND CONSTANCE, WHO TELLS ME A LETTER AWAITS MY RETURN...
TO TELL ME WHEN AND WHERE I'LL MEET HER!
THAT'S EVEN BETTER!
QUIET!
There are many warm thanks to be made and conveyed to you. This evening, around ten o' clock, be in Saint-Cloud, in front of the pavilion standing at the corner of M. d' Estrées' house.
C.B.
KA-CLICK
??
PLANCHET!
I'M HERE...
BLOW!
THANK YOU FOR RECEIVING ME, MONSIEUR DE TRÉVILLE.
LET'S ADMIT THAT OUR MEETING OF YESTERDAY WAS VERY SHORT AND NOT ALL THAT LOQUACIOUS... STARTLING EVEN. YET WE HAD BUT VERY LITTLE TIME.
I FOLLOWED YOU TO THE BALL. EVEN THOUGH I DIDN'T COME HOME ALL THAT LATE, I KNOW THAT THE KING AND THE QUEEN DIDN'T LEAVE THERE BEFORE SIX IN THE MORNING.
THE QUEEN DID, HOWEVER, ABSENT HERSELF FOR A MOMENT AROUND ONE-THIRTY.
A VERY BEAUTIFUL RING THAT IS. "TIMEO DANAOS ET DONA FERENTES."
WHAT?
"DISTRUST THE ENEMY WHO GIVES YOU PRESENTS."
AH, NO! YOU'RE MISTAKEN. THIS RING ISN'T ENGLISH. THE QUEEN HERSELF GAVE ME THIS GIFT WHEN SHE ABSENTED HERSELF.

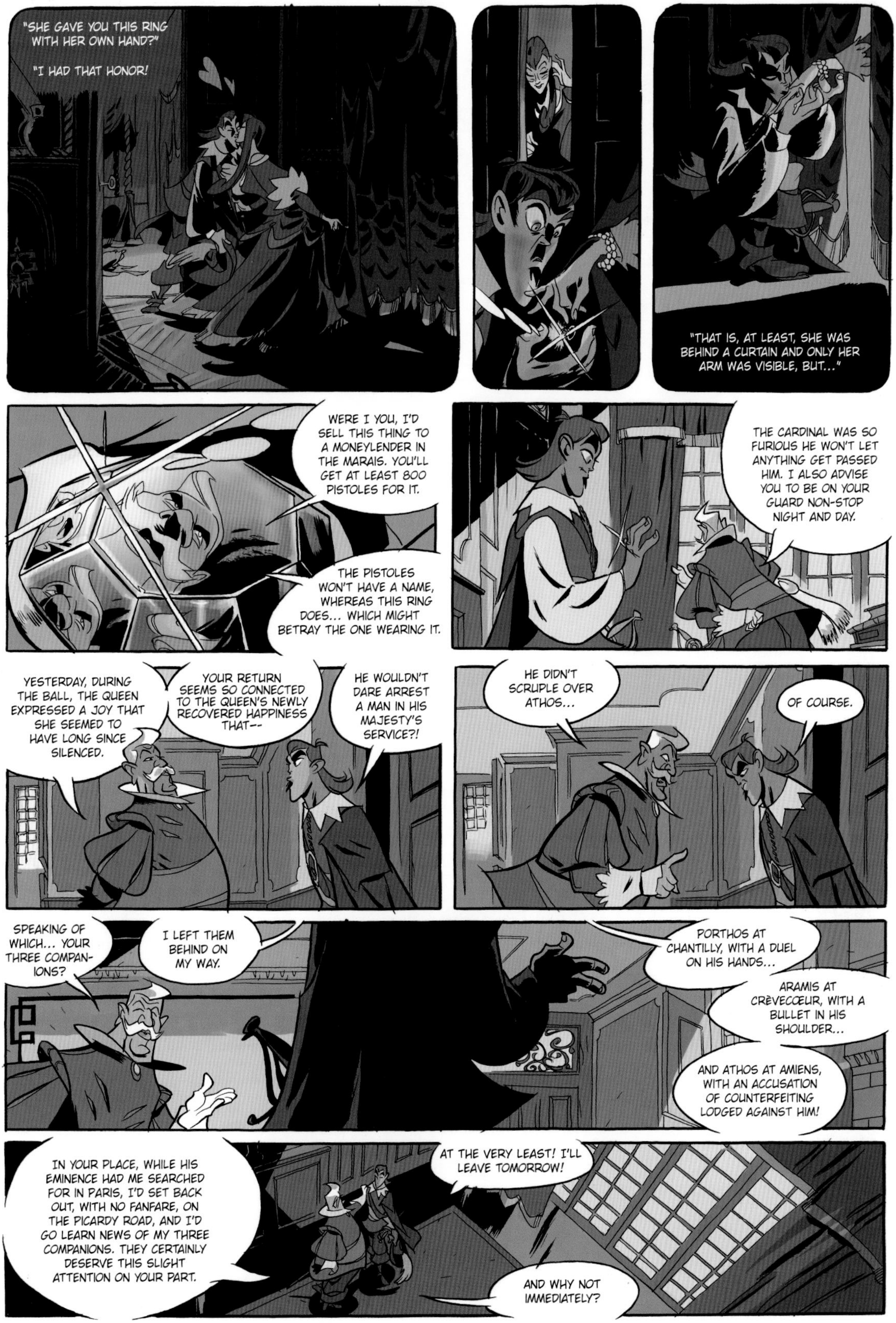
"SHE GAVE YOU THIS RING WITH HER OWN HAND?"
"I HAD THAT HONOR!
"THAT IS, AT LEAST, SHE WAS BEHIND A CURTAIN AND ONLY HER ARM WAS VISIBLE, BUT..."
WERE I YOU, I'D SELL THIS THING TO A MONEYLENDER IN THE MARAIS. YOU'LL GET AT LEAST 800 PISTOLES FOR IT.
THE PISTOLES WON'T HAVE A NAME, WHEREAS THIS RING DOES... WHICH MIGHT BETRAY THE ONE WEARING IT.
THE CARDINAL WAS SO FURIOUS HE WON'T LET ANYTHING GET PASSED HIM. I ALSO ADVISE YOU TO BE ON YOUR GUARD NON-STOP NIGHT AND DAY.
YESTERDAY, DURING THE BALL, THE QUEEN EXPRESSED A JOY THAT SHE SEEMED TO HAVE LONG SINCE SILENCED.
YOUR RETURN SEEMS SO CONNECTED TO THE QUEEN'S NEWLY RECOVERED HAPPINESS THAT--
HE WOULDN'T DARE ARREST A MAN IN HIS MAJESTY'S SERVICE?!
HE DIDN'T SCRUPLE OVER ATHOS...
OF COURSE.
SPEAKING OF WHICH... YOUR THREE COMPANIONS?
I LEFT THEM BEHIND ON MY WAY.
PORTHOS AT CHANTILLY, WITH A DUEL ON HIS HANDS...
ARAMIS AT CRÈVECŒUR, WITH A BULLET IN HIS SHOULDER...
AND ATHOS AT AMIENS, WITH AN ACCUSATION OF COUNTERFEITING LODGED AGAINST HIM!
IN YOUR PLACE, WHILE HIS EMINENCE HAD ME SEARCHED FOR IN PARIS, I'D SET BACK OUT, WITH NO FANFARE, ON THE PICARDY ROAD, AND I'D GO LEARN NEWS OF MY THREE COMPANIONS. THEY CERTAINLY DESERVE THIS SLIGHT ATTENTION ON YOUR PART.
AT THE VERY LEAST! I'LL LEAVE TOMORROW!
AND WHY NOT IMMEDIATELY?

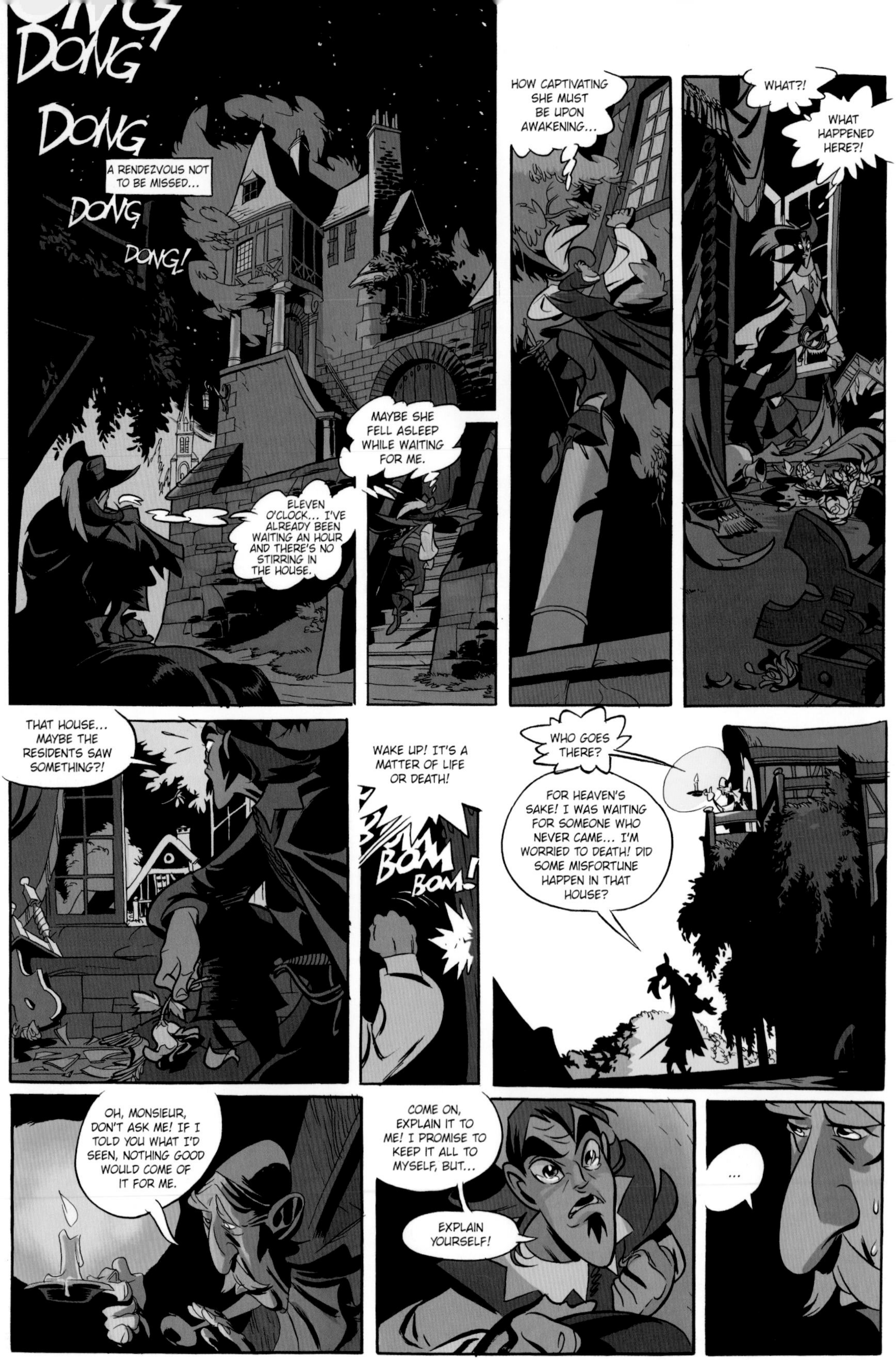
DONG
DONG
A RENDEZVOUS NOT TO BE MISSED...
DONG
DONG!
ELEVEN O'CLOCK... I'VE ALREADY BEEN WAITING AN HOUR AND THERE'S NO STIRRING IN THE HOUSE.
MAYBE SHE FELL ASLEEP WHILE WAITING FOR ME.
HOW CAPTIVATING SHE MUST BE UPON AWAKENING...
WHAT?!
WHAT HAPPENED HERE?!
THAT HOUSE... MAYBE THE RESIDENTS SAW SOMETHING?!
WAKE UP! IT'S A MATTER OF LIFE OR DEATH!
BOM
BOM!
WHO GOES THERE?
FOR HEAVEN'S SAKE! I WAS WAITING FOR SOMEONE WHO NEVER CAME... I'M WORRIED TO DEATH! DID SOME MISFORTUNE HAPPEN IN THAT HOUSE?
OH, MONSIEUR, DON'T ASK ME! IF I TOLD YOU WHAT I'D SEEN, NOTHING GOOD WOULD COME OF IT FOR ME.
COME ON, EXPLAIN IT TO ME! I PROMISE TO KEEP IT ALL TO MYSELF, BUT...
EXPLAIN YOURSELF!
...

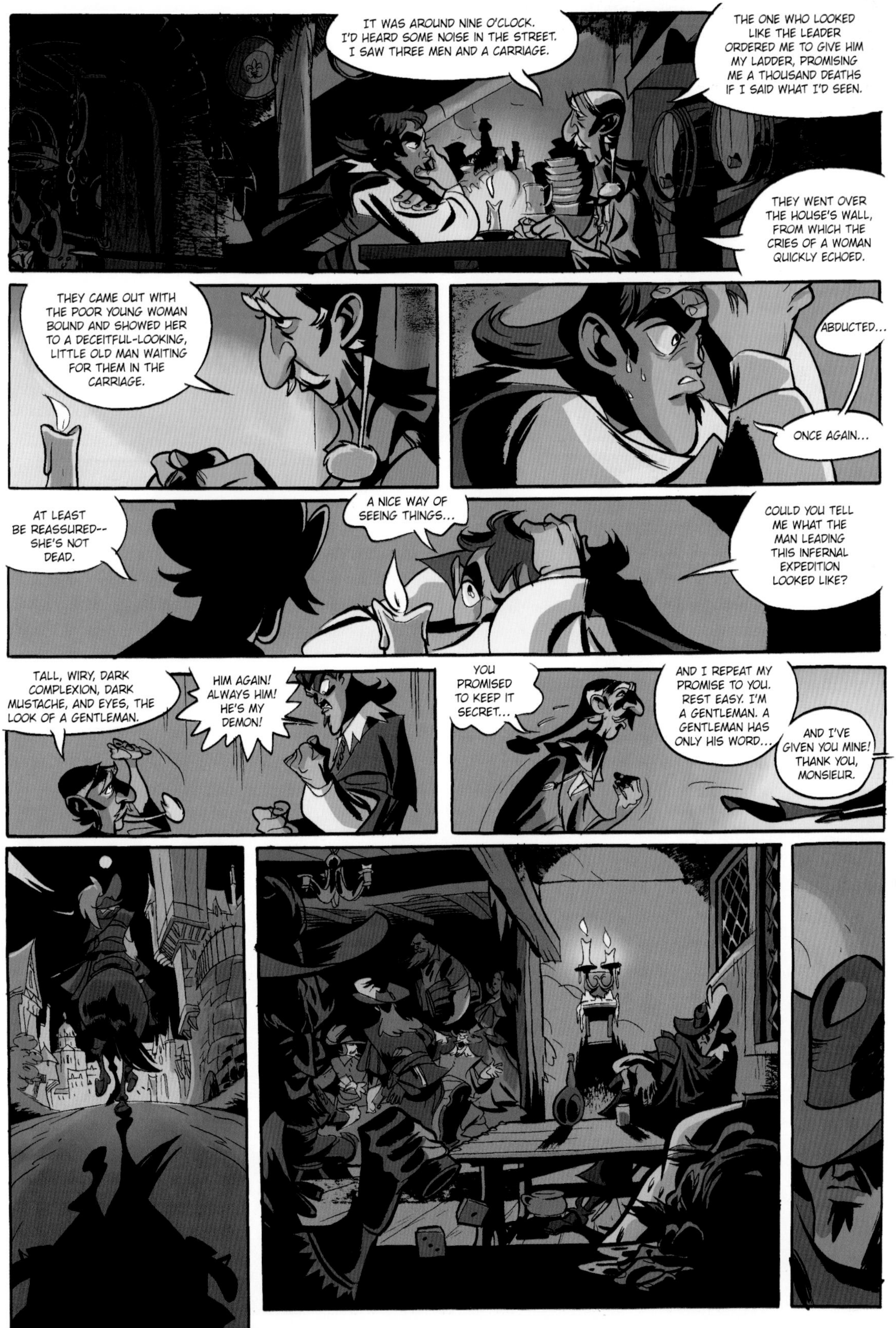
IT WAS AROUND NINE O'CLOCK. I'D HEARD SOME NOISE IN THE STREET. I SAW THREE MEN AND A CARRIAGE.
THE ONE WHO LOOKED LIKE THE LEADER ORDERED ME TO GIVE HIM MY LADDER, PROMISING ME A THOUSAND DEATHS IF I SAID WHAT I'D SEEN.
THEY WENT OVER THE HOUSE'S WALL, FROM WHICH THE CRIES OF A WOMAN QUICKLY ECHOED.
THEY CAME OUT WITH THE POOR YOUNG WOMAN BOUND AND SHOWED HER TO A DECEITFUL-LOOKING, LITTLE OLD MAN WAITING FOR THEM IN THE CARRIAGE.
ABDUCTED...
ONCE AGAIN...
AT LEAST BE REASSURED-- SHE'S NOT DEAD.
A NICE WAY OF SEEING THINGS...
COULD YOU TELL ME WHAT THE MAN LEADING THIS INFERNAL EXPEDITION LOOKED LIKE?
TALL, WIRY, DARK COMPLEXION, DARK MUSTACHE, AND EYES, THE LOOK OF A GENTLEMAN.
HIM AGAIN! ALWAYS HIM! HE'S MY DEMON!
YOU PROMISED TO KEEP IT SECRET...
AND I REPEAT MY PROMISE TO YOU. REST EASY. I'M A GENTLEMAN. A GENTLEMAN HAS ONLY HIS WORD...
AND I'VE GIVEN YOU MINE! THANK YOU, MONSIEUR.

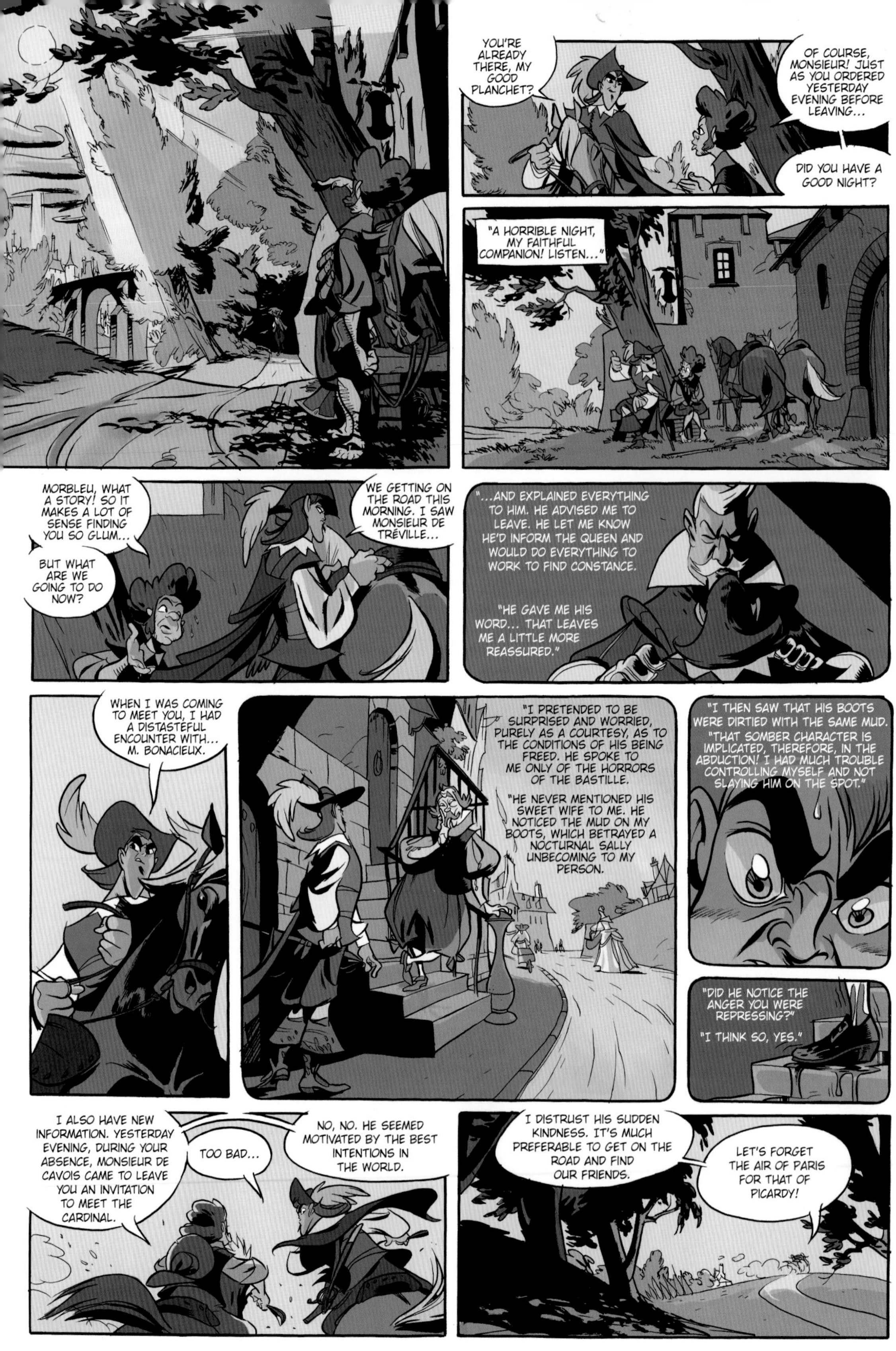
YOU'RE ALREADY THERE, MY GOOD PLANCHET?
OF COURSE, MONSIEUR! JUST AS YOU ORDERED YESTERDAY EVENING BEFORE LEAVING...
DID YOU HAVE A GOOD NIGHT?
"A HORRIBLE NIGHT, MY FAITHFUL COMPANION! LISTEN..."
MORBLEU, WHAT A STORY! SO IT MAKES A LOT OF SENSE FINDING YOU SO GLUM...
BUT WHAT ARE WE GOING TO DO NOW?
WE GETTING ON THE ROAD THIS MORNING. I SAW MONSIEUR DE TRÉVILLE...
"...AND EXPLAINED EVERYTHING TO HIM. HE ADVISED ME TO LEAVE. HE LET ME KNOW HE'D INFORM THE QUEEN AND WOULD DO EVERYTHING TO WORK TO FIND CONSTANCE.
"HE GAVE ME HIS WORD... THAT LEAVES ME A LITTLE MORE REASSURED."
WHEN I WAS COMING TO MEET YOU, I HAD A DISTASTEFUL ENCOUNTER WITH... M. BONACIEUX.
"I PRETENDED TO BE SURPRISED AND WORRIED, PURELY AS A COURTESY, AS TO THE CONDITIONS OF HIS BEING FREED. HE SPOKE TO ME ONLY OF THE HORRORS OF THE BASTILLE.
"HE NEVER MENTIONED HIS SWEET WIFE TO ME. HE NOTICED THE MUD ON MY BOOTS, WHICH BETRAYED A NOCTURNAL SALLY UNBECOMING TO MY PERSON.
"I THEN SAW THAT HIS BOOTS WERE DIRTIED WITH THE SAME MUD.
"THAT SOMBER CHARACTER IS IMPLICATED, THEREFORE, IN THE ABDUCTION! I HAD MUCH TROUBLE CONTROLLING MYSELF AND NOT SLAYING HIM ON THE SPOT."
"DID HE NOTICE THE ANGER YOU WERE REPRESSING?"
"I THINK SO, YES."
I ALSO HAVE NEW INFORMATION. YESTERDAY EVENING, DURING YOUR ABSENCE, MONSIEUR DE CAVOIS CAME TO LEAVE YOU AN INVITATION TO MEET THE CARDINAL.
TOO BAD...
NO, NO. HE SEEMED MOTIVATED BY THE BEST INTENTIONS IN THE WORLD.
I DISTRUST HIS SUDDEN KINDNESS. IT'S MUCH PREFERABLE TO GET ON THE ROAD AND FIND OUR FRIENDS.
LET'S FORGET THE AIR OF PARIS FOR THAT OF PICARDY!

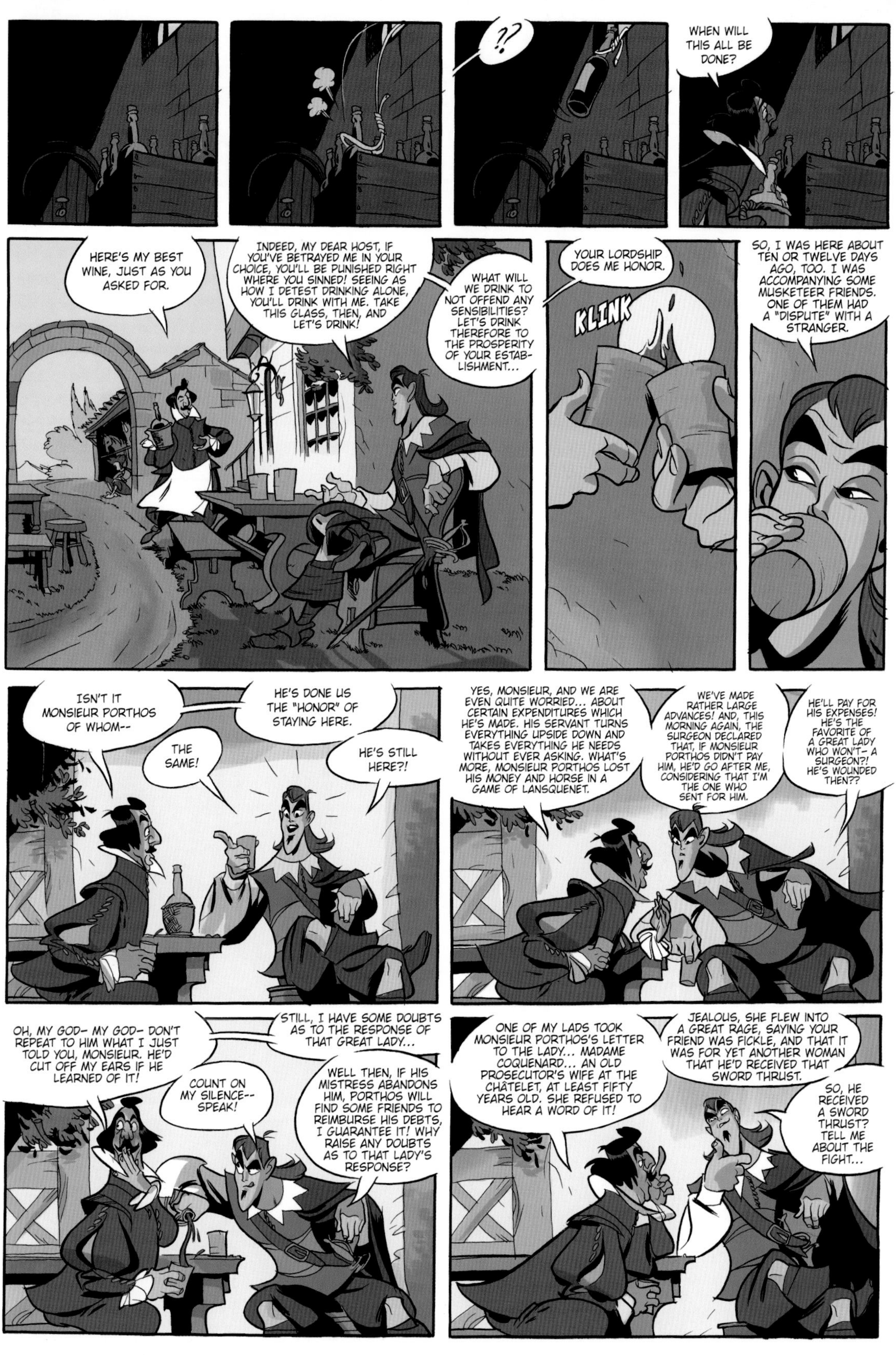
??
WHEN WILL THIS ALL BE DONE?
HERE'S MY BEST WINE, JUST AS YOU ASKED FOR.
INDEED, MY DEAR HOST, IF YOU'VE BETRAYED ME IN YOUR CHOICE, YOU'LL BE PUNISHED RIGHT WHERE YOU SINNED! SEEING AS HOW I DETEST DRINKING ALONE, YOU'LL DRINK WITH ME. TAKE THIS GLASS, THEN, AND LET'S DRINK!
WHAT WILL WE DRINK TO NOT OFFEND ANY SENSIBILITIES? LET'S DRINK THEREFORE TO THE PROSPERITY OF YOUR ESTABLISHMENT...
YOUR LORDSHIP DOES ME HONOR.
KLINK
SO, I WAS HERE ABOUT TEN OR TWELVE DAYS AGO, TOO. I WAS ACCOMPANYING SOME MUSKETEER FRIENDS. ONE OF THEM HAD A "DISPUTE" WITH A STRANGER.
ISN'T IT MONSIEUR PORTHOS OF WHOM--
HE'S DONE US THE "HONOR" OF STAYING HERE.
THE SAME!
HE'S STILL HERE?!
YES, MONSIEUR, AND WE ARE EVEN QUITE WORRIED... ABOUT CERTAIN EXPENDITURES WHICH HE'S MADE. HIS SERVANT TURNS EVERYTHING UPSIDE DOWN AND TAKES EVERYTHING HE NEEDS WITHOUT EVER ASKING. WHAT'S MORE, MONSIEUR PORTHOS LOST HIS MONEY AND HORSE IN A GAME OF LANSQUENET.
WE'VE MADE RATHER LARGE ADVANCES! AND, THIS MORNING AGAIN, THE SURGEON DECLARED THAT, IF MONSIEUR PORTHOS DIDN'T PAY HIM, HE'D GO AFTER ME, CONSIDERING THAT I'M THE ONE WHO SENT FOR HIM.
HE'LL PAY FOR HIS EXPENSES! HE'S THE FAVORITE OF A GREAT LADY WHO WON'T- A SURGEON?! HE'S WOUNDED THEN??
OH, MY GOD- MY GOD- DON'T REPEAT TO HIM WHAT I JUST TOLD YOU, MONSIEUR. HE'D CUT OFF MY EARS IF HE LEARNED OF IT!
STILL, I HAVE SOME DOUBTS AS TO THE RESPONSE OF THAT GREAT LADY...
COUNT ON MY SILENCE-- SPEAK!
WELL THEN, IF HIS MISTRESS ABANDONS HIM, PORTHOS WILL FIND SOME FRIENDS TO REIMBURSE HIS DEBTS, I GUARANTEE IT! WHY RAISE ANY DOUBTS AS TO THAT LADY'S RESPONSE?
ONE OF MY LADS TOOK MONSIEUR PORTHOS'S LETTER TO THE LADY... MADAME COQUENARD... AN OLD PROSECUTOR'S WIFE AT THE CHÂTELET, AT LEAST FIFTY YEARS OLD. SHE REFUSED TO HEAR A WORD OF IT!
JEALOUS, SHE FLEW INTO A GREAT RAGE, SAYING YOUR FRIEND WAS FICKLE, AND THAT IT WAS FOR YET ANOTHER WOMAN THAT HE'D RECEIVED THAT SWORD THRUST.
SO, HE RECEIVED A SWORD THRUST? TELL ME ABOUT THE FIGHT...

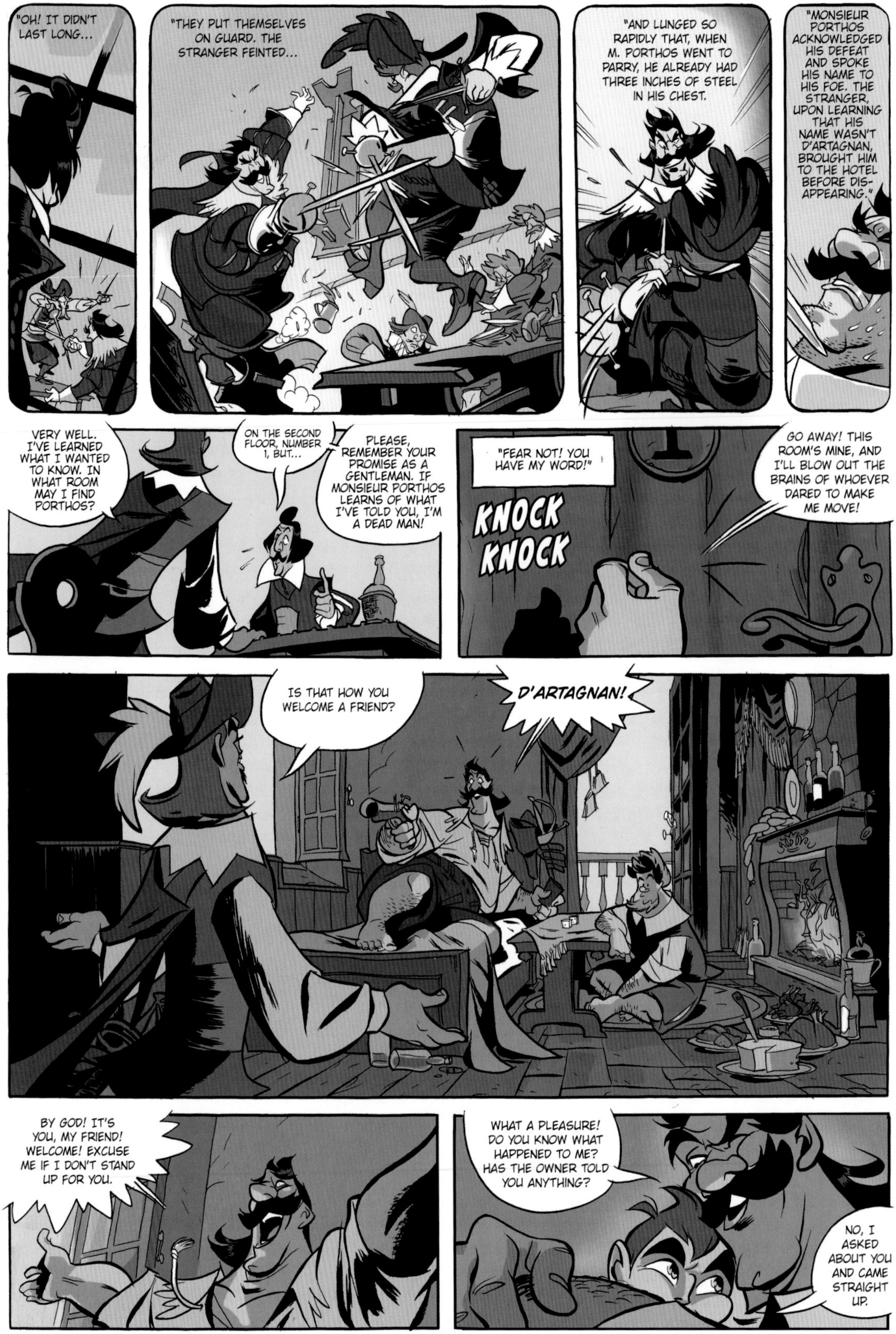
"OH! IT DIDN'T LAST LONG…
"THEY PUT THEMSELVES ON GUARD. THE STRANGER FEINTED…
"AND LUNGED SO RAPIDLY THAT, WHEN M. PORTHOS WENT TO PARRY, HE ALREADY HAD THREE INCHES OF STEEL IN HIS CHEST.
"MONSIEUR PORTHOS ACKNOWLEDGED HIS DEFEAT AND SPOKE HIS NAME TO HIS FOE. THE STRANGER, UPON LEARNING THAT HIS NAME WASN'T D'ARTAGNAN, BROUGHT HIM TO THE HOTEL BEFORE DIS-APPEARING."
VERY WELL. I'VE LEARNED WHAT I WANTED TO KNOW. IN WHAT ROOM MAY I FIND PORTHOS?
ON THE SECOND FLOOR, NUMBER 1, BUT…
PLEASE, REMEMBER YOUR PROMISE AS A GENTLEMAN. IF MONSIEUR PORTHOS LEARNS OF WHAT I'VE TOLD YOU, I'M A DEAD MAN!
"FEAR NOT! YOU HAVE MY WORD!"
KNOCK KNOCK
GO AWAY! THIS ROOM'S MINE, AND I'LL BLOW OUT THE BRAINS OF WHOEVER DARED TO MAKE ME MOVE!
IS THAT HOW YOU WELCOME A FRIEND?
D'ARTAGNAN!
BY GOD! IT'S YOU, MY FRIEND! WELCOME! EXCUSE ME IF I DON'T STAND UP FOR YOU.
WHAT A PLEASURE! DO YOU KNOW WHAT HAPPENED TO ME? HAS THE OWNER TOLD YOU ANYTHING?
NO, I ASKED ABOUT YOU AND CAME STRAIGHT UP.

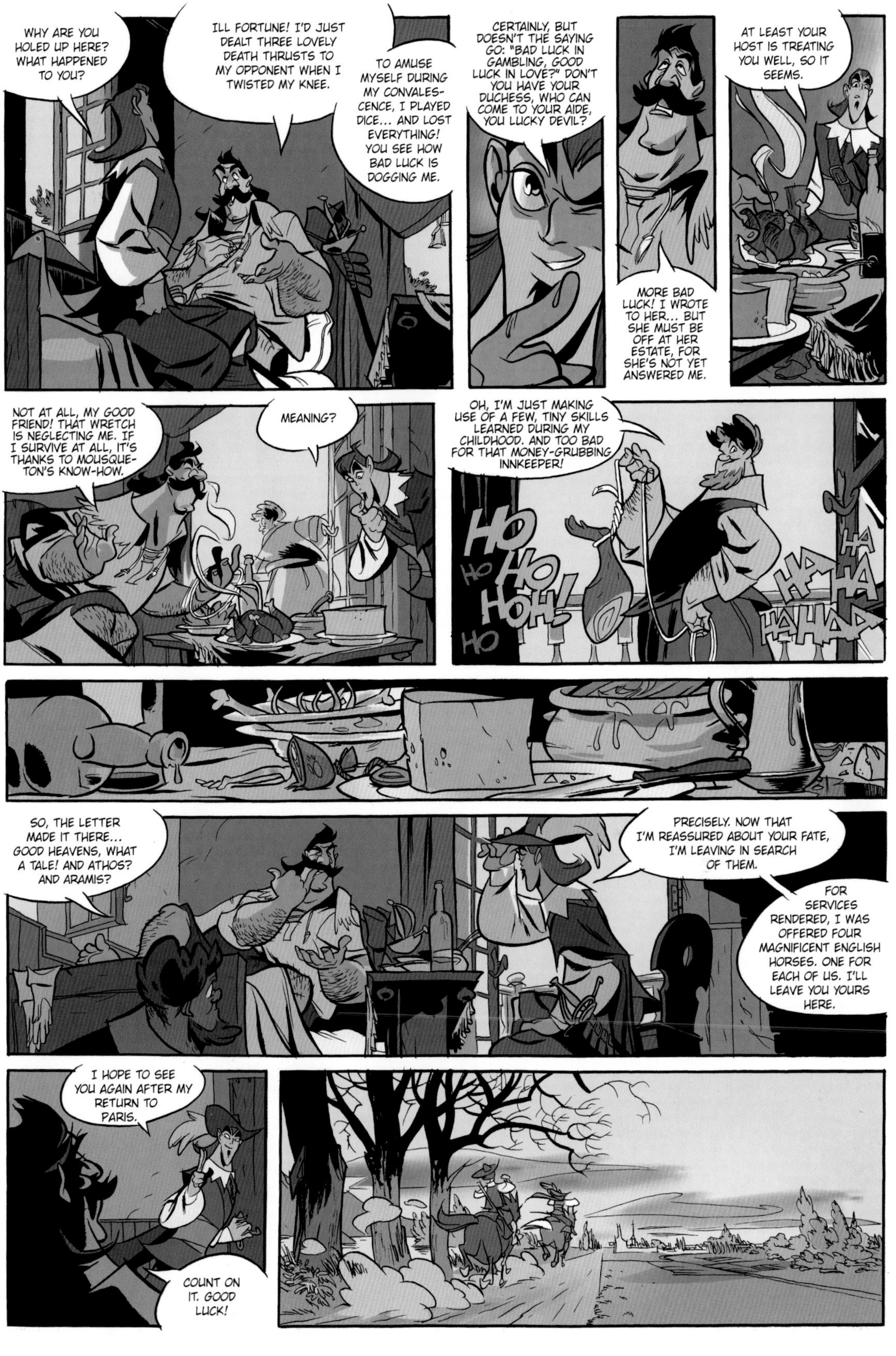
WHY ARE YOU HOLED UP HERE? WHAT HAPPENED TO YOU?
ILL FORTUNE! I'D JUST DEALT THREE LOVELY DEATH THRUSTS TO MY OPPONENT WHEN I TWISTED MY KNEE.
TO AMUSE MYSELF DURING MY CONVALESCENCE, I PLAYED DICE... AND LOST EVERYTHING! YOU SEE HOW BAD LUCK IS DOGGING ME.
CERTAINLY, BUT DOESN'T THE SAYING GO: "BAD LUCK IN GAMBLING, GOOD LUCK IN LOVE?" DON'T YOU HAVE YOUR DUCHESS, WHO CAN COME TO YOUR AIDE, YOU LUCKY DEVIL?
MORE BAD LUCK! I WROTE TO HER... BUT SHE MUST BE OFF AT HER ESTATE, FOR SHE'S NOT YET ANSWERED ME.
AT LEAST YOUR HOST IS TREATING YOU WELL, SO IT SEEMS.
NOT AT ALL, MY GOOD FRIEND! THAT WRETCH IS NEGLECTING ME. IF I SURVIVE AT ALL, IT'S THANKS TO MOUSQUETON'S KNOW-HOW.
MEANING?
OH, I'M JUST MAKING USE OF A FEW, TINY SKILLS LEARNED DURING MY CHILDHOOD. AND TOO BAD FOR THAT MONEY-GRUBBING INNKEEPER!
HO HO HO HOH! HO
HA HA HA HA HAP
SO, THE LETTER MADE IT THERE... GOOD HEAVENS, WHAT A TALE! AND ATHOS? AND ARAMIS?
PRECISELY. NOW THAT I'M REASSURED ABOUT YOUR FATE, I'M LEAVING IN SEARCH OF THEM.
FOR SERVICES RENDERED, I WAS OFFERED FOUR MAGNIFICENT ENGLISH HORSES. ONE FOR EACH OF US. I'LL LEAVE YOU YOURS HERE.
I HOPE TO SEE YOU AGAIN AFTER MY RETURN TO PARIS.
COUNT ON IT. GOOD LUCK!

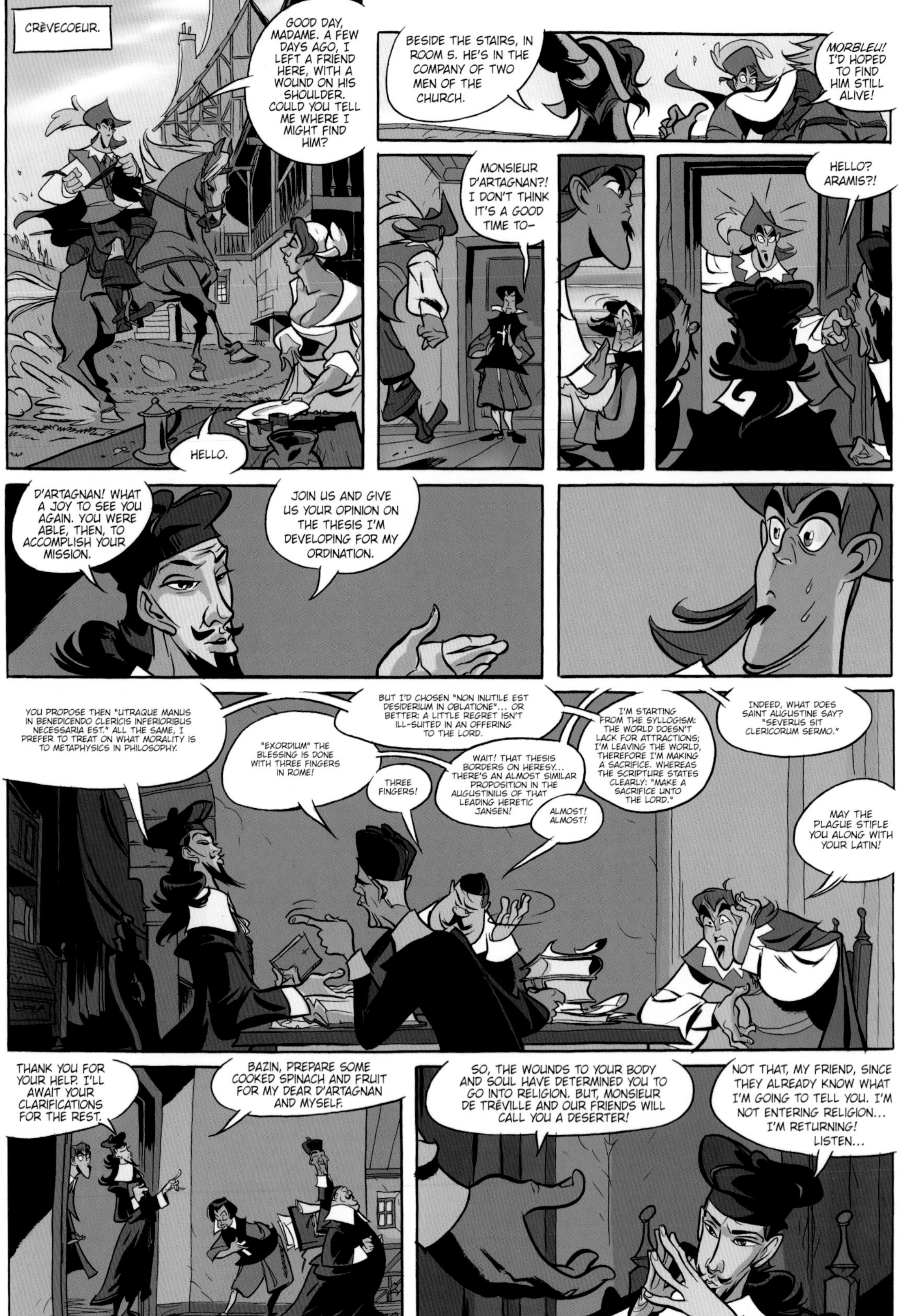

CRÈVECOEUR.
GOOD DAY, MADAME. A FEW DAYS AGO, I LEFT A FRIEND HERE, WITH A WOUND ON HIS SHOULDER. COULD YOU TELL ME WHERE I MIGHT FIND HIM?
HELLO.
BESIDE THE STAIRS, IN ROOM 5. HE'S IN THE COMPANY OF TWO MEN OF THE CHURCH.
MORBLEU! I'D HOPED TO FIND HIM STILL ALIVE!
MONSIEUR D'ARTAGNAN?! I DON'T THINK IT'S A GOOD TIME TO–
HELLO? ARAMIS?!
D'ARTAGNAN! WHAT A JOY TO SEE YOU AGAIN. YOU WERE ABLE, THEN, TO ACCOMPLISH YOUR MISSION.
JOIN US AND GIVE US YOUR OPINION ON THE THESIS I'M DEVELOPING FOR MY ORDINATION.
YOU PROPOSE THEN "UTRAQUE MANUS IN BENEDICENDO CLERICIS INFERIORIBUS NECESSARIA EST." ALL THE SAME, I PREFER TO TREAT ON WHAT MORALITY IS TO METAPHYSICS IN PHILOSOPHY.
"EXORDIUM" THE BLESSING IS DONE WITH THREE FINGERS IN ROME!
THREE FINGERS!
BUT I'D CHOSEN "NON INUTILE EST DESIDERIUM IN OBLATIONE"... OR BETTER: A LITTLE REGRET ISN'T ILL-SUITED IN AN OFFERING TO THE LORD.
WAIT! THAT THESIS BORDERS ON HERESY... THERE'S AN ALMOST SIMILAR PROPOSITION IN THE AUGUSTINIUS OF THAT LEADING HERETIC JANSEN!
ALMOST! ALMOST!
I'M STARTING FROM THE SYLLOGISM: THE WORLD DOESN'T LACK FOR ATTRACTIONS; I'M LEAVING THE WORLD, THEREFORE I'M MAKING A SACRIFICE. WHEREAS THE SCRIPTURE STATES CLEARLY: "MAKE A SACRIFICE UNTO THE LORD."
INDEED, WHAT DOES SAINT AUGUSTINE SAY? "SEVERUS SIT CLERICORUM SERMO."
MAY THE PLAGUE STIFLE YOU ALONG WITH YOUR LATIN!
THANK YOU FOR YOUR HELP. I'LL AWAIT YOUR CLARIFICATIONS FOR THE REST.
BAZIN, PREPARE SOME COOKED SPINACH AND FRUIT FOR MY DEAR D'ARTAGNAN AND MYSELF.
SO, THE WOUNDS TO YOUR BODY AND SOUL HAVE DETERMINED YOU TO GO INTO RELIGION. BUT, MONSIEUR DE TRÉVILLE AND OUR FRIENDS WILL CALL YOU A DESERTER!
NOT THAT, MY FRIEND, SINCE THEY ALREADY KNOW WHAT I'M GOING TO TELL YOU. I'M NOT ENTERING RELIGION... I'M RETURNING! LISTEN...

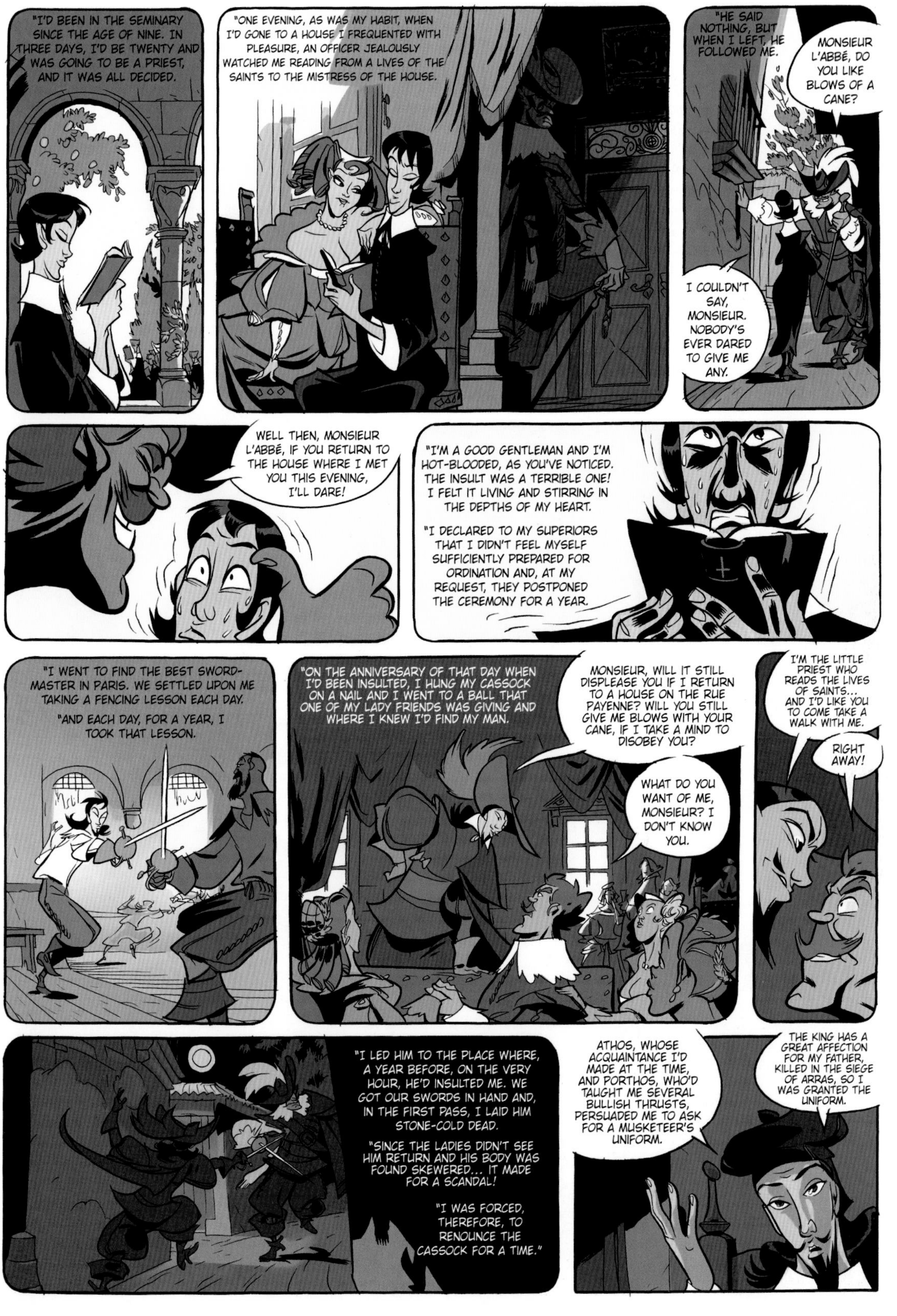
"I'D BEEN IN THE SEMINARY SINCE THE AGE OF NINE. IN THREE DAYS, I'D BE TWENTY AND WAS GOING TO BE A PRIEST, AND IT WAS ALL DECIDED.
"ONE EVENING, AS WAS MY HABIT, WHEN I'D GONE TO A HOUSE I FREQUENTED WITH PLEASURE, AN OFFICER JEALOUSLY WATCHED ME READING FROM A LIVES OF THE SAINTS TO THE MISTRESS OF THE HOUSE.
"HE SAID NOTHING, BUT WHEN I LEFT, HE FOLLOWED ME.
MONSIEUR L'ABBÉ, DO YOU LIKE BLOWS OF A CANE?
I COULDN'T SAY, MONSIEUR. NOBODY'S EVER DARED TO GIVE ME ANY.
WELL THEN, MONSIEUR L'ABBÉ, IF YOU RETURN TO THE HOUSE WHERE I MET YOU THIS EVENING, I'LL DARE!
"I'M A GOOD GENTLEMAN AND I'M HOT-BLOODED, AS YOU'VE NOTICED. THE INSULT WAS A TERRIBLE ONE! I FELT IT LIVING AND STIRRING IN THE DEPTHS OF MY HEART.
"I DECLARED TO MY SUPERIORS THAT I DIDN'T FEEL MYSELF SUFFICIENTLY PREPARED FOR ORDINATION AND, AT MY REQUEST, THEY POSTPONED THE CEREMONY FOR A YEAR.
"I WENT TO FIND THE BEST SWORD-MASTER IN PARIS. WE SETTLED UPON ME TAKING A FENCING LESSON EACH DAY.
"AND EACH DAY, FOR A YEAR, I TOOK THAT LESSON.
"ON THE ANNIVERSARY OF THAT DAY WHEN I'D BEEN INSULTED, I HUNG MY CASSOCK ON A NAIL AND I WENT TO A BALL THAT ONE OF MY LADY FRIENDS WAS GIVING AND WHERE I KNEW I'D FIND MY MAN.
MONSIEUR, WILL IT STILL DISPLEASE YOU IF I RETURN TO A HOUSE ON THE RUE PAYENNE? WILL YOU STILL GIVE ME BLOWS WITH YOUR CANE, IF I TAKE A MIND TO DISOBEY YOU?
WHAT DO YOU WANT OF ME, MONSIEUR? I DON'T KNOW YOU.
I'M THE LITTLE PRIEST WHO READS THE LIVES OF SAINTS... AND I'D LIKE YOU TO COME TAKE A WALK WITH ME.
RIGHT AWAY!
"I LED HIM TO THE PLACE WHERE, A YEAR BEFORE, ON THE VERY HOUR, HE'D INSULTED ME. WE GOT OUR SWORDS IN HAND AND, IN THE FIRST PASS, I LAID HIM STONE-COLD DEAD.
"SINCE THE LADIES DIDN'T SEE HIM RETURN AND HIS BODY WAS FOUND SKEWERED... IT MADE FOR A SCANDAL!
"I WAS FORCED, THEREFORE, TO RENOUNCE THE CASSOCK FOR A TIME."
ATHOS, WHOSE ACQUAINTANCE I'D MADE AT THE TIME, AND PORTHOS, WHO'D TAUGHT ME SEVERAL BULLISH THRUSTS, PERSUADED ME TO ASK FOR A MUSKETEER'S UNIFORM.
THE KING HAS A GREAT AFFECTION FOR MY FATHER, KILLED IN THE SIEGE OF ARRAS, SO I WAS GRANTED THE UNIFORM.

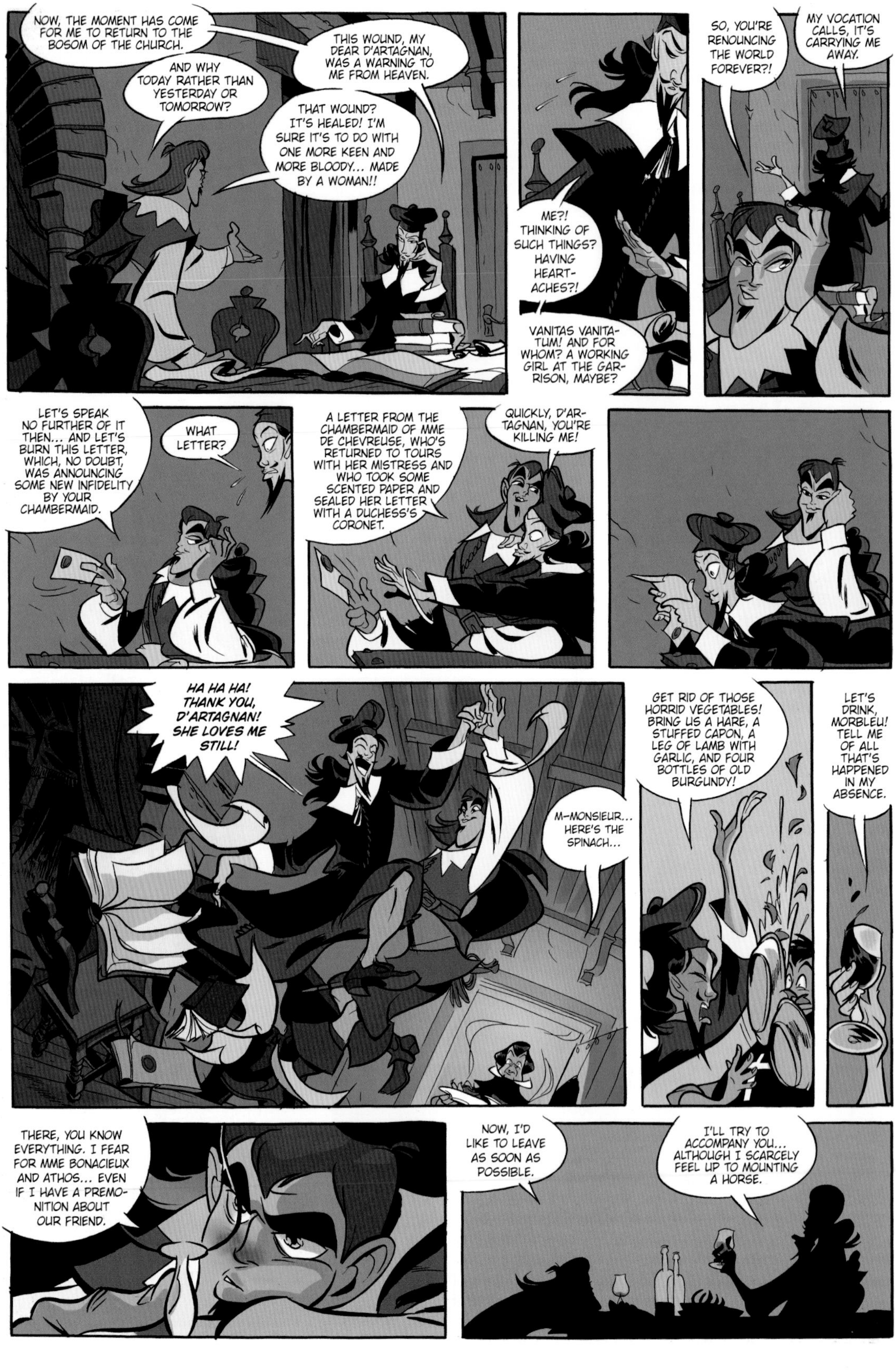
NOW, THE MOMENT HAS COME FOR ME TO RETURN TO THE BOSOM OF THE CHURCH.
AND WHY TODAY RATHER THAN YESTERDAY OR TOMORROW?
THIS WOUND, MY DEAR D'ARTAGNAN, WAS A WARNING TO ME FROM HEAVEN.
THAT WOUND? IT'S HEALED! I'M SURE IT'S TO DO WITH ONE MORE KEEN AND MORE BLOODY... MADE BY A WOMAN!!
ME?! THINKING OF SUCH THINGS? HAVING HEART-ACHES?!
VANITAS VANITATUM! AND FOR WHOM? A WORKING GIRL AT THE GARRISON, MAYBE?
SO, YOU'RE RENOUNCING THE WORLD FOREVER?!
MY VOCATION CALLS, IT'S CARRYING ME AWAY.
LET'S SPEAK NO FURTHER OF IT THEN... AND LET'S BURN THIS LETTER, WHICH, NO DOUBT, WAS ANNOUNCING SOME NEW INFIDELITY BY YOUR CHAMBERMAID.
WHAT LETTER?
A LETTER FROM THE CHAMBERMAID OF MME DE CHEVREUSE, WHO'S RETURNED TO TOURS WITH HER MISTRESS AND WHO TOOK SOME SCENTED PAPER AND SEALED HER LETTER WITH A DUCHESS'S CORONET.
QUICKLY, D'ARTAGNAN, YOU'RE KILLING ME!
HA HA HA! THANK YOU, D'ARTAGNAN! SHE LOVES ME STILL!
M-MONSIEUR... HERE'S THE SPINACH...
GET RID OF THOSE HORRID VEGETABLES! BRING US A HARE, A STUFFED CAPON, A LEG OF LAMB WITH GARLIC, AND FOUR BOTTLES OF OLD BURGUNDY!
LET'S DRINK, MORBLEU! TELL ME OF ALL THAT'S HAPPENED IN MY ABSENCE.
THERE, YOU KNOW EVERYTHING. I FEAR FOR MME BONACIEUX AND ATHOS... EVEN IF I HAVE A PREMONITION ABOUT OUR FRIEND.
NOW, I'D LIKE TO LEAVE AS SOON AS POSSIBLE.
I'LL TRY TO ACCOMPANY YOU... ALTHOUGH I SCARCELY FEEL UP TO MOUNTING A HORSE.

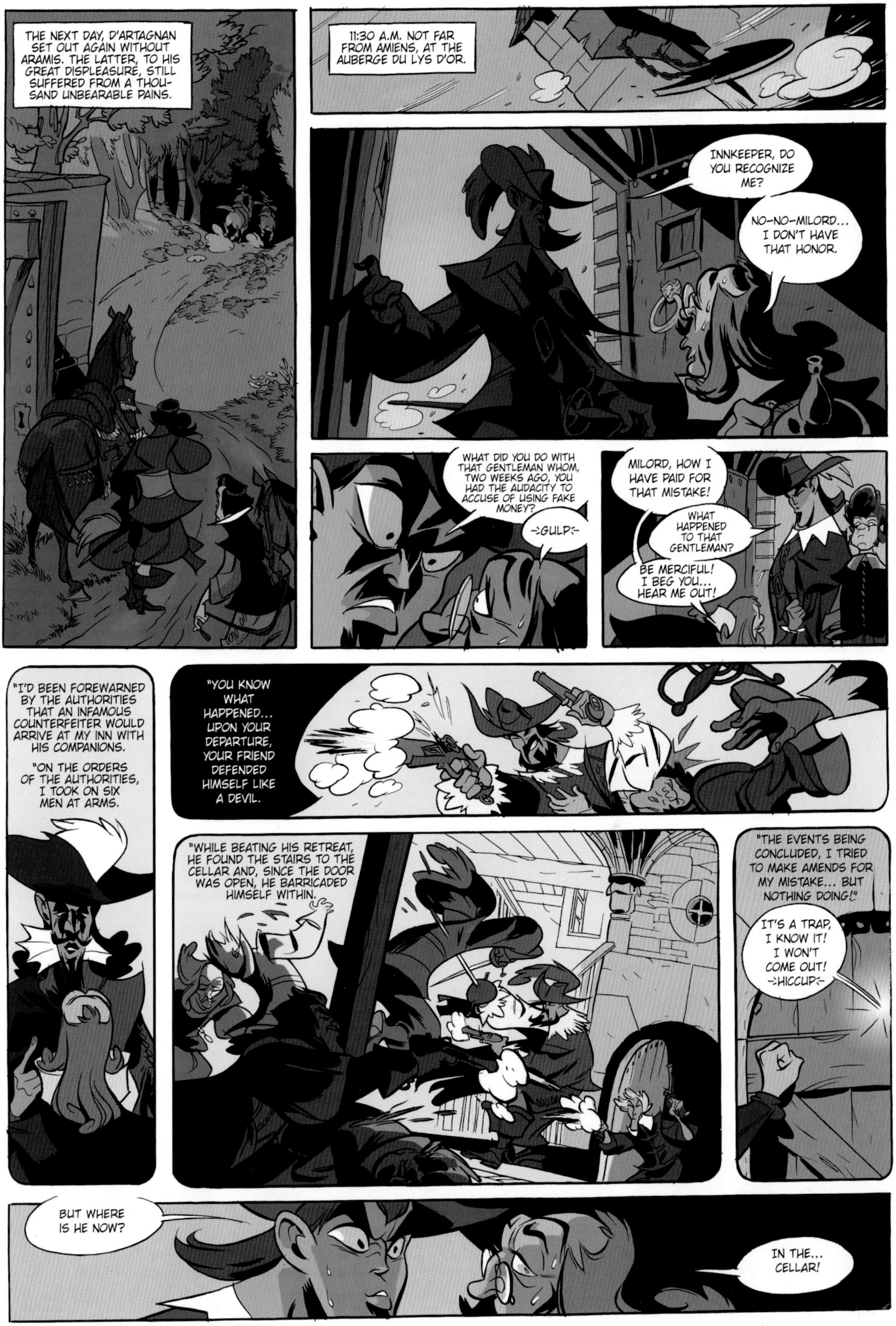

THE NEXT DAY, D'ARTAGNAN SET OUT AGAIN WITHOUT ARAMIS. THE LATTER, TO HIS GREAT DISPLEASURE, STILL SUFFERED FROM A THOUSAND UNBEARABLE PAINS.
11:30 A.M. NOT FAR FROM AMIENS, AT THE AUBERGE DU LYS D'OR.
INNKEEPER, DO YOU RECOGNIZE ME?
NO-NO-MILORD... I DON'T HAVE THAT HONOR.
WHAT DID YOU DO WITH THAT GENTLEMAN WHOM, TWO WEEKS AGO, YOU HAD THE AUDACITY TO ACCUSE OF USING FAKE MONEY?
->GULP<-
MILORD, HOW I HAVE PAID FOR THAT MISTAKE!
WHAT HAPPENED TO THAT GENTLEMAN?
BE MERCIFUL! I BEG YOU... HEAR ME OUT!
"I'D BEEN FOREWARNED BY THE AUTHORITIES THAT AN INFAMOUS COUNTERFEITER WOULD ARRIVE AT MY INN WITH HIS COMPANIONS.
"ON THE ORDERS OF THE AUTHORITIES, I TOOK ON SIX MEN AT ARMS.
"YOU KNOW WHAT HAPPENED... UPON YOUR DEPARTURE, YOUR FRIEND DEFENDED HIMSELF LIKE A DEVIL.
"WHILE BEATING HIS RETREAT, HE FOUND THE STAIRS TO THE CELLAR AND, SINCE THE DOOR WAS OPEN, HE BARRICADED HIMSELF WITHIN.
"THE EVENTS BEING CONCLUDED, I TRIED TO MAKE AMENDS FOR MY MISTAKE... BUT NOTHING DOING!"
IT'S A TRAP, I KNOW IT! I WON'T COME OUT!
->HICCUP<-
BUT WHERE IS HE NOW?
IN THE... CELLAR!

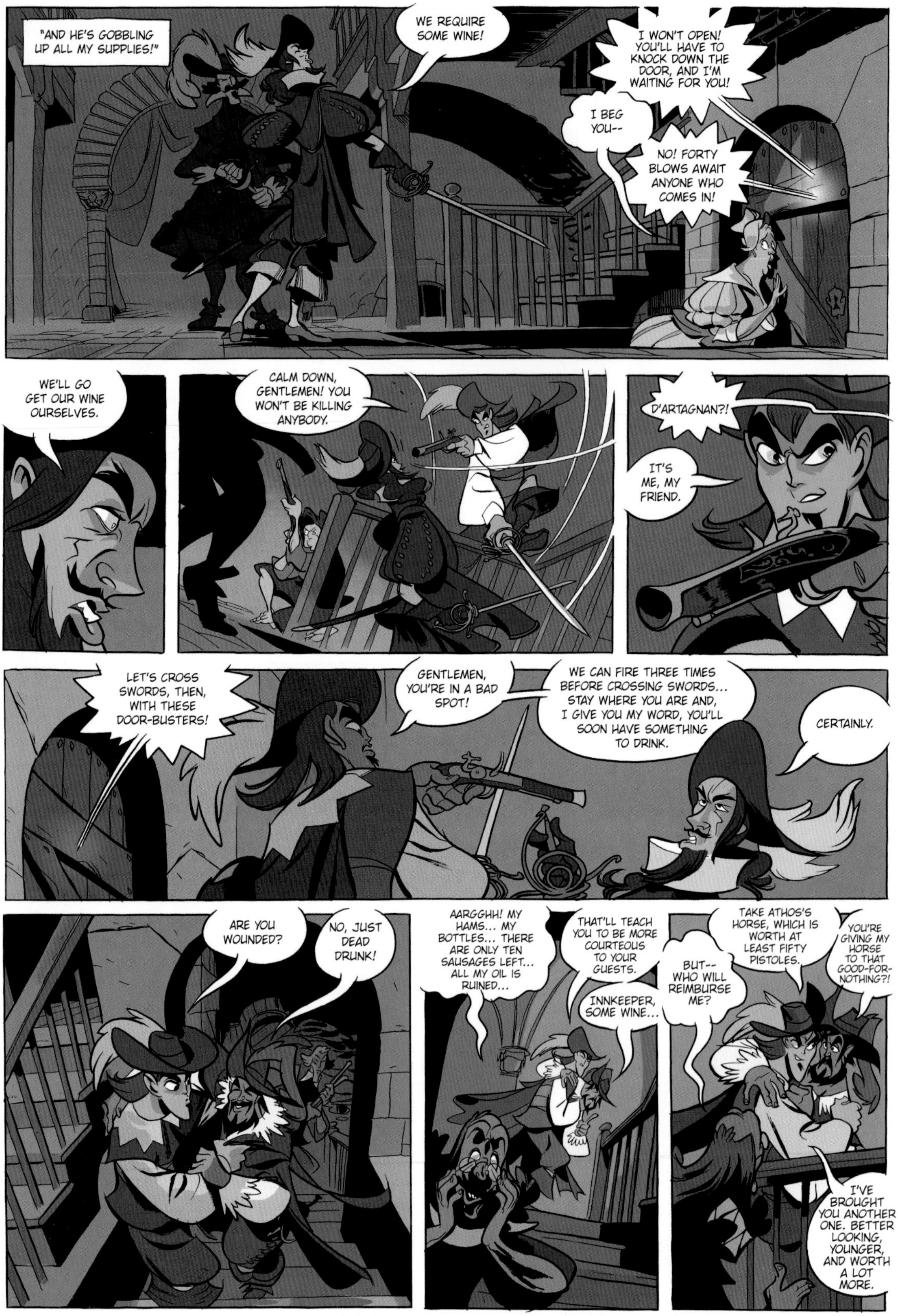
"AND HE'S GOBBLING UP ALL MY SUPPLIES!"
WE REQUIRE SOME WINE!
I WON'T OPEN! YOU'LL HAVE TO KNOCK DOWN THE DOOR, AND I'M WAITING FOR YOU!
I BEG YOU--
NO! FORTY BLOWS AWAIT ANYONE WHO COMES IN!
WE'LL GO GET OUR WINE OURSELVES.
CALM DOWN, GENTLEMEN! YOU WON'T BE KILLING ANYBODY.
D'ARTAGNAN?!
IT'S ME, MY FRIEND.
LET'S CROSS SWORDS, THEN, WITH THESE DOOR-BUSTERS!
GENTLEMEN, YOU'RE IN A BAD SPOT!
WE CAN FIRE THREE TIMES BEFORE CROSSING SWORDS... STAY WHERE YOU ARE AND, I GIVE YOU MY WORD, YOU'LL SOON HAVE SOMETHING TO DRINK.
CERTAINLY.
ARE YOU WOUNDED?
NO, JUST DEAD DRUNK!
AARGGHH! MY HAMS... MY BOTTLES... THERE ARE ONLY TEN SAUSAGES LEFT... ALL MY OIL IS RUINED...
THAT'LL TEACH YOU TO BE MORE COURTEOUS TO YOUR GUESTS.
INNKEEPER, SOME WINE...
BUT-- WHO WILL REIMBURSE ME?
TAKE ATHOS'S HORSE, WHICH IS WORTH AT LEAST FIFTY PISTOLES.
YOU'RE GIVING MY HORSE TO THAT GOOD-FOR-NOTHING?!
I'VE BROUGHT YOU ANOTHER ONE. BETTER LOOKING, YOUNGER, AND WORTH A LOT MORE.

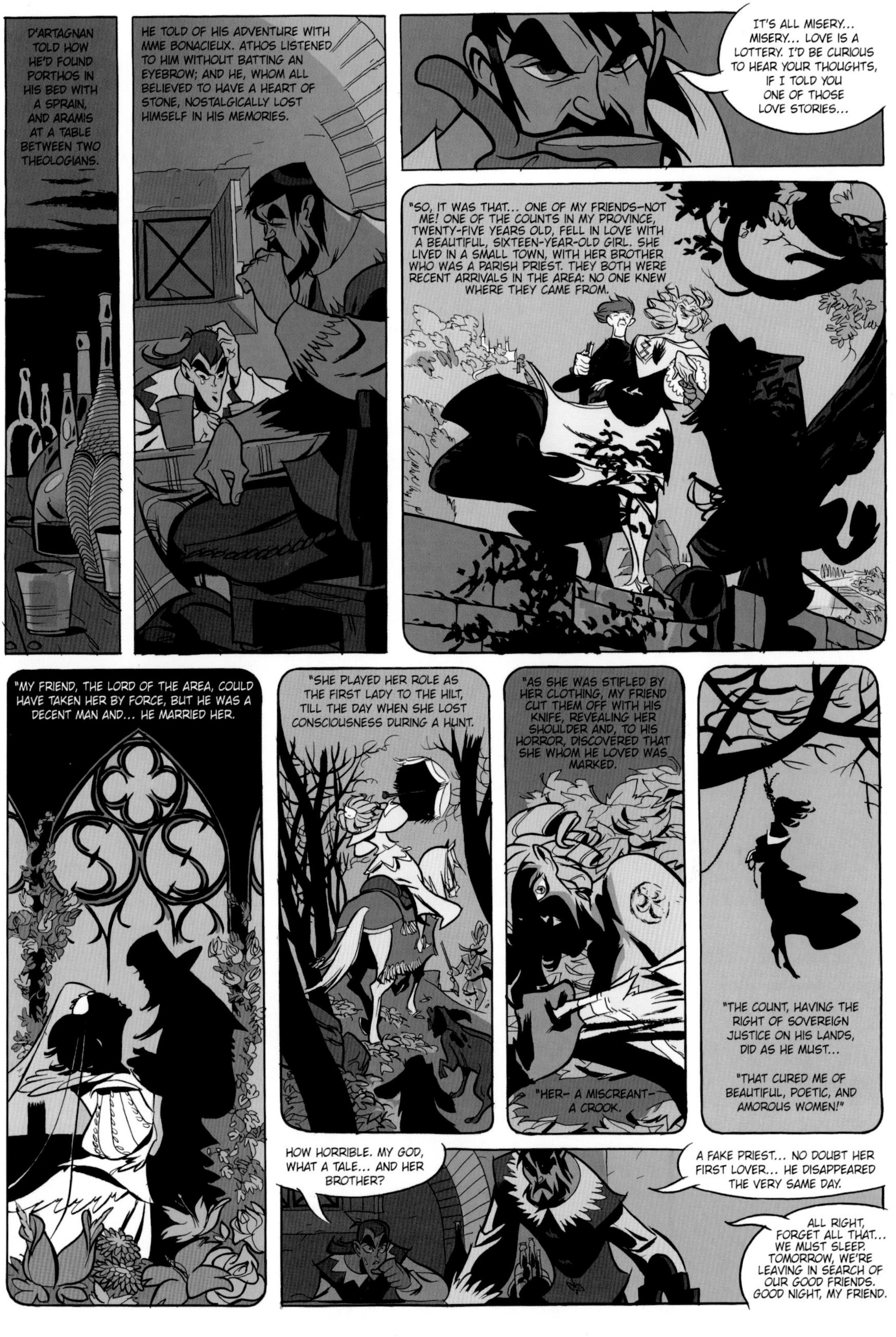
D'ARTAGNAN TOLD HOW HE'D FOUND PORTHOS IN HIS BED WITH A SPRAIN, AND ARAMIS AT A TABLE BETWEEN TWO THEOLOGIANS.
HE TOLD OF HIS ADVENTURE WITH MME BONACIEUX. ATHOS LISTENED TO HIM WITHOUT BATTING AN EYEBROW; AND HE, WHOM ALL BELIEVED TO HAVE A HEART OF STONE, NOSTALGICALLY LOST HIMSELF IN HIS MEMORIES.
IT'S ALL MISERY... MISERY... LOVE IS A LOTTERY. I'D BE CURIOUS TO HEAR YOUR THOUGHTS, IF I TOLD YOU ONE OF THOSE LOVE STORIES...
"SO, IT WAS THAT... ONE OF MY FRIENDS—NOT ME! ONE OF THE COUNTS IN MY PROVINCE, TWENTY-FIVE YEARS OLD, FELL IN LOVE WITH A BEAUTIFUL, SIXTEEN-YEAR-OLD GIRL. SHE LIVED IN A SMALL TOWN, WITH HER BROTHER WHO WAS A PARISH PRIEST. THEY BOTH WERE RECENT ARRIVALS IN THE AREA: NO ONE KNEW WHERE THEY CAME FROM.
"MY FRIEND, THE LORD OF THE AREA, COULD HAVE TAKEN HER BY FORCE, BUT HE WAS A DECENT MAN AND... HE MARRIED HER.
"SHE PLAYED HER ROLE AS THE FIRST LADY TO THE HILT, TILL THE DAY WHEN SHE LOST CONSCIOUSNESS DURING A HUNT.
"AS SHE WAS STIFLED BY HER CLOTHING, MY FRIEND CUT THEM OFF WITH HIS KNIFE, REVEALING HER SHOULDER AND, TO HIS HORROR, DISCOVERED THAT SHE WHOM HE LOVED WAS MARKED.
"HER– A MISCREANT– A CROOK.
"THE COUNT, HAVING THE RIGHT OF SOVEREIGN JUSTICE ON HIS LANDS, DID AS HE MUST...
"THAT CURED ME OF BEAUTIFUL, POETIC, AND AMOROUS WOMEN!"
HOW HORRIBLE. MY GOD, WHAT A TALE... AND HER BROTHER?
A FAKE PRIEST... NO DOUBT HER FIRST LOVER... HE DISAPPEARED THE VERY SAME DAY.
ALL RIGHT, FORGET ALL THAT... WE MUST SLEEP. TOMORROW, WE'RE LEAVING IN SEARCH OF OUR GOOD FRIENDS. GOOD NIGHT, MY FRIEND.

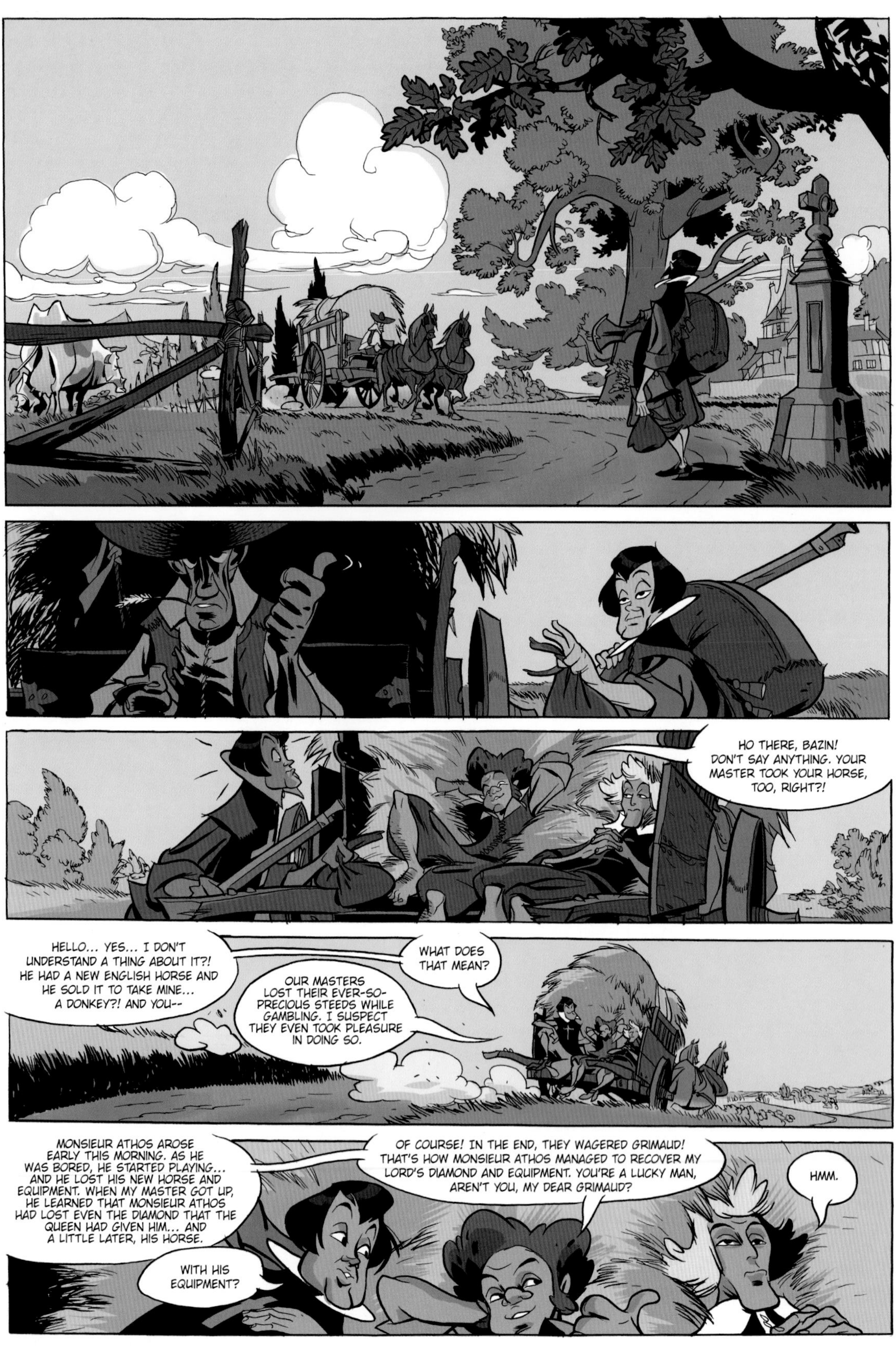
HO THERE, BAZIN! DON'T SAY ANYTHING. YOUR MASTER TOOK YOUR HORSE, TOO, RIGHT?!
HELLO... YES... I DON'T UNDERSTAND A THING ABOUT IT?! HE HAD A NEW ENGLISH HORSE AND HE SOLD IT TO TAKE MINE... A DONKEY?! AND YOU--
WHAT DOES THAT MEAN?
OUR MASTERS LOST THEIR EVER-SO-PRECIOUS STEEDS WHILE GAMBLING. I SUSPECT THEY EVEN TOOK PLEASURE IN DOING SO.
MONSIEUR ATHOS AROSE EARLY THIS MORNING. AS HE WAS BORED, HE STARTED PLAYING... AND HE LOST HIS NEW HORSE AND EQUIPMENT. WHEN MY MASTER GOT UP, HE LEARNED THAT MONSIEUR ATHOS HAD LOST EVEN THE DIAMOND THAT THE QUEEN HAD GIVEN HIM... AND A LITTLE LATER, HIS HORSE.
WITH HIS EQUIPMENT?
OF COURSE! IN THE END, THEY WAGERED GRIMAUD! THAT'S HOW MONSIEUR ATHOS MANAGED TO RECOVER MY LORD'S DIAMOND AND EQUIPMENT. YOU'RE A LUCKY MAN, AREN'T YOU, MY DEAR GRIMAUD?
HMM.

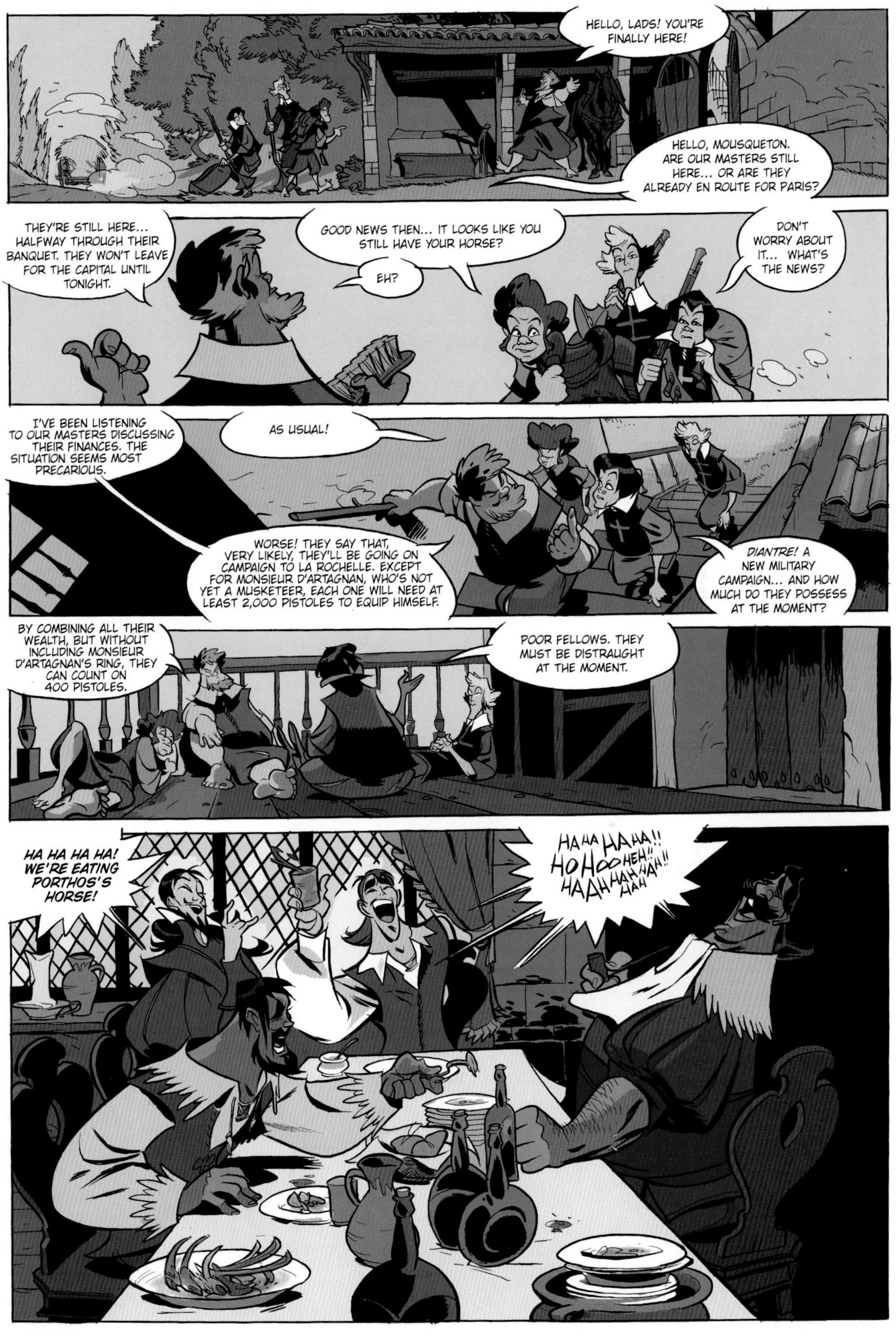
HELLO, LADS! YOU'RE FINALLY HERE!
HELLO, MOUSQUETON. ARE OUR MASTERS STILL HERE... OR ARE THEY ALREADY EN ROUTE FOR PARIS?
THEY'RE STILL HERE... HALFWAY THROUGH THEIR BANQUET. THEY WON'T LEAVE FOR THE CAPITAL UNTIL TONIGHT.
GOOD NEWS THEN... IT LOOKS LIKE YOU STILL HAVE YOUR HORSE?
EH?
DON'T WORRY ABOUT IT... WHAT'S THE NEWS?
I'VE BEEN LISTENING TO OUR MASTERS DISCUSSING THEIR FINANCES. THE SITUATION SEEMS MOST PRECARIOUS.
AS USUAL!
WORSE! THEY SAY THAT, VERY LIKELY, THEY'LL BE GOING ON CAMPAIGN TO LA ROCHELLE. EXCEPT FOR MONSIEUR D'ARTAGNAN, WHO'S NOT YET A MUSKETEER, EACH ONE WILL NEED AT LEAST 2,000 PISTOLES TO EQUIP HIMSELF.
DIANTRE! A NEW MILITARY CAMPAIGN... AND HOW MUCH DO THEY POSSESS AT THE MOMENT?
BY COMBINING ALL THEIR WEALTH, BUT WITHOUT INCLUDING MONSIEUR D'ARTAGNAN'S RING, THEY CAN COUNT ON 400 PISTOLES.
POOR FELLOWS. THEY MUST BE DISTRAUGHT AT THE MOMENT.
HA HA HA HA! WE'RE EATING PORTHOS'S HORSE!
HA HA HA HA!! HO HOO HEH!! HAAHHAHHAH HAH!!

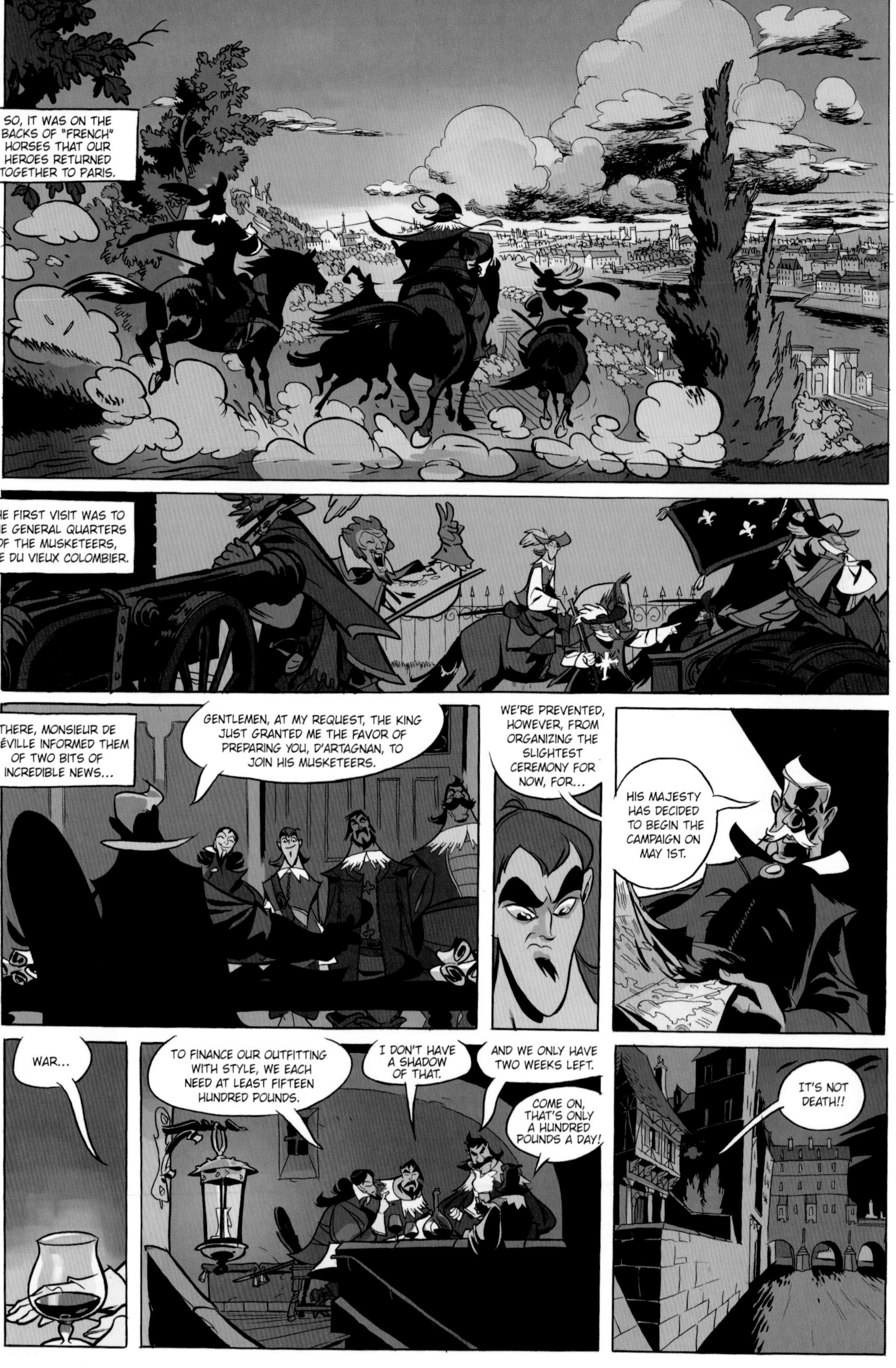
SO, IT WAS ON THE BACKS OF "FRENCH" HORSES THAT OUR HEROES RETURNED TOGETHER TO PARIS.
THE FIRST VISIT WAS TO THE GENERAL QUARTERS OF THE MUSKETEERS, RUE DU VIEUX COLOMBIER.
THERE, MONSIEUR DE TRÉVILLE INFORMED THEM OF TWO BITS OF INCREDIBLE NEWS...
GENTLEMEN, AT MY REQUEST, THE KING JUST GRANTED ME THE FAVOR OF PREPARING YOU, D'ARTAGNAN, TO JOIN HIS MUSKETEERS.
WE'RE PREVENTED, HOWEVER, FROM ORGANIZING THE SLIGHTEST CEREMONY FOR NOW, FOR...
HIS MAJESTY HAS DECIDED TO BEGIN THE CAMPAIGN ON MAY 1ST.
WAR...
TO FINANCE OUR OUTFITTING WITH STYLE, WE EACH NEED AT LEAST FIFTEEN HUNDRED POUNDS.
I DON'T HAVE A SHADOW OF THAT.
AND WE ONLY HAVE TWO WEEKS LEFT.
COME ON, THAT'S ONLY A HUNDRED POUNDS A DAY!
IT'S NOT DEATH!!

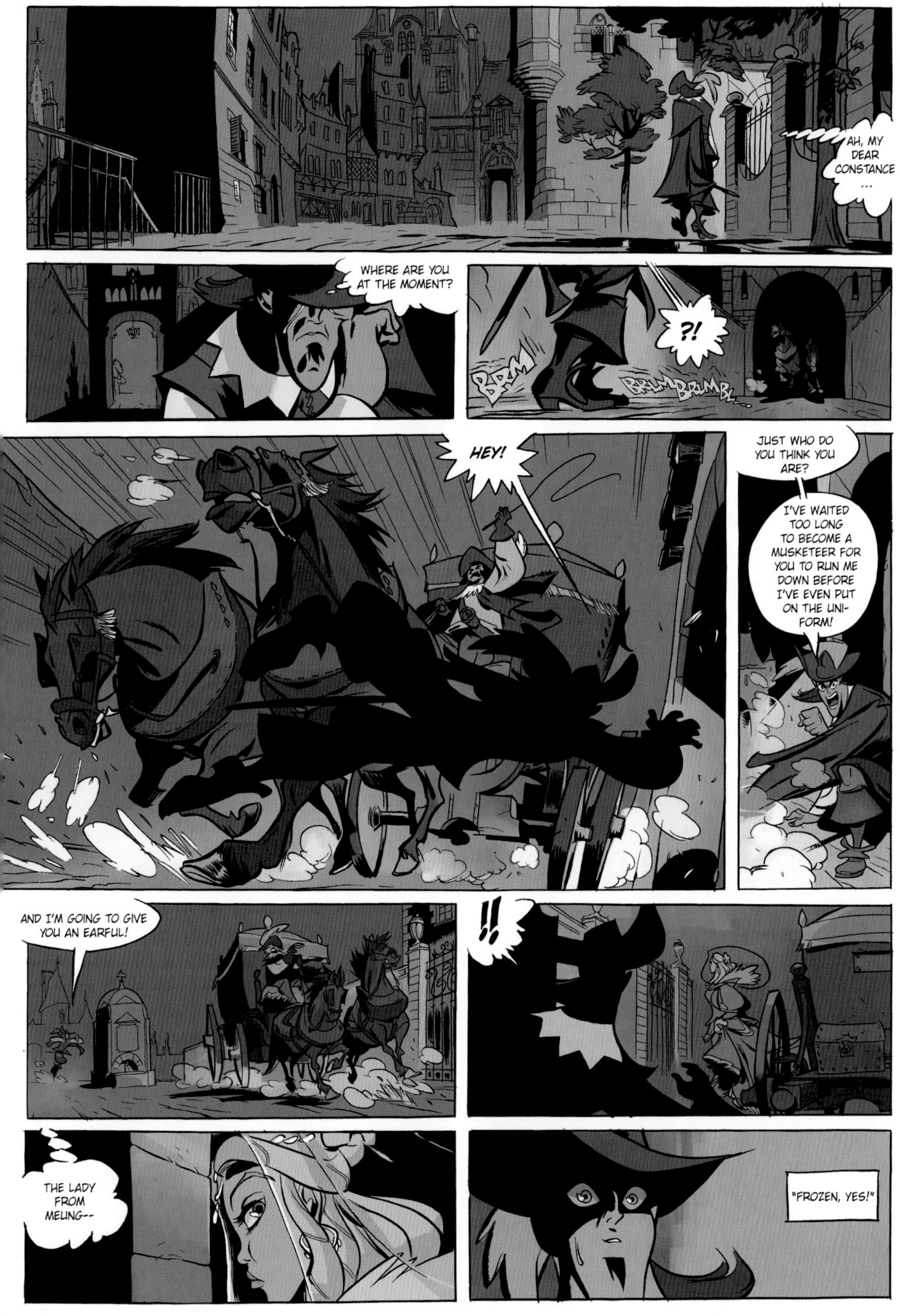
AH, MY DEAR CONSTANCE ...
WHERE ARE YOU AT THE MOMENT?
?!
BRRM
BRRMBRRMBL...
HEY!
JUST WHO DO YOU THINK YOU ARE?
I'VE WAITED TOO LONG TO BECOME A MUSKETEER FOR YOU TO RUN ME DOWN BEFORE I'VE EVEN PUT ON THE UNI-FORM!
AND I'M GOING TO GIVE YOU AN EARFUL!
!!
THE LADY FROM MEUNG--
"FROZEN, YES!"

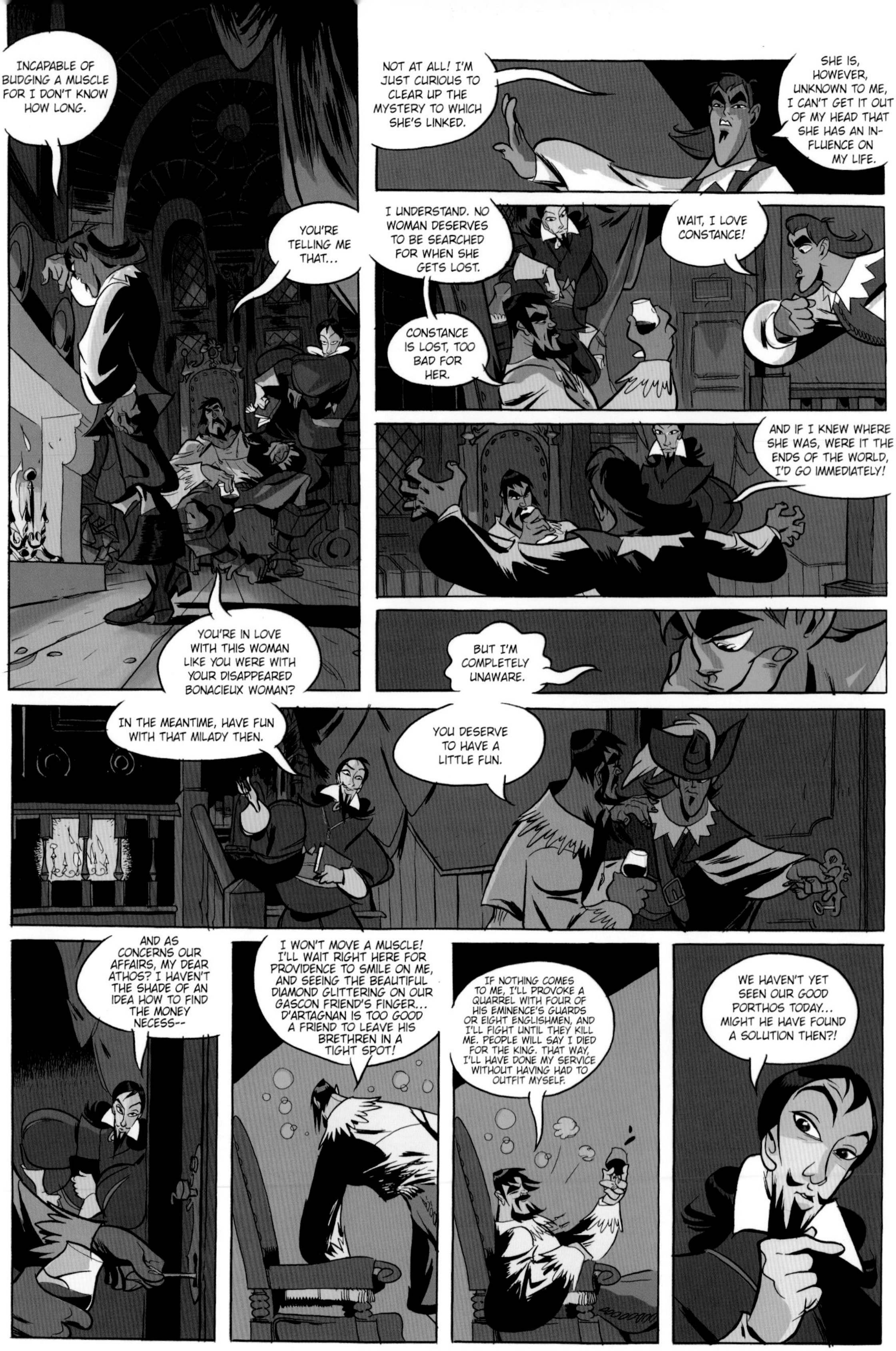
INCAPABLE OF BUDGING A MUSCLE FOR I DON'T KNOW HOW LONG.
YOU'RE TELLING ME THAT...
YOU'RE IN LOVE WITH THIS WOMAN LIKE YOU WERE WITH YOUR DISAPPEARED BONACIEUX WOMAN?
NOT AT ALL! I'M JUST CURIOUS TO CLEAR UP THE MYSTERY TO WHICH SHE'S LINKED.
SHE IS, HOWEVER, UNKNOWN TO ME, I CAN'T GET IT OUT OF MY HEAD THAT SHE HAS AN INFLUENCE ON MY LIFE.
I UNDERSTAND. NO WOMAN DESERVES TO BE SEARCHED FOR WHEN SHE GETS LOST.
CONSTANCE IS LOST, TOO BAD FOR HER.
WAIT, I LOVE CONSTANCE!
AND IF I KNEW WHERE SHE WAS, WERE IT THE ENDS OF THE WORLD, I'D GO IMMEDIATELY!
BUT I'M COMPLETELY UNAWARE.
IN THE MEANTIME, HAVE FUN WITH THAT MILADY THEN.
YOU DESERVE TO HAVE A LITTLE FUN.
AND AS CONCERNS OUR AFFAIRS, MY DEAR ATHOS? I HAVEN'T THE SHADE OF AN IDEA HOW TO FIND THE MONEY NECESS--
I WON'T MOVE A MUSCLE! I'LL WAIT RIGHT HERE FOR PROVIDENCE TO SMILE ON ME, AND SEEING THE BEAUTIFUL DIAMOND GLITTERING ON OUR GASCON FRIEND'S FINGER... D'ARTAGNAN IS TOO GOOD A FRIEND TO LEAVE HIS BRETHREN IN A TIGHT SPOT!
IF NOTHING COMES TO ME, I'LL PROVOKE A QUARREL WITH HIS EMINENCE'S GUARDS OR EIGHT ENGLISHMEN, AND I'LL FIGHT UNTIL THEY KILL ME. PEOPLE WILL SAY I DIED FOR THE KING. THAT WAY, I'LL HAVE DONE MY SERVICE WITHOUT HAVING HAD TO OUTFIT MYSELF.
WE HAVEN'T YET SEEN OUR GOOD PORTHOS TODAY... MIGHT HE HAVE FOUND A SOLUTION THEN?!

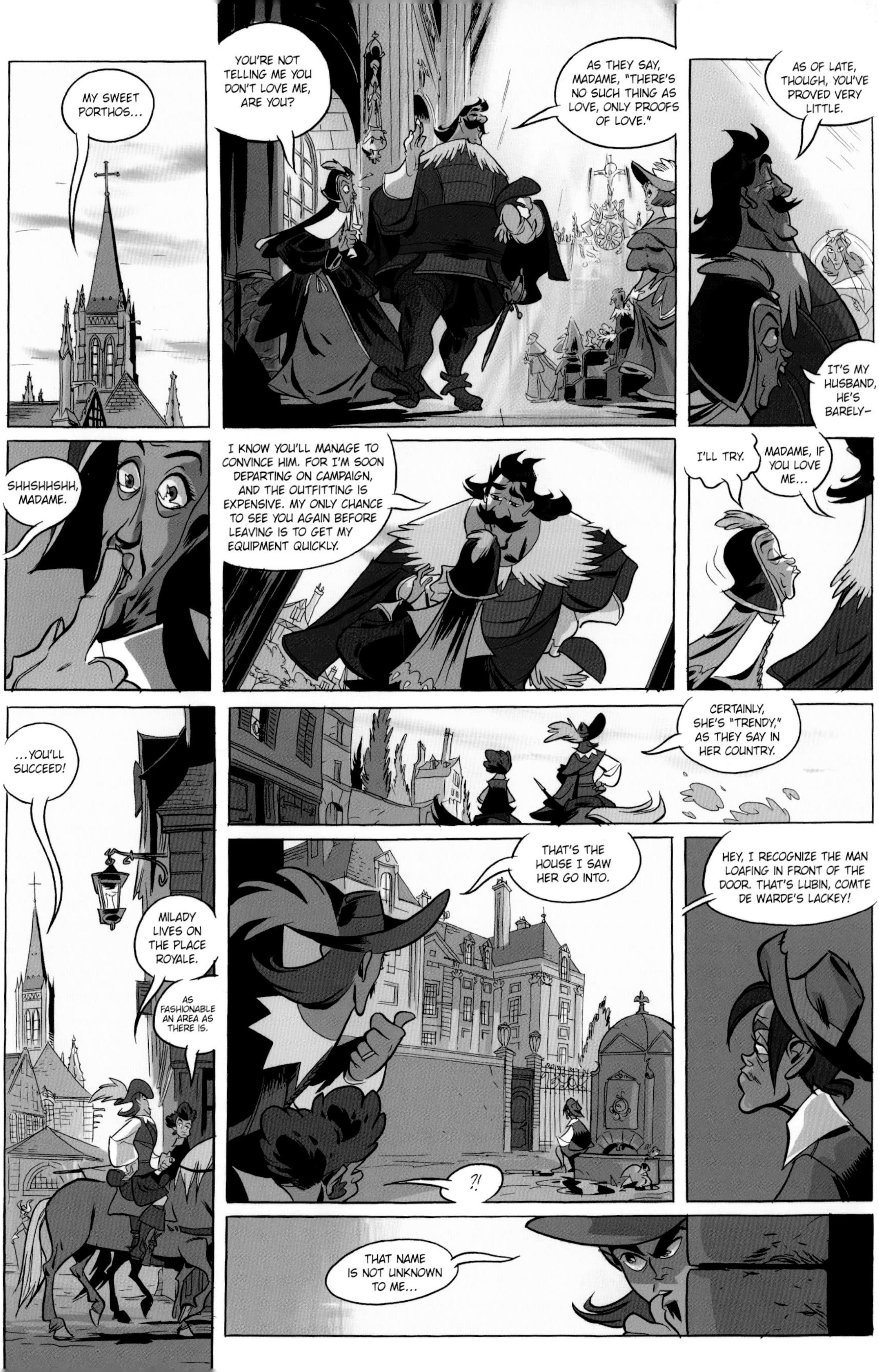
MY SWEET PORTHOS...
YOU'RE NOT TELLING ME YOU DON'T LOVE ME, ARE YOU?
AS THEY SAY, MADAME, "THERE'S NO SUCH THING AS LOVE, ONLY PROOFS OF LOVE."
AS OF LATE, THOUGH, YOU'VE PROVED VERY LITTLE.
IT'S MY HUSBAND, HE'S BARELY-
SHHSHHSHH, MADAME.
I KNOW YOU'LL MANAGE TO CONVINCE HIM. FOR I'M SOON DEPARTING ON CAMPAIGN, AND THE OUTFITTING IS EXPENSIVE. MY ONLY CHANCE TO SEE YOU AGAIN BEFORE LEAVING IS TO GET MY EQUIPMENT QUICKLY.
I'LL TRY.
MADAME, IF YOU LOVE ME...
...YOU'LL SUCCEED!
MILADY LIVES ON THE PLACE ROYALE.
AS FASHIONABLE AN AREA AS THERE IS.
CERTAINLY, SHE'S "TRENDY," AS THEY SAY IN HER COUNTRY.
THAT'S THE HOUSE I SAW HER GO INTO.
?!
HEY, I RECOGNIZE THE MAN LOAFING IN FRONT OF THE DOOR. THAT'S LUBIN, COMTE DE WARDE'S LACKEY!
THAT NAME IS NOT UNKNOWN TO ME...

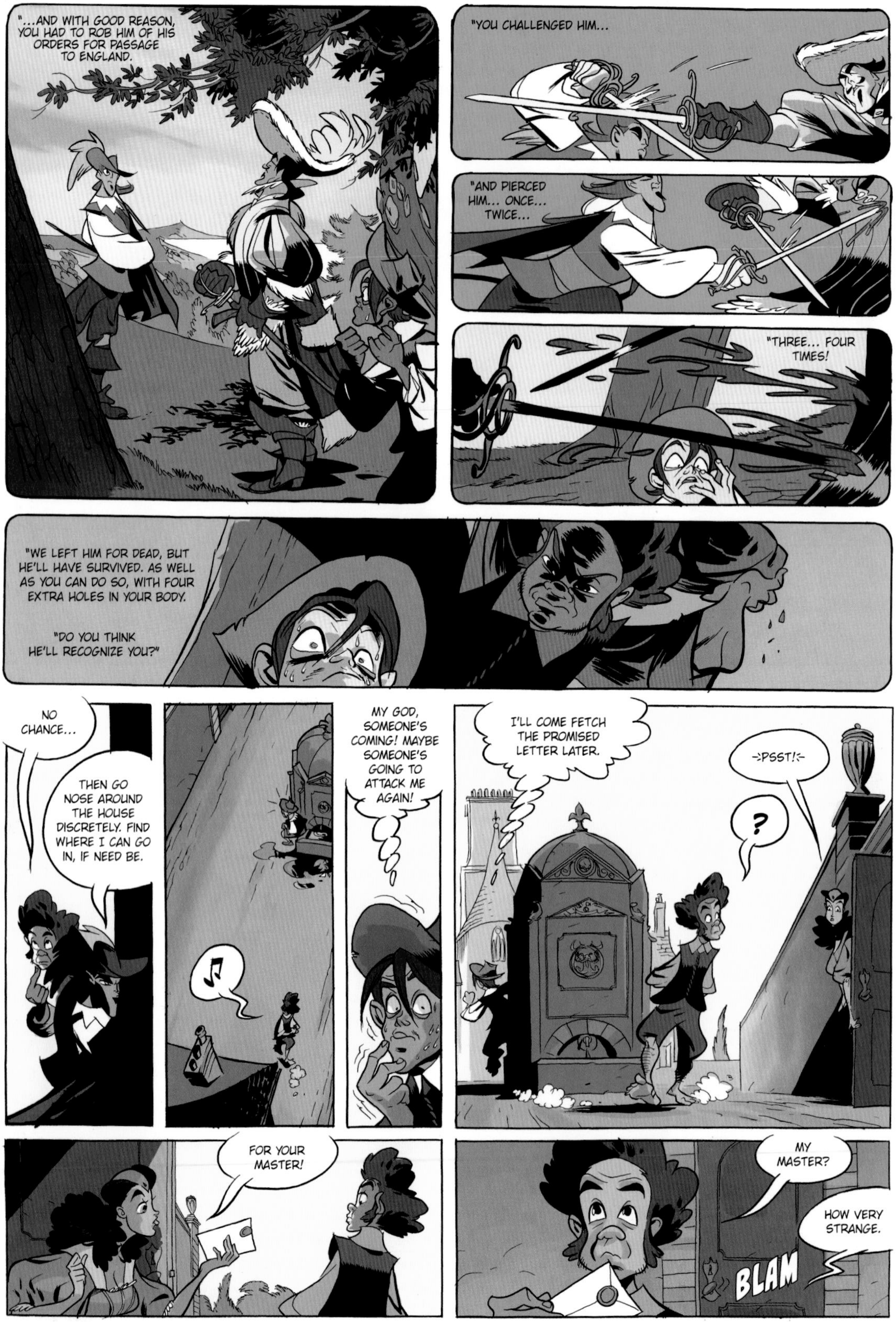
"...AND WITH GOOD REASON, YOU HAD TO ROB HIM OF HIS ORDERS FOR PASSAGE TO ENGLAND.
"YOU CHALLENGED HIM...
"AND PIERCED HIM... ONCE... TWICE...
"THREE... FOUR TIMES!
"WE LEFT HIM FOR DEAD, BUT HE'LL HAVE SURVIVED. AS WELL AS YOU CAN DO SO, WITH FOUR EXTRA HOLES IN YOUR BODY.
"DO YOU THINK HE'LL RECOGNIZE YOU?"
NO CHANCE...
THEN GO NOSE AROUND THE HOUSE DISCRETELY. FIND WHERE I CAN GO IN, IF NEED BE.
♪
MY GOD, SOMEONE'S COMING! MAYBE SOMEONE'S GOING TO ATTACK ME AGAIN!
I'LL COME FETCH THE PROMISED LETTER LATER.
-PSST!-
?
FOR YOUR MASTER!
MY MASTER?
HOW VERY STRANGE.
BLAM

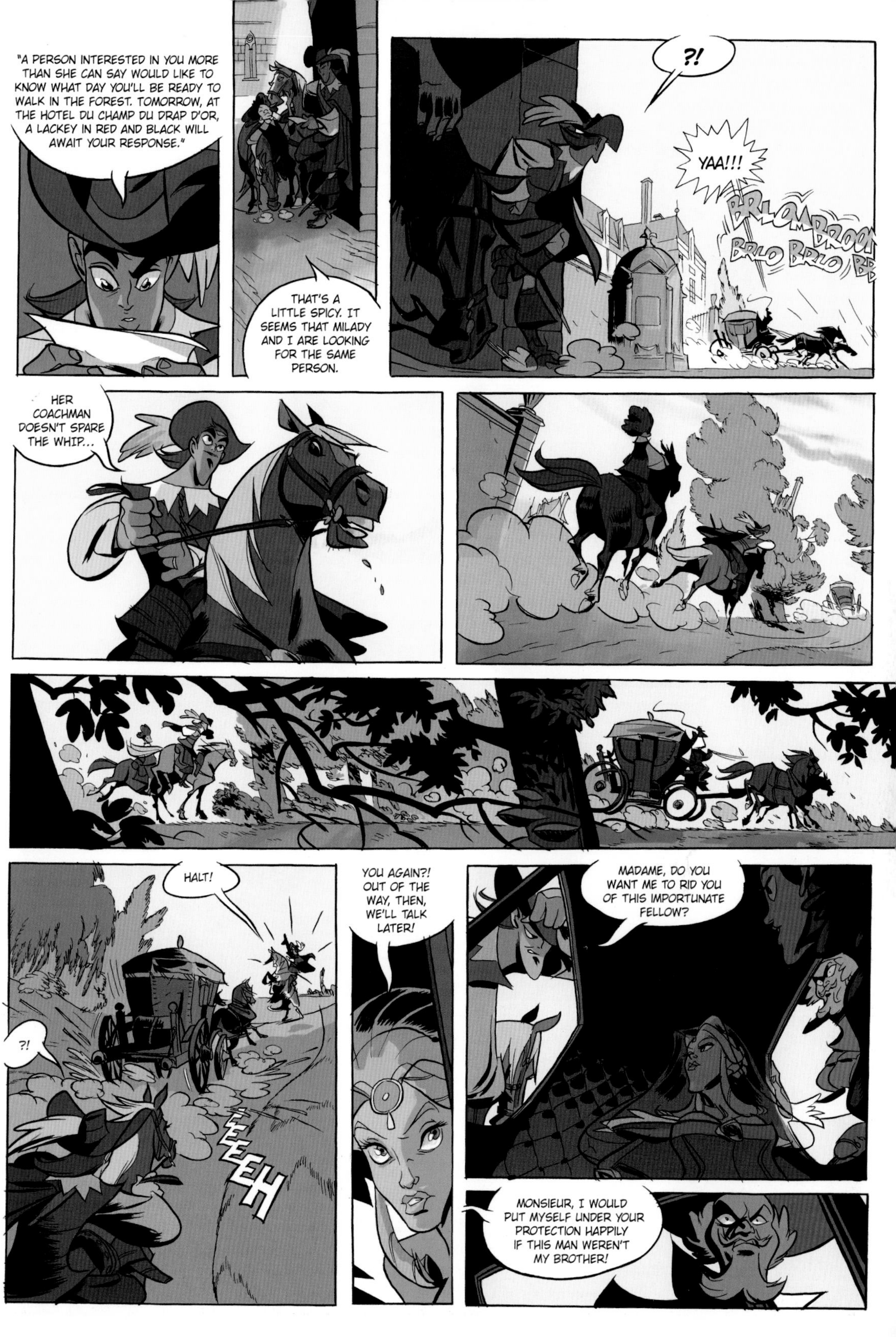
"A PERSON INTERESTED IN YOU MORE THAN SHE CAN SAY WOULD LIKE TO KNOW WHAT DAY YOU'LL BE READY TO WALK IN THE FOREST. TOMORROW, AT THE HOTEL DU CHAMP DU DRAP D'OR, A LACKEY IN RED AND BLACK WILL AWAIT YOUR RESPONSE."
THAT'S A LITTLE SPICY. IT SEEMS THAT MILADY AND I ARE LOOKING FOR THE SAME PERSON.
?!
YAA!!!
BRLOMBROOM
BRLO BRLO BR
HER COACHMAN DOESN'T SPARE THE WHIP...
HALT!
?!
EEEEH
YOU AGAIN?! OUT OF THE WAY, THEN, WE'LL TALK LATER!
MADAME, DO YOU WANT ME TO RID YOU OF THIS IMPORTUNATE FELLOW?
MONSIEUR, I WOULD PUT MYSELF UNDER YOUR PROTECTION HAPPILY IF THIS MAN WEREN'T MY BROTHER!

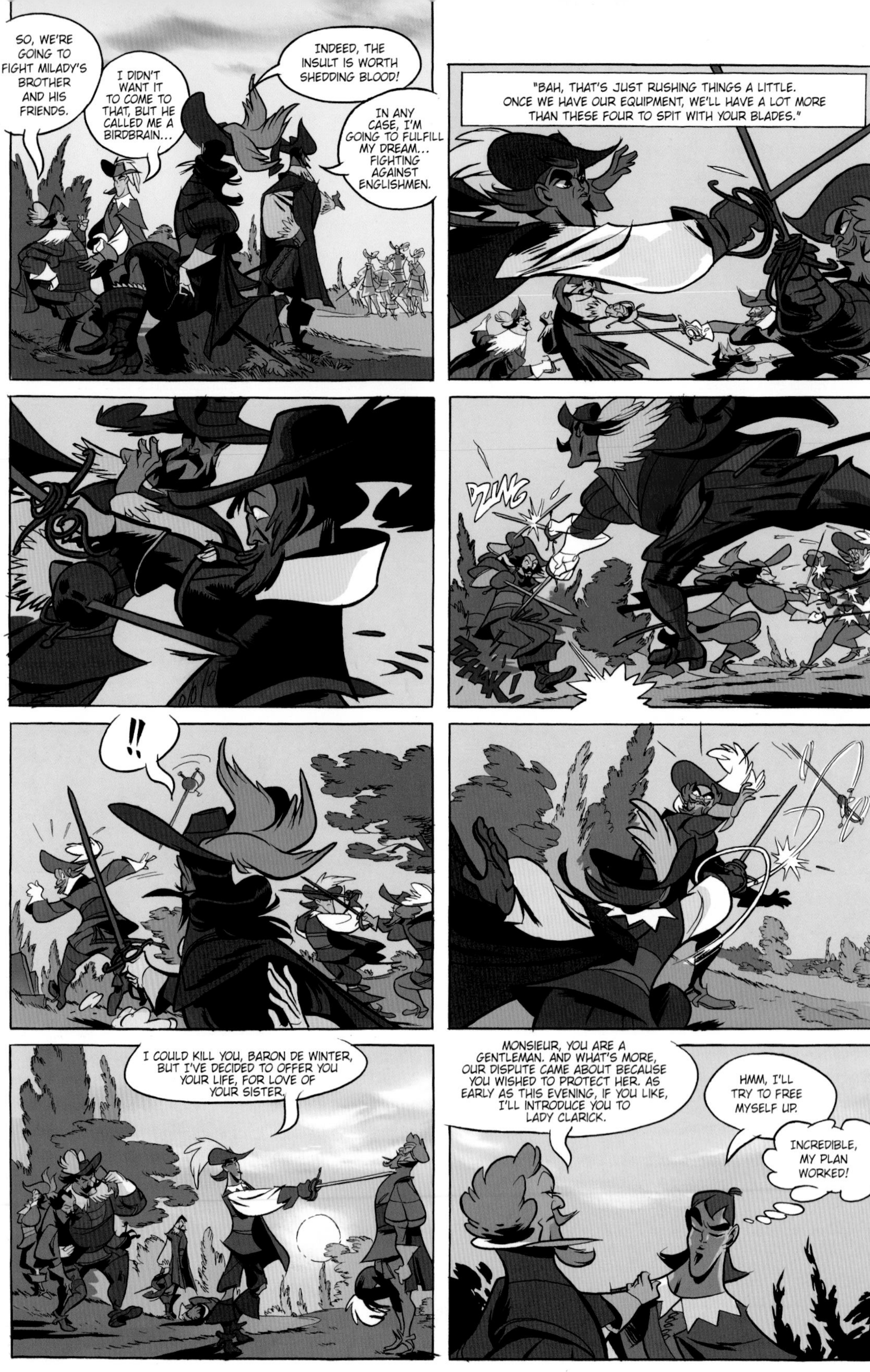
SO, WE'RE GOING TO FIGHT MILADY'S BROTHER AND HIS FRIENDS.
I DIDN'T WANT IT TO COME TO THAT, BUT HE CALLED ME A BIRDBRAIN...
INDEED, THE INSULT IS WORTH SHEDDING BLOOD!
IN ANY CASE, I'M GOING TO FULFILL MY DREAM... FIGHTING AGAINST ENGLISHMEN.
"BAH, THAT'S JUST RUSHING THINGS A LITTLE. ONCE WE HAVE OUR EQUIPMENT, WE'LL HAVE A LOT MORE THAN THESE FOUR TO SPIT WITH YOUR BLADES."
DZING
TCHAK!
!!
I COULD KILL YOU, BARON DE WINTER, BUT I'VE DECIDED TO OFFER YOU YOUR LIFE, FOR LOVE OF YOUR SISTER.
MONSIEUR, YOU ARE A GENTLEMAN. AND WHAT'S MORE, OUR DISPUTE CAME ABOUT BECAUSE YOU WISHED TO PROTECT HER. AS EARLY AS THIS EVENING, IF YOU LIKE, I'LL INTRODUCE YOU TO LADY CLARICK.
HMM, I'LL TRY TO FREE MYSELF UP.
INCREDIBLE, MY PLAN WORKED!

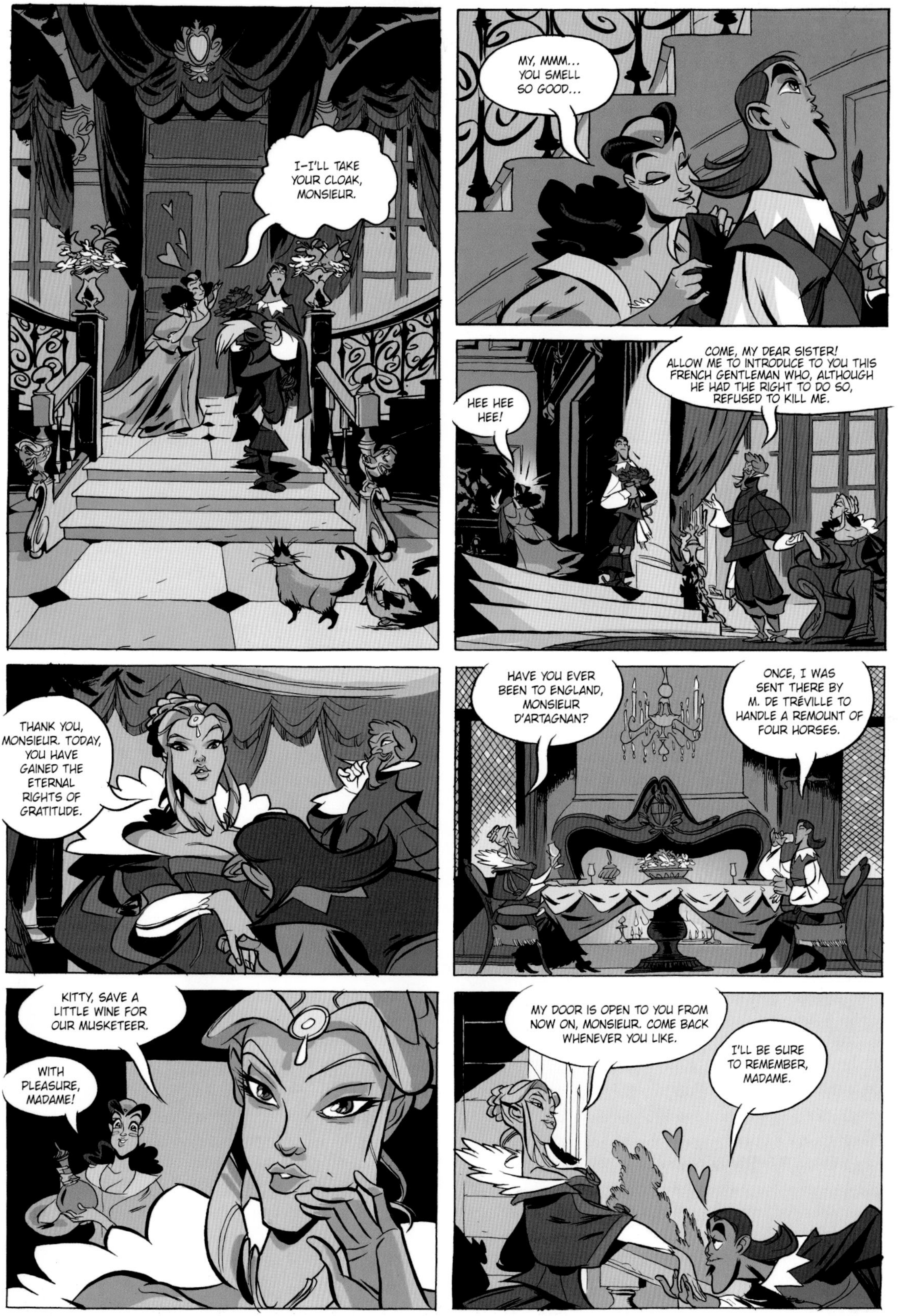
I-I'LL TAKE YOUR CLOAK, MONSIEUR.
MY, MMM... YOU SMELL SO GOOD...
HEE HEE HEE!
COME, MY DEAR SISTER! ALLOW ME TO INTRODUCE TO YOU THIS FRENCH GENTLEMAN WHO, ALTHOUGH HE HAD THE RIGHT TO DO SO, REFUSED TO KILL ME.
THANK YOU, MONSIEUR. TODAY, YOU HAVE GAINED THE ETERNAL RIGHTS OF GRATITUDE.
HAVE YOU EVER BEEN TO ENGLAND, MONSIEUR D'ARTAGNAN?
ONCE, I WAS SENT THERE BY M. DE TRÉVILLE TO HANDLE A REMOUNT OF FOUR HORSES.
KITTY, SAVE A LITTLE WINE FOR OUR MUSKETEER.
WITH PLEASURE, MADAME!
MY DOOR IS OPEN TO YOU FROM NOW ON, MONSIEUR. COME BACK WHENEVER YOU LIKE.
I'LL BE SURE TO REMEMBER, MADAME.

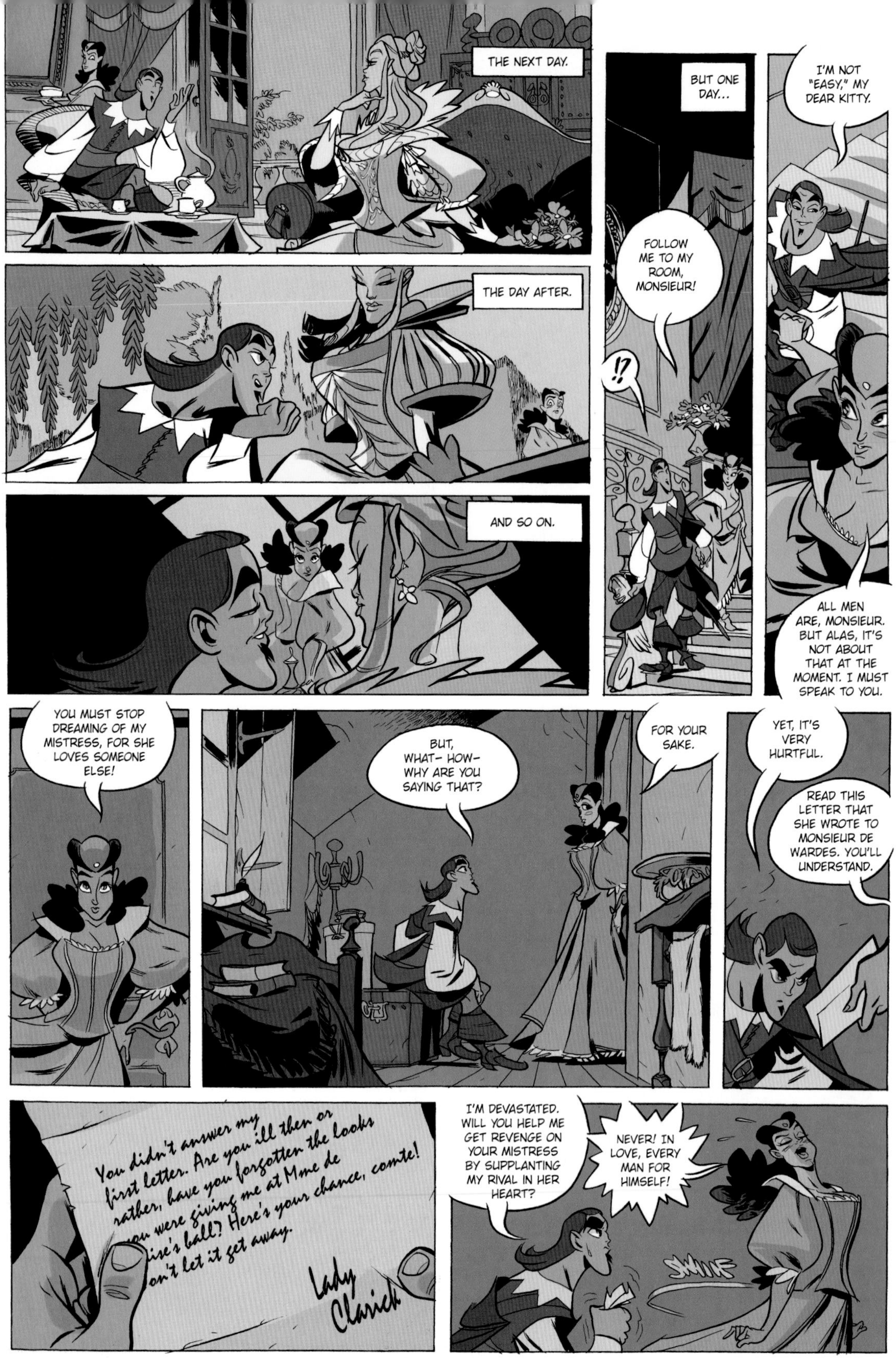
THE NEXT DAY.
THE DAY AFTER.
AND SO ON.
BUT ONE DAY...
FOLLOW ME TO MY ROOM, MONSIEUR!
!?
I'M NOT "EASY," MY DEAR KITTY.
ALL MEN ARE, MONSIEUR. BUT ALAS, IT'S NOT ABOUT THAT AT THE MOMENT. I MUST SPEAK TO YOU.
YOU MUST STOP DREAMING OF MY MISTRESS, FOR SHE LOVES SOMEONE ELSE!
BUT, WHAT- HOW- WHY ARE YOU SAYING THAT?
FOR YOUR SAKE.
YET, IT'S VERY HURTFUL.
READ THIS LETTER THAT SHE WROTE TO MONSIEUR DE WARDES. YOU'LL UNDERSTAND.
You didn't answer my first letter. Are you ill then or rather, have you forgotten the looks you were giving me at Mme de ...ise's ball? Here's your chance, comte! ...on't let it get away.
Lady Clarick
I'M DEVASTATED. WILL YOU HELP ME GET REVENGE ON YOUR MISTRESS BY SUPPLANTING MY RIVAL IN HER HEART?
NEVER! IN LOVE, EVERY MAN FOR HIMSELF!

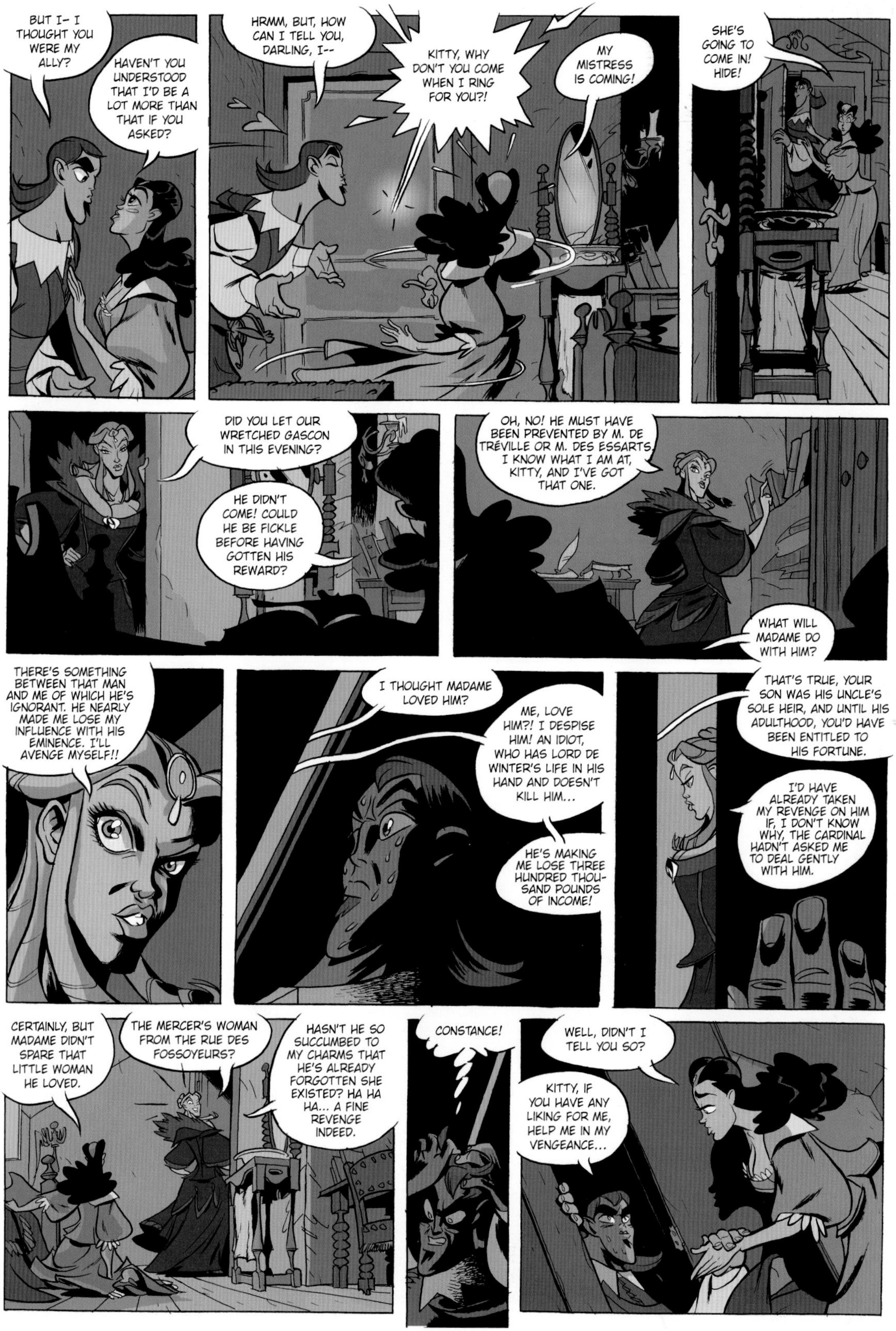

BUT I– I THOUGHT YOU WERE MY ALLY?
HAVEN'T YOU UNDERSTOOD THAT I'D BE A LOT MORE THAN THAT IF YOU ASKED?
HRMM, BUT, HOW CAN I TELL YOU, DARLING, I--
KITTY, WHY DON'T YOU COME WHEN I RING FOR YOU?!
MY MISTRESS IS COMING!
SHE'S GOING TO COME IN! HIDE!
DID YOU LET OUR WRETCHED GASCON IN THIS EVENING?
HE DIDN'T COME! COULD HE BE FICKLE BEFORE HAVING GOTTEN HIS REWARD?
OH, NO! HE MUST HAVE BEEN PREVENTED BY M. DE TRÉVILLE OR M. DES ESSARTS. I KNOW WHAT I AM AT, KITTY, AND I'VE GOT THAT ONE.
WHAT WILL MADAME DO WITH HIM?
THERE'S SOMETHING BETWEEN THAT MAN AND ME OF WHICH HE'S IGNORANT. HE NEARLY MADE ME LOSE MY INFLUENCE WITH HIS EMINENCE. I'LL AVENGE MYSELF!!
I THOUGHT MADAME LOVED HIM?
ME, LOVE HIM?! I DESPISE HIM! AN IDIOT, WHO HAS LORD DE WINTER'S LIFE IN HIS HAND AND DOESN'T KILL HIM...
HE'S MAKING ME LOSE THREE HUNDRED THOUSAND POUNDS OF INCOME!
THAT'S TRUE, YOUR SON WAS HIS UNCLE'S SOLE HEIR, AND UNTIL HIS ADULTHOOD, YOU'D HAVE BEEN ENTITLED TO HIS FORTUNE.
I'D HAVE ALREADY TAKEN MY REVENGE ON HIM IF, I DON'T KNOW WHY, THE CARDINAL HADN'T ASKED ME TO DEAL GENTLY WITH HIM.
CERTAINLY, BUT MADAME DIDN'T SPARE THAT LITTLE WOMAN HE LOVED.
THE MERCER'S WOMAN FROM THE RUE DES FOSSOYEURS?
HASN'T HE SO SUCCUMBED TO MY CHARMS THAT HE'S ALREADY FORGOTTEN SHE EXISTED? HA HA HA... A FINE REVENGE INDEED.
CONSTANCE!
WELL, DIDN'T I TELL YOU SO?
KITTY, IF YOU HAVE ANY LIKING FOR ME, HELP ME IN MY VENGEANCE...

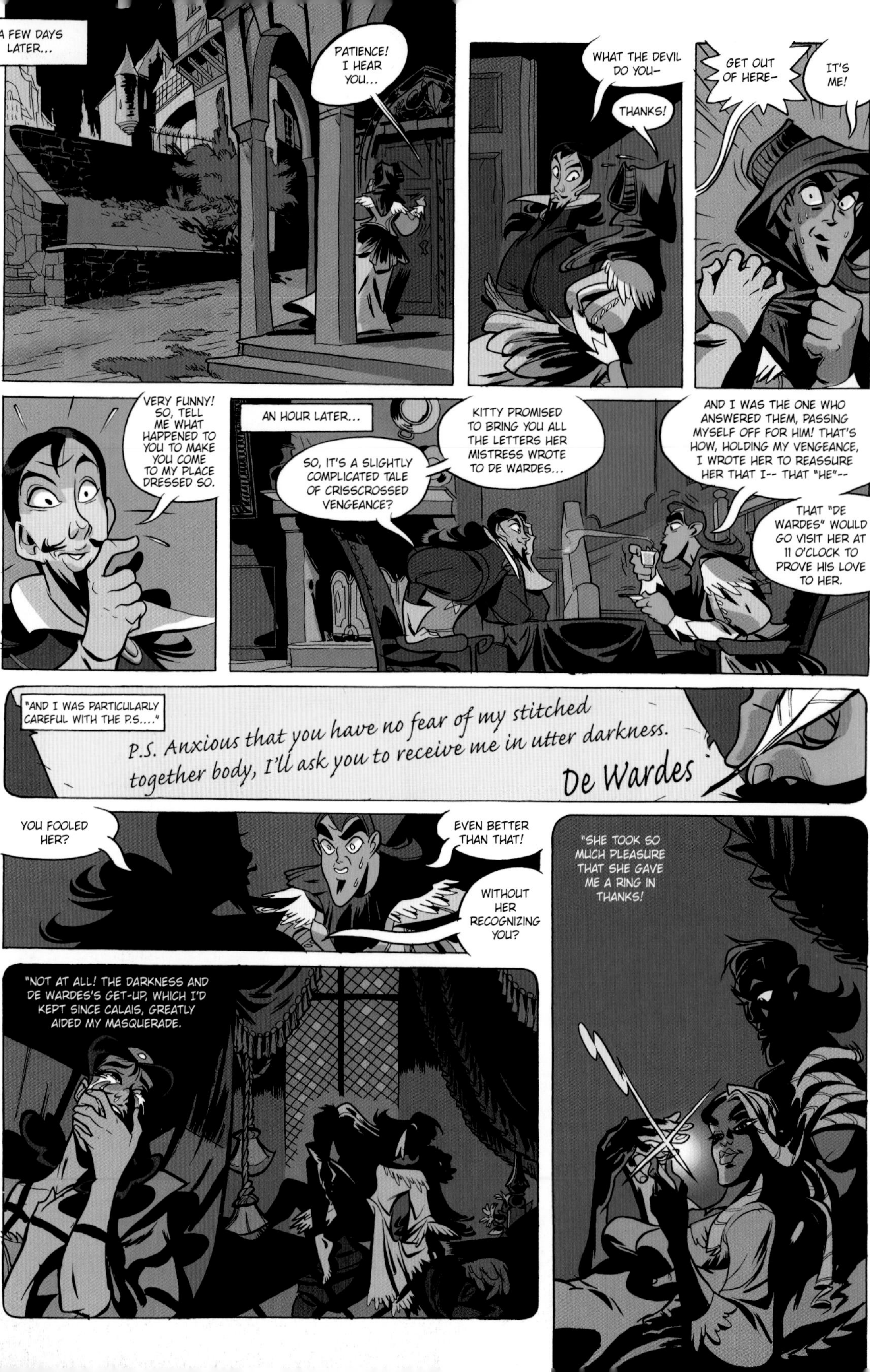

A FEW DAYS LATER...
PATIENCE! I HEAR YOU...
WHAT THE DEVIL DO YOU-
THANKS!
GET OUT OF HERE-
IT'S ME!
VERY FUNNY! SO, TELL ME WHAT HAPPENED TO YOU TO MAKE YOU COME TO MY PLACE DRESSED SO.
AN HOUR LATER...
KITTY PROMISED TO BRING YOU ALL THE LETTERS HER MISTRESS WROTE TO DE WARDES...
SO, IT'S A SLIGHTLY COMPLICATED TALE OF CRISSCROSSED VENGEANCE?
AND I WAS THE ONE WHO ANSWERED THEM, PASSING MYSELF OFF FOR HIM! THAT'S HOW, HOLDING MY VENGEANCE, I WROTE HER TO REASSURE HER THAT I-- THAT "HE"--
THAT "DE WARDES" WOULD GO VISIT HER AT 11 O'CLOCK TO PROVE HIS LOVE TO HER.
"AND I WAS PARTICULARLY CAREFUL WITH THE P.S...."
P.S. Anxious that you have no fear of my stitched together body, I'll ask you to receive me in utter darkness.
De Wardes
YOU FOOLED HER?
EVEN BETTER THAN THAT!
WITHOUT HER RECOGNIZING YOU?
"SHE TOOK SO MUCH PLEASURE THAT SHE GAVE ME A RING IN THANKS!
"NOT AT ALL! THE DARKNESS AND DE WARDES'S GET-UP, WHICH I'D KEPT SINCE CALAIS, GREATLY AIDED MY MASQUERADE.

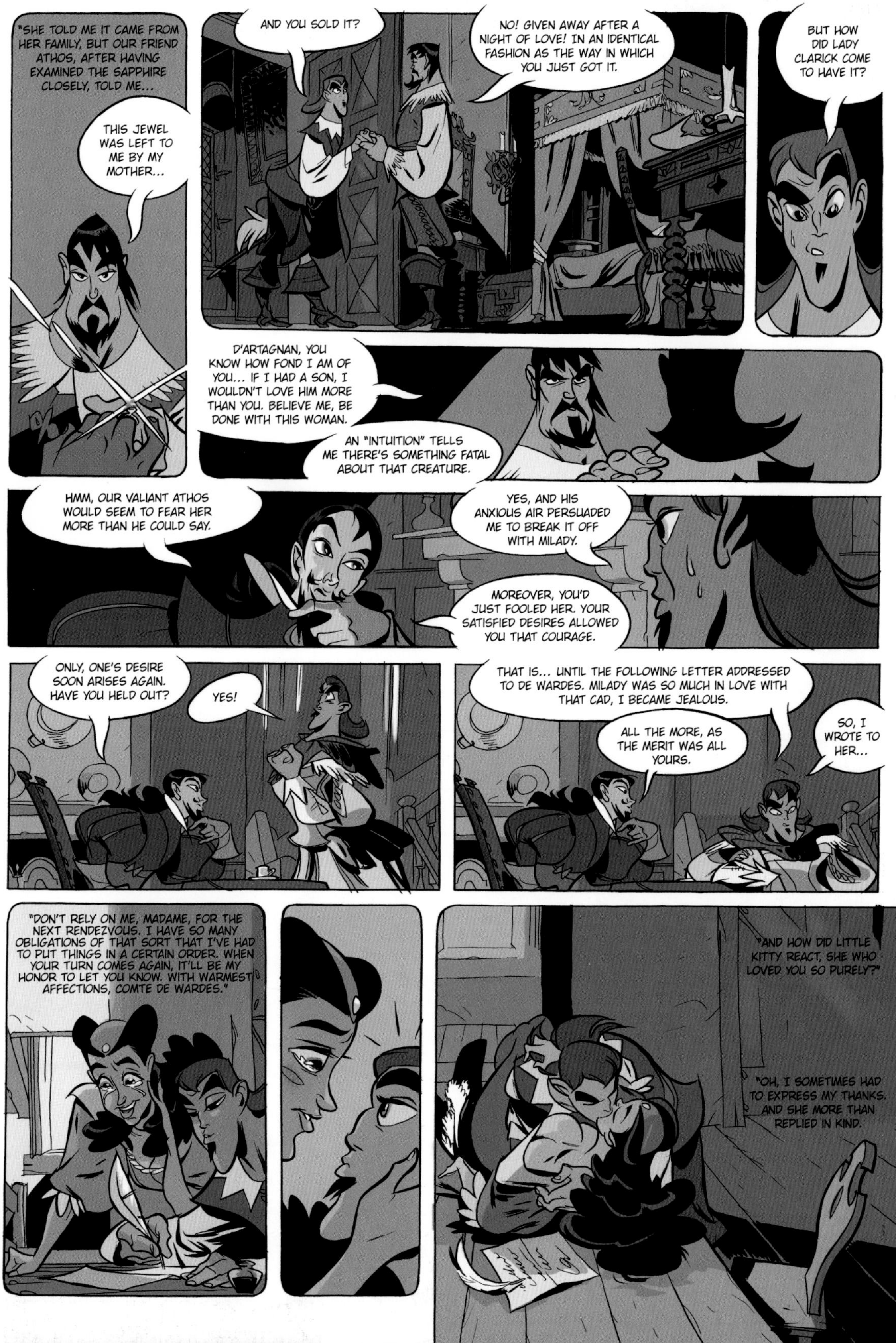
"SHE TOLD ME IT CAME FROM HER FAMILY, BUT OUR FRIEND ATHOS, AFTER HAVING EXAMINED THE SAPPHIRE CLOSELY, TOLD ME...
THIS JEWEL WAS LEFT TO ME BY MY MOTHER...
AND YOU SOLD IT?
NO! GIVEN AWAY AFTER A NIGHT OF LOVE! IN AN IDENTICAL FASHION AS THE WAY IN WHICH YOU JUST GOT IT.
BUT HOW DID LADY CLARICK COME TO HAVE IT?
D'ARTAGNAN, YOU KNOW HOW FOND I AM OF YOU... IF I HAD A SON, I WOULDN'T LOVE HIM MORE THAN YOU. BELIEVE ME, BE DONE WITH THIS WOMAN.
AN "INTUITION" TELLS ME THERE'S SOMETHING FATAL ABOUT THAT CREATURE.
HMM, OUR VALIANT ATHOS WOULD SEEM TO FEAR HER MORE THAN HE COULD SAY.
YES, AND HIS ANXIOUS AIR PERSUADED ME TO BREAK IT OFF WITH MILADY.
MOREOVER, YOU'D JUST FOOLED HER. YOUR SATISFIED DESIRES ALLOWED YOU THAT COURAGE.
ONLY, ONE'S DESIRE SOON ARISES AGAIN. HAVE YOU HELD OUT?
YES!
THAT IS... UNTIL THE FOLLOWING LETTER ADDRESSED TO DE WARDES. MILADY WAS SO MUCH IN LOVE WITH THAT CAD, I BECAME JEALOUS.
ALL THE MORE, AS THE MERIT WAS ALL YOURS.
SO, I WROTE TO HER...
"DON'T RELY ON ME, MADAME, FOR THE NEXT RENDEZVOUS. I HAVE SO MANY OBLIGATIONS OF THAT SORT THAT I'VE HAD TO PUT THINGS IN A CERTAIN ORDER. WHEN YOUR TURN COMES AGAIN, IT'LL BE MY HONOR TO LET YOU KNOW. WITH WARMEST AFFECTIONS, COMTE DE WARDES."
"AND HOW DID LITTLE KITTY REACT, SHE WHO LOVED YOU SO PURELY?"
"OH, I SOMETIMES HAD TO EXPRESS MY THANKS. AND SHE MORE THAN REPLIED IN KIND.

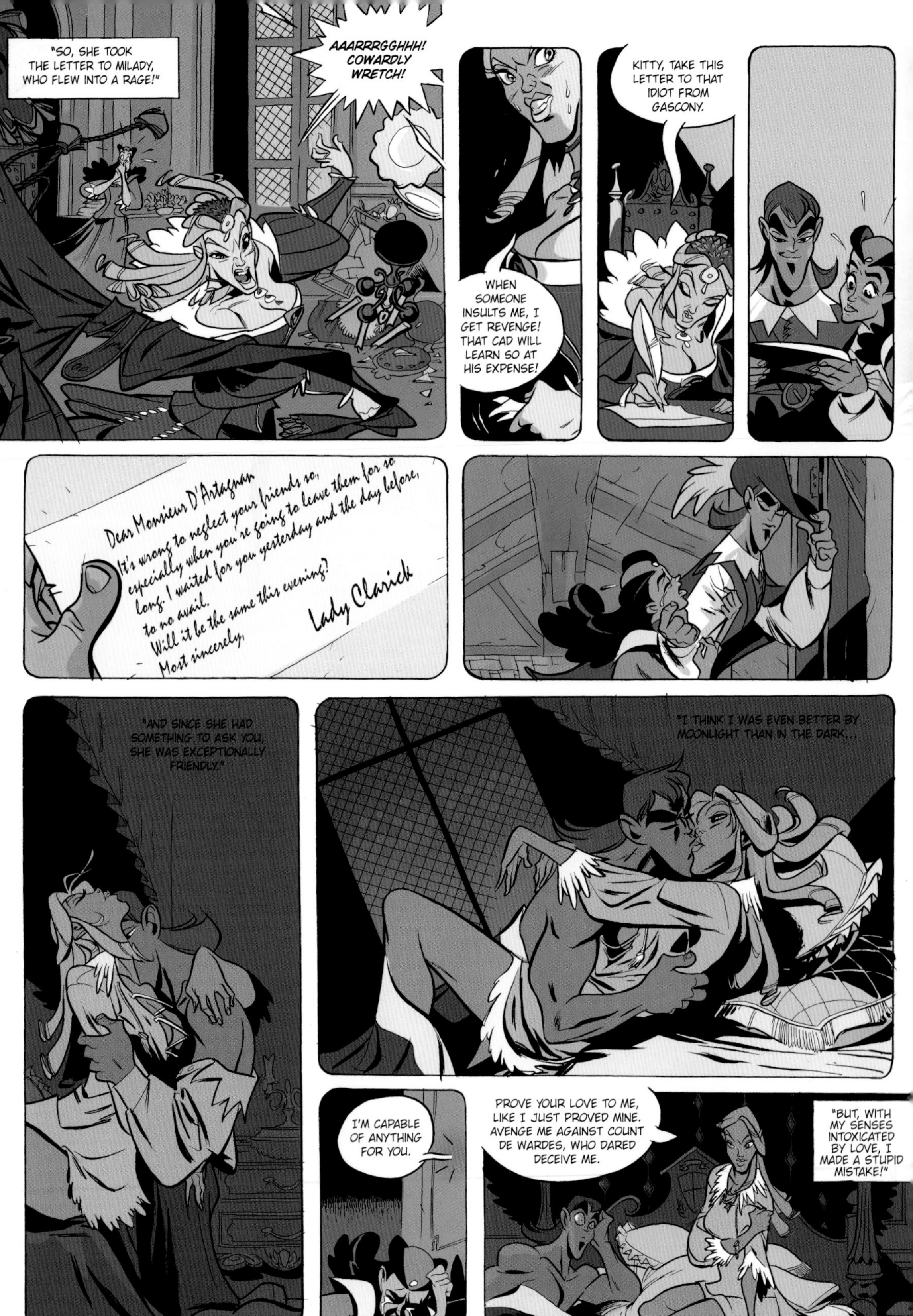
"SO, SHE TOOK THE LETTER TO MILADY, WHO FLEW INTO A RAGE!"
AAARRRGGHHH! COWARDLY WRETCH!
WHEN SOMEONE INSULTS ME, I GET REVENGE! THAT CAD WILL LEARN SO AT HIS EXPENSE!
KITTY, TAKE THIS LETTER TO THAT IDIOT FROM GASCONY.
Dear Monsieur D'Artagnan
It's wrong to neglect your friends so,
especially when you're going to leave them for so
long. I waited for you yesterday and the day before,
to no avail.
Will it be the same this evening?
Most sincerely,
Lady Clarick
"AND SINCE SHE HAD SOMETHING TO ASK YOU, SHE WAS EXCEPTIONALLY FRIENDLY."
"I THINK I WAS EVEN BETTER BY MOONLIGHT THAN IN THE DARK...
I'M CAPABLE OF ANYTHING FOR YOU.
PROVE YOUR LOVE TO ME, LIKE I JUST PROVED MINE. AVENGE ME AGAINST COUNT DE WARDES, WHO DARED DECEIVE ME.
"BUT, WITH MY SENSES INTOXICATED BY LOVE, I MADE A STUPID MISTAKE!"

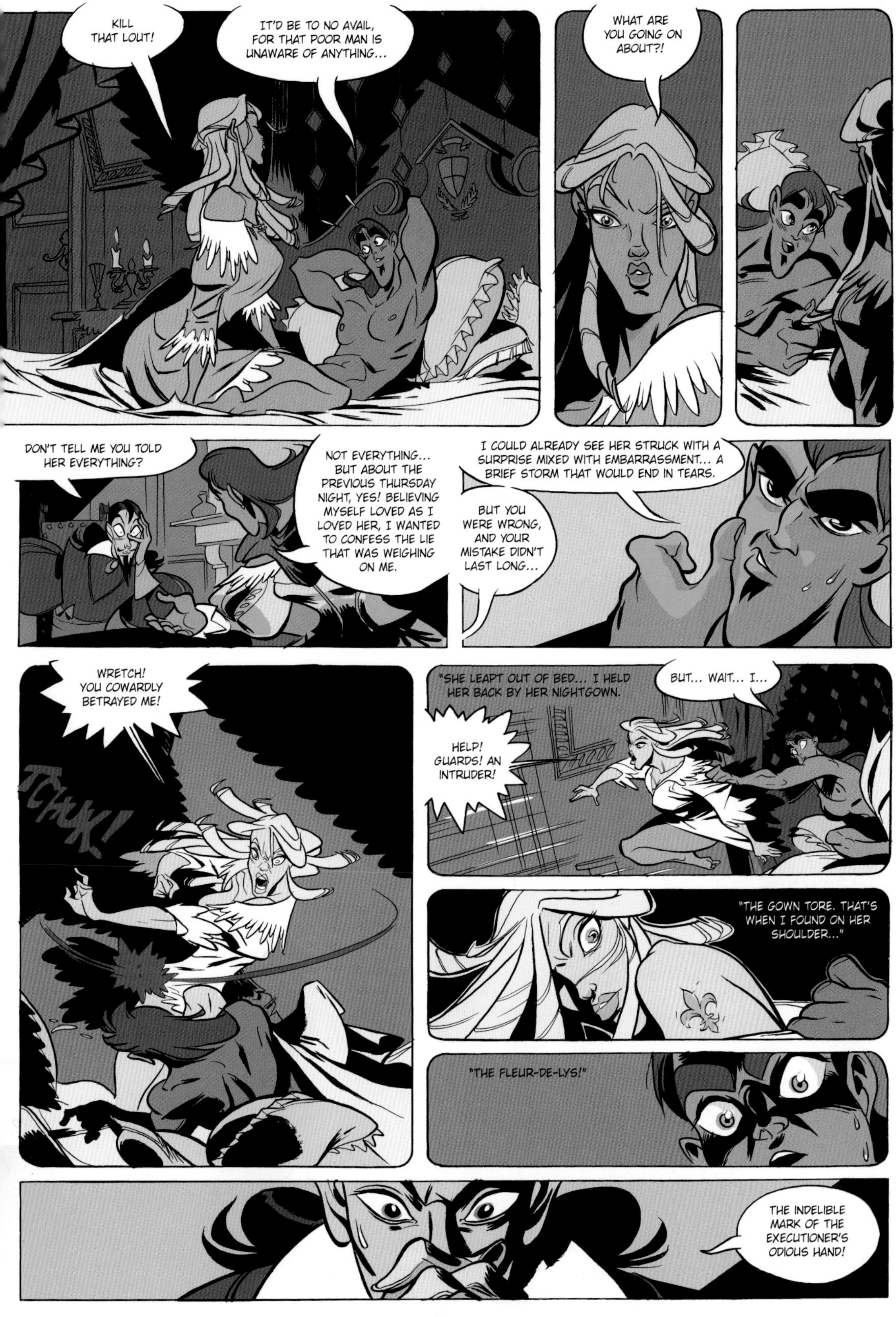
KILL THAT LOUT!
IT'D BE TO NO AVAIL, FOR THAT POOR MAN IS UNAWARE OF ANYTHING...
WHAT ARE YOU GOING ON ABOUT?!
DON'T TELL ME YOU TOLD HER EVERYTHING?
NOT EVERYTHING... BUT ABOUT THE PREVIOUS THURSDAY NIGHT, YES! BELIEVING MYSELF LOVED AS I LOVED HER, I WANTED TO CONFESS THE LIE THAT WAS WEIGHING ON ME.
I COULD ALREADY SEE HER STRUCK WITH A SURPRISE MIXED WITH EMBARRASSMENT... A BRIEF STORM THAT WOULD END IN TEARS.
BUT YOU WERE WRONG, AND YOUR MISTAKE DIDN'T LAST LONG...
WRETCH! YOU COWARDLY BETRAYED ME!
TCHUK!
"SHE LEAPT OUT OF BED... I HELD HER BACK BY HER NIGHTGOWN.
BUT... WAIT... I...
HELP! GUARDS! AN INTRUDER!
"THE GOWN TORE. THAT'S WHEN I FOUND ON HER SHOULDER..."
"THE FLEUR-DE-LYS!"
THE INDELIBLE MARK OF THE EXECUTIONER'S ODIOUS HAND!

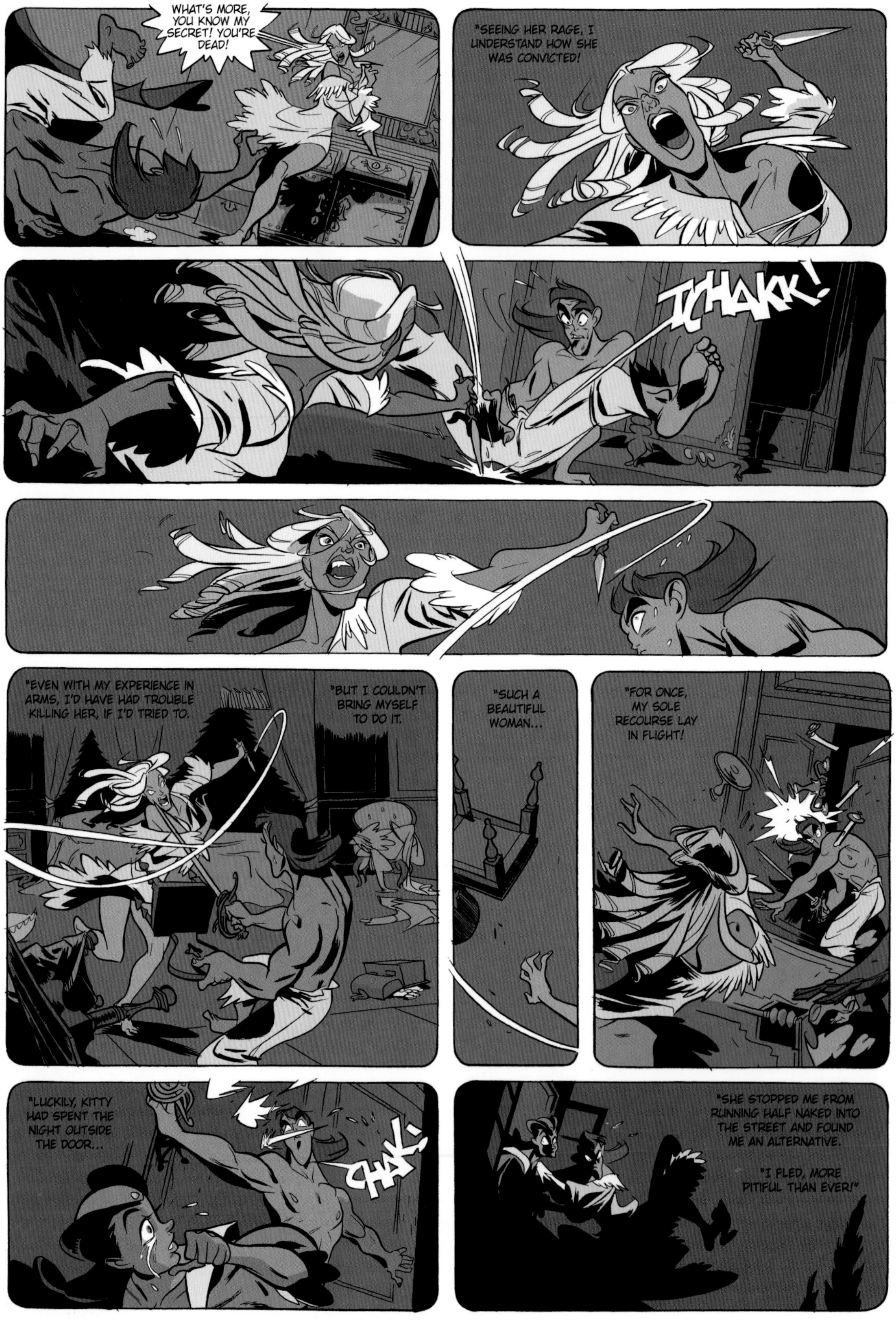
WHAT'S MORE, YOU KNOW MY SECRET! YOU'RE DEAD!
"SEEING HER RAGE, I UNDERSTAND HOW SHE WAS CONVICTED!
TCHAKK!
"EVEN WITH MY EXPERIENCE IN ARMS, I'D HAVE HAD TROUBLE KILLING HER, IF I'D TRIED TO.
"BUT I COULDN'T BRING MYSELF TO DO IT.
"SUCH A BEAUTIFUL WOMAN...
"FOR ONCE, MY SOLE RECOURSE LAY IN FLIGHT!
"LUCKILY, KITTY HAD SPENT THE NIGHT OUTSIDE THE DOOR...
CHAK!
"SHE STOPPED ME FROM RUNNING HALF NAKED INTO THE STREET AND FOUND ME AN ALTERNATIVE.
"I FLED, MORE PITIFUL THAN EVER!"

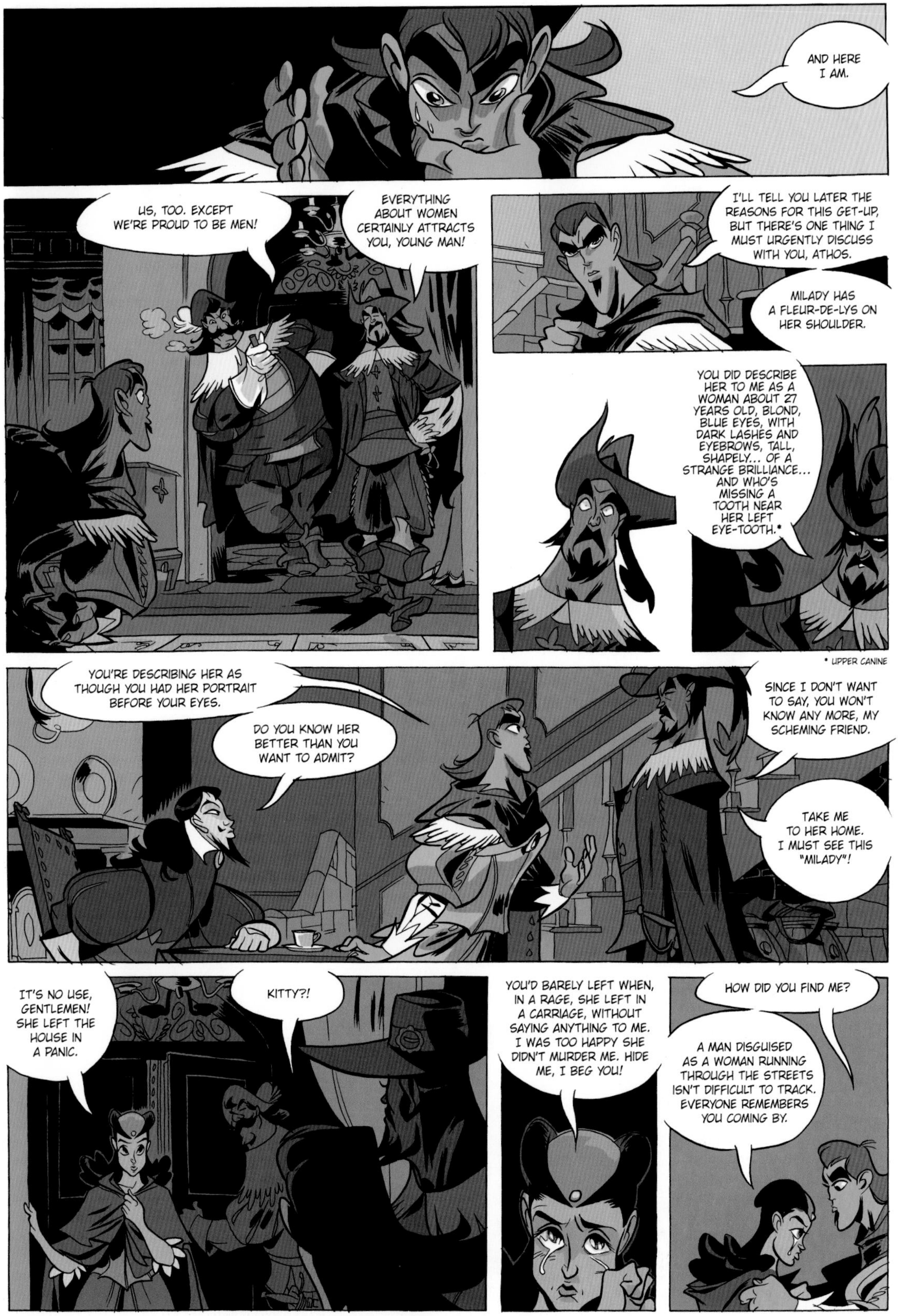

AND HERE I AM.
US, TOO. EXCEPT WE'RE PROUD TO BE MEN!
EVERYTHING ABOUT WOMEN CERTAINLY ATTRACTS YOU, YOUNG MAN!
I'LL TELL YOU LATER THE REASONS FOR THIS GET-UP, BUT THERE'S ONE THING I MUST URGENTLY DISCUSS WITH YOU, ATHOS.
MILADY HAS A FLEUR-DE-LYS ON HER SHOULDER.
YOU DID DESCRIBE HER TO ME AS A WOMAN ABOUT 27 YEARS OLD, BLOND, BLUE EYES, WITH DARK LASHES AND EYEBROWS, TALL, SHAPELY... OF A STRANGE BRILLIANCE... AND WHO'S MISSING A TOOTH NEAR HER LEFT EYE-TOOTH.*
YOU'RE DESCRIBING HER AS THOUGH YOU HAD HER PORTRAIT BEFORE YOUR EYES.
DO YOU KNOW HER BETTER THAN YOU WANT TO ADMIT?
SINCE I DON'T WANT TO SAY, YOU WON'T KNOW ANY MORE, MY SCHEMING FRIEND.
TAKE ME TO HER HOME. I MUST SEE THIS "MILADY"!
IT'S NO USE, GENTLEMEN! SHE LEFT THE HOUSE IN A PANIC.
KITTY?!
YOU'D BARELY LEFT WHEN, IN A RAGE, SHE LEFT IN A CARRIAGE, WITHOUT SAYING ANYTHING TO ME. I WAS TOO HAPPY SHE DIDN'T MURDER ME. HIDE ME, I BEG YOU!
HOW DID YOU FIND ME?
A MAN DISGUISED AS A WOMAN RUNNING THROUGH THE STREETS ISN'T DIFFICULT TO TRACK. EVERYONE REMEMBERS YOU COMING BY.

* UPPER CANINE

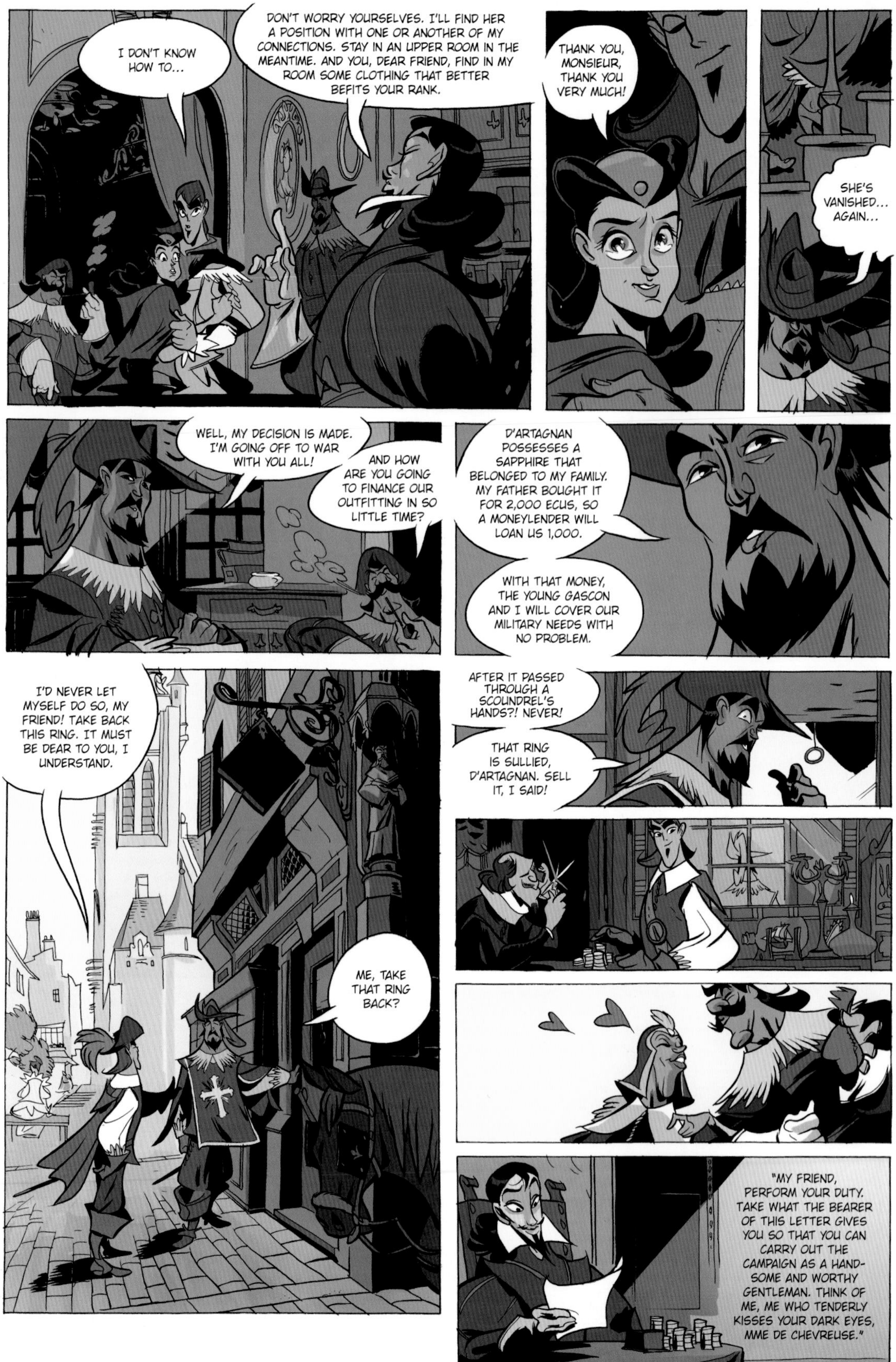
I DON'T KNOW HOW TO...
DON'T WORRY YOURSELVES. I'LL FIND HER A POSITION WITH ONE OR ANOTHER OF MY CONNECTIONS. STAY IN AN UPPER ROOM IN THE MEANTIME. AND YOU, DEAR FRIEND, FIND IN MY ROOM SOME CLOTHING THAT BETTER BEFITS YOUR RANK.
THANK YOU, MONSIEUR, THANK YOU VERY MUCH!
SHE'S VANISHED... AGAIN...
WELL, MY DECISION IS MADE. I'M GOING OFF TO WAR WITH YOU ALL!
AND HOW ARE YOU GOING TO FINANCE OUR OUTFITTING IN SO LITTLE TIME?
D'ARTAGNAN POSSESSES A SAPPHIRE THAT BELONGED TO MY FAMILY. MY FATHER BOUGHT IT FOR 2,000 ECUS, SO A MONEYLENDER WILL LOAN US 1,000.
WITH THAT MONEY, THE YOUNG GASCON AND I WILL COVER OUR MILITARY NEEDS WITH NO PROBLEM.
I'D NEVER LET MYSELF DO SO, MY FRIEND! TAKE BACK THIS RING. IT MUST BE DEAR TO YOU, I UNDERSTAND.
ME, TAKE THAT RING BACK?
AFTER IT PASSED THROUGH A SCOUNDREL'S HANDS?! NEVER!
THAT RING IS SULLIED, D'ARTAGNAN. SELL IT, I SAID!
"MY FRIEND, PERFORM YOUR DUTY. TAKE WHAT THE BEARER OF THIS LETTER GIVES YOU SO THAT YOU CAN CARRY OUT THE CAMPAIGN AS A HANDSOME AND WORTHY GENTLEMAN. THINK OF ME, ME WHO TENDERLY KISSES YOUR DARK EYES, MME DE CHEVREUSE."

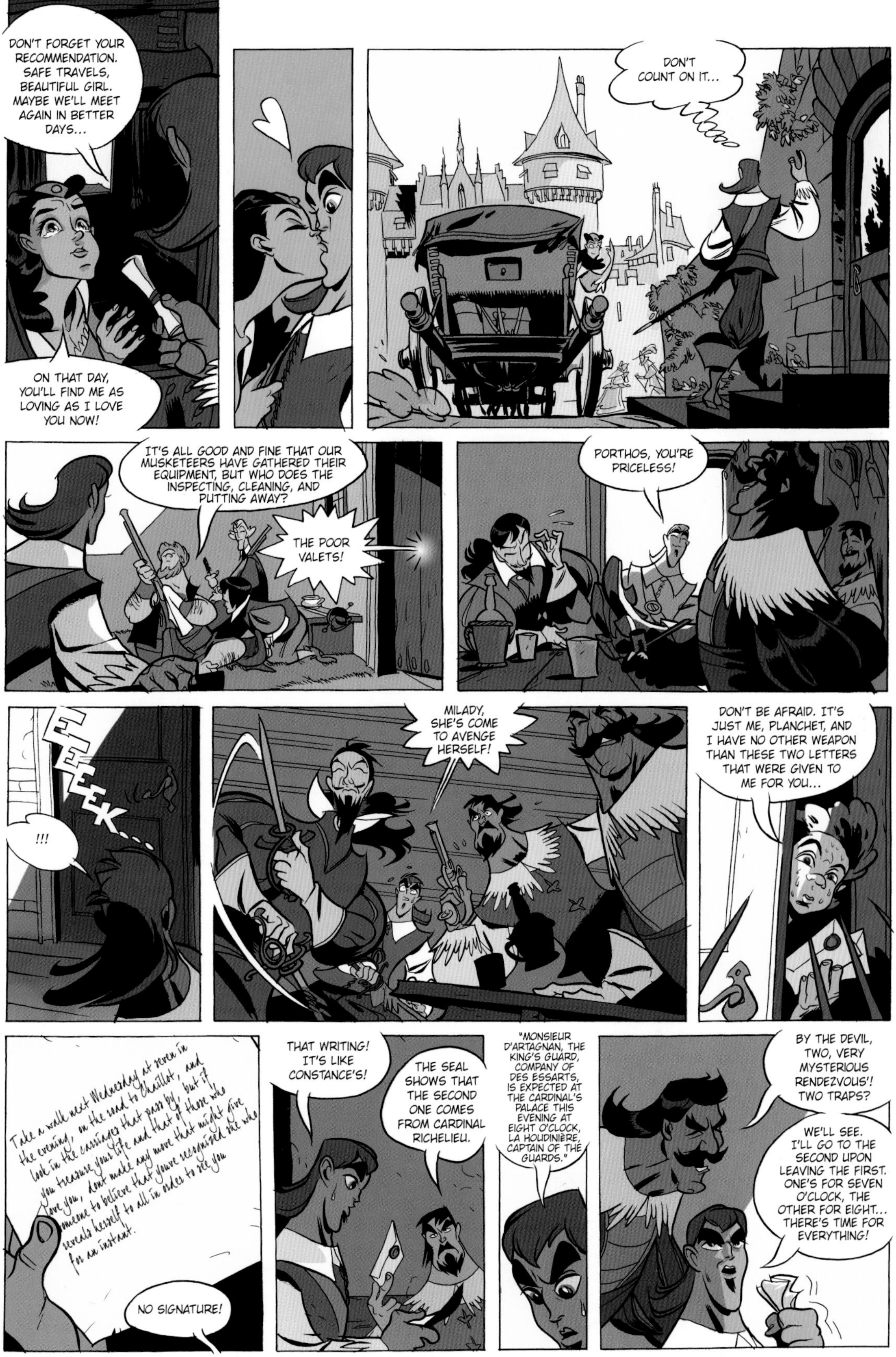
DON'T FORGET YOUR RECOMMENDATION. SAFE TRAVELS, BEAUTIFUL GIRL. MAYBE WE'LL MEET AGAIN IN BETTER DAYS...
ON THAT DAY, YOU'LL FIND ME AS LOVING AS I LOVE YOU NOW!
DON'T COUNT ON IT...
IT'S ALL GOOD AND FINE THAT OUR MUSKETEERS HAVE GATHERED THEIR EQUIPMENT, BUT WHO DOES THE INSPECTING, CLEANING, AND PUTTING AWAY?
THE POOR VALETS!
PORTHOS, YOU'RE PRICELESS!
EEEEEK...
!!!
MILADY, SHE'S COME TO AVENGE HERSELF!
DON'T BE AFRAID. IT'S JUST ME, PLANCHET, AND I HAVE NO OTHER WEAPON THAN THESE TWO LETTERS THAT WERE GIVEN TO ME FOR YOU...
Take a walk next Wednesday at seven in the evening, on the road to Chaillot, and look in the carriages that pass by, but if you treasure your life and that of those who love you, dont make any move that might give someone to believe that youve recognized she who reveals herself to all in order to see you for an instant.
NO SIGNATURE!
THAT WRITING! IT'S LIKE CONSTANCE'S!
THE SEAL SHOWS THAT THE SECOND ONE COMES FROM CARDINAL RICHELIEU.
"MONSIEUR D'ARTAGNAN, THE KING'S GUARD, COMPANY OF DES ESSARTS, IS EXPECTED AT THE CARDINAL'S PALACE THIS EVENING AT EIGHT O'CLOCK, LA HOUDINIÈRE, CAPTAIN OF THE GUARDS."
BY THE DEVIL, TWO, VERY MYSTERIOUS RENDEZVOUS'! TWO TRAPS?
WE'LL SEE. I'LL GO TO THE SECOND UPON LEAVING THE FIRST. ONE'S FOR SEVEN O'CLOCK, THE OTHER FOR EIGHT... THERE'S TIME FOR EVERYTHING!

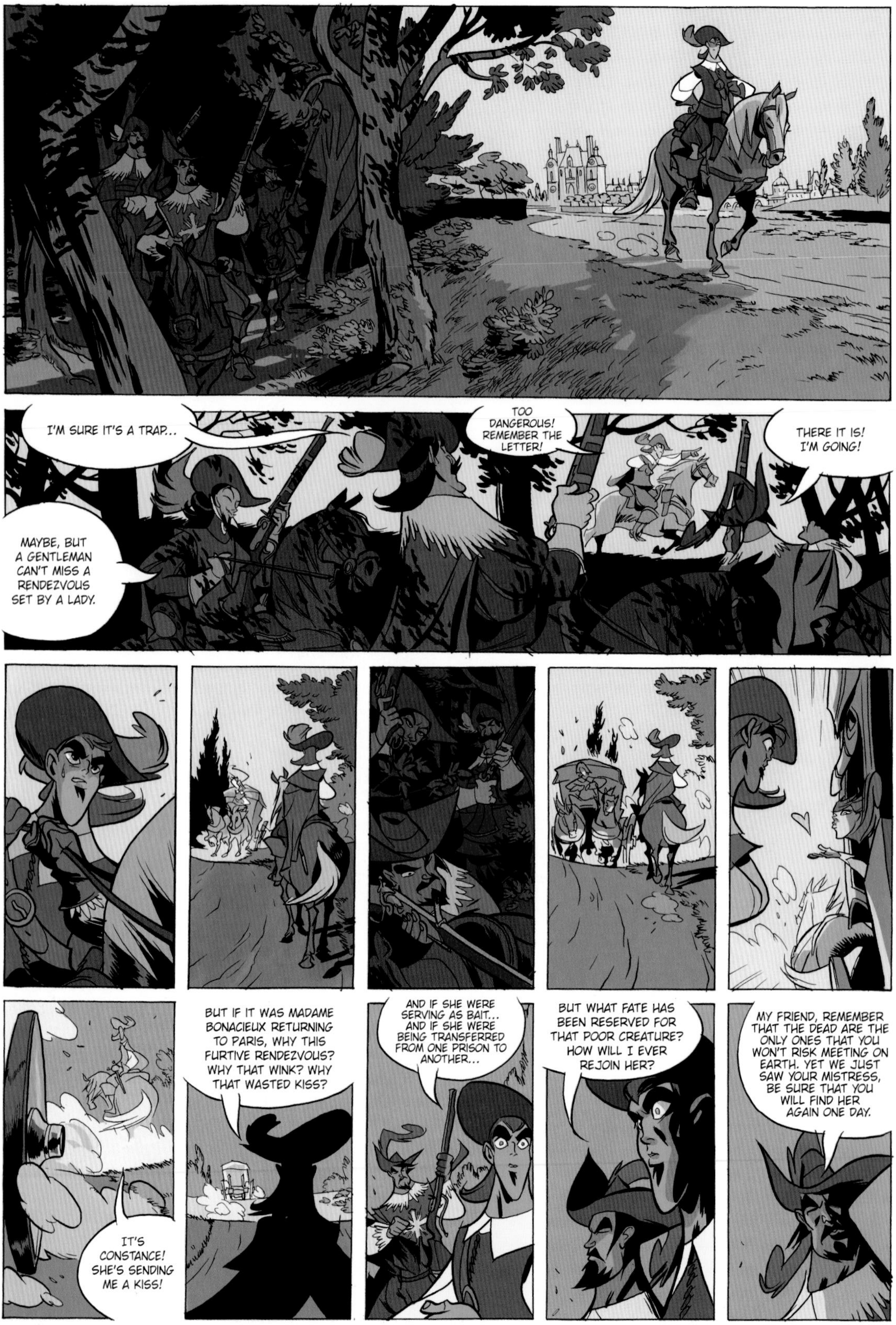
I'M SURE IT'S A TRAP...
MAYBE, BUT A GENTLEMAN CAN'T MISS A RENDEZVOUS SET BY A LADY.
TOO DANGEROUS! REMEMBER THE LETTER!
THERE IT IS! I'M GOING!
IT'S CONSTANCE! SHE'S SENDING ME A KISS!
BUT IF IT WAS MADAME BONACIEUX RETURNING TO PARIS, WHY THIS FURTIVE RENDEZVOUS? WHY THAT WINK? WHY THAT WASTED KISS?
AND IF SHE WERE SERVING AS BAIT... AND IF SHE WERE BEING TRANSFERRED FROM ONE PRISON TO ANOTHER...
BUT WHAT FATE HAS BEEN RESERVED FOR THAT POOR CREATURE? HOW WILL I EVER REJOIN HER?
MY FRIEND, REMEMBER THAT THE DEAD ARE THE ONLY ONES THAT YOU WON'T RISK MEETING ON EARTH. YET WE JUST SAW YOUR MISTRESS, BE SURE THAT YOU WILL FIND HER AGAIN ONE DAY.

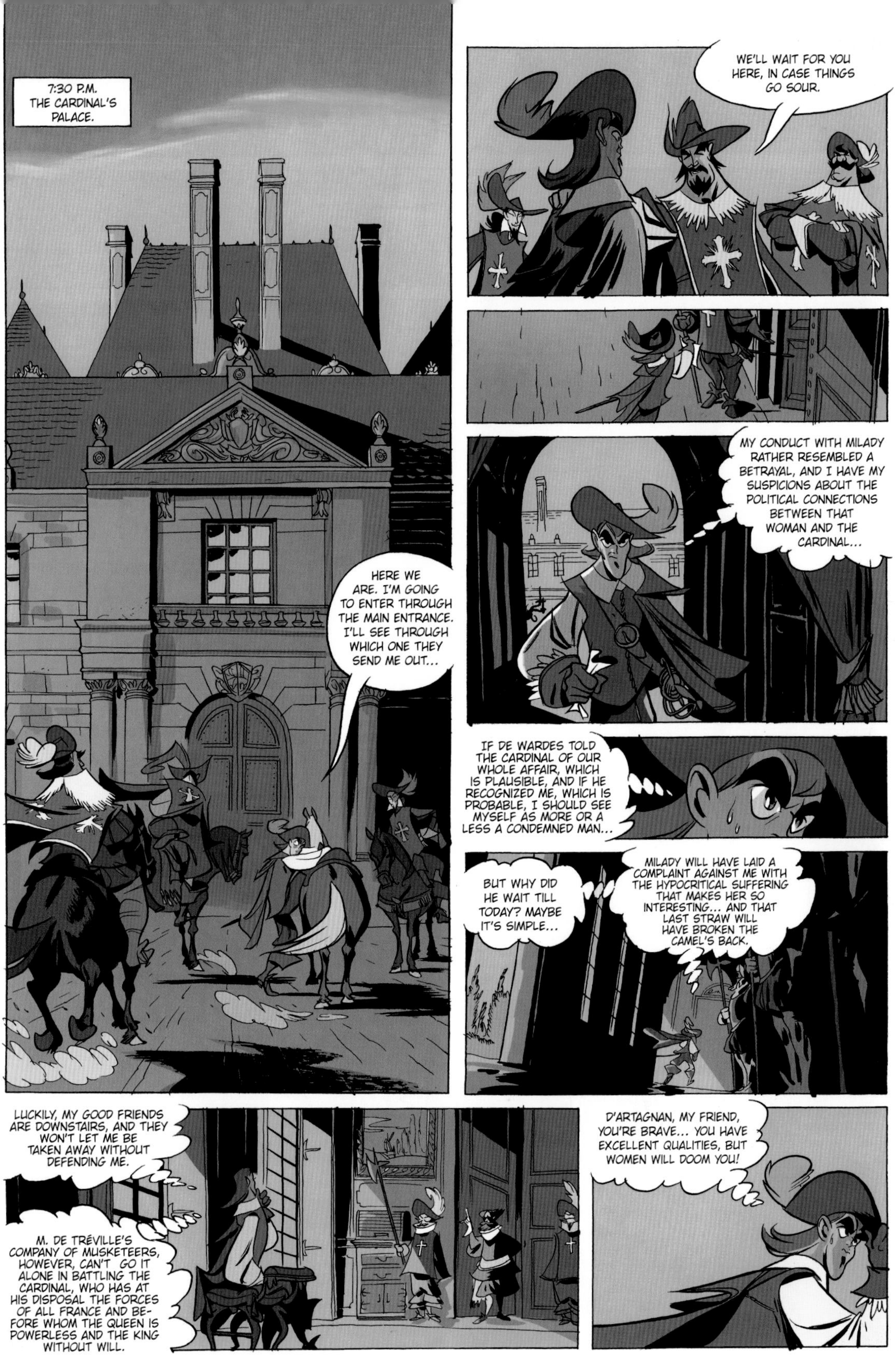

7:30 P.M. THE CARDINAL'S PALACE.
HERE WE ARE. I'M GOING TO ENTER THROUGH THE MAIN ENTRANCE. I'LL SEE THROUGH WHICH ONE THEY SEND ME OUT...
WE'LL WAIT FOR YOU HERE, IN CASE THINGS GO SOUR.
MY CONDUCT WITH MILADY RATHER RESEMBLED A BETRAYAL, AND I HAVE MY SUSPICIONS ABOUT THE POLITICAL CONNECTIONS BETWEEN THAT WOMAN AND THE CARDINAL...
IF DE WARDES TOLD THE CARDINAL OF OUR WHOLE AFFAIR, WHICH IS PLAUSIBLE, AND IF HE RECOGNIZED ME, WHICH IS PROBABLE, I SHOULD SEE MYSELF AS MORE OR A LESS A CONDEMNED MAN...
BUT WHY DID HE WAIT TILL TODAY? MAYBE IT'S SIMPLE...
MILADY WILL HAVE LAID A COMPLAINT AGAINST ME WITH THE HYPOCRITICAL SUFFERING THAT MAKES HER SO INTERESTING... AND THAT LAST STRAW WILL HAVE BROKEN THE CAMEL'S BACK.
LUCKILY, MY GOOD FRIENDS ARE DOWNSTAIRS, AND THEY WON'T LET ME BE TAKEN AWAY WITHOUT DEFENDING ME.
M. DE TRÉVILLE'S COMPANY OF MUSKETEERS, HOWEVER, CAN'T GO IT ALONE IN BATTLING THE CARDINAL, WHO HAS AT HIS DISPOSAL THE FORCES OF ALL FRANCE AND BEFORE WHOM THE QUEEN IS POWERLESS AND THE KING WITHOUT WILL.
D'ARTAGNAN, MY FRIEND, YOU'RE BRAVE... YOU HAVE EXCELLENT QUALITIES, BUT WOMEN WILL DOOM YOU!

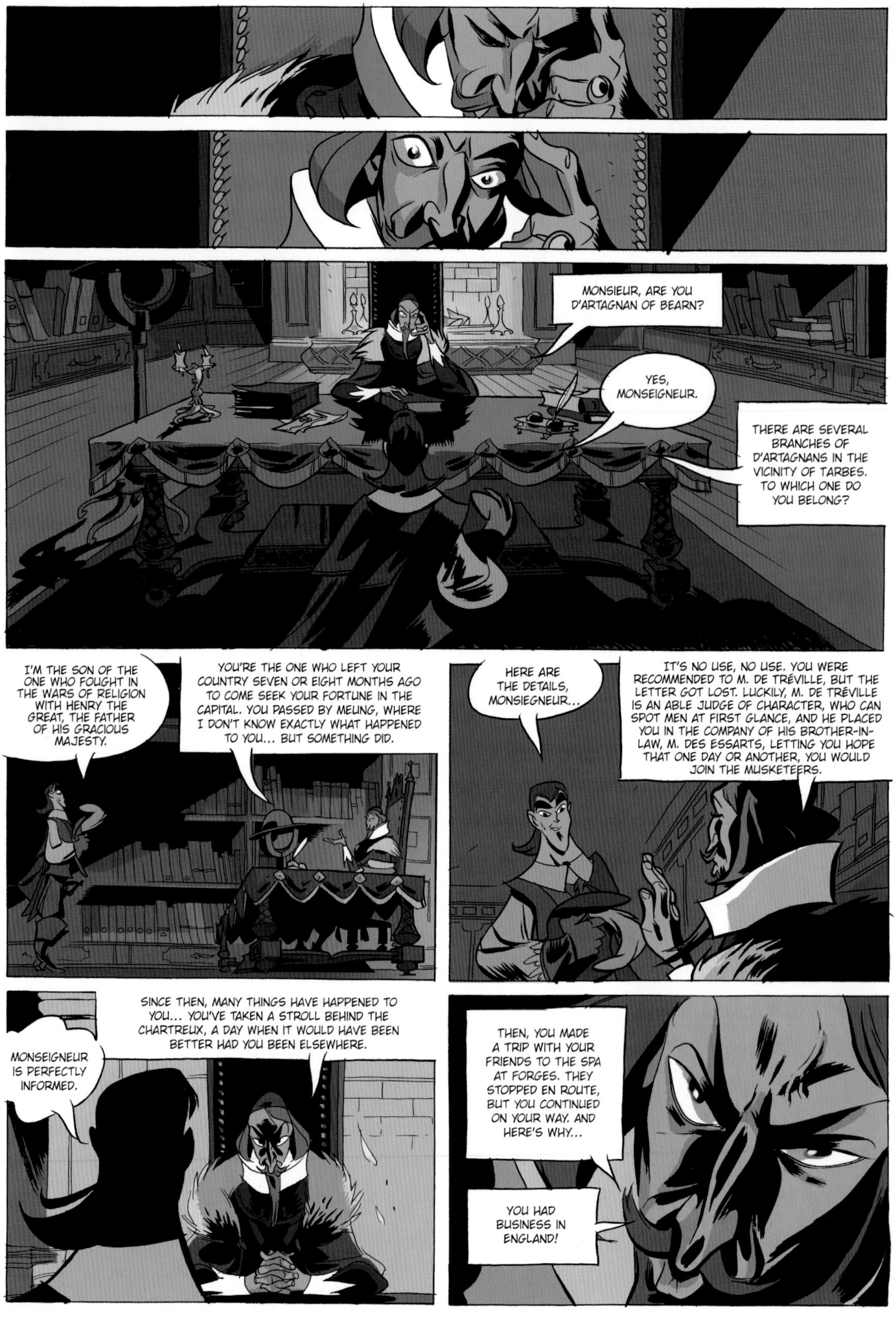
MONSIEUR, ARE YOU D'ARTAGNAN OF BEARN?
YES, MONSEIGNEUR.
THERE ARE SEVERAL BRANCHES OF D'ARTAGNANS IN THE VICINITY OF TARBES. TO WHICH ONE DO YOU BELONG?
I'M THE SON OF THE ONE WHO FOUGHT IN THE WARS OF RELIGION WITH HENRY THE GREAT, THE FATHER OF HIS GRACIOUS MAJESTY.
YOU'RE THE ONE WHO LEFT YOUR COUNTRY SEVEN OR EIGHT MONTHS AGO TO COME SEEK YOUR FORTUNE IN THE CAPITAL. YOU PASSED BY MEUNG, WHERE I DON'T KNOW EXACTLY WHAT HAPPENED TO YOU… BUT SOMETHING DID.
HERE ARE THE DETAILS, MONSIEGNEUR…
IT'S NO USE, NO USE. YOU WERE RECOMMENDED TO M. DE TRÉVILLE, BUT THE LETTER GOT LOST. LUCKILY, M. DE TRÉVILLE IS AN ABLE JUDGE OF CHARACTER, WHO CAN SPOT MEN AT FIRST GLANCE, AND HE PLACED YOU IN THE COMPANY OF HIS BROTHER-IN-LAW, M. DES ESSARTS, LETTING YOU HOPE THAT ONE DAY OR ANOTHER, YOU WOULD JOIN THE MUSKETEERS.
SINCE THEN, MANY THINGS HAVE HAPPENED TO YOU… YOU'VE TAKEN A STROLL BEHIND THE CHARTREUX, A DAY WHEN IT WOULD HAVE BEEN BETTER HAD YOU BEEN ELSEWHERE.
MONSEIGNEUR IS PERFECTLY INFORMED.
THEN, YOU MADE A TRIP WITH YOUR FRIENDS TO THE SPA AT FORGES. THEY STOPPED EN ROUTE, BUT YOU CONTINUED ON YOUR WAY. AND HERE'S WHY…
YOU HAD BUSINESS IN ENGLAND!

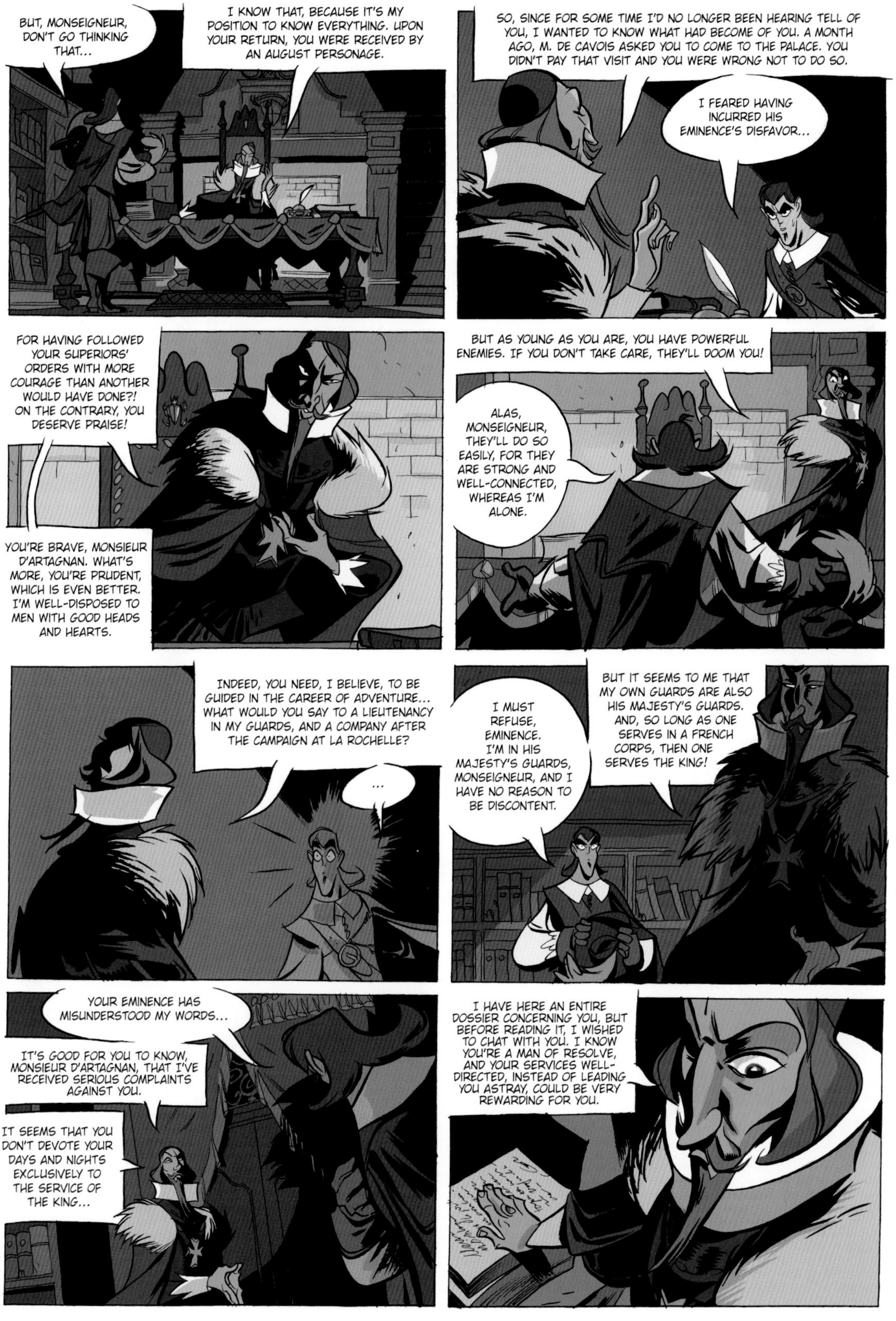
BUT, MONSEIGNEUR, DON'T GO THINKING THAT...
I KNOW THAT, BECAUSE IT'S MY POSITION TO KNOW EVERYTHING. UPON YOUR RETURN, YOU WERE RECEIVED BY AN AUGUST PERSONAGE.
SO, SINCE FOR SOME TIME I'D NO LONGER BEEN HEARING TELL OF YOU, I WANTED TO KNOW WHAT HAD BECOME OF YOU. A MONTH AGO, M. DE CAVOIS ASKED YOU TO COME TO THE PALACE. YOU DIDN'T PAY THAT VISIT AND YOU WERE WRONG NOT TO DO SO.
I FEARED HAVING INCURRED HIS EMINENCE'S DISFAVOR...
FOR HAVING FOLLOWED YOUR SUPERIORS' ORDERS WITH MORE COURAGE THAN ANOTHER WOULD HAVE DONE?! ON THE CONTRARY, YOU DESERVE PRAISE!
YOU'RE BRAVE, MONSIEUR D'ARTAGNAN. WHAT'S MORE, YOU'RE PRUDENT, WHICH IS EVEN BETTER. I'M WELL-DISPOSED TO MEN WITH GOOD HEADS AND HEARTS.
BUT AS YOUNG AS YOU ARE, YOU HAVE POWERFUL ENEMIES. IF YOU DON'T TAKE CARE, THEY'LL DOOM YOU!
ALAS, MONSEIGNEUR, THEY'LL DO SO EASILY, FOR THEY ARE STRONG AND WELL-CONNECTED, WHEREAS I'M ALONE.
INDEED, YOU NEED, I BELIEVE, TO BE GUIDED IN THE CAREER OF ADVENTURE... WHAT WOULD YOU SAY TO A LIEUTENANCY IN MY GUARDS, AND A COMPANY AFTER THE CAMPAIGN AT LA ROCHELLE?
...
I MUST REFUSE, EMINENCE. I'M IN HIS MAJESTY'S GUARDS, MONSEIGNEUR, AND I HAVE NO REASON TO BE DISCONTENT.
BUT IT SEEMS TO ME THAT MY OWN GUARDS ARE ALSO HIS MAJESTY'S GUARDS. AND, SO LONG AS ONE SERVES IN A FRENCH CORPS, THEN ONE SERVES THE KING!
YOUR EMINENCE HAS MISUNDERSTOOD MY WORDS...
IT'S GOOD FOR YOU TO KNOW, MONSIEUR D'ARTAGNAN, THAT I'VE RECEIVED SERIOUS COMPLAINTS AGAINST YOU.
IT SEEMS THAT YOU DON'T DEVOTE YOUR DAYS AND NIGHTS EXCLUSIVELY TO THE SERVICE OF THE KING...
I HAVE HERE AN ENTIRE DOSSIER CONCERNING YOU, BUT BEFORE READING IT, I WISHED TO CHAT WITH YOU. I KNOW YOU'RE A MAN OF RESOLVE, AND YOUR SERVICES WELL-DIRECTED, INSTEAD OF LEADING YOU ASTRAY, COULD BE VERY REWARDING FOR YOU.

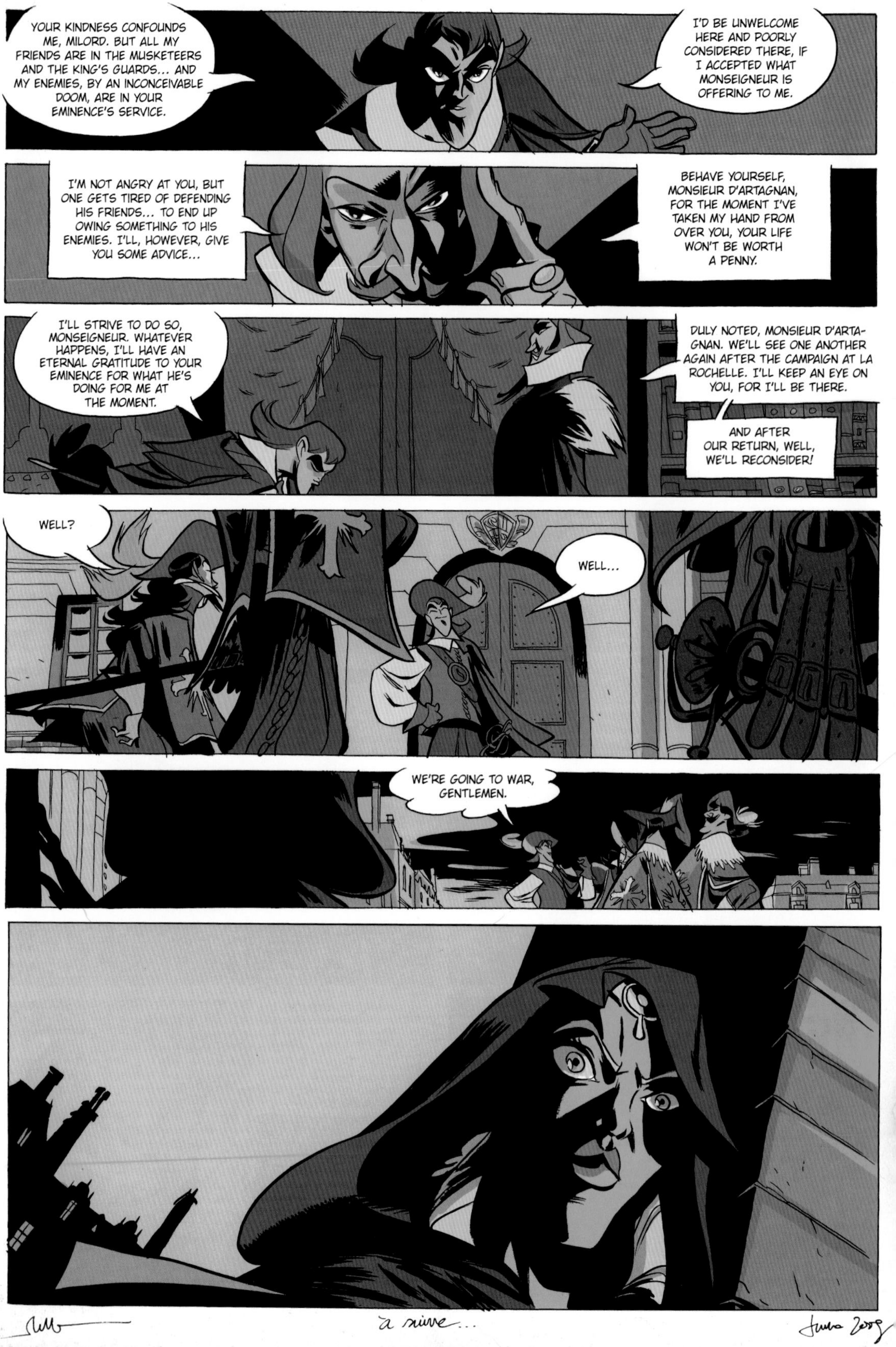
YOUR KINDNESS CONFOUNDS ME, MILORD. BUT ALL MY FRIENDS ARE IN THE MUSKETEERS AND THE KING'S GUARDS... AND MY ENEMIES, BY AN INCONCEIVABLE DOOM, ARE IN YOUR EMINENCE'S SERVICE.
I'D BE UNWELCOME HERE AND POORLY CONSIDERED THERE, IF I ACCEPTED WHAT MONSEIGNEUR IS OFFERING TO ME.
I'M NOT ANGRY AT YOU, BUT ONE GETS TIRED OF DEFENDING HIS FRIENDS... TO END UP OWING SOMETHING TO HIS ENEMIES. I'LL, HOWEVER, GIVE YOU SOME ADVICE...
BEHAVE YOURSELF, MONSIEUR D'ARTAGNAN, FOR THE MOMENT I'VE TAKEN MY HAND FROM OVER YOU, YOUR LIFE WON'T BE WORTH A PENNY.
I'LL STRIVE TO DO SO, MONSEIGNEUR. WHATEVER HAPPENS, I'LL HAVE AN ETERNAL GRATITUDE TO YOUR EMINENCE FOR WHAT HE'S DOING FOR ME AT THE MOMENT.
DULY NOTED, MONSIEUR D'ARTAGNAN. WE'LL SEE ONE ANOTHER AGAIN AFTER THE CAMPAIGN AT LA ROCHELLE. I'LL KEEP AN EYE ON YOU, FOR I'LL BE THERE.
AND AFTER OUR RETURN, WELL, WE'LL RECONSIDER!
WELL?
WELL...
WE'RE GOING TO WAR, GENTLEMEN.
à suivre...

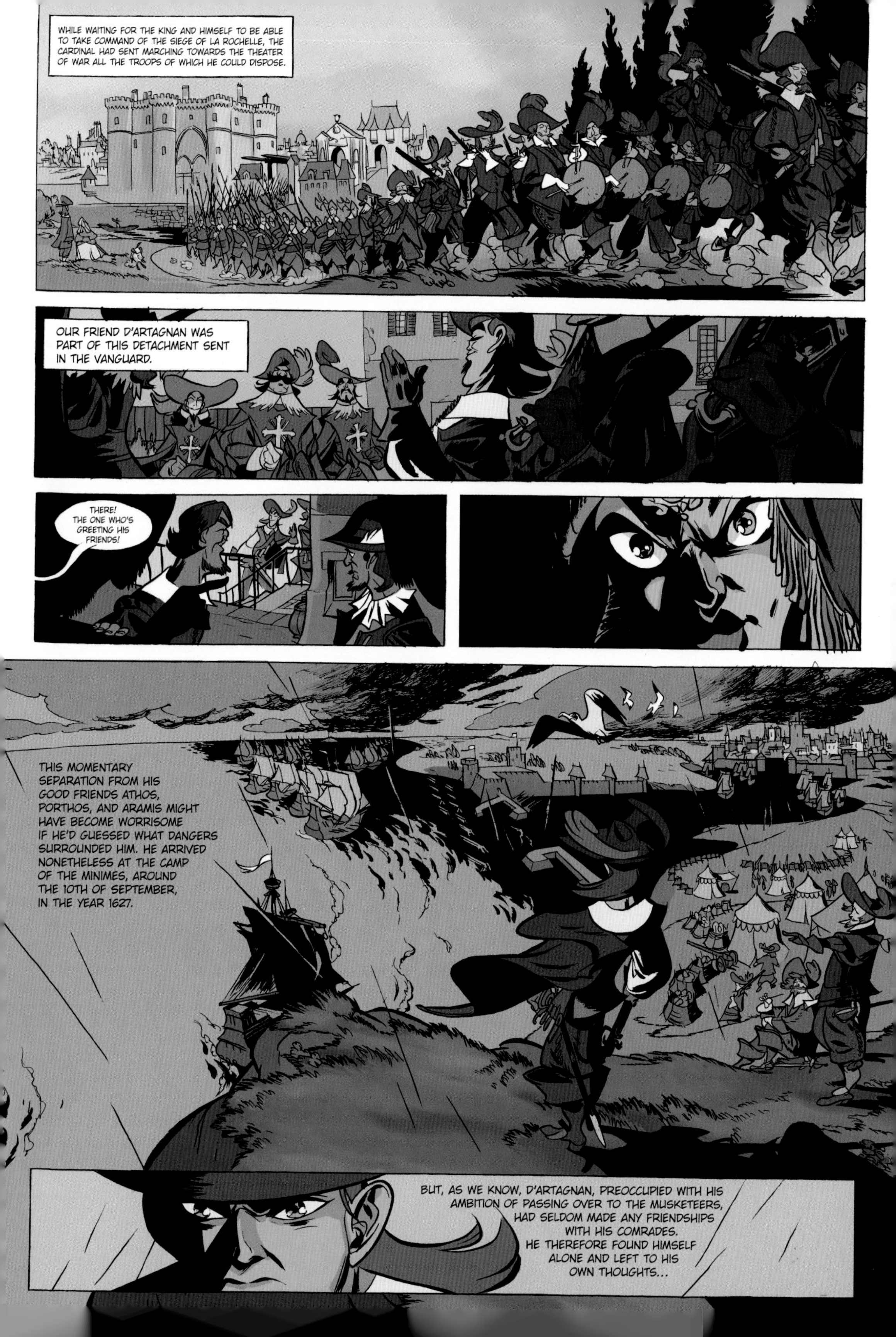
WHILE WAITING FOR THE KING AND HIMSELF TO BE ABLE TO TAKE COMMAND OF THE SIEGE OF LA ROCHELLE, THE CARDINAL HAD SENT MARCHING TOWARDS THE THEATER OF WAR ALL THE TROOPS OF WHICH HE COULD DISPOSE.
OUR FRIEND D'ARTAGNAN WAS PART OF THIS DETACHMENT SENT IN THE VANGUARD.
THERE! THE ONE WHO'S GREETING HIS FRIENDS!
THIS MOMENTARY SEPARATION FROM HIS GOOD FRIENDS ATHOS, PORTHOS, AND ARAMIS MIGHT HAVE BECOME WORRISOME IF HE'D GUESSED WHAT DANGERS SURROUNDED HIM. HE ARRIVED NONETHELESS AT THE CAMP OF THE MINIMES, AROUND THE 10TH OF SEPTEMBER, IN THE YEAR 1627.
BUT, AS WE KNOW, D'ARTAGNAN, PREOCCUPIED WITH HIS AMBITION OF PASSING OVER TO THE MUSKETEERS, HAD SELDOM MADE ANY FRIENDSHIPS WITH HIS COMRADES.
HE THEREFORE FOUND HIMSELF ALONE AND LEFT TO HIS OWN THOUGHTS...

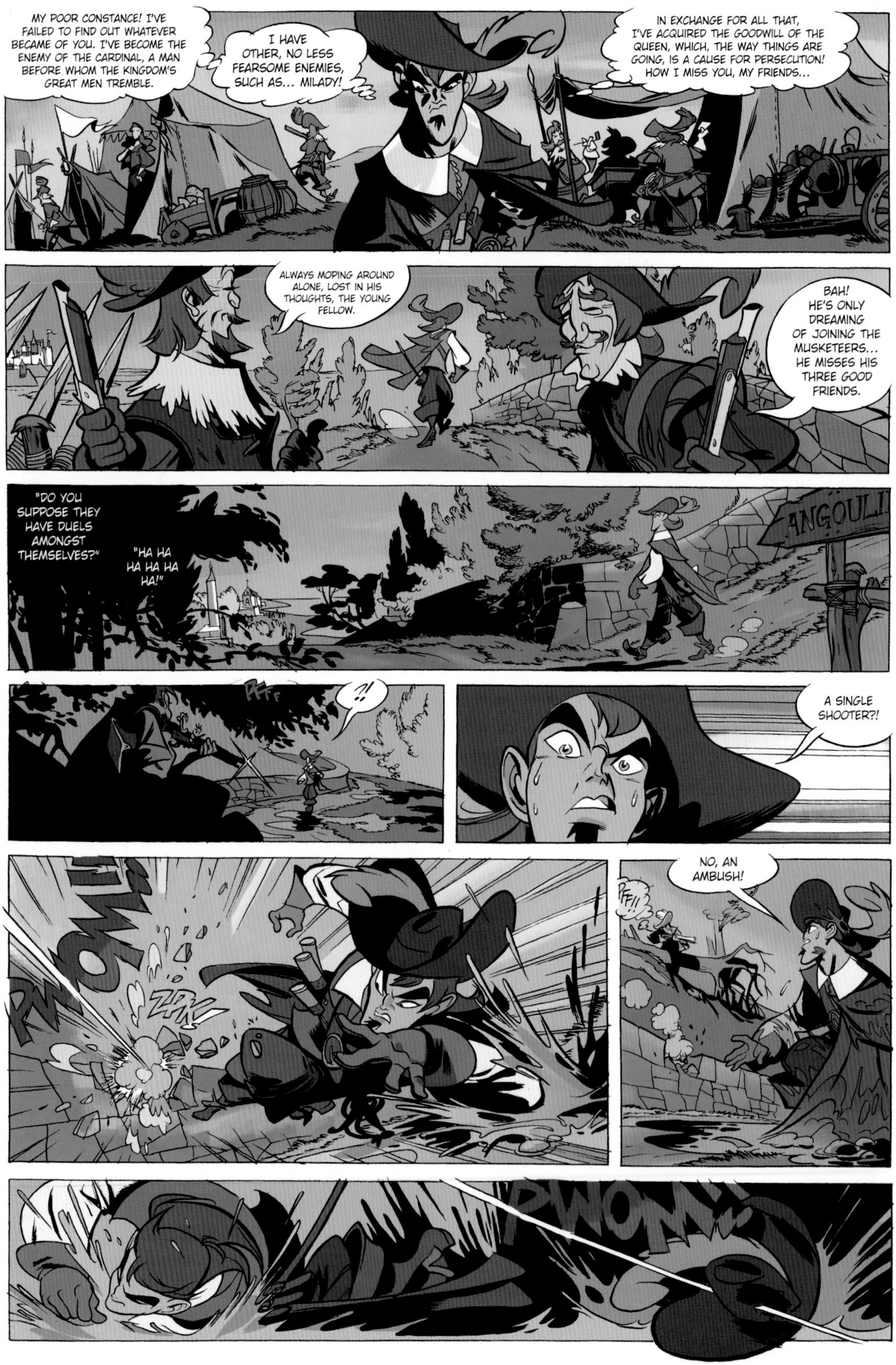
MY POOR CONSTANCE! I'VE FAILED TO FIND OUT WHATEVER BECAME OF YOU. I'VE BECOME THE ENEMY OF THE CARDINAL, A MAN BEFORE WHOM THE KINGDOM'S GREAT MEN TREMBLE.
I HAVE OTHER, NO LESS FEARSOME ENEMIES, SUCH AS... MILADY!
IN EXCHANGE FOR ALL THAT, I'VE ACQUIRED THE GOODWILL OF THE QUEEN, WHICH, THE WAY THINGS ARE GOING, IS A CAUSE FOR PERSECUTION! HOW I MISS YOU, MY FRIENDS...
ALWAYS MOPING AROUND ALONE, LOST IN HIS THOUGHTS, THE YOUNG FELLOW.
BAH! HE'S ONLY DREAMING OF JOINING THE MUSKETEERS... HE MISSES HIS THREE GOOD FRIENDS.
"DO YOU SUPPOSE THEY HAVE DUELS AMONGST THEMSELVES?"
"HA HA HA HA HA HA!"
ANGOUL
PFFF
?!
A SINGLE SHOOTER?!
PWOM
ZPK
NO, AN AMBUSH!
PFF!!
PWOM

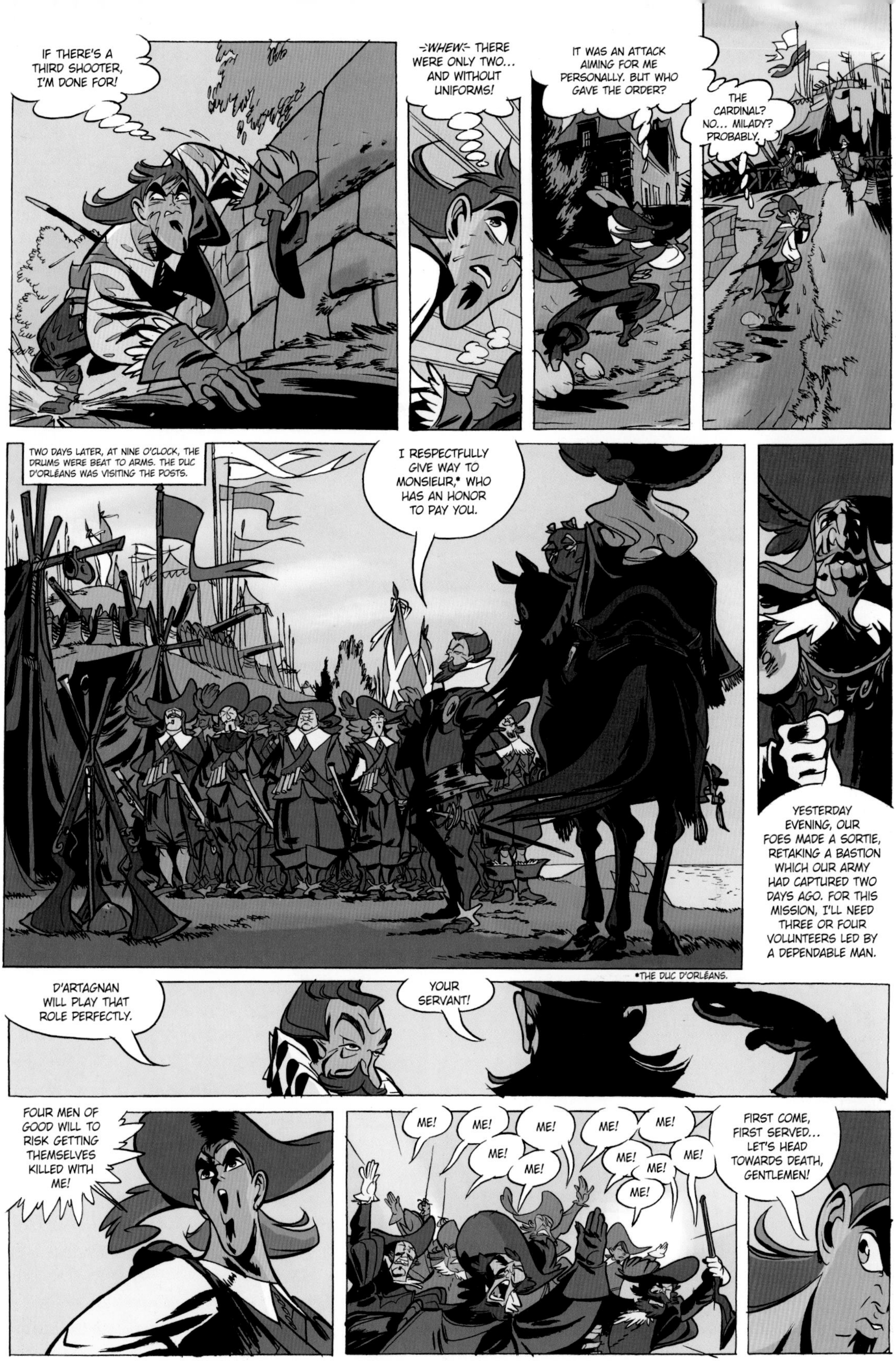

IF THERE'S A THIRD SHOOTER, I'M DONE FOR!
-WHEW- THERE WERE ONLY TWO... AND WITHOUT UNIFORMS!
IT WAS AN ATTACK AIMING FOR ME PERSONALLY. BUT WHO GAVE THE ORDER?
THE CARDINAL? NO... MILADY? PROBABLY.
TWO DAYS LATER, AT NINE O'CLOCK, THE DRUMS WERE BEAT TO ARMS. THE DUC D'ORLÉANS WAS VISITING THE POSTS.
I RESPECTFULLY GIVE WAY TO MONSIEUR,* WHO HAS AN HONOR TO PAY YOU.
YESTERDAY EVENING, OUR FOES MADE A SORTIE, RETAKING A BASTION WHICH OUR ARMY HAD CAPTURED TWO DAYS AGO. FOR THIS MISSION, I'LL NEED THREE OR FOUR VOLUNTEERS LED BY A DEPENDABLE MAN.
*THE DUC D'ORLÉANS.
D'ARTAGNAN WILL PLAY THAT ROLE PERFECTLY.
YOUR SERVANT!
FOUR MEN OF GOOD WILL TO RISK GETTING THEMSELVES KILLED WITH ME!
ME!
ME!
ME!
ME!
ME!
ME!
ME!
ME!
ME!
ME!
ME!
FIRST COME, FIRST SERVED... LET'S HEAD TOWARDS DEATH, GENTLEMEN!

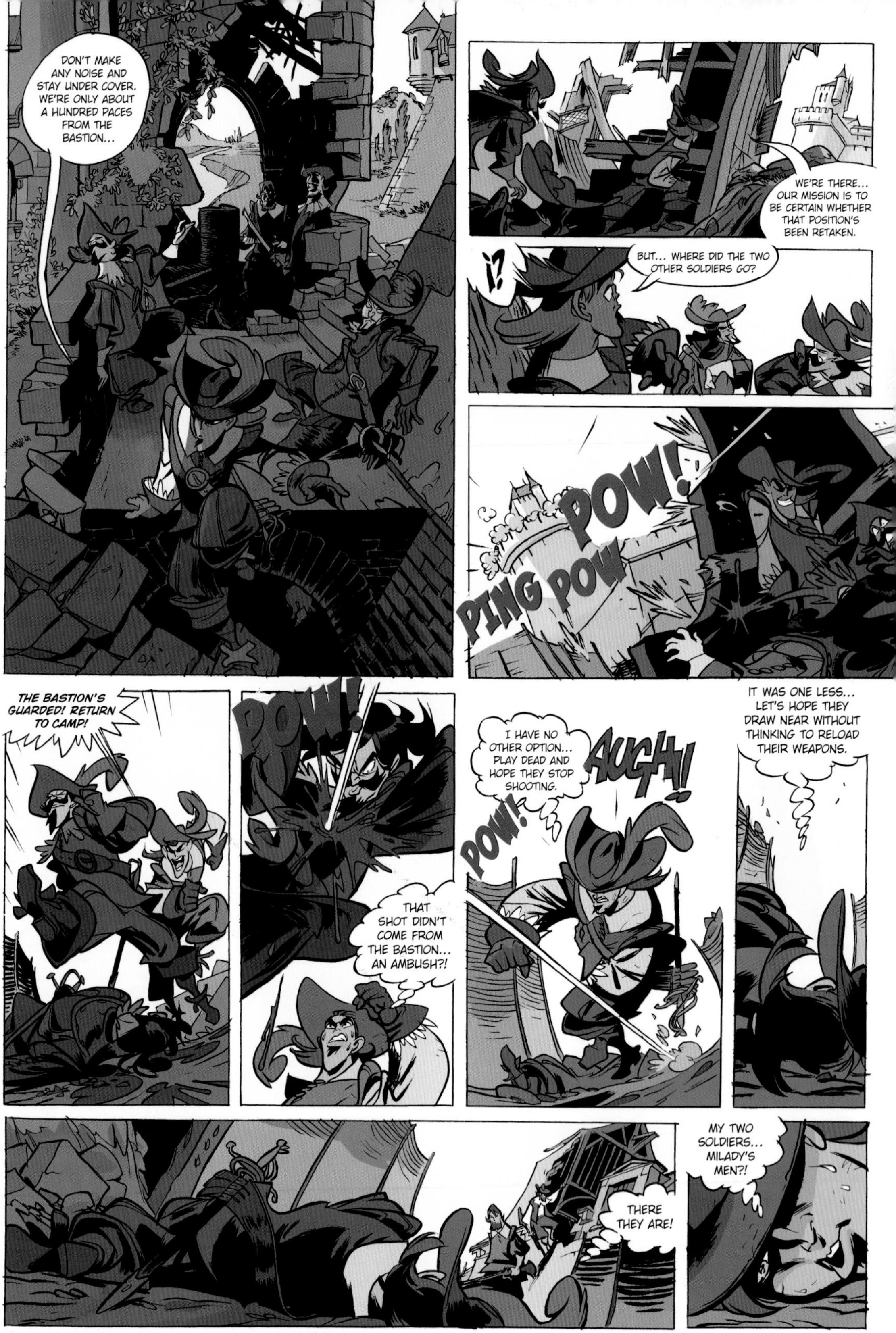
DON'T MAKE ANY NOISE AND STAY UNDER COVER. WE'RE ONLY ABOUT A HUNDRED PACES FROM THE BASTION...
WE'RE THERE... OUR MISSION IS TO BE CERTAIN WHETHER THAT POSITION'S BEEN RETAKEN.
¡?
BUT... WHERE DID THE TWO OTHER SOLDIERS GO?
POW!
PING POW
THE BASTION'S GUARDED! RETURN TO CAMP!
POW!
THAT SHOT DIDN'T COME FROM THE BASTION... AN AMBUSH?!
I HAVE NO OTHER OPTION... PLAY DEAD AND HOPE THEY STOP SHOOTING.
AUGH!
POW!
IT WAS ONE LESS... LET'S HOPE THEY DRAW NEAR WITHOUT THINKING TO RELOAD THEIR WEAPONS.
THERE THEY ARE!
MY TWO SOLDIERS... MILADY'S MEN?!

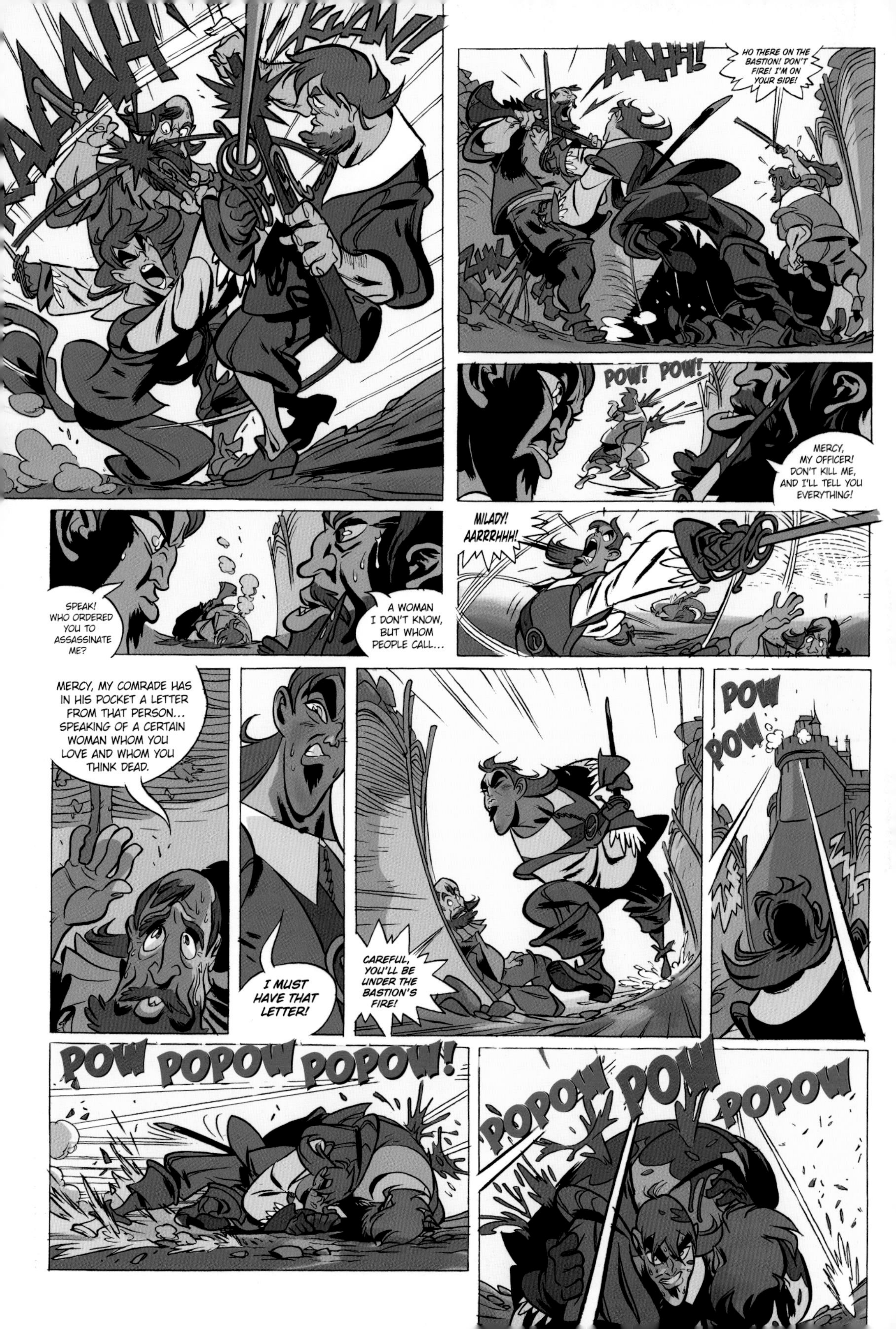
AAAAH!
KLANG!
AAHH!
HO THERE ON THE BASTION! DON'T FIRE! I'M ON YOUR SIDE!
POW! POW!
MERCY, MY OFFICER! DON'T KILL ME, AND I'LL TELL YOU EVERYTHING!
SPEAK! WHO ORDERED YOU TO ASSASSINATE ME?
A WOMAN I DON'T KNOW, BUT WHOM PEOPLE CALL...
MILADY! AARRRHHH!
MERCY, MY COMRADE HAS IN HIS POCKET A LETTER FROM THAT PERSON... SPEAKING OF A CERTAIN WOMAN WHOM YOU LOVE AND WHOM YOU THINK DEAD.
I MUST HAVE THAT LETTER!
CAREFUL, YOU'LL BE UNDER THE BASTION'S FIRE!
POW
POW
POW POPOW POPOW!
POPOW POW POPOW

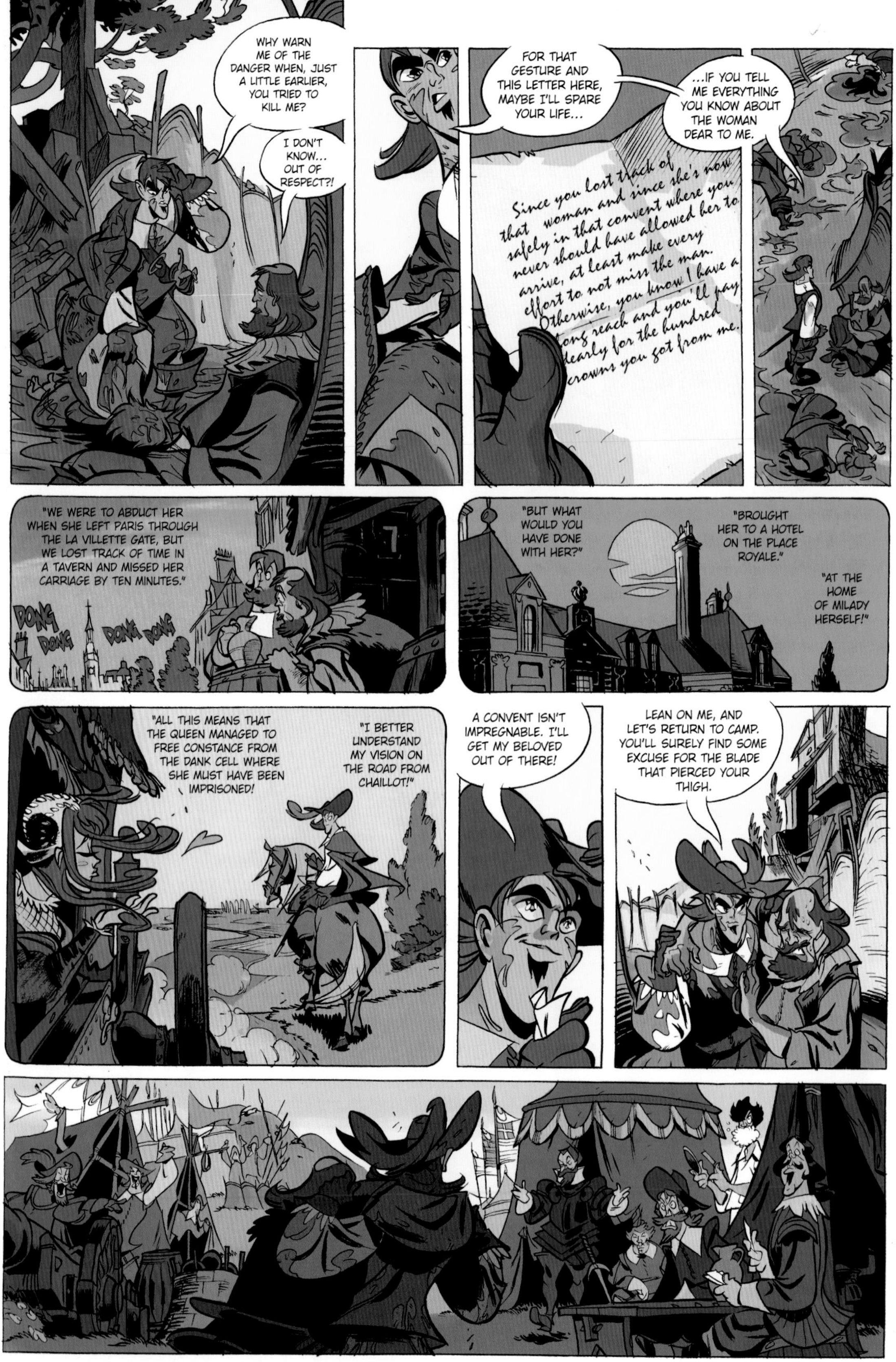
WHY WARN ME OF THE DANGER WHEN, JUST A LITTLE EARLIER, YOU TRIED TO KILL ME?
I DON'T KNOW... OUT OF RESPECT?!
FOR THAT GESTURE AND THIS LETTER HERE, MAYBE I'LL SPARE YOUR LIFE...
...IF YOU TELL ME EVERYTHING YOU KNOW ABOUT THE WOMAN DEAR TO ME.
Since you lost track of that woman and since she's now safely in that convent where you never should have allowed her to arrive, at least make every effort to not miss the man. Otherwise, you know I have a long reach and you'll pay dearly for the hundred crowns you got from me.
"WE WERE TO ABDUCT HER WHEN SHE LEFT PARIS THROUGH THE LA VILLETTE GATE, BUT WE LOST TRACK OF TIME IN A TAVERN AND MISSED HER CARRIAGE BY TEN MINUTES."
DONG DONG DONG DONG
"BUT WHAT WOULD YOU HAVE DONE WITH HER?"
"BROUGHT HER TO A HOTEL ON THE PLACE ROYALE."
"AT THE HOME OF MILADY HERSELF!"
"ALL THIS MEANS THAT THE QUEEN MANAGED TO FREE CONSTANCE FROM THE DANK CELL WHERE SHE MUST HAVE BEEN IMPRISONED!
"I BETTER UNDERSTAND MY VISION ON THE ROAD FROM CHAILLOT!"
A CONVENT ISN'T IMPREGNABLE. I'LL GET MY BELOVED OUT OF THERE!
LEAN ON ME, AND LET'S RETURN TO CAMP. YOU'LL SURELY FIND SOME EXCUSE FOR THE BLADE THAT PIERCED YOUR THIGH.

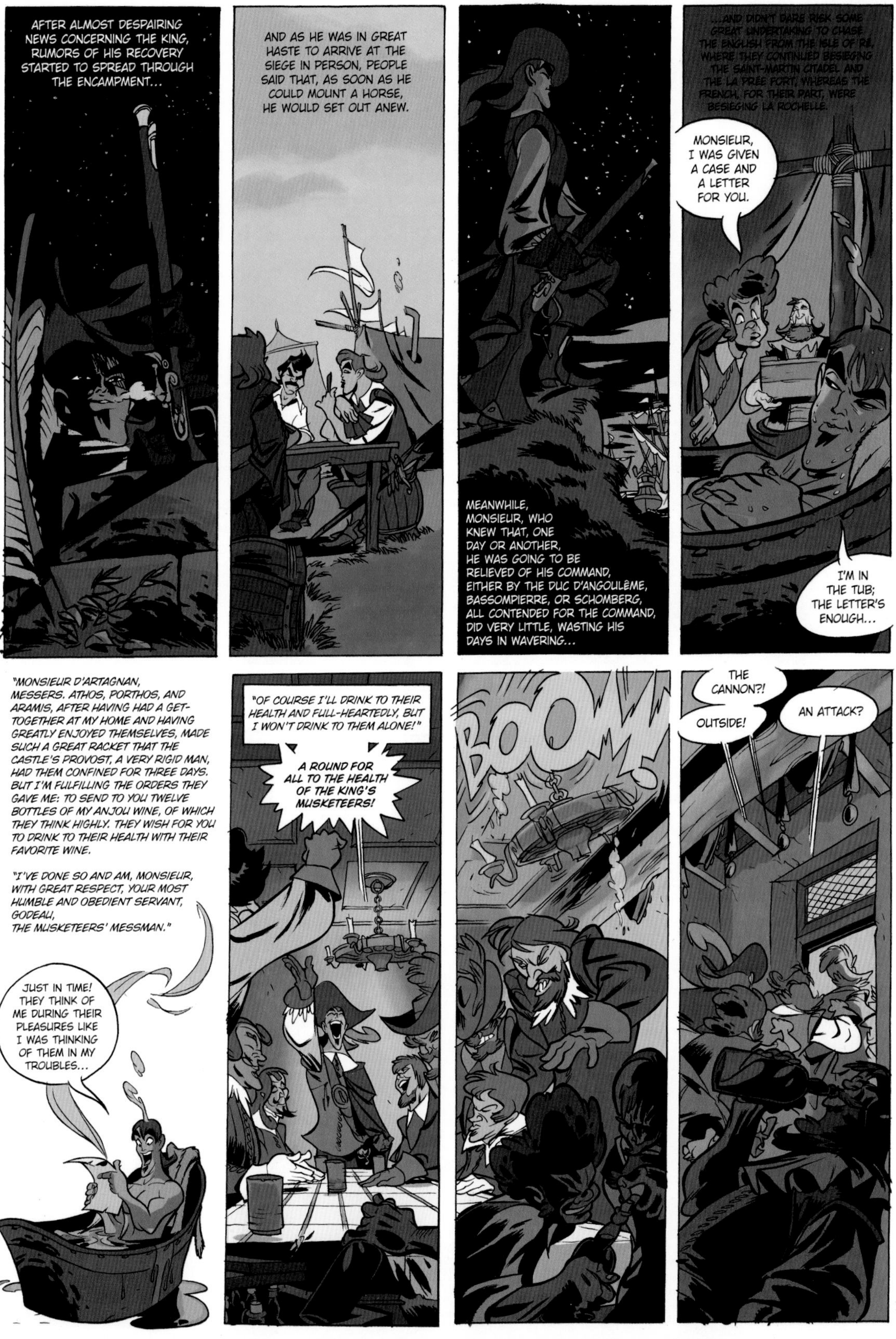
AFTER ALMOST DESPAIRING NEWS CONCERNING THE KING, RUMORS OF HIS RECOVERY STARTED TO SPREAD THROUGH THE ENCAMPMENT...
AND AS HE WAS IN GREAT HASTE TO ARRIVE AT THE SIEGE IN PERSON, PEOPLE SAID THAT, AS SOON AS HE COULD MOUNT A HORSE, HE WOULD SET OUT ANEW.
MEANWHILE, MONSIEUR, WHO KNEW THAT, ONE DAY OR ANOTHER, HE WAS GOING TO BE RELIEVED OF HIS COMMAND, EITHER BY THE DUC D'ANGOULÊME, BASSOMPIERRE, OR SCHOMBERG, ALL CONTENDED FOR THE COMMAND, DID VERY LITTLE, WASTING HIS DAYS IN WAVERING...
...AND DIDN'T DARE RISK SOME GREAT UNDERTAKING TO CHASE THE ENGLISH FROM THE ISLE OF RÉ, WHERE THEY CONTINUED BESIEGING THE SAINT-MARTIN CITADEL AND THE LA PREE FORT, WHEREAS THE FRENCH, FOR THEIR PART, WERE BESIEGING LA ROCHELLE.
MONSIEUR, I WAS GIVEN A CASE AND A LETTER FOR YOU.
I'M IN THE TUB; THE LETTER'S ENOUGH...
"MONSIEUR D'ARTAGNAN, MESSERS. ATHOS, PORTHOS, AND ARAMIS, AFTER HAVING HAD A GET-TOGETHER AT MY HOME AND HAVING GREATLY ENJOYED THEMSELVES, MADE SUCH A GREAT RACKET THAT THE CASTLE'S PROVOST, A VERY RIGID MAN, HAD THEM CONFINED FOR THREE DAYS. BUT I'M FULFILLING THE ORDERS THEY GAVE ME: TO SEND TO YOU TWELVE BOTTLES OF MY ANJOU WINE, OF WHICH THEY THINK HIGHLY. THEY WISH FOR YOU TO DRINK TO THEIR HEALTH WITH THEIR FAVORITE WINE.
"I'VE DONE SO AND AM, MONSIEUR, WITH GREAT RESPECT, YOUR MOST HUMBLE AND OBEDIENT SERVANT, GODEAU, THE MUSKETEERS' MESSMAN."
JUST IN TIME! THEY THINK OF ME DURING THEIR PLEASURES LIKE I WAS THINKING OF THEM IN MY TROUBLES...
"OF COURSE I'LL DRINK TO THEIR HEALTH AND FULL-HEARTEDLY, BUT I WON'T DRINK TO THEM ALONE!"
A ROUND FOR ALL TO THE HEALTH OF THE KING'S MUSKETEERS!
BOOM!
THE CANNON?!
OUTSIDE!
AN ATTACK?

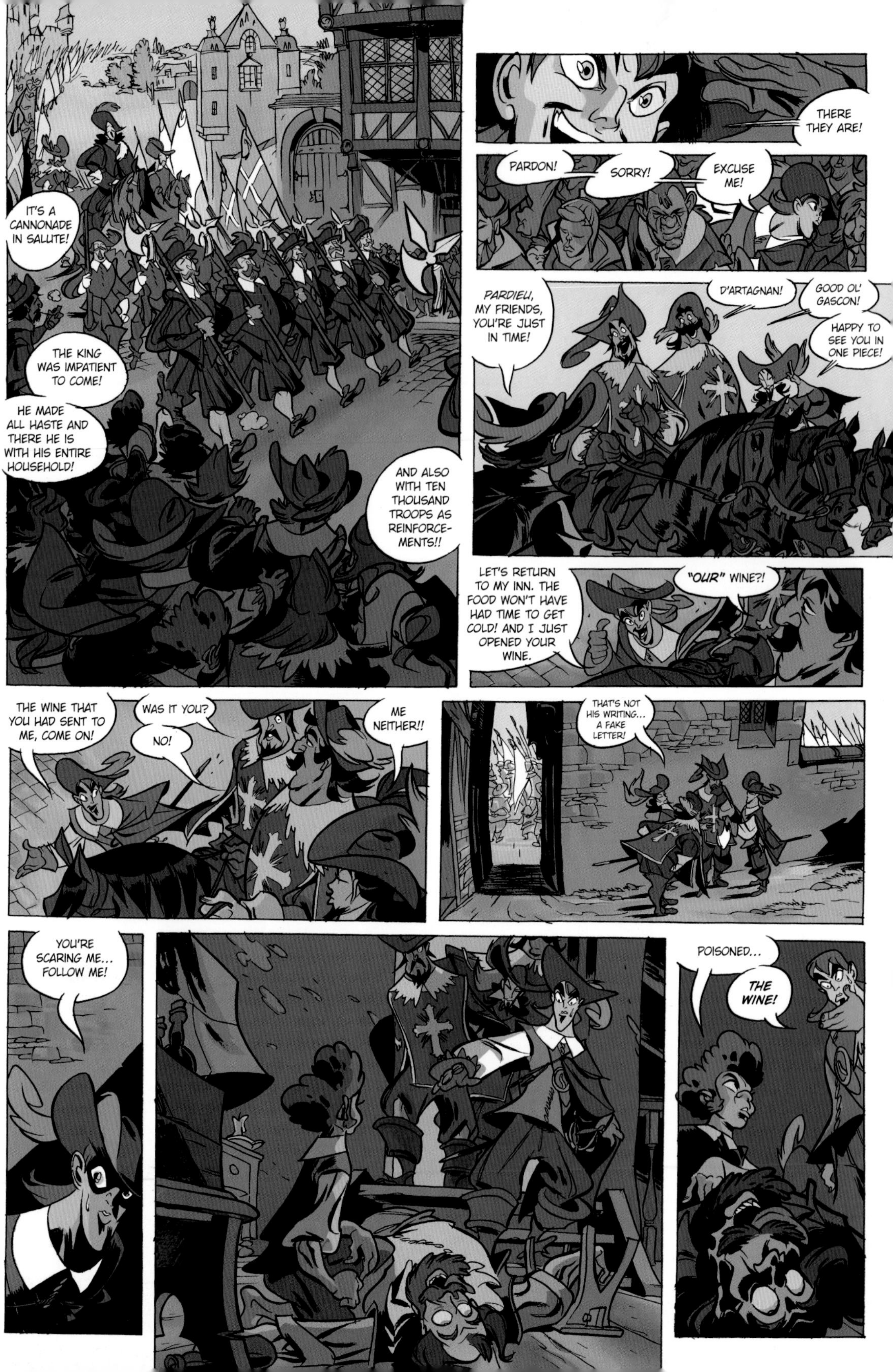
IT'S A CANNONADE IN SALUTE!
THE KING WAS IMPATIENT TO COME!
HE MADE ALL HASTE AND THERE HE IS WITH HIS ENTIRE HOUSEHOLD!
AND ALSO WITH TEN THOUSAND TROOPS AS REINFORCEMENTS!!
THERE THEY ARE!
PARDON!
SORRY!
EXCUSE ME!
PARDIEU, MY FRIENDS, YOU'RE JUST IN TIME!
D'ARTAGNAN!
GOOD OL' GASCON!
HAPPY TO SEE YOU IN ONE PIECE!
LET'S RETURN TO MY INN. THE FOOD WON'T HAVE HAD TIME TO GET COLD! AND I JUST OPENED YOUR WINE.
"OUR" WINE?!
THE WINE THAT YOU HAD SENT TO ME, COME ON!
WAS IT YOU?
NO!
ME NEITHER!!
THAT'S NOT HIS WRITING... A FAKE LETTER!
YOU'RE SCARING ME... FOLLOW ME!
POISONED...
THE WINE!

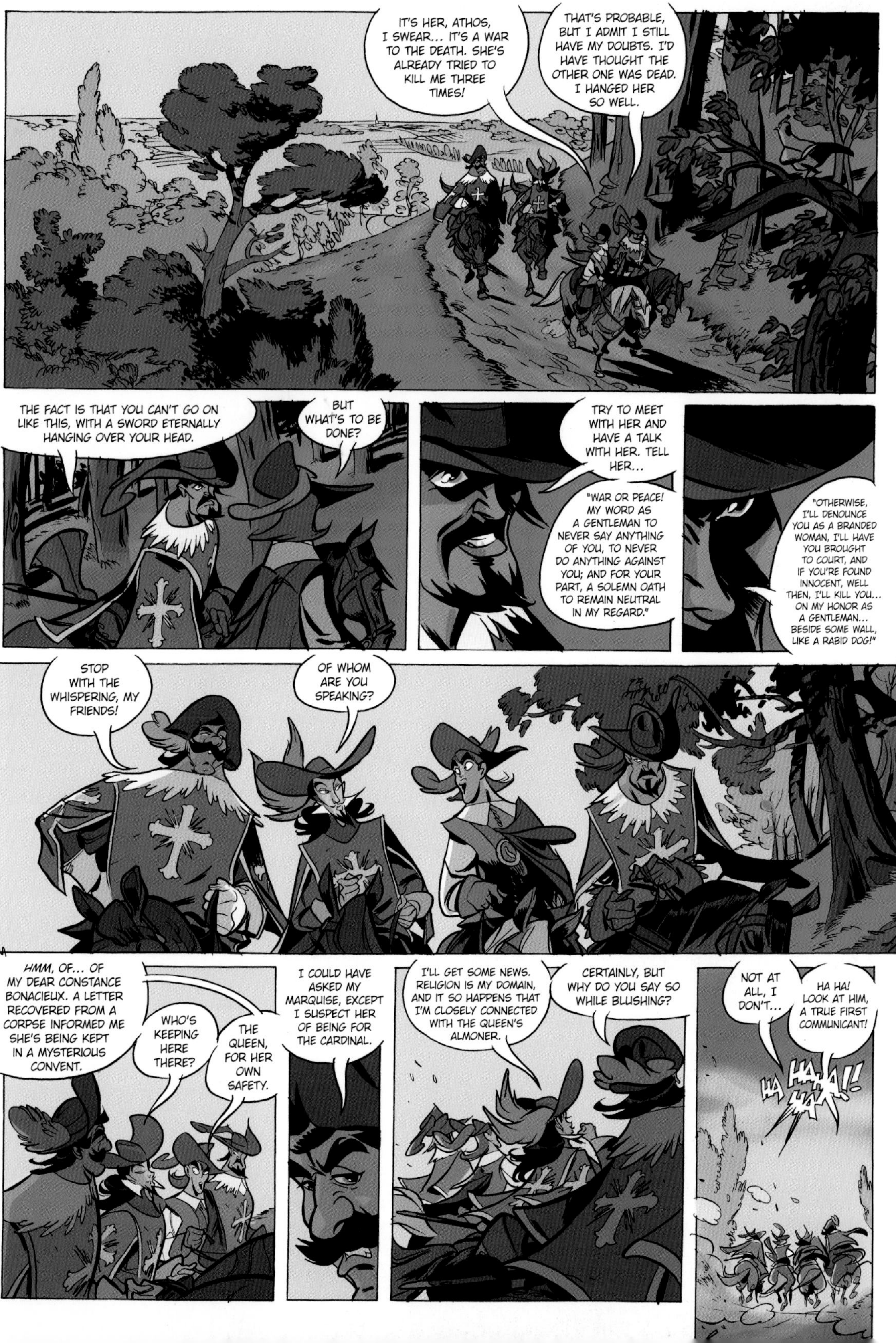
IT'S HER, ATHOS, I SWEAR... IT'S A WAR TO THE DEATH. SHE'S ALREADY TRIED TO KILL ME THREE TIMES!
THAT'S PROBABLE, BUT I ADMIT I STILL HAVE MY DOUBTS. I'D HAVE THOUGHT THE OTHER ONE WAS DEAD. I HANGED HER SO WELL.
THE FACT IS THAT YOU CAN'T GO ON LIKE THIS, WITH A SWORD ETERNALLY HANGING OVER YOUR HEAD.
BUT WHAT'S TO BE DONE?
TRY TO MEET WITH HER AND HAVE A TALK WITH HER. TELL HER...
"WAR OR PEACE! MY WORD AS A GENTLEMAN TO NEVER SAY ANYTHING OF YOU, TO NEVER DO ANYTHING AGAINST YOU; AND FOR YOUR PART, A SOLEMN OATH TO REMAIN NEUTRAL IN MY REGARD."
"OTHERWISE, I'LL DENOUNCE YOU AS A BRANDED WOMAN, I'LL HAVE YOU BROUGHT TO COURT, AND IF YOU'RE FOUND INNOCENT, WELL THEN, I'LL KILL YOU... ON MY HONOR AS A GENTLEMAN... BESIDE SOME WALL, LIKE A RABID DOG!"
STOP WITH THE WHISPERING, MY FRIENDS!
OF WHOM ARE YOU SPEAKING?
HMM, OF... OF MY DEAR CONSTANCE BONACIEUX. A LETTER RECOVERED FROM A CORPSE INFORMED ME SHE'S BEING KEPT IN A MYSTERIOUS CONVENT.
WHO'S KEEPING HERE THERE?
THE QUEEN, FOR HER OWN SAFETY.
I COULD HAVE ASKED MY MARQUISE, EXCEPT I SUSPECT HER OF BEING FOR THE CARDINAL.
I'LL GET SOME NEWS. RELIGION IS MY DOMAIN, AND IT SO HAPPENS THAT I'M CLOSELY CONNECTED WITH THE QUEEN'S ALMONER.
CERTAINLY, BUT WHY DO YOU SAY SO WHILE BLUSHING?
NOT AT ALL, I DON'T...
HA HA! LOOK AT HIM, A TRUE FIRST COMMUNICANT!
HA HA HA HA!!

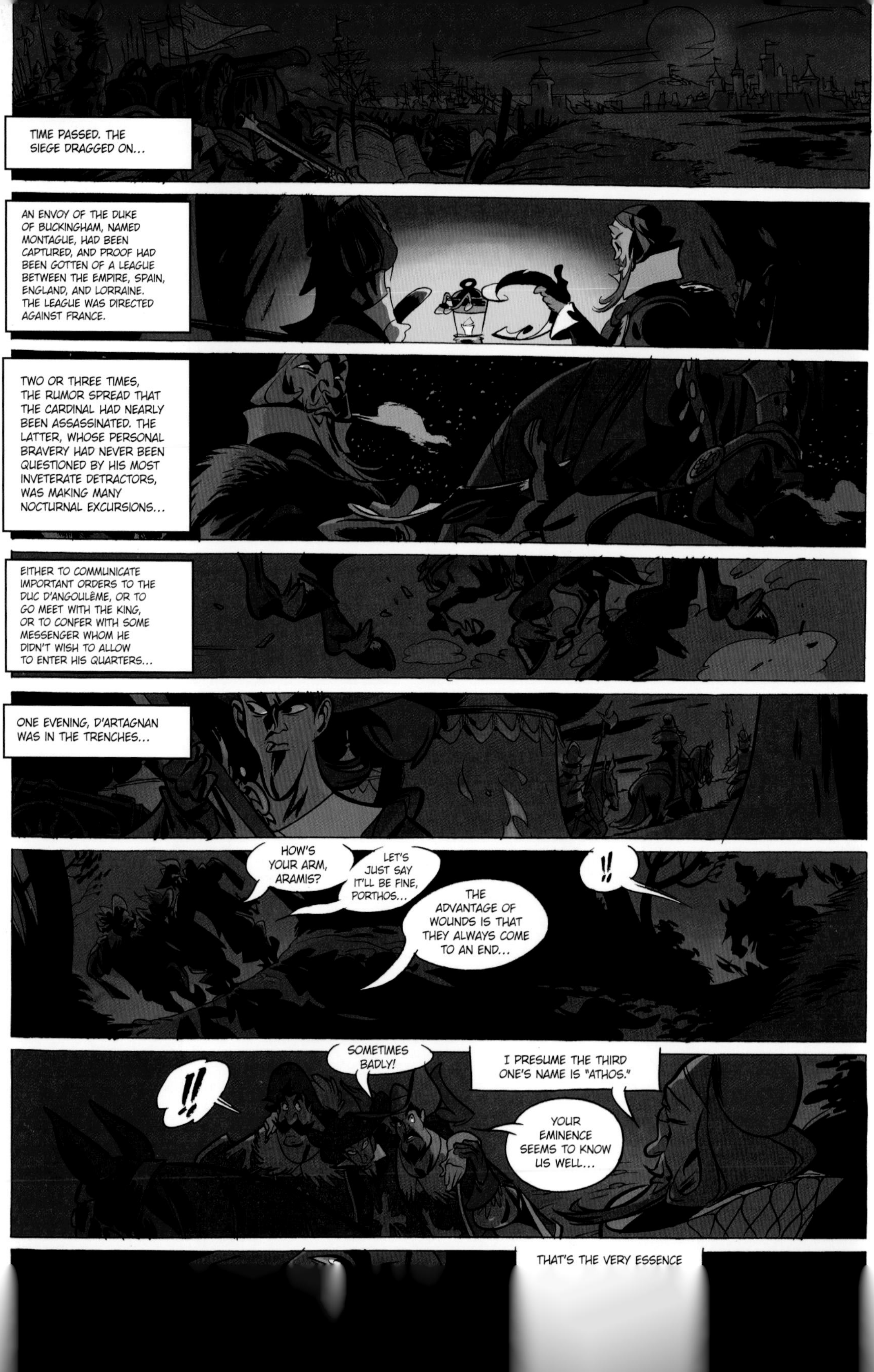
TIME PASSED. THE SIEGE DRAGGED ON...
AN ENVOY OF THE DUKE OF BUCKINGHAM, NAMED MONTAGUE, HAD BEEN CAPTURED, AND PROOF HAD BEEN GOTTEN OF A LEAGUE BETWEEN THE EMPIRE, SPAIN, ENGLAND, AND LORRAINE. THE LEAGUE WAS DIRECTED AGAINST FRANCE.
TWO OR THREE TIMES, THE RUMOR SPREAD THAT THE CARDINAL HAD NEARLY BEEN ASSASSINATED. THE LATTER, WHOSE PERSONAL BRAVERY HAD NEVER BEEN QUESTIONED BY HIS MOST INVETERATE DETRACTORS, WAS MAKING MANY NOCTURNAL EXCURSIONS...
EITHER TO COMMUNICATE IMPORTANT ORDERS TO THE DUC D'ANGOULÊME, OR TO GO MEET WITH THE KING, OR TO CONFER WITH SOME MESSENGER WHOM HE DIDN'T WISH TO ALLOW TO ENTER HIS QUARTERS...
ONE EVENING, D'ARTAGNAN WAS IN THE TRENCHES...
HOW'S YOUR ARM, ARAMIS?
LET'S JUST SAY IT'LL BE FINE, PORTHOS...
THE ADVANTAGE OF WOUNDS IS THAT THEY ALWAYS COME TO AN END...
!!
SOMETIMES BADLY!
!!
I PRESUME THE THIRD ONE'S NAME IS "ATHOS."
YOUR EMINENCE SEEMS TO KNOW US WELL...
THAT'S THE VERY ESSENCE

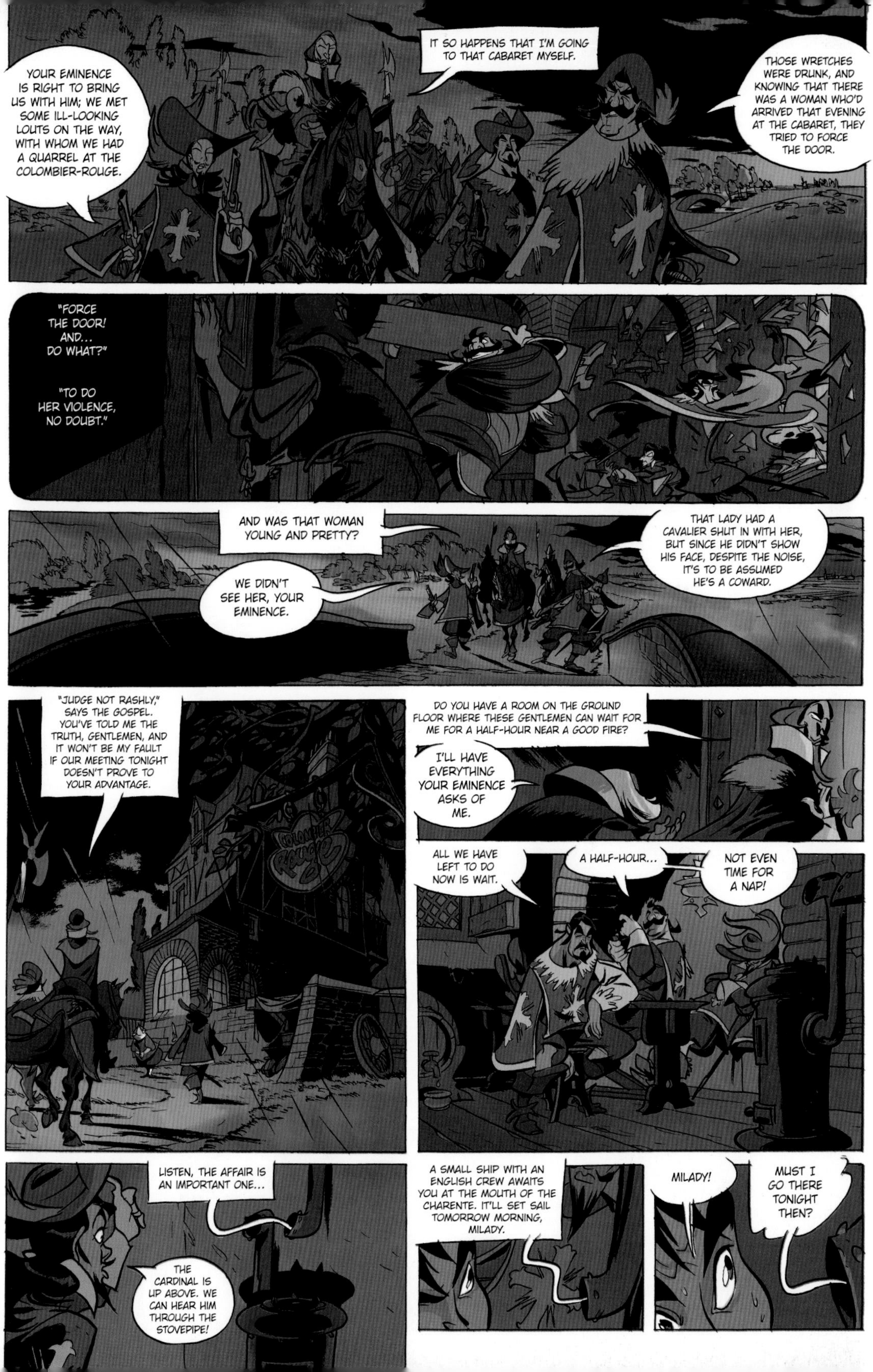
YOUR EMINENCE IS RIGHT TO BRING US WITH HIM; WE MET SOME ILL-LOOKING LOUTS ON THE WAY, WITH WHOM WE HAD A QUARREL AT THE COLOMBIER-ROUGE.
IT SO HAPPENS THAT I'M GOING TO THAT CABARET MYSELF.
THOSE WRETCHES WERE DRUNK, AND KNOWING THAT THERE WAS A WOMAN WHO'D ARRIVED THAT EVENING AT THE CABARET, THEY TRIED TO FORCE THE DOOR.
"FORCE THE DOOR! AND... DO WHAT?"
"TO DO HER VIOLENCE, NO DOUBT."
AND WAS THAT WOMAN YOUNG AND PRETTY?
WE DIDN'T SEE HER, YOUR EMINENCE.
THAT LADY HAD A CAVALIER SHUT IN WITH HER, BUT SINCE HE DIDN'T SHOW HIS FACE, DESPITE THE NOISE, IT'S TO BE ASSUMED HE'S A COWARD.
"JUDGE NOT RASHLY," SAYS THE GOSPEL. YOU'VE TOLD ME THE TRUTH, GENTLEMEN, AND IT WON'T BE MY FAULT IF OUR MEETING TONIGHT DOESN'T PROVE TO YOUR ADVANTAGE.
DO YOU HAVE A ROOM ON THE GROUND FLOOR WHERE THESE GENTLEMEN CAN WAIT FOR ME FOR A HALF-HOUR NEAR A GOOD FIRE?
I'LL HAVE EVERYTHING YOUR EMINENCE ASKS OF ME.
ALL WE HAVE LEFT TO DO NOW IS WAIT.
A HALF-HOUR...
NOT EVEN TIME FOR A NAP!
LISTEN, THE AFFAIR IS AN IMPORTANT ONE...
THE CARDINAL IS UP ABOVE. WE CAN HEAR HIM THROUGH THE STOVEPIPE!
A SMALL SHIP WITH AN ENGLISH CREW AWAITS YOU AT THE MOUTH OF THE CHARENTE. IT'LL SET SAIL TOMORROW MORNING, MILADY.
MILADY!
MUST I GO THERE TONIGHT THEN?

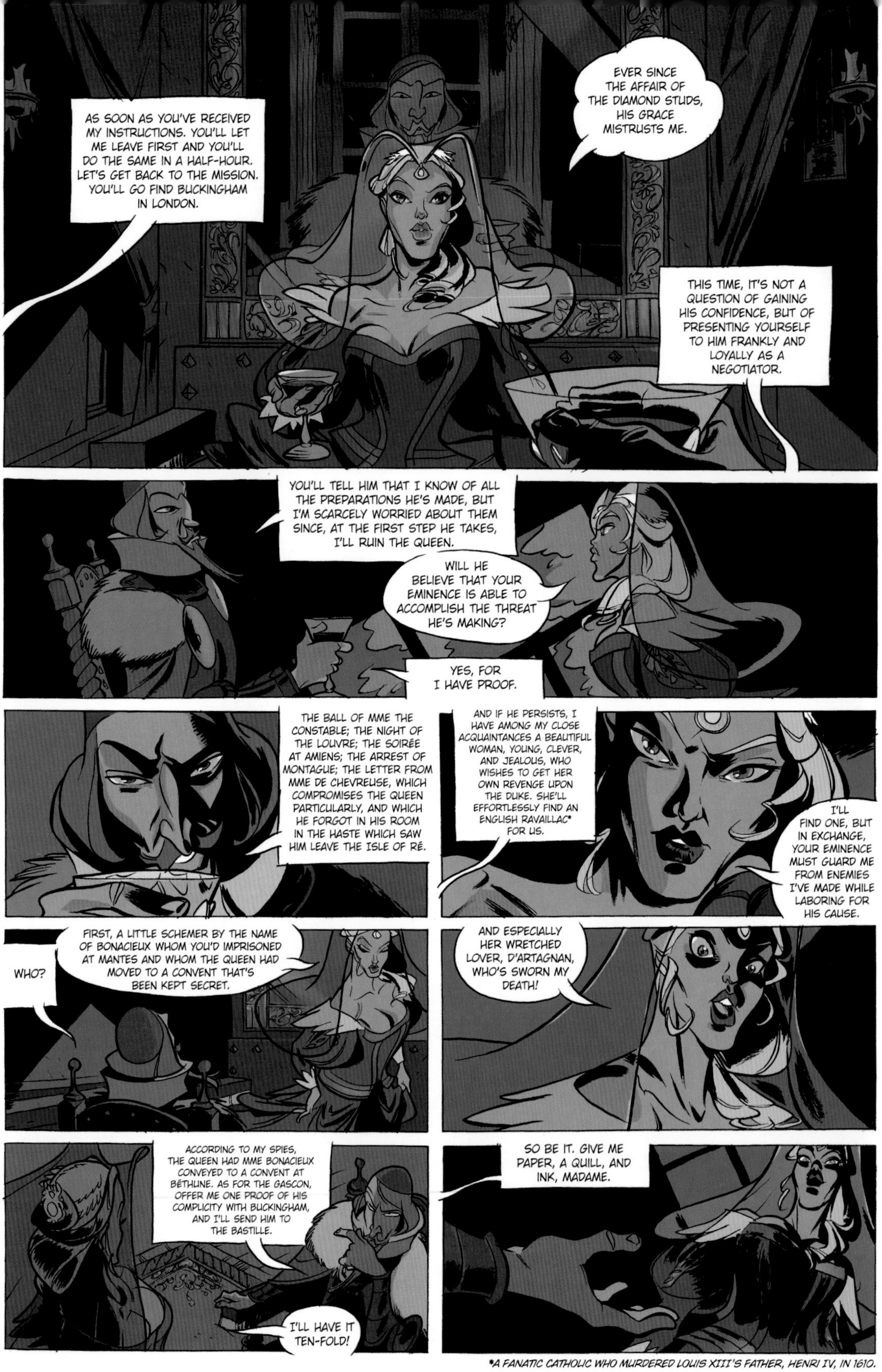
AS SOON AS YOU'VE RECEIVED MY INSTRUCTIONS. YOU'LL LET ME LEAVE FIRST AND YOU'LL DO THE SAME IN A HALF-HOUR. LET'S GET BACK TO THE MISSION. YOU'LL GO FIND BUCKINGHAM IN LONDON.
EVER SINCE THE AFFAIR OF THE DIAMOND STUDS, HIS GRACE MISTRUSTS ME.
THIS TIME, IT'S NOT A QUESTION OF GAINING HIS CONFIDENCE, BUT OF PRESENTING YOURSELF TO HIM FRANKLY AND LOYALLY AS A NEGOTIATOR.
YOU'LL TELL HIM THAT I KNOW OF ALL THE PREPARATIONS HE'S MADE, BUT I'M SCARCELY WORRIED ABOUT THEM SINCE, AT THE FIRST STEP HE TAKES, I'LL RUIN THE QUEEN.
WILL HE BELIEVE THAT YOUR EMINENCE IS ABLE TO ACCOMPLISH THE THREAT HE'S MAKING?
YES, FOR I HAVE PROOF.
THE BALL OF MME THE CONSTABLE; THE NIGHT OF THE LOUVRE; THE SOIRÉE AT AMIENS; THE ARREST OF MONTAGUE; THE LETTER FROM MME DE CHEVREUSE, WHICH COMPROMISES THE QUEEN PARTICULARLY, AND WHICH HE FORGOT IN HIS ROOM IN THE HASTE WHICH SAW HIM LEAVE THE ISLE OF RÉ.
AND IF HE PERSISTS, I HAVE AMONG MY CLOSE ACQUAINTANCES A BEAUTIFUL WOMAN, YOUNG, CLEVER, AND JEALOUS, WHO WISHES TO GET HER OWN REVENGE UPON THE DUKE. SHE'LL EFFORTLESSLY FIND AN ENGLISH RAVAILLAC* FOR US.
I'LL FIND ONE, BUT IN EXCHANGE, YOUR EMINENCE MUST GUARD ME FROM ENEMIES I'VE MADE WHILE LABORING FOR HIS CAUSE.
WHO?
FIRST, A LITTLE SCHEMER BY THE NAME OF BONACIEUX WHOM YOU'D IMPRISONED AT MANTES AND WHOM THE QUEEN HAD MOVED TO A CONVENT THAT'S BEEN KEPT SECRET.
AND ESPECIALLY HER WRETCHED LOVER, D'ARTAGNAN, WHO'S SWORN MY DEATH!
ACCORDING TO MY SPIES, THE QUEEN HAD MME BONACIEUX CONVEYED TO A CONVENT AT BÉTHUNE. AS FOR THE GASCON, OFFER ME ONE PROOF OF HIS COMPLICITY WITH BUCKINGHAM, AND I'LL SEND HIM TO THE BASTILLE.
I'LL HAVE IT TEN-FOLD!
SO BE IT. GIVE ME PAPER, A QUILL, AND INK, MADAME.

*A FANATIC CATHOLIC WHO MURDERED LOUIS XIII'S FATHER, HENRI IV, IN 1610.

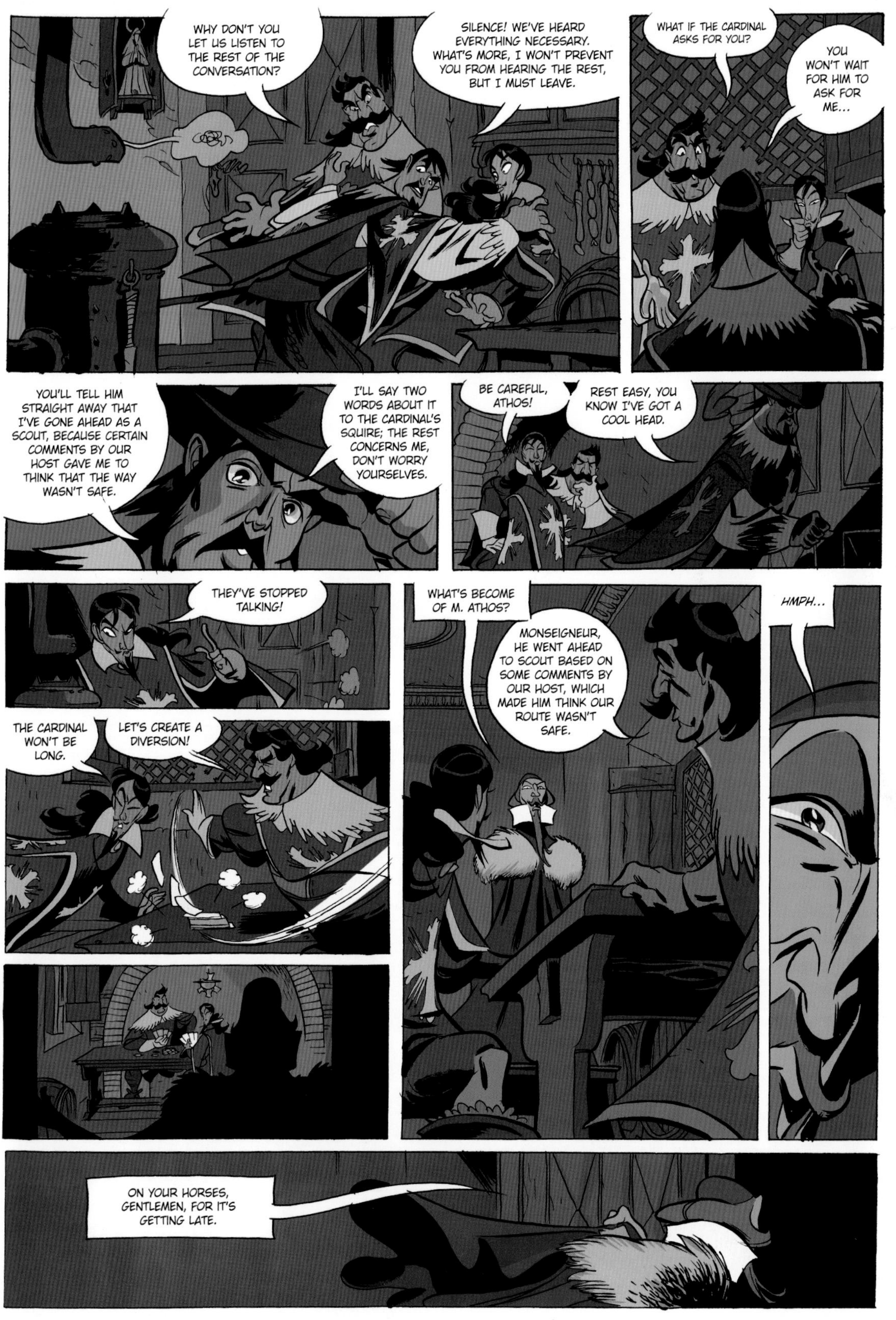
WHY DON'T YOU LET US LISTEN TO THE REST OF THE CONVERSATION?
SILENCE! WE'VE HEARD EVERYTHING NECESSARY. WHAT'S MORE, I WON'T PREVENT YOU FROM HEARING THE REST, BUT I MUST LEAVE.
WHAT IF THE CARDINAL ASKS FOR YOU?
YOU WON'T WAIT FOR HIM TO ASK FOR ME...
YOU'LL TELL HIM STRAIGHT AWAY THAT I'VE GONE AHEAD AS A SCOUT, BECAUSE CERTAIN COMMENTS BY OUR HOST GAVE ME TO THINK THAT THE WAY WASN'T SAFE.
I'LL SAY TWO WORDS ABOUT IT TO THE CARDINAL'S SQUIRE; THE REST CONCERNS ME, DON'T WORRY YOURSELVES.
BE CAREFUL, ATHOS!
REST EASY, YOU KNOW I'VE GOT A COOL HEAD.
THEY'VE STOPPED TALKING!
THE CARDINAL WON'T BE LONG.
LET'S CREATE A DIVERSION!
WHAT'S BECOME OF M. ATHOS?
MONSEIGNEUR, HE WENT AHEAD TO SCOUT BASED ON SOME COMMENTS BY OUR HOST, WHICH MADE HIM THINK OUR ROUTE WASN'T SAFE.
HMPH...
ON YOUR HORSES, GENTLEMEN, FOR IT'S GETTING LATE.

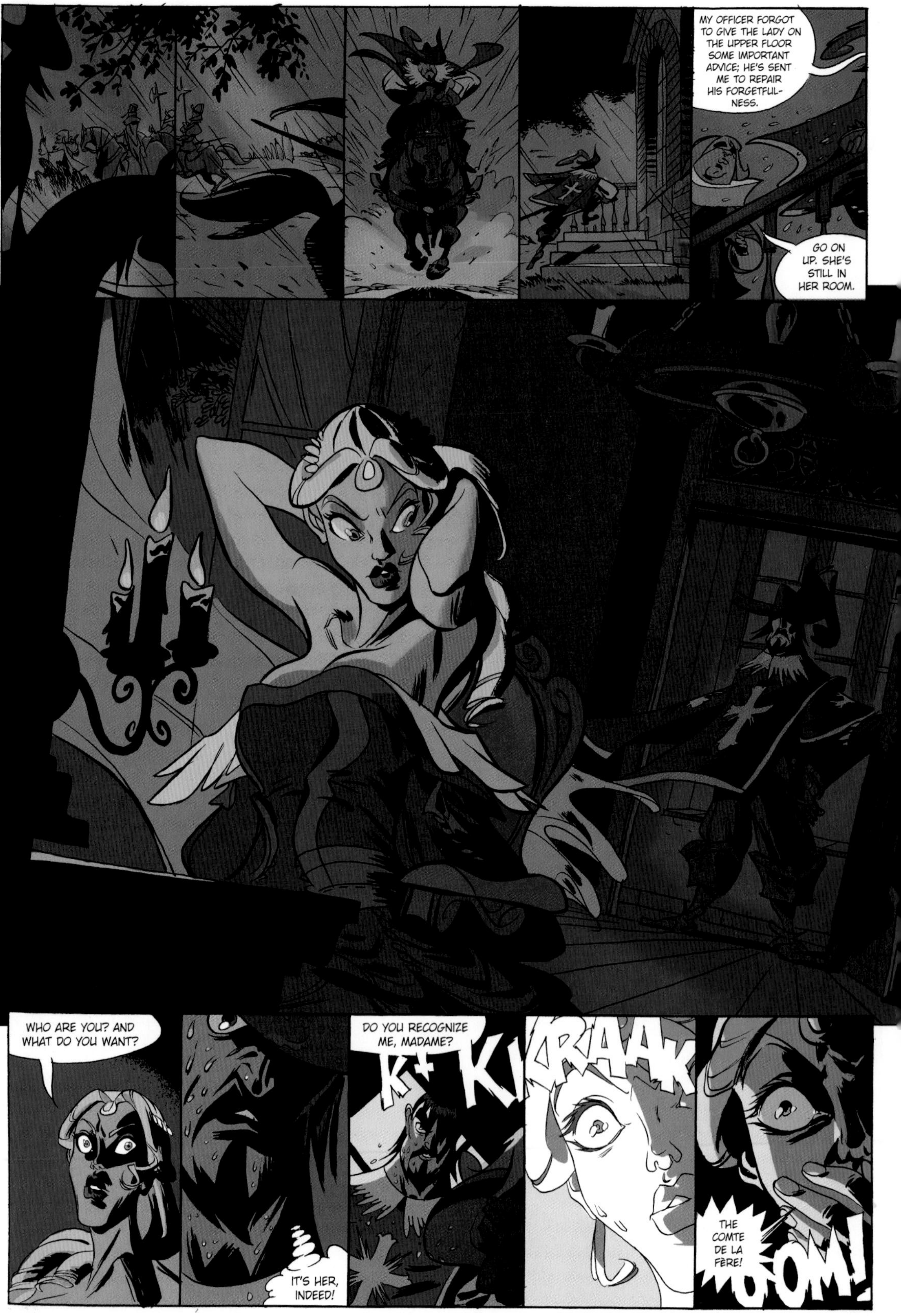
MY OFFICER FORGOT TO GIVE THE LADY ON THE UPPER FLOOR SOME IMPORTANT ADVICE; HE'S SENT ME TO REPAIR HIS FORGETFUL-NESS.
GO ON UP. SHE'S STILL IN HER ROOM.
WHO ARE YOU? AND WHAT DO YOU WANT?
IT'S HER, INDEED!
DO YOU RECOGNIZE ME, MADAME?
THE COMTE DE LA FÈRE!

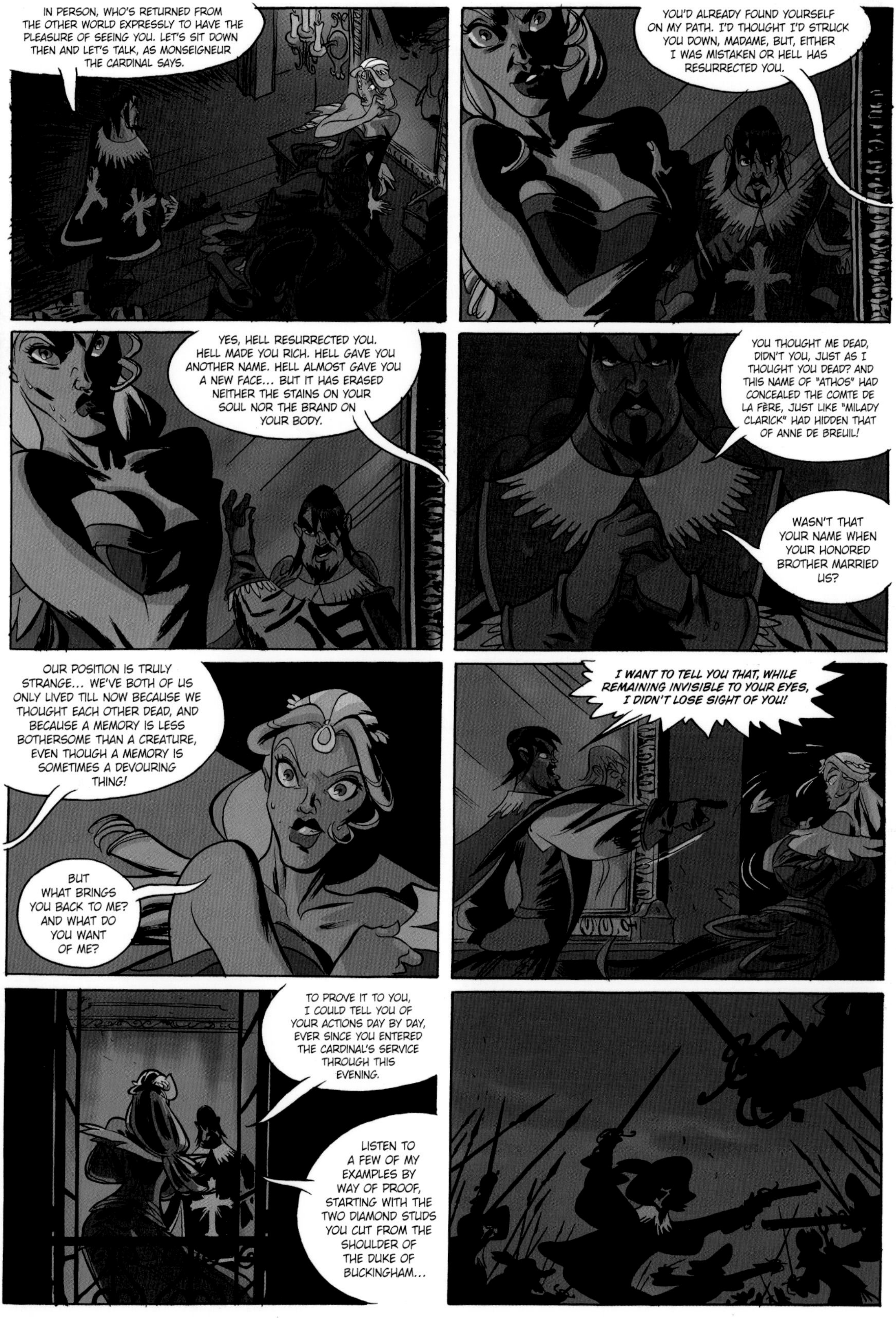
IN PERSON, WHO'S RETURNED FROM THE OTHER WORLD EXPRESSLY TO HAVE THE PLEASURE OF SEEING YOU. LET'S SIT DOWN THEN AND LET'S TALK, AS MONSEIGNEUR THE CARDINAL SAYS.
YOU'D ALREADY FOUND YOURSELF ON MY PATH. I'D THOUGHT I'D STRUCK YOU DOWN, MADAME, BUT, EITHER I WAS MISTAKEN OR HELL HAS RESURRECTED YOU.
YES, HELL RESURRECTED YOU. HELL MADE YOU RICH. HELL GAVE YOU ANOTHER NAME. HELL ALMOST GAVE YOU A NEW FACE... BUT IT HAS ERASED NEITHER THE STAINS ON YOUR SOUL NOR THE BRAND ON YOUR BODY.
YOU THOUGHT ME DEAD, DIDN'T YOU, JUST AS I THOUGHT YOU DEAD? AND THIS NAME OF "ATHOS" HAD CONCEALED THE COMTE DE LA FÈRE, JUST LIKE "MILADY CLARICK" HAD HIDDEN THAT OF ANNE DE BREUIL!
WASN'T THAT YOUR NAME WHEN YOUR HONORED BROTHER MARRIED US?
OUR POSITION IS TRULY STRANGE... WE'VE BOTH OF US ONLY LIVED TILL NOW BECAUSE WE THOUGHT EACH OTHER DEAD, AND BECAUSE A MEMORY IS LESS BOTHERSOME THAN A CREATURE, EVEN THOUGH A MEMORY IS SOMETIMES A DEVOURING THING!
BUT WHAT BRINGS YOU BACK TO ME? AND WHAT DO YOU WANT OF ME?
I WANT TO TELL YOU THAT, WHILE REMAINING INVISIBLE TO YOUR EYES, I DIDN'T LOSE SIGHT OF YOU!
TO PROVE IT TO YOU, I COULD TELL YOU OF YOUR ACTIONS DAY BY DAY, EVER SINCE YOU ENTERED THE CARDINAL'S SERVICE THROUGH THIS EVENING.
LISTEN TO A FEW OF MY EXAMPLES BY WAY OF PROOF, STARTING WITH THE TWO DIAMOND STUDS YOU CUT FROM THE SHOULDER OF THE DUKE OF BUCKINGHAM...

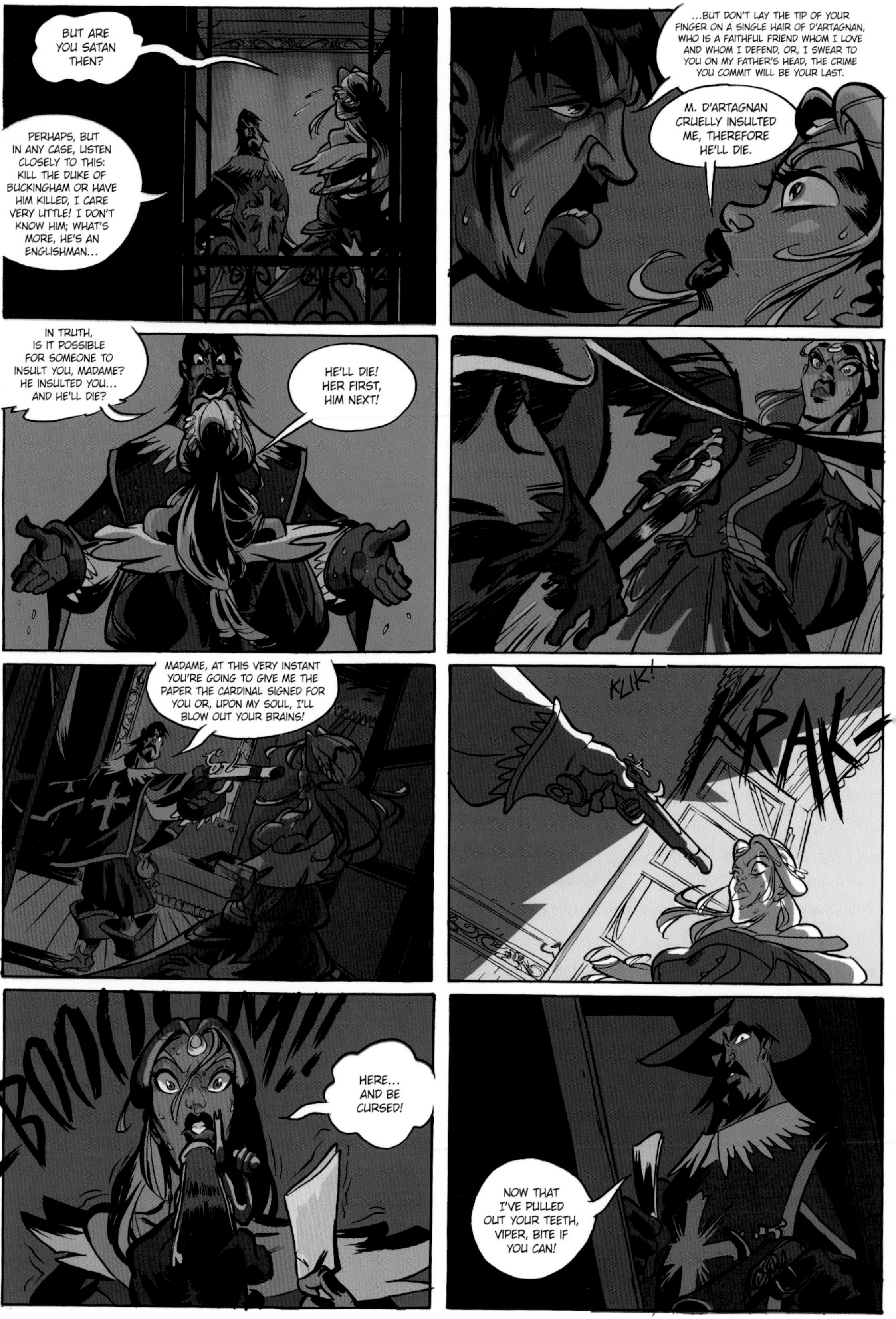
BUT ARE YOU SATAN THEN?
PERHAPS, BUT IN ANY CASE, LISTEN CLOSELY TO THIS: KILL THE DUKE OF BUCKINGHAM OR HAVE HIM KILLED, I CARE VERY LITTLE! I DON'T KNOW HIM; WHAT'S MORE, HE'S AN ENGLISHMAN...
...BUT DON'T LAY THE TIP OF YOUR FINGER ON A SINGLE HAIR OF D'ARTAGNAN, WHO IS A FAITHFUL FRIEND WHOM I LOVE AND WHOM I DEFEND, OR, I SWEAR TO YOU ON MY FATHER'S HEAD, THE CRIME YOU COMMIT WILL BE YOUR LAST.
M. D'ARTAGNAN CRUELLY INSULTED ME, THEREFORE HE'LL DIE.
IN TRUTH, IS IT POSSIBLE FOR SOMEONE TO INSULT YOU, MADAME? HE INSULTED YOU... AND HE'LL DIE?
HE'LL DIE! HER FIRST, HIM NEXT!
MADAME, AT THIS VERY INSTANT YOU'RE GOING TO GIVE ME THE PAPER THE CARDINAL SIGNED FOR YOU OR, UPON MY SOUL, I'LL BLOW OUT YOUR BRAINS!
KLIK!
KRAK-
BOOOOOM!!
HERE... AND BE CURSED!
NOW THAT I'VE PULLED OUT YOUR TEETH, VIPER, BITE IF YOU CAN!

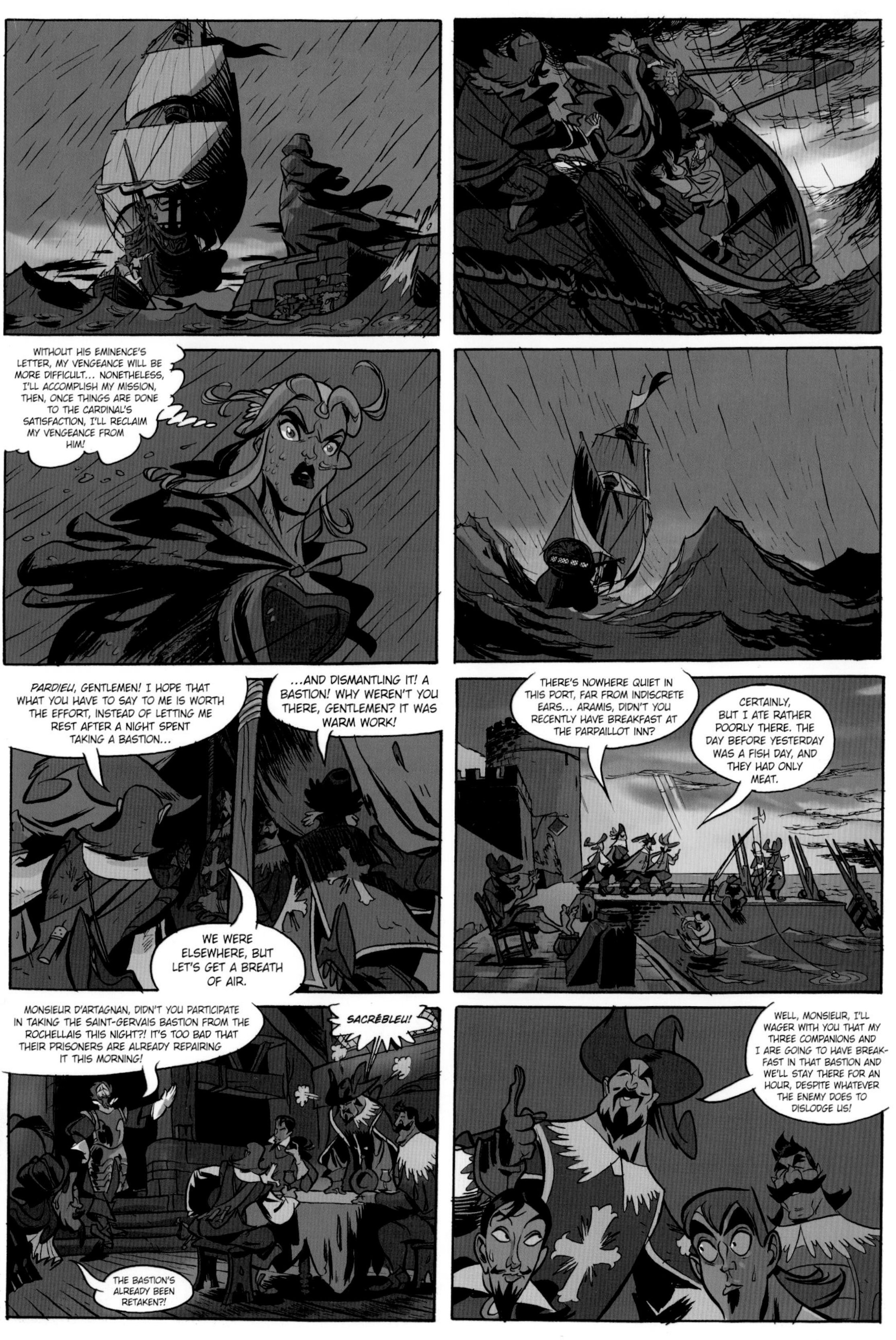
WITHOUT HIS EMINENCE'S LETTER, MY VENGEANCE WILL BE MORE DIFFICULT... NONETHELESS, I'LL ACCOMPLISH MY MISSION, THEN, ONCE THINGS ARE DONE TO THE CARDINAL'S SATISFACTION, I'LL RECLAIM MY VENGEANCE FROM HIM!
PARDIEU, GENTLEMEN! I HOPE THAT WHAT YOU HAVE TO SAY TO ME IS WORTH THE EFFORT, INSTEAD OF LETTING ME REST AFTER A NIGHT SPENT TAKING A BASTION...
...AND DISMANTLING IT! A BASTION! WHY WEREN'T YOU THERE, GENTLEMEN? IT WAS WARM WORK!
WE WERE ELSEWHERE, BUT LET'S GET A BREATH OF AIR.
THERE'S NOWHERE QUIET IN THIS PORT, FAR FROM INDISCRETE EARS... ARAMIS, DIDN'T YOU RECENTLY HAVE BREAKFAST AT THE PARPAILLOT INN?
CERTAINLY, BUT I ATE RATHER POORLY THERE. THE DAY BEFORE YESTERDAY WAS A FISH DAY, AND THEY HAD ONLY MEAT.
MONSIEUR D'ARTAGNAN, DIDN'T YOU PARTICIPATE IN TAKING THE SAINT-GERVAIS BASTION FROM THE ROCHELLAIS THIS NIGHT?! IT'S TOO BAD THAT THEIR PRISONERS ARE ALREADY REPAIRING IT THIS MORNING!
SACRÉBLEU!
THE BASTION'S ALREADY BEEN RETAKEN?!
WELL, MONSIEUR, I'LL WAGER WITH YOU THAT MY THREE COMPANIONS AND I ARE GOING TO HAVE BREAK-FAST IN THAT BASTION AND WE'LL STAY THERE FOR AN HOUR, DESPITE WHATEVER THE ENEMY DOES TO DISLODGE US!

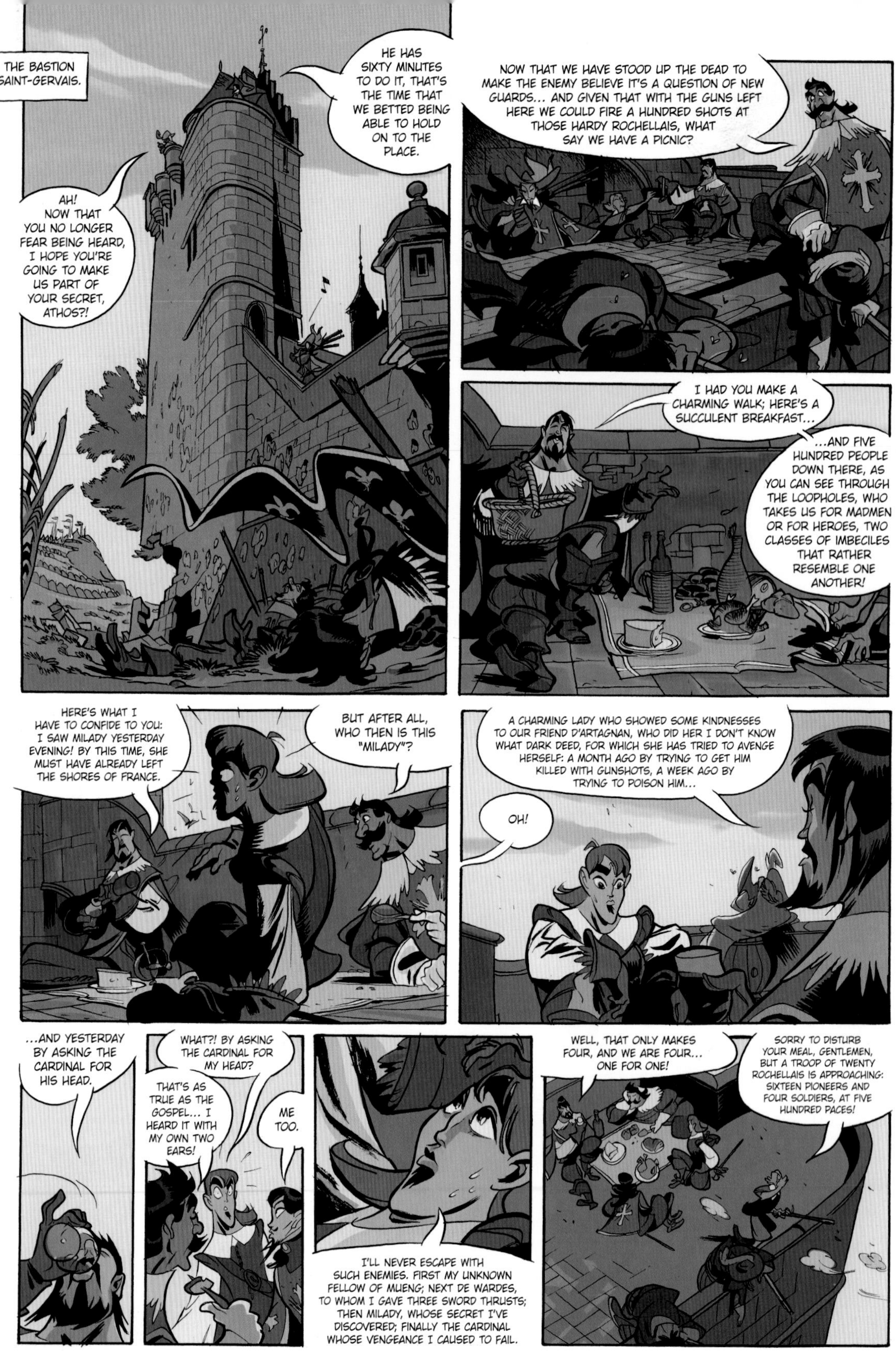
THE BASTION SAINT-GERVAIS.
HE HAS SIXTY MINUTES TO DO IT, THAT'S THE TIME THAT WE BETTED BEING ABLE TO HOLD ON TO THE PLACE.
AH! NOW THAT YOU NO LONGER FEAR BEING HEARD, I HOPE YOU'RE GOING TO MAKE US PART OF YOUR SECRET, ATHOS?!
NOW THAT WE HAVE STOOD UP THE DEAD TO MAKE THE ENEMY BELIEVE IT'S A QUESTION OF NEW GUARDS... AND GIVEN THAT WITH THE GUNS LEFT HERE WE COULD FIRE A HUNDRED SHOTS AT THOSE HARDY ROCHELLAIS, WHAT SAY WE HAVE A PICNIC?
I HAD YOU MAKE A CHARMING WALK; HERE'S A SUCCULENT BREAKFAST...
...AND FIVE HUNDRED PEOPLE DOWN THERE, AS YOU CAN SEE THROUGH THE LOOPHOLES, WHO TAKES US FOR MADMEN OR FOR HEROES, TWO CLASSES OF IMBECILES THAT RATHER RESEMBLE ONE ANOTHER!
HERE'S WHAT I HAVE TO CONFIDE TO YOU: I SAW MILADY YESTERDAY EVENING! BY THIS TIME, SHE MUST HAVE ALREADY LEFT THE SHORES OF FRANCE.
BUT AFTER ALL, WHO THEN IS THIS "MILADY"?
A CHARMING LADY WHO SHOWED SOME KINDNESSES TO OUR FRIEND D'ARTAGNAN, WHO DID HER I DON'T KNOW WHAT DARK DEED, FOR WHICH SHE HAS TRIED TO AVENGE HERSELF: A MONTH AGO BY TRYING TO GET HIM KILLED WITH GUNSHOTS, A WEEK AGO BY TRYING TO POISON HIM...
OH!
...AND YESTERDAY BY ASKING THE CARDINAL FOR HIS HEAD.
WHAT?! BY ASKING THE CARDINAL FOR MY HEAD?
THAT'S AS TRUE AS THE GOSPEL... I HEARD IT WITH MY OWN TWO EARS!
ME TOO.
I'LL NEVER ESCAPE WITH SUCH ENEMIES. FIRST MY UNKNOWN FELLOW OF MUENG; NEXT DE WARDES, TO WHOM I GAVE THREE SWORD THRUSTS; THEN MILADY, WHOSE SECRET I'VE DISCOVERED; FINALLY THE CARDINAL WHOSE VENGEANCE I CAUSED TO FAIL.
WELL, THAT ONLY MAKES FOUR, AND WE ARE FOUR... ONE FOR ONE!
SORRY TO DISTURB YOUR MEAL, GENTLEMEN, BUT A TROOP OF TWENTY ROCHELLAIS IS APPROACHING: SIXTEEN PIONEERS AND FOUR SOLDIERS, AT FIVE HUNDRED PACES!

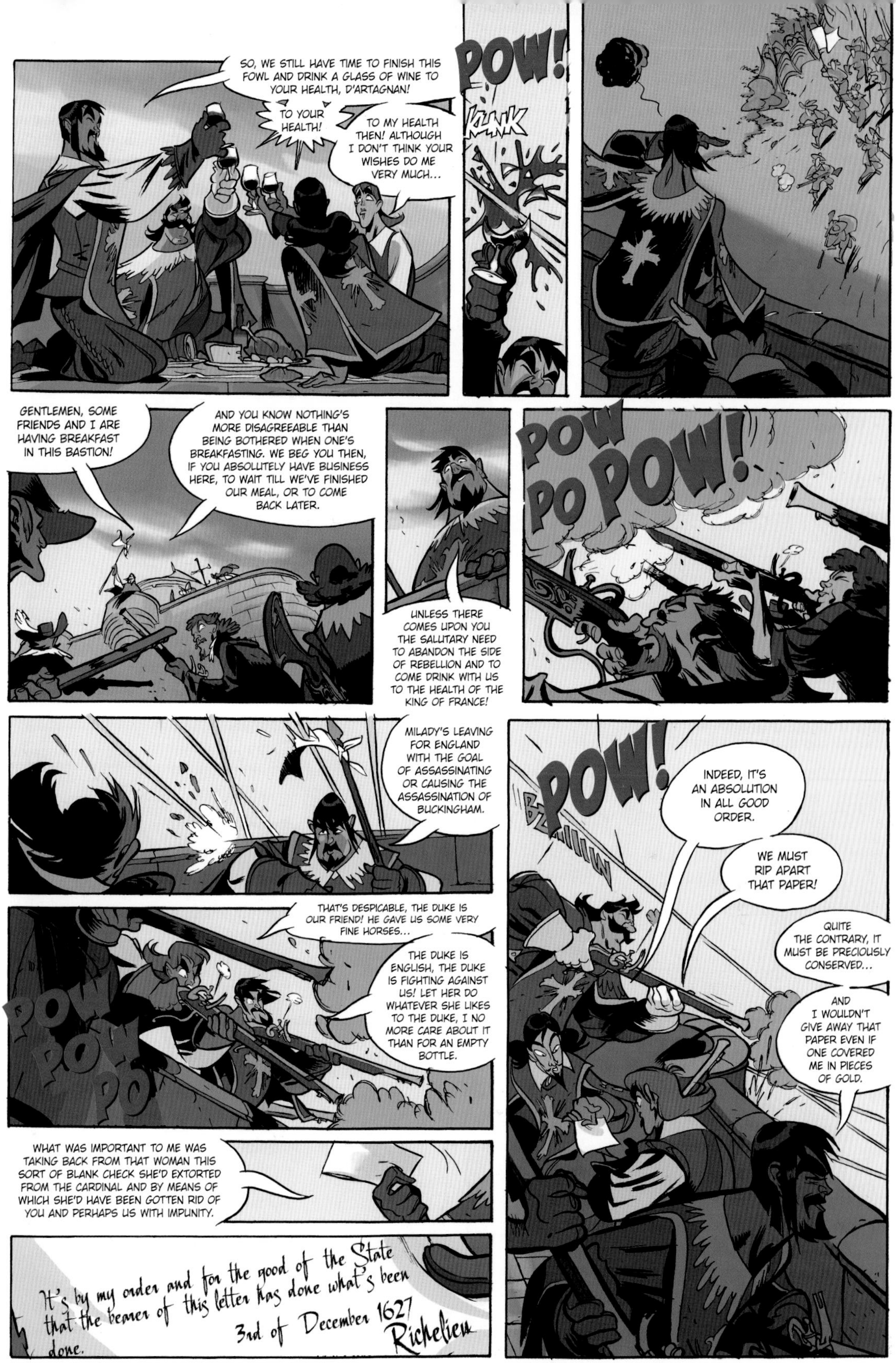
SO, WE STILL HAVE TIME TO FINISH THIS FOWL AND DRINK A GLASS OF WINE TO YOUR HEALTH, D'ARTAGNAN!
TO YOUR HEALTH!
TO MY HEALTH THEN! ALTHOUGH I DON'T THINK YOUR WISHES DO ME VERY MUCH...
POW!
KLINK
GENTLEMEN, SOME FRIENDS AND I ARE HAVING BREAKFAST IN THIS BASTION!
AND YOU KNOW NOTHING'S MORE DISAGREEABLE THAN BEING BOTHERED WHEN ONE'S BREAKFASTING. WE BEG YOU THEN, IF YOU ABSOLUTELY HAVE BUSINESS HERE, TO WAIT TILL WE'VE FINISHED OUR MEAL, OR TO COME BACK LATER.
UNLESS THERE COMES UPON YOU THE SALUTARY NEED TO ABANDON THE SIDE OF REBELLION AND TO COME DRINK WITH US TO THE HEALTH OF THE KING OF FRANCE!
POW PO POW!
MILADY'S LEAVING FOR ENGLAND WITH THE GOAL OF ASSASSINATING OR CAUSING THE ASSASSINATION OF BUCKINGHAM.
THAT'S DESPICABLE, THE DUKE IS OUR FRIEND! HE GAVE US SOME VERY FINE HORSES...
THE DUKE IS ENGLISH, THE DUKE IS FIGHTING AGAINST US! LET HER DO WHATEVER SHE LIKES TO THE DUKE, I NO MORE CARE ABOUT IT THAN FOR AN EMPTY BOTTLE.
PO POW PO
WHAT WAS IMPORTANT TO ME WAS TAKING BACK FROM THAT WOMAN THIS SORT OF BLANK CHECK SHE'D EXTORTED FROM THE CARDINAL AND BY MEANS OF WHICH SHE'D HAVE BEEN GOTTEN RID OF YOU AND PERHAPS US WITH IMPUNITY.
It's by my order and for the good of the State that the bearer of this letter has done what's been done.
3rd of December 1627
Richelieu
POW!
INDEED, IT'S AN ABSOLUTION IN ALL GOOD ORDER.
WE MUST RIP APART THAT PAPER!
QUITE THE CONTRARY, IT MUST BE PRECIOUSLY CONSERVED...
AND I WOULDN'T GIVE AWAY THAT PAPER EVEN IF ONE COVERED ME IN PIECES OF GOLD.

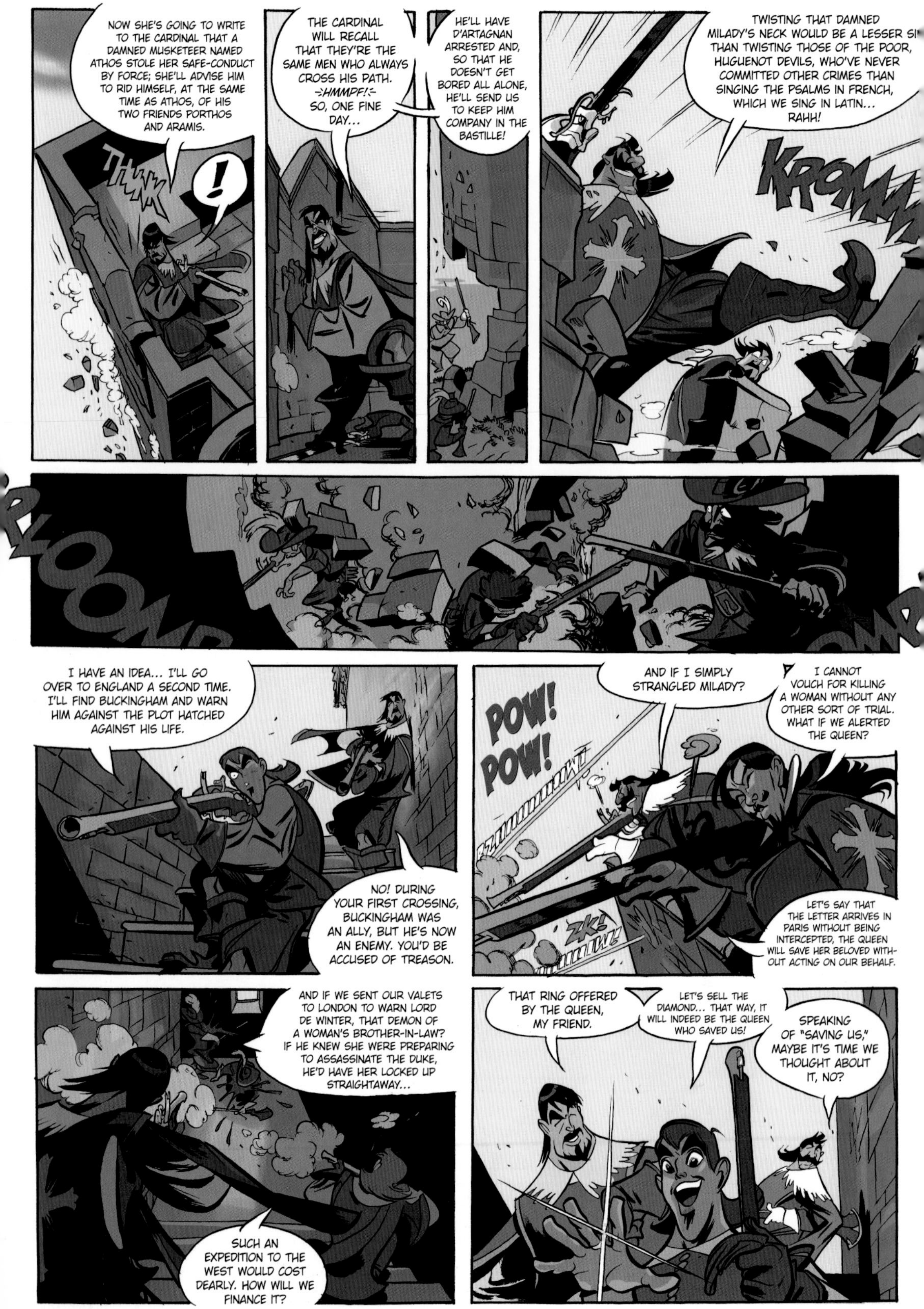
NOW SHE'S GOING TO WRITE TO THE CARDINAL THAT A DAMNED MUSKETEER NAMED ATHOS STOLE HER SAFE-CONDUCT BY FORCE; SHE'LL ADVISE HIM TO RID HIMSELF, AT THE SAME TIME AS ATHOS, OF HIS TWO FRIENDS PORTHOS AND ARAMIS.
THUNK
!
THE CARDINAL WILL RECALL THAT THEY'RE THE SAME MEN WHO ALWAYS CROSS HIS PATH. HMMPF! SO, ONE FINE DAY...
HE'LL HAVE D'ARTAGNAN ARRESTED AND, SO THAT HE DOESN'T GET BORED ALL ALONE, HE'LL SEND US TO KEEP HIM COMPANY IN THE BASTILLE!
TWISTING THAT DAMNED MILADY'S NECK WOULD BE A LESSER SIN THAN TWISTING THOSE OF THE POOR, HUGUENOT DEVILS, WHO'VE NEVER COMMITTED OTHER CRIMES THAN SINGING THE PSALMS IN FRENCH, WHICH WE SING IN LATIN... RAHH!
I HAVE AN IDEA... I'LL GO OVER TO ENGLAND A SECOND TIME. I'LL FIND BUCKINGHAM AND WARN HIM AGAINST THE PLOT HATCHED AGAINST HIS LIFE.
NO! DURING YOUR FIRST CROSSING, BUCKINGHAM WAS AN ALLY, BUT HE'S NOW AN ENEMY. YOU'D BE ACCUSED OF TREASON.
POW! POW!
AND IF I SIMPLY STRANGLED MILADY?
I CANNOT VOUCH FOR KILLING A WOMAN WITHOUT ANY OTHER SORT OF TRIAL. WHAT IF WE ALERTED THE QUEEN?
ZK!
LET'S SAY THAT THE LETTER ARRIVES IN PARIS WITHOUT BEING INTERCEPTED, THE QUEEN WILL SAVE HER BELOVED WITHOUT ACTING ON OUR BEHALF.
AND IF WE SENT OUR VALETS TO LONDON TO WARN LORD DE WINTER, THAT DEMON OF A WOMAN'S BROTHER-IN-LAW? IF HE KNEW SHE WERE PREPARING TO ASSASSINATE THE DUKE, HE'D HAVE HER LOCKED UP STRAIGHTAWAY...
SUCH AN EXPEDITION TO THE WEST WOULD COST DEARLY. HOW WILL WE FINANCE IT?
THAT RING OFFERED BY THE QUEEN, MY FRIEND.
LET'S SELL THE DIAMOND... THAT WAY, IT WILL INDEED BE THE QUEEN WHO SAVED US!
SPEAKING OF "SAVING US," MAYBE IT'S TIME WE THOUGHT ABOUT IT, NO?

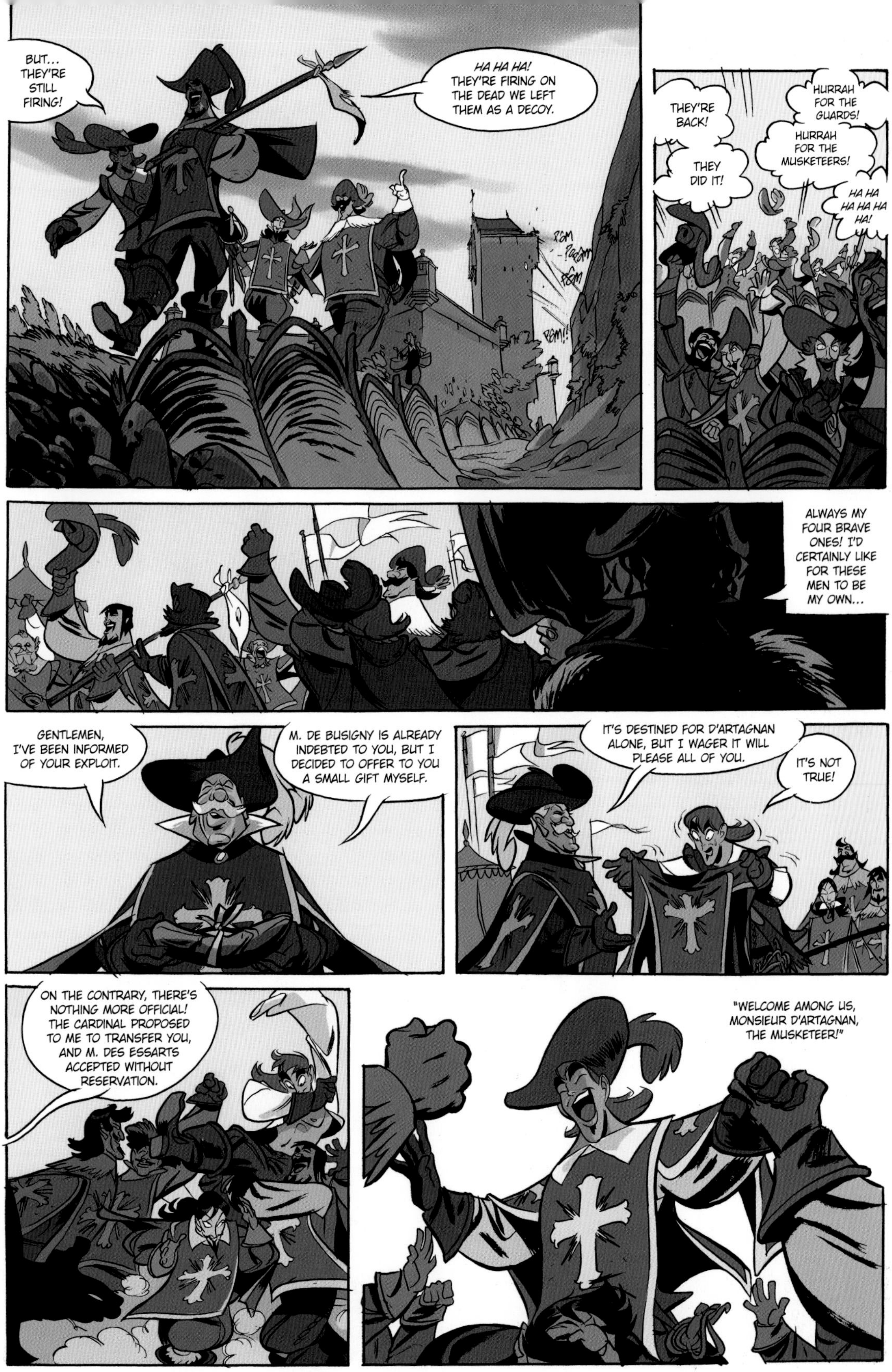

BUT... THEY'RE STILL FIRING!
HA HA HA! THEY'RE FIRING ON THE DEAD WE LEFT THEM AS A DECOY.
PGM PAGAM PGM
PGM!!
THEY'RE BACK!
HURRAH FOR THE GUARDS!
HURRAH FOR THE MUSKETEERS!
THEY DID IT!
HA HA HA HA HA HA!
ALWAYS MY FOUR BRAVE ONES! I'D CERTAINLY LIKE FOR THESE MEN TO BE MY OWN...
GENTLEMEN, I'VE BEEN INFORMED OF YOUR EXPLOIT.
M. DE BUSIGNY IS ALREADY INDEBTED TO YOU, BUT I DECIDED TO OFFER TO YOU A SMALL GIFT MYSELF.
IT'S DESTINED FOR D'ARTAGNAN ALONE, BUT I WAGER IT WILL PLEASE ALL OF YOU.
IT'S NOT TRUE!
ON THE CONTRARY, THERE'S NOTHING MORE OFFICIAL! THE CARDINAL PROPOSED TO ME TO TRANSFER YOU, AND M. DES ESSARTS ACCEPTED WITHOUT RESERVATION.
"WELCOME AMONG US, MONSIEUR D'ARTAGNAN, THE MUSKETEER!"

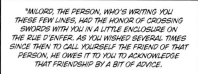

"MILORD, THE PERSON, WHO'S WRITING YOU THESE FEW LINES, HAD THE HONOR OF CROSSING SWORDS WITH YOU IN A LITTLE ENCLOSURE ON THE RUE D'ENFER. AS YOU WISHED SEVERAL TIMES SINCE THEN TO CALL YOURSELF THE FRIEND OF THAT PERSON, HE OWES IT TO YOU TO ACKNOWLEDGE THAT FRIENDSHIP BY A BIT OF ADVICE.

"TWICE YOU'VE NEARLY BEEN THE VICTIM OF A CLOSE RELATIVE WHOM YOU BELIEVE TO BE YOUR HEIRESS, BECAUSE YOU'RE UNAWARE THAT, BEFORE CONTRACTING A MARRIAGE IN ENGLAND, SHE WAS ALREADY MARRIED IN FRANCE. BUT THE THIRD TIME, WHICH IS NOW, YOU MIGHT SUCCUMB.

"YOUR RELATIVE DEPARTED LA ROCHELLE FOR ENGLAND OVERNIGHT. WATCH FOR HER ARRIVAL, FOR SHE HAS GREAT AND TERRIBLE PLANS. IF YOU ARE ABSOLUTELY DETERMINED TO KNOW WHAT SHE'S CAPABLE OF, READ HER PAST ON HER LEFT SHOULDER."

YOU HAVE THE QUILL OF A SECRETARY OF STATE, MY DEAR ARAMIS.

HAVING COMPLETED THE LETTER FOR LORD DE WINTER, I'LL TACKLE ONE FOR MY COUSIN IN TOURS.

"MY DEAR COUSIN, HIS EMINENCE THE CARDINAL, WHOM GOD PRESERVE FOR THE HAPPINESS OF FRANCE AND THE CONFUSION OF THE ENEMIES OF THE REALM, HAS NEARLY DONE WITH THE HERETIC REBELS OF LA ROCHELLE: IT'S PROBABLE THAT HELP FROM THE ENGLISH FLEET WON'T EVEN ARRIVE IN SIGHT OF THE PLACE. I'D EVEN DARE SAY THAT I'M CERTAIN THAT M. DE BUCKINGHAM WILL BE PREVENTED FROM DEPARTING BY SOME GREAT EVENT. HIS EMINENCE IS THE MOST ILLUSTRIOUS POLITICIAN OF TIMES PAST, OF TIMES PRESENT, AND PROBABLY FOR THE TIMES TO COME. HE'D EXTINGUISH THE SUN, WERE IT BOTHERING HIM."

D'ARTAGNAN, DO YOU HAVE THE SUM?

FOURTEEN HUNDRED LIVRES FOR PLANCHET'S ROUND TRIP TO AND FROM ENGLAND. AND SIX HUNDRED FOR BAZIN'S TRIP TO ARAMIS'S COUSIN'S HOME IN TOURS. THE REMAINING FIVE HUNDRED POUNDS WILL COVER OUR INCIDENTAL EXPENSES.

I'LL LEAVE TOMORROW THEN?

RIGHT AWAY! AND YOU'LL GO STRAIGHT TO YOUR GOAL, CONTRARY TO MILADY, WHO MUST MAKE NUMEROUS PRUDENT DETOURS BEFORE ARRIVING SAFE AND SOUND.

AND YOU WILL ALSO STRESS TO LORD DE WINTER: "WATCH AFTER HIS GRACE LORD BUCKINGHAM, FOR THEY WISH TO ASSASSINATE HIM."

"GIVE THESE HAPPY NEWS TO YOUR SISTER, MY DEAR COUSIN. I DREAMT THAT THAT CURSED ENGLISHMAN WAS DEAD. I CAN'T REMEMBER IF IT WERE BY STEEL OR BY POISON; THE ONLY THING OF WHICH I'M SURE IS THAT I DREAMT HE WAS DEAD...

"AND, AS YOU KNOW, MY DREAMS NEVER DECEIVE ME. BE ASSURED OF SEEING ME RETURN SOON."

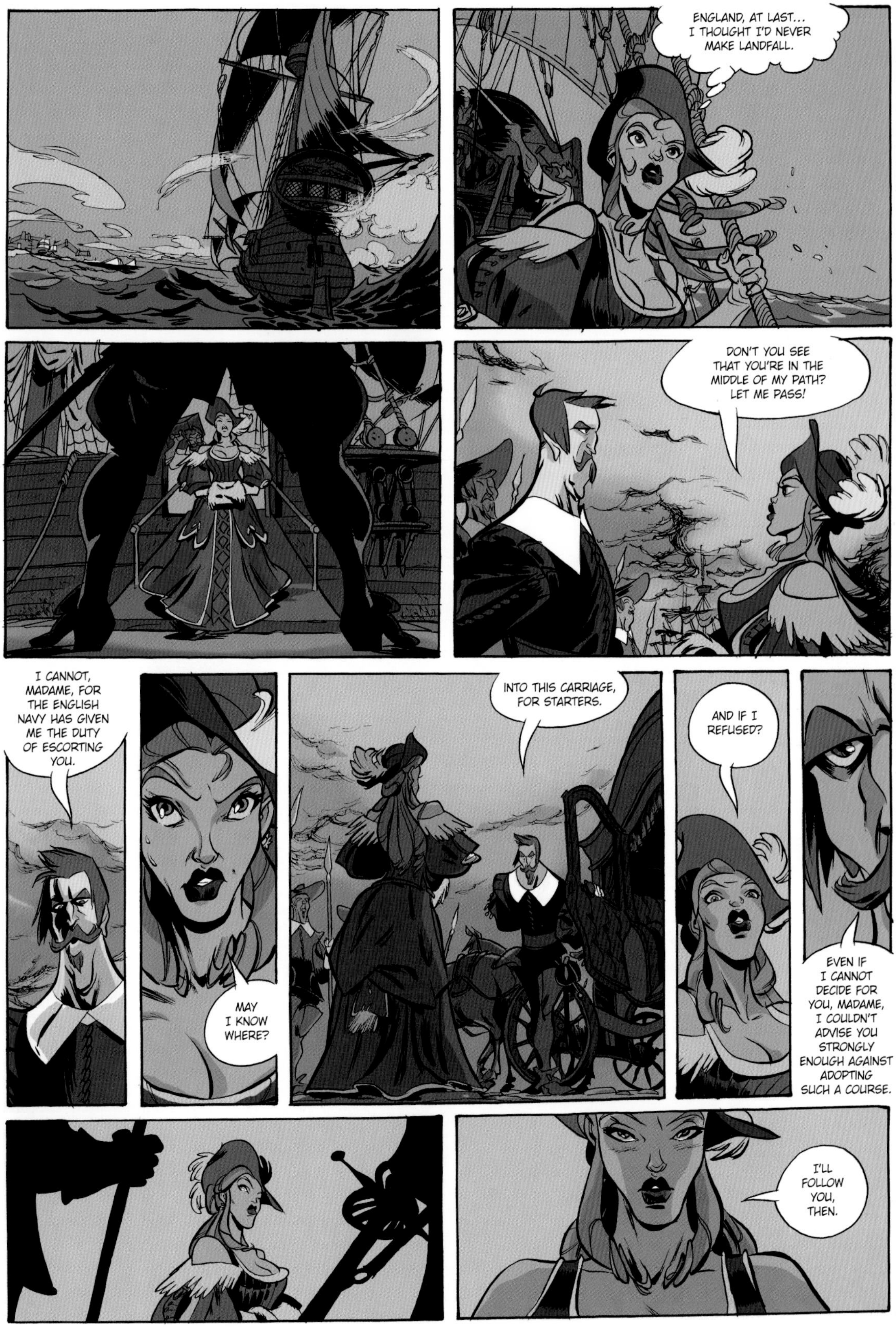
ENGLAND, AT LAST... I THOUGHT I'D NEVER MAKE LANDFALL.
DON'T YOU SEE THAT YOU'RE IN THE MIDDLE OF MY PATH? LET ME PASS!
I CANNOT, MADAME, FOR THE ENGLISH NAVY HAS GIVEN ME THE DUTY OF ESCORTING YOU.
MAY I KNOW WHERE?
INTO THIS CARRIAGE, FOR STARTERS.
AND IF I REFUSED?
EVEN IF I CANNOT DECIDE FOR YOU, MADAME, I COULDN'T ADVISE YOU STRONGLY ENOUGH AGAINST ADOPTING SUCH A COURSE.
I'LL FOLLOW YOU, THEN.

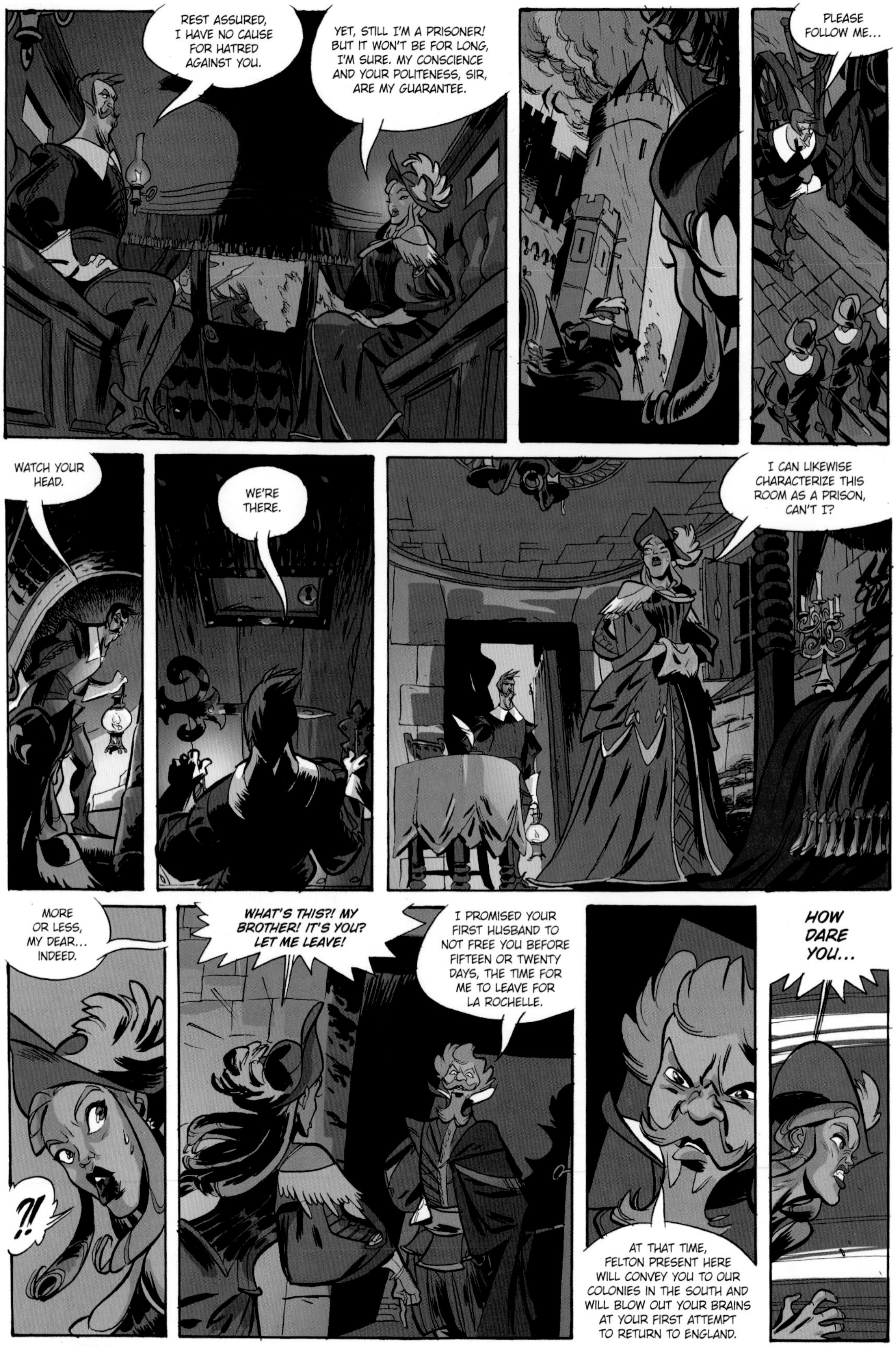

REST ASSURED, I HAVE NO CAUSE FOR HATRED AGAINST YOU.
YET, STILL I'M A PRISONER! BUT IT WON'T BE FOR LONG, I'M SURE. MY CONSCIENCE AND YOUR POLITENESS, SIR, ARE MY GUARANTEE.
PLEASE FOLLOW ME...
WATCH YOUR HEAD.
WE'RE THERE.
I CAN LIKEWISE CHARACTERIZE THIS ROOM AS A PRISON, CAN'T I?
MORE OR LESS, MY DEAR... INDEED.
?!
WHAT'S THIS?! MY BROTHER! IT'S YOU? LET ME LEAVE!
I PROMISED YOUR FIRST HUSBAND TO NOT FREE YOU BEFORE FIFTEEN OR TWENTY DAYS, THE TIME FOR ME TO LEAVE FOR LA ROCHELLE.
AT THAT TIME, FELTON PRESENT HERE WILL CONVEY YOU TO OUR COLONIES IN THE SOUTH AND WILL BLOW OUT YOUR BRAINS AT YOUR FIRST ATTEMPT TO RETURN TO ENGLAND.
HOW DARE YOU...

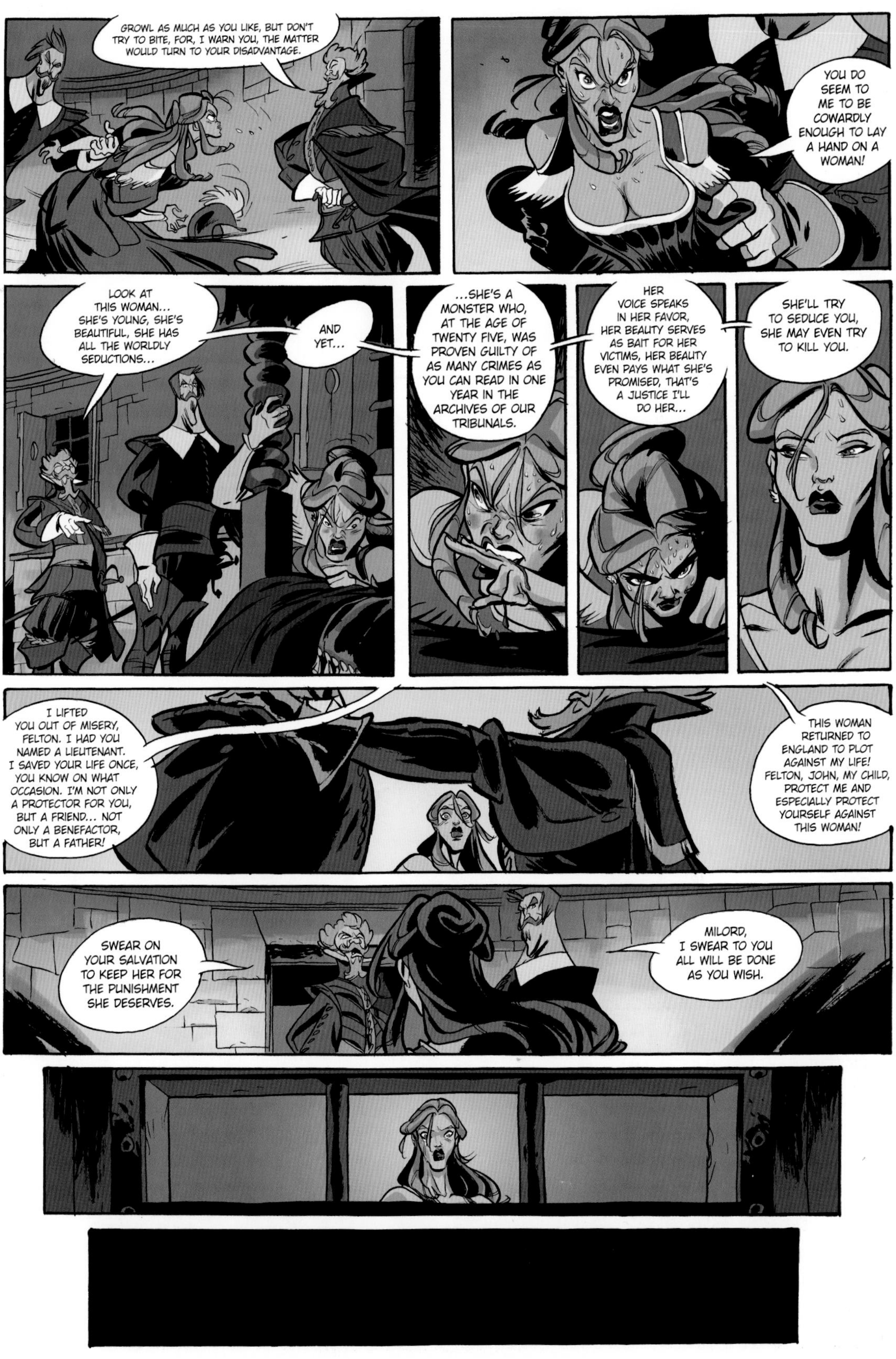
GROWL AS MUCH AS YOU LIKE, BUT DON'T TRY TO BITE, FOR, I WARN YOU, THE MATTER WOULD TURN TO YOUR DISADVANTAGE.
YOU DO SEEM TO ME TO BE COWARDLY ENOUGH TO LAY A HAND ON A WOMAN!
LOOK AT THIS WOMAN... SHE'S YOUNG, SHE'S BEAUTIFUL, SHE HAS ALL THE WORLDLY SEDUCTIONS...
AND YET...
...SHE'S A MONSTER WHO, AT THE AGE OF TWENTY FIVE, WAS PROVEN GUILTY OF AS MANY CRIMES AS YOU CAN READ IN ONE YEAR IN THE ARCHIVES OF OUR TRIBUNALS.
HER VOICE SPEAKS IN HER FAVOR, HER BEAUTY SERVES AS BAIT FOR HER VICTIMS, HER BEAUTY EVEN PAYS WHAT SHE'S PROMISED, THAT'S A JUSTICE I'LL DO HER...
SHE'LL TRY TO SEDUCE YOU, SHE MAY EVEN TRY TO KILL YOU.
I LIFTED YOU OUT OF MISERY, FELTON. I HAD YOU NAMED A LIEUTENANT. I SAVED YOUR LIFE ONCE, YOU KNOW ON WHAT OCCASION. I'M NOT ONLY A PROTECTOR FOR YOU, BUT A FRIEND... NOT ONLY A BENEFACTOR, BUT A FATHER!
THIS WOMAN RETURNED TO ENGLAND TO PLOT AGAINST MY LIFE! FELTON, JOHN, MY CHILD, PROTECT ME AND ESPECIALLY PROTECT YOURSELF AGAINST THIS WOMAN!
SWEAR ON YOUR SALVATION TO KEEP HER FOR THE PUNISHMENT SHE DESERVES.
MILORD, I SWEAR TO YOU ALL WILL BE DONE AS YOU WISH.

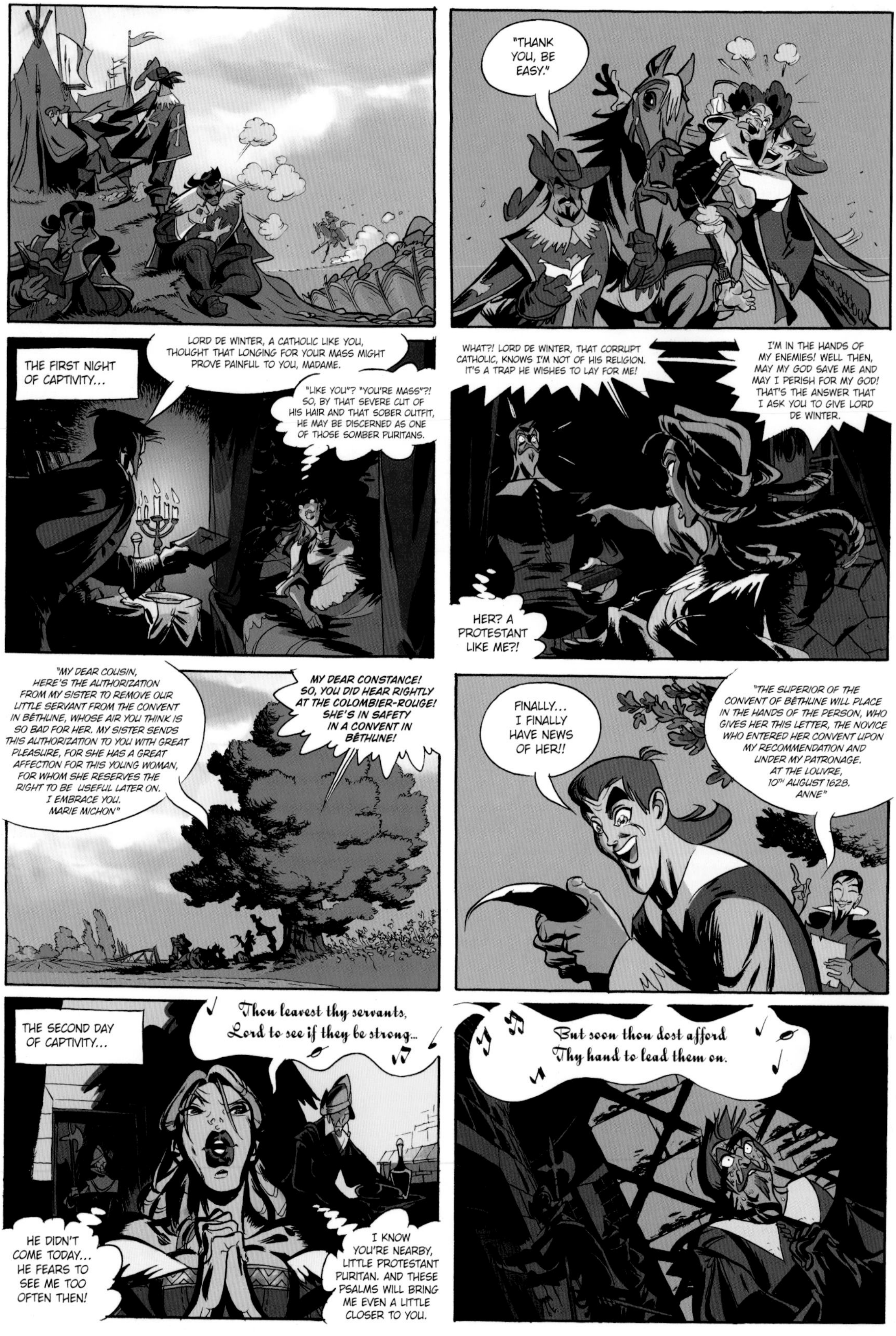
"THANK YOU, BE EASY."
THE FIRST NIGHT OF CAPTIVITY...
LORD DE WINTER, A CATHOLIC LIKE YOU, THOUGHT THAT LONGING FOR YOUR MASS MIGHT PROVE PAINFUL TO YOU, MADAME.
"LIKE YOU"? "YOU'RE MASS"?! SO, BY THAT SEVERE CUT OF HIS HAIR AND THAT SOBER OUTFIT, HE MAY BE DISCERNED AS ONE OF THOSE SOMBER PURITANS.
WHAT?! LORD DE WINTER, THAT CORRUPT CATHOLIC, KNOWS I'M NOT OF HIS RELIGION. IT'S A TRAP HE WISHES TO LAY FOR ME!
I'M IN THE HANDS OF MY ENEMIES! WELL THEN, MAY MY GOD SAVE ME AND MAY I PERISH FOR MY GOD! THAT'S THE ANSWER THAT I ASK YOU TO GIVE LORD DE WINTER.
HER? A PROTESTANT LIKE ME?!
"MY DEAR COUSIN, HERE'S THE AUTHORIZATION FROM MY SISTER TO REMOVE OUR LITTLE SERVANT FROM THE CONVENT IN BÉTHUNE, WHOSE AIR YOU THINK IS SO BAD FOR HER. MY SISTER SENDS THIS AUTHORIZATION TO YOU WITH GREAT PLEASURE, FOR SHE HAS A GREAT AFFECTION FOR THIS YOUNG WOMAN, FOR WHOM SHE RESERVES THE RIGHT TO BE USEFUL LATER ON. I EMBRACE YOU. MARIE MICHON"
MY DEAR CONSTANCE! SO, YOU DID HEAR RIGHTLY AT THE COLOMBIER-ROUGE! SHE'S IN SAFETY IN A CONVENT IN BÉTHUNE!
FINALLY... I FINALLY HAVE NEWS OF HER!!
"THE SUPERIOR OF THE CONVENT OF BÉTHUNE WILL PLACE IN THE HANDS OF THE PERSON, WHO GIVES HER THIS LETTER, THE NOVICE WHO ENTERED HER CONVENT UPON MY RECOMMENDATION AND UNDER MY PATRONAGE. AT THE LOUVRE, 10TH AUGUST 1628. ANNE"
THE SECOND DAY OF CAPTIVITY...
Thou leavest thy servants, Lord to see if they be strong...
HE DIDN'T COME TODAY... HE FEARS TO SEE ME TOO OFTEN THEN!
I KNOW YOU'RE NEARBY, LITTLE PROTESTANT PURITAN. AND THESE PSALMS WILL BRING ME EVEN A LITTLE CLOSER TO YOU.
But soon thou dost afford Thy hand to lead them on.

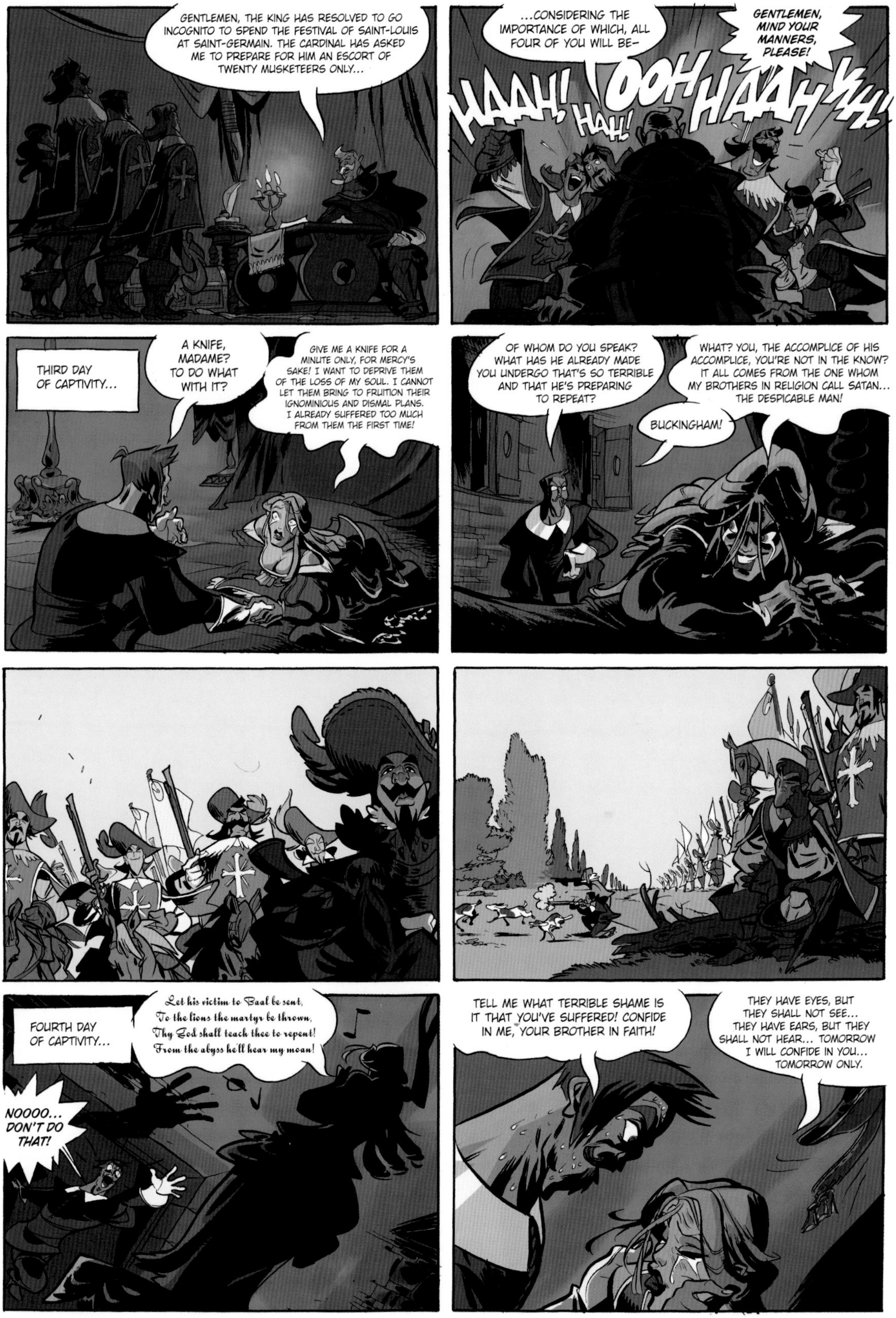

GENTLEMEN, THE KING HAS RESOLVED TO GO INCOGNITO TO SPEND THE FESTIVAL OF SAINT-LOUIS AT SAINT-GERMAIN. THE CARDINAL HAS ASKED ME TO PREPARE FOR HIM AN ESCORT OF TWENTY MUSKETEERS ONLY...
...CONSIDERING THE IMPORTANCE OF WHICH, ALL FOUR OF YOU WILL BE–
GENTLEMEN, MIND YOUR MANNERS, PLEASE!
HAAH! HAH! OOH HAAHHH!
THIRD DAY OF CAPTIVITY...
A KNIFE, MADAME? TO DO WHAT WITH IT?
GIVE ME A KNIFE FOR A MINUTE ONLY, FOR MERCY'S SAKE! I WANT TO DEPRIVE THEM OF THE LOSS OF MY SOUL. I CANNOT LET THEM BRING TO FRUITION THEIR IGNOMINIOUS AND DISMAL PLANS. I ALREADY SUFFERED TOO MUCH FROM THEM THE FIRST TIME!
OF WHOM DO YOU SPEAK? WHAT HAS HE ALREADY MADE YOU UNDERGO THAT'S SO TERRIBLE AND THAT HE'S PREPARING TO REPEAT?
WHAT? YOU, THE ACCOMPLICE OF HIS ACCOMPLICE, YOU'RE NOT IN THE KNOW? IT ALL COMES FROM THE ONE WHOM MY BROTHERS IN RELIGION CALL SATAN... THE DESPICABLE MAN!
BUCKINGHAM!
FOURTH DAY OF CAPTIVITY...
Let his victim to Baal be sent, To the lions the martyr be thrown, Thy God shall teach thee to repent! From the abyss he'll hear my moan!
NOOOO... DON'T DO THAT!
TELL ME WHAT TERRIBLE SHAME IS IT THAT YOU'VE SUFFERED! CONFIDE IN ME, YOUR BROTHER IN FAITH!
THEY HAVE EYES, BUT THEY SHALL NOT SEE... THEY HAVE EARS, BUT THEY SHALL NOT HEAR... TOMORROW I WILL CONFIDE IN YOU... TOMORROW ONLY.

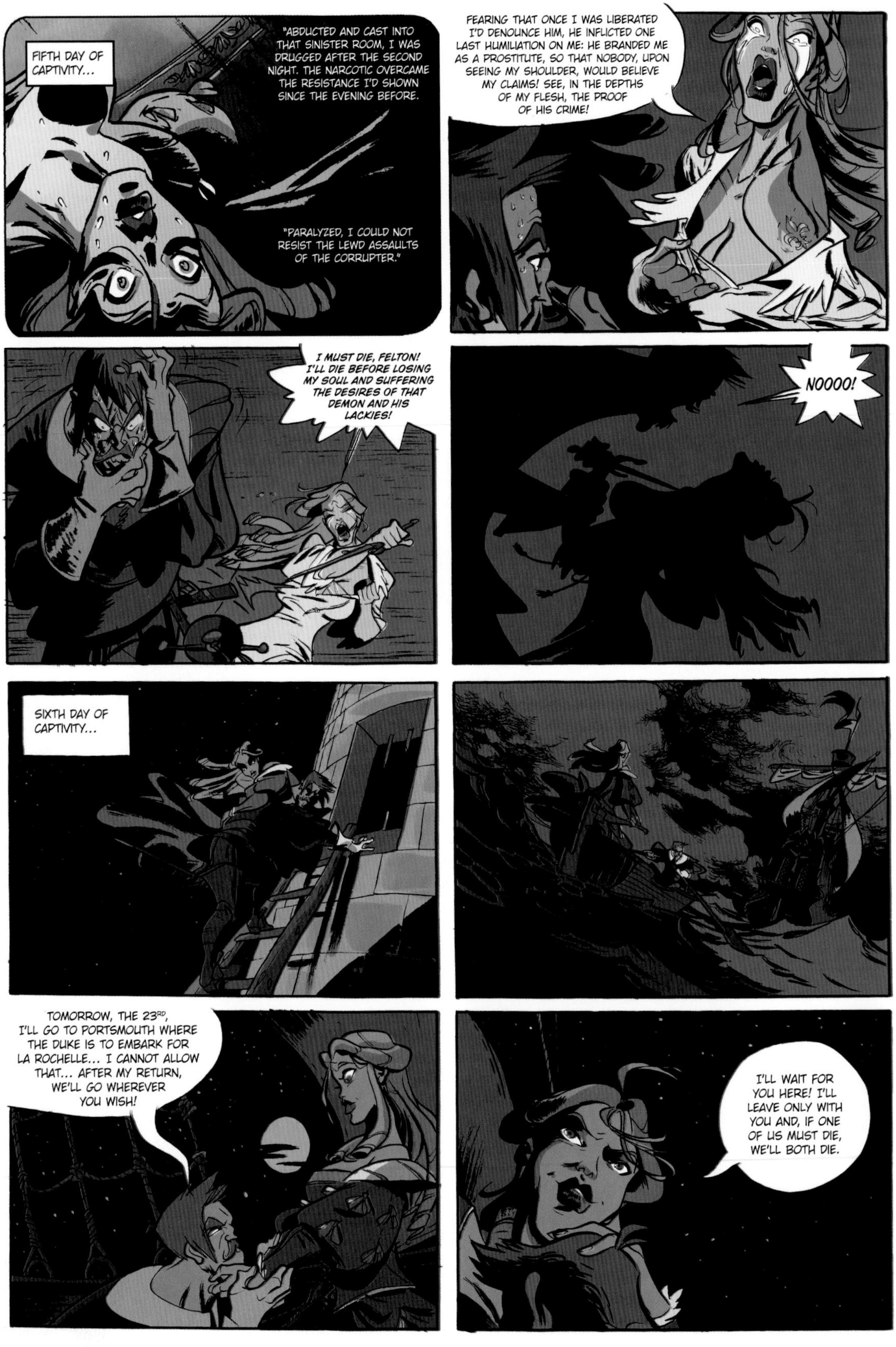
FIFTH DAY OF CAPTIVITY...
"ABDUCTED AND CAST INTO THAT SINISTER ROOM, I WAS DRUGGED AFTER THE SECOND NIGHT. THE NARCOTIC OVERCAME THE RESISTANCE I'D SHOWN SINCE THE EVENING BEFORE.
"PARALYZED, I COULD NOT RESIST THE LEWD ASSAULTS OF THE CORRUPTER."
FEARING THAT ONCE I WAS LIBERATED I'D DENOUNCE HIM, HE INFLICTED ONE LAST HUMILIATION ON ME: HE BRANDED ME AS A PROSTITUTE, SO THAT NOBODY, UPON SEEING MY SHOULDER, WOULD BELIEVE MY CLAIMS! SEE, IN THE DEPTHS OF MY FLESH, THE PROOF OF HIS CRIME!
I MUST DIE, FELTON! I'LL DIE BEFORE LOSING MY SOUL AND SUFFERING THE DESIRES OF THAT DEMON AND HIS LACKIES!
NOOOO!
SIXTH DAY OF CAPTIVITY...
TOMORROW, THE 23RD, I'LL GO TO PORTSMOUTH WHERE THE DUKE IS TO EMBARK FOR LA ROCHELLE... I CANNOT ALLOW THAT... AFTER MY RETURN, WE'LL GO WHEREVER YOU WISH!
I'LL WAIT FOR YOU HERE! I'LL LEAVE ONLY WITH YOU AND, IF ONE OF US MUST DIE, WE'LL BOTH DIE.

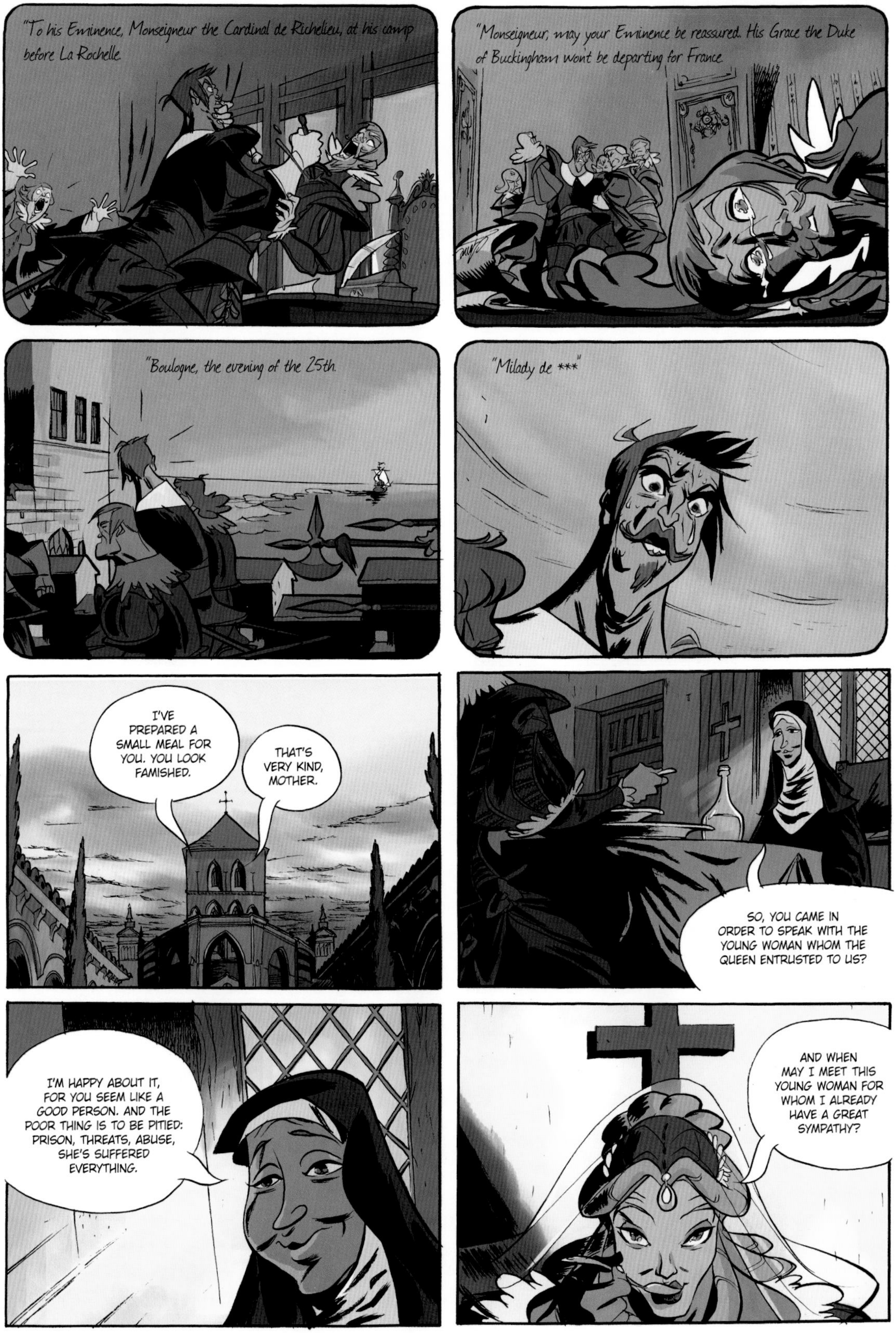
"To his Eminence, Monseigneur the Cardinal de Richelieu, at his camp before La Rochelle.
"Monseigneur, may your Eminence be reassured. His Grace the Duke of Buckingham won't be departing for France.
"Boulogne, the evening of the 25th.
"Milady de ***"
I'VE PREPARED A SMALL MEAL FOR YOU. YOU LOOK FAMISHED.
THAT'S VERY KIND, MOTHER.
SO, YOU CAME IN ORDER TO SPEAK WITH THE YOUNG WOMAN WHOM THE QUEEN ENTRUSTED TO US?
I'M HAPPY ABOUT IT, FOR YOU SEEM LIKE A GOOD PERSON. AND THE POOR THING IS TO BE PITIED: PRISON, THREATS, ABUSE, SHE'S SUFFERED EVERYTHING.
AND WHEN MAY I MEET THIS YOUNG WOMAN FOR WHOM I ALREADY HAVE A GREAT SYMPATHY?

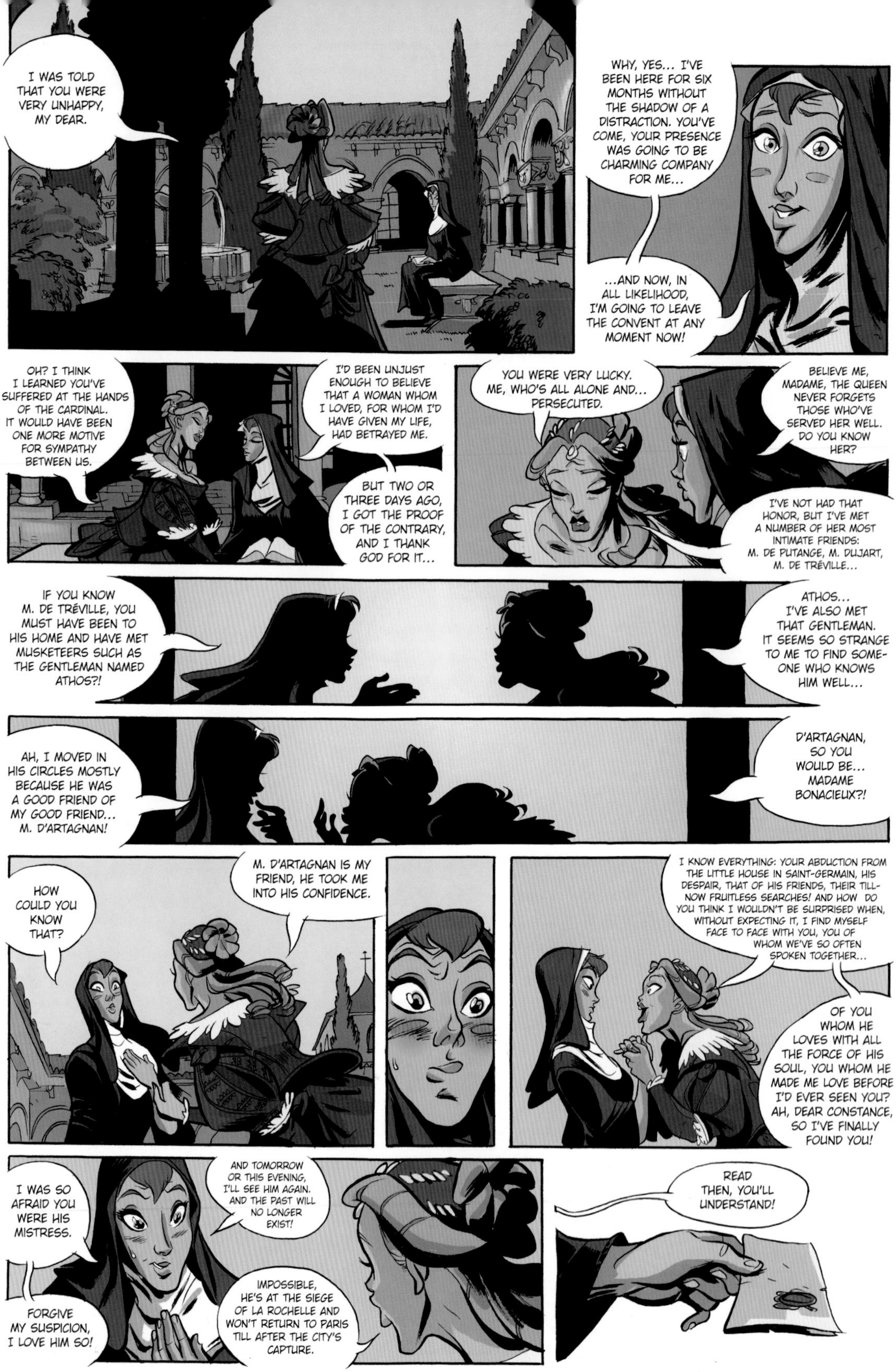
I WAS TOLD THAT YOU WERE VERY UNHAPPY, MY DEAR.
WHY, YES... I'VE BEEN HERE FOR SIX MONTHS WITHOUT THE SHADOW OF A DISTRACTION. YOU'VE COME, YOUR PRESENCE WAS GOING TO BE CHARMING COMPANY FOR ME...
...AND NOW, IN ALL LIKELIHOOD, I'M GOING TO LEAVE THE CONVENT AT ANY MOMENT NOW!
OH? I THINK I LEARNED YOU'VE SUFFERED AT THE HANDS OF THE CARDINAL. IT WOULD HAVE BEEN ONE MORE MOTIVE FOR SYMPATHY BETWEEN US.
I'D BEEN UNJUST ENOUGH TO BELIEVE THAT A WOMAN WHOM I LOVED, FOR WHOM I'D HAVE GIVEN MY LIFE, HAD BETRAYED ME.
BUT TWO OR THREE DAYS AGO, I GOT THE PROOF OF THE CONTRARY, AND I THANK GOD FOR IT...
YOU WERE VERY LUCKY. ME, WHO'S ALL ALONE AND... PERSECUTED.
BELIEVE ME, MADAME, THE QUEEN NEVER FORGETS THOSE WHO'VE SERVED HER WELL. DO YOU KNOW HER?
I'VE NOT HAD THAT HONOR, BUT I'VE MET A NUMBER OF HER MOST INTIMATE FRIENDS: M. DE PUTANGE, M. DUJART, M. DE TRÉVILLE...
IF YOU KNOW M. DE TRÉVILLE, YOU MUST HAVE BEEN TO HIS HOME AND HAVE MET MUSKETEERS SUCH AS THE GENTLEMAN NAMED ATHOS?!
ATHOS... I'VE ALSO MET THAT GENTLEMAN. IT SEEMS SO STRANGE TO ME TO FIND SOME-ONE WHO KNOWS HIM WELL...
AH, I MOVED IN HIS CIRCLES MOSTLY BECAUSE HE WAS A GOOD FRIEND OF MY GOOD FRIEND... M. D'ARTAGNAN!
D'ARTAGNAN, SO YOU WOULD BE... MADAME BONACIEUX?!
HOW COULD YOU KNOW THAT?
M. D'ARTAGNAN IS MY FRIEND, HE TOOK ME INTO HIS CONFIDENCE.
I KNOW EVERYTHING: YOUR ABDUCTION FROM THE LITTLE HOUSE IN SAINT-GERMAIN, HIS DESPAIR, THAT OF HIS FRIENDS, THEIR TILL-NOW FRUITLESS SEARCHES! AND HOW DO YOU THINK I WOULDN'T BE SURPRISED WHEN, WITHOUT EXPECTING IT, I FIND MYSELF FACE TO FACE WITH YOU, YOU OF WHOM WE'VE SO OFTEN SPOKEN TOGETHER...
OF YOU WHOM HE LOVES WITH ALL THE FORCE OF HIS SOUL, YOU WHOM HE MADE ME LOVE BEFORE I'D EVER SEEN YOU? AH, DEAR CONSTANCE, SO I'VE FINALLY FOUND YOU!
I WAS SO AFRAID YOU WERE HIS MISTRESS.
FORGIVE MY SUSPICION, I LOVE HIM SO!
AND TOMORROW OR THIS EVENING, I'LL SEE HIM AGAIN. AND THE PAST WILL NO LONGER EXIST!
IMPOSSIBLE, HE'S AT THE SIEGE OF LA ROCHELLE AND WON'T RETURN TO PARIS TILL AFTER THE CITY'S CAPTURE.
READ THEN, YOU'LL UNDERSTAND!

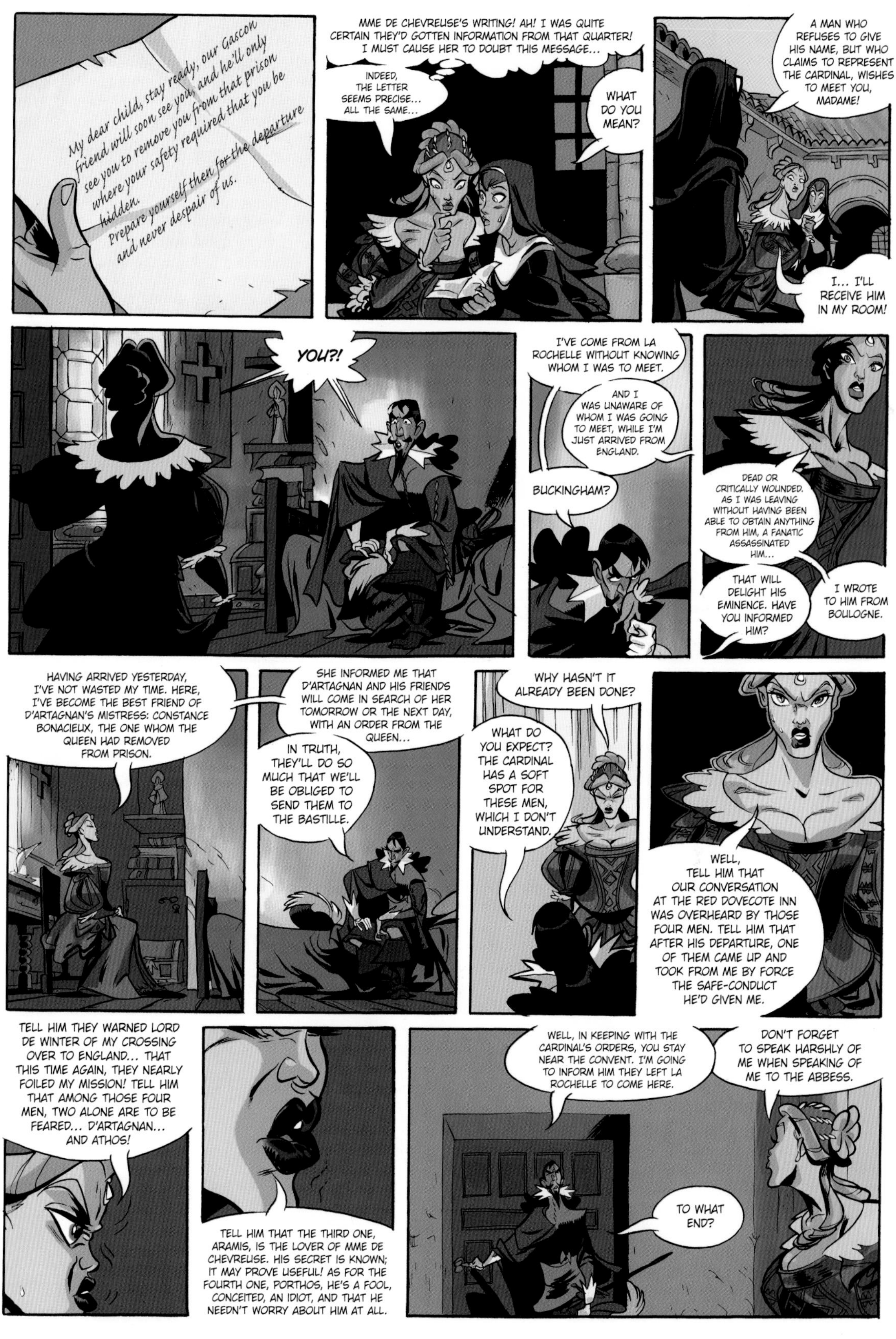
My dear child, stay ready, our Gascon friend will soon see you, and he'll only see you to remove you from that prison where your safety required that you be hidden.
Prepare yourself then for the departure and never despair of us.
MME DE CHEVREUSE'S WRITING! AH! I WAS QUITE CERTAIN THEY'D GOTTEN INFORMATION FROM THAT QUARTER! I MUST CAUSE HER TO DOUBT THIS MESSAGE…
INDEED, THE LETTER SEEMS PRECISE… ALL THE SAME…
WHAT DO YOU MEAN?
A MAN WHO REFUSES TO GIVE HIS NAME, BUT WHO CLAIMS TO REPRESENT THE CARDINAL, WISHES TO MEET YOU, MADAME!
I… I'LL RECEIVE HIM IN MY ROOM!
YOU?!
I'VE COME FROM LA ROCHELLE WITHOUT KNOWING WHOM I WAS TO MEET.
AND I WAS UNAWARE OF WHOM I WAS GOING TO MEET, WHILE I'M JUST ARRIVED FROM ENGLAND.
BUCKINGHAM?
DEAD OR CRITICALLY WOUNDED. AS I WAS LEAVING WITHOUT HAVING BEEN ABLE TO OBTAIN ANYTHING FROM HIM, A FANATIC ASSASSINATED HIM…
THAT WILL DELIGHT HIS EMINENCE. HAVE YOU INFORMED HIM?
I WROTE TO HIM FROM BOULOGNE.
HAVING ARRIVED YESTERDAY, I'VE NOT WASTED MY TIME. HERE, I'VE BECOME THE BEST FRIEND OF D'ARTAGNAN'S MISTRESS: CONSTANCE BONACIEUX, THE ONE WHOM THE QUEEN HAD REMOVED FROM PRISON.
SHE INFORMED ME THAT D'ARTAGNAN AND HIS FRIENDS WILL COME IN SEARCH OF HER TOMORROW OR THE NEXT DAY, WITH AN ORDER FROM THE QUEEN…
IN TRUTH, THEY'LL DO SO MUCH THAT WE'LL BE OBLIGED TO SEND THEM TO THE BASTILLE.
WHY HASN'T IT ALREADY BEEN DONE?
WHAT DO YOU EXPECT? THE CARDINAL HAS A SOFT SPOT FOR THESE MEN, WHICH I DON'T UNDERSTAND.
WELL, TELL HIM THAT OUR CONVERSATION AT THE RED DOVECOTE INN WAS OVERHEARD BY THOSE FOUR MEN. TELL HIM THAT AFTER HIS DEPARTURE, ONE OF THEM CAME UP AND TOOK FROM ME BY FORCE THE SAFE-CONDUCT HE'D GIVEN ME.
TELL HIM THEY WARNED LORD DE WINTER OF MY CROSSING OVER TO ENGLAND… THAT THIS TIME AGAIN, THEY NEARLY FOILED MY MISSION! TELL HIM THAT AMONG THOSE FOUR MEN, TWO ALONE ARE TO BE FEARED… D'ARTAGNAN… AND ATHOS!
TELL HIM THAT THE THIRD ONE, ARAMIS, IS THE LOVER OF MME DE CHEVREUSE. HIS SECRET IS KNOWN; IT MAY PROVE USEFUL! AS FOR THE FOURTH ONE, PORTHOS, HE'S A FOOL, CONCEITED, AN IDIOT, AND THAT HE NEEDN'T WORRY ABOUT HIM AT ALL.
WELL, IN KEEPING WITH THE CARDINAL'S ORDERS, YOU STAY NEAR THE CONVENT. I'M GOING TO INFORM HIM THEY LEFT LA ROCHELLE TO COME HERE.
DON'T FORGET TO SPEAK HARSHLY OF ME WHEN SPEAKING OF ME TO THE ABBESS.
TO WHAT END?

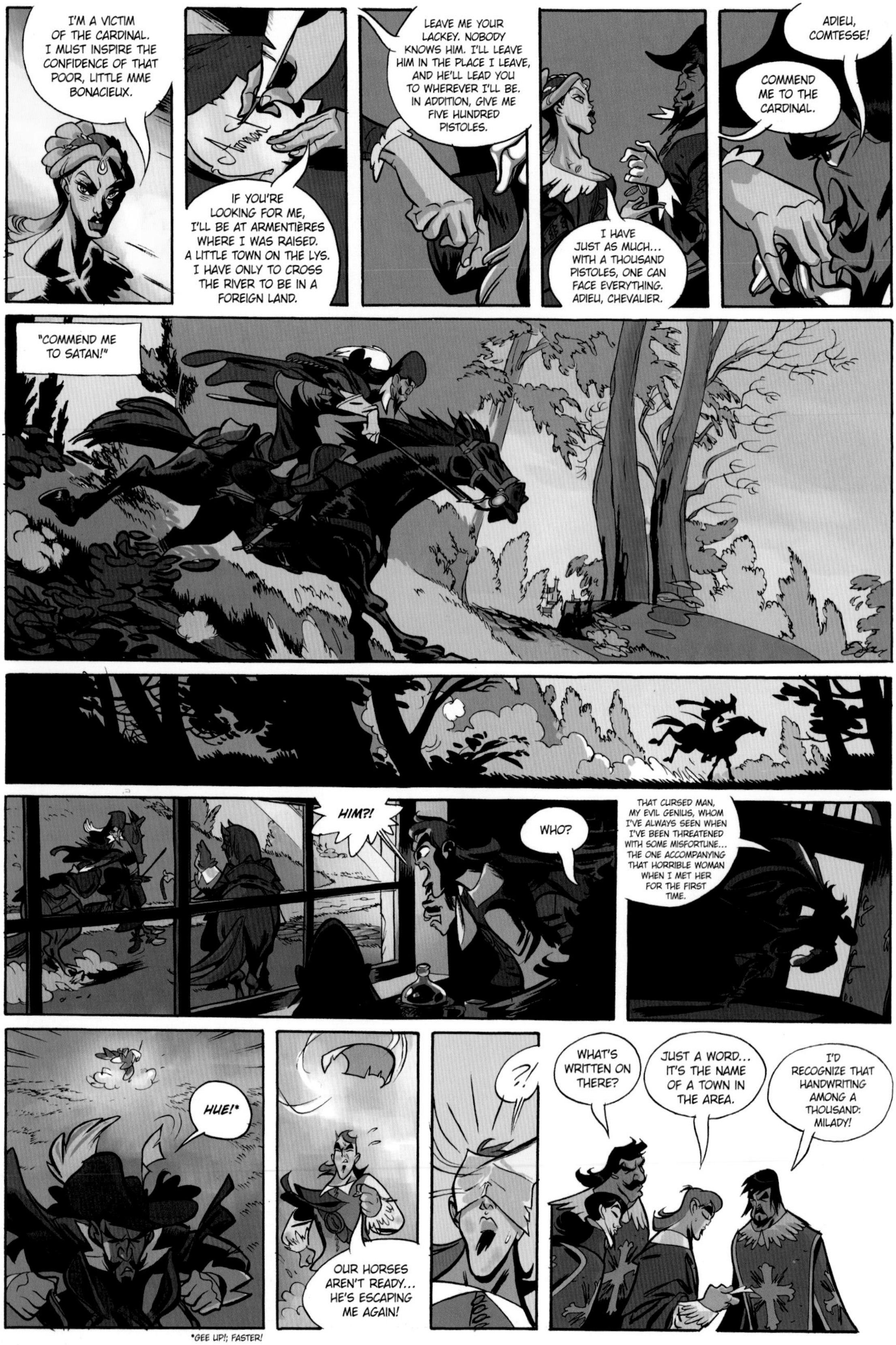
I'M A VICTIM OF THE CARDINAL. I MUST INSPIRE THE CONFIDENCE OF THAT POOR, LITTLE MME BONACIEUX.
IF YOU'RE LOOKING FOR ME, I'LL BE AT ARMENTIÈRES WHERE I WAS RAISED. A LITTLE TOWN ON THE LYS. I HAVE ONLY TO CROSS THE RIVER TO BE IN A FOREIGN LAND.
LEAVE ME YOUR LACKEY. NOBODY KNOWS HIM. I'LL LEAVE HIM IN THE PLACE I LEAVE, AND HE'LL LEAD YOU TO WHEREVER I'LL BE. IN ADDITION, GIVE ME FIVE HUNDRED PISTOLES.
I HAVE JUST AS MUCH... WITH A THOUSAND PISTOLES, ONE CAN FACE EVERYTHING. ADIEU, CHEVALIER.
ADIEU, COMTESSE!
COMMEND ME TO THE CARDINAL.
"COMMEND ME TO SATAN!"
HIM?!
WHO?
THAT CURSED MAN, MY EVIL GENIUS, WHOM I'VE ALWAYS SEEN WHEN I'VE BEEN THREATENED WITH SOME MISFORTUNE... THE ONE ACCOMPANYING THAT HORRIBLE WOMAN WHEN I MET HER FOR THE FIRST TIME.
HUE!*
OUR HORSES AREN'T READY... HE'S ESCAPING ME AGAIN!
?!
WHAT'S WRITTEN ON THERE?
JUST A WORD... IT'S THE NAME OF A TOWN IN THE AREA.
I'D RECOGNIZE THAT HANDWRITING AMONG A THOUSAND: MILADY!

*GEE UP!; FASTER!

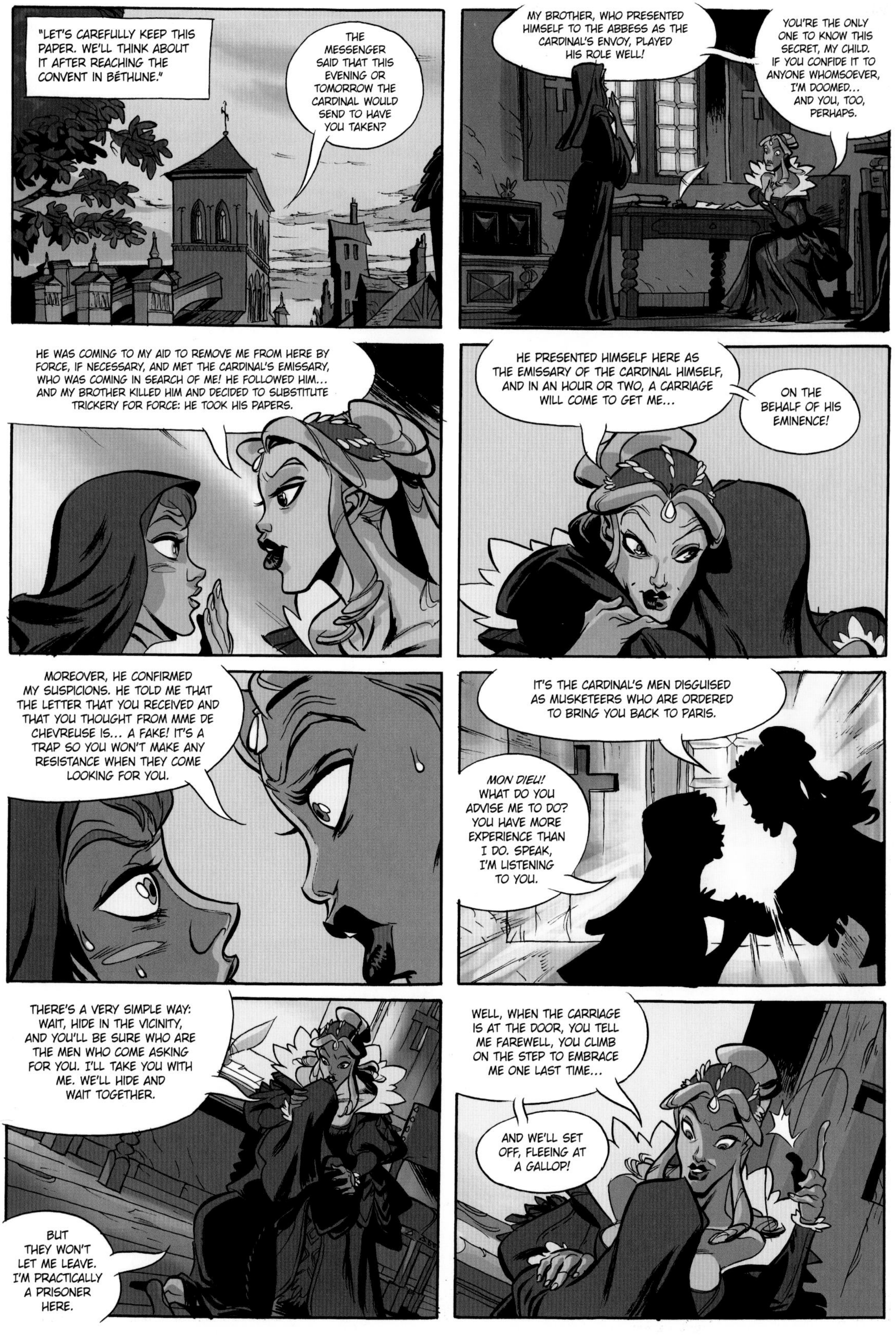
"LET'S CAREFULLY KEEP THIS PAPER. WE'LL THINK ABOUT IT AFTER REACHING THE CONVENT IN BÉTHUNE."
THE MESSENGER SAID THAT THIS EVENING OR TOMORROW THE CARDINAL WOULD SEND TO HAVE YOU TAKEN?
MY BROTHER, WHO PRESENTED HIMSELF TO THE ABBESS AS THE CARDINAL'S ENVOY, PLAYED HIS ROLE WELL!
YOU'RE THE ONLY ONE TO KNOW THIS SECRET, MY CHILD. IF YOU CONFIDE IT TO ANYONE WHOMSOEVER, I'M DOOMED... AND YOU, TOO, PERHAPS.
HE WAS COMING TO MY AID TO REMOVE ME FROM HERE BY FORCE, IF NECESSARY, AND MET THE CARDINAL'S EMISSARY, WHO WAS COMING IN SEARCH OF ME! HE FOLLOWED HIM... AND MY BROTHER KILLED HIM AND DECIDED TO SUBSTITUTE TRICKERY FOR FORCE: HE TOOK HIS PAPERS.
HE PRESENTED HIMSELF HERE AS THE EMISSARY OF THE CARDINAL HIMSELF, AND IN AN HOUR OR TWO, A CARRIAGE WILL COME TO GET ME...
ON THE BEHALF OF HIS EMINENCE!
MOREOVER, HE CONFIRMED MY SUSPICIONS. HE TOLD ME THAT THE LETTER THAT YOU RECEIVED AND THAT YOU THOUGHT FROM MME DE CHEVREUSE IS... A FAKE! IT'S A TRAP SO YOU WON'T MAKE ANY RESISTANCE WHEN THEY COME LOOKING FOR YOU.
IT'S THE CARDINAL'S MEN DISGUISED AS MUSKETEERS WHO ARE ORDERED TO BRING YOU BACK TO PARIS.
MON DIEU! WHAT DO YOU ADVISE ME TO DO? YOU HAVE MORE EXPERIENCE THAN I DO. SPEAK, I'M LISTENING TO YOU.
THERE'S A VERY SIMPLE WAY: WAIT, HIDE IN THE VICINITY, AND YOU'LL BE SURE WHO ARE THE MEN WHO COME ASKING FOR YOU. I'LL TAKE YOU WITH ME. WE'LL HIDE AND WAIT TOGETHER.
BUT THEY WON'T LET ME LEAVE. I'M PRACTICALLY A PRISONER HERE.
WELL, WHEN THE CARRIAGE IS AT THE DOOR, YOU TELL ME FAREWELL, YOU CLIMB ON THE STEP TO EMBRACE ME ONE LAST TIME...
AND WE'LL SET OFF, FLEEING AT A GALLOP!

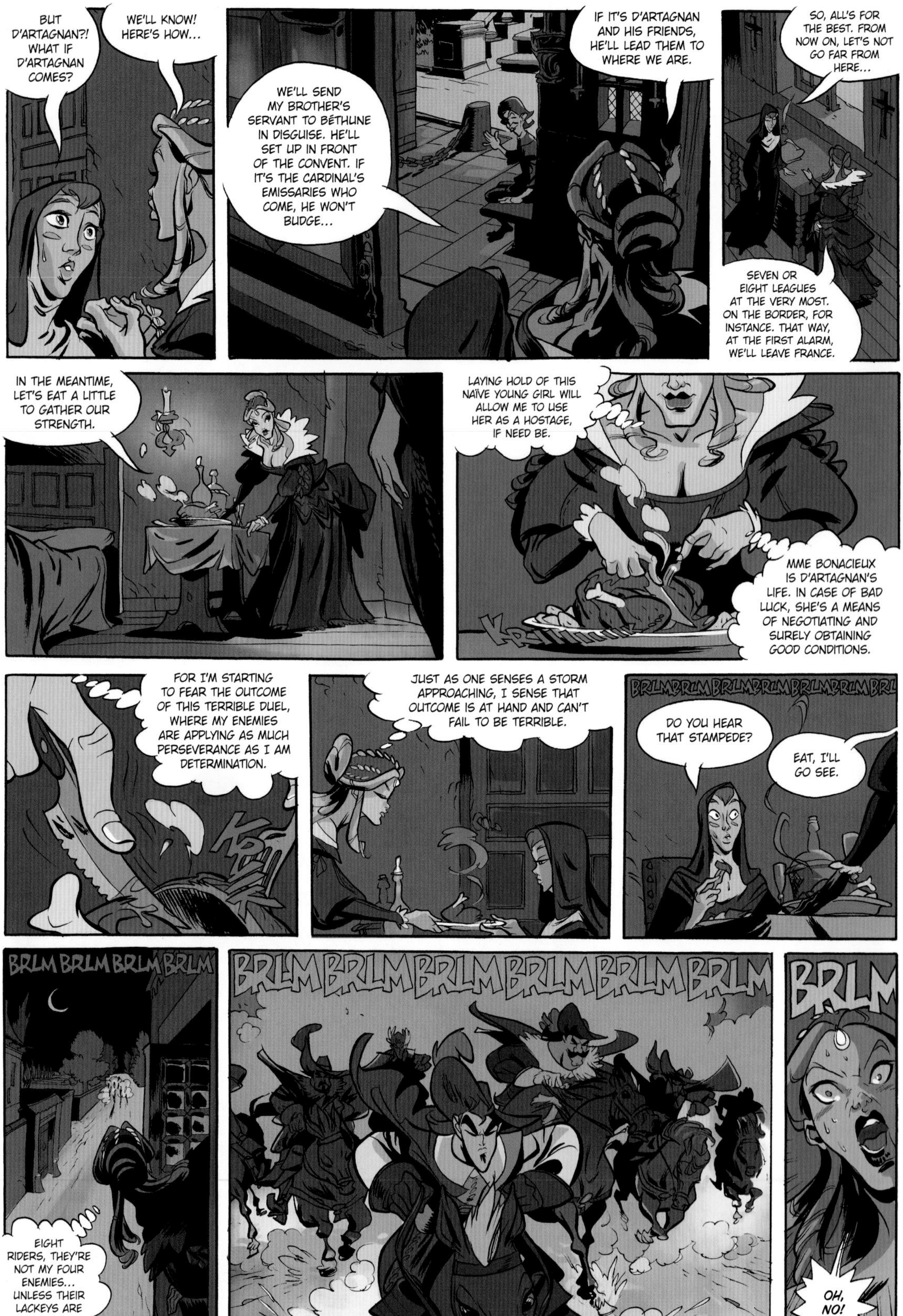
BUT D'ARTAGNAN?! WHAT IF D'ARTAGNAN COMES?
WE'LL KNOW! HERE'S HOW...
WE'LL SEND MY BROTHER'S SERVANT TO BÉTHUNE IN DISGUISE. HE'LL SET UP IN FRONT OF THE CONVENT. IF IT'S THE CARDINAL'S EMISSARIES WHO COME, HE WON'T BUDGE...
IF IT'S D'ARTAGNAN AND HIS FRIENDS, HE'LL LEAD THEM TO WHERE WE ARE.
SO, ALL'S FOR THE BEST. FROM NOW ON, LET'S NOT GO FAR FROM HERE...
SEVEN OR EIGHT LEAGUES AT THE VERY MOST. ON THE BORDER, FOR INSTANCE. THAT WAY, AT THE FIRST ALARM, WE'LL LEAVE FRANCE.
IN THE MEANTIME, LET'S EAT A LITTLE TO GATHER OUR STRENGTH.
LAYING HOLD OF THIS NAÏVE YOUNG GIRL WILL ALLOW ME TO USE HER AS A HOSTAGE, IF NEED BE.
MME BONACIEUX IS D'ARTAGNAN'S LIFE. IN CASE OF BAD LUCK, SHE'S A MEANS OF NEGOTIATING AND SURELY OBTAINING GOOD CONDITIONS.
FOR I'M STARTING TO FEAR THE OUTCOME OF THIS TERRIBLE DUEL, WHERE MY ENEMIES ARE APPLYING AS MUCH PERSEVERANCE AS I AM DETERMINATION.
JUST AS ONE SENSES A STORM APPROACHING, I SENSE THAT OUTCOME IS AT HAND AND CAN'T FAIL TO BE TERRIBLE.
BRLM BRLM BRLM BRLM BRLM BRLM BRLM
DO YOU HEAR THAT STAMPEDE?
EAT, I'LL GO SEE.
BRLM BRLM BRLM BRLM
EIGHT RIDERS, THEY'RE NOT MY FOUR ENEMIES... UNLESS THEIR LACKEYS ARE ACCOMPANY--
BRLM BRLM BRLM BRLM BRLM BRLM
BRLM
OH, NO!

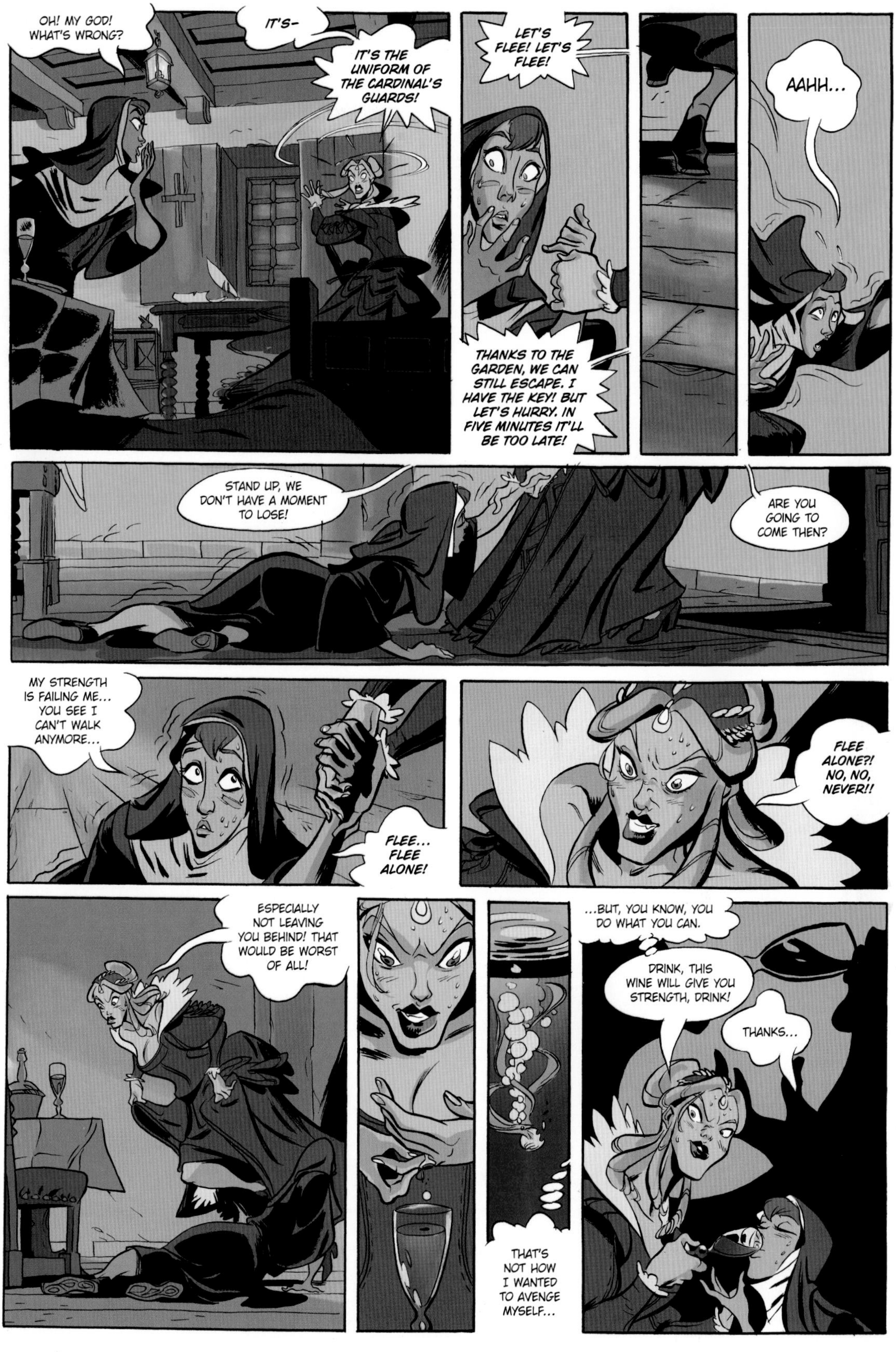
OH! MY GOD! WHAT'S WRONG?
IT'S-
IT'S THE UNIFORM OF THE CARDINAL'S GUARDS!
LET'S FLEE! LET'S FLEE!
THANKS TO THE GARDEN, WE CAN STILL ESCAPE. I HAVE THE KEY! BUT LET'S HURRY. IN FIVE MINUTES IT'LL BE TOO LATE!
AAHH...
STAND UP, WE DON'T HAVE A MOMENT TO LOSE!
ARE YOU GOING TO COME THEN?
MY STRENGTH IS FAILING ME... YOU SEE I CAN'T WALK ANYMORE...
FLEE... FLEE ALONE!
FLEE ALONE?! NO, NO, NEVER!!
ESPECIALLY NOT LEAVING YOU BEHIND! THAT WOULD BE WORST OF ALL!
THAT'S NOT HOW I WANTED TO AVENGE MYSELF...
...BUT, YOU KNOW, YOU DO WHAT YOU CAN.
DRINK, THIS WINE WILL GIVE YOU STRENGTH, DRINK!
THANKS...

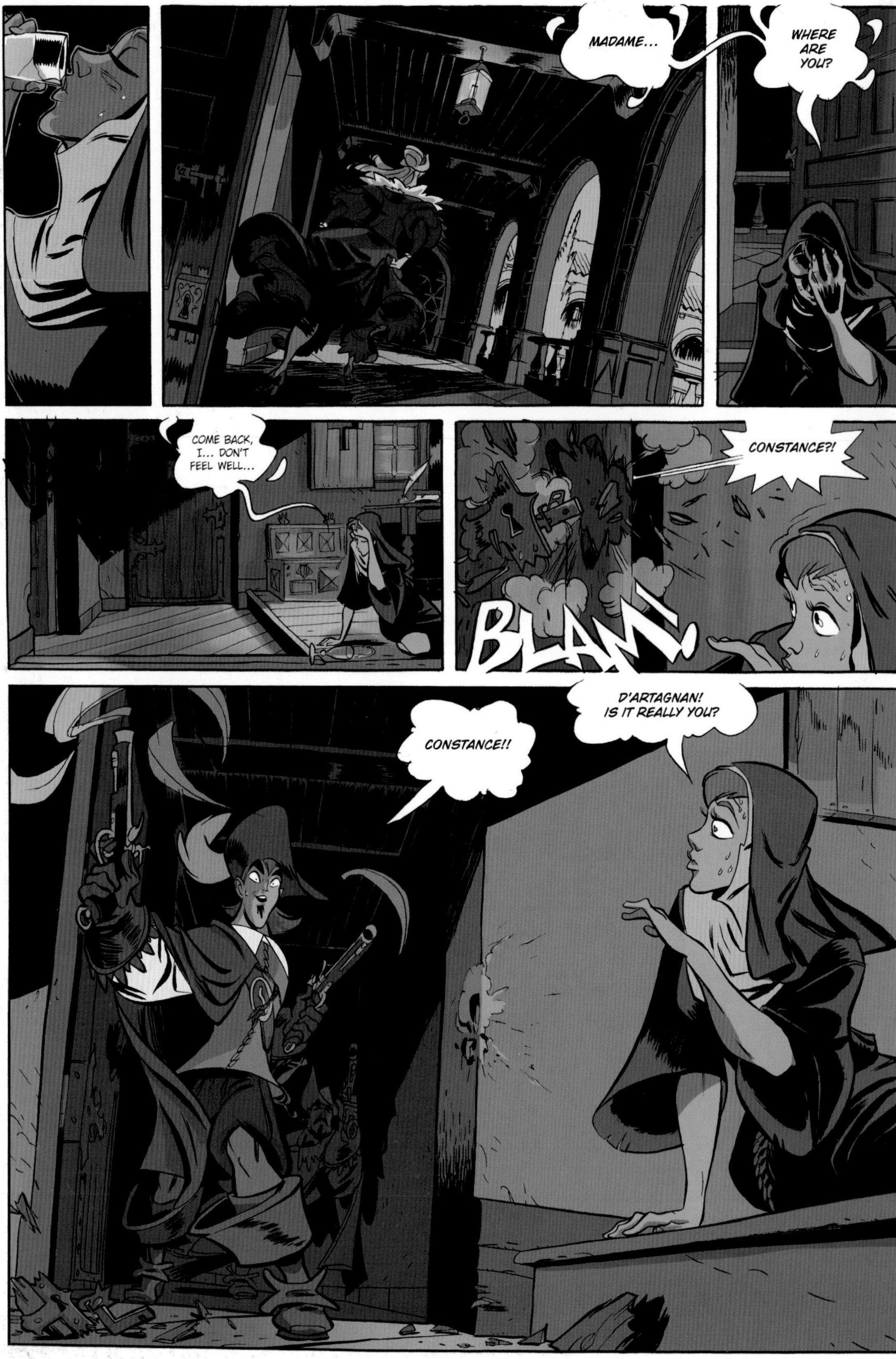
MADAME...
WHERE ARE YOU?
COME BACK, I... DON'T FEEL WELL...
CONSTANCE?!
BLAM!
CONSTANCE!!
D'ARTAGNAN! IS IT REALLY YOU?

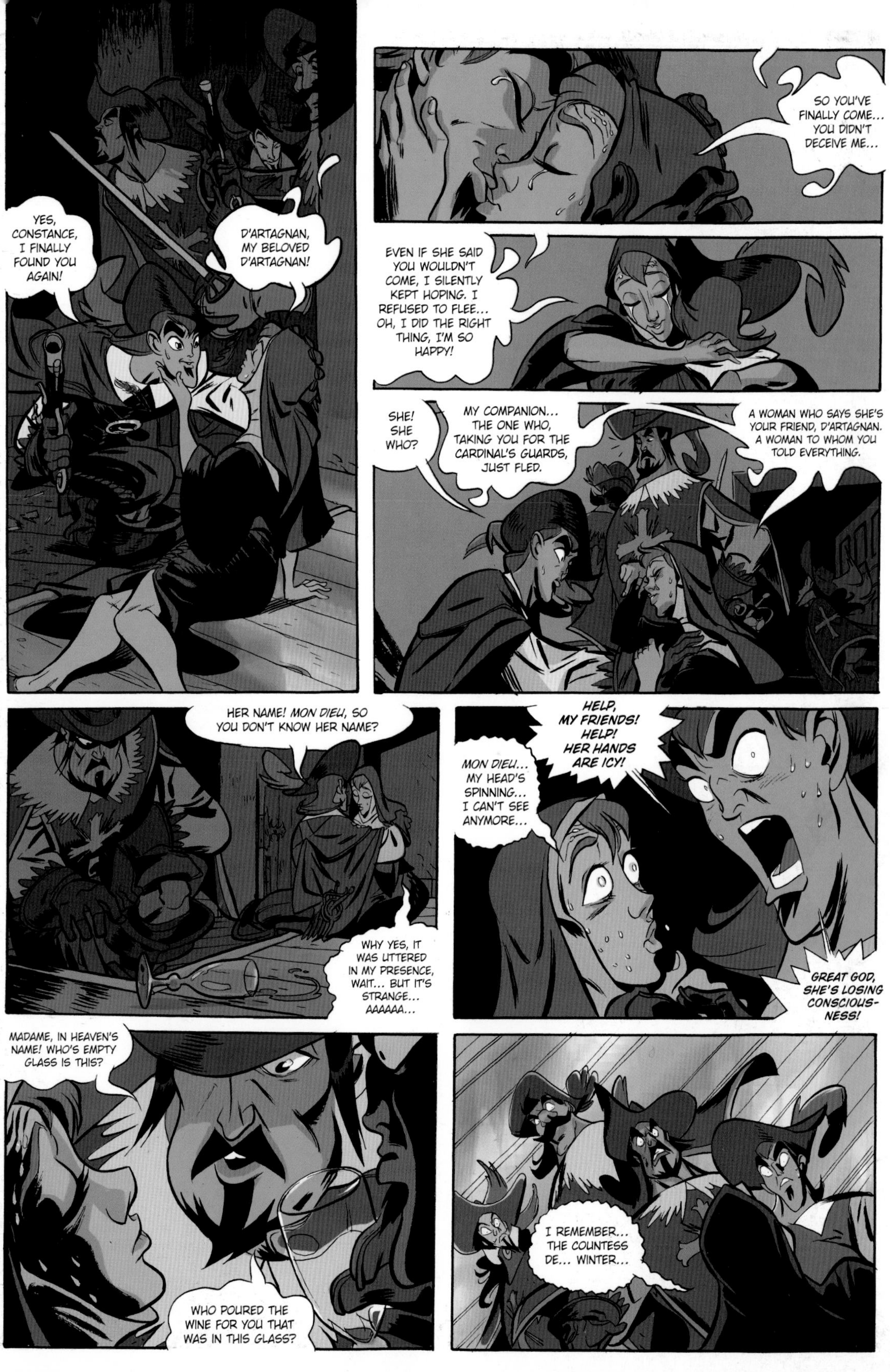
YES, CONSTANCE, I FINALLY FOUND YOU AGAIN!
D'ARTAGNAN, MY BELOVED D'ARTAGNAN!
SO YOU'VE FINALLY COME... YOU DIDN'T DECEIVE ME...
EVEN IF SHE SAID YOU WOULDN'T COME, I SILENTLY KEPT HOPING. I REFUSED TO FLEE... OH, I DID THE RIGHT THING, I'M SO HAPPY!
SHE! SHE WHO?
MY COMPANION... THE ONE WHO, TAKING YOU FOR THE CARDINAL'S GUARDS, JUST FLED.
A WOMAN WHO SAYS SHE'S YOUR FRIEND, D'ARTAGNAN. A WOMAN TO WHOM YOU TOLD EVERYTHING.
HER NAME! *MON DIEU*, SO YOU DON'T KNOW HER NAME?
WHY YES, IT WAS UTTERED IN MY PRESENCE, WAIT... BUT IT'S STRANGE... AAAAAA...
MON DIEU... MY HEAD'S SPINNING... I CAN'T SEE ANYMORE...
HELP, MY FRIENDS! HELP! HER HANDS ARE ICY!
GREAT GOD, SHE'S LOSING CONSCIOUS-NESS!
MADAME, IN HEAVEN'S NAME! WHO'S EMPTY GLASS IS THIS?
WHO POURED THE WINE FOR YOU THAT WAS IN THIS GLASS?
I REMEMBER... THE COUNTESS DE... WINTER...

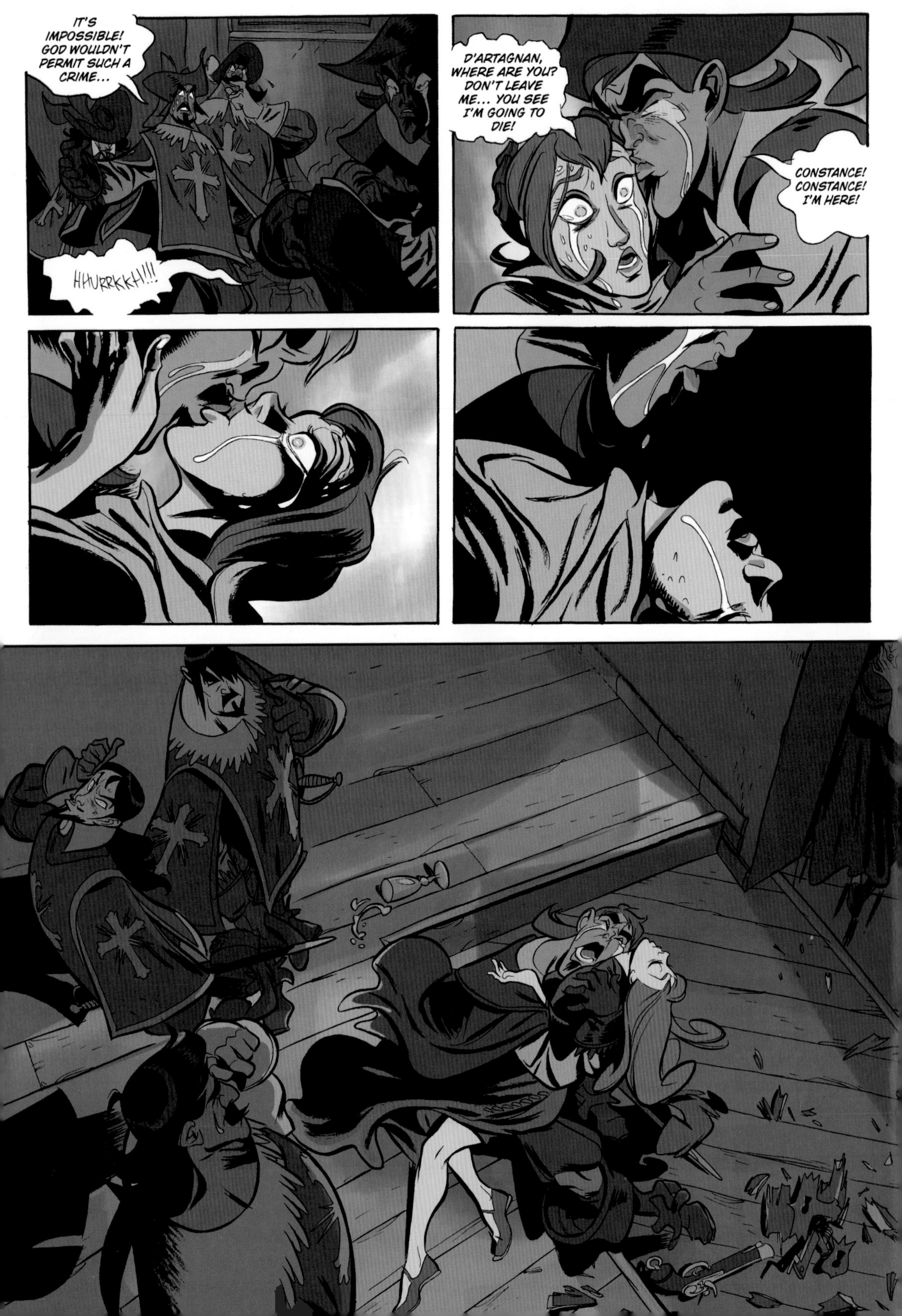
IT'S IMPOSSIBLE! GOD WOULDN'T PERMIT SUCH A CRIME...
HHURRKKH!!!
D'ARTAGNAN, WHERE ARE YOU? DON'T LEAVE ME... YOU SEE I'M GOING TO DIE!
CONSTANCE! CONSTANCE! I'M HERE!

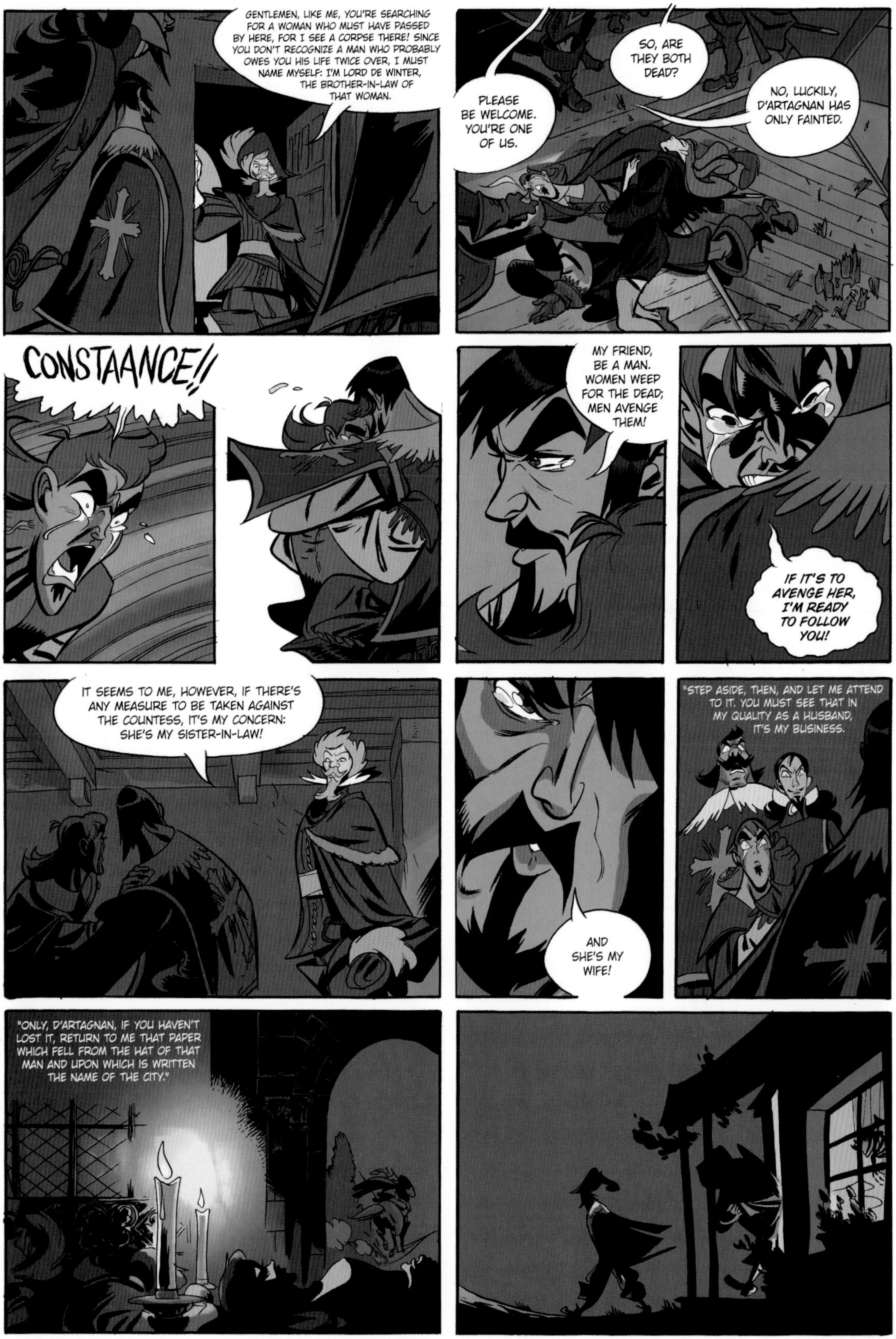
GENTLEMEN, LIKE ME, YOU'RE SEARCHING FOR A WOMAN WHO MUST HAVE PASSED BY HERE, FOR I SEE A CORPSE THERE! SINCE YOU DON'T RECOGNIZE A MAN WHO PROBABLY OWES YOU HIS LIFE TWICE OVER, I MUST NAME MYSELF: I'M LORD DE WINTER, THE BROTHER-IN-LAW OF THAT WOMAN.
PLEASE BE WELCOME. YOU'RE ONE OF US.
SO, ARE THEY BOTH DEAD?
NO, LUCKILY, D'ARTAGNAN HAS ONLY FAINTED.
CONSTAANCE!!
MY FRIEND, BE A MAN. WOMEN WEEP FOR THE DEAD; MEN AVENGE THEM!
IF IT'S TO AVENGE HER, I'M READY TO FOLLOW YOU!
IT SEEMS TO ME, HOWEVER, IF THERE'S ANY MEASURE TO BE TAKEN AGAINST THE COUNTESS, IT'S MY CONCERN: SHE'S MY SISTER-IN-LAW!
AND SHE'S MY WIFE!
"STEP ASIDE, THEN, AND LET ME ATTEND TO IT. YOU MUST SEE THAT IN MY QUALITY AS A HUSBAND, IT'S MY BUSINESS.
"ONLY, D'ARTAGNAN, IF YOU HAVEN'T LOST IT, RETURN TO ME THAT PAPER WHICH FELL FROM THE HAT OF THAT MAN AND UPON WHICH IS WRITTEN THE NAME OF THE CITY."

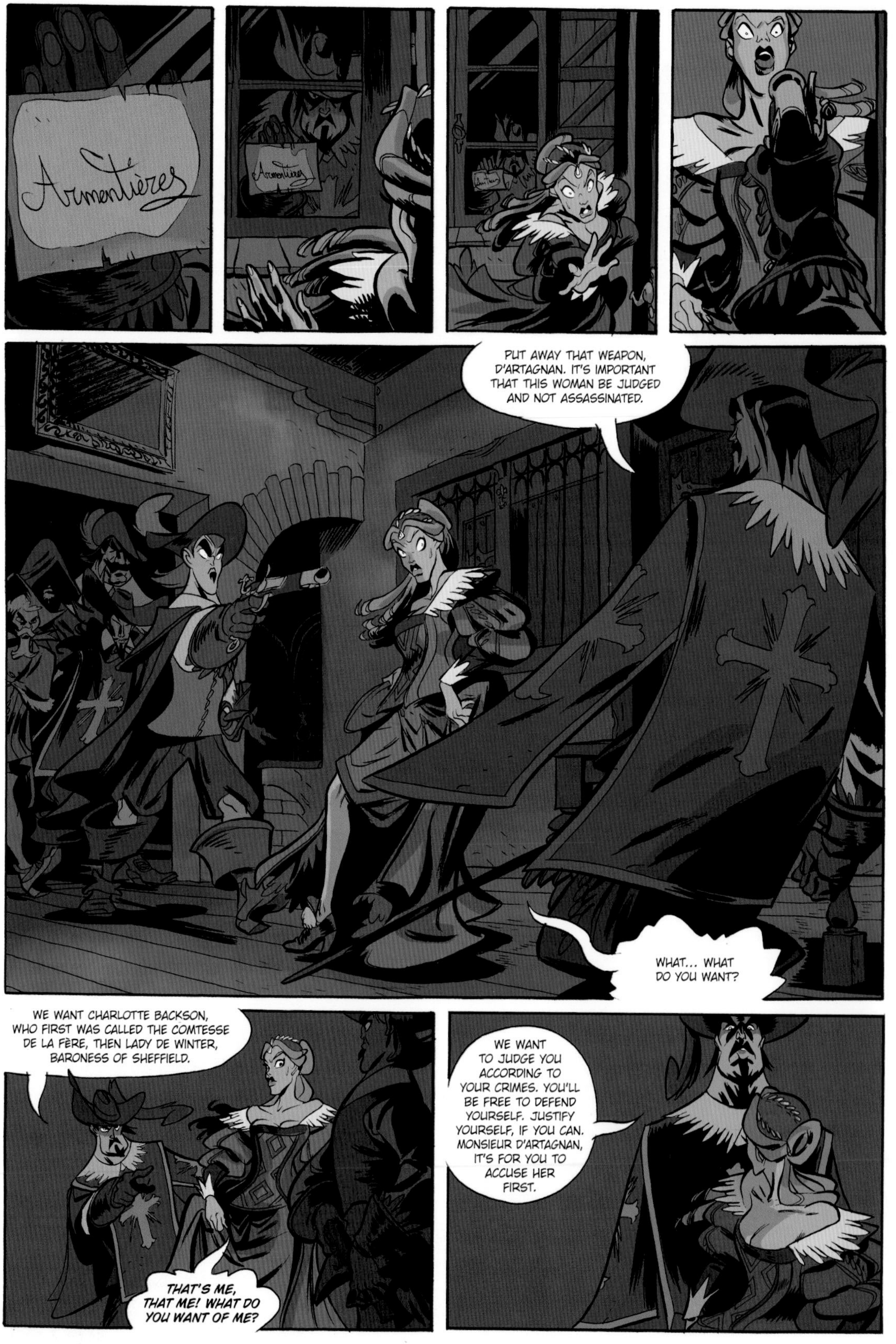
Armentières
PUT AWAY THAT WEAPON, D'ARTAGNAN. IT'S IMPORTANT THAT THIS WOMAN BE JUDGED AND NOT ASSASSINATED.
WHAT... WHAT DO YOU WANT?
WE WANT CHARLOTTE BACKSON, WHO FIRST WAS CALLED THE COMTESSE DE LA FÈRE, THEN LADY DE WINTER, BARONESS OF SHEFFIELD.
THAT'S ME, THAT ME! WHAT DO YOU WANT OF ME?
WE WANT TO JUDGE YOU ACCORDING TO YOUR CRIMES. YOU'LL BE FREE TO DEFEND YOURSELF. JUSTIFY YOURSELF, IF YOU CAN. MONSIEUR D'ARTAGNAN, IT'S FOR YOU TO ACCUSE HER FIRST.

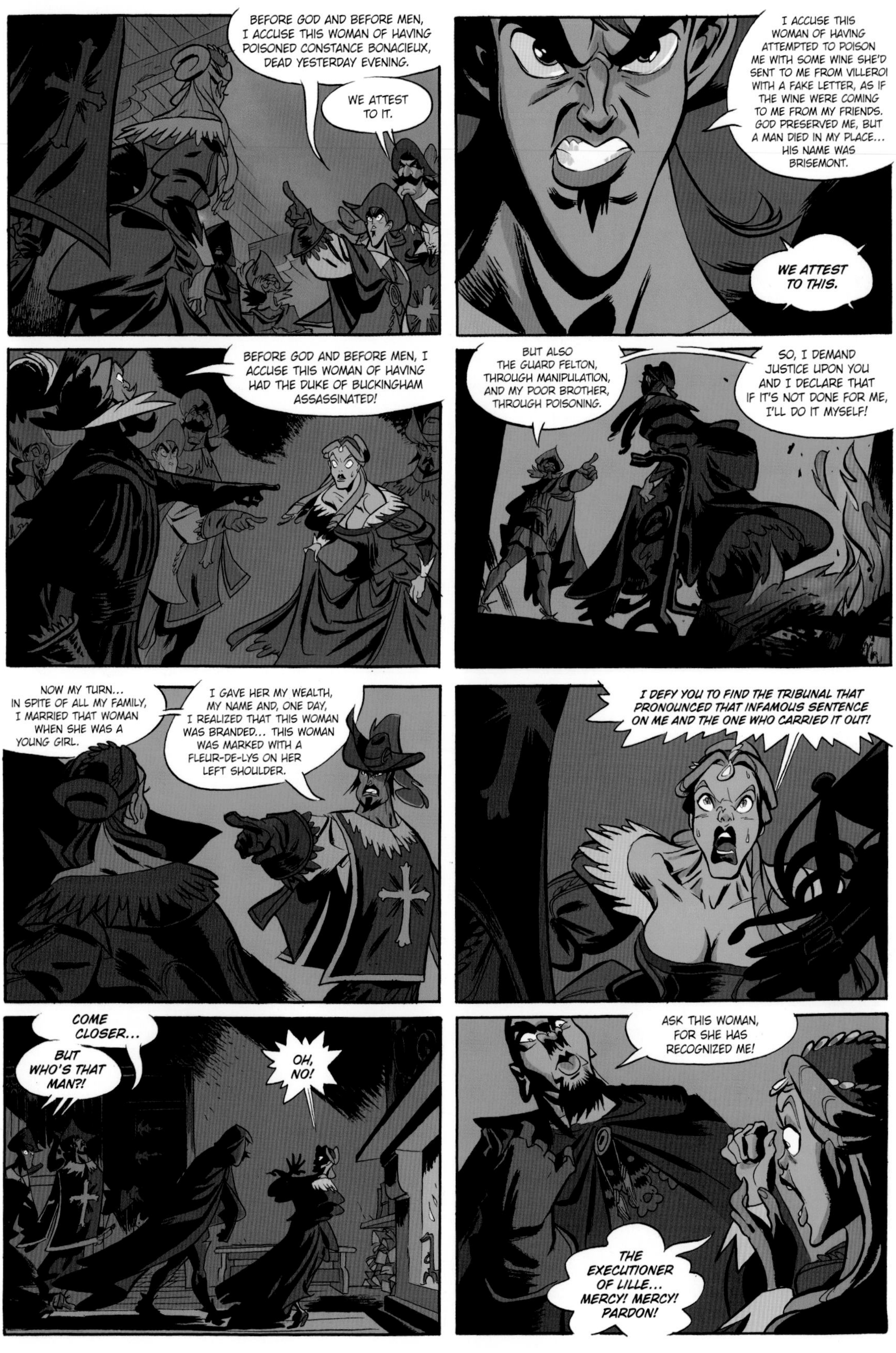
BEFORE GOD AND BEFORE MEN, I ACCUSE THIS WOMAN OF HAVING POISONED CONSTANCE BONACIEUX, DEAD YESTERDAY EVENING.
WE ATTEST TO IT.
I ACCUSE THIS WOMAN OF HAVING ATTEMPTED TO POISON ME WITH SOME WINE SHE'D SENT TO ME FROM VILLEROI WITH A FAKE LETTER, AS IF THE WINE WERE COMING TO ME FROM MY FRIENDS. GOD PRESERVED ME, BUT A MAN DIED IN MY PLACE... HIS NAME WAS BRISEMONT.
WE ATTEST TO THIS.
BEFORE GOD AND BEFORE MEN, I ACCUSE THIS WOMAN OF HAVING HAD THE DUKE OF BUCKINGHAM ASSASSINATED!
BUT ALSO THE GUARD FELTON, THROUGH MANIPULATION, AND MY POOR BROTHER, THROUGH POISONING.
SO, I DEMAND JUSTICE UPON YOU AND I DECLARE THAT IF IT'S NOT DONE FOR ME, I'LL DO IT MYSELF!
NOW MY TURN... IN SPITE OF ALL MY FAMILY, I MARRIED THAT WOMAN WHEN SHE WAS A YOUNG GIRL.
I GAVE HER MY WEALTH, MY NAME AND, ONE DAY, I REALIZED THAT THIS WOMAN WAS BRANDED... THIS WOMAN WAS MARKED WITH A FLEUR-DE-LYS ON HER LEFT SHOULDER.
I DEFY YOU TO FIND THE TRIBUNAL THAT PRONOUNCED THAT INFAMOUS SENTENCE ON ME AND THE ONE WHO CARRIED IT OUT!
COME CLOSER...
BUT WHO'S THAT MAN?!
OH, NO!
ASK THIS WOMAN, FOR SHE HAS RECOGNIZED ME!
THE EXECUTIONER OF LILLE... MERCY! MERCY! PARDON!

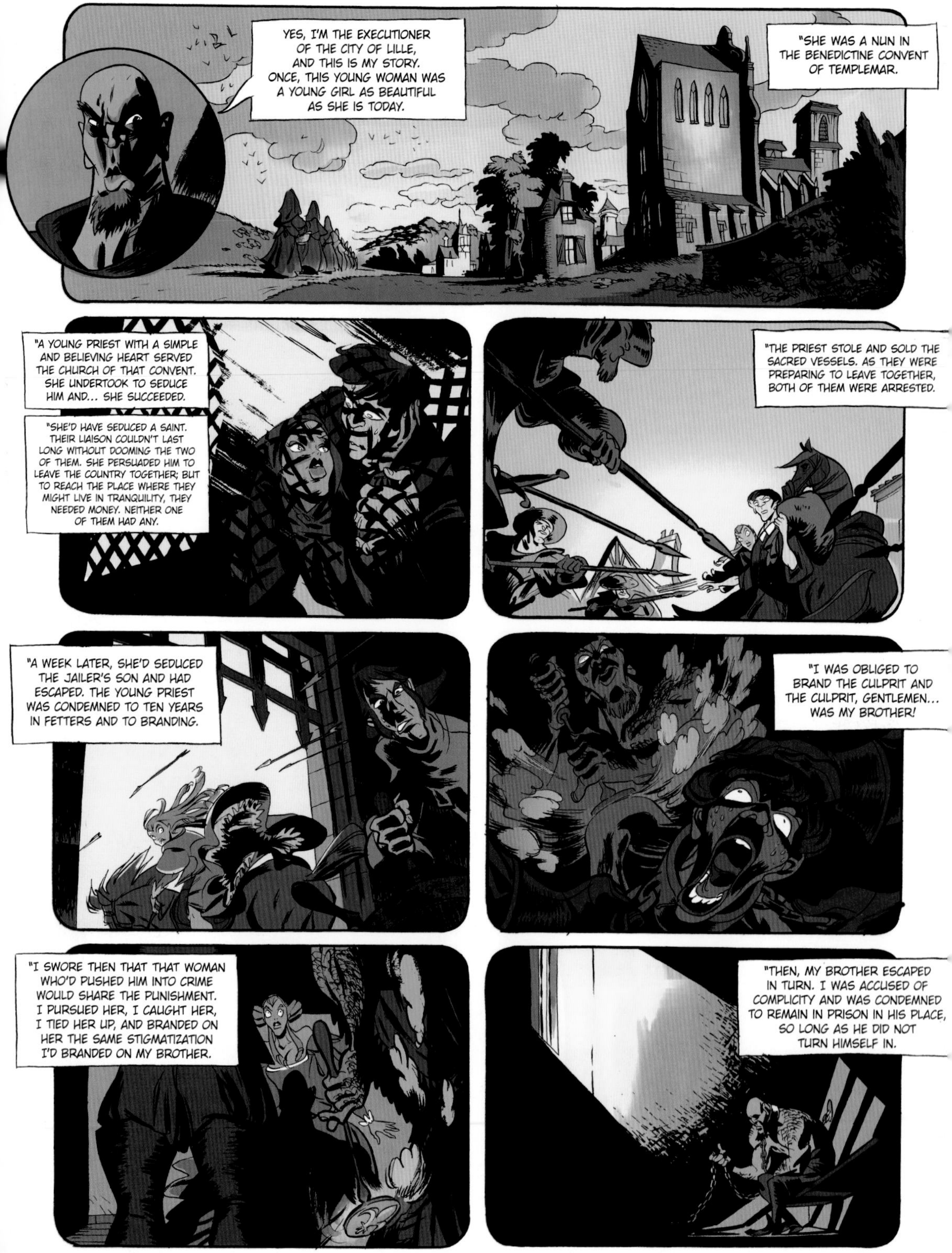
YES, I'M THE EXECUTIONER OF THE CITY OF LILLE, AND THIS IS MY STORY. ONCE, THIS YOUNG WOMAN WAS A YOUNG GIRL AS BEAUTIFUL AS SHE IS TODAY.
"SHE WAS A NUN IN THE BENEDICTINE CONVENT OF TEMPLEMAR.
"A YOUNG PRIEST WITH A SIMPLE AND BELIEVING HEART SERVED THE CHURCH OF THAT CONVENT. SHE UNDERTOOK TO SEDUCE HIM AND... SHE SUCCEEDED.
"SHE'D HAVE SEDUCED A SAINT. THEIR LIAISON COULDN'T LAST LONG WITHOUT DOOMING THE TWO OF THEM. SHE PERSUADED HIM TO LEAVE THE COUNTRY TOGETHER; BUT TO REACH THE PLACE WHERE THEY MIGHT LIVE IN TRANQUILITY, THEY NEEDED MONEY. NEITHER ONE OF THEM HAD ANY.
"THE PRIEST STOLE AND SOLD THE SACRED VESSELS. AS THEY WERE PREPARING TO LEAVE TOGETHER, BOTH OF THEM WERE ARRESTED.
"A WEEK LATER, SHE'D SEDUCED THE JAILER'S SON AND HAD ESCAPED. THE YOUNG PRIEST WAS CONDEMNED TO TEN YEARS IN FETTERS AND TO BRANDING.
"I WAS OBLIGED TO BRAND THE CULPRIT AND THE CULPRIT, GENTLEMEN... WAS MY BROTHER!
"I SWORE THEN THAT THAT WOMAN WHO'D PUSHED HIM INTO CRIME WOULD SHARE THE PUNISHMENT. I PURSUED HER, I CAUGHT HER, I TIED HER UP, AND BRANDED ON HER THE SAME STIGMATIZATION I'D BRANDED ON MY BROTHER.
"THEN, MY BROTHER ESCAPED IN TURN. I WAS ACCUSED OF COMPLICITY AND WAS CONDEMNED TO REMAIN IN PRISON IN HIS PLACE, SO LONG AS HE DID NOT TURN HIMSELF IN.

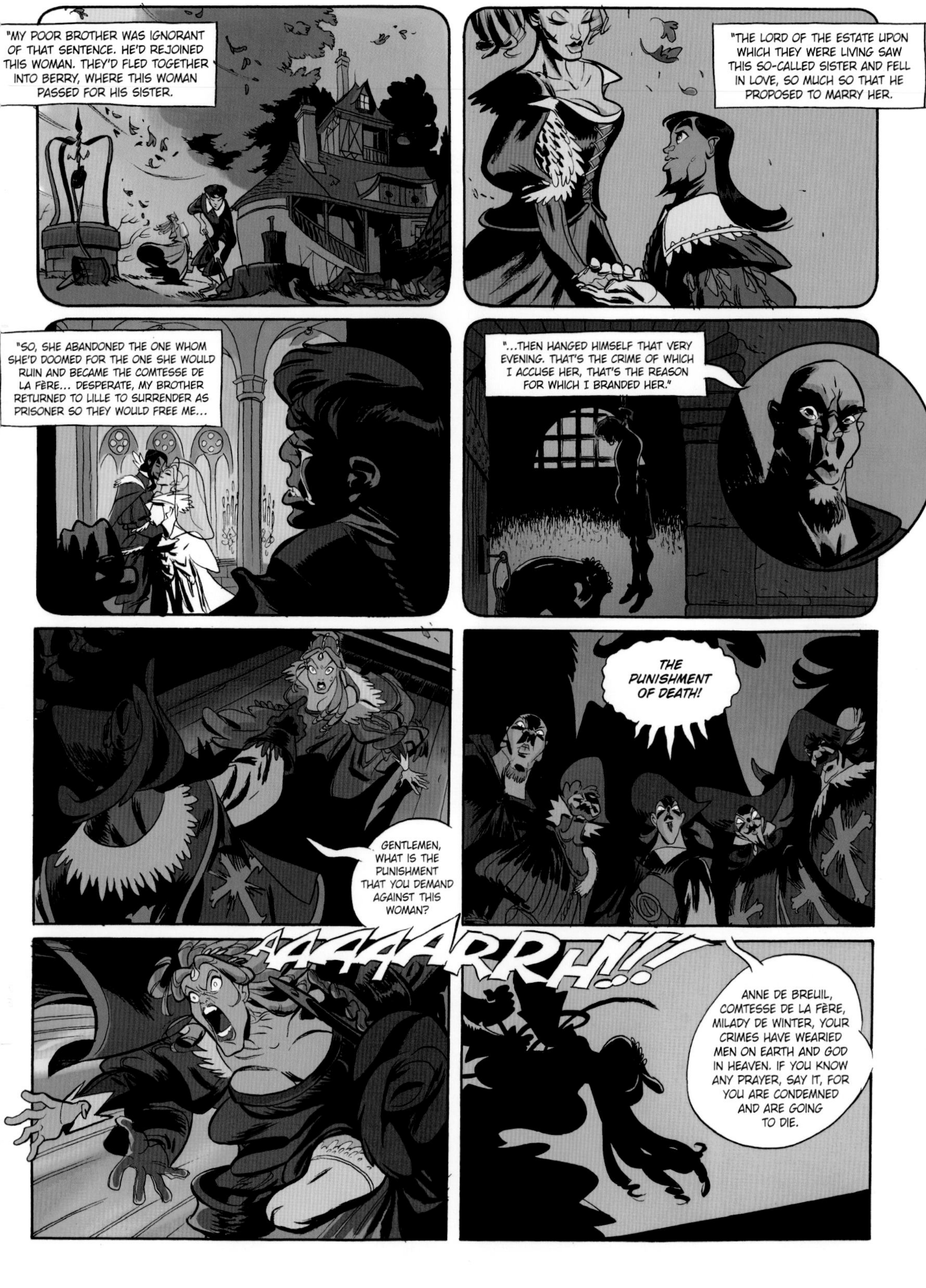
"MY POOR BROTHER WAS IGNORANT OF THAT SENTENCE. HE'D REJOINED THIS WOMAN. THEY'D FLED TOGETHER INTO BERRY, WHERE THIS WOMAN PASSED FOR HIS SISTER.
"THE LORD OF THE ESTATE UPON WHICH THEY WERE LIVING SAW THIS SO-CALLED SISTER AND FELL IN LOVE, SO MUCH SO THAT HE PROPOSED TO MARRY HER.
"SO, SHE ABANDONED THE ONE WHOM SHE'D DOOMED FOR THE ONE SHE WOULD RUIN AND BECAME THE COMTESSE DE LA FÈRE... DESPERATE, MY BROTHER RETURNED TO LILLE TO SURRENDER AS PRISONER SO THEY WOULD FREE ME...
"...THEN HANGED HIMSELF THAT VERY EVENING. THAT'S THE CRIME OF WHICH I ACCUSE HER, THAT'S THE REASON FOR WHICH I BRANDED HER."
GENTLEMEN, WHAT IS THE PUNISHMENT THAT YOU DEMAND AGAINST THIS WOMAN?
THE PUNISHMENT OF DEATH!
AAAAARRH!!
ANNE DE BREUIL, COMTESSE DE LA FÈRE, MILADY DE WINTER, YOUR CRIMES HAVE WEARIED MEN ON EARTH AND GOD IN HEAVEN. IF YOU KNOW ANY PRAYER, SAY IT, FOR YOU ARE CONDEMNED AND ARE GOING TO DIE.

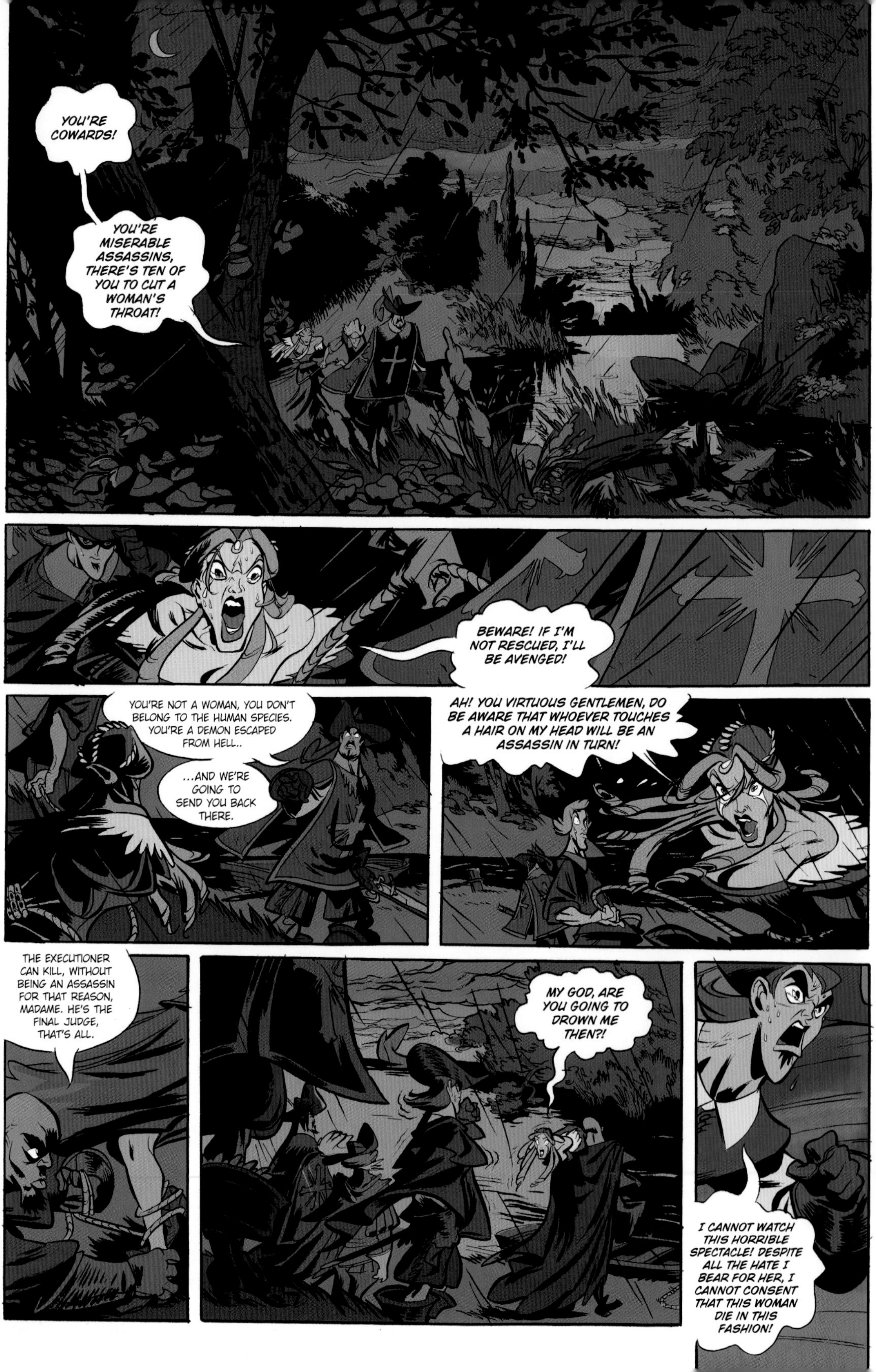
YOU'RE COWARDS!
YOU'RE MISERABLE ASSASSINS, THERE'S TEN OF YOU TO CUT A WOMAN'S THROAT!
BEWARE! IF I'M NOT RESCUED, I'LL BE AVENGED!
YOU'RE NOT A WOMAN, YOU DON'T BELONG TO THE HUMAN SPECIES. YOU'RE A DEMON ESCAPED FROM HELL..
...AND WE'RE GOING TO SEND YOU BACK THERE.
AH! YOU VIRTUOUS GENTLEMEN, DO BE AWARE THAT WHOEVER TOUCHES A HAIR ON MY HEAD WILL BE AN ASSASSIN IN TURN!
THE EXECUTIONER CAN KILL, WITHOUT BEING AN ASSASSIN FOR THAT REASON, MADAME. HE'S THE FINAL JUDGE, THAT'S ALL.
MY GOD, ARE YOU GOING TO DROWN ME THEN?!
I CANNOT WATCH THIS HORRIBLE SPECTACLE! DESPITE ALL THE HATE I BEAR FOR HER, I CANNOT CONSENT THAT THIS WOMAN DIE IN THIS FASHION!

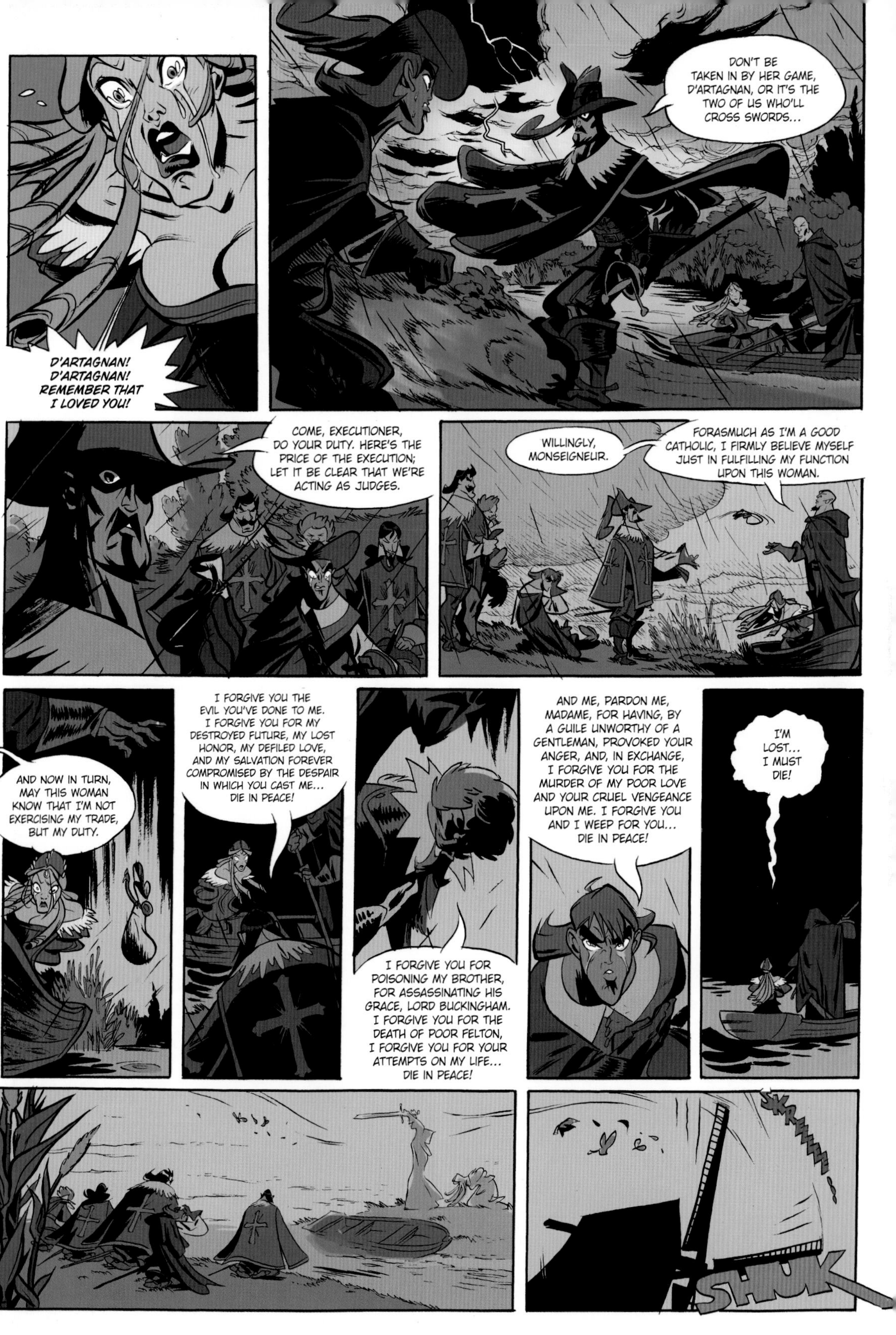
D'ARTAGNAN! D'ARTAGNAN! REMEMBER THAT I LOVED YOU!
DON'T BE TAKEN IN BY HER GAME, D'ARTAGNAN, OR IT'S THE TWO OF US WHO'LL CROSS SWORDS...
COME, EXECUTIONER, DO YOUR DUTY. HERE'S THE PRICE OF THE EXECUTION; LET IT BE CLEAR THAT WE'RE ACTING AS JUDGES.
WILLINGLY, MONSEIGNEUR.
FORASMUCH AS I'M A GOOD CATHOLIC, I FIRMLY BELIEVE MYSELF JUST IN FULFILLING MY FUNCTION UPON THIS WOMAN.
AND NOW IN TURN, MAY THIS WOMAN KNOW THAT I'M NOT EXERCISING MY TRADE, BUT MY DUTY.
I FORGIVE YOU THE EVIL YOU'VE DONE TO ME. I FORGIVE YOU FOR MY DESTROYED FUTURE, MY LOST HONOR, MY DEFILED LOVE, AND MY SALVATION FOREVER COMPROMISED BY THE DESPAIR IN WHICH YOU CAST ME... DIE IN PEACE!
I FORGIVE YOU FOR POISONING MY BROTHER, FOR ASSASSINATING HIS GRACE, LORD BUCKINGHAM. I FORGIVE YOU FOR THE DEATH OF POOR FELTON, I FORGIVE YOU FOR YOUR ATTEMPTS ON MY LIFE... DIE IN PEACE!
AND ME, PARDON ME, MADAME, FOR HAVING, BY A GUILE UNWORTHY OF A GENTLEMAN, PROVOKED YOUR ANGER, AND, IN EXCHANGE, I FORGIVE YOU FOR THE MURDER OF MY POOR LOVE AND YOUR CRUEL VENGEANCE UPON ME. I FORGIVE YOU AND I WEEP FOR YOU... DIE IN PEACE!
I'M LOST... I MUST DIE!
SHUK

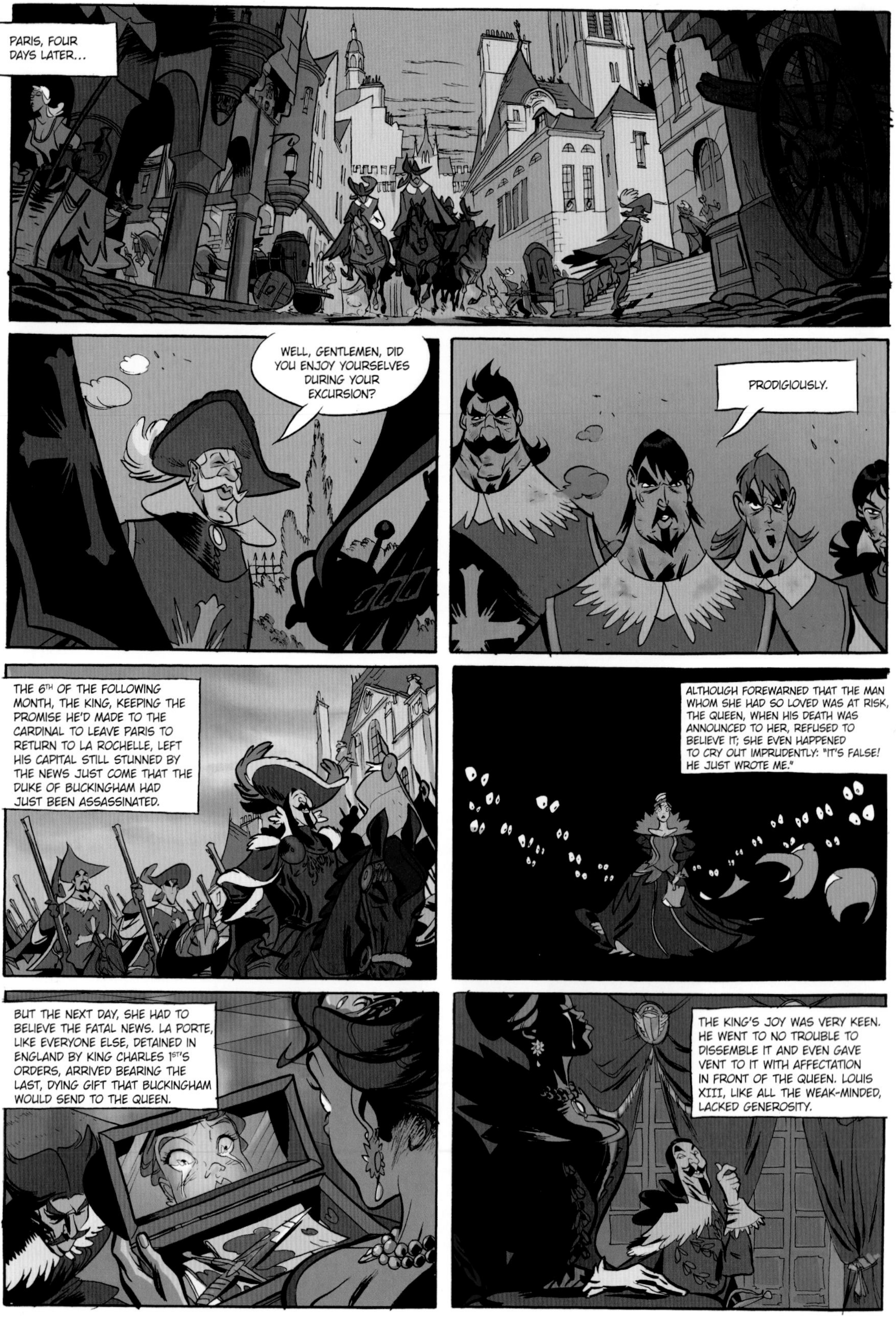
PARIS, FOUR DAYS LATER...
WELL, GENTLEMEN, DID YOU ENJOY YOURSELVES DURING YOUR EXCURSION?
PRODIGIOUSLY.
THE 6TH OF THE FOLLOWING MONTH, THE KING, KEEPING THE PROMISE HE'D MADE TO THE CARDINAL TO LEAVE PARIS TO RETURN TO LA ROCHELLE, LEFT HIS CAPITAL STILL STUNNED BY THE NEWS JUST COME THAT THE DUKE OF BUCKINGHAM HAD JUST BEEN ASSASSINATED.
ALTHOUGH FOREWARNED THAT THE MAN WHOM SHE HAD SO LOVED WAS AT RISK, THE QUEEN, WHEN HIS DEATH WAS ANNOUNCED TO HER, REFUSED TO BELIEVE IT; SHE EVEN HAPPENED TO CRY OUT IMPRUDENTLY: "IT'S FALSE! HE JUST WROTE ME."
BUT THE NEXT DAY, SHE HAD TO BELIEVE THE FATAL NEWS. LA PORTE, LIKE EVERYONE ELSE, DETAINED IN ENGLAND BY KING CHARLES 1ST'S ORDERS, ARRIVED BEARING THE LAST, DYING GIFT THAT BUCKINGHAM WOULD SEND TO THE QUEEN.
THE KING'S JOY WAS VERY KEEN. HE WENT TO NO TROUBLE TO DISSEMBLE IT AND EVEN GAVE VENT TO IT WITH AFFECTATION IN FRONT OF THE QUEEN. LOUIS XIII, LIKE ALL THE WEAK-MINDED, LACKED GENEROSITY.

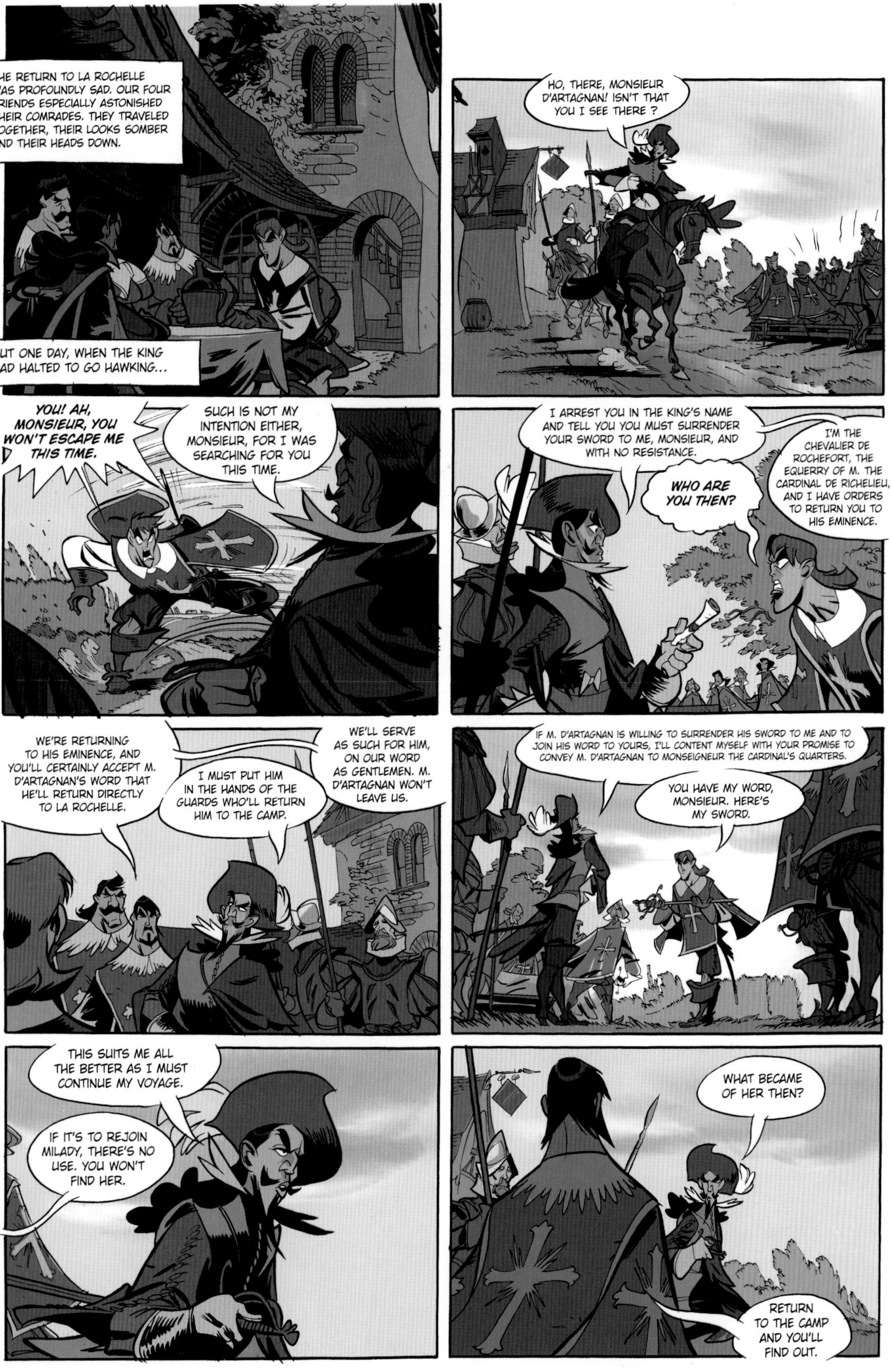
THE RETURN TO LA ROCHELLE WAS PROFOUNDLY SAD. OUR FOUR FRIENDS ESPECIALLY ASTONISHED THEIR COMRADES. THEY TRAVELED TOGETHER, THEIR LOOKS SOMBER AND THEIR HEADS DOWN.
BUT ONE DAY, WHEN THE KING HAD HALTED TO GO HAWKING...
HO, THERE, MONSIEUR D'ARTAGNAN! ISN'T THAT YOU I SEE THERE ?
YOU! AH, MONSIEUR, YOU WON'T ESCAPE ME THIS TIME.
SUCH IS NOT MY INTENTION EITHER, MONSIEUR, FOR I WAS SEARCHING FOR YOU THIS TIME.
I ARREST YOU IN THE KING'S NAME AND TELL YOU YOU MUST SURRENDER YOUR SWORD TO ME, MONSIEUR, AND WITH NO RESISTANCE.
WHO ARE YOU THEN?
I'M THE CHEVALIER DE ROCHEFORT, THE EQUERRY OF M. THE CARDINAL DE RICHELIEU, AND I HAVE ORDERS TO RETURN YOU TO HIS EMINENCE.
WE'RE RETURNING TO HIS EMINENCE, AND YOU'LL CERTAINLY ACCEPT M. D'ARTAGNAN'S WORD THAT HE'LL RETURN DIRECTLY TO LA ROCHELLE.
I MUST PUT HIM IN THE HANDS OF THE GUARDS WHO'LL RETURN HIM TO THE CAMP.
WE'LL SERVE AS SUCH FOR HIM, ON OUR WORD AS GENTLEMEN. M. D'ARTAGNAN WON'T LEAVE US.
IF M. D'ARTAGNAN IS WILLING TO SURRENDER HIS SWORD TO ME AND TO JOIN HIS WORD TO YOURS, I'LL CONTENT MYSELF WITH YOUR PROMISE TO CONVEY M. D'ARTAGNAN TO MONSEIGNEUR THE CARDINAL'S QUARTERS.
YOU HAVE MY WORD, MONSIEUR. HERE'S MY SWORD.
THIS SUITS ME ALL THE BETTER AS I MUST CONTINUE MY VOYAGE.
IF IT'S TO REJOIN MILADY, THERE'S NO USE. YOU WON'T FIND HER.
WHAT BECAME OF HER THEN?
RETURN TO THE CAMP AND YOU'LL FIND OUT.

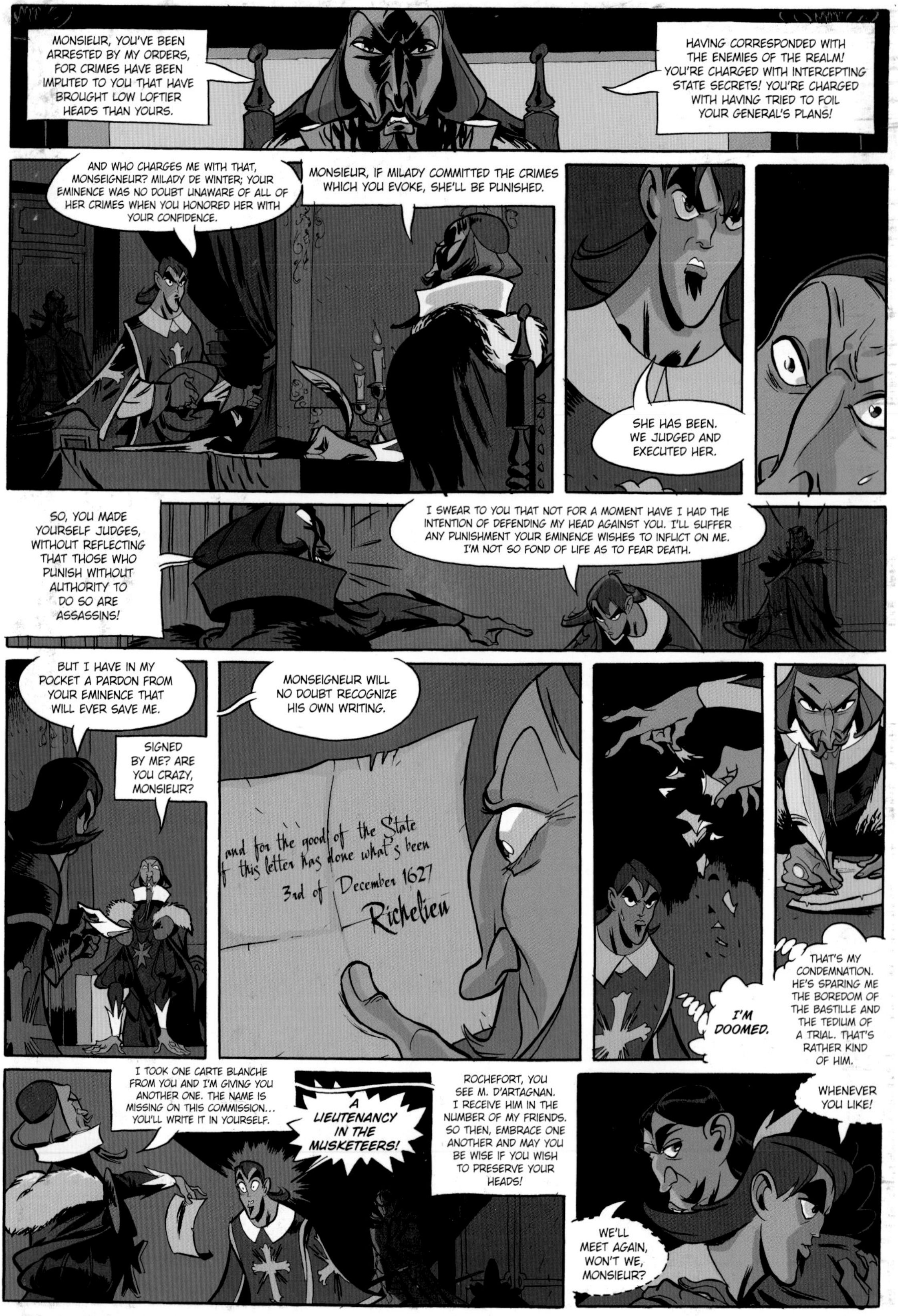
MONSIEUR, YOU'VE BEEN ARRESTED BY MY ORDERS, FOR CRIMES HAVE BEEN IMPUTED TO YOU THAT HAVE BROUGHT LOW LOFTIER HEADS THAN YOURS.
HAVING CORRESPONDED WITH THE ENEMIES OF THE REALM! YOU'RE CHARGED WITH INTERCEPTING STATE SECRETS! YOU'RE CHARGED WITH HAVING TRIED TO FOIL YOUR GENERAL'S PLANS!
AND WHO CHARGES ME WITH THAT, MONSEIGNEUR? MILADY DE WINTER; YOUR EMINENCE WAS NO DOUBT UNAWARE OF ALL OF HER CRIMES WHEN YOU HONORED HER WITH YOUR CONFIDENCE.
MONSIEUR, IF MILADY COMMITTED THE CRIMES WHICH YOU EVOKE, SHE'LL BE PUNISHED.
SHE HAS BEEN. WE JUDGED AND EXECUTED HER.
SO, YOU MADE YOURSELF JUDGES, WITHOUT REFLECTING THAT THOSE WHO PUNISH WITHOUT AUTHORITY TO DO SO ARE ASSASSINS!
I SWEAR TO YOU THAT NOT FOR A MOMENT HAVE I HAD THE INTENTION OF DEFENDING MY HEAD AGAINST YOU. I'LL SUFFER ANY PUNISHMENT YOUR EMINENCE WISHES TO INFLICT ON ME. I'M NOT SO FOND OF LIFE AS TO FEAR DEATH.
BUT I HAVE IN MY POCKET A PARDON FROM YOUR EMINENCE THAT WILL EVER SAVE ME.
SIGNED BY ME? ARE YOU CRAZY, MONSIEUR?
MONSEIGNEUR WILL NO DOUBT RECOGNIZE HIS OWN WRITING.
and for the good of the State
f this letter has done what's been
3rd of December 1627
Richelieu
I'M DOOMED.
THAT'S MY CONDEMNATION. HE'S SPARING ME THE BOREDOM OF THE BASTILLE AND THE TEDIUM OF A TRIAL. THAT'S RATHER KIND OF HIM.
I TOOK ONE CARTE BLANCHE FROM YOU AND I'M GIVING YOU ANOTHER ONE. THE NAME IS MISSING ON THIS COMMISSION... YOU'LL WRITE IT IN YOURSELF.
A LIEUTENANCY IN THE MUSKETEERS!
ROCHEFORT, YOU SEE M. D'ARTAGNAN. I RECEIVE HIM IN THE NUMBER OF MY FRIENDS. SO THEN, EMBRACE ONE ANOTHER AND MAY YOU BE WISE IF YOU WISH TO PRESERVE YOUR HEADS!
WHENEVER YOU LIKE!
WE'LL MEET AGAIN, WON'T WE, MONSIEUR?

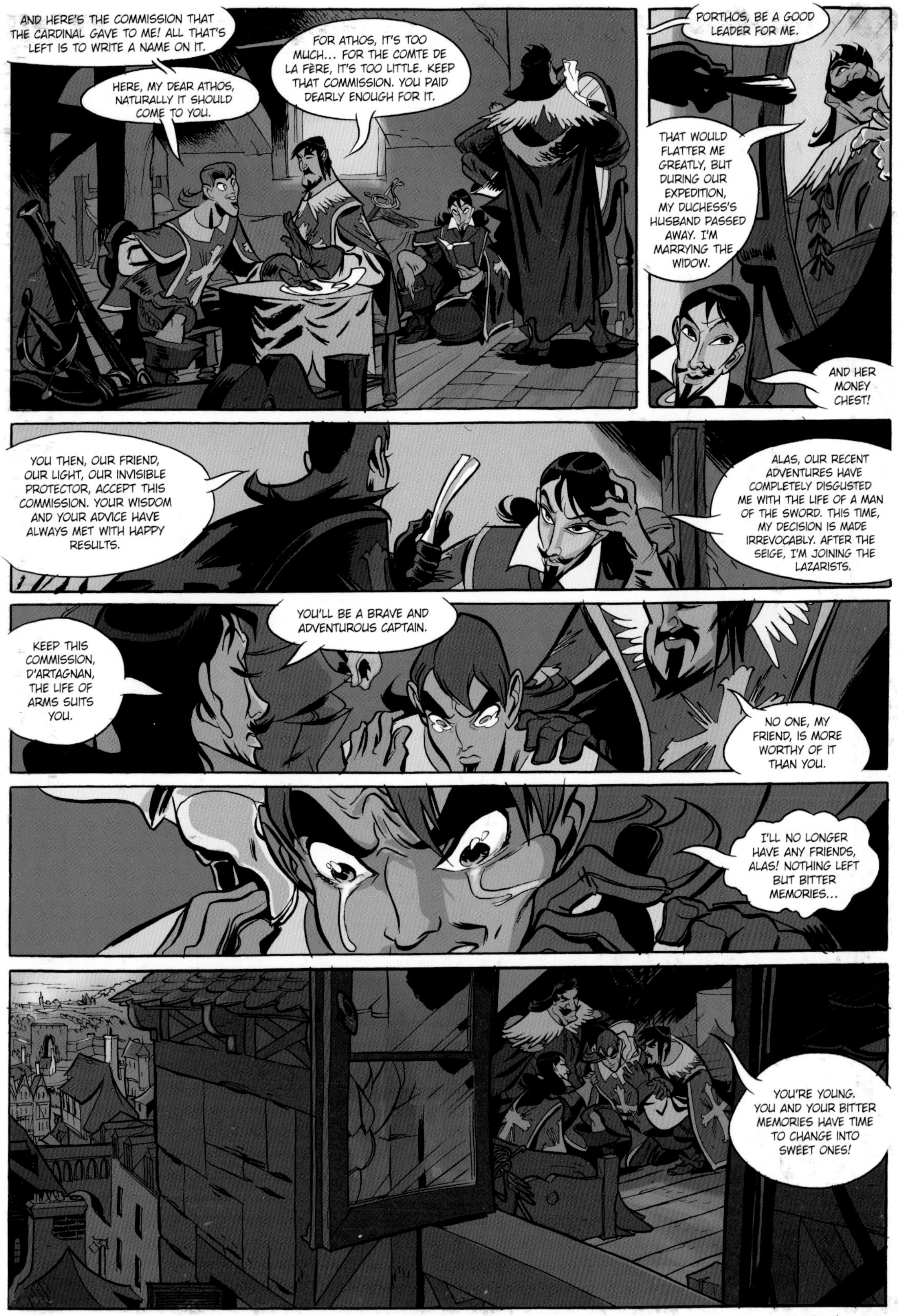
AND HERE'S THE COMMISSION THAT THE CARDINAL GAVE TO ME! ALL THAT'S LEFT IS TO WRITE A NAME ON IT.
HERE, MY DEAR ATHOS, NATURALLY IT SHOULD COME TO YOU.
FOR ATHOS, IT'S TOO MUCH... FOR THE COMTE DE LA FÈRE, IT'S TOO LITTLE. KEEP THAT COMMISSION. YOU PAID DEARLY ENOUGH FOR IT.
PORTHOS, BE A GOOD LEADER FOR ME.
THAT WOULD FLATTER ME GREATLY, BUT DURING OUR EXPEDITION, MY DUCHESS'S HUSBAND PASSED AWAY. I'M MARRYING THE WIDOW.
AND HER MONEY CHEST!
YOU THEN, OUR FRIEND, OUR LIGHT, OUR INVISIBLE PROTECTOR, ACCEPT THIS COMMISSION. YOUR WISDOM AND YOUR ADVICE HAVE ALWAYS MET WITH HAPPY RESULTS.
ALAS, OUR RECENT ADVENTURES HAVE COMPLETELY DISGUSTED ME WITH THE LIFE OF A MAN OF THE SWORD. THIS TIME, MY DECISION IS MADE IRREVOCABLY. AFTER THE SEIGE, I'M JOINING THE LAZARISTS.
KEEP THIS COMMISSION, D'ARTAGNAN, THE LIFE OF ARMS SUITS YOU.
YOU'LL BE A BRAVE AND ADVENTUROUS CAPTAIN.
NO ONE, MY FRIEND, IS MORE WORTHY OF IT THAN YOU.
I'LL NO LONGER HAVE ANY FRIENDS, ALAS! NOTHING LEFT BUT BITTER MEMORIES...
YOU'RE YOUNG. YOU AND YOUR BITTER MEMORIES HAVE TIME TO CHANGE INTO SWEET ONES!

03 Janvier 2010

WATCH OUT FOR PAPERCUTZ

Welcome to the special 70th Anniversary edition of the all-new CLASSICS ILLUSTRATED DELUXE series from Papercutz. I'm your swash-buckling editor-in-chief, Jim Salicrup, here to talk a little about "The Three Musketeers" and CLASSICS ILLUSTRATED DELUXE.

To celebrate the 70th Anniversary of CLASSICS ILLUSTRATED, originally called CLASSICS COMICS, started in October 1941, we thought it would be fun to revisit the subject of CLASSIC COMICS's premiere-- Alexandre Dumas's "The Three Musketeers." Albert Lewis Kanter, the visionary publisher and the man who conceived CLASSICS ILLUSTRATED, was clearly attempting to attract the young audience of the early 1940s then flocking to the comicbook exploits of Superman and his colorful ilk, with literary works that contained ample amounts of action and adventure. The only real limitation Kanter faced, was attempting to adapt a novel nearly 600 pages long in a 68-page comicbook. This all-new adaptation by Jean David Morvan, Michel Dufranne, and Rubén is the longest comics adaptation yet published. The idea of a comicbook longer than a 100 pages just seemed impractical, for many reasons, back when comics sold for a dime. The best that could be hoped for was an adaptation focused on the main action, while dropping many story elements deemed "non-essential." There clearly is a reason the suggestion to not "miss the added enjoyment of reading the original, obtainable at your school or public library" appears at the end of CLASSICS ILLUSTRATED adaptations.

CLASSICS Illustrated
THE THREE MUSKETEERS
Alexandre Dumas
Featuring Stories by the World's Greatest Authors
No. 1
15¢

A reprint of the revised version of CLASSIC COMICS #1, with George Evans and Reed Crandall artwork was published by Jack Lake Productions.

Even at 68 pages, it was tough to maintain that 10 cent price, and later printings of CLASSIC COMICS/CLASSICS ILLUSTRATED #1 saw price increases. Back when most comics were just 12 cents, the entire CLASSICS ILLUSTRATED line sold for 25 cents each, due to the higher page counts. But now, it's not uncommon to see graphic novels featuring hundreds of pages of original material.

It should also be noted, that works such as "The Three Musketeers" and "Great Expectations" were originally serialized when originally published, which may explain their sprawling length. If a particular serialized story was popular, there may have been pressure from publishers to keep the story going for as long as possible.

The popular appeal of "The Three Musketeers" has not gone unnoticed by Hollywood. Many major stars have portrayed Musketeers over the years, even Charlie Sheen played a Musketeer, in the 1993 film adaptation. There have been excellent film adaptations—in fact, there are two all-new adaptations in the works right now. One, directed by Paul W.S. Anderson, starring Milla Jovovich, Logan Lerman, Christopher Waltz, and Mads Mikkelsen, and another to be directed by Doug Liman. Perhaps, my favorite film adaptation was "The Three Musketeers," "The Four Musketeers," and "The Return of the Musketeers*," all directed by Richard Lester. Lester knew he needed more than one movie to do just to "The Three Musketeers," and by adapting the book into two movies, he created one three and a half hour movie masterpiece.

We hope you enjoyed the Morvan, Dufranne, and Rubén comics adaptation, because the whole point behind CLASSICS ILLUSTRATED DELUXE is to allow more pages for better adaptations. That's why we're excited to announce that CLASSICS ILLUSTRATED DELUXE # 8 "Oliver Twist" will be our longest adaptation yet! Visit www.papercutz.com for more information on CLASSICS ILLUSTRATED DELUXE as well as on everything else we're publishing at Papercutz. Let us know what you think—you can email me at salicrup@papercutz.com, or send a letter to me at Papercutz, 40 Exchange Pl., Ste. 1308, New York, NY 10005..

Thanks,

Jim

*"The Return of the Musketeers" was based on the Alexandre Dumas sequel, "Twenty Years Later," which has yet to be adapted into comics.

NOW THAT YOU HAVE READ THE CLASSICS Illustrated EDITION, DON'T MISS THE ADDED ENJOYMENT OF READING THE ORIGINAL, OBTAINABLE AT YOUR SCHOOL OR LIBRARY.

EPILOGUE

La Rochelle, deprived of help from the English fleet and the army promised by Buckingham, surrendered after a one-year siege. On October 28, 1628, the Capitulation was signed.

The King made his entrance into Paris on December 23rd of the same year. His triumph was celebrated as though he were returning from vanquishing the enemy and not French people. He entered via the Faubourg Saint-Jacques, under verdant arches.

D'Artagnan took charge of his new position.

Porthos left military service and married Mme Coquenard in the middle of the following year; the long-desired chest contained eight hundred thousand livres.

Mousqueton got a magnificent livery and, what's more, the satisfaction, for which he'd been ambitious his entire life, of climbing on the rear of a gilded carriage.

Aramis, after a trip to Lorraine, disappeared entirely and stopped writing to his friends. They later learned, by way of Mme de Chevreuse, who said so to two or three of her lovers, that he'd taken the habit in a convent in Nancy.

Bazin became a lay brother.

Athos remained a Musketeer under d'Artagnan's orders until 1633, the period at which, following a trip he made to Touraine, he, too, left military service on the pretext that he'd just collected a small inheritance in Roussillon.

Grimaud followed Athos.

D'Artagnan battled Rochefort three times and wounded him three times. "I'll probably kill you on the fourth try," he told him, while stretching out his hand to lift him up.

"It's better then, for you and me, that we leave it there," answered the wounded man. Corbleu! I'm more your friend than you think, for, from our very first encounter, by saying a word to the Cardinal, I could have had your throat cut."

They embraced that time, but goodheartedly and with no afterthoughts.

Planchet got from Rochefort the rank of sergeant in the Guards.

M. Bonacieux was living quite tranquilly, perfectly ignorant of what had become of his wife and scarcely worrying over it. One day, he had the imprudence to recall himself to the Cardinal's memory; the Cardinal responded to him that he would see that Bonacieux would never again lack for anything.

Indeed, the next day, M. Bonacieux, having left at seven in the evening from his home in order to go to the Louvre, never reappeared again at the Rue des Fossoyeurs; the opinion of those who appeared the best informed was that he was nourished and lodged in some royal castle at the expense of his generous Eminence.

ALEXANDRE DUMAS

Alexandre Dumas (1802-1870), the son of a general of the French Revolution, raised by his mother, Alexandre Dumas receives a rather mediocre education and neglects his studies. He works in a notary clerk's office, all the while drafting his first theatrical works. Joining the service of the Duc d'Orléans, he moves to Paris and, in 1829, realizes his first success with the staging by the Comédie Française of his play *Henri III and His Court*. In 1844, Alexandre Dumas finds himself in a precarious financial situation. Theatrical successes are far between, and the box office receipts don't cover the expenditures of an author, who loves living life to the fullest. Luckily for him, there comes a revolution in the world of writing: the serial novel. Meant to boost sales of newspapers —*La Presse, Le Siècle, the Journal des débats* and *Le Constitutionnel*— these breathless tales managed to touch the petty bourgeoisie and made famous the phrase "Continued in the next issue." After Eugène Sue, Frédéric Soulié or Paul Féval, it's Alexandre Dumas's turn to enjoy success with his trilogy *The Three Musketeers, Twenty Years Later* (1845), and *The Vicomte of Bragelonne* (1848-1850).